# THE WOLVES AND THE GREYHOUNDS

# A NOVEL OF THE GREAT WAR

# THE WOLVES AND THE GREYHOUNDS

## ROBERT SCHREINER

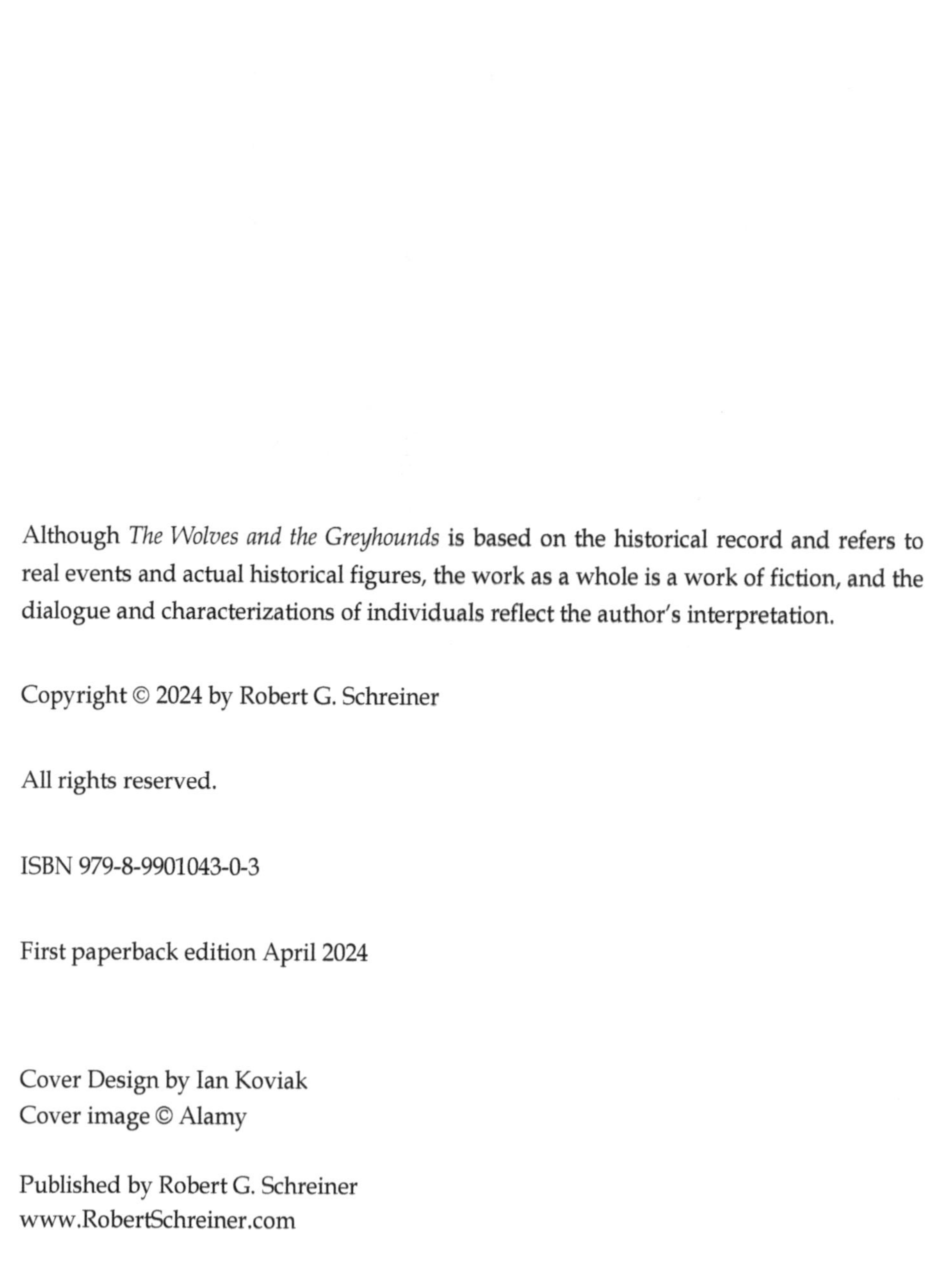

Although *The Wolves and the Greyhounds* is based on the historical record and refers to real events and actual historical figures, the work as a whole is a work of fiction, and the dialogue and characterizations of individuals reflect the author's interpretation.



ISBN 979-8-9901043-0-3

First paperback edition April 2024

Cover Design by Ian Koviak
Cover image © Alamy

Published by Robert G. Schreiner
www.RobertSchreiner.com

For Diane,
who sees the things I cannot see.

"God forbid that I should do this thing,
and flee away from them;
if our time be come,
let us die manfully for our brethren,
and let us not stain our honour."

*I. Maccabeas ix. 10*


From the Cradock Memorial, York Minster

# PROLOGUE

## All Saints Day

*Sunday, November 1, 1914*
*Pacific Ocean, 50 Miles West of Coronel, Chile*

HMS *Good Hope* rose upon a massive swell, her hull groaning and straining against its force, before plunging into the inky trough beyond. The heavy sea hammered her bows, and howling winds lashed the big warship's superstructure. The clear night sky belied the maelstrom on the surface, as towering whitecaps pounded the beleaguered cruiser and drenched her decks with torrents of seawater.

As the warship labored up the face of another swell, wailing shrieks from the darkness above announced the arrival of another salvo of falling German shells. Most of the incoming rounds plunged into the dark ocean near the ship, throwing up towering columns of foaming spray—but one of the shells struck the warship near the stern, rocking it with a thunderous explosion.

Rear-Admiral Sir Christopher Cradock, standing in what remained of his stricken flagship's bridge compartment, knew the old vessel could not endure much more. The enemy's rate of fire had increased, and armor-piercing shells were falling almost continuously now, like steel rain from the starlit sky. The entire ship was ablaze. On the foredeck below the bridge, from the gaping hole where the ship's forward gun turret had once been, a vortex of flame roared ten feet into the night air.

Cradock watched as a score of men staggered on the pitching deck near the blazing hole. With hand-pumped hoses, they directed meager streams of water into the fiery cauldron—having little effect upon the source of the inferno, several decks below.

The warship crested another huge swell and plummeted into a cavernous trough. Foaming green water washed over the forecastle and sent a swirling cataract of brine into the burning chasm. Rather than dousing the flames, the explosive mix of fire and water ejected a geyser of scalding steam high above the deck. The firefighters recoiled and stumbled back as the fire raged back to life before them.

A comingled stench of burning oil and seared human flesh hung heavily in the air, and clouds of putrid black smoke poured in through the shattered windows of the wheelhouse. Cradock coughed and gagged on the smoky air as he tried, in vain, to pinpoint the location of the enemy ships upon the dark sea to the east. The enemy cruisers were visible for only brief seconds—when their gun batteries fired yet more deadly salvos of shells toward Cradock's harrowed line.

For the past forty minutes, the Germans had relentlessly pummeled *Good Hope* and the other ships of his small, overmatched squadron. From bow to stern, the heavy rounds remorselessly punched through the cruiser's steel armor, detonating below decks in passageways, wardrooms, coal bunkers, and machine spaces. Each successive impact sent rumbling tremors through the ship, sparking fires, and sowing death within.

The enemy vessels were steaming on a nearly parallel southward course, a few miles to the east, along the rugged Chilean coastline. Unfortunately, since the setting of the sun, the German cruisers had been cloaked in darkness. They were impossible to see—and therefore impossible to target with *Good Hope's* guns.

Even if his spotters could see the enemy ships, Cradock's options were diminishing quickly. *Good Hope's* forward turret was gone, destroyed in the opening moments of the battle. The wireless room below the bridge was a burning husk—its crew and equipment incinerated. Fires raged out of control in at least a dozen compartments throughout the ship, and men were dead or dying on almost every deck. Several corpses lay nearby within the wheelhouse itself, including the mangled body of the captain, and the pitching deck beneath Cradock's feet was slick with a slurry of blood and seawater.

The other ships of his ravaged squadron, the armored cruiser *Monmouth* and the light cruiser *Glasgow*, were faring no better. Following directly astern, *Monmouth* was also burning fiercely, and she was taking a beating as terrible as that of the flagship. *Glasgow* was at the rear of the line, difficult to see in the darkness, but Cradock assumed that she too was enduring a withering hail of gunfire. To make matters worse, the German gunlayers were having no trouble targeting the British ships in the gloom, because the bright fires burning within them were glowing beacons visible for miles.

In his forty years of Royal Navy service, Cradock had never faced a situation so dire; and he realized that until that moment, he had never truly experienced fear. However, it was that fear that focused Cradock's resolve and brought him an unexpected sense of clarity and calm. He saw an opportunity—one small sliver of a chance to turn despair into triumph, even if it became his last living act. He measured his breathing and tightly gripped a handrail as the big ship rumbled through another trough and the deck pitched beneath his feet.

"Damage report from the engineering spaces, sir," said the senior navigation officer. "Explosions in the port side boiler array have cut power to the port propeller shaft. Fire and steam are preventing engineers from entering the space to assess the damage."

"Understood," replied Cradock grimly. "What is our current..." He was interrupted as more explosions threw up huge columns of seawater around the ship—the latest salvo of incoming shells was falling upon them. One of the rounds struck the ship somewhere aft. A rumble reverberated through the ship, and the deck of the wheelhouse trembled momentarily as the towering bulk of the severed aft wireless mast toppled into the black swells to starboard.

"What is our current speed?" he finished as the thunderclap faded.

"Down to sixteen knots, sir."

Cradock had few choices left. He could no longer retreat, and *Good Hope's* guns were useless against a distant foe that his spotters could not see. Now the ship was losing power to her engines. If the damage to the boilers was severe, she could be dead in the water in minutes. At this range, the Germans could just continue to pound away at them with impunity. Only one weapon remaining in his arsenal had a slim hope of sinking any of the powerful enemy ships. He needed to close the distance between them before all was lost.

"Helmsman, four more points to port," he said. "Full speed. Give us everything the engines have left."

"Aye, sir," replied the helmsman hesitantly. "Four points to port. Full speed."

Cradock turned to the senior gunnery officer. "Tell your men to ready both torpedoes. We're turning into their line. We must close the distance with whatever engine power remains—and get in under their big guns. At two thousand yards, launch those torpedoes at the first target the spotters see."

"Aye, sir." The gunnery officer passed his instructions on to his men through the voice pipe array.

The British flagship labored into the eastward turn, pitching more severely as the surging southerly wind and sea now buffeted her starboard beam. The large cruiser steamed ponderously toward the unseen enemy vessels lurking somewhere in the blackness before them. The remaining officers on the bridge peered anxiously over the dark seascape and braced themselves as the deck rolled dramatically beneath their feet.

"Enemy ships firing again," announced the gunnery officer, noting the ripple of yellow muzzle flashes ahead of them to the east—closer now than they had been before. Another wave of shells was streaking toward them in the night sky.

"Distance to those flashes?" asked Cradock.

"At least five thousand yards, sir."

They were still much too far away.

"Helmsman, what is our current speed?" He coughed again as tendrils of greasy smoke blew into the wheelhouse from the fires raging outside.

"Fourteen knots and falling, sir. We're getting nothing from the port engine."

Come on, old girl, thought Cradock, his jaw rigid—as he tried to will *Good Hope* to greater speed. Just a bit closer. If we can come in fast enough, their gunners may not be able to rapidly depress their barrels to hit us before we can launch our torpedoes.

With a mournful wail, the shells tore through the air overhead.

It was working, thought Cradock. They had overshot their target, sending the salvo too high. *Good Hope* was approaching the Germans faster than their gunlayers could react in the darkness.

Almost.

Six of the incoming shells had flown long, exploding harmlessly in the sea beyond *Good Hope's* stern, but two of them found their mark.

The first shell struck the outer hull on the port quarter—the force of its oblique impact deflected by the thick belt of armor plate that ran the length of the ship, just above the waterline.

The second shell met no such resistance. As it fell, its trajectory took it down through a ragged hole in the armored decking amidships, just aft of the main mast—where a previous impact had torn apart the steel plates. The shell screamed downward into the great belly of the warship, unimpeded until it punched cleanly through a steel bulkhead, bursting into the large compartment beyond. That compartment was *Good Hope's* main magazine, which was packed end to end with more than a thousand cordite propellant charges and high explosive lyddite rounds.

There the German shell finally detonated.

And HMS *Good Hope* ceased to exist.

# PART ONE

# The Drums of War

# ONE

*Sunday, August 2, 1914*
*Port of Rio de Janeiro, Brazil*

AS IT TURNED OUT, the parrots would get to stay, but the dog had to go. Captain Luce knelt down and gave the speckled cream and tan spaniel an affectionate scratch behind his ears. The dog responded by pressing his head into Luce's palm and nuzzling him, urging more attention. Instead, the captain stood and handed the looped end of the leather leash to a man in a dark gray suit and hat.

"He's a miserable excuse for a hunting dog," Luce said with a smile. "If you hope to actually bring home any ducks on your next outing, Mister Robertson, you'll leave this wild fellow at home." The two men and the dog stood on the freshly washed deck of the light cruiser HMS *Glasgow*. The late afternoon sun had begun to dip toward the western hills above the port city of Rio de Janeiro, lengthening the shadows cast upon the smooth gray steel.

The British diplomat took the leash and looked down, addressing the dog playfully. "Well, I doubt we'll be doing much hunting for a while now. You'll just have to keep yourself busy chasing pigeons around the legation grounds." The dog tilted his head quizzically but seemed unconcerned by this development. The minister turned back to Luce, his smile fading back to seriousness. "It appears you may be doing a bit of hunting yourself, Captain. As we discussed, we'll keep you apprised by wireless as we hear any further developments." Robertson led the spaniel toward the opening in the starboard gunwale—where a stair-like ladder descended steeply from the deck, along the outer hull of the ship to his waiting boat. The eager dog strained happily at the leash, fixated on the bobbing boat below and the rare trip ashore it represented. Robertson paused at the top and turned back. With a slight nod, he said, "Good luck, Captain."

Luce watched Robertson lead the dog awkwardly down the steep metal steps to the floating platform. Tied up beside the ship was a twenty-foot steam launch, with a small engine and smokestack amidships. Two of the junior legation officers—also in dark suits—were already aboard, and one of them reached across the narrow space between the boat and platform to give the minister a hand. The captain had to smile again when the dog leapt exuberantly into the boat, almost pulling the diplomat off his feet. Robertson took his assistant's hand, clambered awkwardly aboard, and sat down among the boxes and crates already loaded in the boat. Two of *Glasgow's* sailors cast off the lines and gave the boat a push. Behind the smokestack, the pilot turned the wheel and released a lever. The chugging engine coughed bursts of gray smoke from the stack, and the launch pulled slowly away. From his makeshift seat on a crate, Robertson looked up once more and tipped his hat to the captain as the boat began its short trip to the inner harbor and wharf.

Luce noticed that several sailors working on deck had paused to watch the small boat move off with the dog, which was vigorously wagging its tail and tilting its head into the breeze. The captain could imagine what those men must be thinking, for he was feeling the same way. As silly as it might seem on this surreal day, the departure of that incorrigible animal, his dog—the ship's dog—made all of these unbelievable events more real and made their preparations all the more ominous.

He watched for a moment longer before turning and making his way back toward the bridge. All around him, men were engaged in the innumerable tasks required to prepare HMS *Glasgow* for war. Near the port lifting boom, four sailors wrestled a large wooden cabinet up a ladder onto the deck. The bulky piece of furniture had previously resided in the junior officers' mess. Although it was now empty of dishware and cutlery, it was still extremely heavy, and all four of the men were perspiring heavily in the tropical heat. On the quarterdeck, men were furling canvas awnings and stacking them in bundles, awaiting the next lighter from the shore. Farther aft, a petty officer directed a serpentine chain of junior ratings carrying crates and boxes to be added to the stacks near the starboard gunwales. Other petty officers were meticulously cataloging each piece that would be sent ashore, hopefully ensuring that when all of this was over, the ship's furnishings and each man's personal effects could be appropriately reclaimed.

◆

THEY HAD ARRIVED in Rio de Janeiro two weeks earlier from Montevideo. Like his officers and crew, Captain Luce had been in high spirits. After two years patrolling South American waters, *Glasgow* was finally heading home to Portsmouth. During her commission, Luce's ship had been the only Royal Navy vessel assigned to patrol and protect British interests in the South Atlantic from the coast of Brazil south to the tip of Cape Horn and eastward well past the Falkland Islands. More than eight thousand miles of coastline, millions of square miles of open ocean, and countless merchant vessels had been their responsibility—and now that responsibility was to be passed on to a new ship, a new crew, and a new captain.

The prospect of soon seeing family and home had infected the entire crew with a festive giddiness as they had made their way northward along the South American coast for the last time. When the distinctive rounded green peaks above Rio de Janeiro came into view, the crew had let out a cheer. Rio was their last official South American stop before heading north to St. Vincent, then on to Portsmouth. Home and family were only a few weeks away.

Captain John Luce was forty-four years old and had achieved his current rank six years earlier. He had commanded both the depot ship HMS *Hecla* and the old battleship *Hibernia* before taking command of *Glasgow* and the South American station in 1912. The assignment had been a mixed blessing. Sole command of the station was certainly an honor—and it reflected the Admiralty's high regard for the promising officer. However, the South American station was remote, and his absence during the two-year commission had been hard on his young family. He had been married for twelve years and, not surprisingly, had spent much of that time at sea. It was no coincidence that three of his four boys were conceived before he made captain, while he was assigned to the Admiralty in the Naval Intelligence Department. His wife, Mary, still jokingly referred to those fleeting home-bound years as their "honeymoon," the real thing having been an impossibility when they first married. Although Mary had been able to visit him once on station the previous October, Luce had not seen his young sons in almost two years.

He knew that most of the officers and men aboard were similarly homesick, whether they were married or single. Their tour of duty had, by his estimation, been a great success, but now home and family beckoned. Luce had not yet been assigned his next commission, although the Far East was a possibility. Hopefully he would be able to spend at least a few months close to home before the next command and the next assignment took him far away again.

Upon *Glasgow's* arrival at the outer harbor and the customary exchange of salutes, Luce granted extended shore leave to the crew. Rio was a beautiful, busy, welcoming place with an active British community supporting a thriving trade between Brazil and Britain. Those crew members who were eligible were enthusiastically enjoying their last port of call before the homeward journey.

Many officers and men purchased gifts for their wives, mothers, and children. A chief stoker had happened upon a bird vendor in the *Mercado* near the old naval arsenal and purchased a pair of emerald and crimson parrots in a decorative wicker cage. "A gift for the missus," he had explained proudly. The obvious brilliance of his idea was soon copied by many of the ratings and officers alike, and within a few days, more than sixty of the beautiful but surprisingly noisy parrots were chattering to each other from cages all over the ship. Luce briefly considered—then rejected—the notion of buying a couple of the parrots for his boys, realizing that their interest would likely be fleeting, and the climate in Wiltshire was probably less than ideal for the tropical birds.

For the first week of their stay, the crew had enjoyed themselves ashore and even took in a thrilling football match between the newly formed Brazilian national team and the Exeter City club, which was finishing up a goodwill tour of South America. However, during the second week, the festive atmosphere began to erode.

Late on Tuesday afternoon, a British legation courier had arrived unexpectedly on a launch from shore. The young man insisted on delivering the message to Captain Luce personally and stated plainly that he—and the small boat tethered alongside—would stay and await a response. It was a formal but curt request, on crisp diplomatic stationery:

> *Captain John Luce, RN*
> *HMS Glasgow*
>
> *Captain Luce, your presence is requested at the Office of the British Legation, Rio de Janeiro, Brazil, on Wednesday, the twenty-first of July, 1914, for a private meeting with Minister Malcolm A. Robertson. A motor car and driver will be provided at Pier 2 at 10:00 am.*
>
> *Office of the British Legation*
> *Rio de Janeiro, Brazil*
> *Chargé d'Affaires, Malcolm A. Robertson*

After quickly reviewing the message, Luce had summoned the first officer to his stateroom. Luce had poured two small glasses of vintage port and was absently inhaling the rich aroma of the liquor as he watched his first officer, Lieutenant-Commander Will Thompson, read over the message. The young commander, a tall slender man with sandy hair, leaned casually against the edge of Luce's writing desk and sipped from his glass as he perused the paper.

"It's from the British Minister to Brazil himself," observed Thompson, apparently impressed. "Why do you suppose he wants to meet you tomorrow morning? It doesn't look like he's just inviting you for a spot of tea." He handed the note back to Luce.

"I was actually hoping you could tell me, Will," Luce replied. He genuinely liked and respected Thompson—an officer who, like himself, was not afraid to speak his mind. "I thought it might be a disciplinary matter with one of the men," Luce continued. "Some incident ashore, perhaps at the football match yesterday?" As first officer, Thompson was responsible for dealing with any men who were "on report." Whenever necessary, the master-at-arms would deliver a list of any men who had committed a particular infraction punishable under standard naval regulations. During such a "commander's report," Thompson would review each case, ask the man on report for an explanation, then determine an appropriate punishment, usually involving extra work during the sailor's off-duty hours. It was a tiresome but necessary function, and Luce thought that Thompson handled it well, with good humor and understanding.

Thompson shook his head. "Heard nothing from the MA this morning. As far as I know, it was a good day all around, even with the excitement of the match and so many men off the ship. From what I heard, everyone was on their best behavior."

The captain nodded and took another sip of his port. The truth was that *Glasgow's* crew was rather well disciplined. Luce respected the sacrifices made by every man aboard, regardless of rank—and in turn he had high expectations of everyone under his command. As he had mentioned to the men on several occasions, among his expectations was that the personal conduct of each man on his ship represented Britain, the Royal Navy, and—most importantly—the captain himself. He believed that his firm-but-fair approach was generally successful, if not perfect. While many ships had daily "commander's reports" and even "captain's reports" for more serious offenses, such occurrences were far less common aboard *Glasgow*. Furthermore, this close to the end of their commission, it would be particularly foolish for anyone to act up and risk disciplinary action. So, if the reason for this unusual summons was not an issue with the crew, what could it be?

"Although I'm acquainted with him," said Luce, "I'm afraid I don't know Minister Robertson well enough to read anything into this note, such as it is."

"You've met him?" Thompson asked.

"Yes, about two years ago in Montevideo. An official function at the German embassy. Do you remember when we met SMS *Bremen* there in port?"

"Yes, of course," Thompson replied, smiling. "I remember giving those German chaps a tour of the ship and having to listen to them prattle on about how the engineering of their ship was so superior to ours, with their steam radiators in the cabins and such. I, of course, countered with a comparison of our 6-inch guns to their little battery of fours." Thompson leveled a mock accusatory glare and a pointed finger in his captain's direction. "As I recall, you were conspicuously absent during all of this—and I could have used some reinforcements. Those cheeky blokes even commented on the diameter of the bolts in our deck plating!"

Luce smiled, "While you were playing your game of 'whose is bigger,' I found myself unable to wriggle out of a diplomatic invitation that was a bit more cordial than this one here," he said, gesturing with Robertson's note. "The Germans threw quite the party, as I recall. Music and plenty of beer and wine. Unfortunately, I spent the better part of the evening listening to *Bremen's* captain extol the virtues of the Parsons turbine engine to some equally captive members of the Uruguayan navy. I was finally rescued by our Mister Robertson, who was then Minister to Uruguay." Luce drained the last few drops in his glass and set it on the desk. "He and I chatted for a few minutes about the local hunting, I believe. Then he was called away to meet some other minister of something-or-other, and I was able to quietly slip away and return to the ship. Beyond that encounter, I don't know much about him. He did seem like a decent fellow—perhaps not your typical diplomat."

"Well, it certainly isn't typical to summon the captain of a Royal Navy warship at a moment's notice."

"True, but he is, after all, the Crown's representative here in Brazil." Luce stood and gestured toward the door. "We'll need to let the courier know that the legation will be having a guest in the morning."

◆

THE NEXT MORNING, Captain Luce, escorted by a young petty officer, made his way down the pier from *Glasgow's* cutter. Although the reason for his summons was still a mystery, any meeting with a British diplomatic officer was formal enough for the full-dress white uniform. The brilliant morning sun glinted off the gold stitching on Luce's epaulets and cap. The petty officer walking beside him was also in his dress white uniform. Luce was of average height and build, and his neatly trimmed light brown hair had only recently begun to gray. Unlike some of his fellow senior officers, he preferred to remain clean-shaven, thinking privately that facial hair was rarely a positive affectation.

The pier was nearly deserted. Most of the fishermen had departed hours earlier, leaving only a handful of children mending nets and a few elderly men tending to crab traps. Unlike their breezy anchorage in the outer harbor, here the air was heavy with odors of fish, seaweed, and machine oil. A black and silver motor car was parked upon the cobblestones at the end of the pier, and a smartly dressed young Brazilian man stood beside the door, as if at attention. He greeted the two officers politely and ushered them into the vehicle.

Under a brilliant blue sky, Rio's lush green peaks towered over the tiled red roofs of the city. Upon leaving the port, the driver turned southeast onto the wide, tree-lined expanse of the *Avenida Rio Branco*. In contrast to the relative quiet of the pier, the crowded avenue was bustling with activity. Electric trolleys, horse-drawn carriages, sputtering automobiles, and pedestrians appeared to enjoy equal rank on the busy street. Whenever the car briefly stopped because some person, cart, or mule had gotten in the way, it was besieged by throngs of street urchins, clamoring for handouts from its finely dressed occupants. The driver yelled colorful curses in Portuguese at those impeding their progress and made good time picking his way through the chaos—although Luce wondered if the car's continually bleating horn would wear out by the conclusion of the trip. Soon they had turned off the *Avenida* and passed through the large, open gates of the British legation grounds. Two armed soldiers saluted the captain as he rode past in the car. This was the first time Luce had been to the British diplomatic mission in Rio. The main building resembled a stately older mansion of mixed European and South American architectural design. Before its many windows, large white columns supported eaves and rooflines tiled in terra cotta. The vehicle continued past the polished steps of the building's large public entrance and came to a stop on the gravel drive before another doorway on the far side.

As they climbed down from the car, a diplomatic aide appeared at the top of the stairs, holding open the large wooden door. "Good morning, gentlemen. Please come in." The petty officer was shown to a modest sitting room to wait while the captain was escorted down a wide hall, passing doorways that opened into large, well-appointed rooms. Numerous people bustled about, and Luce could hear the clicking of wireless chatter emanating from another room. The aide directed him into an anteroom, where another legation officer was seated at a desk, talking on a telephone. The seated man looked up and simply nodded as they passed. He continued talking—using a cumbersome amalgam of English and broken Portuguese. The escort walked past the desk, stopped at the interior door, knocked twice, and entered. He stood aside and announced, "Captain Luce of HMS *Glasgow* has arrived, sir."

The wood-paneled room beyond was spacious, with a large window overlooking a beautifully manicured garden. The British Minister had been sitting behind a glossy rosewood desk. He stood as they entered, smiling broadly. At thirty-seven, Malcolm Robertson was young to hold a Minister position, let alone his second one. He looked even younger than his years, particularly with his shirtsleeves rolled up and his collar unbuttoned in his current casual state of dress.

"Good morning, Captain. Good to see you again." Robertson shook Luce's hand.

"Good morning, Minister."

"Please, have a seat," said Robertson, directing Luce toward two large overstuffed chairs near the window. "How long has it been since that dreadful function at the German embassy in Montevideo? Nearly two years?"

Luce nodded. "I believe so."

"Amazing how time slips by. I regret that you and I have yet to go on that duck-hunting trip we discussed."

"It's a shame," agreed Luce, who was surprised that the Minister had remembered their brief conversation from so long ago. "We still have three days before we depart for Portsmouth. Perhaps you and I could squeeze in a half-day's hunt before I have to shove off. I'd like to make it a longer outing, but if I risk delaying our departure for home even another day, I might have a mutiny on my hands."

Robertson chuckled, but then his expression changed—becoming more serious. "That's why I called you here this morning. Unfortunately, I doubt that we'll have time for that hunt, because I've received some information that will likely change your travel plans."

Luce frowned, wondering what information the minister might have that could have any effect upon his orders. A legation staffer appeared at the door, bearing a tray with a teapot and two cups. The staffer placed the tray on a low table between the two, turned, and left, closing the office door behind him. Robertson filled both cups and handed one upon its saucer to Luce.

"Thank you," said Luce. "You have some information that concerns me or *Glasgow*?"

"I'm afraid so." Robertson took a sip of his tea. "I assume you've been reading the news reports of the growing uneasiness in Europe?"

Luce nodded. He had briefly skimmed a local newspaper the day before. Most of the coverage had been of the Brazilian football victory over Exeter City, but he had read another story hinting at the possibility of war between Austria-Hungary and Serbia. It was true that relations between those nations had grown increasingly strained in recent weeks since the assassination of Archduke Ferdinand and his wife in Sarajevo. However, he had seen no mention of the European political situation in any of the standard naval communications. Aside from noting that Germany appeared to be meddling in the tense political affair, Luce had not, frankly, given it much thought. "There's something to this story about the chance of war?" he asked.

Robertson nodded gravely. "Several international treaties have set up a precarious row of dominoes. Germany has allied itself politically and militarily with the Austro-Hungarian government. The Austrians are doggedly provoking a conflict with the Serbians, using the assassination as a pretext. Little Serbia, however, is an ally of Russia, which has pledged to protect Serbia militarily. Therefore, if Serbia is attacked, Russia will go to war against Austria and Germany. As you know, Russia is also bound by treaty to both France and Britain. Therefore, if Russia goes to war, so must France and Britain. The enemy of one is the enemy of us all. These treaties are complicated but quite clear. One domino topples, and the rest must follow."

"Good lord," said Luce, the true enormity of the realization hitting him with sickening force. "Germany and Austria know exactly what they're doing."

For the captain, it made sense in a simple, inevitable way. Even before he had joined the service, the path toward this confrontation was being laid. For decades, the Royal Navy, the undisputed ruler of the world's oceans, had watched as Germany built a navy to rival that of Britain. Every year of Luce's career, Britain's shipbuilders, armorers, engineers, and gunnery experts would peer across the Channel and see some new development or advancement that needed to be countered. Naval forces were only one part of the picture. Kaiser Wilhelm had also been building his powerful land armies and steadily expanding a formidable empire of colonies worldwide. Russia and France, knowing that they were increasingly seen as impediments to German imperial growth, had been bolstering their armed forces as well, and Britain had followed suit. The armed forces of the world had never been so prepared for conflict. Luce continued, almost in a whisper, "It's madness. Now that they finally have their excuse, they're going to provoke a war."

"It appears so. I take it the Admiralty haven't yet said anything official?"

Luce shook his head. "Not a word. Perhaps these events are moving faster than they expected."

"Perhaps so. It certainly has thrown all of us here into a bit of a fuss. Last evening, I met with the Brazilian trade secretary and had to explain that Britain could very likely be drawn into this war, should it actually happen. Although Brazil has pledged neutrality in such a circumstance, President Fonseca is understandably concerned about what effect a conflict between Britain and Germany might have upon to his nation's foreign trade. Britain and Germany are Brazil's two largest trading partners. In fact, in most areas, Brazil's trade with Germany exceeds their volume of trade with Britain."

"In a war, however," said Luce, "the Royal Navy would be tasked with interdicting all German-flagged shipping in international waters — and that would include ships traveling to and from Brazil."

Robertson nodded. "Even if they remain neutral, Brazil would likely suffer considerably. I am doing my best to assuage their concerns and assure them that Britain will remain a steadfast partner, regardless of what happens."

Luce considered the far-reaching implications. "Of course, the neutrality of foreign ports comes with its own complications."

"You'd have some restrictions on where and how often you could put into port, correct?"

"Yes. Under international rules governing neutral ports in time of war, the Royal Navy's ability to come and go as we please in this part of the world would be severely restricted. It could render even routine operations considerably more complicated. I do not envy my successor on this station."

"Well, that is one of the reasons I wanted to speak to you," said Robertson hesitantly. "Although you've not yet received official word from the Admiralty, my sources indicate that all Royal Navy ships on station in the Caribbean and South America will be staying on for some time. Of course, I have heard this through our diplomatic channels, not your military ones."

Luce thought for a moment. Although he had heard nothing yet from the Admiralty, with rising tensions and the threat of war, extending *Glasgow's* commission was certainly possible, perhaps even likely. He nodded. "The Admiralty are aware that we plan to leave for St. Vincent in three days. If they intend to keep us here on station, they will probably inform me before then."

"Probably so. I thought you should know, even if that makes me the bearer of bad news," Robertson said with a resigned smile.

"My men won't be happy, but I certainly appreciate your candor. It looks like the next few days will be busy ones for us."

"There is one more thing," the minister added. "We are aware that a number of agents of the German government are operating here in Rio under the guise of civilian and commercial enterprises. It is also possible that they may have influence within the Brazilian government. Until now, their activities have been seen as benign. However, if we're at war…"

"Have you identified any of them?" Luce asked.

"A few, but nothing we could act upon. Most importantly, we believe that several agents are in positions of authority with the local German shipping companies. We have yet to see any unusual activity in the port, but that may change. There are more than a dozen German-registered vessels here at the moment. I wanted to let you know so that your men can watch for anything unusual."

"We'll keep an eye out for anything out of the ordinary. I'd certainly appreciate hearing anything you come across as well."

"Certainly. I just wish I could be of more help, Captain."

"Actually, Mister Robertson, I appreciate your help already. If we do go to war, the more eyes and ears we have looking out for us, the better." Luce knew for certain that it would now be a long time before *Glasgow* returned to Portsmouth.

◆

THE ADMIRALTY notified him even sooner than he had expected. The next morning, after the Exeter City team's ship had left the port with much fanfare, a brief encrypted wireless message to the captain informed him that *Glasgow's* commission on the South American station was being extended for a minimum of six more months. The officers and crew were understandably shocked and dismayed by this news, and a cloud of quiet melancholy settled over the ship.

Luce spent the next two days considering options and making preparations. On Friday, July 24th, Luce received a private message from Minister Robertson that an Austrian ultimatum had been delivered to Serbia.

The first relevant message from the Admiralty did not come in for another three days—a general wireless signal stating simply that relations between Britain and Germany were strained. By then, the local papers were boldly reporting that not only had Austria declared war on Serbia, but that Russian, German, and French forces were beginning to mobilize. The dominos were starting to fall. The reality was that if Britain were to go to war, *Glasgow's* operations patrolling the South American station would be drastically altered. For the past two years, Luce and his crew had made a circuit of ports of call in Brazil, Uruguay, Argentina, Chile, and the Falkland Islands—the only British possession in the region. They had freely docked, coaled, and provisioned at will, and as they showed the flag, they had been welcomed universally by their hosts.

The captain knew well, however, that under the rules of the Hague Conventions, operations would be very different during wartime. With the exception of the Falkland Islands, which were sovereign British territory, every other port of call on the South American station would be neutral. Combatant warships could coal in the port of a neutral nation only once every three months and could stay no longer than twenty-four hours for a visit of any purpose. These constraints would necessitate a complete change in *Glasgow's* operations.

The most critical issue would be coal. All steam ships were dependent upon adequate supplies of coal; but warships, with their powerful, coal-hungry turbines and limited fuel storage space, were particularly vulnerable to any interruption in coal supply. Customarily, they had been able to purchase coal whenever they docked in any of the ports of Brazil, Uruguay, or Argentina—but that was during peacetime. If war were to be declared, *Glasgow* would rarely be able to coal in port—and probably only under extreme circumstances, because they would then not be able to return to that port for three months. Although they could dock and coal whenever they wanted at Port Stanley in the Falklands, the British possession was simply too remote for them to use as their only coaling base on station. Instead, coaling would have to be accomplished at sea, directly from a collier ship, something neither Luce nor his crew had attempted in the open ocean.

Ship-to-ship coaling itself was a routine exercise, and Luce's crew had done it many times, whenever dockside coaling with proper cranes and winches was not possible. However, almost all of those ship-to-ship coaling operations had been conducted in sheltered water, usually while moored in port. Even then, a medium swell could bring two hulls crashing together, potentially damaging the ships and possibly injuring members of the crew. The prospect of having to routinely coal at sea, in unknown conditions, was daunting.

Luce knew that if they were to go to war, he would need another local coaling base besides the Falklands. He needed a secure, sheltered spot where his ship could rendezvous with colliers at will and he could refuel without worrying about breaching the rules of neutrality. He believed he knew of such a place, but he would have to bend those rules a bit.

He authorized the purchase of enough food, provisions, and supplies to last at least a month at sea, not knowing where or how they would be deployed. He also sent a cable to charter a British collier, which was to be dispatched from Cardiff specifically to rendezvous with *Glasgow*. The mood aboard the ship was increasingly somber, as shore leave was cancelled and preparations began for the grim possibility of war.

On the morning of August 1st, Luce was in his wardroom eating his breakfast while he reviewed the latest wireless messages from the Admiralty and from Minister Robertson at the British legation. In brief, matter-of-fact language, the messages described an ominous chain of events. After Austria's declaration of war upon Serbia, Russia had mobilized against Austria in defense of their Serbian allies. Germany had then declared war against Russia. France was mobilizing as well, apparently ignoring Germany's ultimatum to stand down. Luce marveled that none of these nations seemed interested in defusing this rapidly escalating confrontation. The nations of Europe appeared to be eagerly, recklessly marching to war — and Britain would likely soon be embroiled as well. He realized he was no longer hungry, leaving the rest of his breakfast uneaten. As he set his plate aside, a whistle trilled and Commander Thompson's voice echoed through the voice pipe mounted on the bulkhead near his desk.

"Excuse me, sir. Sorry to bother you. There's something going on in port I think you should see."

"Very well, I'll be there in a moment." Luce stood, plucked his hat from its shelf, and headed topside.

When he reached the bridge, Thompson and Gunnery Commander Backhouse were standing at the railing outside the wheelhouse and both had binoculars trained on the inner harbor area.

"Good morning, gentlemen," Luce said. "So, what have you got?"

"Morning, sir." Commander Backhouse nodded and stepped to the side, giving Luce his position at the rail.

Thompson turned and handed his field glasses to the captain. "Take a look at the two German merchantmen moored there, near the railyard." He pointed west toward a line of large merchant ships anchored alongside the railroad tracks in the inner harbor. "The passenger steamer and the old collier beside it. There's some unusual activity aboard."

Luce trained the lenses toward the harbor. He quickly found the ships to which Thompson was referring. The smaller of the two vessels was a squat, unremarkable, single-funneled ship, probably twenty or more years old. While it may have hauled all manner of goods at some point in its career, it was now obviously a collier. He could see dockside steam cranes in action and men on deck loading coal from railcars beside the ship. A thin gray fog of coal dust hung over the deck as the men worked to fill the collier's hold with the filthy black cargo. That alone was not unusual, although the men aboard the collier did appear to be working hastily.

He panned over to the adjacent ship, a newer and much larger vessel of perhaps nine or ten thousand tons. It was a passenger steamer, also one-funneled, with three white-painted passenger decks rising above its long, black hull. This ship, by contrast, had much less apparent activity. Luce could see no passengers aboard the ship at all, and the only visible crew members on deck were all near the bow. Another dockside crane and winch had just deposited a large bundle on the deck, and more than a dozen men were gathered around it. As he watched, four men hoisted what looked to be a large, thick, finished piece of lumber, twice as long as the height of a man. They moved it several yards forward, lowered it with some difficulty, and positioned it on an otherwise clear area of the foredeck. Another group of men did the same with an identical piece of wood, placing it near the first.

"How long has this been going on?" asked Luce, watching as the activity continued.

"They've been at this for about an hour now, on both the collier and the steamer," Thompson replied. "We're not sure about the collier, but the passenger liner has been here in port since we arrived. They just moved it down next to the railyard yesterday."

"These are both German ships?" Luce asked. Neither ship was currently flying any flag. He swept his view aft along the larger ship, pausing at the bridge area, where he thought he could make out a dark-clad figure standing near a railing, apparently looking back at him with field glasses as well, but at this distance, he could not be sure.

"Yes, sir," said Backhouse. "The collier is the *Lotte*, and we don't know much about her. She tied up there early this morning, just before they began loading the coal. The passenger steamer is *Cap Vilano*. When we arrived in Rio, she was already moored north of here, in the newer area of the port."

"So, she's been here more than two weeks but hasn't taken on any passengers," observed Luce, handing the binoculars back to Thompson. "Has she been undergoing any repairs?"

"Not that we're aware of," said Thompson. "However, in truth we hadn't been paying much attention until she showed up next to the railyard and they started bringing all that wood aboard. Unusual activity for a passenger ship, I'd say."

"Agreed. Keep an eye on them. If I had to guess, they're bringing those timbers aboard to reinforce their deck for a gun mount. It looks like they're planning to convert *Cap Vilano* into an armed auxiliary cruiser."

The Royal Navy was well aware of *Kaiserliche Marine* contingency plans to convert German merchant ships to armed cruisers in time of war. The basic concept was to take a larger merchant ship, often a passenger liner, and mount a few smaller guns on deck, usually no larger than 4-inch caliber. Such a converted ship would be of no practical threat against an actual warship such as *Glasgow*, but it could be very effective against unarmed enemy merchant vessels. It was likely, he thought, that in ports all over the world, German-flagged vessels like *Cap Vilano* were now being prepared in just such a manner, under orders from the various German embassies and consulates. These ships, once converted, could conceal their newly installed guns under tarps and would appear to a casual observer to be no different than before—until they got within range of a foreign-flagged vessel, at which time they could fire upon and capture or sink their surprised target. The concept was simple and brilliant—so brilliant, in fact, that the Admiralty had drawn up plans to convert some of Britain's passenger liners, if necessary, to counter this German threat and act as clandestine armed escorts for British merchant ships.

Most of the process necessary to convert a merchant ship for auxiliary military use could be accomplished in any reasonably equipped port. Activities such as reinforcing areas of the upper deck for gun mountings, stripping extraneous fittings, and installing or upgrading onboard wireless systems did not require military oversight. However, one part of the process would require direct *Kaiserliche Marine* intervention: delivering the guns themselves. Luce knew that if *Cap Vilano* or any other German merchant ship currently in Brazilian waters were to be converted for military use, it would need naval guns, and those guns would be carried aboard German warships. That was the ominous implication of this activity—if they were converting this ship, they were doing so in the hope that a nearby German warship would be able to equip them with armaments. Just where, he wondered, would that warship be?

"Let me know if you see any other unusual activity, or if any German ship attempts to leave port," he said, turning and making his way down the ladder toward the wireless room just below the bridge. He needed more information about the disposition of German naval assets in the Atlantic. Hopefully the Admiralty or the British legation would know something.

Later that day, *Glasgow* loaded more than eight hundred tons of coal from a Brazilian collier, filling each of the warship's bunkers. As the crew labored with the grimy, backbreaking work of coaling, officers kept watch on the German merchant ships in the harbor. The activity among all of those vessels had increased substantially, not just aboard *Lotte* and *Cap Vilano*. Crews were loading substantial amounts of supplies, and many ships were—just like *Glasgow*—filling their bunkers with coal. The activity near the bow of *Cap Vilano* was apparently complete, but a comparable operation was taking place astern, near the aft wireless mast. They were bringing aboard other supplies as well. As night fell, the Germans continued to work under yellow lights—and the watchful eyes of *Glasgow's* officers.

◆

THE LAST SUNDAY of peacetime was anything but peaceful. Luce had arisen early and had not yet considered breakfast when the first wireless message from the Admiralty arrived and was delivered to his quarters. It stated quite simply:

ADMIRALTY TO ALL SHIPS:

PREPARE FOR WAR.

After briefing his senior officers, Luce began preparations in earnest. He distributed orders throughout the ship. All non-essential items, any unnecessary trappings of relaxed peacetime operations, anything flammable—particularly wooden fittings and furniture—had to go. Objects even partially obstructing a passageway, door, or hatch had to be relocated or removed from the ship. Anything that might hinder combat operations or might throw dangerous splinters or debris among the crew could not remain.

Throughout the ship; on every deck; in every hold, cabin, and passageway, the officers and crew worked throughout the day. With efficient determination, they systematically stripped the ship of anything not directly related to the waging of war. Books, photographs, china, glassware, tables, chairs, carpets, and souvenirs from more than a dozen ports of call began to accumulate in crates, boxes, and bags on deck.

That afternoon, as arranged with the British legation, two lighters from shore began making trips to and from the ship, taking the crates, boxes, and furniture to waiting carriages and lorries on the dock. As Luce surveyed the strange collection being loaded aboard the boats, he was amazed at all of the superfluous cargo they had gathered during the past two years. He also noted the determined but somber mood of the crew around him.

He, too, had packed up many of his personal effects, leaving only the framed photograph of his wife, Mary, that he kept upon his writing desk—a photograph in which she looked much more serious than he knew her to be, but it was his favorite of her nonetheless. In light of his own unexpected emotional reaction to packing up his personal belongings, he had issued a modified order to his officers and crew. Rather than relinquishing every non-essential item among the men's personal effects, he ordered that only the most fragile and flammable of their personal items should be taken ashore. Everything else—personal photographs, keepsakes, and the like were allowed to remain. Most of the books unfortunately had to go, but personal diaries and bibles were exempt. He knew, of course, that many of the men would probably tuck away several banned items despite the prohibition.

He had not, however, expected the request from one of his lieutenants and a chief petty officer that the men be permitted to keep all of the caged parrots they had purchased during the previous fortnight, before their commission was extended. Apparently, the original vendors would not take the birds back under any circumstances, and the British legation had no means to house or take care of all of the squawking and chirping parrots. The crew had become quite attached to the birds, and one of the little feathered noisemakers had already been taught to whistle the chorus of *Rule, Britannia!* Realizing that there was little harm in keeping them aboard—and thinking that their presence on the ship might provide a small boost to the men's morale—Luce agreed to the request.

The ship's dog, Dhobey, was another matter altogether. He had never acquitted himself well as a hunting dog, despite numerous attempts to train him on hunts over the past two years. The spaniel was simply too wild, too playful—and Luce surmised, probably not the smartest pup in his litter. The poor animal also suffered terrible frights from the noises of the guns, and after every gunnery practice, Dhobey could be found cowering under a cot or berth, usually having urinated copiously all over himself. No, this was not an animal suited for the rigors of naval combat. The dog would have to be turned over to the legation.

Luce had received word via wireless that Minister Robertson wanted to meet with him again in person and had planned to come out to the ship later that day. By mid-afternoon, the bustling activity had reached a crescendo. The starboard lifting boom had to be repaired after two bolts at its base cracked. A man was slightly injured when a poorly arranged stack of crates toppled onto his foot and ankle. Soon thereafter, Luce unfortunately found himself intervening between the assistant paymaster and three contract Maltese canteen personnel who were now terrified to find themselves employed aboard a ship heading off to war. They demanded to be put ashore immediately, and the captain acquiesced, much to the chagrin of many of the crewmen who had come to appreciate their culinary skills. At the height of the chaos, a lieutenant informed the captain that a steam launch had arrived alongside with the British minister and two aides.

Luce and Robertson met in the senior officers' wardroom, which now seemed austere with most of its wooden paneling and furniture removed. The room's largest table and chairs remained, but little else.

"And I thought the Germans knew how to throw a party," quipped Robertson with a smile.

"Only the best for our diplomatic corps," replied Luce. "I'd offer you some tea, but amid all this disorder, I'm sure someone has sent it ashore, along with something else we'll be wanting in a few days."

"This visit will be all business, I'm afraid." Robertson was dressed more formally than at their last meeting, wearing a dark suit and tie, his hat tucked under one arm. "After your message yesterday, I made some discreet inquiries of my own. Firstly, regarding the German steamer *Cap Vilano*—it turns out she was recently purchased by the *Hamburg-Amerika* line. She was supposed to return to Germany three weeks ago but instead has been sitting here in port. She has no new passenger manifests that we're aware of, nor has her captain filed any paperwork with the harbormaster, other than to extend her stay another week. As you noticed, she was moved yesterday near the railyard, where she took on coal, food, water, supplies, and several loads of timber.

"Additionally," Robertson continued, "what you probably could not have seen was that two German embassy officers and some otherwise unidentified men, possibly local German agents, also went aboard and spent most of the day there. We believe that two or more of the unidentified men remained aboard the ship and intend to leave with her."

"That does seem to confirm my suspicions that they're planning to refit her as an auxiliary cruiser," Luce nodded. "They were interested in our activities as well. They watched us throughout the day."

Robertson walked over to the porthole, looking out westward toward the inner harbor. "We couldn't confirm that *Lotte* had been chartered by *Cap Vilano* as her collier, but it probably wouldn't matter. A number of other German ships here in Rio could fulfill the same duty. All of them are currently loaded with coal and fresh supplies."

"Mr. Robertson, if *Cap Vilano* is being refitted as an auxiliary cruiser, that means that somewhere, somehow, they must rendezvous with a German warship to transfer naval guns aboard. Thus far, the Admiralty have provided no precise information, other than to say that the German light cruisers *Dresden* and *Karlsruhe* met up at Port au Prince a week ago.

Quite frankly, the location of either of those warships is much more of a concern to me than the possibility that these chaps are refitting this passenger liner for military use." The reality was that a large, slow, armed merchant ship would be much easier to track and neutralize than actual German naval vessels. Luce knew that although *Glasgow* was more than a match for either *Karlsruhe* or *Dresden*, finding them before they could inflict serious damage on British trade could be difficult.

Robertson turned back from the porthole. "Unfortunately, I have no information about *Karlsruhe*, but we did hear from one of our colleagues in St. Thomas that *Dresden* coaled there two days ago."

"That's good to know," Luce replied. "St. Thomas is more than three thousand miles from here. *Dresden* couldn't be meeting up with any German merchant ships near here for at least a week, if this is even where they are headed, of course." He could not imagine that a rendezvous with a German merchant vessel could possibly be *Dresden's* first priority. Instead, it was much more likely that the German warship would begin looking for targets of opportunity among the hundreds of British or French merchantmen heading to and from the Americas. Either of those cruisers could be anywhere from the coast of the United States to the mouth of the Amazon.

"If Britain declares war," Luce continued, "finding one or both of those German warships will become our immediate priority."

"Understood. Of course, we will pass on any information we come across. The legation is at your disposal to help you hunt them down in any way we can. I'm just sorry I couldn't be of more help at this moment."

"Actually," Luce replied, "this information is helpful. At least we know that we don't yet have German cruisers on our doorstep. We can continue our preparations without worrying about an immediate naval engagement."

"Speaking of your preparations," said Robertson, "is there anything else my office can do to assist you and your men?"

"You've done so much already, thank you. Because of the efforts of you and your staff, by this evening we'll have offloaded nearly everything that is to go ashore to be stored. We have provisions for a month of operations, and we're also fully coaled. About the only item of business that remains is finding an appropriate new home for our dog."

Robertson smiled. "Yes, one of my aides mentioned that we'd be taking your spaniel back with us. I'd appreciate the honor of escorting him myself."

◆

THE FOLLOWING DAY was strangely quiet. As *Glasgow* waited, moored offshore in the outer harbor, the weather in and around Rio de Janeiro was still, with no wind, no waves, and not a cloud in the sky—as if the entire world was taking a deep breath before plunging into some unseen depth. The officers and men soberly completed the routines of their watches, with little chitchat. The messes were quiet. Even the dozens of parrots aboard the ship were oddly silent, perhaps sensing the somber mood of the men around them. Here and there throughout the day, someone found an odd piece of superfluous wood or canvas that had been overlooked the day before. These items were simply tossed overboard, and in the still waters of the harbor, random pieces of debris floated lazily about the ship.

The one area aboard *Glasgow* that was not quiet was the wireless room. All day, new telegrams arrived continuously. Each message that Luce read carried more dire news than the last. Germany had declared war upon France, and its forces were already advancing rapidly into Belgium. Britain issued an ultimatum to Germany to withdraw its forces by midnight or a state of war would exist between the two nations. Around noon, a message arrived from the Admiralty:

ADMIRALTY TO ALL SHIPS:

THE BRITISH ULTIMATUM TO GERMANY WILL EXPIRE AT MIDNIGHT GMT, AUGUST 4. NO ACT OF WAR SHOULD BE COMMITTED BEFORE THAT HOUR, AT WHICH TIME THE TELEGRAM TO COMMENCE HOSTILITIES AGAINST GERMANY WILL BE DISPATCHED FROM THE ADMIRALTY.

Later that afternoon, with *Glasgow's* boilers fired up and smoke curling from her four funnels, the crew prepared to leave port. Sailors secured the ship's boats, furled awnings, darkened lights, and manned their stations. As the sun slipped over the western hills, Luce ordered the anchors raised and for the ship to proceed out to sea beyond the three-mile territorial limit—to await the final telegram. As they got underway, the wireless room began picking up messages sent out by several moored German merchant ships, each warning of *Glasgow's* departure from the port. At nine in the evening in Rio, the midnight deadline passed in London. Shortly thereafter, the telegram arrived:

ADMIRALTY TO ALL SHIPS:

COMMENCE HOSTILITIES AGAINST GERMANY.

Luce read the message again, marveling at how much could be conveyed in so few words. He directed the helmsman to steer northeast, and HMS *Glasgow* slipped through the gentle swells under a canopy of brilliant stars.

T W O

*Thursday, August 6, 1914*
*Ponapé Island in the Caroline Islands, Pacific Ocean*

FOR THE MEN of Germany's East Asia Squadron, war had come to them in paradise. From behind the starboard bridge railing of the armored cruiser SMS *Gneisenau*, Captain Julius Maerker looked out over the shimmering blue surface of the placid lagoon. Where the water met the crescent-shaped shore, a rich cascade of green foliage swayed and danced over the lapping azure ripples. No beach marked the transition; rather the jungle met the sea directly, its coiled vines and broad fronds leaning expectantly over the water, unable to continue their creeping advance. Behind that shoreline, a tropical forest, thick with soaring palms and tangled mangroves, formed an emerald canopy that climbed steeply upward. Scores of silvery waterfalls cascaded from the misty green heights. Above it all, a dark stone monolith, the remnant of an ancient volcano, towered over the island. Ponapé was truly one of the most beautiful places Maerker had ever seen.

Five ships were moored within the large, reef-encircled lagoon. Three were warships—their light gray paint gleaming almost white in the tropical sun. Near *Gneisenau* lay her sister ship, the nearly identical armored cruiser SMS *Scharnhorst*, flagship of Vice-Admiral Maximilian Graf von Spee, the squadron's commander. The light cruiser *Nürnberg* was moored farthest out toward the reef, having arrived only that morning from Hawaii. Beside her was the chartered Japanese collier *Fukoku Maru*. The fifth and smallest ship was *Titania*, a lightly armed supply ship attendant to the squadron. The presence of these vessels, particularly the massive twin armored cruisers, was an incongruous contrast to the tranquil beauty of their surroundings.

Most of the activity in the lagoon centered on *Nürnberg*, as her crew labored to simultaneously coal the ship, bring on fresh supplies, and strip it of its woodwork, flammable furnishings, and other extraneous peacetime fittings. Both Maerker's ship and that of his admiral had completed their wartime preparations days before, as they awaited *Nürnberg's* arrival. They had sent the items ashore to the small colonial village, where a representative of the local German trading company had been contracted to store the cargo. All hands aboard *Nürnberg* now worked in haste, and each of the other ships had lent a number of sailors to help, for the admiral planned to leave the island the next day.

As Maerker watched the activity at the far end of the broad lagoon, his first officer, Commander Hans Pochhammer, walked up briskly beside him and stood at attention. He held an envelope in one hand.

"I have a message from the admiral, sir," Pochhammer said, formally presenting the envelope. "A courier from *Scharnhorst* just delivered it, sir." He remained standing stiffly, as Maerker opened the envelope and pulled out a single sheet of the admiral's personal stationery.

"Thank you. At ease, Commander," replied Maerker, looking over the paper. The first officer seemed to relax, but only slightly. The message was a personal request from Admiral von Spee to Maerker, asking that the admiral's son, Heinrich, be granted shore leave in the morning to attend a church service with the admiral. One of the curiosities of Maerker's new command was that one of his junior lieutenants was Graf Heinrich von Spee, the younger of the admiral's two sons. The admiral's other son, Otto, was a lieutenant aboard *Nürnberg*.

Thus far, having a young *graf*, or count, among the crew had not been an issue at all, even though this particular count was also the son of their admiral and squadron commander. Maerker had found that Lieutenant Heinrich von Spee was a humble, unassuming, and hard-working young officer who eschewed any notion of celebrity or privilege. Only Pochhammer appeared to show any deference at all to Heinrich. The usually rigid and demanding first officer softened a bit when dealing with the admiral's son, occasionally reserving more choice duty assignments for the young man. Maerker had slowly become aware of this preferential treatment and intended to say something to Pochhammer—but their sudden preparations for war had taken precedence over such mundane matters.

The admiral's request was not unreasonable. *Nürnberg* had been gone for several months, tending to German interests along the coast of Central America. Now that she had returned to the squadron and the admiral had his two sons together, however briefly, he wanted to see them before they all put to sea again.

"Thank you, Commander," he said again, nodding to his first officer. "I will talk to the courier and send my reply to the admiral." Maerker paused thoughtfully, then added, "Could you check with the paymaster to ensure that we have received all of the provisions requisitioned from the colony?" Maerker had found that Pochhammer's usually stiff demeanor had actually worsened since the declaration of war, and keeping him busy overseeing the stripping of the ship and their preparations for departure was an effective outlet for his energies — and helped keep him from unduly aggravating the other senior officers while they waited here at Ponapé.

"Yes, sir." Pochhammer nodded curtly, turned crisply on his heel, and left the bridge.

Across the water, a cheer went up from the men aboard *Nürnberg*. Apparently, their coaling was complete. Before heading to the signals bridge, Maerker paused to look back up at the looming volcanic mountain once more, knowing that the war would take them far from beautiful places such as this.

◆

THE ORIGINAL PLAN had been much different. The German East Asia Squadron was based in Tsingtao, China, the port from which Germany oversaw its diverse empire in the Pacific. Not only did their presence at Tsingtao provide Germany with invaluable direct access to rich Chinese mines and bountiful trade, but from that port, their warships could also protect economically critical German shipping and maintain order among the dozens of island possessions under their control.

That summer, the ships of the squadron were to embark upon a cruise throughout the southwest Pacific, visiting each of the island colonies, speaking with local German magistrates and native officials, delivering supplies, and generally reminding everyone who ultimately was in charge. Maerker had heard the admiral refer to this planned Pacific cruise as "tending to the fences of the empire."

Although Captain Maerker was a seasoned officer, this was his first time in the Pacific. In fact, he had taken command of *Gneisenau* only two months earlier. Previously, he had been the captain of the light cruiser *Magdeburg*, a fast, experimental torpedo ship operating out of Kiel. As a rising officer, he had served once before under Admiral von Spee, then Chief of Staff of the North Sea Command. When the previous commander of *Gneisenau* rotated back to the High Seas Fleet, Graf Spee specifically requested that the promising and innovative Captain Maerker join him in Tsingtao.

The schedule had been hectic. Less than three weeks after assuming command, Maerker and *Gneisenau* had left Tsingtao for Nagasaki, coaling there and retrieving messages for the admiral from the German consulate. After meeting up with *Scharnhorst* for brief stops at the German possessions of Saipan and Truk, where they received word of the worsening political situation in Europe, the timetable for the original cruise had to be abandoned. The ships had been moored here at the Ponapé colony for two weeks, awaiting further orders from the *Admiralstab* in Berlin.

Maerker realized that there were certainly worse places to have to wait. The island was spectacularly beautiful, blanketed in lush green vegetation and ringed by coral reefs that protected the calm blue waters of multiple lagoons. This German colonial possession, which had been purchased from Spain only sixteen years earlier, had quite a few German residents, many of whom had come to Ponapé because of the booming trade in copra. In addition to the governor and his administrators, this remote island was now home to a number of German businessmen, farmers, traders, and their families. The governor maintained a small garrison of colonial troops to keep order, and a handful of priests at the Catholic mission ministered to as many natives as they could reach. This small German community was honored to host the admiral and his squadron, and they ensured that the crews of the warships had plenty of food, livestock, fresh water, and even bathing facilities—which may have been the greatest luxury of all.

Germany's possession of this colony had gotten off to a rocky start. The island's native inhabitants had long chafed under Spanish governance and were no happier with their new German masters. Their resistance to colonial rule festered and grew into a full-blown rebellion that had turned violent in 1910. During the resulting clash between the native warriors and the settlers, several German citizens were killed, including the governor, and ships from the East Asia Squadron had to ultimately crush the rebel stronghold by shelling it from beyond the reef. In the years since then, the natives assumed a grudging acceptance of German rule, and the colony had been relatively quiet and peaceful.

The day after the arrival of the German ships, Admiral von Spee presided over a solemn ceremony on the grounds of the mission. Beneath the bell tower of the church, he placed a small stone memorial that had been brought from Tsingtao. It commemorated the colonists and soldiers who had lost their lives in the uprising four years earlier. Maerker was impressed with the quiet, reverential manner in which the admiral handled the affair, speaking of the sacrifices made for the Fatherland by all German citizens in remote corners of the empire—and that he wished to ensure that those sacrifices were never forgotten.

Later that same day, the senior officers of the squadron were invited to a banquet in their honor, hosted by the native tribes of the surrounding villages. Whether the motive for this ceremonial welcome was derived more from fear than diplomatic protocol was unknown to Maerker, but it appeared to him that the native leaders welcomed them with sincere warmth and hospitality. The elders of each village, in fact, treated the captains and the admiral as if they were the chiefs of a visiting tribe.

The admiral and each of the ships' captains sat at places of honor and were presented with woven garlands of flowers and leaves. They and the senior officers dined on roast fowl, barbecued reef fish, and an array of fruits and vegetables while they watched tribal dancers cavort by firelight. The initial dances were more warlike, with the men clashing spears and thumping their heels into the earth. Later, the dances became more ceremonial and somber—the remnants of some ancient ritual. Maerker noted that his officers were particularly appreciative of the copper-skinned female dancers, who wore naught but short flowing skirts of palm fronds, with their breasts bared and their legs adorned with ornate tattoos. Maerker reveled in the entire evening, thinking it was like a magnificent exotic scene right out of a novel by Defoe or Stevenson.

◆

IN THE DAYS TO COME, the news from Europe worsened with each new message relayed from Tsingtao by the powerful wireless station on the German-administered island of Yap. War appeared to be imminent. Realizing that the scheduled Pacific cruise was going to be canceled outright, the admiral had recalled *Nürnberg*, instructing her captain to meet them in Ponapé after a coaling stop at the American possession of Hawaii.

Curiously, although the news reports were getting worse, the squadron received no definitive news from the *Admiralstab* in Berlin. A brief message on July 22nd simply told the admiral to remain where he was and await further orders. Maerker attempted to alleviate the monotony of the routine aboard the moored *Gneisenau* by allowing shore leave for the men to sightsee on the island, attend church services, visit with the local German populace, and engage in whatever other constructive activity they could devise. One morning, a few of the men even commandeered some local native canoes for competitive races in the lagoon. Soon, however, even these diversions seemed inadequate. Ironically, even a tropical paradise could eventually feel like a prison.

On July 29th, Maerker accepted an invitation from Admiral von Spee to accompany him on a hike to the top of Sokehs Peak, the impressive black rock looming over the lagoon. Maerker knew the admiral to be an avid naturalist, an interest he shared as well. With no word yet from the *Admiralstab* and no definite plans for their departure, a chance to leave the moored ship and break the daily cycle of inactivity was welcome.

The following morning, they met on the shore beneath the peak, across the bay from the colonial village. Admiral von Spee and Captain Maerker were joined by Captain Otto Filietz, the admiral's chief of staff. The three officers were accompanied by an equal number of seamen bearing packs and rifles and two local native guides who had been recommended by the governor.

Maerker had first met Captain Filietz on his long voyage aboard *Patricia* when he joined the East Asia Squadron in June. Maerker was initially buoyed by the presence aboard the transport of another newly assigned captain to the squadron—hoping to strike up a friendship. However, Filietz was strangely aloof, keeping to his cabin for most of the trip. Consequently, Maerker knew little about him, other than he had spent most of his career in the offices of the *Admiralstab*, working on various administrative issues with the fleet. Since their arrival, he had encountered Filietz only a few times in the past two months, and it seemed that the reclusive officer's time was spent either attending directly to the admiral or sequestered in his cabin.

Inexplicably, for today's expedition, Filietz was dressed in his standard shipboard uniform—and with his slight frame and sallow complexion, Maerker thought he looked ill-suited for any type of strenuous activity, particularly a hike to a jungle mountaintop. By contrast, both Maerker and the admiral wore khaki and white tropical gear, broad straw hats to guard against the sun, and sturdy leather boots. Both Maerker and Graf Spee were tall, the tallest officers in the squadron. The admiral was a striking and regal figure, even in this less-than-official garb, with piercing blue eyes and a close-cropped, pointed white goatee and moustache. Maerker had a more casual bearing, and he wore his brown hair and mustache slightly longer than most of his peers would have thought appropriate. He disdained the formal dress that was so often required for official functions, so this tropical attire was much more to his liking. Maerker's wife, Ilsa, had often teased him about his relaxed approach to uniformed protocol, in a playful attempt to convince him to "try to at least look the part of a naval captain." Thus far, however, his lack of interest in the sartorial aspects of the job had not overshadowed his skills as a commander.

Filietz uneasily shifted his weight from foot to foot and sniffed the air with disapproval. Although the morning was still cool, he was perspiring around his temples—and he dabbed at his face intermittently with a handkerchief.

Graf Spee turned to his chief of staff with a smile. "I finally get you out of your cabin and into the sunshine, and you look as happy as a condemned man. The least you could do is make an attempt to have a good time."

Filietz nodded, but his dour expression did not change. "Of course, sir." Apparently, coming along on this outing had not been his idea.

The admiral turned back toward Maerker. "Gentlemen, let's go see what this island looks like from up there." The men gazed up at the black cliff looming above them, then started off along the trail, following the two native guides.

As the path wound southwest from the periphery of the village, it became a narrow but well-worn track through ever-thickening foliage. The men were forced to follow single-file behind their diminutive, barefooted guides. Among the Germans, the admiral was in the lead, followed by Maerker and then Filietz. The armed seamen brought up the rear, bearing packs laden with food and water. As they traveled, ferns and fronds brushed against their legs, and soon the canopy above was thick enough that much of the direct sunlight no longer reached the ground, instead casting a diffuse green glow over them.

Maerker had never heard such a cacophony of birds and insects as they made their way through the dense, humid undergrowth. Occasionally, the admiral would pause to examine an unusual flower, a fern, or an unknown species of butterfly; then they would resume their trek. The path began to tilt upward as it slowly turned toward the sloping southeastern side of Sokehs Peak. As the path became steeper, Maerker could hear Filietz's breathing behind him become more labored. He began to drift farther behind Maerker and was ultimately overtaken by two of the three seamen, who were determined to maintain the pace set by the guides and not let the admiral out of their sight. The third sailor, in deference to Filietz's rank, slowed down and walked more slowly, trailing the fatigued officer.

An hour into their climb, the canopy over their heads thinned as the trail approached the top of the volcanic cone. The guides, followed by Graf Spee, Maerker, and the two sailors, stepped into brilliant tropical sunshine once again as the ascent became more gradual. Filietz and his escort were still trailing some distance behind them. Up here, instead of the mulchy, leaf-carpeted soil, the path became dark and rocky. The guides abruptly stopped, muttering nervously to each other in their native tongue. Gesturing, they indicated that they would proceed no farther.

Ahead, the trail led upward into a ragged clearing on the ridge. In its center were the remnants of a crude fortification. A walled stone enclosure, roughly oval in shape and perhaps thirty meters across, dominated the space. The stones were of different shapes and sizes, and the walls themselves looked as though they had been hastily or haphazardly built. In some places, a wall still stood as it had originally been built, about the height of a man. However, in many places, the stones had collapsed and were slowly being consumed by the creeping green carpet of the jungle.

Around this ruin, the jagged stumps of dead trees reached up from the foliage—their lifeless, twisted shapes trailing vines and tendrils. A few other large, jumbled piles of volcanic rock lay about the area, partly covered with greenery—perhaps the toppled remnants of other structures.

"What is this place?" Maerker asked, peering over the nearest section of wall into the leafy, overgrown interior of the oval.

"The rebellion, four years ago. This is where the native rebels made their last stand," answered Graf Spee, "before our ships' guns bombarded this ridge and our troops were finally able to take their position." He paced around the eastern perimeter of the wall. "I have always wanted to see this place."

"They probably hadn't counted on an artillery barrage when they came up here." Maerker tilted one of the loose stones with two hands, then let it slip back into its spot on the old wall. He looked back down the trail from which they had come. Their two native guides were sitting at the edge of the forest, determined not to venture any closer. The two sailors stood nearby, chatting quietly while they waited. Maerker evaluated the surrounding area, thinking that it was well suited for such a retreat. "It looks like the route we took is the only way up here. Defending it was probably relatively easy. This rock is a perfect natural fortress."

"I agree," replied the admiral, walking to the edge of the ridge and looking down at the steep slope below. His presence startled a flock of small brown starlings, which took flight and soared off toward the treetops below. "Choosing this spot was tactically brilliant. It was nearly impregnable, even though their construction here was crude, and many of the rebels had outdated weapons. Of course, our army commander made the most critical mistake in warfare. He foolishly underestimated his enemy, thinking that such backward native savages couldn't possibly withstand a modern military assault. These 'savages' had probably been using this rock as a fort and sanctuary for centuries before they ever saw a white man. Our commander got three of his men killed and twice as many wounded trying to fight his way up here. Had our ships not intervened with direct artillery fire upon this fort, the locals might have held out for weeks instead of days. Many more of our countrymen would have perished needlessly."

"How many of the natives died here, defending this spot?" Maerker asked.

"A few dozen. Of course, after our shells began landing up here, most of the warriors fled, somehow making it down the mountainside over there." Graf Spee gestured toward the western slope of the ridge, which looked just as steep and forbidding as the other sheer faces. "Eventually, as you probably know, they were all captured. The leaders were tried and executed, and everyone else from that tribe was relocated to Palau. Some four hundred people, I believe."

At that moment, Captain Filietz and his escort finally reached the clearing. He was breathing heavily and sweating profusely. He must have lost his handkerchief, because he now used his sleeve to mop sweat from his brow. His white uniform was drenched with moisture, and he had slightly torn his left pant leg. He paused and bent over, resting his hands on his knees. The third sailor joined his seated companions, and Maerker noticed that they shared a silent smirk between them.

"Glad you could join us, Mister Filietz," bellowed the admiral with a broad smile. "I was beginning to wonder if we would have to send a search party back for you. Captain Maerker and I were just about to climb onward to the summit. It is only a few meters farther. Would you care to join us?"

Filietz looked up with narrowed eyes. "Thank you, sir, but I'd prefer to sit for a few minutes. Please go on without me." He shuffled to a nearby pile of rocks and sat down with an audible sigh. "I need some water," he said pointedly to the sailors. The man who had arrived with Filietz held out a canteen, and the officer drank in loud gulps.

"As you wish. We shouldn't be too long." The admiral turned back toward Maerker and they began walking upward again, this time clambering up the rock slab itself. "I definitely need to get that man out in the fresh air more often," he said, quietly enough that only Maerker could hear him. "I asked the *Admiralstab* for a new chief of staff, and instead they sent me a bookkeeper." He shook his head, and they continued climbing.

The rocky path continued upward for another forty meters or so, finally reaching the broad round summit. The view was extraordinary. Both men simply stood and took it in.

To the north lay the shimmering lagoons, one of which currently sheltered their ships. Beyond these relatively placid pools were the reefs, upon which pounded a strong surf, inaudible to them from this distance. Past the reefs lay the open sea. Their visibility extended for more than a hundred kilometers in every direction. Below them to the east lay the rooftops of the colonial village, which from this vantage point looked like little more than a few tiny dwellings scattered among a rippling green carpet of treetops. Ever so small, the German flag fluttered above the trees, indicating the position of the governor's offices near the center of the village. The mountains to their south, which dominated the bulk of the island, were a brilliant emerald, and a feathery mist drifted about the peaks. Maerker counted at least ten more waterfalls visible from this elevation and reflected that this truly was paradise. Then his attention was drawn to the western horizon.

"Weather coming in," noted Maerker, looking westward at a roiling gray cloud bank forming some forty kilometers away.

"Indeed," agreed Graf Spee, appraising the developing weather system. Storms and squalls were a daily occurrence here, with powerful driving rains and even occasional lightning. Usually, after the furious storms had passed, the sun would reemerge, shining as if not a drop of rain had ever fallen. "We probably have just enough time for some lunch."

The admiral called down to the men below, telling them to bring the food to the summit. Two of the sailors clambered up the rock and helped set out a simple meal of bread, cheese, and some white wine for the two officers. Filietz chose to stay below, eating his lunch without moving from his chosen rocky seat.

When the sailors had once again retreated out of earshot, the admiral turned to Maerker and asked, "So, how is your command thus far? Is everything well aboard *Gneisenau*, now that you have a couple of months under your belt?"

"Honestly, it is the finest ship I have ever been on—truly an engineering wonder. The crew, of course, is first-rate. I am still getting to know many of them, but it is coming along nicely. They, like the rest of the men in the squadron, are probably better trained and focused than any in the home fleet. Even the fresh recruits who came with me on *Patricia* have acclimated well. The crew is already a cohesive unit." He paused, thinking of the rumblings of war from Europe. "I think they will be well prepared for whatever the Kaiser has in store for us."

"Good to hear. It may be that the Kaiser will send us to sink some Russian or French warships," replied Graf Spee, matter-of-factly. "The prospect of war appears more likely with each new message from Berlin."

"Neither the Russians nor the French would pose much of a threat against our squadron," noted Maerker. The obsolete Russian Pacific Fleet, since their devastating loss to the Japanese at Tsushima nearly ten years earlier, had become an afterthought, as Moscow concentrated on its naval deployments in the Baltic and Black Seas. The French had but two warships in the whole Pacific—the aging armored cruisers *Montcalm* and *Dupleix*. Neither of these nations could oppose the powerful East Asia Squadron in any meaningful way. Maerker knew, however, that these forces were not the squadron's greatest threat. "But what if it is not just the Russians and the French?" he asked.

Graf Spee paused briefly before replying. "If we must fight against the British as well, that will be another matter altogether. Hopefully it will not come to that." He finished the last sip of his wine. "Although they are our rivals, the British are a vastly more civilized people than either the Russians or the French. Perhaps London will ultimately decide to let this conflict pass."

"Yes, we can hope they do." Maerker replied quietly, thinking that such a hope was wishful at best.

The wind picked up, swirling over the exposed rock outcrop and rustling the jungle canopy below. The gray cloudbank had darkened considerably and was advancing rapidly toward the island. Both officers packed up the remnants of their meal and made their way down toward the rest of the group.

"I believe our lunch break is officially over," said the admiral to the waiting men below and gesturing to the roiling clouds above. "Time to head back down the hill."

Filietz looked up at the admiral, shook his head slowly, and let out an exasperated sigh. As he stood stiffly and began to make his way back down the path, the first raindrops began to fall.

◆

WHEN THE OFFICERS finally returned to their ships later that afternoon, soaked from the downpour, awaiting them were wireless messages from Berlin. The messages stated simply that Austria-Hungary and Serbia were now at war.

Shortly thereafter, signal flags were raised on *Scharnhorst*: "ALL SHIPS MAKE READY FOR DRILL." Maerker gathered his officers, exhorting them to ensure that each area of the ship was prepared, from the weather decks and guns, to the messes and infirmary, to the coal bunkers and weapons magazines, to the boiler rooms and engines. This was the closest they had yet come to full preparations for war.

After long days of routine boredom and idleness, the men relished the new orders and the rush of activity. Every square centimeter of the ship was cleaned and examined. Shells and charges were counted and checked. Guns were lubricated and tested. All of the ship's armor plating was inspected. Every item aboard, large or small, fixed or movable, was cataloged. By afternoon of the next day, *Scharnhorst*, *Gneisenau*, and even little *Titania* were ready for inspection by the admiral.

In the evening of August 1st, they received word from Berlin of *Kriegsgefahr Zustand*, a threatened state of war. Russia had mobilized against Germany. As dictated by standard *Kaiserliche Marine* protocol, each captain ordered that his ship be stripped for wartime duty. Maerker decided that *Gneisenau's* grand piano was a necessary exception to the wartime rules, so it remained in the main officers' wardroom, looking smaller and smaller as the room was steadily emptied of its other amenities. In the days that followed, as the crews continued to remove all other flammable and nonessential furnishings and personal belongings from the warships, they received official word that Germany had declared war upon Russia, then France. The war had begun.

Spirits among the men were high as they diligently prepared the ship for combat. Here and there, Maerker overheard sailors and even officers speaking of their desire to strike at the Russians and the French. All were energized at the prospect of fighting the enemies of the Kaiser and the Fatherland. This was an extraordinary group of men, thought Maerker proudly. They were a credit to the *Kaiserliche Marine*. Soon they would have the opportunity to put to good use all of their training and discipline. All that remained was to gather the other ships of the squadron.

In addition to the large armored cruisers *Scharnhorst* and *Gneisenau* currently at Ponapé, the East Asia Squadron comprised three other ocean-going warships, the light cruisers *Nürnberg*, *Emden*, and *Leipzig*. At that moment, these smaller ships were inconveniently scattered across the Pacific. The admiral had already recalled *Nürnberg*, and she was due to arrive at Ponapé within the next few days. *Emden* had been left behind at Tsingtao to oversee the port while the other ships were on their Pacific cruise. For now, the admiral needed to leave *Emden* where she was, in case the Russians or French made any moves toward Tsingtao. The final ship in the squadron, *Leipzig*, had just relieved *Nürnberg* of duty along the American coast and was currently anchored off Mazatlán, Mexico. Germany's Mexican allies were unfortunately embroiled in a bitter civil war, and Berlin wanted to keep at least one warship nearby to protect local German interests. For now, *Leipzig* was waiting there for a chartered collier—and for further orders from the admiral.

They did not yet know the deployments of their enemies' warships, but it was highly unlikely that any Russian or French vessels were within even three thousand kilometers of their current location. The Russian Pacific Fleet no longer ventured far from Vladivostok or the Sea of Japan. The French ships, having no permanent harbor of their own, usually operated in the vicinity of the British port of Hong Kong. If the East Asia Squadron wanted to sink any of them, they would likely have to go hunting.

◆

ON THE AFTERNOON of August 5th, Maerker was feeling refreshed and confident, certainly better than he had felt in many days. *Gneisenau* and *Scharnhorst* had just returned from the open sea through the narrow break in the foaming reef to anchor once again in the lagoon. The admiral had agreed to Maerker's suggestion that the armored cruisers should conduct target practice. Although the men's spirits were up, keeping them focused on the serious business of preparing for war was critical for morale as they awaited further orders from Germany.

The target practice had gone exceptionally well. *Titania* had towed behind her an old fishing vessel from the colony, upon which they had erected a large, rectangular, canvas-spanned frame. This towed vessel served as the target for the warships, in much the same way that the squadron customarily conducted gunnery practice with towed target barges in the waters off Tsingtao. One of the men who had helped refit the fishing boat for this purpose, a known prankster, had scrawled "*Russische Schweine*" in large black letters on the canvas.

The gunners aboard *Scharnhorst*, steaming in the vanguard ahead of *Gneisenau*, fired first at the towed target, six and a half kilometers away. They had shot well—holing the canvas twice on their second salvo with the solid practice rounds from their large main guns. *Gneisenau's* gunners had also performed splendidly, finding their range quickly. Spotters reported three hits to the target from their second salvo. In fact, after they had made their planned turn behind the flagship and were once again steaming parallel to the target for another broadside pass, the spotters in the foretop piped down that a fourth round must have gone through the hull of the towed sailboat itself, because it was clearly taking on water. Both ships dropped several more practice shells directly on the target with their second pass, sinking it promptly.

On their way back to the island, the admiral had signaled, "WELL DONE. EXCELLENT SHOOTING." Maerker was pleased. The ships of the East Asia Squadron already had quite a reputation in the fleet, having won the Kaiser's Cup for marksmanship in each of the past two years. Although more than a third of the current crew was as new to the ship as he was, Maerker was gratified to see that in the short time he had been captain, their discipline and gunnery were at peak form.

*Titania*, having completed her temporary duty as a towboat, had also returned, and all of the ships were now once again anchored in the lagoon. Aboard *Gneisenau*, crews were cleaning the guns, lubricating the ammunition hoists, and checking the magazines to return the ship to wartime readiness.

Maerker was on deck near the forward main turret with Lieutenant-Commander Johann Busch, his senior gunnery officer. "Outstanding work,

Mister Busch," said Maerker. "Your spotters and gun crews performed beautifully. We even outshot the flagship."

"Thank you, sir, but we still have some work to do before we're ready to punch holes in any actual Russians," replied Busch. "One of the rangefinders was initially miscalibrated, and this exercise didn't really test our ability to conduct sustained salvo fire."

"We'll just have to find a more challenging trial of your capabilities then, won't we?" said Maerker with a smile. Busch was his most trusted officer. He was young for his rank, with a boyish face and short cropped dark hair. In the brief period of his command, Maerker had found the lieutenant-commander to be dedicated, competent, and intuitive. Men like him had a bright future in the *Kaiserliche Marine*.

"I'll look forward to that," Busch replied, "but before we fire another shot at anything, in practice or otherwise, I'm having my men reorganize the main magazines to provide better access to the armor-piercing shells. That should help improve our rate of fire in a real battle"

Maerker nodded, then gestured toward the turret beside them. "Were you able to finish the overhaul of…"

A young lieutenant rushed up to the two men, stopped, and saluted. Maerker paused and turned to him, recognizing him as one of the wireless operators.

"Yes, Mister Picht?" Maerker asked, quietly pleased with himself that he had remembered the man's name.

"Excuse me, sir," he stammered. The young sailor was obviously flustered. "We just received a wireless message from the Yap station, sir. Commander Pochhammer requested that you come to the bridge immediately."

This was probably not good news. Maerker cut short his briefing with the gunnery officer and made his way back up to the bridge. When he got there, the first officer was ranting.

"Unbelievable!" Pochhammer shouted, to no one in particular. All of the officers on the bridge had stopped their activities and were looking at him with wide eyes. He stalked across the wheelhouse and slammed a fist onto a metal panel. "This changes everything! Never would I have imagined that…"

"Mister Pochhammer," Maerker interrupted, "What has gotten you into such a boil?"

Pochhammer turned abruptly, apparently surprised to find the captain already standing there. "Captain, sir! The British! Look at this." He held out a wireless transcript. "The British have declared war on us. Germany has done nothing to them, yet they have sided with the Russians…" He shook his head in disbelief. "…And the French!"

It was true. Britain had issued an ultimatum to Germany to demobilize and withdraw all troops from Belgium. Receiving no response, Britain had declared war on Germany. The squadron was now to regard all British ships as hostile and all British territory as enemy ground. Furthermore, now that Britain was committed to war, it was now possible that Japan may also enter on the side of Britain, Russia, and France. This was disastrous. In one afternoon, they had gone from the prospect of fighting two easily vanquished foes to suddenly facing overwhelming global naval superiority.

For the last two decades, the *Admiralstab* had warily regarded Britain's Royal Navy and its centuries-long global domination of the seas. That domination had become an obstacle to an emergent and truly powerful German empire. The *Kaiserliche Marine* had been steadily building, growing, and innovating. They were now powerful enough that no nation on earth could oppose them—except, of course, for Britain. In fact, the Kaiser's goal had been to build a naval force so daunting that even the British would not risk a catastrophic confrontation with such a powerful opponent. Apparently, however, the Brits were not to be so easily intimidated.

Ironically, they had recently hosted British naval officers in Tsingtao. In fact, just days after Captain Maerker had taken command of *Gneisenau*, the British armored cruiser HMS *Minotaur* had steamed into Kiaochow Bay to pay a visit to the East Asia Squadron. *Minotaur* was the flagship of Vice-Admiral Martyn Jerram, commander of the Royal Navy's China Station, based in Hong Kong. The visit to Tsingtao was a friendly one, of course, but Admiral von Spee had been most displeased with its timing. He was fully engaged in preparations for the long Pacific cruise, and nearly half of his squadron's personnel had just left on the transport *Patricia*, the same ship that had brought their replacements, including Captain Maerker.

The admiral voiced his suspicions to Maerker and the other officers that Jerram had chosen the timing of his visit deliberately, knowing the Germans would be embroiled in the chaos of integrating hundreds of new crewmen while simultaneously preparing for their summer cruise. Grudgingly, they had suspended their trip preparations during the four-day British visit. After all, there had been a long, cooperative, and friendly association between the Royal Navy and *Kaiserliche Marine* in China. British and German sailors and soldiers had even fought alongside each other only fourteen years earlier against Chinese rebels during the Boxer uprising.

Much of the British visit was taken up with sightseeing ashore, games of football, boat races, and other diversions. The evenings involved sumptuous dinners, parties, and even a formal ball at the governor's residence. Two of those dinners, and even a dance, were held aboard *Scharnhorst* and *Gneisenau*, which had been moved alongside *Minotaur* in the inner harbor as a matter of protocol. During those shipboard events, the British officers displayed a keen interest in the two German armored cruisers. They had asked many questions about the guns, armor, engines, and other systems; and they requested a tour of as much of the ships as was permitted. While the British officers claimed that all of this interest in the German ships was only friendly curiosity—they had provided reciprocal tours of *Minotaur* as well—Maerker could not help but feel that a potential opponent was sizing them up. Now that potential had become reality, and those formerly friendly British sailors were suddenly their enemies.

"Sir? Excuse me, sir."

The voice beside him brought him back to the present. Maerker realized that a signals lieutenant was standing beside him on the bridge. "Yes?" he replied, hoping he had not just been standing there like some dazed fool.

"Sir, another message from the flagship." The officer handed over the transcript. The other men on the bridge had resumed their duties, but the murmurs had already begun. News, particularly bad news, traveled at flank speed throughout a warship. Deck by deck, the crew was finding out that they were at war with not only Russia and France, but Britain as well.

Graf Spee's latest message made no mention of the British declaration, for *Gneisenau's* wireless operators had received the message from Yap just as clearly as had the operators on *Scharnhorst*. Instead, it noted that *Nürnberg* had confirmed that she would arrive at Ponapé in the morning, and that upon her arrival, all captains of the squadron were to convene aboard the flagship to plan their departure.

◆

*NÜRNBERG* APPEARED on the horizon at dawn, as predicted. Soon after anchoring in the lagoon, the men of all the ships pitched in to help prepare the new arrival for action. *Nürnberg's* crew would not have the leisure and shore leave opportunities enjoyed by the men of the other ships. The squadron could wait at Ponapé no longer. Within the hour, Maerker was aboard *Scharnhorst* as the captains gathered with their admiral in his stateroom.

"Welcome back, Captain Schönberg." The admiral smiled broadly and shook hands with *Nürnberg's* captain as he entered the room. "You're looking fit and healthy, as always."

"Thank you, sir. It is good to be back, and not a moment too soon. Seems I can't leave even for a few months without a war starting in my absence," he said with a laugh. He then looked to Maerker. "I've been away long enough that I have not yet had the opportunity to meet our newest commander." He extended his hand to Maerker.

"Of course," said the admiral, turning to address both men. "Karl von Schönberg, this is Julius Maerker, *Gneisenau's* new captain"

"Good to finally meet you," said Maerker, shaking the other officer's hand. Captain Schönberg was not as tall as Maerker, but he was a handsome, solidly built man with large, deeply tanned hands and a powerful grip. He wore a slightly graying pointed goatee and mustache in a fashion similar to the admiral's, and his gray eyes glinted with intelligence and rigid determination.

"Welcome aboard, Julius," said Schönberg. "I look forward to serving with you as we smite some enemies of the Kaiser."

Graf Spee motioned to the man in the far corner. "Also, you have not yet met Captain Filietz, my new chief of staff."

"Pleased to meet you, Captain," said Schönberg to the taciturn chief of staff, who simply nodded curtly as the two men shook hands. Schönberg then proceeded to greet the other two men in the room, whom he obviously had known for some time. Captain Felix Schultz, a thoughtful and quiet officer, was technically *Scharnhorst's* commander, although as the admiral's flagship, her command truly belonged to Graf Spee. Schönberg shook his hand warmly, then that of Lieutenant-Commander Friedrich Vogt, commander of the little auxiliary steamer *Titania*.

The admiral's stateroom looked oddly bare and even larger now that most of the wooden furnishings had been removed. In clearing the room, the admiral had made an exception for the long, heavy teak dining table, until recently used for formal dinners but now employed to hold an array of maps and charts. The officers took chairs around the table, facing the admiral, who remained standing, leaning over a large chart of the western Pacific.

"Now that you are back with us, Mister Schönberg," continued Graf Spee, "we must plan for our departure from this place as soon as possible—tomorrow afternoon at the latest. Not only are the British now our enemies, but we must be suspicious of Japan as well. Their neutrality may not hold much longer. Unfortunately, we were sighted by a Japanese fishing vessel several days ago. Although she had no wireless, it is only a matter of time before her captain mentions our encounter to someone. Additionally, this harbor was a well-known, planned stop on our Pacific cruise. Ponapé will be on Admiral Jerram's short list of places to look for us."

"What about Müller and *Emden*?" asked Schönberg.

"He is in Tsingtao, making final preparations to leave," replied Graf Spee. "He's been busy converting two armed merchant cruisers, using the guns from the old *Cormoran*. I have ordered him to meet us in Pagan, hopefully with at least one collier."

"Pagan?" Captain Schultz was concerned. "But Pagan is *closer* to Japan—and probably closer to the British as well."

"True, but it is also closer to Tsingtao, and therefore easier for *Emden* and the colliers to reach without blundering into an enemy ship. Additionally, Pagan is but an insignificant dot in the ocean." He pointed to a spot on the map, about eighteen hundred kilometers from their current location. "The British would dismiss it as an unreasonable anchorage and are unlikely to search for us there. It is one of the few secret bases we've been able to keep from them."

"What about *Fukoku Maru*?" Maerker asked. He was referring to the chartered Japanese collier that was, at that moment, only a few hundred meters away, pulling alongside the anchored *Nürnberg* to begin the coaling process. "Having a Japanese ship contracted to our squadron now seems like a dangerous liability."

"True," answered the admiral. "She has no wireless, but we still cannot trust her captain or crew. Although we have no other collier at this time, we can't risk bringing her with us."

"Could we keep her here on some bureaucratic pretense?" asked Filietz, speaking for the first time. He smiled thinly. "Perhaps the local governor could find some issue with her paperwork, seize her, and hold her here until…"

"And risk a direct provocation of Japan?" interjected Graf Spee. "Japan may not stay neutral forever, but we need not push them over the edge. In any case, the local governor would have no such jurisdiction. No, we'll need to find something else for *Fukoku Maru* to do, while she is still under our charter."

"Perhaps a wild goose chase," suggested Maerker "Some mission that will keep her occupied for a while."

Graf Spee nodded. "I think we can come up with something. However, now we must be on to other matters. Captain Schönberg, can your ship be stripped, coaled, and ready by noon tomorrow?"

"Absolutely, sir. In fact, any member of my crew who isn't ready will find himself left here on this island when we depart."

"Good, good," said the admiral. He leaned back over the chart and explained the remaining details of the departure plan to his captains.

◆

THE FOLLOWING MORNING, the admiral and his two sons went ashore and attended a service at the Catholic mission. No one else was granted shore leave this close to their scheduled departure, so missionaries came out to the ships to hear confessions from those crew members who were Catholic. Not to be outdone, Chaplain Rost, the protestant minister to the squadron, also disembarked *Gneisenau* to briefly visit each of the other ships to provide words of encouragement and faith to the men.

The local governor had seen to it that each ship received a supply of livestock, fruit, vegetables, and fresh water. Cooks had already slaughtered several pigs; the squadron's refrigerated compartments were full of hanging meat; and on every ship, dozens of chickens clucked from small cages.

When the admiral was back aboard the flagship and his sons had returned to their stations on their respective ships, the squadron weighed anchor and steamed out to sea, beyond the foaming reefs.

The collier *Fukoku Maru* was left behind, with orders to depart that afternoon for Samoa to acquire more coal for the squadron, then return to Ponapé. The admiral had arranged with the governor's office to send a German official along to ensure that the collier completed her mission appropriately. If it went as planned, *Fukoku Maru* would be harmlessly occupied for at least two more weeks. The Japanese captain did not know the squadron's current destination, and he had no way of knowing that they would not be at Ponapé when he returned.

As Captain Maerker looked back at the diminishing mountains of the island, dark thunderheads of another squall were forming to the west. He reflected on the extraordinary privilege it was that his naval career permitted him to both serve the Fatherland and travel to far-flung locales around the world. How he would love to bring Ilsa to a place such as this. When they were younger, Julius and Ilsa had been fortunate to travel to some of the great cities of Europe—Vienna, Venice, and even Paris—but Ilsa had certainly never been anywhere like this. Maerker knew she would be awestruck by the pristine beauty of the island and the exotic, almost prehistoric culture of its native inhabitants.

Ponapé steadily receded from his view, becoming little more than a shimmering speck on the horizon. He returned his attention to the helm and looked out over the unfamiliar waters that lay ahead.

# THREE

*Friday, August 7, 1914*
*South Atlantic Ocean, Bahia Coast, Brazil*

FROM *GLASGOW'S* BRIDGE, the senior navigation officer saw the yellow glow of the lighthouse on the northern horizon just before dawn—confirming what the spotter above had seen a few minutes earlier. From this distance, perhaps still fifteen miles away, the light was just a tiny pinprick, but it was unmistakable. They had reached their destination. He piped down to inform the captain.

"Thank you, Mister Portman," Luce replied through the voice pipe. "I'll be there in a moment." The captain was sitting at the desk in his cabin and had just finished reading through a handful of transcribed wireless messages from the Admiralty. The messages had been relayed, encrypted, from Rio de Janeiro and had confirmed that the light cruisers *Dresden* and *Karlsruhe* were the only German warships in the West Indies. Regrettably, the Admiralty did not know the location of either enemy ship.

The trip northward had been mostly uneventful. In fact, the one ship they had encountered was an amazing stroke of good luck. A large British collier, *Wayfarer*, was bound for Rio with its holds brimming with coal destined for the Brazilian railways. When stopped by *Glasgow*, the collier's exuberantly patriotic Welsh captain had enthusiastically complied with Luce's new orders to proceed to a rendezvous point several hundred miles north.

*Glasgow* had then conducted her first wartime drill for action stations. Afterward, multiple officers reported operational or procedural concerns that were already being addressed and corrected. Luce was impressed with the manner in which the crew was committed to becoming as battle-ready as possible. Later that afternoon, he issued an order for all hands to assemble on the aft weather deck, and he took a position above on the quarterdeck rail where he could be seen by everyone. It was an odd and rare sight to witness this gathering of the entire crew—more than four hundred men—standing in silence, looking up at him expectantly.

He unfolded a sheet of paper. "I would like to read a message," he began, speaking loudly so as to be heard even by those men standing far to the rear. "I received it this morning. The message is from His Royal Highness, King George himself, to all of the commanders in the fleet:

> *'At this grave moment in our national history, I send to you and through you to the officers and men of the fleets of which you have assumed command, the assurance of my confidence that under your directions this will renew the old glories of the Royal Navy and prove once again the sure shield of Britain and her empire in the hour of trial.'"*

Luce looked up from the paper at the faces of his men. He was not one for long, formal speeches, but he knew that this occasion called for him to say something to his crew. Luce took a breath and began. "Officers and men of HMS *Glasgow*, the last time that the Royal Navy was required to defend our nation in battle was long ago, before any of our grandfathers were born. I actually believe that His Royal Highness is only partly right. Yes, once again, we are to be the shield of Britain; however, our success will not be because of our commanders, our captains, or our admirals," he said, raising his voice even louder. "Our triumph will be because of you— the officers and men of *Glasgow*. We have served together for two years, and I have come to know and respect every one of you. Now, our peacetime cruise has come to an end, and we find ourselves at war against a powerful enemy—an enemy who will surely test our resolve and our courage. It has been more than a century since Britain has fought a sea-borne war, and the Kaiser's navy may be the most dangerous and capable enemy in our nation's long history. However, you men are just as brave and certainly better trained than the men who fought in Nelson's time. You are an excellent crew aboard a fine ship, and I know that each of you will do his best for our king and our country." He paused, then said, "Three cheers for His Majesty!"

Hearty cheers went up from all the men, then someone in the crowd off to starboard yelled, "Three cheers for the captain!" Four hundred voices cheered in unison, as loudly as they had for their king.

◆

THEY STEAMED NORTHWARD through that day and night, finally reaching their destination at dawn. Luce arrived on the bridge as the waxing daylight began to illuminate the whitewashed pillar of the distant lighthouse, still several miles away.

This place was called the Abrolhos Rocks, a tight collection of five tiny rocky islands that inexplicably rose from the Atlantic some fifty miles from the Brazilian coast. The name Abrolhos, derived from a Portuguese warning to "open your eyes," was an appropriate one, for the barren rocky outcrops and their surrounding reefs and shallows were a deadly hazard to any unsuspecting vessel. Some fifty years earlier, the Brazilian government had erected a lighthouse on the largest of the small islands to help warn ships away. Now the only human inhabitant of this lonely and desolate place was the sole lighthouse keeper himself.

The Abrolhos Rocks technically belonged to Brazil, but they were far beyond the three-mile coastal territorial limit, and this place was nowhere near any regular patrol area for the small Brazilian navy. Luce had thought of this godforsaken spot as soon as war had become imminent. It had no proper anchorage, but the small landforms and the shallows of the reefs provided some shelter from heavy winds and seas. It was not ideal, but it would be enough.

The reefs, although dangerous, were spectacularly beautiful. In many places, the clear blue waters afforded views of the multicolored depths greater than sixty feet. Glittering shoals of reef fish swirled and darted beneath the surface, and an occasional steel-gray shark languidly hunted among the corals. The rocks themselves could hardly be considered islands, with only the sparsest scraps of low vegetation clinging to the wind-scoured promontories. Numerous sea birds made these barren islets their home, strutting and preening on the rocky shores.

The best feature of this place was its proximity to the shipping lanes that ran along the Brazilian coastline. From here, Luce thought, *Glasgow* could coal in relative shelter and operate as if the islands were a base, venturing into the shipping lanes to help warn and protect Allied ships—and, if they were lucky, perhaps catch *Dresden* or *Karlsruhe* if they tried to slip through.

For now, however, coal was their first priority. *Glasgow* had consumed about two hundred tons of coal, nearly a quarter of her capacity, on their way from Rio. Some of that had burned up when Luce briefly took the engines up to their maximum rated speed of twenty-five knots while the ship was conducting its preparatory drills farther out to sea. The engineering commander had reported that they might even be able to squeeze a few more knots out of her, but Luce declined. For now, twenty-five knots was enough to best either *Dresden* or *Karlsruhe*, and he wanted to avoid any unnecessary wear on the engines and boilers.

While they had detoured to conduct their drills, the collier *Wayfarer* had proceeded directly to the rendezvous as ordered. As *Glasgow* neared the islands, her officers spotted the large vessel anchored about three miles southeast of the reefs. After sending lamp and flag signals that initially were misinterpreted by the civilian ship, *Glasgow* was finally able to get the collier to pull alongside in the lee of the largest of the islands. The swell was slight and the winds were virtually still, but even those relatively favorable conditions could not prevent their first open-ocean ship-to-ship coaling exercise from going awry.

*Wayfarer*, at eleven thousand tons, was more than twice the size of *Glasgow*. As the two ships drifted at anchor beside each other, the collier's deck loomed several feet above the warship's, slowly rising and falling on the swells. Neither vessel had proper fenders, and the men's efforts to keep the two ships from colliding were largely in vain. Repeatedly, the hulls met forcefully, the metal surfaces scraping and groaning. Fortunately, none of the cruiser's port side 4-inch gun turrets, which ran along the outboard edges of the upper deck, were damaged in the encounter. However, the engineers reported that in two places, the cruiser's hull plating had been bent enough to require minor repairs.

As the men used the collier's large booms to clumsily swing the sacks of coal aboard *Glasgow* while trying to keep their ship from being rattled to pieces by the adjacent behemoth, they were being watched. From the lighthouse above, the lonely keeper had taken a keen interest in their activities. He used a lamp to signal down to them in jumbled syntax, asking repeatedly what they were doing and insisting that they stop their illegal activities and leave immediately. Luce knew that the lighthouse had no wireless, and therefore the keeper could not alert the Brazilian authorities to their presence. The sailors simply ignored the signals, determined to finish the coaling process as quickly as possible.

After the warship's bunkers were once again full and the men had scrubbed and washed off the residual black grime from all of the outer surfaces of the cruiser, *Wayfarer* returned to her anchorage a few miles from the rocks. Until another collier arrived, she was their only immediate source of fuel.

The engineers finished the minor repairs to the port side hull plating in less than two hours. There was ample time for the men to receive their daily rum ration before the duty rosters were updated and each crewman had his new wartime assignment. The boilers were stoked, the anchors raised, and Luce ordered the helmsman to steer northwest. It was time for *Glasgow* to get to business.

Between their current position and the coast ran one of the busiest sea lanes in the Atlantic. Several hundred miles to the north, off the bustling Pernambuco coast of Brazil, the shipping routes from Europe and North America converged and continued southward toward Rio and ultimately to the key ports of Montevideo and Buenos Aires at the mouth of the *Rio de la Plata*. Merchant vessels from Argentina, Uruguay, Brazil, Mexico, the United States, Britain, Germany, France, Spain, Portugal, and at least a dozen other nations regularly steamed through these waters. Every conceivable cargo transited this route—coffee, hardwood, meat, grain, sugar, nitrates, coal, iron, industrial parts, and machinery. As an island nation, Britain depended upon this nautical lifeline, and the responsibility of protecting these waters fell upon John Luce and the crew of HMS *Glasgow*.

Abrolhos was near the northernmost limit of their designated area of responsibility. Northward, from Pernambuco up into the Caribbean and along the east coast of the United States, British interests were under the protection of the numerous ships of the Royal Navy's Fourth Cruiser Squadron under Rear-Admiral Cradock. Down here, however, *Glasgow* was on her own. If *Dresden* or *Karlsruhe* were to try to intercept Allied shipping, Luce knew this was as good a place as any. With so many potential prizes, so much ocean in which to hide, and only one designated British warship patrolling the area, the merchant shipping off this coast might prove to be too irresistible of a target.

On their first full day of active patrol, they encountered three vessels, none of which was British or German. Luce chose not to board any of them—a French sailing ship, a tiny American merchant steamer, and a coastal Brazilian merchantman. Instead, by signal lamp, *Glasgow* warned each crew of the danger of German warships possibly operating in the area—and of the particular risks near the port of Recife, in Pernambuco to the north. Only the crew of the Brazilian ship was even aware that war had been declared.

On the morning of August 9th, they received a small bit of useful news. An encrypted Admiralty message informed them that two days earlier, a ship in Admiral Cradock's squadron had sighted *Karlsruhe* near the Bahamas and had given chase. Although the German ship had escaped, Luce was assured that at least one of the two German cruisers was nowhere nearby. Unfortunately, *Dresden* had not been sighted in a week, and by now she could be anywhere along the northern Brazilian coast.

On the bridge, Luce was briefing Thompson about this latest development when a thin smoke trail appeared on the southern horizon. Within a few minutes, the spotter above identified the ship as a merchant steamer.

"Helmsman, two points to starboard," Luce said. "Three-quarters speed. Eighteen knots." The warship turned southwest, and the merchantman came steadily into view as they neared.

"She's sporting a Union Jack, sir," said Thompson, looking through binoculars at the fluttering British flag on the steamer's forward mast. "She's a bit smaller than us. A freighter of some sort."

"Well," replied Luce, "let's make sure she's flying that flag for the right reasons." It was a known practice for merchant ships—and even warships—to occasionally fly a false flag to deceive an enemy, to avoid capture, or even to mount a surprise assault. "Signal her to heave-to and prepare to be boarded."

After receiving the signal, the merchant ship did begin to slow, its bow wave slackening, and returned a signal of "Come aboard." Thus far, they were behaving as if their flag were genuine. Luce turned to his first officer. "We'll take their word for it. Prepare your boarding party, Will. You have the honor of conducting our first wartime boarding."

"Thank you, sir," Thompson replied with a smile. "Hopefully we'll remember how to do this properly."

*Glasgow* circled around astern of the steamer and assumed a parallel course three hundred yards to starboard. The merchant ship was of average appearance; in fact, she looked a bit shabby. Faded yellow letters on her stern spelled *Hyades* and "British & South American Steam Nav. Co. - Liverpool". Her black hull was streaked and rusted, and she was in desperate need of a good painting. Several men were on deck, waving to the warship as they pulled alongside and matched speed with the steamer. One of *Glasgow's* small wooden boats was lowered, and Thompson, along with the ship's intelligence officer and three seamen, clambered in. They pushed off and made their way toward the steamer. With two men at the oars, it took only a few minutes for them to reach the merchant ship. Fortunately, the swell was still gentle and they were able to tie up and mount the ladder to the steamer's deck without any difficulty.

Up close, the steamship was no prettier than she had been from afar. The weather deck was a patchwork of bleached wooden planks and riveted metal plating. The single red and black funnel above the peeling superstructure had an obvious crack along a previously repaired seam. As Thompson and the others came aboard, an older man stepped out of the wheelhouse and approached the British sailors. He wore a woolen cap and a black pea coat, his full beard was completely gray, and his thick eyebrows were a haphazard, wiry tangle over his eyes. He walked with a slight hitch in his gait.

"Welcome aboard the good ship *Hyades*," he said, holding out a weathered hand and looking up at the much taller naval officer. "I'm the captain. Morrison's the name. What can I do for His Majesty's Royal Navy this morning?"

"Good to meet you, Captain Morrison." Thompson shook the man's hand. "I'm Lieutenant-Commander Thompson of HMS *Glasgow*. We'll need to conduct an inspection. What's your course and cargo?"

"I've got forty-five hundred tons of Argentine corn headed to Essen via Rotterdam. We left Rosario a fortnight ago. It is all by the numbers, Commander. If there is a problem, I can show you our bill of lading." Although he was being polite enough, the old captain seemed annoyed at being questioned about his business.

"I'm sure it's all correct, Captain, but if you could have one of your men show the paperwork to Mister Hirst, here," Thompson said, gesturing to the intelligence officer at his side, "we'll just check everything out to be sure. We'll also need to inspect your cargo holds."

"Samuels, go show these men our papers," the captain barked at one of his crew, a younger man with close-cropped hair and wire-frame spectacles. The man appeared to be a junior officer, although the attire of this crew was so informal, it was difficult to tell. "Then give 'em all a good look at the holds." Captain Morrison turned back to Thompson with a stern look. "Now, what the hell is this all about—the Royal Navy stopping us out here and treating us like we're smugglers or something?"

Thompson did not answer the question, instead asking, "Essen, you say? As in Essen, Germany?"

"Of course Essen, Germany! What kind of daft question is that? It's not bloody Essen, Ireland. We were chartered by *Nordwesten Liefernd*, a German company, to ship corn from Rosario to Rotterdam. From there it goes on to Essen by rail. They don't have enough damned ships of their own, so they hire ours. Why is this any concern of the Royal Navy, for God's sake? This is good business, and our charter is all in order." The angry merchant captain was apparently unaccustomed to being questioned in this manner.

Thompson smiled and held up his hand as if to reassure the irate man. "I'm certain everything is in order, Captain. The problem is that there's a war on—a war with Germany."

Morrison's expression went from annoyed to perplexed, his eyebrows knitting together. "A war? Seriously? A real war between us and the Germans? When the hell did this happen?"

"Five days ago. The Germans are already fighting the Russians and the French. From what we hear, they've mobilized hundreds of thousands of men. Now we've joined the party as well. Out here we have orders to stop any German shipping. This war is the real thing, Captain." He glanced upward at the ship's mast above them, confirming *Hyades* had no wireless aerial. "You don't have wireless, so if you left Argentina two weeks ago, you couldn't have known."

"Jesus Christ. A fucking war against Germany? Well, I'll be damned..." Morrison paused, then spoke forcefully, pointing an index finger at the commander. "But we're no bloody German ship. This here's a British registered vessel out of Liverpool."

"True," answered Thompson. "But your cargo was headed for Germany. Although a shipment of corn might not be classified as war-related materiel, I highly doubt the German navy would give a damn what you're carrying if you tried to steam right in to Rotterdam, flying the Union Jack, in the middle of a war."

"But we're a British ship. What the hell are we supposed to do with forty-five hundred tons of German corn?"

"Well, I suppose it's British corn, now," replied Thompson. "I would suggest you turn around and make for Rio. Then you can contact your company in Liverpool and get new orders."

"Rio?" Morrison was aghast. "Are you mad, commander? That's five hundred miles and three days backward out of our way. No, no, we'll continue on to Recife, then talk to the home office from there. At least that would still be on our way north, if they reroute us to an English port."

"I'm sorry, Captain, but we've been warning ships away from Recife—and the Pernambuco coast in general. The Germans may have a warship in the area, and we're concerned that they'll be targeting Allied shipping there."

"Jesus fucking Christ! Now the Germans have a goddamn warship here, too?" The old captain was shaking his head and muttering as much to himself as he was to anyone else. "What are we supposed to do now, just steam around in circles with our holds full of German corn, or British corn, or whoever-the-hell it belongs to?"

"Actually, Captain, Rio should be reasonably safe for now. We just came from there, and we have seen no reports of German naval activity in the region. If you can get to Rio, you should be able to receive new orders from your offices back home. After we eliminate the threat posed by the German warships, these sea lanes should be safe again."

Moments later, officer Hirst and the sailor returned from their brief inspection, escorted by Samuels. "Everything seems to be in order, sir," stated Hirst. "Their charter, bill of lading, ship's log, and cargo all appear to be correct. It's all a bit messy, but it looks to be accurate."

Morrison rolled his eyes at the young officer, then turned back to Thompson. "So, Commander, can we now take our load of 'British' corn and our messy paperwork and be on our way?"

"Yes, of course. I'm sorry to have been the bearer of bad news, Captain Morrison. Again, I would strongly urge you to stay clear of the Pernambuco area until we can find that German warship. The British legation in Rio should be able to help you make arrangements with your company officials back home. Good day, Captain." Thompson and the rest of the boarding party made their way back down the ladder to the boat below.

From the deck of *Hyades*, Morrison and his first mate watched the British sailors row back to the waiting *Glasgow*. Samuels turned to his captain with an expectant smile. "Sir, they say that Rio is a beautiful city. It's probably not a bad place to wait while the home office sorts out all of this mess."

"Yeah," replied Morrison. "Too bad we're not going to Rio."

◆

HMS *Glasgow* spent the next several days and nights alternately coaling from *Wayfarer* at Abrolhos and crisscrossing the nearby shipping lanes to warn passing merchantmen of the potential danger northward near Recife. The weather remained favorable, and the clear skies made for easy spotting of passing ships. However, the tropical heat made the nights almost unbearable, because the crew had to keep all hatches battened as part of the standard wartime darkened ship protocol.

Unfortunately, the Admiralty had no further news of *Dresden*, and *Karlsruhe* had disappeared from under Admiral Cradock's nose. Luce began to wonder if Berlin had abandoned its plans to use cruisers to attack merchant shipping and had instead called its warships home.

They received an unexpected but welcome gift from Malcolm Robertson. The British minister had dispatched a small collier from Rio to Abrolhos, which brought not only additional coal, newspapers, and supplies, but also four volunteer recruits from the British community. *Glasgow's* officers and crew welcomed aboard the new men and got them settled into their duties.

The lighthouse keeper had apparently become resigned to their presence near his rocky islands, and he no longer signaled warnings and admonitions to them while they coaled. Occasionally, pods of leaping and blowing humpback whales would visit the ships as they congregated near the reefs and outcrops.

Each day, *Glasgow* intercepted and warned several merchantmen regarding the danger posed by *Dresden* lurking to the north. Luce sent parties to board some of the ships, but none was German. Messages from the legation indicated that most of the German-registered merchant ships in these waters—lacking any formal naval protection—were choosing to stay in port rather than risk capture by the Royal Navy. As the days passed, the anxiety of *Glasgow's* crew increased. The news stories out of Brazil were full of rumor, speculation, and even wild falsehoods—including a claim that German naval forces had sunk nine British capital ships in the North Sea. This story they knew to be completely fabricated, but that fact was of little solace to the men as they hunted—and waited, growing more nervous. Without reliable news of *Dresden's* location, every new streak of funnel smoke on the horizon could be the approaching German warship. Each time, however, the vessel turned out to be yet another merchantman from Brazil, America, France, or Britain.

The messages from the Admiralty did little to assuage their concern. If the five ships of Cradock's squadron could not find *Karlsruhe* in the Caribbean, how was *Glasgow* alone supposed to find *Dresden* in the entirety of the South Atlantic? On August 13th, Luce received word that he would be receiving some assistance. The armored cruiser HMS *Monmouth* had been dispatched with a collier to rendezvous with *Glasgow* at Abrolhos in about a week and would be placed under Luce's command. While their chances of finding the elusive German warship were still slim, two ships were certainly better than one.

The next day, *Glasgow* finally encountered its first German vessel. Just after noon, a spotter reported smoke to the northwest. As they drew near, Luce could see that the oncoming ship was a small commercial steamer with a black hull and white superstructure, heading due south. *Glasgow* moved to an intercept course and sent the customary signal to heave-to. Surprisingly, however, the ship did not slow her engines.

Luce lifted a pair of field glasses to take a look at the unresponsive ship, still two miles away. "Signal them again, Mister Stuart. Perhaps they weren't paying attention the first time." The ship, at least when viewed bow-on, bore no obvious flags or marks of identification.

In a few minutes, the signals officer reported essentially what Luce could already see through the binoculars. The steamer had actually increased her speed and had adjusted course a few degrees away from the oncoming warship.

"Mister Backhouse, let's deliver the message in a different manner. Perhaps we need to speak another language." The two ships were now closing rapidly, less than a mile apart. Black smoke was pouring from the vessel's single funnel, and she was likely steaming at the limit of her speed.

"Certainly, sir," replied the gunnery commander with a wry expression. "I know just how to phrase it for them." Backhouse looked every bit the part of a gunnery officer, big and barrel-chested, with a full brush of a reddish-brown moustache and a broad, square jaw. Luce had often thought that the gunnery commander looked a bit like a bull walrus that had somehow been stuffed into the uniform of a naval officer. Backhouse passed along the orders to his men.

In response to the commander's instructions, a two-man crew armed one of the port side Vickers three-pound guns—a small, auxiliary, deck-mounted gun with a modern, semi-automatic firing system. Unlike *Glasgow's* larger turreted 4-inch and 6-inch guns, these relatively new weapons were too small for real ship-to-ship warfare. They had been designed to enhance the cruiser's capabilities in close-quarters combat, far inside the range of larger naval artillery. The concept was reasonably sound, although in an engagement with another warship, the larger guns would decide the outcome at a range of several miles, long before they would be close enough to use the Vickers guns. Thus far, *Glasgow* had only used them to fire salutes, either to passing warships or as the customary entry signal at foreign ports. Today, however, the gun was loaded with actual explosive shells. "Two rounds, a hundred yards ahead of her bow," said Backhouse sternly. "Fire."

The Vickers fired, sounding from the bridge like a loud crack. Two seconds later, it fired again. A five-foot high splash erupted some ninety yards ahead of the steamship's bow, then a second one slightly closer.

"Give them a moment," said Luce, still watching. Sure enough, the ship's bow wave lessened and the vessel began to noticeably slow its pace. "Good. Looks like that didn't need a translation. Helmsman, bring us about on her starboard side. Let's keep this distance." The men at the three-pounder still had their weapon trained on the steamship. Commander Backhouse had ordered other men on deck with rifles, and they took up positions along the port gunwales. Two other men crewed a port side machine gun and kept its barrel leveled at the deck of the steamer.

The merchant ship was now moving at a slow crawl, with just enough power to maintain control, as *Glasgow* swept around behind her. Her stern read in large white letters, "*Santa Catharina* – Hamburg". Definitely a German ship. *Glasgow* assumed a parallel course and dropped her speed to match that of the steamship. "Two boats and twice the men this time—armed," Luce said. "Mister Hirst, this may be our first German prize of the war. I want everything by the book."

"Yes, sir." the intelligence officer left to assemble his boarding parties. The wartime prize rules as defined by established maritime law were very specific. If a warship stopped a merchant vessel belonging to an enemy nation and determined that the vessel was transporting any cargo that could aid the enemy in its war-fighting effort, the crew of the warship could take possession of the ship, remove the crew for transport to a neutral port, and confiscate or destroy any war-related materiel or cargo aboard. The ship itself and any incidental cargo or goods aboard could then essentially be ransomed back to the country of origin. Most importantly to *Glasgow's* crew, according to Admiralty policies, some portion of that ransom money would be shared as a prize bonus among the men—assuming, of course, that the crew did not violate any of the rules or unnecessarily damage the captured vessel.

Luce was not concerned about collecting prize money, although he knew some of his men might feel otherwise. He thought that prizes and ransoms were archaic throwbacks to a bygone era—and had no place in the modern, professional navy. However, if the capture of an enemy merchant ship were to be poorly handled, especially if the captured ship were to be unnecessarily damaged or sunk, it could cause a serious political flap—and no naval captain wanted that kind of scrutiny.

Luce watched as the boats were lowered and then made their way across to the German ship. A few of *Santa Catharina's* crewmen had gathered on the deck, but they showed no signs of belligerent activity. They just watched as the small British boats crossed the gap between the two ships. The boarding parties tied up alongside, and the sailors climbed ladders and went aboard. Through the lenses, Luce could see Lieutenant Hirst greet and shake hands with three men who must have been the German ship's officers. The armed sailors took up positions on the deck, and the captured crew members were ordered to assemble on deck. HMS *Glasgow* had captured her first prize of the war.

*Santa Catharina* was a relatively new ship and was carrying a mixed cargo of valuable goods from New York to Santos, Brazil. Some of the cargo was exempt under the rules of wartime capture, but many items were on the banned list—certainly enough to justify taking her as a prize. Like many of the other vessels currently transiting the area, *Santa Catharina* had left port before the start of the war and had no wireless. Therefore, the officers and crew had no idea that a war had begun. Needless to say, none of these men were particularly happy to find themselves brought aboard a British warship under armed guard.

As British sailors painstakingly cataloged every piece of cargo aboard *Santa Catharina,* Captain Luce and Commander Thompson took the opportunity to speak to the steamer's officers in one of *Glasgow's* wardrooms. The master at arms stood by as the three German merchant officers were ushered into the room by several Royal Marines.

"Good afternoon, gentlemen," Luce began. "Welcome aboard HMS *Glasgow.* I am Captain John Luce, and this is my first officer, Commander Thompson. Do any of you speak English?"

"We do, although hopefully you'll pardon my pronunciation. I am Hans Reiter, captain of the *Santa Catharina.*" He was a tall, broad-shouldered man in his forties, with close-cropped light brown hair. His English was heavily accented but understandable. Reiter gestured to his right. "These are my senior officers, *Herr* Becker *und Herr* Kämpfer." Luce thought that Becker looked to be the youngest of the three, probably in his thirties. He seemed to be nervous, shifting anxiously on his feet. Kämpfer was an older man, with a full, graying beard and large, wild-looking eyes. He stood stiffly and openly glared at the two British officers.

Luce nodded. "I am sorry that we are not meeting under more pleasant circumstances."

"I was told by your officer Hirst that Britain and Germany are now at war," continued Reiter. "Is this correct?"

"Yes, I'm afraid it is," replied Luce.

"Britain has actually sided with France against Germany? That is hard to believe," said Reiter with a contemplative frown. "Even if it is as you say, by what authority do you seize my ship and crew? We are not a ship of war."

"True. However, you are carrying cargo that may be of material value to the German war effort. Therefore, we are authorized by Hague Conventions to take possession of your ship."

"But surely you can see that we have nothing to do with the war. As you know, we were not even aware that the war had started. No one on board is a soldier or government official, and our cargo is all simple items—common goods of peacetime trade."

Thompson raised an eyebrow and interjected, "If you were only ferrying simple cargo, why didn't you stop or even respond to our repeated signals to heave-to? In fact, you actually increased your speed and attempted to evade us."

Reiter paused and looked over his shoulder disapprovingly at the glowering Kämpfer, who did not react. "One of my senior officers had the helm at that time, while I was attending to a matter with the chief engineer." Reiter paused and shook his head. "I believe that he... misunderstood your intentions and attempted to avoid a collision. I went to the bridge when I realized that we had increased our speed, and that is when you began shooting at us—so I ordered a stop."

Luce could tell that there had already been some cross words exchanged between these men over this incident, and that this version of their story was only partly true.

"In point of fact," Thompson corrected him, "we weren't shooting at you. We were just trying to get your attention. Had we been shooting *at* you, your ship would now have several holes in it."

Reiter stiffened but maintained his polite demeanor. "As I said, we are a peaceful ship carrying routine cargo. We have no weapons; we have no 'war materials.' We were not trying to escape from you. This was just a misunderstanding. Surely you can see that this was a simple error."

Luce noted the emotion in Reiter's face. It was obvious that the German captain had nothing to hide—and certainly he had been surprised to have been intercepted by a foreign warship in international waters.

Reiter continued, "Captain, your men who are searching my ship are undoubtedly confirming what I have said. Our voyage has no connection to this war. Surely you can permit us to continue on to our destination?"

"I am sorry," Luce replied, with genuine sympathy. "It's a bit of bad luck, but unfortunately my orders are quite clear. We are to stop and seize any German commercial vessels. However, I am also duty-bound to ensure your safe passage to a neutral port. You and your crew will be transferred to the next available commercial vessel that can take you. I assure you; no harm will come to anyone, and we will do our best to keep you as comfortable as possible while you are our guests."

The German captain looked crestfallen. "So, I have lost my ship? There is nothing I can do to appeal this seizure?"

"I'm afraid not, Captain Reiter." Luce felt truly sorry for the man. Had the German captain known of the war, he could have put into a safe, neutral port before *Santa Catharina* had ever encountered *Glasgow*.

"*Verdammte Arsch!*" shouted Kämpfer, suddenly striding forward and startling the master-at-arms, who stepped in front of the angry German and prevented him from getting any closer to the British officers. "*Lügner!* You are all liars and thieves. You steal like pirates!"

"That is enough, *Herr* Kämpfer," admonished his captain.

The irate German was not finished, however. "You will lose this war, of course. The Kaiser's armies will crush you…"

"*Genug! Schließen Sie ab!*" Reiter snapped at the older man, who snorted in disgust and stepped back to where he had been standing. Reiter turned back to the British officers. "I am sorry, Captain. Hopefully you can understand how difficult this is for us. Please forgive my officer's outburst."

"Absolutely," replied Luce with a sympathetic nod. "If I were in your position, I'm sure I would have similar things to say, and I might not have been as polite about it. As I said, you and your men will be put aboard the next commercial ship we encounter that can take you to a neutral port. Until that occurs, I will see to it that all of you have food, drink, and a place to sleep—although I'm afraid that aboard a warship, none of those amenities will be luxurious."

The British sailors adhered to the rules meticulously, ensuring that everything aboard *Santa Catharina* was documented and inventoried. Nothing was removed from the ship, although undoubtedly some of the men were tempted by the two hundred bottles of fine ale found in one of her storage lockers. As it turned out, *Glasgow's* crew only had to hold *Santa Catharina's* officers and men for one night, because the next morning they intercepted a small British tramp steamer whose captain agreed to take the prisoners to Buenos Aires to be released.

*Glasgow* could now return to the business of trying to find *Dresden*. Over the next few days, they encountered several more commercial ships, none of which was German. They did have one disconcerting false alarm, when they pursued a thick smoke trail on their southern horizon. The spotter identified the vessel as a man-o'-war, and Luce ordered the ship to action stations. The battle ensigns were raised. Men scrambled to their positions all over the ship—at the boilers, the engine rooms, the signal deck, the munitions magazines, the hoists, and the gun turrets. They waited tensely as they closed on their target, which then was identified as the small Brazilian gunboat *Tiradentes*. Luce ordered everyone to stand down, and *Glasgow* slowed and abandoned the pursuit. However, the incident must have been harrowing for the crew of the Brazilian ship, for even though they received the British signal of greeting, they abruptly turned and fled the scene at full steam.

Although the alert had turned out to be false, the senior officers agreed that it had been a useful drill for everyone aboard. After all, at some point they would be doing this for real—and they could all use some extra practice.

Luce wondered, however, if they would do it for real. He knew that the chances of finding *Dresden* in the open ocean were remote at best. She could be anywhere within a thousand miles of their current location.

He had no way of knowing how close *Dresden* actually was.

◆

FROM THE WHEELHOUSE of the freighter *Hyades*, Captain Morrison watched the sun rise, deep crimson, on the eastern horizon. The sky was already brightening to a brilliant, hazy blue; and the captain inhaled deeply, savoring the crisp morning sea air. After clearing Recife's outer harbor, he adjusted course, heading northeast through a gently rolling sea toward the open ocean. Another cargo ship was leaving the port at the same time, trailing a few miles astern. Morrison imagined that the captain of that other ship was probably enjoying this moment as much as he was. It was a perfect morning to put out to sea.

With smug satisfaction, he turned to his first officer, who was checking the charts once more, reviewing their new course. "Samuels, one day maybe you'll have your own ship. By then, you might know a thing or two about keeping The Company happy. If we'd listened to that damned Royal Navy commander, we'd only be leavin' Rio now, a week farther away down the bloody coast—farther away from unloading this damned orphaned corn and getting paid what we're owed."

Samuels looked out the window at the ever-lightening sea and sky. He adjusted the spectacles on his nose. "Yes, I suppose you're right, sir," he replied with a wistful smile and a resigned nod. "My trip to Rio will just have to wait."

After their brief encounter with HMS *Glasgow*, Morrison had waited until the warship disappeared over the horizon, then adjusted his course northward. Their voyage to the port of Recife in Pernambuco had, of course, been completely uneventful. They had seen no other warships, German or otherwise. Morrison had even begun to wonder if the Royal Navy had collectively gone mad and had fabricated all of this war nonsense. He had put in at Recife anyway just to check in with the home offices in Liverpool, and soon enough he received confirmation by cable— Britain truly was at war with Germany. He noticed that multiple German steamers were moored there in the port, apparently unwilling to leave for fear that they might encounter one of the patrolling British warships.

The home office of the British & South American Steam Navigation Company was initially unsure of their next course of action. They could not very well let *Hyades* continue to her original destination, and the previous charter agreement was with a company in a nation that was now their enemy. After a half-day's debate, they declared the original contract in default. They told Morrison to bring the steamship and her cargo home, assuming that in the two weeks or so that it would take for *Hyades* to reach Liverpool, the company could find another buyer somewhere who would be willing to accept a heavily discounted shipment of fine Argentine corn.

Morrison was pleased. Not only was his cargo not going to be a total loss, but he would get back to England significantly earlier than had originally been planned. After a few days spent at home with the old wife or sampling the fare at his favorite pub on Fenwick Street, he could get another assignment and put back out to sea, hopefully somewhere far from the bloody war.

*Hyades* continued on her northward course as the day progressed. In the early afternoon, Samuels had returned to the wheelhouse after having a quick smoke. He casually mentioned to the captain, "Looks like they're following the same course."

"Following the same course? Who is?"

"The German steamer that left port this morning right after we did. She's still behind us, six miles astern. It looks like she's headed on the same course as we are."

"Really? German, you say?" Morrison realized that he had not really paid much attention to the other departing ship when they both had left port that morning. "Well, I doubt that they're headed all the way to Liverpool," he said with a laugh. "For now, though, if a German ship is brave enough to leave Recife, that should be a good sign for us. They must have heard that the British warships are too far away to bother them, so they've decided to make a run for it. At least that means we won't have to worry about that damned *Glasgow* showing up again and telling us our business." Definitely a good sign, he thought. Not having to worry about dodging that infernal British warship made an already beautiful day that much better.

"True. That would be…" Samuels paused as he looked out dead ahead. Where the sea met the sky was a growing black smudge and the silhouette of a ship. "Hmmm… Perhaps that German steamer behind us is in for a surprise." He plucked a pair of binoculars from their rack on the bulkhead and peered at the distant ship. It was nearly bow-on to his view, so he could see little above the vessel's foaming spray except the forecastle, superstructure, and the foremost funnel. It was definitely a warship—probably a light cruiser. "It looks like *Glasgow* isn't that far away after all, sir. Those Germans astern are not going to be happy."

"Let me have a look." Morrison stepped aside to give Samuels the wheel. He took the field glasses and leveled them at the oncoming ship. She was a warship, but something struck him as odd about her appearance. As the vessel came closer into view, he realized what it was. "Oh, bloody hell," he said. "Hard to port! Now, you fucking idiot! We need full speed!"

Samuels manhandled the wheel, and the heavily loaded ship tilted ponderously as its forward inertia strained against the turning rudder. Morrison gave the engine room the signal for full speed, and the men below did their best to stoke the boilers and get the most out of their aged engine.

"Sir?" Samuels was holding the wheel tightly as the sluggish freighter lumbered slowly through the turn. "Why are we…?"

"That's not the *Glasgow*, boy," said Morrison in response. "That there ship's got only three funnels. I think those fucking Germans from Recife have given us up to their goddamned navy."

Sure enough, Samuels could now see that the oncoming warship had three funnels, not *Glasgow's* four. He could make out other differences as well. This ship was smaller, and her lines were different. A sickening knot tightened in his stomach. This was not a British ship at all.

To emphasize that point, an amber flash and brown puff of smoke erupted from the deck of the oncoming cruiser. The shell detonated in a foaming white column about thirty yards off their starboard bow.

A flashing lamp blinked from the deck of the warship. "Now they're signaling us, sir," said Samuels, agape. "I think they want us to stop."

"And I think you've got a mastery of the obvious, Samuels. They're not inviting us to breakfast." Morrison shook his head. "Bloody fucking hell. Engine room, all stop. Samuels, straighten her out, nice and easy." He looked out at the warship, which was rapidly closing. Through the binoculars, he could now see the colors she was flying. The fluttering flag on her forward mast was a black, white, and red tricolor emblazoned with a black iron cross—the jack of the *Kaiserliche Marine*. "Dammit," he muttered, "I knew this was going to be a bad day."

◆

CAPTAIN MORRISON'S bad day had only just begun. After *Hyades* had come to a stop, as ordered, the German warship moved alongside. A gruff boarding party of ten armed men and two officers rowed over and came aboard. The senior officer spoke only rudimentary English, but he was able to convey that the steamer's crewmen were now their prisoners. Everyone aboard the British freighter was transported to the German ship and unceremoniously herded at gunpoint into an otherwise empty compartment below decks. Although the German sailors could not understand the words of Captain Morrison's profanity-laced tirade, his meaning was certainly clear to them.

From the small porthole in the compartment that was now their prison, they could see *Hyades* anchored nearby, with a number of the German sailors walking about on her deck. After more than an hour, an armed German sailor opened the metal door to their compartment and stepped in, along with a young blond officer.

"Good afternoon, gentlemen," said the officer in slightly accented English. "My name is *Kapitänleutnant* Canaris. You are aboard His Imperial Majesty's Ship *Dresden*. My captain would like to speak with your captain, please."

"And I have a few fucking words to say to him, too," replied Morrison, stepping forward and glaring into the lieutenant's eyes. "Well, are you going to take me to the son-of-a-bitch or not?"

Canaris suppressed a smile. "Then you would be Captain Morrison?"

"No, boy, I'm the goddamned queen of Egypt. Take me to your captain, already."

"A pleasure to meet you, sir. Please follow me, Captain Morrison," Canaris said with a respectful nod. He then turned over his shoulder and addressed the remaining men in the compartment. "Please accept our apologies for the cramped accommodations. Someone will bring food and drink to you shortly." The armed sailor led Morrison and Canaris through the door and then closed it behind them.

Morrison was led topside into the afternoon sunlight. The captain of the German warship was standing on the quarterdeck. He was speaking with another officer who was gesturing in an animated fashion, although Morrison could not understand what they were saying. He looked out toward his ship. The Germans had completed their search of *Hyades*, and it now seemed that they were in a hurry to leave. Officers were barking orders and directing men to return to two small boats that were tied up alongside the rusted hull of the freighter.

On *Dresden's* port side, another steamer was pulling alongside the warship, and it was the actions of this newly arrived vessel that the German captain was apparently discussing with his officer. Morrison recognized this ship immediately. It was one of the German colliers that had been moored in Recife when they arrived. It was also the same ship that had left that morning right behind *Hyades*. The crews of both ships were preparing to coal the warship, and the decks of both vessels were bustling with activity as the collier moved gingerly closer. The German collier was larger than both *Hyades* and *Dresden*, and Morrison noted with dismay that she had a wireless aerial strung between her masts. He shook his head, realizing what had happened. This collier had been dispatched, probably by German agents in Recife, to rendezvous with *Dresden*. Unfortunately for him, she had departed right after *Hyades* and had shadowed the British steamer, all the while in contact with *Dresden*, which moved in to intercept. Now the Germans had their coal and a handy prize as well.

Canaris was speaking to his captain in German. *Dresden's* captain was a slightly built man who spoke softly, in measured tones. They paused, and then Canaris turned to Morrison. "Captain Lüdecke says he is sorry that we have to take your men prisoner, and he assures you that according to international law, you and your crew shall be sent to a neutral port aboard the first available merchant vessel."

"How about sending us on our way aboard our own ship?" asked Morrison indignantly.

"I'm afraid that will not be possible." Canaris and Lüdecke exchanged a few more words.

"Why the hell not?"

"Because we are going to sink it."

For a split second, Morrison was actually at a loss for words. "What? Sink her? For what goddamned bloody reason? The whole damned ship is full of corn that was supposed to go to Germany, for Christ's sake! Why in the hell would you sink a ship full of corn?"

"Because we are at war, Captain," Canaris answered plainly. "Our orders are to sink any ships belonging to enemies of the Kaiser. Yours is a British ship, and your cargo is irrelevant. I am very sorry, Captain, but it must be so. Again, you and your crew will be kept safe and returned to a neutral port as soon as possible."

"Are you and your captain deaf, Lieutenant? *Hyades* is full of corn. Not bombs, not guns, not coal, or any other goddamned thing that could be used against your precious fucking Kaiser."

Captain Lüdecke said a few more words to the lieutenant, then turned away and strode off toward the bridge area, leaving Morrison with Canaris and the armed sailor.

"I am sorry, but we have no more time, Captain Morrison. We must finish our business here before someone sees us and reports our position to your navy. Please return to your crew, and we will have some food and drink brought to you." The armed sailor led Morrison back to the holding compartment.

The Germans were true to their word. A simple but edible meal of roast pork, bread, and cheese was brought to the men—most of whom ate in stunned silence after they heard the fate that awaited their ship. Two hours later, they heard *Dresden's* steam turbines begin to growl beneath them, and then the German ship was moving. From the porthole, they watched *Hyades*, illuminated by the fading afternoon sun, recede until she was out of their view.

After a few minutes, the German ship made a half turn, then settled back into a straight course. Outside their compartment, they could hear orders being given and loud footfalls beside and above them. An electric buzzer sounded somewhere. Suddenly, they were startled by a loud boom, followed in rapid succession by four more loud percussions that rattled the bulkheads and rang in their ears. They could see only empty ocean from the porthole—whatever was going on was happening on the other side of the ship. The series of explosions rang out again and again, vibrating the whole ship.

After at least twenty of the reports, the noise stopped, and they could feel the ship being swung around in a tight arc, the deck beneath them pitching dramatically. As she came about and again straightened out, a horrific sight came into view through the porthole. *Hyades* was about a mile away, and she was burning. Ragged holes had been torn in her hull, and smoke was pouring from her stern.

"Dear God," whispered Samuels, "they're using her for target practice."

The buzzers sounded again, and then the loud booms, this time directly overhead, rattling their compartment. The men jostled and shoved each other to watch through the small porthole. The few men with a decent view saw the first starboard salvo miss *Hyades*, throwing up a line of white splashes several hundred feet beyond the doomed freighter.

The second salvo was more accurate. Three splashes erupted in front of the black hull, and two shells exploded on the steamer's upper works. The red and black funnel pitched over, trailing its severed support wires. The third and fourth salvos sent more shells into the hull, and thick black smoke swirled upward from multiple wounds. The stricken freighter was taking on water, settling lower as flames consumed her upper deck.

After at least forty shells had been fired, the guns above finally fell silent. The stern of the freighter was almost completely submerged, as smoke and steam vented violently from her aft deck. As *Dresden* pulled away, the crew of SS *Hyades* watched as their ship slipped beneath the gray surface and was gone.

# FOUR

*Wednesday, August 12, 1914*
*Pagan Island in the Marianas Islands, Pacific Ocean*

"EXCUSE ME, CAPTAIN," said the young signals officer. "I have a message from *Titania*, sir. They have sighted two approaching ships, identified as *Emden* and a support ship."

"Excellent. Thank you, Mister Picht," replied Maerker. He was standing near *Gneisenau's* rearmost funnel, observing the men below and aft as they transferred coal from the adjacent collier *Mark*. The much-anticipated arrival of SMS *Emden* and the armed merchant cruiser *Prinz Eitel Friedrich*—a converted passenger liner—would bring the total number of ships moored in Pagan Bay to fourteen.

A motley collection of supply ships and colliers had straggled in, one by one, since the day before. Some large and some small, some old and some new, they were the only German-flagged merchant vessels to have escaped the noose that the Royal Navy was closing around Tsingtao. The newest arrivals were moored haphazardly in the small bay, along with *Scharnhorst*, *Gneisenau*, and *Nürnberg*. Little *Titania* was stationed out beyond the reef, about a kilometer away, acting as a sentry.

Undoubtedly this was the greatest number of ships to have ever visited this sorry excuse for a harbor, thought Maerker. It was no wonder that Admiral von Spee thought that Pagan would be low on the list of places for the British to search. The island was tiny, no more than sixteen kilometers long and only some five kilometers across at its widest spot. At each end of the small landmass rose a volcanic peak, and the larger of these two volcanoes, at the north end of the island, appeared to be active, with wisps of steam curling lazily from its summit. Palm trees and other vegetation covered much of the island, but the top of the northern peak was scarred and barren, ringed with ash and volcanic ejecta. A thin strip of land connected the two volcanic mounds, and the bay in which they rested was within the curve of that low saddle. Interestingly, the sand along the crescent-shaped beach was brownish-black, unlike any shore he had ever seen.

Pagan had but a few native inhabitants, and their crude huts were the only structures on the island. Much like Ponapé in the Carolines, Germany had recently purchased this and other islands of the Northern Marianas from Spain but thus far had not considered it valuable enough to install a proper colonial presence. Therefore, it remained unimproved, without even a dock or pier. The bay itself, although protected by a reef, was barely large enough to contain all of the recently arrived ships, and maneuvering the colliers about in the cramped area to service the warships had proven awkward and difficult. Nonetheless, early that morning, they had managed to bring *Mark* alongside and had begun the coaling process.

For the men's sake, Maerker had hoped to have the bulk of the work completed before the tropical sun was at its zenith, but the collier's crew was inexperienced, and the coaling had proceeded slowly. Unfortunately, they had discarded the ship's flammable deck awnings back at Ponapé. Now, as mid-day approached, the sailors toiled without a scrap of shade, in unremitting sunshine and oppressive heat.

For all of our modern technological advancements, thought Maerker, this fueling process was still maddeningly primitive. Coal had to be brought aboard the warship by crane in large canvas sacks that were hoisted over to *Gneisenau's* deck. The contents of the sacks, which could weigh as much as a hundred kilograms when filled, were then dumped upon the deck near the coal chute hatches. Men would then use shovels to scoop the crumbling hunks and fragments of black fuel into the chutes. It was backbreaking work, made even more unpleasant by the clouds of dust that arose each time the coal was moved, dumped, or shoveled. The more experienced men knew to wrap their noses and mouths with moistened strips of linen to keep out at least some of the airborne particles, but everyone involved in the process continually coughed and wheezed in the heavy cloud of dust.

The gritty black grime settled on every exposed surface, including the sweat-dampened skin and clothing of the men as they worked. In short order, those wielding the shovels were tinted black from head to foot, accentuating the gleaming whites of their eyes. Considering how unpleasant this part of the process was, it was worse for the men below. At the bottom of those coal chutes lay the long narrow spaces of the cavernous coal bunkers themselves, positioned on either side of the ship's vital interior spaces. Men were down there also, furiously shoveling the falling piles of coal outward from the chute, piling it against the bulkheads to fit as much fuel as possible into the bunker. As the black chunks slowly filled the space, those men below had to keep stepping up to stand on the rising level of coal in the bunker, being careful not to be crushed and buried by the falling black avalanche as it rumbled down the chute. The temperature in the dark, stifling bunkers below was even higher than out in the direct sunlight, so those men had to change shifts frequently to avoid being overcome by the heat and choking dust.

During this arduous process, almost everyone aboard turned their attention to the coaling procedure in some way. Most of the crewmen made up the shifts working the booms, shoveling on deck, and packing the bunkers. Junior lieutenants would direct these operations, timing each shift and recording the amounts of coal transferred. Each shift's tally was noted on slate for all to see, encouraging successive shifts to better the mark of their predecessors. Men with musical talents took shifts playing in the ship's band, which sported an odd assemblage of horns, fiddles, and even a cello. The band was positioned on the quarterdeck, playing rousing tunes to keep the men in high spirits as they worked. Other crewmen kept busy running fresh cool water to the thirsty laborers and providing clean linen face scarves to replace those clogged with grime. Sometimes the band would temporarily break up as some of its members cycled out to other duties. During those lulls between tunes, men from the wireless room would come aft and take turns reading aloud the latest bulletins relayed from the Yap wireless station. These snippets of news from Europe seemed to provide a morale boost to the men, helping them feel less isolated so far from home.

The band had recently finished playing a rendition of *Die Wacht am Rhein* and had temporarily dispersed. It was time for the morning bulletin. A young signals officer stepped up to the railing and began to loudly read the transcript of the most recent message relayed from Yap. The report was a lengthy description of the German siege of the fortifications at Liege. Apparently, the Belgians, led by the valiant and capable General Gerard Leman, had put up stubborn resistance, fiercely guarding the forts and the Meuse River. The Kaiser's armies, however, led by the crafty and relentless General Otto von Emmich, were overwhelming the Belgians. German artillery had mercilessly pounded the walls and buildings for days, and General von Emmich planned to have the fortifications reduced to rubble within a matter of hours. At this news, the men cheered heartily before returning to their labors.

Belgium and all of that death and destruction were so very far away, thought Maerker. However, the battlefront was only three hundred kilometers from Ilsa and the children, who were in Herford—a thought that chilled him. For the men of the squadron moored here at this remote island, their families and friends back home were the only tangible connection to the raging conflict on the other side of the world. To hear the progress of the war relayed in the daily dispatches was more like reading chapters of a serial novel than hearing about actual events. It all seemed so distant. Maerker realized, however, that this war was like a plague—a rapidly spreading contagion that was relentlessly and inevitably infecting every continent, ocean, and island on the globe. Soon enough, he knew, this war would be brought to them, wherever they might be.

◆

ADMIRAL MARTYN JERRAM, commanding the Royal Navy's China Squadron based in Hong Kong, wanted desperately to bring the war directly to the East Asia Squadron, if he could find them. That was already proving to be maddeningly difficult. By a miserable stroke of bad luck, Admiral Graf von Spee had already left on his damnable Pacific cruise when war was declared. The light cruiser *Emden* had also slipped out of port a week ago, before any of his ships could get there. Had the German squadron been bottled up in the harbor at Tsingtao, Jerram's ships could have neutralized them quickly. Now, however, the Germans could be anywhere within two thousand miles.

The German possessions in the Pacific were numerous and far-flung, including islands in the Carolines, the Marianas, the Marshalls, Samoa, and New Guinea. Graf Spee could be hiding in any of those places. He would have access to plenty of provisions, fresh water, and supplies. Much to Admiral Jerram's chagrin, he now knew that Graf Spee would also have plenty of coal, because several laden German colliers were known to have escaped from Tsingtao and Yokohama before his ships could cut them off.

"Not a blasted one of them is here," said Jerram with a sigh, looking at the small harbor of the Yap Island colony through field glasses. Standing on the bridge of HMS *Minotaur*, he swept the glasses in a slow, steady arc across the horizon beyond the island. No, the East Asia Squadron was definitely not here. Looking back toward the harbor, only one small steamship, the noncombatant German survey vessel *Planet*, was tied up at the quay. The harbor was deserted, but some activity on the beach drew his eye. "What do you make of that, Mister Kiddle?"

"It looks like they are trenching the beachhead, sir; probably trying to prevent an armed landing," replied the flagship's captain. A dozen men were furiously digging along a line near the top of the beach. Some appeared to be packing sandbags and reinforcing the position. "A few are armed with rifles, but I don't see anything heavier," added the captain.

"Well, they can dig as many trenches as they like, because we don't have the time or the manpower to land anyone here today." Jerram lowered the glasses and shook his head with frustrated resignation. "Until we can get a proper troop ship here, we won't be able to take possession of the island. In fact, we don't have the luxury of waiting around any longer, either. Those blasted German warships aren't here, so God only knows where they might be. Now our priority must be to get back and protect the shipping lanes closer to home."

They had steamed southeast from Hong Kong for five days in a desperate attempt to intercept and catch the German squadron at anchor. Not knowing where Graf Spee might be, the admiral had gambled that *Emden* and at least one collier were going to try to rendezvous with the rest of the squadron at the nearest German possession of any major strategic importance. The island of Yap, with its key cable station and powerful wireless transmitter, was the most likely spot. Jerram had split his force, sending the light cruiser *Yarmouth*, the old battleship *Triumph*, and the French armored cruiser *Dupleix* to secure Tsingtao. While those ships headed north, the armored cruiser *Hampshire* and the light cruiser *Newcastle* accompanied *Minotaur* as they set out for Yap. Unfortunately, the German-held island was more than eighteen hundred miles from Hong Kong, near the outer limit of their range, and *Hampshire* already had to turn back for lack of sufficient coal.

In an encouraging stroke of good luck, they happened upon and captured the German collier *Elsbeth*, loaded with coal from Tsingtao and, curiously, bundles of mail addressed to the crews of the armored cruisers *Scharnhorst* and *Gneisenau*. This coincidence suggested that Jerram's instinct was correct, so after taking the German crew prisoner and scuttling the collier, he resumed course for Yap as quickly as possible. However, when *Minotaur* and *Newcastle* finally arrived at Yap, they found no German warships and no colliers.

"Captain Kiddle," the admiral continued with a sigh, "our little jaunt out here won't be entirely for naught. At least we can shut out the lights before we leave. Give them half an hour to evacuate."

"Certainly, sir," replied Kiddle. He turned to the senior officers beside him. "Mister Harrold, signal them that all personnel must get away from the buildings immediately. Also let Captain Powlett aboard *Newcastle* know that we will begin shelling the station in thirty minutes. Mister Talbot, target the cable station building first, then the wireless mast itself. High explosive rounds." The signals officer and gunnery officer relayed their orders to the men.

The next thirty minutes passed slowly as they waited in position, a mile out, with their port beam toward the beach. From their vantage point, the

British officers could not see the doorway to the small, white cable station building, so they did not know if the Germans had heeded their warning to evacuate. The only indication they had of any response at all was relayed by the wireless room, which reported that the enemy station had stopped transmitting. Lieutenant-Commander Talbot gave the order, and two of *Minotaur's* port 7.5-inch guns fired with a loud reverberating rumble. Through binoculars, the admiral and the captain watched as the men digging the trenches on the beach toiled on, seemingly unperturbed, until the first two lyddite shells exploded several hundred feet behind them. One shell detonated in the grassy yard beside the cable station, ejecting a plume of brown earth and vegetation. The other shell struck the building directly, shattering the seaward wall and throwing roofing tiles skyward. At this, the men in the trench scattered in a panic. The second pair of shells was just as accurate, and the British officers could now see orange flames curling from the demolished frame of the building.

The two-hundred-foot-tall steel wireless mast itself rose from a slope slightly farther inland. Within moments, *Minotaur's* high-explosive shells were landing at its base, tearing up palm trees and spouting sprays of earth and rocks. After three salvos, the metal latticework of the mast shuddered and crumpled, tipping and falling mightily into the underbrush below. The entire attack had lasted less than fifteen minutes.

Only partly satisfied, Admiral Jerram issued the order to depart. *Minotaur* and *Newcastle* turned about and headed back toward Hong Kong.

◆

THE EAST ASIA SQUADRON'S first true council of war had begun with most unfortunate news. In the hour before they gathered in the admiral's stateroom, each of the captains had been informed that the Yap wireless station had abruptly stopped transmitting. In the middle of a report detailing the deployment of the Russian First Army near Königsberg, the transmission simply ended, mid-word — and had not resumed.

"The British have apparently reached Yap," stated the admiral plainly. "They have either taken the island or destroyed the wireless station." Graf Spee was seated at the middle of the long teak table. He looked regal in his dress uniform, and his silvery-white hair, moustache, and goatee were impeccably groomed. To his left sat his chief of staff, Captain Filietz, and *Scharnhorst's* commander, Captain Schultz. To his right sat Captain Schönberg of *Nürnberg*. Maerker was seated directly across from the admiral, with Captain Müller of *Emden* to his left. To his right sat Friedrich Vogt and Max Thierichens, the commanders of the armed merchant vessels *Titania* and *Prinz Eitel Friedrich*. Maps and charts were laid out before them on the table, with the familiar chart of the western Pacific Ocean on the top.

They had greeted the recently arrived Captain Müller warmly. He was the youngest of all the commanders—a bright and well-respected member of the squadron. They discovered upon his arrival that, surprisingly, Müller had already captured the squadron's first prize of the war, the Russian passenger steamer *Ryazan*, which had blundered too close to Kiaochow Bay as *Emden* was preparing to depart. The admiral and Müller's fellow captains congratulated the young commander on his early catch but playfully chided him for already making the rest of them look slothful by comparison. In another bit of encouraging news, *Markomannia*, one of the colliers that Müller had sent on ahead from Tsingtao, had arrived in Pagan a few hours earlier, delayed slightly because her captain had misinterpreted the rendezvous instructions. Her presence brought the total number of ships at Pagan to fifteen, but regrettably, Müller had sent the other collier, *Elsbeth*, down to Yap to await further instructions. It was now likely that she had been captured by the British.

Graf Spee had quickly dispensed with the pleasantries of welcoming Müller. Although having four of his five cruiser captains back together was a cause for celebration, the fall of Yap had put the admiral in a troubled mood, and he wanted to get on with planning their next steps.

"With the Yap transmitter gone, we are now cut off from direct contact with the *Admiralstab*," Graf Spee went on. "Therefore, as the representatives of His Imperial Majesty's naval forces in the Pacific, we in this room must decide upon a course of action. I have gathered all of you for your counsel, and I expect that each of you will speak freely." The admiral paused, his blue eyes scanning the faces of his commanders. "As you all know, our standing orders in the event of war with Britain state that our warships on foreign station are to engage in *Kreuzerkrieg*—attacking and disrupting British merchant shipping wherever we can. Britain is utterly dependent upon seaborne trade, and any significant disruption of their maritime lifeline could be devastating to their economic well-being and their ability to fight a war, not to mention the emotional and social effects of such deprivation upon the British people."

Graf Spee looked grave. "However," he continued, "I believe that our circumstances require the discussion of other alternatives that the *Admiralstab* may not have considered. First, we not only face the British, but we must also now contend with the Japanese, who may have already entered the war against us as well."

"Opportunistic Jap bastards," mumbled Schönberg as he traced the tip of his pointed beard with his finger and thumb. "This isn't their war at all, but they'd love to jump in and take possession of Tsingtao."

"Probably true," answered the admiral. "Unfortunately, we'll have to leave it to them. We would be hard-pressed to try to defend Tsingtao from the British alone, but against Japan's navy as well, such an effort would be a suicidal stand. No, we are vastly more useful to the Kaiser as an offensive force."

Despite his earlier gloomy demeanor, Maerker could now see a familiar gleam in the old man's eyes, much like the mischievous look of a scheming schoolboy. He was sure that for the admiral, the exhilaration of presiding over a council of war with his trusted captains was surpassed only by actual combat itself.

Graf Spee continued, "Inherent to the concept of *Kreuzerkrieg* is the presumption that individual German cruisers on foreign station around the world would operate alone, slashing into sea lanes to interdict British or Allied merchant vessels, then disappear before being intercepted by enemy naval assets. Thus, *Königsberg* currently off the coast of East Africa, *Dresden* and *Karlsruhe* operating in the West Indies, and even our own *Leipzig* now off the Mexican coast will be expected to wreak as much havoc as possible in their respective regions before they are either sunk or are forced to be interned in a neutral port."

The admiral was becoming more animated as he went on. He stood and gestured to all of his captains. "We, however, represent a somewhat different opportunity. The East Asia Squadron is a formidable naval force unto itself, not just a collection of individual cruisers. As a squadron, we essentially match the firepower and speed of the British China Squadron in Hong Kong. We are, for all intents and purposes, a 'fleet in being'. Because of that, our very existence is a threat to the naval powers of the region. If we keep the squadron together, we compel our enemies to concentrate their forces to deal with us. As long as they have no idea where we are, they must assume that they could encounter our full squadron all at once. They are searching for four needles in several million square kilometers of haystack. They must mass their resources here to deal with us, which otherwise they might be able to move to Europe to bolster their fleets blockading the English Channel and the North Sea. The question, then, gentlemen, is where we should operate where we can simultaneously do the most damage and operate most effectively?"

He continued without waiting for a response, pointing to a region of the map west of their current location. "We cannot operate in the waters off the China coast. Between Jerram's squadron and the Japanese, not to mention the Russians and the French, this region is crowded with our enemies. Their combined naval strength far exceeds our own, and there are simply no friendly or neutral ports of call available to us." He moved his hand southward on the map, toward New Guinea and Australia. "South of us is no better. The Australian fleet is commanded by Admiral Patey, whose flagship battlecruiser *Australia* alone is probably more than a match for our entire squadron. I would not be surprised if at this very moment, Patey and his ships are hunting for us near our colony at Rabaul."

"That leaves us with two options," he went on. "We can either head farther west, into the Indian Ocean, or we can go east across the Pacific to the west coast of South America. In either case, we would have the opportunity to disrupt critical British and Allied shipping routes. Of the two—although the journey is longer—I think that going east to South America is preferable."

"I respectfully disagree, sir," said Captain Müller. "The Indian Ocean is a critical conduit of goods, supplies, and even troops to Europe, either through the Suez Canal or around the Cape of Good Hope. Were we to attack British shipping there, they would feel it almost immediately. We could effectively shut down transit through the canal and force all of their shipping to go around the Cape. Much of their shipping, from the Far East, Australia, South Asia, and even East Africa, transits some portion of the Indian Ocean. Attacking British targets there could paralyze commerce to and from multiple continents at once."

"True enough," replied Graf Spee, nodding thoughtfully. "However, operating in the Indian Ocean would be far from easy. Finding enough coal would be the main problem. While we currently have enough coal for the squadron for perhaps a month, eventually our colliers will be empty. Of course, any enemy ships we capture may augment our coal supplies, but this squadron is hungry. We use up an extraordinary amount of fuel every day. We may also need to put in at neutral ports to coal. Unfortunately, the only neutral ports in that direction are the Dutch East Indies, and the Dutch are anything but friendly to us. They will strictly enforce the twenty-four-hour rule, and they will report our presence to the British. Additionally, in that region, we have few German agents in place who could help us secure additional coal supplies." The admiral paused, his eyes drifting over the map below. He shook his head. "We could make an initial impact, but then we might find ourselves out of fuel and out of options."

Maerker agreed with the admiral's assessment, but he admired young Müller's audacity and his astute analysis of the situation. Striking British shipping in the Indian Ocean would surely have a profound effect upon Allied commerce and British morale. He did not, however, relish the thought of being bottled up there without coal, supplies, or even a reliable neutral port.

Graf Spee continued, "Although you're correct that we would have a great many targets from which to choose, the Indian Ocean is essentially a

British lake. I fear that we'd be sailing into a box, and as soon as the Royal Navy could muster enough ships to the area, they'd close the lid on us." He gestured toward the map again, this time sweeping his arm across the Pacific. "However, if we head east, the South American coast is a hunting ground that is nearly as rich. Those trade routes are also critical to Britain, but unlike the Indian Ocean, the Royal Navy's presence there is weak. Additionally, Chile and Argentina are friendly neutrals. We may be able to convince them to look aside when it comes to the rules governing port calls. Finally, our South American embassies can help us reestablish direct communication with Berlin, and we have many agents already in place who can help secure coal supplies."

"I like the idea," offered Maerker, "but we'll have to plan our route carefully. We will have to coal every three or four days as we hopscotch across the Pacific—and many of the islands where we might stop along the way belong to our enemies. We will have to choose our…"

"I'm afraid I don't like it at all," interjected Captain Schultz testily. "So many of our enemies are right here, in the Far East. I think that our circumstances give us a unique opportunity to strike a blow that will be felt all over the world."

"What do you mean, Felix?" asked the admiral, apparently surprised by the loud determination in the voice of *Scharnhorst's* usually quiet captain.

"I am suggesting that we use the firepower of this squadron to attack and destroy a major British installation, perhaps even the port in Hong Kong. With their ships out God-knows-where hunting for us, a surprise assault on the Hong Kong harbor would be devastating to them. I am sure that the Kaiser would be proud to see a newspaper headline that read, 'Hong Kong Burns after Daring German Naval Attack'. Just think of the effect that would have upon our arrogant British enemies."

Graf Spee smiled, "Yes, I suppose the Kaiser would be pleased to read that over his morning coffee. However, even if we could pull that off without bringing both the British and Japanese fleets down upon us, what then? We would be out of coal and probably out of ammunition as well, with no neutral port in which we could seek refuge. We would then be surrounded and slaughtered like sheep in a pen. That is not a headline I would want His Imperial Majesty to see."

"And even if Hong Kong burned," added Müller. "I doubt that it would have much of an effect upon British commerce. We would have sacrificed ourselves to shout a loud but ultimately irrelevant insult at the British king."

"True," agreed Schönberg across the table, "but I understand what you mean, Felix. I would also like to strike a decisive blow against our enemies; However, I don't think that the Far East can be our target."

Schultz was unconvinced. "But there are no major British naval bases or significant installations anywhere on the route you propose. Where will we be able to strike this decisive blow?"

"I think that perhaps we have lost sight of something in this discussion," intervened Graf Spee. "While the idea of striking the British in some large, audacious show of force sounds appealing, I think we actually are initially more of a threat to British commerce and their naval operations simply by existing. The longer our whereabouts are unknown to our enemies, the more time, effort, and resources they must expend to find us while they also must protect their lanes of commerce." He turned to Schultz directly. "We will get our chance to strike at the enemy, but we must be patient and prudent. We must remain operational as long as possible so that we can capture or destroy as many British and Allied targets as we can. An ongoing atmosphere of fear and trepidation will keep their merchant ships cowering in port and will do the most damage to our enemies' commercial interests." He looked down and took a deep breath. "Admittedly, I would much rather fight a true naval battle against British warships than simply skulk about plucking at the occasional unarmed merchant steamer. I would prefer us be the wolves that confront a bear than mere foxes that raid a chicken coop. However, we must do what is best for the Fatherland and for our squadron."

"Along those lines, sir," asked Müller, "is it possible that we might amplify the effect of this 'fear and trepidation' if we were able to strike in more than one place at once?"

"Possibly," answered the admiral with apparent curiosity. "What do you have in mind?"

Müller continued. "You are, of course, correct that the Indian Ocean may be a difficult place to operate with the full squadron. The limited coal supplies and lack of neutral ports could be problematic for all of us. However, what if the main body of the squadron was to continue on as you suggest to South America, but one cruiser were to be dispatched westward? *Emden* uses considerably less coal than *Scharnhorst* or *Gneisenau*. Operating with a single collier, I would have potentially several months of coal. Anything beyond that I could capture from enemy merchant vessels. *Emden* is the fastest of our ships, so she would be harder to catch, even if they do find us." Müller was speaking quickly now, with an infectious enthusiasm and energy. Those around the table were listening attentively. "If simultaneously we could strike at enemy merchant shipping off the coast of South America and in the Indian Ocean, not only would the British have to contend with two threats at once, but the economic and psychological effects of those attacks would be greatly increased."

Everyone was silent for a few moments. Each of the captains looked to the admiral, who was deep in thought.

Filietz, the admiral's chief of staff, was the first to speak. He pressed his spectacles higher on his nose and looked directly at the young commander. "Captain von Müller, are you telling us that you wish to recklessly embark upon this mission of yours in the Indian Ocean, regardless of the effect that it would have upon the squadron that you would leave behind? To remove a ship and its firepower from the squadron, simply so that you can seek individual glory is, frankly, a foolish and selfish…"

"Enough, Filietz," interjected Graf Spee sternly. "In truth, Captain Müller's plan has some merit. We would dearly love to inflict some damage on British trade in the Indian Ocean, but operating with our entire squadron there is out of the question. This plan might actually work, but I must give it some thought." He turned toward Filietz with an admonishing stare. "And I do not believe that Captain Müller was suggesting this plan to pursue personal glory, certainly not at the risk of the lives of anyone in his crew or in the squadron as a whole." He looked back at Müller. "I will consider your proposal."

Müller nodded respectfully.

Maerker thought that the young commander's plan was brilliant, if risky, and he thought it could use some additional support. "If it is of any consideration, sir," he said to the admiral, "Were *Emden* to depart westward, we could offset her absence with *Leipzig*, which is currently along the Central American coast. Were she to rejoin the squadron when we cross the Pacific, we would still have two heavy armored cruisers and two faster light cruisers, as well as the armed steamers *Titania* and *Prinz Eitel Friedrich*. Such a squadron would still be quite potent."

"True," replied Graf Spee thoughtfully. "The trick will be finding a way to communicate with *Leipzig* to let her know of our intentions." He paused, drumming his fingers on the table as he looked over the map, then continued. "We are here at Pagan," he pointed. "The route that I think would serve us best would take us east here, to the Marshall Islands. It is doubtful that either the British or the Japanese will be able to get any ships out there for some time. Our small colony at Eniwetok could provide us with some supplies, and we can coal in the shelter of the reefs there." He then indicated a tiny dot in the ocean farther to the southeast. "From Eniwetok, we could make it to Christmas Island, which I understand is uninhabited. We should be able to coal in relative safety, even though the island is a British possession. The intriguing opportunity offered by that route is that the Hawaiian Islands are within range of Eniwetok as well. We could dispatch one of the cruisers there while the main squadron goes on to Christmas Island. The cruiser at Hawaii could purchase coal and send messages to the *Admiralstab* about our intentions, including instructions for *Leipzig* to meet us somewhere along the South American coast. After leaving Hawaii, that ship could rejoin the squadron at Christmas Island, and we could all proceed onward to the southeast."

"I believe I should take *Nürnberg* to Hawaii, sir," offered Captain Schönberg. "We were just there two weeks ago, and the Americans would likely not think much of our return. For all they know, we've simply been operating between there and the American coast. Our presence would still be reported to the British, of course, but they would have no way of knowing that *Nürnberg* was connected with the main body of the squadron."

"Excellent," agreed Graf Spee, nodding. "I will begin working on the messages we will send. Berlin must be informed of our intentions, and they can hopefully get in touch with Captain Haun on *Leipzig*. The *Admiralstab* can inform our agents in Chile that we will need coal and other supplies when we arrive on the South American coast. They can then begin making the necessary preparations without arousing too much suspicion." He looked up at his captains. "Are there any objections to this course of action?"

Each man shook his head and offered his support for the plan in its current rudimentary form.

"Very well," the admiral continued, "we must get all ships up to steam and make ready to leave this evening by seventeen thirty hours. If the British are at Yap, they are only eleven hundred kilometers away. We need to quickly put as much ocean between us and them as possible."

◆

THAT AFTERNOON, the squadron made its way out of Pagan Bay, one by one, through the gap in the reef. At sea, they formed two columns, with the flagship leading the cruisers and *Titania* in the first column. The nine merchant steamers, led by the larger *Prinz Eitel Friedrich*, comprised the second column, steaming off the warships' starboard quarter. As they formed up and began traveling eastward, a thick gray overcast blanketed the sky, and a heavy wind whipped the waves into whitecaps and sent rain slashing down in blowing sheets.

As he watched the two columns of ships leave the island behind them, Captain Maerker thought that it was a remarkable display, looking every bit the "fleet-in-being" referenced by the admiral. Unfortunately, the weather continually worsened as they traveled on through the night, and the merchant ships, whose crews were unaccustomed to the discipline required to maintain positions in a convoy, had become a disorganized mess. By dawn, the second column was unrecognizable as any type of formation.

"Unbelievable," exclaimed Pochhammer, looking out from the bridge at the scattered merchant ships. "Even ducklings can swim in a straight line. These merchant captains need some lessons in seakeeping discipline."

"Well, I believe that today is their first day of class," replied Maerker. "None of them has ever had to steam in a convoy before, and certainly not in this kind of weather. They'll learn soon enough or they will be left behind."

"I can barely see *Holsatia*, *Mark*, and *Longmoon*. We're not even steaming at ten knots; you'd think it wouldn't be this difficult." Pochhammer shook his head in disbelief.

As gusts of driving rain pelted the windows of *Gneisenau's* wheelhouse, the flagship, steaming ahead of them, raised a series of signal flags that simply stated, "*Emden* detached. Good luck."

"Detached?" asked Pochhammer, surprised. "Where is *Emden* going?"

"Captain von Müller has requested that he be allowed to operate independently in the Indian Ocean," answered Maerker.

"The Indian Ocean? And the admiral granted this request?" Pochhammer was incredulous. "Why would he let Captain Müller desert our squadron in such a manner?"

"He isn't deserting us, Mister Pochhammer. In fact, his plan is quite daring. He will be attacking enemy commerce while evading an ocean potentially full of Royal Navy ships. His presence there may well draw some attention away from us here in the Pacific. I do not envy his task. He will likely need all the luck he can get."

A few moments later, *Emden* sent a return signal, stating, "My dutiful thanks for the confidence placed in me. Success to the squadron and good journey to all." A second signal from *Scharnhorst* simply stated, "*Markomannia*, follow *Emden*." With that, the small cruiser left the line and began steaming southwest, followed by the collier, which hopefully would provide the warship with at least two months of fuel. Maerker watched the two ships depart through the rolling seas and pictured the long and hazardous route they must take to reach the Indian Ocean. Good luck and Godspeed, Captain Müller, he thought. He wondered grimly if *Emden* would ever make it there.

# FIVE

*Saturday, August 22, 1914*
*South Atlantic Ocean, Pernambuco Coast, Brazil*

HMS *Monmouth* belonged in a museum — or perhaps more appropriately in a scrapyard. In fact, had war not been declared, she likely would have been dismantled and sold as scrap. Instead, here she was off the Brazilian coast, newly arrived to help bolster John Luce's search for *Dresden*. *Glasgow* had steamed northward to the Pernambuco area to meet *Monmouth* and escort her back to Abrolhos. When they first saw her late that morning, every man on *Glasgow's* bridge was taken aback by the decrepit appearance of the old armored cruiser.

"I'm not exactly sure what they do with our ships in the Reserve Fleet," said Luce to his first officer, "but I'm guessing it isn't a whole lot of maintenance. She's probably being held together mostly by rust." Although the old ship had received a hasty repainting before she left Plymouth, much of her hull was now streaked with oxidation.

Commander Thompson lowered his binoculars. "They recommissioned her? Are you sure they didn't just raise her from the bottom of the Channel?" He shook his head, frowning. "What a sight. I don't think she has any business being afloat in a bathtub, let alone steaming six thousand miles to Brazil."

"Yet, here she is," said Luce. He turned to the signals officer. "Mister Stuart, please send the following message to Captain Brandt, 'Welcome to South America. Happy to see some friendly faces. Please follow to coaling base'." He turned back to Thompson. "Of course, we're just seeing the outside. God only knows what kind of shape the rest of her is in. We'll have to make an assessment after they've coaled."

*Glasgow* assumed a southward course, and *Monmouth* fell in behind her. The old armored cruiser was a strangely designed ship. She was about the same length as *Glasgow*, but *Monmouth* was much wider and more than twice as heavy. Launched in 1901, she was a relic of an era of shipbuilding that now was hopelessly obsolete. Unlike most modern armored cruisers, she had no main battery of heavy guns. Instead, she sported fourteen smaller 6-inch guns—four in turrets on deck and the rest in a series of swiveling casemates that protruded from the side of her hull, just above the waterline. Many of those casemates, it was well known, were placed so low on the hull that in anything but the calmest sea they would be swamped with water and rendered useless. In addition to being under-gunned, she had been designed with relatively thin armor in a misguided attempt to cut down on additional weight and marginally improve her speed. All in all, thought Luce, *Monmouth* represented a class of warships that was woefully ill-suited for modern warfare.

*Glasgow*, by comparison, was one of the Royal Navy's newer ships, launched only four years earlier. A Town-Class light cruiser, she was sleek and fast, slicing through the sea in an almost effortless manner that made *Monmouth* look ungainly and plodding. Light cruisers generally had little or no armor, relying instead on swiftness and agility, and *Glasgow* was no exception. She was, however, well-armed for a smaller ship, with two turreted 6-inch guns on deck, one fore and one aft, and ten 4-inch gun turrets—five mounted along each flank. She was not expected to directly engage bigger, more heavily armed and armored ships. Instead, her task was to perform fast scouting duties and to chase and destroy enemy light cruisers and coastal vessels—and in that category, no German ship was yet her equal. Luce had come to love *Glasgow*, and unlike the larger, more cumbersome ships upon which he had served earlier in his career, she felt responsive, agile, and alive.

When they reached Abrolhos, *Monmouth* pulled alongside *Wayfarer* and began coaling. While that process was taking place, Captain Brandt came aboard *Glasgow*. They met in the senior officers' wardroom. Frank Brandt was a couple of years younger than Luce. Brandt was a thin man with wide-set eyes; he was of average height, with close-cropped black hair. Because Luce had several years of command seniority, he was now, by default, Brandt's commanding officer.

"Welcome aboard, Captain," said Luce, shaking Brandt's hand. "It's good to see you again." They had encountered each other a few times when Luce had been assigned to the Admiralty.

"Likewise. I'm glad to finally be serving with you, John, even if these circumstances are… unfortunate."

Luce introduced his first officer. "Frank, this is Will Thompson."

"Good to meet you, Will," said Brandt, shaking his hand as well.

"We're happy to have you with us, Captain," replied Thompson. "Even though this is shaping up to be a bit of a wild goose chase."

"My last command was HMS *Maidstone*, a depot ship, so the opportunity to get out here and do something meaningful was certainly appealing. Better than sitting on my backside in Portsmouth, tending to submarines. Of course, *Monmouth* isn't exactly fresh out of the shipyard." Brandt rolled his eyes and smiled. "I take it you've noticed the bucket of bolts I've brought to reinforce you?"

Luce and Thompson chuckled. "How seaworthy is she?" Luce asked seriously.

"Not as bad as she looks, which is a good thing. She had only been decommissioned for about five months, so much of what you see is superficial deterioration only. We certainly have some maintenance problems, and most of her machinery works about as well as you would expect for a ship of her age. The engines are functional, but she's unlikely to make her rated twenty-three knots," he said with a grin. "In fact, on the way from St. Vincent, I briefly took her up to eighteen knots, just to knock off some of the cobwebs, and I thought my engineering commander was going to drop dead of worry. We might squeeze twenty out of her for a short stretch, if necessary." He paused and sighed. "My problem isn't so much with the ship—it's the crew."

"How green are they?" asked Luce.

"Mostly a scratch crew, unfortunately—reservists and coastguardsmen. We have a few cadets, too—just boys, really." Brandt sighed deeply. "They're about as green a crew as we could find and still be able to run a ship. In fact, we haven't yet been able to conduct any true action drills because no one knows their stations well enough yet." He paused, a concerned look on his face. "It is fortunate that of all the places we could have been sent, we were assigned here. Anywhere else, where we might see some actual combat, and this would have been a disaster."

Luce was silent for a moment. An aging ship crewed by old men and untrained boys? What was the Admiralty thinking? He tried to offer some reassurance to Brandt. "If we do see any combat down here, it will likely entail us firing a few shots at *Dresden* while we chase her into a Brazilian port to be interned."

"Hopefully," added Thompson, "with your help, we can find *Dresden* more quickly. She's around here somewhere—just sank a British freighter near Recife last week. Of course, we warned that crusty old fool Morrison to stay away from there, but there's no telling some people."

"Speaking of Recife," replied Brandt, seemingly happy to talk about something other than the sorry state of his ship and crew, "I heard a big

German passenger steamer, *Blucher*, managed to sneak in there just before we joined you. The rumor has it she was carrying gold bullion."

"Gold bullion? If that's true," offered Luce, "the gold is probably to fund German agents here in Brazil. I understand they have quite an established network."

"Too bad you couldn't have intercepted her on your way down," added Thompson. "Sounds like she would have made an excellent prize."

"I suppose, but that might have required us to fire a gun or two, and that's something this crew has yet to attempt," Brandt said soberly. "Besides, we received word from the Admiralty that the prize rules have been abolished. We're not to bother with any of it—the Germans certainly aren't taking prizes."

"Just as well," commented Luce. "We have a German cruiser to find before she sinks any more of our ships." He smiled, "we also need to get your crew ready for some wartime operations, Captain."

◆

UNFORTUNATELY, Captain Brandt's assessment of his crew's lack of readiness was spot on. *Monmouth's* first coaling at Abrolhos was a clumsy debacle, making *Glasgow's* early efforts look elegant by comparison. Almost none of *Monmouth's* crewmen had ever attempted any type of coaling at sea, and although *Wayfarer* and *Monmouth* were more closely matched in size, the coaling took the better part of a day and resulted in three slight injuries to sailors aboard the cruiser.

Several of *Glasgow's* officers and men visited *Monmouth* to help gauge her readiness and offer any assistance they could render. When they returned, their reports were less than encouraging. All of the boilers and condensers needed maintenance, the engines were barely holding together, one of the ammunition hoists was inoperable, and at least two of her gun casements were so rusted and poorly maintained that they could barely move. Engineers from both ships attended to these issues as best they could, and by the next day, Captains Luce and Brandt agreed that *Monmouth* was reasonably prepared for operations—at least as ready as she could be without a six-month refit in a proper dockyard.

As they were setting out, a wireless message from Rio confirmed that, as expected, Japan had declared war on Germany and was sending ships to Tsingtao to join the British blockade of the German port. The Admiralty also informed Luce that the West Indies Squadron under Admiral Cradock was to spare another warship to be sent southward under Luce's command. His wireless attempts to reach Cradock to confirm this plan had thus far been unsuccessful.

*Glasgow* continued to receive wireless reports of sightings of *Dresden* near Recife, although none of those reports could be substantiated. The sinking of *Hyades* was definitely having an effect. Many nearby Allied ships were now either remaining in port or avoiding the Pernambuco coast altogether. Just the possibility that *Dresden* might still be lurking nearby was having a crippling effect on local shipping.

The two British warships began their search by moving northward from Abrolhos toward the last confirmed location of *Dresden*, where *Hyades* now lay on the bottom of the sea. *Glasgow* and *Monmouth* steamed in parallel, five miles apart, increasing the swath of ocean they could visually sweep for any signs of distant funnel smoke. They began to pick up encrypted German wireless signals, faint at first, but getting steadily stronger as they moved northward. Luce surmised that German merchant ships and shore stations were exchanging the signals, but it was possible that *Dresden* was part of the exchange as well. The two cruisers searched fruitlessly for several days; the only other vessel they encountered was *Turakina*, a passenger liner from New Zealand, whose captain relayed that he also had seen no further sign of any German warships.

Life aboard a Royal Navy warship was, by necessity, governed by schedules and repetition. From the regular bells and watch schedules to the duty rosters and the mess rotations, every man on board worked, ate, and slept according to a schedule. On a precise daily timetable, the decks were washed down, gun mounts and capstans were lubricated, and metal fittings were polished with sand and oil. Meals were prepared, laundry was washed, and garbage and waste were thrown or pumped into the sea. However, now that war had been declared and they were hunting for *Dresden*, the schedules of the men aboard *Glasgow* and *Monmouth* began to take on a different air.

Their daily routine became a frustrating combination of tension and tedium. Each man at every duty post had to be ready at a moment's notice in case the spotters found *Dresden*, and Luce could see that the constant state of near-readiness brought on a wearying agitation among the crew. Each successive day they found nothing, and the frustration of that perpetual futility made the crew's unrest even worse. The edgy atmosphere among the men was compounded by the heat, especially in the evenings—when the stillness of the air and the mandatory closed hatches and blocked portholes of wartime operation left the ship's interior spaces stifling. Even the usually raucous parrots in their cages throughout the ship seemed less talkative, as if numbed by the daily monotony and the unrelenting heat. Petty officers reported that men in every area of the ship were becoming agitated. Scuffles had broken out among off-duty seamen, usually following the distribution of the men's daily rum ration.

Captain Luce decided that the men needed a break in this maddening daily routine. He ordered the two warships to take half a day to conduct some gunnery drills, which was a new experience for *Monmouth's* crew. Getting each man to his assigned station in a reasonable amount of time, loading the guns, operating the hoists, and responding to commands from the gunnery officers all proved awkward and difficult for *Monmouth's* untrained men. Hours went by before Captain Brandt was confident enough in his crew that they might be able to attempt a live fire exercise. The first result was ragged at best, with only two of the starboard gun crews able to fire their guns at all. The second and third attempts went better, with enough coordination that the firing sequences vaguely resembled salvos. Still, thought Luce as he observed from *Glasgow's* bridge, they had a long way to go. Getting the guns to fire was one thing; actually hitting a target was something else altogether.

A wireless message finally came in from Admiral Cradock, directing Luce farther north to the bleak, uninhabited Rocas Atoll, near the Brazilian penal colony on the island of Fernando de Noronha. There they found waiting the enormous Orient Line passenger ship SS *Otranto*, which had been refitted with six 4.7-inch guns to serve as an armed merchant cruiser. At more than twelve thousand tons, she was a large, slow, and cumbersome ship. Now dubbed HMS *Otranto*, she had also been assigned to Luce's command to help find *Dresden*.

*Otranto's* new captain, Herbert Edwards, seemed like a smart and decent enough fellow, but he had little relevant naval experience, and Luce was concerned about his adequacy as a wartime commander. He also worried that the addition of this ungainly ship would be more of a hindrance than a help.

"You're commanding quite the little fleet now, Captain," quipped Thompson as they watched the immense and lumbering *Otranto* fall in line behind *Monmouth* and *Glasgow* as they headed back south toward Abrolhos. "If we added a paddleboat and a garbage scow, you'd have a complete order of battle."

"I hope they do assign us a garbage scow," replied Luce drily, "so I can make you her captain."

"Seriously, sir, what can Cradock and the Admiralty be thinking? We're trying to hunt down a fast light cruiser, and they send us an obsolete reserve ship and this converted monstrosity? What's next, a canoe?"

"Their priorities are elsewhere. Cradock is tasked with patrolling the Caribbean and the Atlantic coast of North America. Back home, the Admiralty are staring across the North Sea at the entire German High Seas Fleet, waiting for them to come charging out. They're not keen to spare any of their best ships to help us find one light cruiser way down here. At least they've sent us a couple of ships, regardless of their condition; we can extend our visual search line a bit farther." Luce was trying to see the situation in the best possible light—although he had serious doubts of his own.

Satisfied that *Otranto* was following them in good order, Luce returned his attention to a chart laid out before him. A pattern of red dots on it represented known or presumed sightings of *Dresden*; the latest one had been entered eleven days earlier. He reflected grimly that the German cruiser could have traveled a significant distance in eleven days.

"I wish they had sent us a supply ship as well," Thompson said. "According to the canteen, by the time we get back to Abrolhos to coal again, we'll be low on food."

"True," replied Luce. "We haven't been in port for nearly a month, and I'm sure that anything that was fresh is probably long gone."

Customarily, a supply ship had been dispatched to them every three months. However, because *Glasgow* had been near the end of her commission, no such resupply vessel had been scheduled. Even with the food they had hastily brought aboard in Rio before their departure, their stores had been nowhere near capacity—and in the chaos of the first days of the war, Luce's requests for supplies had thus far gone unanswered.

Luce continued, "Brandt says *Monmouth* isn't doing any better. If they can't get a supply ship to us, I'm inclined to start asking some of these merchant ships for whatever food they can spare."

"Wonderful," said Thompson. "Now the Royal Navy, ruler of the seas, is reduced to begging for food."

◆

THE TRIP BACK to Abrolhos was as frustratingly uneventful as each of their previous voyages through the shipping lanes. The makeshift squadron searched in vain for two days as the three warships worked steadily southward. They encountered only one passing vessel, a French steamer, *Parana*. The French captain was a militant and excitable fellow who was incensed at the "imperialistic" Germans and quite happy that the Royal Navy was so aggressively protecting these waters. He gratefully provided as much of his ship's food stores as he could spare. Unfortunately, the few crates of fruit and vegetables did not last long when distributed among more than a thousand men aboard the three British ships. In fact, most of it was gone in the first day.

They arrived at Abrolhos at dawn on September 1st and began the tiresome process of coaling. Blessed with calm seas and light winds, the refueling went a little more smoothly. Unfortunately, however, *Wayfarer's* vast holds were now less than half full of coal, and Luce knew he would soon have to find additional colliers to supply his growing flotilla. Thus far, they had been spectacularly unsuccessful in their search for *Dresden*, they were low on food, and now they were running out of coal. It was a miserable situation.

It was about to get worse.

"Come in," said Luce in reply to the knock at his stateroom door.

"Good morning, Captain." It was Thompson, looking flushed. "You're not going to believe this."

"What is it?"

"This just came in from Rio." Thompson held a wireless transcript in his hand. "The bastards got past us somehow."

"*Dresden*?" asked Luce.

"Yes, bloody *Dresden*," he confirmed sourly. Thompson handed the pages to Luce. "Yesterday, a tramp steamer arrived in Rio carrying the crew of *Holmwood*, a British-flagged collier contracted to the Brazilian railways, like our *Wayfarer*. Apparently, *Dresden* surprised her two hundred miles off the coast of *Rio Grande do Sul*."

"Oh no." Luce exhaled heavily and looked over the transcript. *Rio Grande do Sul* was near the southern end of the Brazilian coast, some twelve hundred miles south of their current position. "The location of *Holmwood's* sinking explains a lot. If they were two hundred miles off the coast, they must have thought it was safer to travel outside the regular shipping lanes. If that's where *Dresden* found her, that means that the Germans went around us, far out to sea, then headed south."

"Apparently so, sir. It looks like it was simply bad luck for *Holmwood* that they happened along in just the wrong spot."

"Bad luck indeed. It says here that *Dresden* sank the collier with charges after disembarking the crew. *Dresden* didn't even bother taking any of the coal."

"They must have a collier with them," offered Thompson.

"And they look to be in a hurry. They got down there awfully quickly, considering they took the long way around. This happened a few days ago. By now, they might already be at the mouth of the River Plate." His words hung ominously in the air. The key ports of Montevideo and Buenos Aires sat on opposite shores of the immense delta where the *Rio de la Plata*, referred to in Britain as the River Plate, met the South Atlantic. An extraordinary amount of critical British and Allied shipping transited the area — which was now completely unprotected.

"Get messages off to the Admiralty and the legation in Rio so that they can pass warnings along," Luce continued. He and Thompson left the stateroom and headed out into the passageway. "Tell Brandt and Edwards to finish coaling as quickly as possible. We must get to Montevideo immediately." He was sure, however, that they were already too late.

The last of the coaling was finally finished during the night. The three ships departed before dawn, heading south at fifteen knots, which was nearly *Otranto's* top speed. *Wayfarer* trailed behind, unable to keep up with even that modest pace, with orders to rendezvous with the navy vessels near Montevideo whenever she could get there.

On the second day of the voyage, as they headed south along the coast, Luce received an Admiralty message announcing that Admiral Cradock had been given command along the South American coast. Cradock was heading south, leaving Admiral Stoddart in charge of the West Indies squadron to patrol the coast of North America and continue the hunt for *Karlsruhe*. With *Holmwood's* sinking and *Dresden's* rapid southward movement, the hunt for the German Cruiser had taken on a new urgency.

As the three British ships traveled southward, the weather worsened. Cold winds whipped the growing swells into whitecaps, and a chill rain lashed the ships. Although the cool air was initially preferable to the sweltering heat they had endured for weeks, the damp chill in every interior space soon became as irritating as the heat had been. When the three warships finally arrived off Montevideo on the evening of September 8th, the weather was bitterly cold, with a gusting wind that blew rain in snapping sheets. Although their visibility was extremely limited, Luce ordered his small squadron to search the area, hoping they would find *Dresden* coaling or at anchor. Several German merchant vessels were moored in port, but there was no sign of the enemy light cruiser.

The cold and rain were not their only annoyances. Each ship was now nearly out of coal, and the food stores were critically low. Although his rank customarily afforded him some unique luxuries, including his own private pantry, Luce thought it unseemly to maintain such amenities in an atmosphere of wartime deprivation. In fact, he had not stocked his private pantry since the outbreak of the war, sending the remaining supplies therein to the ship's cooks for general distribution. It was not until now, however, that somehow word began to pass among the crew that the captain, like them, was eating the same meager meals of canned gray bully beef, salt pork, and ship's biscuits.

Surprisingly, there had been no sightings of *Dresden* near Montevideo or Buenos Aires, so the whereabouts of the German ship was still a mystery. Luce had assumed that after sinking *Holmwood*, the Germans would naturally continue southward to the target-rich River Plate region. The stated goal of *Kreuzerkrieg* was to attack and disrupt the merchant shipping of the enemies of the Kaiser — and there were few better places to do so than the mouth of the River Plate. Strangely, however, *Dresden* was nowhere to be found. Either the German cruiser had bypassed the area on its way even farther south, or she was lying in wait somewhere out to sea.

Admiral Cradock was headed to Montevideo aboard his flagship, HMS *Good Hope*, to rendezvous with Luce. Cradock sent word via wireless, instructing Captain Luce and his ships to stay there until he arrived. While they waited, Luce intended to resupply and refuel his ships. The captain sent his intelligence officer ashore to meet with the British legation in Montevideo to secure some food, supplies, and coal for the three warships.

When they could operate during lulls in the foul weather, colliers and supply ships refueled and resupplied *Glasgow*, *Monmouth*, and *Otranto*. Members of the local British community came out in boats alongside *Glasgow* just to say hello and offer words of support and encouragement. The news from the war in Europe was distressing. German forces had surrounded and destroyed the advancing Russian Second Army at Tannenberg in East Prussia, and by some estimates, the Russians had lost a quarter of a million men—an astonishing number of casualties. On the western front, the Germans were also advancing toward Paris, and the British and French armies had launched a counterattack as they fell back toward the Marne River. The results of that battle were not yet known. Luce found it disheartening that not only was the German navy proving to be extremely elusive, the German armies in Europe appeared to be unstoppable.

◆

MOORED just outside Uruguay's three-mile territorial limit, Luce could dimly see Montevideo's outer harbor. As he looked out through the mist and rain at the lights along the distant waterfront, Luce recalled the decidedly different atmosphere surrounding their trip to this port a year earlier, in October of 1913. Of course, it was peacetime then; but more importantly, Mary had just arrived. Perhaps the greatest benefit accorded to captains on foreign station was the occasional privilege of having their wives visit them on station. Mary had arrived in Montevideo aboard a passenger steamer. Unlike today, Luce remembered, the weather that day had been glorious, with brilliant sunshine filtered through high, wispy clouds.

The long voyage from England seemed to have had no effect on her, and Mary looked radiant and happy as she was piped aboard her husband's ship. She was so much prettier than the photograph of her he kept in his stateroom. Even now, in her mid-thirties, she still had the same glittering hazel eyes and playful smile that had captivated him so many years before.

They spent three glorious weeks together, during which time Mary endeared herself to everyone she met. John was impressed that she knew so many of the officers by name, considering that she had heard of them only in her husband's letters. By the time she finally had to leave—aboard a steamer out of Buenos Aires—she had spoiled the entire ship's company with her mischievous sense of humor, musical laughter, and generous nature.

That had been such a different time, he thought now as he looked over at *Monmouth* and *Otranto* moored nearby, occasionally obscured by curtains of driving rain. The entire world was embroiled in war, and Mary's hazel eyes and infectious laugh seemed all the more distant.

A young petty officer stepped up to the railing beside him. "Message from the admiral, sir," he said, handing a sheet of paper to the captain.

"Thank you, Mister Hobbs." Luce looked over the transcript of the message. HMS *Good Hope* was having some engine problems that had slowed her down, but the admiral still expected to reach Montevideo within half a day. Upon his arrival, Luce and the captains of *Monmouth* and *Otranto* were to meet Admiral Cradock aboard the flagship. Their new commanding officer was about to arrive, and it was time for his South American squadron's first council of war.

# SIX

*Sunday, September 6, 1914*
*Christmas Island (Kiritimati), Pacific Ocean*

THE SMALL BOATS from the ships of the squadron nosed up to *Nürnberg's* hull like suckling pigs to a great gray sow. The light cruiser had arrived earlier in the morning, meeting up with the rest of Graf Spee's ships a few kilometers from Christmas Island. The admiral had ordered the squadron to anchor in the calm sea for a while to conserve coal, and the ships had dispatched boats to retrieve their share of the fruits, vegetables, newspapers, and other supplies that *Nürnberg* had brought back from Hawaii. Men on the cruiser's deck lowered crates and bundles to the sailors waiting in the boats below.

Captain Maerker watched the scene from a porthole in the admiral's stateroom aboard *Scharnhorst*. The admiral had called for a council of his captains, and all but Schönberg were already waiting in the room. *Nürnberg's* captain had apparently been delayed by the chaos in and around his ship. Maerker hoped that the distribution of the food, supplies, and some news from the world would help buoy the men's morale, which had become frightfully low since they had left Pagan.

The isolation, the routine, and their precarious military situation were taking a toll upon the men. After the departure of *Emden*, a palpable depression had settled over the crew as they steamed toward Eniwetok. Maerker mentioned his concerns to Chaplain Rost, who tried to inspire the men with a sermon about great German heroes, including their ship's namesake, Field Marshal Gneisenau. Not surprisingly, a minister droning on about long dead generals had little resonance with the crew. Maerker personally visited every compartment and watch on the ship, speaking to the men and trying to keep their spirits up. He attempted to assuage their concerns about the naval forces arrayed against them—reminding them that the squadron still remained undiscovered and was a potent and formidable fighting force.

Their daily action drills helped focus the men's efforts and hone the fighting efficiency of the ship. Clearing the decks for battle, preparing and loading the guns, transporting ammunition from the magazines, communicating orders from the bridge and the conning tower, and all of the procedures necessary to carry the fight to an enemy were repeated to the point that each man could probably have done his duty with his eyes shut. The newer crewmen were now fully integrated into the workings of the ship, and Maerker was confident that if they did have to fight, all of the crew would be ready. Unfortunately, some of the necessary drills, such as the protocols for repairing leaking bulkheads, putting out fires, and transporting wounded men to the infirmary, reminded the men of the brutal realities of combat—and of the possibility that they might all still perish under a rain of enemy shells.

The squadron had stopped as planned at Eniwetok Atoll in the Marshall Islands to coal and resupply from their support vessels. Unfortunately, when the coaling was complete, the holds of two of the squadron's colliers, *Prinz Waldemar* and *Mark*, were empty. Those ships were dismissed in the hopes that they might find a safe neutral harbor. Then *Nürnberg* had departed for Hawaii, and the sense of isolation was amplified for everyone remaining in the squadron. They traveled steadily east toward Christmas Island, stopping only once, at Majuro Atoll. There they emptied the remaining provisions from two of the supply ships, released them from service, and sent them to Hawaii, where they might be safe. The squadron was becoming steadily smaller as they headed farther east into the vast openness of the Pacific.

On their way to Christmas Island, the two armored cruisers conducted another round of firing exercises, with *Titania* once again towing the target. Even the successful exercise did nothing to improve the mood of the men aboard. Maerker passed on his concerns to the admiral, who agreed that they would have to do something to shake up the routine and inspire the men.

Now, with the squadron moored at Christmas Island, *Nürnberg* had finally rejoined them. An expectant murmur of excitement traveled through the ship as the prospect of fresh provisions and some news from home encouraged the men ever so slightly. Maerker knew, however, that some fresh food and a few newspapers could only lift the men's spirits for a short while.

When he joined the admiral and Captains Schultz, Filietz, Vogt, and Thierichens aboard *Scharnhorst*, Maerker confirmed that the malaise among the men was occurring on every ship. The crews of the squadron were becoming more miserable with every passing day. For them, the war itself had become a distant abstraction—and its only tangible manifestations were tedium, deprivation, isolation, and anxiety.

After a half-hour delay, Captain Schönberg was finally piped aboard *Scharnhorst*, and he entered the stateroom with a flourish.

"Aloha!" he boomed with a broad smile. Beside him stood a young sailor, straining under the weight of a large sack. He motioned to the young man, who set the bundle down. "Just a few gifts from the Hawaiian Islands," he said with a laugh. Schönberg reached into the sack and began pulling out immense greenish-gold pineapples. He playfully tossed one to each of the captains in the room. Maerker caught the heavy pineapple deftly and thanked Schönberg, smiling. Filietz was apparently unaccustomed to having large spiky objects tossed at him, and he fumbled his catch, allowing the pineapple to hit the decking with a thud. He was not amused. After Schultz, Vogt, and Thierichens had caught their gifts, Schönberg wisely chose to place the admiral's pineapple on the table rather than toss it toward his commanding officer. "Two of our freshly conscripted reservists had been working at one of the Americans' pineapple plantations," offered Schönberg, "and I arranged to have about a ton of the fruits brought aboard before we left Honolulu. I've eaten so much of it on the way here that I think I might begin to grow spikes myself." He turned and dismissed the sailor, who closed the door behind him.

The admiral turned the pineapple over in his hands. "I've heard that this fruit has a beneficial effect on the blood. Thank you and welcome back, Captain," he said to Schönberg. "I take it that all went according to plan?"

"Not entirely, but our mission was a success," replied Schönberg. "The Americans are such lackeys of the Brits. At first, they denied our request for coal, claiming that as a warship from a belligerent nation in time of war, we were prohibited under the Hague Conventions from coaling at the same neutral port more than once in a three-month period. I had to file a formal appeal, noting that the last time *Nürnberg* was there, war had not yet been declared. After a day's delay, they relented, and we were able to load all but fifty tons of the coal we had requested. Although maddening, the delay provided me plenty of time to ensure that all of our messages were delivered to the consulate."

"Excellent work, Karl," said Graf Spee. "Those messages were a critical element of our preparations." The *Admiralstab* was now informed of the movements of the squadron thus far, their coaling and supply issues, the communication problems caused by the capture of the Yap wireless station, and the detachment of *Emden* to the Indian Ocean. They also now knew of Graf Spee's intentions to operate off the South American coast.

"I believe that we can proceed in good faith toward South America," continued the admiral. "By the time we reach Valparaiso, awaiting us should be coal, supplies, and hopefully some useful information about the disposition of any British naval assets in the region. Also, God willing, Captain Haun and *Leipzig* will receive orders from the *Admiralstab* to join us off the Chilean coast."

"What news of the war?" asked Captain Schultz.

"It goes well for us, of course," replied Schönberg. "Our troops had encircled a whole Russian army at Tannenberg and were on the brink of a great victory. We are also pushing the French and British back in the west on the way to Paris. Some in the German community in Hawaii are saying that the war might be over by Christmas." He paused, adding, "Of course, in our colonies, things are going a bit differently. Japan, as you know, has laid claim to Tsingtao—and the Japanese and British have blockaded Kiaochow Bay. I heard no news of the smaller colonies, but Samoa has fallen to an invasion force from New Zealand."

"An invasion force?" asked Graf Spee. "Do you know any details?"

"Not much, I'm afraid. A number of ships, including troop carriers, sailed to Samoa under the protection of Admiral Patey's squadron. From what I gathered, the New Zealanders had our colony under their control in a matter of hours."

"Did you hear anything of casualties?"

"I did not. The accounts, if they are accurate, indicate that the colony was taken without any significant resistance."

Everyone mulled this over silently. Samoa was home to hundreds of German citizens and had been one of the scheduled stops on their planned summer cruise of the Pacific colonies. Now, quite abruptly, it belonged to their enemies.

"Of course," offered Schönberg, "if you believe all of the preposterous newspaper accounts from Hawaii, both *Scharnhorst* and *Gneisenau* were damaged in a great gun battle and were towed triumphantly into Hong Kong harbor by the British."

There were a few half-hearted chuckles among the officers.

"Hopefully no one believes that absurd propaganda," said Filietz with a sneer.

"I got the impression from our consul that the general populace in Britain and America believe whatever they are told by their journalists, even if those stories change each day."

"Ah, that is the way of war," said Graf Spee with a dismissive wave of his hand. "There are always three stories: ours, the enemy's, and the truth.

In my experience, the truth, if told at all, is the last story to be heard. That is of little consequence to us now. I am more concerned about the well-being and morale of our men. Captain Maerker and I have discussed the fact that the men of the squadron are restless, fearful, and generally miserable. The war for them has thus far been only a long, lonely, uncomfortable journey—while our countrymen on the other side of the world are actually fighting for our Kaiser and the Fatherland. I believe we must do something decisive to shake things up a bit and show our men that they have a role in winning this war."

Maerker noticed that Schönberg glanced in his direction. Curiously, that brief look from *Nürnberg's* captain seemed to be tinged with malice; but as startling as that momentary glance initially had been, Schönberg's demeanor now appeared to be completely normal. Maerker dismissed it, realizing that he did not yet really know his fellow captain and must have misread his expression.

The admiral went on. "Now that the New Zealanders have taken Samoa, I would assume that Patey and his fleet have left the area, probably still searching for us. It is possible, however, that they have left a warship and some supply ships behind with the troops who now occupy the colony at Apia. While the rest of our squadron continues on to the Marquesas, I believe that we should detach *Scharnhorst* and *Gneisenau* on a detour to Samoa. Hopefully we can surprise one or more of their ships at anchor and sink them right in Apia harbor."

"Excellent plan, sir," offered Captain Schultz. "If we're truly fortunate, Patey's flagship *Australia* will be sitting there in port, helpless and vulnerable."

"Unlikely," replied Graf Spee. "Patey has no reason to babysit Samoa. That's what all those New Zealand troops are for. No, he'll take his battlecruiser elsewhere. It's just as well, as far as I'm concerned—that one big ship could destroy us all. I'd prefer to keep several thousand kilometers between us and Patey's *Australia*."

"Sir?" Schönberg interjected, "I agree that we should do something decisive. It is well past time that we actually strike our enemies—and to that end, I have an additional idea." He pointed to a spot on the chart and continued. "On our voyage here from Hawaii, we passed not far from Fanning Island. In fact, we heard their wireless transmissions from time to time as we drew near. Fanning is a British possession and is the location of a cable relay station. It is a perfect target and a key communications relay for the British in the south Pacific. I propose that *Nürnberg* and *Titania* divert to Fanning, which is only two hundred and fifty kilometers from here. We can destroy the cable station—and *Titania* has equipment aboard than can cut the British undersea cable leading to the island. If our enemies can bring down Yap, we can certainly bring down Fanning. We could accomplish the mission in a single day, perhaps even before you set off for Samoa."

Graf Spee smiled. "I like it, Karl," he said, nodding. "Fanning is likely to be unguarded, and destroying the station will certainly damage some of Britain's communications network in the Pacific. Because that relay is one of the ways they communicate with the Australians and New Zealanders, cutting the cable may even hamper their search for us. When can you be ready?"

"We are ready. When we're finished coaling and offloading the supplies we brought back for the squadron, we can be on our way—possibly this afternoon." He turned to Commander Vogt. "Friedrich, is *Titania* ready?"

"Fully coaled and ready," replied Vogt. "Just say the word."

"We'll have to make some preparations before we set off for Apia," said Graf Spee, "But I would like to leave as soon as possible. If you and Commander Vogt can complete your mission to Fanning and return by the morning of the ninth, I think we can do it. The flagship and *Gneisenau* will then head southwest to Samoa, and you can escort the supply ships east to the Marquesas and wait for us there." He indicated the routes on the chart. "When our mission in Samoa is accomplished, we will head back east to join you—and then the full squadron will make the long trip to Easter Island."

Schönberg was smiling proudly, and each of the other captains was nodding with approval. Maerker could feel a decisive and determined energy infusing the room. Finally, the East Asia Squadron was truly going to war.

◆

THE MORNING of September 7th had begun much like every other morning on Fanning Island. The first rays of sunlight dappled the shimmering blue arc of the atoll's small lagoon. A light breeze rustled the palm fronds above and warmed the air—a portent of the hot day to come.

Wireless operator Thomas Bender paused outside the small cable station building—little more than a modest, white-walled shack—and took a final drag on his cigarette. Inhaling deeply, he discarded the butt onto the white sand at his feet and crushed it with the toe of his shoe. For much of the day, he would be cooped up in the small wireless room within, so he took another look out over the glittering lagoon before heading inside.

Something out beyond the reef caught his eye. At first, he could not be sure of what he was seeing, and he assumed the morning light was playing tricks on his eyes. Then he saw it more distinctly and was sure. It was a ship. Not just any ship—a warship. It had three funnels and was painted light gray, and it was making its way around the outer reef toward the nearest opening in the ring of coral.

What was a warship doing out here? He looked at it intently as it drew nearer. It was certainly not the largest naval vessel he had seen, but he could not determine what kind it was. Bender knew little about warships, but he knew enough to realize that this was big news for their little island. He trotted to the entrance of the cable station building and swung the door open. Inside, two operators sat at consoles within the small room, working intently to transcribe the previous night's cable traffic. A third man, a supervisor named Hemming, was busily pinning sheaves of papers to a cork board on the wall.

One of the operators, a young man named Rogers, looked up and grinned as he saw Bender standing at the open door. "There you are, Tommy boy. Mister Hemming here was just asking about you, and I was telling 'im you'd be right along. Probably saying your morning prayers with breakfast, I said." He winked at his friend.

"Morning, Rogers," Bender replied with a smile. "Morning, Smith," he addressed the other operator—then gestured with his head toward the lagoon. "Come take a look at this."

"Mister Bender," interjected supervisor Hemming testily, "we have no time for any of your sophomoric games this morning. In case you were not aware, there's a war on—and the cable traffic doesn't stop just because you'd like us to take a break."

"Well, I'm guessing this has something to do with the war," replied Bender. "It's a ship, just outside the reef. Come look."

The men inside exchanged glances, then got up and made their way out the door. On the sandy grass clearing between the building and the top of the beach, they paused. Sure enough, there was a warship out beyond the reef—perhaps a mile away. It appeared to have come to a stop.

"Is it one of ours?" asked Rogers, to no one in particular.

"I don't know," replied Hemming. "Could be, I suppose, but we weren't told to expect any Royal Navy visitors." He frowned, visibly perturbed at this unexpected breach of protocol.

"Maybe it's American," offered Smith.

"If they bothered to come all the way out here, it is probably one of ours," said Rogers. "Maybe they have some rum on board," he added hopefully.

"There's one way to find out who they are," said Bender. He ran back to the building, ducked inside, and emerged with a pair of binoculars. He returned to the group and raised the glasses. "Let's get a closer look."

Through the lenses, Bender could see the ship a bit more clearly. Uniformed men were moving about on deck, apparently preparing a boat to be lowered. "I think they are going to send a boat," he said.

"What flag she flyin', Tommy?" asked Rogers.

Curiously, the warship was flying no flags at all. "I… I don't think she has any," said Bender, although he was not sure if he was looking in the right places.

"No flags? Ridiculous," snapped Hemming. "Give me those glasses, Bender. Navy ships always fly flags. Otherwise, how would they know who is a friend and who is an enemy?" Hemming took the binoculars and scanned the ship. It had no visible flags. "This isn't a Royal Navy vessel— I'm sure of it. Not flying a flag is highly irregular, you know." He sniffed derisively. "I believe we should report this via cable and over the wireless. Bender, come with me."

Hemming handed the glasses to Smith, then turned and walked back to the building. Bender followed, although he would have preferred to watch from outside. Smith and Rogers remained on the beach, taking turns peering at the mysterious ship. Once inside the building, Bender sat at the console, put the earphones around his neck, and waited. Hemming paused as if deep in thought.

"What would you like me to say?" asked Bender.

"For now, just send the following: 'Unidentified warship sighted'," said Hemming. "Send it general dispatch, both cable and wireless."

"Will do." Bender donned the headphones, adjusted the settings on the console, and began tapping out the message. He was finished in a few moments.

Smith called from outside, "They've got a boat in the water now. It looks like they're coming ashore."

Bender stood, and he and Hemming both looked out the open seaward window of the small building. Sure enough, a cutter was heading through the break in the reef, into the lagoon, with a number of men aboard. Eight oars were dipping and pulling in unison.

Smith turned and called back again. "They've got a flag on the boat. It looks French."

"French?" asked Hemming from inside. "You mean three stripes? Red, white, and blue?"

"Yes, definitely French."

"That's certainly unusual," commented Hemming. He looked at Bender. "All right then, we'll have to amend our earlier message. We don't want to unnecessarily alarm anyone. Send a new general dispatch that says, 'French warship sighted'." He looked out at the approaching boat. "I wonder why the French navy would be paying us a visit?"

Bender finished sending the message, then stood and also looked out the window. The boat was nearing the shore. A small French *tricolore* was flapping from the bow. Rogers and Smith had begun to walk down the beach to greet their new guests.

"These Frenchmen are going to be disappointed if they were expecting a welcoming party in their honor," said Bender. "Unless they fancy a sip of coconut milk, we don't have much to offer them."

"I'm sure they are just paying us a courtesy visit. They're our allies, after all. In fact, if I had to guess, I'd say that..." Hemming stopped, mid-sentence, his mouth agape.

The boat had reached the sand, and several sailors leapt into the shallow water. They were all armed with rifles, which they immediately pointed at Rogers and Smith. The two men hesitated, obviously confused. One of the sailors said something that Bender could not hear, and both Rogers and Smith raised their hands above their heads. There were now a total of ten sailors on the beach, and two of them were setting up a machine gun on a tripod. The sailor who had spoken—apparently the leader of the group—began yelling orders at his men, who fanned out along the beach and began advancing toward the cable station building.

"Oh, dear God," said Hemming.

"Perhaps these Frenchmen need to be reminded that they are our allies," offered Bender.

"Quickly, send out another message." Hemming's face was drained of color. "It should say, 'Warship is not French. Armed men have come ashore...'"

A firm, loud knock at the door interrupted Hemming, who looked at Bender, unsure of what to do.

"I think you should probably answer the door," suggested Bender. "They do have guns, after all—and they did knock."

Hemming took a deep breath, walked to the door, and pulled it open. A foreign naval officer took a step into the doorway and leveled a pistol at Hemming's chest.

"*Guten Morgen*," he said. "My name is *Oberleutnant* Haas from His Imperial Majesty's ship *Nürnberg*. Who is the commander of this installation?" The officer spoke with an accent, but his English was quite clear.

"I am, uh... the senior cable supervisor for this station," stammered Hemming, who was staring wide-eyed at the barrel of the pistol.

"And your name is?" asked the German officer.

"Nigel Hemming, of the Cable and Wireless Company. What do you want from us?"

"*Herr* Hemming, we do not wish to harm anyone here. We have come to destroy the station. How many men to you employ here?"

"Destroy it?" Hemming asked in disbelief.

"How many men, *Herr* Hemming?" asked Haas more sternly.

"Eight, including myself and our Fijian cook."

"Assemble all of your men on the beach, away from this installation. Both of you, please step outside." He gestured with the pistol, and both Hemming and Bender made their way out of the building with their hands above their heads. The German sailors now had six men under guard. As they were walked a short way down the beach, more armed sailors escorted the remaining two men from the barracks building to join the group. When the station staff was assembled, they were told to sit on the sand with their hands on their heads. Two of the sailors stood by with rifles, guarding the captives warily.

During the next hour, the rest of the Germans then went to work with determined efficiency. Bender could hear them smashing equipment and batteries inside the station. One man cut the wireless aerial from the building, while another sailor busily swung an axe at the base of the wooden wireless mast itself. It soon fell, trailing its support lines and crashing into the yard in front of the station. The Germans then moved on to the storage sheds behind the main building, and although Bender could not see them, he could hear more smashing and breaking. They were destroying the spare equipment as well.

Bender could see that other men were carrying crates, files, and boxes from the buildings, including the company cash box. After the Germans had removed everything that they intended to take, Haas gave orders to his men, all but two of whom then moved farther away down the beach. The two remaining sailors then took petrol canisters and liberally poured fuel in and around the main building. One of them threw something inside the station, and both men ran down the beach. A muffled explosion startled Bender and his fellow prisoners, and thick black smoke and curling orange flames enveloped the station building.

Out to sea, a second, smaller ship rounded the point beyond the reef and steamed through the opening into the lagoon. This vessel had a black hull and looked to be a typical merchant steamer—although it did have what looked like small naval guns mounted on the forecastle and the stern. The sailors on shore signaled to the second ship, and it began to move parallel to the beach about a hundred yards away. Bender could see that it was dragging lines or chains from booms on either side of the ship. After a few minutes, the small ship slowed to a stop, and men began to hoist the lines. It then became obvious what they were doing, for the chains had hooks on them and had brought up the submerged communication cables.

The black cables were as thick as a man's arm, but somehow the men on board the second ship were able to quickly cut them, and the severed ends splashed back into the lagoon.

*Oberleutnant* Haas approached the seated men, who were still under armed guard. Bender realized soberly that there was nothing they could do if these Germans intended to shoot them, and from the terrified looks of his compatriots, he assumed they were all thinking the same thing. Beside him, Hemming was shaking and staring vacantly at the sand.

Haas smiled at them and said, "We will be leaving now, gentlemen. We appreciate your cooperation. *Auf Wiedersehen.*" The officer turned and strode away. The sailors guarding them raised their rifles, and all of the Germans made their way back to their boat, pushing off and clambering inside.

Bender stood and exhaled in relief as he watched the enemy sailors depart. He looked down and noticed that Hemming had not moved. He was still sitting, trembling, and staring. The incident had apparently been a bit much for him. The Germans were rowing quickly back out across the lagoon, as the smoke from the burning station drifted up and over the island. The Germans had been ashore for less than two hours.

The employees of the Fanning Island Relay Station stood near their burning buildings watched in silence as the small, black-hulled ship followed the cutter out through the gap in the reef. The cutter was hoisted back aboard the cruiser, and the two ships steamed out around the southwest curve of the reef until they were both out of sight.

◆

"THIS IS WHAT I GET for choosing this rendezvous point sight unseen," muttered Admiral von Spee gruffly.

He and Captain Maerker stood on *Scharnhorst's* forecastle, looking out at Suvarov Atoll. The admiral had chosen this spot because it lay directly between Samoa and the Marquesas, where he had planned to rejoin the rest of the squadron. The admiral had previously arranged for the collier *Ahlers* to detach from the squadron, head south, and meet them at Suvarov. The collier had been waiting there as planned—and she was now anchored half a kilometer off the flagship's port quarter. However, no one in the squadron had ever been to the small, bleak island, which turned out to have no accessible harbor and offered scant protection from the ocean swells. Attempting to coal in such a spot would have been hazardous and foolish. While anchored outside the reef at Suvarov, the admiral had called Maerker over to the flagship to discuss their options.

"I shouldn't be surprised, Julius," continued von Spee. "Although we're running out of everything else, we don't seem to be running out of problems."

Maerker smiled. "No, sir. It would seem not."

"This ridiculous spit of land is utterly worthless for coaling or anything else. I'm not surprised they named it after a Russian." On deck, the wind was a pleasant breeze, but large swells surged past the anchored ship, driven by some distant tempest. The bow rose and fell dramatically with the waves as the two men looked out at the small, sparsely vegetated smear of land off to starboard. The powerful surf pounded noisily on the nearby reef, throwing up towering fans of foaming spray. Both men wore their white tropical uniforms, and the admiral—ever polished—also wore a bicorn hat with its characteristic gold-braided trim. Maerker's head, as usual, was unadorned, and his long brown curls swirled about his face in the breeze. The admiral turned away from the island in disgust. "We still need to coal, of course, now that we've nearly emptied our bunkers during our little sightseeing tour of the Samoan islands."

The admiral's bitterness was understandable. Their detour to Samoa from Christmas Island had taken five days of steady steaming. Initially, the men had been in great spirits, following the return of *Nürnberg* and *Titania*. News of the successful attack upon the Fanning Island station had raced through the squadron. Although not a single shot had been fired, the crews were buoyed by the cleverness of the assault and the knowledge that at least one significant portion of Britain's vaunted network of worldwide communications cables—their "All Red Line"—had been destroyed. *Scharnhorst* and *Gneisenau* had departed southwest for Samoa that afternoon, leaving *Nürnberg* to escort the remaining ships of the squadron east toward the Marquesas.

Unfortunately, when they arrived at the Apia harbor on the Samoan island of Upolu, they found it empty. New Zealand's flag flew above the colonial offices that had so recently belonged to Germany, but no enemy warships were in sight. Because at least several hundred New Zealand troops were likely now garrisoned in the colony, sending a landing party like *Nürnberg* had done at Fanning was out of the question. Shelling the captured colony was also not an option, because they did not want to risk harming any German colonists who might still be there—and the colony's wireless station was too far inland to target with their guns.

Disappointed, the admiral had ordered both armored cruisers to steam on slowly past the harbor, along the coast of the island, in full view of anyone ashore who might be watching. This was the only part of the admiral's original plan they could now achieve—a standard old naval trick intended to fool a gullible enemy into believing they were leaving in a false direction. Of course, their next rendezvous point at Suvarov lay nearly a thousand kilometers to the east, but the German ships could wait until they were well out of sight from land before turning back in that direction.

Some useful information came to them, surprisingly, in the form of two German colonists who managed to launch a steam cutter from the shore and, flying a defiant German flag, raced out to intercept the flagship. The admiral slowed to allow the men to come board. The colonists were ardent patriots who volunteered on the spot and breathlessly recounted the invasion and occupation of Samoa by the New Zealanders. The enemy had arrived under the protection of a squadron of cruisers led by Patey's great battlecruiser *Australia*. Also among the fleet was the French cruiser *Montcalm*. The force was overwhelming, and the colony had been forced to surrender or face a devastating naval bombardment. Fifteen-hundred New Zealand troops then landed, after which the naval fleet departed—probably, the admiral surmised, to continue the hunt for the East Asia Squadron.

Fifteen-hundred soldiers were an overwhelming force. The German garrison at Apia had comprised only a few dozen colonial soldiers and fewer than a hundred native troops—little more than a police force, really. The colony would have had no chance, had they resisted.

According to the two men, the colony's German governor, Erich Schultz, had been courageously defiant to the end, even ordering his personnel to try to disable the colony's new wireless station as the enemy soldiers came ashore. After a confrontation at the main colonial offices, the New Zealanders had unceremoniously taken the governor into custody. Governor Schultz had actually been led in manacles to one of the warships that subsequently departed, taking the captive governor God-knows-where.

Admiral von Spee was incensed at this outrage. If this story were true, it would be an unthinkable breach of diplomatic protocol. He and Governor Schultz were friends, and such an egregious violation of decency could not go unpunished.

It was clear to Maerker that the admiral was still seething, several days later, as they discussed their plans while overlooking Suvarov's forbidding reefs.

"From here, we still have enough coal to easily reach Humphrey Island or Penrhyn Island," said Maerker, "although they are both a bit out of our way to the north. However, we don't know that the coaling conditions there will be any better than here. Few of these isolated atolls offer much protection from the sea or wind."

"True. We would truly be in a bind if we steamed all the way to either of those places and then still couldn't coal. No, I have another idea."

"Sir?"

"Those uncivilized cretins took our governor of Samoa away in chains. In chains, Julius, like some common criminal! There must be retribution for this outrage. I'd dearly love to strike a blow of revenge upon the New Zealanders, but there aren't any of them way out here—so we'll have to do the next best thing."

"Which is?"

"The French, Julius!" The admiral paused and inhaled a lungful of sea air before continuing. "The French cruiser *Montcalm* accompanied Patey's invasion force—and later escorted the ship in which Governor Schultz was imprisoned. In return for their complicity in this crime against the Kaiser's representative in our colony, I believe we should strike a blow against those miserable French barbarians at one of their colonies." The admiral had begun to pace back and forth on the deck, gesturing demonstratively as he spoke. His blue eyes had taken on a steely glint. He continued, "Instead of heading directly northeast to the Marquesas from here, a slight detour to the southeast will take us into the heart of French Polynesia. The jewel of their colonies in the South Pacific is Tahiti. Therefore, Papeete harbor in Tahiti shall be our target. The port is probably lightly defended. We will arrive with an overwhelming show of force and demand the surrender of the colony. Then we can land armed parties to take possession of their coal stores and anything else that might be of use to us. We may even make a prisoner of *their* colonial governor. After we have sacked Papeete, we can resume our course northward to the Marquesas to rejoin the rest of the squadron. Perhaps our rendezvous with the squadron will be delayed by an extra day or two, but I think the prize of striking Papeete will justify our tardiness."

Maerker pondered this revelation and had to smile. "Sir, your plan does not disappoint for its audacity. However, if I may speak freely, I can think of two problems with this scheme—and a possible solution."

The admiral nodded. "Please go on."

Maerker continued. "First, your 'slight detour' to Tahiti is what, fifteen hundred kilometers? Although we now have *Ahlers* with us, we cannot coal in these conditions here—forcing us to go on with what fuel we still carry. My stokers estimated this morning that we had coal in our bunkers sufficient for perhaps eleven or twelve hundred more kilometers of steady steaming, which would leave us still short of our objective. Secondly, you yourself have said that a military commander's greatest mistake is to underestimate his opponent. Although it may be that Tahiti is lightly defended, we truly know nothing of the disposition of French naval forces in the area, nor do we know anything of possible French defenses at Papeete. We are now in an area of the ocean where our knowledge is, sadly, rather limited."

The admiral was listening intently.

"There may be a way we can glean some valuable information about Papeete, while we also fill our bunkers in a sheltered anchorage. French Polynesia has dozens of islands, correct? One of those islands, Bora Bora, is less than twelve hundred kilometers from here, just within our current range, if we steam conservatively. Bora Bora, in turn, is less than three hundred kilometers from Tahiti. Although we have not yet been there, Bora Bora is known to have a decent anchorage—so coaling there should not be a problem. I also believe that they have no wireless capability, so if we steam to Bora Bora first, they will have no way of warning Tahiti of our arrival. If we're lucky, they might not yet have any knowledge of the war—so we may be able to coal there without raising any undue suspicions. Additionally, while we're there, we can also make some discreet inquiries as to the state of French defenses at Papeete."

The Admiral smiled. "Perhaps so, if they're willing to provide us with that information."

"They may be, especially if we engage in a bit of deception. After all, do they need to know that these are German warships?"

The admiral raised an eyebrow. "What are you scheming, Julius?"

"Several of my senior officers are multi-lingual. How many aboard *Scharnhorst* speak fluent French or English?"

"Perhaps a dozen, I would guess," replied the admiral with a wry smirk.

PART TWO

A Gathering of Wolves

# SEVEN

*Monday, September 14, 1914*
*South Atlantic Ocean, Santa Catarina Coast, Brazil*

PERHAPS IT WAS ONLY FITTING that the flagship of the motley British squadron was aging and trouble-ridden herself. Luce had received word via wireless that one of *Good Hope's* engines had broken down, and Admiral Cradock had stopped near Santa Catarina, Brazil, to make repairs. Rather than meeting in Montevideo, as originally planned, *Glasgow*, *Monmouth*, and *Otranto* were summoned north to rendezvous with their new commander. The weather was no better as they traveled northward, enduring driving rain, biting wind, and rough seas.

When they reached the flagship, it was mid-day, although the churning purple skies mimicked an angry dusk. The large armored cruiser was anchored a few miles off shore, rolling slightly in the whitecaps. Other than the lack of smoke emanating from her funnels, the only sign that anything was amiss was a sizeable tarp that had been erected abaft the rear wireless mast, over one of the stern hatches. Luce could see men working in that area of the deck. The canvas was billowing and snapping in the wind, and Luce doubted that it was providing much shelter from the cold, slanting downpour. He instructed his signalmen to send the customary greetings, and the flagship replied with instructions for him and his fellow captains to come aboard immediately.

HMS *Good Hope* was a large ship—more than fourteen thousand tons and some five hundred thirty feet long. She was also old—older even than *Monmouth*, whose initial appearance had so appalled *Glasgow's* officers. Back in her day, *Good Hope* had briefly held the distinction of being the fastest armored cruiser afloat, but that had been thirteen years ago. Luce thought that it might as well have been one hundred and thirteen years—

and even when her engines were working, it was unlikely that this old relic would now make much more than twenty knots. Cradock's previous flagship had been HMS *Suffolk*, a sister ship to *Monmouth*. So, by moving to the larger *Good Hope*, Cradock had gained more spacious accommodations and perhaps a slight increase in speed, but he had only marginally improved his potency in battle. By modern standards, *Good Hope* was undergunned for her class, with a main battery of only two 9.2-inch guns, each in a separate upper deck turret—one on the foredeck below the wheelhouse and the other aft of the fourth and last of her funnels. Her secondary battery of 6-inch guns was placed in antiquated casemates along her hull—much like *Monmouth*'s unfortunate gun array. Those guns, protruding from the hull only a few feet above the waterline, would also be useless in all but the calmest of seas. HMS *Good Hope* had also been sitting idle in the reserve fleet and would have been scrapped had war not been declared. So now, with a crew of reservists and cadets, this old cruiser had become Admiral Cradock's "new" flagship.

The council of officers was to take place in the dining compartment of the admiral's spacious stateroom. Luce had brought with him Commander Thompson and his young intelligence officer, Lieutenant Hirst. Also in attendance were *Good Hope's* captain, Philip Francklin; Frank Brandt of *Monmouth*; Brandt's first officer, Commander Forbes; and Captain Edwards of *Otranto*. After brief introductions, Cradock bade them to take a seat at the long, polished, wooden table. Luce noticed that *Good Hope*, unlike his own ship, had retained at least some of her pre-war wooden furnishings, including the glossy rosewood paneling in the admiral's stateroom.

Rear-Admiral Sir Christopher Cradock was well known and well regarded throughout the Royal Navy. He had an exemplary record of distinguished service and had received his knighthood two years earlier. He had also written several well-known books on naval matters. Luce had met him a number of times before, and he genuinely liked the older man. He had often thought that Cradock was a throwback to the classic naval commanders from Nelson's days—men who were colorful, brash, and courageously reckless—the kind of men who seemed to be in short supply in the cautious, political, modern Royal Navy. Cradock was a small man, always impeccably dressed and coiffed, with a neatly trimmed beard of salt and pepper gray. He was a lifelong bachelor and, at fifty-two, still had a reputation in diplomatic circles as quite a ladies' man. He was sociable and gracious, and he appeared to genuinely enjoy the company of his fellow officers.

"Welcome aboard, gentlemen," Cradock began. "I do apologize for the slight change in our meeting plans. Unfortunately, this old girl has thrown a shoe, but I am assured by our engineers that we will be up and running again sometime before the end of the war." The captains chuckled, and Cradock shook his head in mock exasperation and straightened a short stack of papers before him. "Let's get straight to business, shall we? As you all know, since the beginning of August, our primary naval objective in the Atlantic has been to search for the light cruisers *Dresden* and *Karlsruhe*. Thus far, we've done a piss-poor job of finding either one. We do know that *Karlsruhe* is still operating in the Caribbean. Since her sinking of *Bowes Castle*, she has captured or sunk at least two other ships off the Venezuelan coast. We believe that she's still in that region, and Admiral Stoddart is searching for her there. *Dresden* is another matter altogether. We know that she's been moving steadily southward, and now we may know why."

He pulled two sheets of paper from the stack before him. "I have some intelligence from the Admiralty. The German East Asia Squadron, commanded by Vice-Admiral Maximilian von Spee, left their base in Tsingtao just before the declaration of war—and their precise whereabouts is currently unknown, other than they are somewhere in the Pacific. One of the cruisers from that squadron recently coaled in Hawaii. While there, her captain met with the German consul and was able to send some messages to the *Admiralstab* in Berlin. We do not know the nature of these messages; however, we have just learned that the German Naval Attaché in Washington recently made covert arrangements with German agents in South America to gather a collection of colliers and other supply ships near the Strait of Magellan. As we know, *Dresden* has been heading farther south—and by now she could be near the Strait. The arrangements being made by the agents, however, suggest a far greater number of support vessels than would be required to support a single light cruiser such as *Dresden*. In short, the Admiralty believes that von Spee may be bringing his entire squadron to South American waters."

For a moment, the officers were silent as they considered this surprising revelation.

"What is the current makeup of his squadron?" asked Luce. He had heard of the East Asia Squadron before—they were regarded as a crack outfit. With the thought that his next posting may have been in the Far East, he had assumed that at some point he would have made the acquaintance of Admiral Graf von Spee and his captains.

"The backbone of the squadron is a pair of new armored cruisers, *Scharnhorst* and *Gneisenau*," replied Cradock. "These are big, powerful ships, each of which has a main battery of eight 8.2-inch guns, plus a secondary battery of six 5.9-inch guns. They are well armored, and we believe they can make at least twenty-two knots. Our boys got a good look at them back in June, when Admiral Jerram paid them a visit in Tsingtao.

Those are two damn fine warships, with crews as well trained as any in the Kaiser's navy. The rest of the squadron comprises the light cruisers, *Emden*, *Nürnberg*, and *Leipzig*. Those cruisers are relatively lightly armed—in fact, *Emden* is a sister ship to our elusive *Dresden*, so you are already familiar with her specifications. Basically, all of them have a uniform battery of ten 4.1-inch guns. The light cruisers aren't particularly powerful warships, but they are all relatively new and they can all reach at least twenty-two knots. We believe he may also have one or more auxiliary cruisers among his support ships."

"Why would this German admiral bring his squadron half-way around the world?" asked Edwards. "I'm sorry if I'm missing something, sir, but it doesn't make a bit of sense to me."

"Perhaps not at first glance," said Cradock, "but I know Admiral von Spee. In fact, we served together once, years ago, on a joint force in China. He has a brilliant naval mind—perhaps the best in the Kaiser's whole damned navy. I believe von Spee has done the math and determined that the forces he would face in the western Pacific are overwhelming. In addition to two Royal Navy squadrons, he would have to contend with the French, the Russians, and the entire Japanese navy. Staying there would be suicidal. If I were him, I might do the same thing and come to South America, where he has fewer enemies—and where he has a lot more friends. He can still threaten Allied trade here, and all of the various German communities and their agents will do their best to help him."

"This von Spee has quite the reputation," agreed Francklin. "From what I've heard, he's thought of as a sharp and focused fellow—one of the Kaiser's favorites. I doubt he'd do anything without thinking it through. If he's bringing that bang-up squadron of his eastward, he's definitely tallied up the positives and negatives."

"What was their last known position?" asked Luce.

"Well, that's a bit of a mixed bag, unfortunately. The two big ships haven't really been seen since they left Tsingtao in late June, although *Gneisenau* did stop briefly in Nagasaki. Since the declaration of war, neither armored cruiser has been sighted at all. It's as if they simply vanished. We have a little more information on the light cruisers, but not much. *Nürnberg* has coaled twice in Honolulu, most recently last week. *Emden* was the last ship to leave Tsingtao, but she hasn't been seen since the first week of August. *Leipzig* was known to be somewhere along the Mexican coast as recently as six days ago."

"So, the full squadron probably isn't yet together," stated Luce.

"True," replied Cradock. "At the very least, we know that *Leipzig* hasn't joined them yet, but she may be on her way as we speak. I am also assuming that *Dresden* has orders to join von Spee's squadron, and that is why she has been heading south so rapidly—and why the *Admiralstab* wants colliers and supply ships waiting near the Strait of Magellan."

"Like wolves gathering before a hunt," said Brandt quietly, as if he were speaking to himself. He raised his eyes and looked at the admiral. "That would give them a squadron of six new warships, plus their auxiliaries. We have three warships, two of them elderly, plus *Otranto*..." Brandt trailed off, letting his words hang in the air. He looked extremely troubled.

He had every reason to be troubled, thought Luce. Not only did it sound like the German armored cruisers were more than a match for both *Good Hope* and *Monmouth* in gunnery and speed, but also the German crews were known to be extremely good. By contrast, the hastily mustered reserve crews of *Good Hope* and *Monmouth* were anything but combat-ready. *Glasgow's* men were the only crew in their squadron with an appropriate amount of training and experience—but *Glasgow* certainly could not fight *Scharnhorst* or *Gneisenau*. Luce also knew that if he had to go it alone against the four remaining German light cruisers, *Glasgow* might be able to sink one or two of them—but surviving a sustained fight against all four would be nearly impossible.

"The Admiralty are sending us two more ships to bolster our squadron," said Cradock, sensing the mounting anxiety in the room. "They've told me that *Defence* is being sent from the Mediterranean, and *Canopus* is on her way down as well. *Defence* is a new ship, a fine armored cruiser on par with the big German ships—so she should be able to give them a run for their money. *Canopus*, however, is a frightfully old battleship. I'm honestly not sure what we can do with her, but we'll have to think of something."

"What are our orders?" asked Luce. "A missing German squadron in the Pacific is one thing—what the Admiralty expect us to do about it is something else altogether."

"There's the rub." Cradock sighed and picked up a sheet of paper and scanned it. He found the relevant passage and said, "the Admiralty have told us to do the following: 'Leave a sufficient force to deal with *Dresden* and *Karlsruhe*. Concentrate a squadron strong enough to meet *Scharnhorst* and *Gneisenau*, making Falkland Islands your coaling base. Until *Defence* joins, keep at least *Canopus* and one County-class cruiser with your flagship. As soon as you have superior force, search Strait of Magellan, being ready to return and cover the Plate, or search north as far as Valparaiso. Break up German trade and destroy German cruisers'." Cradock set the sheet back on the table and clasped his hands. "There you have it, Gentlemen—our orders."

Luce was not surprised at the tinge of sarcasm in the admiral's voice. These orders were astonishingly naïve. At the very least, the Admiralty's expectations spectacularly disregarded the reality of their situation. Even with the addition of two ships, they still would not have enough vessels to simultaneously find and neutralize *Dresden* and *Karlsruhe*, protect the River Plate area, search the Chilean coast from the Strait up to Valparaiso, break up German trade, and—last but not least—find and destroy the enemy's most powerful cruiser squadron. What could Churchill, First Lord of the Admiralty, and Battenberg, First Sea Lord, be thinking?

As if his first officer had been hearing his thoughts, Thompson interjected, "With all due respect, sir, does the Admiralty believe all that nonsense is possible?"

"Actually, Commander," replied Cradock, smiling, "I think they do. Absurd as it sounds, the Admiralty seem to believe that all of this is possible—and they expect us to do it."

"Even with *Defence*, sir," said Luce, "our squadron would still be less than a match for the Germans, if we can find them. Even that is assuming that we could bring our whole squadron to bear on them at once, without leaving any of our ships behind to cover the Plate or to try to find *Dresden*."

"I agree, Mister Luce," said Cradock. "So, we're not going to do all of it—at least not all at once."

The officers looked expectantly at the admiral, who stood and straightened the lapels of his jacket. He stepped to the paneled bulkhead behind him, where a large chart of the South American continent was affixed. He pointed to an area of the map north of Brazil.

"First off, Admiral Stoddart is chasing *Karlsruhe* about in the Caribbean." His finger traced the northernmost portion of the South American coastline. "Because *Karlsruhe* has shown no indication that she is heading southward, we'll assume her orders are to stay in that region and interfere with Allied shipping there—so for now, she'll remain Stoddart's responsibility." He moved his hand down to the southern tip of the continent. "*Dresden* bypassed the River Plate area altogether and appears to be headed to the Strait—hell, she may already be there—so for now, we won't have to leave any ships patrolling in the Atlantic to search for her here. Initially, I believe that we should steam for the Strait and search there. Hopefully, we will find *Dresden* hiding somewhere in the area and we can destroy her before the East Asia Squadron is anywhere near. When *Defence* arrives, we can more assuredly move through the Strait, into the Pacific, and up the Chilean coast toward Valparaiso. I've ordered *Bristol* to move down to Montevideo. She should be here shortly, and perhaps we'll leave old *Canopus* behind with her, so the two of them can keep an eye on the Plate for us. While we're over on the west coast, we can interfere with any German merchant ships that are attempting to set up for von Spee's arrival. Perhaps by doing so, we can discourage him from heading down here and maybe drive him elsewhere."

"And if we can't keep von Spee from coming to the Chilean coast?" asked Brandt.

"Then we'll have to try to sink him," replied Cradock.

◆

AFTER *Good Hope's* engine had been satisfactorily repaired, the four ships of Cradock's squadron returned to Montevideo, where the weather promptly worsened to gale force conditions, preventing their departure for several more days. During their infuriating delay at Montevideo, as the ships pitched and rolled in the heavy seas and driving rain, they received a series of messages that were both troubling and perplexing. A message from the Admiralty to Cradock regarding a sighting of the East Asia Squadron had finally prompted the admiral to call his captains together, so each of them had made the unpleasant journey over to the flagship in cutters that were decidedly ill-suited for the heavy sea conditions.

Despite the coverage provided by his greatcoat and the admirable efforts of the oarsmen to efficiently steer the cutter through the rain-slashed peaks and troughs of the whitecapped swells, every square inch of Luce's body was soaking wet when he finally came aboard *Good Hope*. A steward took his sodden outer garments and provided a warm blanket before ushering him to the admiral's stateroom.

Captain Edwards of *Otranto* was the only squadron captain absent. He had attempted to cross in the rough sea, but he and his oarsmen had thought better of it and had returned to his ship—sending his regrets via signal lamp. Luce was seated in a chair next to Brandt of *Monmouth*, across from the admiral and Francklin of *Good Hope*. Each officer had passed around and reviewed a copy of the latest dispatch from the Admiralty.

Admiral Cradock had apologized for calling for a meeting in such miserable conditions, but he had felt it was necessary, considering the circumstances. As a peace offering to his damp captains, Cradock had poured liberal amounts of fine brandy and had offered cigars from his impressive store—and now a rich aromatic smoke hung heavily in the compartment as the four men sipped the warm amber liquid. The stateroom was listing back and forth as the big ship rode the angry swells outside, and the syrupy brandy in Luce's glass tilted slowly to and fro.

"I think they're damned fools if they believe that," said Cradock. "It must have been a trick—and not a very complicated one at that."

"True. It seems obvious to me as well," agreed Luce, wondering why any seasoned commander would fall for such a common ruse. The message detailed the sudden alarming appearance of Admiral von Spee's armored cruisers off the Samoan port of Apia, now held by New Zealand troops. Luckily, no Royal Navy ships had been in port at the time. The Germans had not fired a shot; instead, they simply left, steaming northwest. The direction of their departure had somehow convinced the Admiralty that von Spee was no longer heading east toward the South American coast. Cradock now had revised orders to simply search the Strait and the Chilean coast up to Valparaiso for *Dresden* and to break up any German trade that might be occurring in the region.

"If I were him," continued the admiral, "I'd still be headed this way. The South American coast is still the safest and friendliest place for him to operate. And there are simply too many coincidences—too much unusual activity down there to be anything but preparations for a gathering of his squadron. I'm certain that von Spee is still headed to South America."

"Which means that we still have to prepare for him, even though the Admiralty thinks the Germans are headed elsewhere," said Luce.

"And that also means we're down one armored cruiser as well," said Cradock ominously. Luce, Brandt, and Francklin looked at him, surprised. Cradock exhaled a swirl of silvery smoke and continued. "As you know, we had been told that *Defence* would be joining us, but the Admiralty no longer believes that von Spee's squadron is headed this way, so now they intend to send *Defence* elsewhere—thinking we no longer need her."

Brandt shook his head. "So now we're faced with the possibility that von Spee may still be headed to South America, but we have fewer ships than our earlier estimates—which were less than favorable to begin with?"

"Precisely," replied Cradock. "I hope I'm wrong about that—and perhaps the Admiralty will reconsider and still send *Defence* our way. I also hope that our men in London are right and von Spee is keeping his ships on the other side of the Pacific. But I won't make decisions based on hopes—so either way, we can't wait around to find out. At least the Admiralty are still sending us *Canopus*," he said with a smile and a shake of his head. "For now, we still have to search the Strait. If nothing else, we need to know where *Dresden* is hiding. If we can find and sink her, then we can scratch one of the myriad duties off our list."

"True," replied Luce. "Unfortunately, our next problem will be food stores. We are running low again aboard all of the ships. I don't know how *Good Hope* is doing, but *Glasgow* will be out of food within a month, and *Monmouth* and *Otranto* will run dry in as few as three weeks. If we cannot replenish our stores in Punta Arenas, we may have to wait until we reach Valparaiso, which will be cutting it close."

"We're low as well," said Francklin. "Only three or four weeks left."

"It isn't just the food, either," added Brandt. "*Monmouth's* engines and boilers are badly in need of a refit. My engineers are holding things together for now, but we're getting low on spare machine parts."

"Regrettably," replied Cradock, "there was a bit of a foul-up and our scheduled store ship was apparently emptied by *Bristol* and *Cornwall* up north—I shall have a word with Admiral Stoddart about that. For now, Captain Brandt, see if the engineers aboard the other ships can spare any necessary parts that might fit your equipment. As far as some of the food is concerned, we should be able to partially resupply at Punta Arenas. While we're there, we'll try to get some meaningful intelligence regarding *Dresden's* location. As soon as the weather clears, we will make for the Strait."

They waited several more frustrating days, moored near Montevideo, for the weather to ease up and then were finally able to coal the ships and begin the slow trip southward in only slightly more hospitable seas. The morale on board was low—with limited food supplies, poor weather, and the apparent futility of their mission all dragging on the men's spirits. *Glasgow*, because of her crew's experience in these waters, was in the vanguard, with *Good Hope*, *Monmouth*, and *Otranto* trailing. The weather and *Otranto's* slower engines often limited the squadron to less than ten knots, so their progress down the Argentine coast was plodding. They encountered no other shipping of any sort along the way, and the first indication of any other vessels in the area came by wireless as they neared the eastern mouth of the Strait of Magellan.

Four days into the voyage, the wireless room was surprised to receive a brief message from a British passenger liner that was making its way east through the Strait. The passenger ship *Ortega* claimed to have encountered a German cruiser seven days earlier and was making for Montevideo as quickly as possible. *Glasgow* responded and arranged to meet the liner as the ships passed each other near the mouth of the Strait.

The possibility that someone had finally seen *Dresden*—and had survived to tell the tale—was the first remotely positive sign or message they had received in more than a week.

*Ortega's* story was remarkable. After being briefly pursued by a German light cruiser that must have been *Dresden*, the captain of the steamer—a likeable, no-nonsense fellow named Kinnier—escaped by fleeing into a narrow channel that the Germans must have found too dangerous to try to navigate. *Ortega* then slowly made her way through the previously uncharted Nelson Strait, feeling along behind lifeboats that took continual soundings of the treacherous, winding course ahead of the large passenger ship. Kinnier then made his way south through Smyth Channel, finally reaching the Strait of Magellan after a slow and nerve-wracking detour of some one hundred miles. Thompson commended Kinnier for his bravery and resourcefulness and assured him that his passage to Montevideo would be safe from German warships. *Ortega's* captain provided *Glasgow's* navigating officers with charts they had made during their harrowing journey, in case the British ships should have to take a similar route in their quest to hunt down *Dresden*.

After a chorus of hearty cheers and songs from her French passengers and English crew, *Ortega* left them, continuing on her way north. The squadron resumed its course southward, soon entering the eastern mouth of the Strait of Magellan. Here at its Atlantic end, the Strait was immense — a sizeable gulf so broad that they could not yet see the southern shore. Only after they had proceeded more than fifty miles westward did the rocky southern shoreline come into view, at first hazy and indistinct. Soon the waterway narrowed dramatically, and in some places the bleak, craggy shores narrowed to less than three miles apart. Slowly, steadily, they wound their way southwest toward Punta Arenas; and with each mile they traveled, the shrill wind became colder.

Luce thought that *Ortega's* story had been both encouraging and disconcerting. On one hand, they now had direct confirmation that their quarry was operating in the vicinity of the Strait. On the other hand, they still did not know *Dresden's* precise location — and the thousands of channels, inlets, bays, and islands on the western end of the Strait offered the German ship innumerable potential hiding places and points of ambush.

The squadron reached Punta Arenas before noon on September 28th. *Glasgow* had last visited this small city — the southernmost in the world — in February. Luce recalled that during that previous trip, the officers and crew had enjoyed themselves immensely. The duck hunting had been fabulous, despite Dhobey's shortcomings as a hunting dog. An exciting football match between *Glasgow's* crew and a local club had resulted in a surprising three-to-one victory for the ship's team. He reflected that while they had been moored in Punta Arenas on that earlier visit, they had received a long-awaited mail delivery — ironically delivered by a German steamer out of Montevideo.

Luce had always thought that Punta Arenas was pretty, in a rustic sort of way. The town's brightly painted buildings dotted shoreline around the large natural harbor. Here they were somewhat sheltered from the driving winds that had buffeted the squadron since their entrance into the Strait. Punta Arenas was customarily a busy place — the only significant port and coaling spot for the merchant ships that transited the Strait between the

Atlantic and Pacific. Still, he thought, this seemed to be a remote and unforgiving place to call home.

The four ships of the squadron anchored in the port, and immediately they were met by representatives from the small British community, as well as local Chilean port officials who reminded them curtly of the twenty-four-hour limit on their stay. Admiral Cradock arranged a quick meeting with the British consul, and the fruit of that meeting was some troubling but useful information.

Apparently, *Dresden* had bypassed Punta Arenas and in fact had avoided the Strait of Magellan altogether. Instead, she had sailed farther south around Cape Horn and, according to accounts from local seamen, was using the remote Orange Bay as a coaling base. Additionally, only two weeks earlier, two Chilean merchant ships under unknown charter had mysteriously departed from Punta Arenas, and the dockside rumors had them heading for Orange Bay. This activity appeared to confirm Cradock's suspicions that *Dresden* was establishing a base of operations in the region and was awaiting the arrival of von Spee's squadron.

The admiral told his captains to prepare to depart again, to head south and sweep into Orange Bay — with the hope that they might catch the German cruiser and her supply vessels there. Cradock's sense of urgency was amplified by the second piece of troubling news passed on by the British consul. The ships of the German East Asia Squadron had made another appearance, this time some fifteen hundred miles closer to South America than their last sighting at Samoa.

Admiral von Spee had attacked Tahiti.

# EIGHT

*Monday, September 21, 1914*
*Pacific Ocean, 35 Kilometers West of the Island of Bora Bora, French Polynesia*

THE RAGGED, emerald-clad twin peaks of the island of Bora Bora, crowned by a diaphanous haze of thin white clouds, were now clearly visible above the eastern horizon, dead ahead of *Gneisenau*. Captain Maerker turned to his bridge officers. "All hands to battle stations. No visible flags."

"All hands to battle stations," repeated Commander Pochhammer, who then distributed the captain's orders throughout the ship with electric bells and voice pipe commands.

"All flags are stowed," confirmed the signals officer.

"Remember, gentlemen," Maerker admonished, "This alert status is only a precaution. We hope to steam right up to the reef without firing a shot or even arousing any suspicion. If this works, we'll stand down."

"Yes, sir," said Pochhammer.

With *Ahlers* trailing behind, they had steamed slowly and steadily southeast from Suvarov, attempting to burn their coal as efficiently as possible. On Maerker's orders, men had already slathered a coat of light gray paint over the name *Gneisenau* on the stern, and they had adequately covered and camouflaged the large crest adorning the prow of the ship. A similar operation had occurred aboard *Scharnhorst* to help cloak her identity as well.

Maerker had determined that eleven of the officers on his ship spoke either fluent English or French, and each of these men had preliminary orders, should their linguistic services be required. *Scharnhorst* had a comparable number of officers fluent in those languages as well. All of the flags of the *Kaiserliche Marine* were safely stowed as they approached the

French-administered island of Bora Bora. If anyone was to do any signaling by flag or otherwise, it would be the admiral from the flagship. Maerker scanned the reef-encircled island. He could see a few small boats, probably fishing vessels, moored in the lagoon. Beyond them were the simple buildings and huts of the small town. No warships were in sight, and thus far he saw no signs of suspicious or hostile behavior.

So far, so good, he thought. Hopefully they would be able to stand down from their battle stations and steam up to their anchorage as if everything was completely normal. All that remained now was to see what reaction they would receive from the local populace.

◆

SO, IT WAS TRUE, thought Brigadier Philippe Fournier as he looked out through binoculars at the approaching ships. France must truly be at war. What other reason could there be for the sudden appearance off their western reef of these two immense warships and their supply vessel?

Just three weeks earlier, a cargo ship headed to Fiji from Panama had made an unscheduled stop at Bora Bora to disembark a gravely ill crewman. Fournier recalled that the captain had been a decent enough fellow and had hoped that someone on the island could help his sick sailor. The ship was already overdue in Fiji, so the merchant captain simply left the ailing man in the care of the island's only "doctor" — a priest who also directed the colony's small Christian mission. Before the steamer departed, the captain mentioned ominously that France was newly at war with Germany and that somehow all of Europe had risen up in armed conflict. Fournier remembered thinking that it seemed to be a fanciful story. Unfortunately, the sick sailor had died the next morning. In fact, he was now buried on the grounds of the mission. The simple marker on his grave was blank because in his haste, the merchant captain had neglected to mention the poor man's name.

A week later, a small supply ship from Papeete had arrived on its regular monthly trip. The crew confirmed the story that France had sided with Russia against the invading Germans and that Britain had also allied itself with the French Republic against the Kaiser. It had all sounded so extraordinary and unbelievable, but suddenly here were these impressive warships steaming right up to the island. What reason could they possibly have to visit this remote colony? Perhaps the Germans were planning to attack, and these warships were here to protect the islands.

Fournier had been the senior officer of the small island *gendarmerie* on Bora Bora for four years. During that time, he had seen only two French warships, the old cruiser *Dupleix*, which had stopped by on a courtesy visit more than two years earlier, and the small gunboat *Zélée*, which made occasional trips throughout the islands from its home port of Papeete. These two approaching ships were much larger, newer, and more formidable than any warships he had ever seen. He nodded in satisfaction. Surely, the Germans would not dare attack if French Polynesia were defended by such fearsome vessels.

The two massive gray warships had now slowed to a stop a few hundred meters beyond the opening in the reef. The support vessel also stopped, some distance farther away. The lead warship raised a series of small colored flags on the ship's forward mast. Fournier had no idea what they might signify, but he assumed it must be a greeting—and perhaps a summons. People were assembling on the quay to take in the unusual sight, and Brigadier Fournier's heart swelled with patriotic pride. The arrival of these majestic ships and their brave crews was certainly an exciting event for their little colony, he thought. Fournier lifted his uniform jacket from the hook behind his desk and put it on, carefully smoothing out the creases in the fabric.

"Laurent?" he asked.

"Yes, sir?" asked the young policeman, who was gazing at the fascinating spectacle out beyond the reef.

"Please inform Tama and Matareka that we have guests. Have Matareka make the boat ready immediately. He will need to find rowers, for I will be going out to the ships to speak with their captains. Also, I need a token of some sort—a gift of welcome and thanks to these men in recognition of their duty to France." Fournier paused, then looked to Officer Laurent. "Any ideas?"

"Perhaps some of those hibiscus flowers, sir?" offered the young policeman. "Surely they will appreciate a bouquet of the beautiful local flowers."

Fournier agreed immediately. "Yes, Laurent, hibiscus flowers! Perfect! Have them brought to me at the dock. Quick, quick!"

Minutes later, Fournier and Laurent were seated in the prow of a canoe as six hastily conscripted, bare-chested natives seated behind them dug into the water with their oars. A large sheaf of brilliant pink hibiscus blooms lay across Fournier's lap, and he fiddled with the top button of his jacket, trying to ensure that it would remain in place. They were headed slowly but steadily across the lagoon to the opening in the reef. Matareka, one of Fournier's promising native Polynesian trainees, sat in the rear of the boat and exhorted the rowers in their native tongue to put their backs into the effort. He looked up at Fournier and beamed a broad white smile. He seemed to be as excited as the brigadier to be welcoming their honored guests.

They cleared the gap in the reef without incident. Beyond its perimeter, the swells were slightly higher but still navigable. Fournier decided that they should steer for the lead warship—the one upon which the signal flags were fluttering gaily. He motioned to Matareka, who dutifully directed the rowers to steer toward the great ship.

As they approached, Fournier could see crewmen aboard the warship lowering a ladder from a portion of a lower deck that was only a few meters off the water line. They drew alongside the giant vessel, and Fournier was awed by the great wall of gray steel that loomed over them. The armored hull rose above him in giant stair-like steps, like the battlements of a floating metal fortress. Fearsome-looking cannons jutted from multiple turrets along its flank.

"It's huge," whispered Laurent, as if he could read this commander's mind.

"Huge indeed," agreed Fournier, humbled by the staggering size of the ship and the sheer numbers of guns protruding from its decks. "Remember, Laurent," he admonished, "I will greet the captain and make the formal introductions and welcome. You need not say anything unless I ask it of you directly."

"Yes, sir." Laurent nodded, wide-eyed, clearly relieved that he would not have to say anything under such intimidating circumstances.

The canoe drew alongside the ladder—at the top of which stood several uniformed sailors. Gingerly, Fournier stood up and saluted formally as the rowers kept the canoe steady. He addressed the nearest of the men aboard the ship, saying loudly, "I am Brigadier Philippe Fournier. I request permission to come aboard."

"Please come aboard, sir," replied a young, brown-haired officer, in an accent of French that sounded to Fournier as if it was tinted with Alsatian or Franconian.

Fournier clambered out of the rocking canoe and climbed the steep steps, awkwardly carrying the large bouquet of flowers. Laurent also stood and began to follow, but he nearly slipped as he made the short leap to the bottom rung of the metal stair. He regained his balance and made his way up the ladder behind Fournier. As instructed, Matareka kept the canoe waiting for them below. They reached the small, narrow lower deck, and the young naval officer nodded and gestured to a stairway that ascended to what must have been the main deck above. They made their way up this second ladder more easily. When Fournier finally reached the top, he could see that half a dozen officers in crisp white dress uniforms had gathered on the deck in a smart line. A whistle heralded his arrival, and he immediately clicked his heels—coming to attention and saluting again. All of the officers returned his salute, including one officer who immediately drew Fournier's eye. He was the tallest man present, with a regal bearing and piercing blue eyes. His graying, pointed beard was neatly trimmed, his unusual hat was edged with white feathers, and he wore gold braiding upon his shoulders. Fournier thought that he, certainly, must be the captain of this vessel. Fournier took a half step forward toward the captain and began his hastily rehearsed speech.

"I am Brigadier Philippe Fournier of the *Gendarmerie* of Bora Bora," he began. "As the local representative of the government of the Republic of France, I hereby welcome you to our humble island. Please accept this small token of our hospitality and…" Gold braids, thought Fournier, realizing suddenly that he had made his first mistake. This man was not a captain at all. Gold braids! He froze, mid-sentence, then recovered as best he could. "… and our welcome to the *admiral* and his men. We are at your disposal." He held the large bouquet of flowers awkwardly toward the admiral, who nodded and smiled but did not move or speak. One of the other officers approached, took the flowers, and stepped back into his previous position. You are such an idiot, Fournier thought to himself. How could you possibly have missed—even for a second—that this man was an admiral and not a captain? He hoped that these officers had not noticed his clumsy pause and hesitation. Most of them looked stern but cordial. These were serious men—brave warriors who likely had little time for foolish stuttering. He inhaled deeply and attempted to act as normal as possible. Laurent stood stiffly beside him in silence. Hopefully, Laurent had not noticed his stumble, either.

The admiral then exchanged a few quiet words with another officer standing beside him. This man, who was somewhat younger but obviously also a senior officer, turned to Fournier and said, "Thank you for your gracious welcome, Brigadier. Have you any news of the war here in Polynesia?" The man's French was also slightly accented—but Fournier could not quite place the origin.

"No, sir, none. We only recently learned of the war from a passing ship. Is it true that we have declared war upon Germany?"

"Yes, it is. France marches with us and the Russians against the German threat."

With us? Fournier frowned, trying to understand what the officer meant by that. His accent was so maddeningly familiar, but he still could not place it. Then, suddenly, it all made sense and he had the sickening realization that he had made his second terrible mistake in as many minutes. Dear God, these were not French ships at all.

They were British.

The officer continued. "We originally planned to coal and provision at Tahiti, but we had no way of knowing if Papeete had already fallen to the

Germans. A squadron of German ships is known to be operating in this vicinity. Have they yet been sighted here?"

Fournier swallowed hard, hoping he did not look as foolish as he felt for mistaking the identity of these British ships. He regained his composure enough to answer the officer. "Oh, good gracious, no," he said. "We have not seen any enemy ships, sir." It occurred to him that he might be able to make up for his earlier missteps by at least appearing to be authoritative about *something*. He continued, his chin held up with confidence. "Of course, we are gratified to see your mighty Royal Navy vessels here, because the defenses at Papeete would likely be inadequate against a German attack."

The British officer looked concerned. "Papeete is undefended?"

"No, not completely," replied Fournier, "but they are ill-equipped for war. The island has a garrison of some twenty-five soldiers and one officer. They have some policemen, like myself, but again not many."

"Can they at least defend the port with artillery?" asked the British officer.

"There are some old shore batteries, but I don't believe they have fired a shot in decades. I heard two weeks ago that the garrison was preparing to defend the port by moving the guns from the *Zélée* ashore."

"The *Zélée*?"

"She is a small gunboat; nothing like your grand ships. *Zélée* is the only French warship permanently stationed here in Polynesia. Of course, if they have removed her guns, she won't be of much use in combat."

"Of course," replied the British officer, who smiled at his compatriots. "It is good that we arrived when we did. Papeete is obviously vulnerable, and there is no way to know when the German squadron might show up."

"Indeed," gushed Fournier, "we are grateful for your service against our common enemy." He thought for a moment, hoping these British officers had not noticed his earlier confusion and foolishness. Perhaps a more specific offer of hospitality would ensure that their recollection of this visit was positive. "Of course," he continued, "we do not have the coal stores that they keep at Papeete, but we would gladly help with any provisions that the admiral and his men would require before you depart."

"In truth," said the officer, gesturing over his shoulder, "our supply ship has plenty of coal. For now, we simply would like the use of these lovely, calm waters outside your port so that we may replenish our coal supplies from our own collier. I'm sure we can acquire more coal when we arrive in Tahiti. However, we would like to purchase some provisions. It has been a long voyage from Hong Kong. Do you have any livestock, fruits, or vegetables here in Bora Bora that we might buy?"

"Of course, of course. I will return to the port and summon our local businessmen, who can provide you with everything you need."

"That would be excellent," said the British officer. "Just have them send out whatever fresh food and livestock they can spare. We will handle all payment when the goods are delivered to the ship." He nodded toward a young officer who was standing beside a small table, upon which sat a sizeable metal box. Stenciled lettering on the front of the box read, "*C & W - Fanning*", which meant nothing to Fournier. The young British officer unclasped and opened the lid, and Fournier heard Laurent audibly gasp behind him. The box was filled with British gold sovereigns and half-sovereigns. "I trust that our sovereigns will suffice as payment?" he asked.

"Oh, absolutely. I'm certain that your gold will be most readily accepted." Fournier made a mental note to ensure that a few of the coins would find their way into his own pocket.

"Superb! It seems we were quite fortunate to have stopped here at your beautiful island, Brigadier Fournier. You have been most gracious. Now, with your permission, we would like to begin coaling our ships. It is time-consuming and messy work, and the sooner we can begin, the sooner we can be on our way to Tahiti to make sure everything is in order."

"Absolutely, sir." Fournier saluted again, and Laurent followed suit. The policeman turned to the admiral and said, "Good luck to you, Admiral, and all of your men. We are in your debt." The admiral and his officers returned Fournier's salute, then two officers ushered Fournier and Laurent back down the ladders to their waiting canoe. Matareka, smiling as always, helped them back aboard. The rowers churned the water with their paddles, and soon the boat was slipping back through the gap in the reef into the lagoon. Only when he was back aboard the small craft did Fournier realize that although he had introduced himself aboard the ship, in his nervousness and excitement he had neglected to introduce Laurent and had not asked the names of any of the British officers. You are such a fool, Philippe, he thought. No wonder you are assigned here to the most remote speck of French soil on Earth. Anywhere else and you would probably cause so much diplomatic damage that you might start a war all by yourself.

When they finally reached the dock, Fournier began barking orders to Laurent and Matareka, who immediately ran off to spread the word among the local farmers, fishermen, and businessmen.

Later that morning, as the two great gray warships maneuvered to opposite sides of their supply vessel to coal, a flotilla of small boats and canoes began their journeys out to the visiting ships. The boats were laden with fruits, vegetables, chickens, baskets of eggs, and even pigs. One farmer, after returning from his first trip, indicated that he had received a special request from the crew aboard one of the ships. He then marched two cows onto the deck of a larger fishing boat and had the fisherman take him and his cattle out to the waiting warships. The ships' crews butchered the animals immediately on the deck, sending the cuts of meat below for cold storage. Many local proprietors on Bora Bora had quite a profitable day, courtesy of their new guests. Brigadier Fournier looked on with satisfaction throughout the afternoon as the canoes went to and from the huge ships anchored just outside the reef.

As the waning afternoon light lengthened the shadows along the bank of the lagoon, Fournier was still standing at the window of the small police hut looking out at the big ships. He lowered his binoculars as he heard Matareka enter the room. The broad-shouldered Polynesian looked exhausted. He and Laurent had spent most of the day directing traffic on the dock, keeping the peace among the local businessmen who had scrambled to send boatloads of goods out to the waiting navy ships. Matareka had even accompanied some of the boat and canoe trips, particularly those with skittish livestock, to ensure that the loading and unloading went as smoothly as possible. The big man sank onto a bench and pushed coils of long black hair out of his eyes.

"Sir, I believe the British have bought everything they wanted. The last canoes are returning now."

"Thank you Matareka. You've done well." Fournier pointed to the warships. "See that? They have finished the coaling, and now they are cleaning the ships. I find the whole process truly fascinating."

Matareka seemed less than enthralled by the goings-on aboard the visiting ships. He stretched his neck and massaged the base of his skull, trying to relieve some of the tension in his exhausted muscles. He frowned, then looked up at Fournier. "What does *Gineesenahoo* mean in English?"

"Excuse me?"

"The word *Gineesenahoo*. What does it mean in English?"

"Unfortunately, I don't know much English, and this word is unfamiliar to me. How is it spelled?"

Matareka enunciated the letters. "G... N... E... I... S... E... N... A... U."

"I'm afraid I don't know that word, Matareka, although I'm fairly certain you're not pronouncing it correctly. Where have you seen it?"

"On our last trip out there to the ships, I was helping old Hoanui because he can't row so well anymore. After we got outside the reef, he got a bit off-course, and we drifted behind one of the big ships before we could come back around to the side. The ship's name was written on the back, but it was covered over with gray paint. I could see the letters, and they spelled out the word *Gineesenahoo*. I just wondered what that meant in English, that's all."

Fournier shook his head. "I'm afraid I don't know much about English ships or how they title them, sorry. Perhaps it is the name of an admiral or a king?"

"Yes, perhaps," agreed Matareka.

"You did well today," Fournier said again. "I am proud that we were able, in our own small way, to help out the war effort by providing supplies to these valiant allies of ours." He paused, bringing the binoculars to his eyes once more. The warships had moved away from the supply vessel and were raising steam. Clouds of smoke now wafted from the ships' funnels, and all of the ladders had been raised. "I think they are preparing to leave. We should send them off with a proper salute. Where is that large *drapeau tricolore*, the one we've never used?"

"Still in the cabinet, I believe. Over there." He gestured toward a large piece of furniture near the door.

"Excellent. Fetch it and come with me to the dock. We must find a proper pole for it." Fournier hurriedly left the building, and Matareka stood stiffly and walked to the cabinet to find the flag.

Out on the dock, Fournier had selected a long wooden pole, of the type that the natives customarily lashed together to make floats for fishing seines. Matareka arrived, carrying the folded flag. Together, they affixed the flag to one end of the pole as a group of fishermen sat nearby, watching them skeptically. Fournier grasped the pole near the base end and motioned for Matareka to do the same.

"Lift it, Matareka. We will wave it as a salute to our departing guests." He and the Polynesian heaved on the long, heavy pole, struggling to lift the attached flag skyward. Matareka barked at the closest of the idle fishermen, and two of them scrambled to their feet and rushed over to help the policemen. With four men pushing upward on the pole, the large red, white, and blue flag was soon flapping jauntily above them in the evening breeze.

"Wave it back and forth," instructed Fournier breathlessly as he looked over his shoulder at the departing warships. The men beside him complied, awkwardly pushing the tall pole back and forth to impart more motion to the French flag flying above.

The warships were moving off, toward the northern tip of the island, with their supply vessel following behind. In the waning light, Fournier could see that the admiral's ship was also raising a flag to return his salute. The flag was striped black, white, and red, with a black cross in its center — the unmistakable flag of the *Kaiserliche Marine*.

◆

ALTHOUGH an overnight rain had limited their visibility and slightly hampered their navigation from Bora Bora, the German cruisers drew within visual range of the island of Tahiti shortly after dawn. The weather had cleared before sunrise, offering a calm sea and a cloudless light blue morning sky. They approached Tahiti from the northwest, passing the small neighboring island of Moorea. The sharp green mountaintops of Tahiti first came into view, then the details of the town of Papeete below. By now, the islanders had also seen the approaching ships, and this time the reaction of the locals was less than welcoming. Maerker could see a growing plume of thick black smoke rising from one end of the port area, curling upward like the trunk of a great black tree before drifting off on the prevailing wind.

"They're burning their coal stocks," noted Maerker as he viewed the activity through binoculars. "It looks like they've identified us more accurately than their compatriots at Bora Bora."

"Expecting us, it seems," agreed Gunnery Officer Busch, who was also observing from the bridge, along with the first officer. "They probably heard via wireless about our little visit to Samoa."

"Cowards," muttered Pochhammer. "Even if they burn their coal, there are other supplies we can salvage from their pitiful colony. Shall I assemble the landing parties, sir?"

"Not yet, Commander," replied Maerker. "We'll await orders from the flagship." Thus far, the only signal from *Scharnhorst* had been to *Ahlers*—the collier had dutifully dropped astern to wait as the warships neared the island.

The two cruisers, with *Scharnhorst* in the vanguard, were now less than two thousand meters from the mouth of the harbor, off their starboard bow. Maerker could clearly see that only two seagoing ships lay at anchor. The smaller vessel, an old, white-painted, single-funneled warship, was undoubtedly the gunboat *Zélée*. Maerker could see no guns on the small craft—corroborating the account of the brigadier at Bora Bora who had said that her guns had been removed and placed elsewhere. Men were scrambling about on her deck and were preparing to cast off—for what purpose, he did not know. The other, larger vessel was a freighter flying a large French *tricolore* and, curiously, was festooned with festive bunting and numerous small flags. Maerker could see no one aboard the freighter.

The town itself teemed with frenzied activity. Scores of people clogged the streets; some were running. The populace was in a state of panic, with most attempting to flee the waterfront area. The coal depot to the north of the town was now burning furiously, and a thick column of black smoke loomed over the buildings of the colony, most of which were small, single-room dwellings.

As the warships crossed the entrance to the port, Maerker noticed that the customary harbor markers and buoys were missing. He guessed that the French had removed them to make any entry into the harbor—or a potential armed landing—more difficult and hazardous. Yes, they definitely were expecting us, he thought, wondering if submerged mines also lurked in the unmarked channel.

As planned, *Scharnhorst* raised a series of signal flags and simultaneously broadcast a wireless signal demanding the peaceful surrender of the colony. Several minutes passed as the two ships steamed threateningly past the harbor, their ominous presence amplifying the panic ashore. Maerker watched as a horse-drawn cart laden with barrels, driven by a wildly gesticulating man, simply charged through the throng, tossing people aside and under hoof. After that brutish trampling, Maerker was relieved to see some of the persons knocked down by the careening cart get to their feet and resume their flight. Why was the colony not surrendering? Surely their leaders could appreciate the futility of either flight or resistance. A uniformed policeman was trying to funnel the chaotic flow of humanity down a side street, but many of the terrified residents ignored him in their rush to vacate the waterfront.

At last, the cruisers received an unexpected reply to their demand for surrender. Two puffs of white smoke appeared on the lush green hillside above the town. Moments later, two small splashes of foam rose up on either side of *Scharnhorst's* bow.

"They've fired at us!" exclaimed Pochhammer, astonished. "Do they really think they can sink us with those little pea-shooters?"

"Probably not, but that was a pretty accurate first salvo," commented Busch with an appreciative nod. "They straddled *Scharnhorst* on their first try."

The flagship immediately turned to port and increased her speed. Maerker ordered his helmsman to follow suit, putting more distance between the cruisers and the heavily forested hillside that concealed the French guns. Another two puffs of smoke sent two more shells into the water, ninety meters astern of *Gneisenau*.

"Mister Busch, do you have the position of those guns?" asked Maerker.

"Yes, sir. High-explosive rounds loaded and ready. Permission to fire on them?

"Not yet. We'll await orders from the flagship."

Another salvo from the hill dropped splashes even farther behind the cruisers. They were now well out of range of whatever small guns the French had hidden in the jungle canopy. At a distance of about seven thousand meters, *Scharnhorst* came about and signaled that *Gneisenau* should fall in line for a run across the harbor to shell targets. The two warships began to once again traverse the harbor mouth—beyond the reach of the hidden artillery but well within the range of the cruisers' port guns.

"When the flagship fires, Mister Busch, fire upon those hidden shore batteries." Maerker scanned the shore. The waterfront area was clearing out, and only a few stragglers remained. He could see a young boy frantically pedaling a bicycle away from the wharf and various people on horseback and in motorcars heading out of the little town.

With a rippling series of booms, *Scharnhorst's* port guns opened fire ahead of them. Busch gave the order and *Gneisenau's* port batteries roared as well, belching billowing cones of brown smoke. Both ships' gun crews had targeted the emplacements on the hill, which erupted in a flashing cascade of explosions that sent tree limbs, rocks, and earth flying upward. No puffs of white smoke answered from the scarred and smoking hillside. The shore batteries were silenced.

"Mister Busch, let's turn our attention to that gunboat." Maerker was eyeing *Zélée* as she slowly maneuvered away from her slip toward the mouth of the harbor. "Without guns, about all they can do with her now is try to scuttle her in the channel mouth to block the entrance. Let's keep that from happening."

"Yes, sir." Busch was smiling—obviously enjoying the opportunity to finally do his job. He barked orders through the voice pipes to the gun crews, who retargeted their weapons.

*Scharnhorst* fired first, another salvo thundering from her flank. *Gneisenau's* gunners followed suit. *Zélée* was struck immediately, as two explosions tore open her foredeck and three more struck along the waterline—causing the small ship to shudder violently. Both cruisers began to fire independently, and plumes of roiling foam sprang up within the harbor. Both *Zélée* and the large freighter beyond were struck multiple times. The bow of the gunboat began to sink, and soon the forecastle was entirely submerged. Maerker could see several crewmen leap from the stricken ship. Their exit was timely, for within moments *Zélée* rolled over and disappeared into the lagoon.

The freighter was now lower in the water as well, but the large ship was moored closer to shore, in what was likely shallower water. The punctured steamer's stern settled on the floor of the bay, unable to sink any farther. The bow of the ruined cargo ship still protruded from the water, listing slightly to starboard.

Both cruisers had completed their transit across the harbor and had come about again to begin another run, should additional shelling be necessary. Again, *Scharnhorst* led as the German ships traveled slowly in front of the bay—their starboard guns aimed and ready. However, a signal from the flagship was not forthcoming.

Maerker scanned the area. The shore batteries had been destroyed. Both enemy ships were sunk. A handful of buildings behind the wharf were ablaze. Neither cruiser had intended to hit any structures on shore, but at this short distance, the shallow trajectories of their shells had resulted in a few errant shots skimming over the targeted ships and exploding in the town. Maerker could see no fire crews attending to the blazes, some of which had caught upon thatched roofs and were now burning brightly. Undoubtedly, the people of Papeete were expecting further bombardment and were loath to venture out, even to quench the spreading fires.

The two warships again crossed the bay, this time without firing a shot. *Scharnhorst* turned about to make another pass, with *Gneisenau* behind her in tight formation. Maerker assumed the admiral was debating the continuation of their original plan, which had been to convince the colony to surrender, then send ashore several hundred armed men to requisition coal and supplies. Of course, now the coal was destroyed, the colony had refused to surrender, and the harbor entrance was unmarked—and possibly mined as well. Even if they were able to send landing parties safely ashore, it appeared that the local populace would likely resist an armed landing—and the prospect of trying to secure the waterfront under fire from French sharpshooters was unappealing.

Through the glasses, Maerker saw that a series of flags was being raised above one of the buildings in the town. At first, he assumed that the colony was surrendering, but the message was something altogether different.

"Does that say what I think it says?" asked Maerker, incredulous.

"It is a bit jumbled, sir," said his senior signals officer, who had stepped up beside the captain to get a better view with his own binoculars, "but it says something about German hostages in peril and a German merchant ship. I believe it is a threat, sir."

"They're threatening to harm German hostages if we don't withdraw?"

"It looks that way, sir."

"The French are animals," offered Pochhammer sourly. "As uncivilized a race as has ever trod upon the earth."

Maerker realized then why the moored freighter had been so gaily decorated. "That cargo ship we just sank—it must have been German."

"Sir?" asked Busch, who was also reviewing the flag signal.

"Even though the people back at Bora Bora knew little about the war, the French here at Tahiti have been prepared for some time. That steamer, however, had no wireless aerial. If she was German, she probably had no news of the war and blundered into their clutches. The French captured her and were keeping her as a prize. From the way they had decorated her, it looks like they were quite proud of their little trophy."

"So, we've sunk one of our own ships?" asked Pochhammer.

"Well, she belongs to France now," replied Busch. "Every waterlogged ton of her."

"And the hostages they are threatening were most likely the crew of that ship," added Maerker.

"Despicable," said Pochhammer. "Dear God, do you think any of them were aboard the steamer when we hit it?"

"Unlikely," replied Maerker. "I saw no activity on board her before or during our attack. They must have the crew in captivity somewhere in the town. I think we can assume that if these Frenchmen are using the hostages as bargaining chips, then they are probably unharmed."

"For now," added Pochhammer soberly. "These French mongrels cannot be trusted. I can have landing parties assembled in minutes, sir."

"No, I don't believe the admiral will want to land now. There is no coal to take; our entrance through the harbor mouth will be too treacherous; and the colonists seem to be intent on perpetuating this miserable little conflict, even if it means their complete ruin. No, I am guessing that we'll be leaving shortly."

"Even with German citizens in the custody of these cruel bastards?"

"Commander, in many places around the world there are German citizens now in the custody of someone who considers themselves our enemy. What do you think will become of our compatriots back in Tsingtao? As uncomfortable as it may be, we cannot save them all. In fact, we may not be able to save any of them. Getting ourselves killed for foolish heroics is not what the Kaiser has in mind."

To corroborate his point, a signal from *Scharnhorst* indicated that they were to depart, first heading westward in their customary misdirectional ruse. After they were out of sight of the islands, the cruisers would resume their original course northeast toward the Marquesas. The two big ships headed out to sea, with *Ahlers* trailing after them. Receding astern, the burning town of Papeete smoldered under a churning stormcloud of black and gray smoke.

# NINE

*Tuesday, September 29, 1914*
*Cockburn Channel, Patagonian Coast, Southern Chile*

THE SCENERY SURROUNDING the British squadron was as beautiful as it was treacherous. Soaring, snow-capped mountains and massive glaciers loomed over both rocky shores of the twisting, jagged channel as the four warships steamed slowly southward under a clear sky that was somehow still more gray than blue.

For Luce, the squadron's lack of quality charts of the convoluted Chilean coast had become a serious liability, especially if they were now expected to hunt down an enemy cruiser among the countless islands, fjords, bays, and passages of this remote territory. They had few maps of the area, all of which were simply reproductions of old charts drawn by the few scientific expeditions that had explored the region decades before.

Of some small consolation to Luce was the knowledge that the Germans possessed charts of no greater accuracy. They were likely blundering about just as blindly, he thought. Mile by plodding mile, with the spotters helping to continually adjust their course, they made their way through the glacier-scoured landscape. By late afternoon, the British ships had safely reached the southwest terminus of the channel, finally emerging into the blustery gray emptiness of the Pacific Ocean. From there, the squadron steamed southeast through choppy seas along the tangled, wind-lashed coast. The weather remained hospitable but cold, and they encountered no other ships of any sort as they neared Cape Horn.

Their destination was Orange Bay, a remote angular slash carved into the rocky shore of one of the southernmost islands of Tierra del Fuego. The mouth of the bay was relatively large — several miles across, and Cradock's plan called for the four ships of the squadron to approach the entrance from different directions simultaneously—charging in with guns at the ready—in the hope that they might catch *Dresden* unprepared. The squadron rounded the jutting tip of the Hardy Peninsula and moved north under the cover of darkness to take up positions outside the bay just before dawn.

Luce turned to Thompson and said, "Time we got to work."

"Action stations," said Thompson, and the first officer's order was repeated by the bridge officers as they relayed commands throughout the ship.

As usual, *Glasgow's* experienced crew was ready and in position long before the other three ships. They waited for some time while the rest of the squadron positioned itself. The amber dawn bloomed astern, and Luce finally received the signal from the flagship to proceed.

"Ahead three quarters, Mister Alison," said Luce. "Let's bring her up to eighteen knots."

The fast cruiser steamed quickly up to speed as they swept into the northern reach of Orange Bay. The spotters in the foretop and the officers on the bridge scanned the rocky coastline for any sign of the German warship. On the weather deck out ahead of him, Luce watched the forward 6-inch gun turret swivel slightly to starboard as the crew within prepared to engage the enemy ship, wherever she might be. The crews of the 4-inch turrets along *Glasgow's* flanks also prepared their guns. As the ship steamed onward, the wedge-shaped bay became narrower, and Luce could see that they were steadily converging on *Good Hope* to their south as the coastline funneled the British ships closer and closer. Soon they could see details of the coastline at the far western end of the bay.

*Dresden* was nowhere to be seen. Other than the British squadron, the bay appeared to be empty.

"Looks like she's given us the slip," said Luce, disappointed that the German cruiser had eluded them yet again. Within minutes, signals from the rest of the squadron confirmed that the German warship had not been sighted anywhere within the bay. "Resume normal duty stations, but keep those men on the three-pounders in case there is anyone ashore who might cause trouble."

"Aye, sir," said Backhouse sourly, disappointed that they had not caught *Dresden* in her hiding place.

"Well, I'd say the 'Battle of Orange Bay' was a bit of a bust," said Thompson. "Doubtful that anyone will be writing about this one in the naval journals."

Luce turned to his senior signals officer. "Mister Stuart, send the following message to the flagship: 'Request permission to send boats ashore to search for signs of *Dresden*'."

Over the next few hours, boats from *Glasgow* and *Good Hope* took landing parties to various spots along the shoreline. In addition to seals and penguins, this remote, barren spot near the bottom of the world had surprisingly hosted a number of human visitors over the years, many of whom had left some memento of their passing. The sailors found remnants of what looked to have been a long-abandoned camp of some sort, including the footings for what had been rudimentary buildings on stilts. The buildings themselves had long ago been scoured away by wind and sea, but a nearby sandstone slab was carved with the inscription, *"Expédition Romanche 1882"*. Half a mile away was a large, heavily weathered wooden plank wedged between two rocks as if it were an incongruously placed tavern sign. Carved decoratively into the front was *"SMS Bremen 1912"*. On that same sign, scratched more crudely along the bottom of the plank, were the words, *"11 September 1914 - SMS Dresden"*. The German cruiser had certainly been here, but the British squadron had missed her by nearly three weeks.

◆

"THUS FAR, she's kept at least two steps ahead of us at every turn," muttered Admiral Cradock around the bit of a well-worn pipe. Wisps of lazy silver smoke curled up from the bowl and out through the partially opened porthole in the admiral's spacious cabin. He had summoned Luce, his senior captain, to the flagship for a brief meeting after their fruitless search of Orange Bay.

"True," replied Luce, "but she's bound to trip up eventually, especially if she's lingering in this area waiting for von Spee to arrive." He was standing, leaning on the high back of a leather-clad chair, upon which he had recently draped his greatcoat. Cradock sat in an identical chair next to the outer bulkhead beneath the porthole, his booted feet propped upon a low table. The admiral's small terrier, his constant companion, was curled in his master's lap, sleeping soundly. Luce marveled that Cradock always seemed to exude calmness, even when faced with frustration or disappointment.

The admiral's quarters, like much of the rest of the interior spaces aboard *Good Hope*, had not been stripped down for war as drastically as *Glasgow* had been. Here, the glossy wood paneling lent an appearance of warmth that Luce's cabin unfortunately lacked. Still, Luce was surprised at the austerity of the space. Cradock had no photographs or paintings in the room. The only object of decoration was a porcelain vase nestled in a felt-lined box upon his writing desk. It was beautiful—delicately translucent and hand-painted in shades of blue—but it had been broken. A large jagged shard was missing from its rim, and an obvious crack wound downward toward its base.

"Brought that back from China," Cradock said, noticing the object of Luce's glance. "More than a decade ago—about the same time I met our Graf von Spee. It was a gift from the widow of a colonel in the Chinese imperial army—a lovely woman. She promised that it would bring me luck." He paused, smiling, apparently reflecting on a happy memory. "So many years ago... I've kept it with me since—on every ship, every command. Silly, I suppose. But who am I to say, really? I've had quite a successful career—and I've managed some narrow scrapes that I could certainly attribute to luck—so perhaps she was right about it after all." The dog shifted restlessly in his lap, and Cradock stroked the nape of its neck. "Then, regrettably, several weeks ago—when the stewards were moving my personal effects from *Suffolk* to *Good Hope*—it fell and was broken." He chuckled. "I suppose it was bound to happen eventually. Hopefully this doesn't mean my luck has run out."

"I doubt it, sir," said Luce. "I've always thought that we make our own luck. Our decisions place us in fortune's path, or not."

"In my case, Luce, you'd be giving me too much credit," said Cradock with a laugh. "My decisions certainly haven't gotten us a lucky break in finding this blasted German cruiser. Unfortunately, von Spee has many sympathizers and agents in Argentina and Chile—certainly more friendly allies than we can muster up hereabouts. While we might get an occasional rumor or some anonymous hint about where *Dresden* might have been weeks ago, I'm sure her captain is getting specific reports of our current whereabouts, how many ships we have, and probably what I've eaten for supper."

"Which, if your meals are anything like my mine lately, wouldn't make for a very interesting intelligence report."

Cradock's smile turned into a scowl. "Actually, I wouldn't be surprised if *Dresden* has moved on altogether, especially if her captain knows we're here."

"Where would she go?" asked Luce. "Even if von Spee is headed here, his last reported location at Tahiti is still a few weeks' distance from the Strait or the Cape—and that's assuming he doesn't stop anywhere else along the way to coal and provision, which he'll certainly need to do. If *Dresden* has been ordered to meet the rest of the German ships down here, she still needs to wait somewhere safe for at least a few weeks, perhaps a month."

"She's probably operating farther up the coast. Knowing that we're hunting her, she'll lay low for a while in some uncharted inlet."

"That's what I would do," agreed Luce.

"Of course, the Admiralty don't think she's doing that at all. They believe her sole purpose here is to interfere with Allied shipping—and maybe even protect some German merchant ships. They still want us to find her, of course. While I disagree with their assessment of the overall situation, for once I agree with them on finding *Dresden*. Regardless of what she's doing here, catching her sooner than later is critical. They've ordered me to move our squadron north, up the Chilean coast. We're to stamp out any signs of resurgent German trade and find and sink *Dresden*." Cradock tamped another pinch of tobacco into his pipe and inhaled in a series of short puffs, causing the mouth of the bowl to glow warmly. He glanced at the broken vase. "Maybe our luck—or the Germans'—will change and we'll find her."

"Maybe," said Luce, "but if she's moved north, our task doesn't get any easier, especially if it takes us a while to find her hiding place. From the western mouth of the Strait north along the Chilean coast there are a thousand miles of empty coastline before we get to Coronel and a usable port facility. If we're actively searching for *Dresden*, we won't be able to operate without coal supplies."

Cradock nodded. He had anticipated Luce's concern. "From here, I'll send *Otranto* back to Punta Arenas to charter a collier. The British office there was confident that they could arrange one for us. We'll take the rest of the squadron to the Falklands, coal there, then meet up with *Otranto* and the newly-chartered collier at Punta Arenas to continue through the Strait and head north."

"We need a coaling base," said Luce.

"A coaling base?" Cradock repeated. "A harbor?"

"Yes, someplace secluded. As you know, our makeshift coaling base at Abrolhos served us adequately during the first weeks of the war. It was deserted, out of the way, and offered just enough shelter from the swells to coal at sea. Similarly, the southern Chilean coast is virtually unpopulated, and there are hundreds of sheltered coves and bays to choose from. If we found an appropriate spot, we could station colliers there as we did at Abrolhos—and from that clandestine coaling base we could operate along the coast, from the Cape to… how far north does the Admiralty want us to go?"

"No farther than Valparaiso. They don't want to take the chance that *Dresden*—or any other German ship—could slip past us around the Cape and into the Atlantic while we're too far north to do anything about it."

"That works. With the right location, our ships could coal in seclusion, then be within a couple days' steaming of Valparaiso or the Cape— wherever we're needed."

Cradock nodded. "A secret coaling base is an excellent idea, Luce, so we won't have to keep dragging our colliers around with us—as long as the Chileans don't find out. Of course, *Dresden* is already violating the neutrality rules as much as we would be by setting up camp in one of their bays."

"I doubt that we need to worry about the Chileans," said Luce. "Their navy is small, and they don't spend a great deal of time searching the southern coast. In fact, we've yet to see a single Chilean naval vessel since the war began. They're probably staying close to their ports for now."

"I'm sure von Spee knows this as well—another reason this very same coast is an attractive stopping point for him." Cradock was staring across the cabin at the opposite bulkhead as if lost in thought. He was silent for a few moments, then said, "He's headed this way, I'm sure of it. I don't give a damn what Churchill and Battenberg believe. The attack on Tahiti puts him more than half-way across the Pacific now. He wouldn't drag his whole squadron, with all those support ships, thousands of miles across the ocean if they were simply going to turn back. Admiral Maximilian Graf von Spee is not a man to sail around in circles. Inexplicably, London seems to think that's just what he's doing, especially now that *Emden* has shown up in the Indian Ocean and is attacking Allied shipping. The Admiralty believes that von Spee has broken up his squadron to attack us in multiple places at once—and that belief has paralyzed them with indecision." Cradock rang his fingers through the short gray hairs of his beard. "I think *Emden* was detached alone to throw us off his actual trail."

"The attack on Tahiti certainly didn't achieve any great strategic goal," agreed Luce. He realized that Cradock was right; the evidence was overwhelming, yet the Admiralty could not—or would not—see it.

"No indeed. Lobbing a few shells into Papeete harbor isn't worth a damn unless he's steaming right by the poor French bastards anyway. It was simply a target of opportunity. Unfortunately, the Admiralty don't see it that way."

"What about *Defence*? Have they reconsidered sending her to us?" asked Luce hopefully, although he realized that he probably already knew the answer.

Cradock sighed deeply and shook his head. "It now looks like they will be sending her to the West Indies."

"Surely, they're concerned about *Dresden* operating down here, and the suspicious activity among the German agents at Punta Arenas?" Luce was baffled that the Admiralty were so oblivious to these glaring signals.

"They're convinced the Germans are only trying to resume trade along the west coast of the Americas—safely out of our reach. Despite the information that we've passed long, they believe *Dresden* is operating alone. The only acknowledgement they've made to the possibility that von Spee might still be heading to South America is to remind me that *Canopus* is on her way to join us, as if that will make a damned bit of difference."

"When's *Canopus* due?"

Cradock shrugged. "Another week, perhaps. They've instructed me to wait until *Canopus* has arrived before proceeding up the coast in force. Of course, they also want us to find and destroy *Dresden* as soon as possible. If only I had as many ships as I have contradictory orders..." He set his pipe in a pewter tray and looked directly at Luce. "We can't really wait for *Canopus* to arrive or for the Admiralty to pull their heads out of their arses. We'll need that coaling base sooner than later. I'll wait at the Falklands for *Canopus* to arrive. When I have the old relic with me, I'll then join you, Brandt, Edwards, and the collier at whatever spot you've chosen. From there, hopefully we can find *Dresden*, wherever she's hiding."

Unless of course, thought Luce ruefully, the entire German squadron finds us first.

◆

ON THE MORNING of October 11th, *Glasgow*, *Monmouth*, and *Otranto* were anchored in a secluded bay hidden among a network of channels and islands on the southern Chilean coast. It was a beautiful spot—to the east, a distant saw-toothed wall of formidable mountains reached for a brilliant, cloud-dappled sky. All around them, sage-hued folds of undulating rocky coastline dropped steeply into the mirrored surface of the bay. In many ways, thought Luce, it resembled a pristine highland loch.

Their remote location on the western side of the Patagonian Andes prohibited wireless communication with Admiral Cradock, who was now anchored in the Falklands. Therefore, the precise planning of the remainder of their mission was now in Captain Luce's hands.

He had invited Commander Thompson and his fellow captains Brandt and Edwards for a breakfast meeting aboard *Glasgow*, the first such opportunity for all of the men to speak in person since they had left Punta Arenas several days earlier. While in Punta Arenas, Edwards had chartered the sturdy collier *Maston*, which was, at that moment, transferring coal to *Monmouth* on the southern end of the small bay.

The four officers sat at one end of the long table in the starkly empty wardroom. The fare, by necessity, was simple: tinned kippers, biscuits, and marmalade that tasted vaguely of metal—and could conceivably have been canned before any of the four officers had begun their naval careers. Supplies were again dwindling aboard all of the ships of the squadron.

After everyone was seated and served, Luce's steward poured tea for the officers and left the room.

"It's a pleasant change to eat a stationary breakfast," said Thompson, "without having to chase the cups and plates about on a pitching tabletop."

"Yes, we should enjoy it while we can," agreed Luce. The weather had been atrocious for nearly every day since their abrupt departure from the Falklands a week earlier. As planned, after their search of Orange Bay, *Glasgow* and *Monmouth* had steamed to Port Stanley to coal, while *Otranto* returned to Punta Arenas to gather more intelligence, charter a collier, and await the return of the rest of the squadron. Cradock had searched southern Tierra del Fuego for a few more days before heading toward the Falklands himself.

For Luce and much of *Glasgow's* crew, Port Stanley in the Falklands had become their "home away from home" during the two years of their commission. The islands were sparsely populated—less than a thousand permanent human residents were outnumbered at least one hundred to one by sheep—but those relative few Falkland Islanders had always welcomed *Glasgow's* crew warmly. The locals, mostly transplanted Scots, were a friendly, hard-working, and fiercely patriotic lot. If it were not for the penguins and other strange fauna of the windswept islands, a visitor might have thought that a wee bit of Scotland had been magically transported to the middle of the South Atlantic.

Any of the officers and crew who were hoping to enjoy the hospitality of the few pubs in town were to be disappointed, however. The newly arrived *Glasgow* had barely finished coaling when a wireless message to Luce from Admiral Cradock directed *Glasgow* and *Monmouth* to return immediately to Punta Arenas. The wind and sea were so rough that at first it seemed they were making no headway at all, and the powerful swells made their navigation along the eastern portion of the Strait of Magellan additionally hazardous. They had finally arrived in Punta Arenas two days later, meeting up with *Otranto* and *Maston*.

From the western mouth of the Strait, the small squadron labored north along the Chilean coast through heavy seas, making slow, punishing progress. The angry ocean tossed the British ships about like toy boats, and even some the most seasoned sailors aboard *Glasgow* fell ill to seasickness. Fortunately, their charts of the Chilean coastline north of the Strait were marginally better than their charts of the Cape area, and Luce identified several possible locations that might provide adequate shelter from the elements. After surveying a few inlets, channels, and fjords, he finally selected this secluded bay in a region dubbed "Vallenar" on their old maps. As the morning light confirmed, it would likely serve quite well as their clandestine coaling base.

"So, gentlemen," Luce said, "what do you think of our new home for the time being?"

"Nice enough spot, I suppose," replied Edwards between mouthfuls of biscuit. "The question is *how long* will this lovely little corner of Chile be our home?"

"Unknown," said Luce. "The Admiralty have heard rumors that German trade has resumed out of Valparaiso and Coronel, so they want us to head up there and break up whatever is going on. Of course, there is also the vexing matter of finding *Dresden*—which we've been trying to do, unsuccessfully, for the better part of two months now. We could be operating from here for weeks."

"Until von Spee's squadron arrives," said Brandt solemnly. "Then what?"

The men were silent for a moment.

"I have to admit that none of this makes much sense," said Luce. "From what I can tell, our orders are a symptom of the Admiralty being too far away and relying too much on hearsay, rumor, and speculation. For some reason, they believe that the Germans have blissfully resumed seaborne trade down here, as if there wasn't a war on. Of course, we haven't seen a sea-going German ship since we left Abrolhos. The four of us know full well that all German-flagged merchant ships are tucked snugly into ports throughout South America, afraid to venture out for now—but Admiral Cradock has his orders from the Admiralty," Luce paused and scanned the faces of his commanders, "so we will dutifully investigate, even if there is nothing to find. I also think it is highly unlikely that we'll encounter *Dresden*. Her potential hiding places are too numerous, the local German intelligence network is too good, and she can probably stay a step ahead of us no matter where we travel along the coast."

"The problem is that by using our three ships on this fool's errand," said Brandt, "we put ourselves at grave risk should von Spee actually show up. We're no match for either of his big cruisers, and neither *Monmouth* nor *Otranto* is fast enough to evade them. At least *Glasgow* could outrun them if you sighted the German squadron and had to escape."

"I agree," said Luce with a sigh. "However, Cradock wants to keep us together because of *Dresden*. Together, we would overwhelm her quickly without much risk to ourselves. But you're right, Frank—to von Spee and his armored cruisers, our three ships would just be a collection of targets. We'd be outgunned and outclassed immediately. Sending all of us north to Valparaiso with the possibility of the German squadron arriving in force is unnecessarily risky."

"Good thing we don't have to worry about them headed this way then," offered Thompson sarcastically. "The Admiralty have assured us that old Graf Spee and his scary squadron are headed anywhere but here."

Brandt was not amused. He scowled and continued. "We know damned well he's headed this direction. The Admiralty are dangling us out here—for what? To stamp out nonexistent German trade? To find one light cruiser that is probably already a thousand miles away? Meanwhile, they ignore the actual threat that is on its merry way eastward."

Luce was concerned as well, but he knew that they had to fulfill the Admiralty's orders as relayed by Admiral Cradock. Perhaps, he thought, they could quickly accomplish what the Admiralty wanted and try to remove themselves from harm's way, should the German squadron arrive. He looked at the three men at the table and laid out his plan. "For now," he said, "I believe we're reasonably safe. Admiral von Spee is probably still two or more weeks away, given his last known position in Tahiti and the fact that he's probably dragging a train of slow supply ships with him. If we move quickly, I think we can probably investigate as far north as Valparaiso, then fall back here to await the arrival of *Good Hope* and *Canopus*. Captain Edwards, you and *Otranto* will remain here with our collier for the time being. Captain Brandt, you and I will take *Monmouth* and *Glasgow* north to have a look at Coronel and Valparaiso. Without *Otranto*, we can move faster, and we'll still have overwhelming firepower should we encounter *Dresden*. We'll stay no longer at either port than the time it takes to contact the local British offices and to see what kind of activity is taking place among the Germans. Then we return here as quickly as possible and pass on our findings to Admiral Cradock, who should then be on his way with *Canopus*."

"And when Cradock gets here—then what?" asked Brandt.

"I'm afraid I don't know," replied Luce honestly.

# TEN

*Saturday, September 26, 1914*
*Eiao Island in the Marquesas Islands, French Polynesia, Pacific Ocean*

AFTER THEIR ATTACK on Papeete, *Scharnhorst* and *Gneisenau* had steamed northeast for three days, finally reaching the cluster of islands known as the Marquesas. Like Bora Bora and Tahiti, these remote island colonies were administered by France. *Nürnberg* had arrived a few days earlier, having escorted *Titania*, *Prinz Eitel Friedrich*, and the remaining support vessels of the squadron from Christmas Island. As ordered, Captain Schönberg had guided the other ships to a hidden anchorage at one of the remote, unpopulated islands—where they awaited the rendezvous with the two armored cruisers.

The morning after the return of the big ships, Schönberg was summoned for a meeting with the admiral aboard *Scharnhorst*. He boarded *Nürnberg's* steam pinnace, and a seaman piloted the small boat across the bay. As the boat made its way toward the flagship, Schönberg looked forward to the opportunity to speak with the admiral alone for the first time in many weeks.

He had grudgingly accepted the fact that the two armored cruisers had been the best choice for the mission to Samoa. After all, had any Royal Navy vessels been present at Apia, the firepower of the big ships would have been critical in a gun battle. He knew also that at least one true warship would have to remain with the armed auxiliaries, colliers, and supply ships on their way eastward, which meant that *Nürnberg* had—by default—been temporarily relegated to escort duty. Schönberg had hoped, however, that when the squadron was back together that the admiral would be able to assign him some responsibilities and authority more commensurate with his obvious abilities. After all, his brilliantly conceived and flawlessly executed attack on the Fanning cable station had been the first real strike against their enemies.

He was piped aboard the flagship and ushered to the admiral's stateroom. As he walked in, he was disappointed to find that Captain Maerker was already there, seated across from Graf Spee's desk, as well as Captain Schultz of *Scharnhorst*. At least that humorless lackey Filietz was not in attendance.

"Good to see you again, Karl," said Graf Spee warmly. He stood and shook Schönberg's hand.

"And you as well, sir," replied Schönberg. "I heard that you destroyed the French colony at Papeete. Well done, sir."

"In truth, those foolish Frenchmen basically destroyed their own colony. Set fire to the coal stocks and took to the hills. Quite a waste, really." Graf Spee nodded toward Maerker, "Julius and I only fired a few salvos. The French did the rest."

"Well, we did sink one of our own merchant ships in the harbor," quipped Maerker, "so our mission wasn't a total loss." Both Graf Spee and Maerker chuckled at the apparent joke. Schönberg coolly appraised them both, not knowing what to say. Maerker shook Schönberg's hand, as did Schultz.

"We missed you on our little jaunt, Karl" said the admiral, gesturing for the men to be seated around the low table. "You would have enjoyed fooling those Frenchies in Bora Bora more than anyone. It was surprisingly good sport." Graf Spee's demeanor then changed, becoming more serious. "But enough about all that—we can tell you the stories another time. For now, we have another French colony to plunder."

Graf Spee unrolled a chart showing the dozen or so islands that comprised the Marquesas. He pointed to one of the northernmost islands, where they were now anchored. "Like the island off our port bow, gentlemen, most of the Marquesas are uninhabited. We believe the French have colonial offices only on these two islands, Nuku Hiva and Hiva Oa." He indicated two islands on the chart. "We know that the anchorage at Nuku Hiva can accommodate most of our squadron, but this old chart suggests that the port at Hiva Oa may not be as large. Consequently, I propose temporarily splitting the squadron again during our stay here. Captain Maerker, I'd like you to take *Gneisenau* to Hiva Oa under the cover of darkness tonight. *Scharnhorst* and *Nürnberg* will steam to Nuku Hiva. At dawn, we sweep in and take both settlements. I'll leave it up to you to decide how you want to execute the mission, Julius, but I believe we should be able to trick them into letting us come ashore. As far as we know, neither settlement has wireless, so they should have received no advanced warning of our approach. Hopefully we can take control of both colonial villages without firing a shot."

Schönberg could hardly believe his ears. The admiral was directing Maerker to take one of these islands *by himself*. Schönberg could not let this opportunity be taken from him. This was *his* chance. "Pardon me, Admiral," he interjected, "but might I respectfully suggest an alternative plan?"

"What do you have in mind?"

"Sir, because we know so little about the port area or anchorage at Hiva Oa, might it not make more sense for *Nürnberg* to take that port? She is smaller and more maneuverable than *Gneisenau*, and *Nürnberg* has a shallower draft. If these depth soundings are inaccurate..."

"The soundings are probably accurate enough," interrupted Graf Spee with a wave of his hand. "I'm not suggesting that Captain Maerker get so close to the shore that his men can hop off the gunwales onto the sand. I assume that all of our ships will remain some distance from the port. I am more concerned about potential shore batteries like the ones we destroyed at Papeete. If the French resist us and we must use our guns, I want overwhelming firepower—which means having one of the armored cruisers at each island."

"But sir," Schönberg persisted, "it is highly probable that we can take this colony by trickery, much as I did at Fanning Island. Whether the French have shore batteries will then be irrelevant. In fact, if *Titania* were to accompany *Nürnberg* again on this mission, we could..."

"Karl, I appreciate your enthusiasm," interrupted Graf Spee again curtly, "but this is a mission best suited for *Gneisenau*. Now, on to other business—namely the re-provisioning of this worn and weary squadron."

With that, the matter was settled. Schönberg was stunned that the admiral had not taken his suggestion seriously at all. As Graf Spee continued to outline his plans for acquiring food and supplies from the colonial storehouses and mandating squadron-wide repairs, Schönberg seethed quietly. Somehow, somewhere, he thought, he would take his opportunity. He would find some way to reveal Maerker for the disheveled poseur that he surely was. How this untested newcomer had already insinuated himself into the admiral's favor so quickly was an infuriating mystery.

The admiral was now talking about shore leave. "I'll leave it to your discretion, gentlemen, but I am certain that all of our crews could use some time ashore, once we've established ourselves and coaled the ships."

"Agreed," said Maerker with a grin. "If I don't let my men off the ship soon, I'll surely have a mutiny on my hands."

The other officers laughed with knowing nods. Schönberg simply glared at Maerker. He found himself despising the other man's relaxed smile, his long hair, his rumpled uniform, and even his moustache. Mostly he despised the curiously instant friendship that this bedraggled excuse for a sea captain had somehow struck up with the admiral. Schönberg's left hand began to twitch slightly, and he tightly grasped the armrest of his chair to try to calm himself. You'll take your opportunity, Karl, he thought. Soon enough, you'll take your opportunity.

◆

*GNEISENAU* arrived off the shallow southern bay at dawn. Maerker had chosen to fly only a small French *tricolore* for identification. The tiny colonial town of Atuona, with its mixed roofs of red tile and brown thatch, lay directly beneath a towering green forested ridge, the top of which was hidden by a thick mantle of clouds tinged orange by the rising sun. Only a handful of vessels—all small, crudely fashioned native craft—were moored in the bay.

The simple false flag ruse worked perfectly. As four cutters of armed men rowed toward the colony, a small crowd of perhaps twenty people gathered dockside. The colonists waved enthusiastically to the men in the boats, thinking the sailors were their countrymen.

Only when the men landed was the deception revealed—and then it was too late. The shocked colonists were led off at gunpoint, and teams of sailors fanned out into the town. Within half an hour, the French flag flying above the largest building in the town—the administrative seat of the colony—was lowered. That was the signal that the colony had been taken.

Maerker was grateful that the admiral had decided to use their stop in the Marquesas to resupply the squadron, repair the ships as much as possible, and to grant the men some much needed shore leave.

Months at sea without access to proper port facilities had taken a toll upon the squadron, and all of the ships were in a sorry state of disrepair. Layers of gray and white linoleum covering many of the decks and gangways had peeled and cracked or had been worn away altogether— revealing the bare steel beneath. Many of the electric lamps had burned out, and many other simple fixtures were showing signs of wear. Without access to replacements that could have easily been obtained in Tsingtao or any other friendly port, countless items on every ship were simply wearing out. Brooms and mops had been worn down to nubs, buckets were cracked or dented beyond repair, and supplies of even the most mundane articles, such as soap and matches, were exhausted.

Over the next several days, Maerker's crew were able to restock the ship's stores with meat and produce, purchased at fair prices from the local farmers and businessmen. They bought these goods with some of the ten thousand francs seized from the French colonial treasury. Needless to say, the colonial governor was mightily displeased, especially after his curiously abundant private storehouse was raided as well—yielding a variety of goods such as cases of wine, aged cheese, dried vegetables, tobacco, and even a fine German sewing machine.

During the next week, as the ship was being repaired and restocked, Maerker allowed rotating shifts of men to go ashore for a half-day of leave, under the strict admonition that they were to treat the local populace with respect and that nothing was to be damaged or stolen. Eventually, nearly every man had enjoyed a significant amount of time ashore—exploring the lush jungle, bathing in the streams, visiting with the friendly natives, and even chatting amiably with the local French police officials—who, after their initial terror abated, turned out to be quite hospitable. The ship's officers organized hunting excursions for pigs, which roamed freely among the farming huts rather than being confined to pens. Within days, the ship's meat lockers were full once again, and a sty had been constructed on the aft deck to accommodate more captured pigs to be slaughtered later. A number of feisty chickens also received makeshift coops, and parts of the cruiser's weather deck began to resemble more a barnyard than a warship.

During their stay at Hiva Oa, Maerker himself did not leave the ship, preferring instead to spend his days conducting inspections throughout the cruiser. He had never kept a ship under his command at sea this long without a stop at a fully equipped port. He was concerned that the prolonged wear upon the ship's hardware and machinery would soon begin to tell upon her performance—which could be a deadly liability if they were to encounter any capable enemy warships. For the next few days, he toured every operational area aboard *Gneisenau*, focusing his attention in particular upon the engineering spaces, where the men were busily scrubbing condensers, cleaning boilers, lubricating fittings, tightening or replacing steam lines, and making the innumerable small repairs that would have been difficult or impossible while the ship was at sea.

In the evenings, he wrote letters to his wife. After their stop in Bora Bora, Maerker had abandoned his cabin altogether, moving his clothes and other necessities into the ready room near the bridge—a small space previously occupied only by the ship's charts. There he had a simple cot, a metal chair, and a small fold-down steel writing desk hinged to the bulkhead. The austerity of the space was oddly comforting—as if more luxurious lodgings would have been inappropriate, considering their circumstances. Mostly, he liked being closer to the bridge, because the chances of encountering their enemy increased with each passing day. As he sat and wrote, he could look out on the darkened island from the compartment's starboard porthole. He could hear the voices of the duty officers in the nearby wheelhouse, the chatter from the wireless room below, and the music of the nightly concerts on the quarterdeck.

Although he continued to keep his official daily log, his letters to Ilsa had taken the place of a personal journal. Each evening he would draft a new letter, recalling for her the day's events — without, of course, dwelling too much upon the atmosphere of isolation that he felt more acutely with each passing day. Instead, he would try to inject as much humor as he could into his letters. He knew that the children would laugh uproariously at his tales of errant piglets running amok on the deck as sailors scrambled to get the squealing escapees back into their pens. He also wrote of the men and what an exceptional crew they were — a true inspiration to the Kaiser and the German people.

Of course, until they could call on a port with a German diplomatic mission, actually sending any of these letters would be impossible. Like the rest of the officers and men of the squadron, he had been unable to send or receive any mail since their departure from Tsingtao in June. With the war still raging in Europe, Maerker worried for the safety of his family — and he hoped that Ilsa would not lose faith, although she had no way of knowing if her husband was even still alive.

Julius sometimes pictured Ilsa sitting in the parlor of their small house in Herford. He imagined her reading each of the letters in turn, pulling them one by one from a single large bundle — because undoubtedly they would all be delivered at once. She would smile at his funny stories as she pushed a drifting strand of her auburn hair back over her ear.

Thinking of his wife sitting in a quiet parlor on the other side of the world would invariably jolt him back to his own grim reality. Although the enemy had not yet found them, the truth was that his ship was now the prey in a massive, global hunt to the death. With each kilometer that they steamed eastward, the squadron's future became more tenuous. Admiral von Spee intended to reach the west coast of South America — but then what? The squadron might strike at Allied merchant ships and perhaps call at a friendly port or two in Chile. Even then, Maerker knew, their options would be limited. It was only a matter of time before the British would send warships into the Pacific to stop them. Perhaps, he thought, we might be able to elude the British patrols, round Cape Horn, and make our way north through the Atlantic. Perhaps we could even make it home. Such hopes, however, seemed remote and foolish. More likely, he knew, he might never reach a German port—and Ilsa would simply never hear from him again.

◆

"OUTSTANDING!" exclaimed Commander Pochhammer. "The *Admiralstab* understands our situation and is supporting us even out here, so far from home. With *Dresden* and *Leipzig*, soon we shall be a squadron of such power that the British dare not challenge us."

"Well, Commander, I don't know about that," offered Busch as he sipped his steaming coffee. "I doubt that the sailors of the Royal Navy are going to run crying to their mothers just because our squadron has added two more light cruisers."

They were in *Gneisenau's* spacious main officers' wardroom, seated along the heavy table that stood opposite the ship's gleaming black piano—the only other remaining object in the large room. The nearby senior officers' wardroom, a smaller space where the captain usually held meetings with his senior staff, was being repainted that morning—so the captain had moved this meeting to the larger, seemingly emptier, space. Maerker sat at the end of the table, which was laid out for breakfast. The ship's cooks were still enjoying the spoils of their stay in Hiva Oa, and the plates before the officers were laden with boiled eggs, cheese, ham, and freshly baked bread.

After their weeklong stay at the Marquesas, the squadron had resumed their long journey—and they had been steadily steaming southward for several days. The officers and men of *Gneisenau* had been in good spirits since hearing that *Dresden* and *Leipzig* were to meet the squadron at Easter Island. This meeting of Maerker's senior officers fell upon an auspicious day, for earlier that morning, the squadron had steamed southeast past the Tropic of Capricorn—leaving the warmth and familiarity of the equatorial regions behind. In addition to the captain, first officer, and the gunnery commander, at the table were also seated the senior navigating officer, the senior signals officer, the engineering commander, and Doctor Nohl.

Pochhammer gave Busch an exasperated look. "Where has the fearsome Royal Navy been so far, Lieutenant-Commander? With a dozen slow merchant ships in tow, we have sailed freely about the Pacific. We steamed unchallenged to the Brits' doorstep in Samoa; we fooled those idiot Frenchmen in Bora Bora; we shelled Papeete; and we took over their Marquesas colony and used it as our private resort for a week. What have our enemies done to stop us?"

"Just because they haven't found us yet doesn't mean they haven't been trying," replied Busch. "There are millions of square kilometers of ocean for them to search. It is simply a matter of time."

"Hah! If they are so unfortunate as to find us, they will rue that day. We will have five of the Kaiser's finest warships, each crewed by the best men to ever set foot upon a ship." Pochhammer smiled to himself in satisfaction, as if he had settled the argument once and for all. He returned his attention to the ham on his plate.

"Mister Born," said Maerker, addressing the senior navigating officer, "what is our estimated time of arrival at Easter Island?"

"Two days, sir. Maintaining our current course and speed, we should arrive at Easter Island before dawn on October 12th."

"Very well. *Dresden's* last confirmed position was closer to Easter Island, so she may well arrive there ahead of us. The admiral has also sent *Titania* on ahead to scout the area, in case the British are lying in wait for us."

"I hope they are," murmured Pochhammer quietly.

"Actually," replied Maerker to the group—although he cast a glance directly at his first officer, "if we must fight the British, I'd prefer to meet them on *our* terms—when we can choose the time and place of the battle and when our entire force is assembled."

The engineering commander spoke up. "And I'd like to have a look at the boilers again before we go charging into battle. Since we adjusted them back at the islands, I haven't been happy with the pressure on boilers two and four. It may be just a valve problem, but I'd like to be sure."

"And," added Busch with a smile, "we could use another round of gunnery practice. We can't have everyone all soft after a week's holiday."

"Agreed," said Maerker. "We'll likely be spending several days at Easter Island. We should have time for further combat preparations, maintenance, and even some gunnery exercises—assuming the British haven't yet caught our scent."

# ELEVEN

*Tuesday, October 13, 1914*
*Pacific Ocean, Off the Chilean Coast, 169 Miles South of Coronel, Chile*

"I WAS BEGINNING to think that someone had emptied the Pacific of all its ships," commented Thompson as he confirmed the sighting of a thin brown smudge of funnel smoke on the northern horizon. "Good to see there's at least one still left." The morning wind was blowing from astern, sending *Glasgow's* funnel smoke ahead of them like a fluttering veil, partially obscuring their view to the north.

"A merchant steamer," said Luce, holding binoculars steadily on the distant but approaching vessel. "Single funnel. From her lines, I'd say she's a passenger ship."

This was the first vessel they had sighted since *Glasgow* and *Monmouth* had left the slower *Otranto* and their collier behind at their secluded coaling base at Vallenar. After the bruising and difficult trip northward from the Cape, the seas farther up the coast were considerably calmer and the weather much clearer, but still quite cold. For much of the two-day voyage northward, the pair of British warships had kept the Chilean coastline just in sight in the eastern distance. Luce did not want to take the chance that *Dresden* might elude them by hugging the coast or ducking into one of the countless bays and inlets along their route. Mile after mile of lush green forests, rocky islands, and glittering river mouths slid by them on the starboard horizon — beautiful and utterly uninhabited.

The rolling gray sea had been deserted as well, which Luce found intriguing. Customarily, this would have been a well-traveled shipping lane — with numerous vessels sailing from Valparaiso southward or making their way north along the coast from Punta Arenas or ports around the Cape in the Atlantic. Instead, they had seen no sign of any ships until early in the morning of the second day, when a spotter noticed the single trail of smoke to the north.

"Mister Stuart," said Luce, lowering his glasses, "signal them to heave-to and prepare to be boarded for an inspection." Turning to Thompson, he said, "Commander, prepare the boarding parties."

The steamer visibly slowed as *Glasgow* and *Monmouth* approached. A signal lamp aboard the other vessel flashed, "Are you British ships?"

"Hmmm, it looks like they've recognized our ensign," said Thompson. "Do you suppose that if we say 'yes' they'll prepare us a spot of tea?"

"I don't care if they have tea, crumpets, and gooseberry jam," said Luce. "I just want that ship boarded and searched. I wish to be on our way as soon as possible."

Within a few minutes, they were close enough to see the vessel clearly in the steadily brightening morning sunlight. She was indeed a small, one-funneled passenger steamer. Her hull was black, with a white stripe running along her forward gunwales. On that stripe was stenciled the name *Oropesa*. A Chilean flag fluttered at the forward mast, beneath which a small crowd of men and women had gathered on her deck.

*Monmouth* took up a position half a mile to the west as *Glasgow* sent two boats over to *Oropesa*. As the boats approached the drifting ship, the crowd on board began to cheer, their shouts increasing in volume as the rowers brought the small white craft alongside. After securing the boats at the base of the ladders, sixteen men boarded swiftly. When they reached the weather deck amidships, the crowd appeared to envelop them. Luce could see exuberant handshakes, back-slapping greetings, and he could hear cheering across the water.

"Well, that's a good sign," said Thompson, as he and the captain observed from the bridge. "Perhaps you'll get those crumpets after all."

In less than an hour, the boarding parties had completed their work and returned to the warship. Lieutenant Hirst reported that *Oropesa* was, in fact, a British mail steamer. The Chilean flag was a ruse in case they ran into any Germans. They had left Valparaiso in a rush two days earlier, after her captain heard rumors passed along by some of the Chileans in port that a great number of the Kaiser's warships would soon be arriving. The ship was empty, other than some bundled mails and a couple of dozen British passengers who were extremely happy to see Royal Navy ships in the area.

"So even this little steamer's captain has heard that old von Spee is on his way to Chile," mused Thompson. "As far as operational secrets go, this one's not very well kept. It's a shame the Admiralty don't yet believe it."

"True," replied Luce. "All the more reason we need to get in and out of Coronel and Valparaiso as quickly as possible. The Germans could be here within a fortnight. I'd like to be gone in half that time. By then, hopefully Admiral Cradock will be at Vallenar with *Good Hope* and *Canopus*."

Luce looked out at the British steamship, reflecting on how comforting it was to make even this brief connection with a few of their countrymen so far from home. He continued, "We need to let *Oropesa* get on her way. See if any of our men have mails to send with her, but tell them to make it quick. We resume our course within half an hour."

Several dozen crewmen took advantage of the opportunity—hastily stuffing their homebound letters into mailbags that were then swung over to the smaller ship. As the two vessels got back up to steam and began to diverge, the passengers and crew of *Oropesa* gathered beside the near railing, waving and cheering in farewell. *Glasgow* and *Monmouth* resumed their course northward. *Oropesa* also got underway, heading south, with her passengers still waving from the deck as the steamer disappeared over the horizon.

By mid-afternoon, *Glasgow* and *Monmouth* had arrived outside the small port city of Coronel, some two hundred and fifty miles south of Valparaiso. Although he was sure that the German squadron could not yet have made it all the way to the Chilean coast, Luce led both ships in a full reconnaissance sweep of the semicircular gulf in which Coronel was nestled. Reasonably satisfied that the enemy squadron was nowhere near, Luce directed *Monmouth* to stay outside the harbor and conduct a few action drills before nightfall. The more practice her crew could get, the better, he thought.

As the crimson sun began to set astern, *Glasgow* made her way into the harbor, which seemed to be extremely quiet. Luce had never been to Coronel before, and what he saw was not impressive. The port facilities were rudimentary at best, with a few wooden piers jutting out into the shallow harbor. He could see only two cranes on the wharf, neither of which was steam-driven. With the exception of a handful of modest warehouses, few of the structures in the town rose higher than a single story. The tiled roofs of the simple brick and timber buildings stretched across an unremarkable waterfront. A few men were unloading crates from a motor lorry in front of a storehouse, but that was the only modern vehicle in sight—elsewhere, mule-drawn carts made their way along the wharf road. The shores of the bay around them were muddy flats, and odors of rotting fish and stagnant brine wafted from the marshy shallows. He scanned the motley collection of ships moored in the bay. Two German ships—a small merchant steamer and an older single-funnel passenger liner—were anchored a few hundred yards to starboard, and their crews took an immediate interest in the British cruiser—gathering on deck and observing through binoculars. The remaining few vessels appeared to be Chilean coastal craft—fishing boats, barges, and two small colliers.

*Glasgow* dropped anchor in the middle of the bay, and Luce sent Commander Thompson ashore with a half-dozen men to find and meet with the local British consul and to send a cable to Admiral Cradock updating their current position and providing the location of the new coaling base at Vallenar. Thompson returned several hours later, and he reported that the brief meeting had been marginally fruitful. The consul had passed along what little information he had gleaned, which was mostly that German and Chilean wireless activity had been steadily increasing during the past two weeks. As Luce had suspected, there was no resurgence of German sea-borne trade activity in Coronel, but mounting evidence indicated that the Germans had developed a sophisticated communications network along the Chilean coast. Additionally, a growing percentage of their communications were now being encrypted. Other than unsubstantiated rumors, the consul had no specific news of the imminent arrival of the enemy squadron. Thompson had then sent the cable to Cradock at Port Stanley and returned to *Glasgow*.

At midnight, Luce ordered the anchors to be weighed and for the helmsman to set an initial course to the southwest. When they reached the deeper water of the bay, *Monmouth* fell in behind them, and in the darkness the two ships steamed out past a small island at its western opening. When the few dim lights of Coronel were finally out of sight, he ordered a course change to the north, and the cruisers resumed their journey toward Valparaiso.

Before retiring to his quarters, Luce stepped out of the wheelhouse onto the port side flying bridge and inhaled the cool sea air. The evening was unusually mild, but the wind was picking up, rustling the flags fluttering above and foretelling the chill that would accompany an October night on these seas. The moon was a thin amber arc, hanging low in the sky and casting minimal light onto the sea below. Looking aft, he could just discern the dark outline of *Monmouth*, plowing through the swells half a mile astern. He noted that the older ship was, for a change, adequately maintaining her station in the darkness—a task that had been a consistent problem for her inexperienced helmsmen.

Luce was genuinely concerned for *Monmouth*, her officers, and her men. Captain Brandt was a capable enough leader, but his ship was barely serviceable—and his inexperienced crew, although eager, had yet to show that they were ready to engage in anything resembling combat. Unfortunately, the Admiralty seemed to be intent on putting them in a position in which the possibility of combat was becoming increasingly more likely.

He was certain that the German nationals here in Chile were making preparations for the arrival of their squadron. In both Punta Arenas and Coronel, the activity of the locals had been suspicious and troubling. Of course, Luce had no way of knowing precisely what Admiral von Spee might be planning, but he could envision the most likely scenarios. It was possible that the German squadron would try to operate from the Chilean coast for a while, harassing Allied shipping and using the neutral but friendly Chilean ports for shelter and coaling stops. Such a plan would have a limited lifespan, however. Although Britain had no significant naval presence on this coast, surely Admiral von Spee would expect the Royal Navy to eventually confront him directly and flush him from his new lair.

Luce believed that more likely, the German admiral had something else in mind. Chile was probably just another brief stop on their long journey from Tsingtao. They could pause here just long enough to coal, provision, refresh their men, and send and receive communications with Berlin. From here, they would likely try to elude the British naval net, heading south around the Cape and into the Atlantic, where the hunting would be rich—and where they might even contemplate making a break for their home waters in Germany.

It was so clear to him. That had to be it—the Germans must be heading for the Atlantic. He wondered how the Admiralty in London could see it any differently.

Soon von Spee would probably try to add *Dresden* and *Leipzig* to his squadron, if he had not summoned them already. Either *Scharnhorst* or *Gneisenau* alone would be more than a match for *Good Hope* and *Monmouth* put together. With an additional light cruiser or two, Admiral von Spee would have a fast, flexible squadron with an ideal combination of speed and firepower. Luce knew that their own patchwork squadron under Admiral Cradock—with or without the old battleship *Canopus*—would be no match for this threat.

◆

"AT LEAST they've changed the script for this one," muttered Thompson as he looked over the transcript. The wireless operators had picked it up only minutes after the spotters first sighted the port of Valparaiso around nine in the morning. It was simple and to the point:

TWO     BRITISH     NAVY     CRUISERS     SIGHTED APPROACHING VALPARAISO PORT 0900 OCTOBER 15.

"I will personally have a word with our consul as soon as we can get ashore," replied Luce. "He and the foreign minister in London can then file formal complaints with the appropriate Chilean authorities." Luce doubted, however, that his complaint—or London's—would have much effect upon the Chilean government, which was proving to be decidedly pro-German, much to the dismay of the British foreign office.

"I certainly hope so, sir," said Lieutenant Stuart. "This is another clear violation of the laws of neutrality."

*Glasgow's* wireless room had heard a similar message broadcast from Coronel the night before, announcing their departure right after midnight.

"Perhaps they'll have a parade waiting for us when we dock," offered Thompson with a wink. He scanned the port as they drew steadily closer. "I do love a good parade."

"The damned Chileans are letting every Hun for three hundred miles around know that we're here," muttered Backhouse—who had apparently gotten little sleep and was in a particularly foul mood.

Luce sighed. "Violation or not, that announcement is as much of a welcome as we're going to get, gentlemen, so let's not waste any time. Mister Stuart, let Captain Brandt know we're going in straight away."

"Fortunately, it's unlikely there are any German warships in wireless range yet," said Thompson, "but we certainly don't need the Chileans to be the damned town criers every time we steam in or out of a port somewhere along their coast."

"And I'd wager it isn't just the wireless," said Luce. "You can be sure that the German consulate is providing regular cabled updates on our whereabouts to Berlin as well." Luce surveyed the harbor mouth. "It doesn't really matter who they tell, really. We'll be staying in Valparaiso no more than a few hours—just as long as it takes me to meet with our consul. Then we'll be gone, and they can go and announce our departure as well."

The two British warships steamed slowly into the harbor. Valparaiso was much larger than Coronel and was a bustling center of commerce. The bay opened northward in a deep semicircle, accentuated by the steep hillsides around it. The buildings of the city clambered up the hills in a jumble of white, brown, and cream-colored boxes perched precariously on the slopes, overlooking the sea. Stately older buildings, many of them three or four stories tall, rose from a densely built-up downtown area near the waterfront, which teemed with people and activity. Luce observed that the city was shaped much like an old Roman amphitheater, with the busy harbor as the stage below.

Dozens of ships lay at anchor, including two small Chilean destroyers. As was customary practice when entering a foreign port with a military presence, *Glasgow's* gunners fired a saluting round from one of the three-pounders on the foredeck. A few minutes later, one of the destroyers answered with a similar cannon shot.

"At least their navy is polite," said Thompson, "even if they've already blabbed to the whole world that we're here."

The two British cruisers dropped anchor in the outer harbor, half a mile from the wharf and farther out than any other moored ships. Luce wanted to ensure that no other vessel could impede their departure, should they need to leave more quickly than was planned.

"Looks like we have at least six German merchantmen at anchor here," said Backhouse, scanning the port. "Maybe more. Can't tell with some of them. A few local boats, too—and at least one passenger liner."

Thompson was scanning the waterfront as well. He added, "One large ship dockside. Looks to be loading lumber. Might be American. Overall, nothing here looks too suspicious—except of course, for us."

"Those German ships are suspicious enough," said Backhouse, huffing derisively through the brush of his mustache. "Too bad they're all too frightened to come out and play with us. My crews could do with a little more target practice."

"Just as well," offered Luce. "We don't have time to be chasing any of them about. He addressed Thompson, "Will, you have the bridge. I'm going ashore to meet with the consul. At least we know now that he'll be expecting us." He stood and turned to the other officers present. "Speaking of which, Mister Stuart, we'll need to have the consulate send a car for us at the wharf, if they haven't already. Also, inform Captain Brandt that I am leaving by cutter in ten minutes and that I'll meet him on the dock."

"Right away, sir." Stuart nodded and left the bridge.

Luce continued. "Mister Backhouse, keep your men sharp—in case we have to leave in a rush. Mister Hirst, you are with me in the cutter, but rather than riding to the consulate with Captain Brandt and myself, I'd like you to go into town and arrange to purchase whatever provisions you can get your hands on. Coordinate with *Monmouth's* paymaster to see what they need. Make any arrangements necessary to get whatever you can out to both ships as soon as possible. Everyone to be back on board by noon."

"Of course, sir," said Hirst. "I'll muster the shore party."

The two steam cutters took less than fifteen minutes to make the trip from the anchored warships to the waterfront. Two petty officers and four Marines accompanied Captain Luce and Lieutenant Hirst, and a comparable number of men occupied Brandt's cutter, which trailed a few yards astern. Their route across the still waters of the harbor passed within a hundred yards of one of the anchored German merchant ships, an aging steamer with the name *Mariana* painted on her hull. Half a dozen of

*Mariana's* crewmen were standing at the ship's near railing, shouting insults and making rude gestures as the British cutters passed. Luce and his men ignored the catcalls, and soon the shouting faded behind them.

As they neared the wharf, Luce could see that a small crowd had gathered at the end of the nearest pier. "Gentlemen," he said warily, "we might have a bit of a sticky situation on the pier. Just keep it together. We don't want an incident. They probably just want to shout a few choice words at us, which should be harmless enough. Once we've cleared the waterfront, I expect they'll disperse." The pilot of the cutter throttled back the thumping steam engine slightly and steered the boat toward the nearest usable jetty. With the engine noise reduced, Luce could now hear the group on the pier ahead, and to his surprise he did not hear German insults. Instead, he heard the unmistakable sound of cheering—in English. The small crowd of forty or fifty people, both men and women, were apparently members of the small British community in Valparaiso and had come out to welcome their visiting countrymen.

"That's a pleasant surprise," said Hirst as the cutters pulled alongside the pier. In moments, the men had the boats tied up and all of the sailors were disembarking to a warm and noisy welcome. A few ragged verses of "God save the King" ushered *Glasgow's* and *Monmouth's* men ashore. Luce noted with a smile that the gathering was not unlike a parade after all—Thompson would surely be jealous. The British citizens were enthusiastically shaking the sailors' hands and patting their backs. Some of the women had brought items for the sailors: baskets of fruit, jars of pickles, tobacco, and even coats and gloves.

Luce shook hands with Brandt, who seemed just as surprised at the unexpected welcome. After a few minutes, they were able to slip away from the main group. Taking only a petty officer and one burly Marine with them, the two captains walked to the foot of the pier, leaving the crowd behind—and Lieutenant Hirst with the task of arranging the provisioning of the ships. As expected, a small black motorcar and driver awaited them, parked on the cobblestone road that ran along the waterfront. Within minutes, they were riding through the narrow, bustling streets of Valparaiso.

The British consulate was less than a mile from the harbor, nestled in a row of houses belonging to the wealthiest of Valparaiso's residents. It was a stately brick building of three stories, trimmed in white and black, with a gray slate roof. The premises, having no fence or gate, fronted the street, and the driver of the car simply parked the vehicle before the broad steps of the building's entrance. A young Chilean doorman ushered the captains inside, while the two sailors remained with the car and driver.

Luce thought that the interior of the building looked more like a residence than a consular office. The foyer was modestly sized, with a tile floor and several unremarkable landscapes in gilded frames upon the walls. The interior was quiet, unlike the noisy bustle of the consulate in Rio. Only one person waited for them inside, a small older Chilean man in formal attire. The diminutive man bowed deeply and took their overcoats. He asked them to wait there, then disappeared down the hall.

Minutes later, a portly gentleman in a rumpled brown suit walked into the foyer. The man had a luxuriant mop of curly red hair that descended in thick muttonchops along either side of his face toward his chin. He bore no other facial hair, and his plump cheeks were liberally speckled with freckles.

"Good morning, gentlemen," said the man warmly, "I am Charles Newman, His Majesty's Consul to Valparaiso. Welcome to our little corner of Chile."

"Good morning, Mister Newman," replied Luce. "I am John Luce, of HMS *Glasgow*, and this is Captain Frank Brandt of HMS *Monmouth*. Thank you for seeing us on such short notice."

"Not at all, gentlemen. It is entirely my pleasure." The men shook hands, and Newman gestured to a sitting room off the main foyer. "Please, come in and make yourselves comfortable." The three men sat on large plush chairs positioned around a low table that had already been set with urns of tea and coffee and an assortment of fresh pastries. The small man who earlier had run off to fetch the consul now reemerged and served each of the men before discreetly withdrawing to the foyer once again.

"It is quite the treat to have such honored guests, gentlemen," said Newman. "Despite the amount of trade with Britain that travels through this port, visits from our Royal Navy are rare. With this war on, we seem to have found ourselves on the wrong side of the continent." Newman tore the end from a croissant and popped it delicately into his mouth before continuing. "I realize that your ships will not be able to stay long—neutrality rules and all that—but how might I be of service while you are here?"

"We're primarily interested in information," answered Luce. "You are correct, of course, that we cannot stay here long. Although we could, technically, remain in port until this time tomorrow, I intend to leave within a few hours. I would prefer not to linger with so many hostile eyes watching our every move."

"Yes," agreed the consul, who was picking at another pastry on his plate. "There's a German around every bend in this city. Our former head of the household staff was German, you know. A solid, dependable woman. Of course, we had to let her go at the start of the war. A shame, really. The place has been in a bit of a shambles since then."

"Well, someone—German, Chilean, or probably both—has been broadcasting our every move on the wireless since we left Coronel yesterday," said Luce.

"And that's the last thing we need," interjected Brandt testily, "with a whole damned German squadron headed this way."

Newman nodded. "I have already lodged a complaint with the local Chilean governor, who unfortunately is a bit of a lap-dog for the Gerrys. As you may already know, they run almost everything here, including the wireless station, of course. I will have the British Foreign Office call the Chilean ambassador to task as well, although I doubt much will change." Newman leaned forward in his chair, suddenly serious. "For every pound we spend here, the Germans triple that in Marks. For every British citizen in Valparaiso, there are ten Germans. In many ways, Chile might as well be one of their blasted colonies. Here in Valparaiso, for example, other than the English Club, there isn't a single proper pub in the city—but there are at least five German beer halls. You can find bratwurst in half a dozen places in the city, but you'll be hard-pressed to find a decent mince pie..." He trailed off, temporarily lost in thought, then spoke again. "Enough about all that. You're here for *useful* information about the Germans. I believe I can help you." He reached into an attaché case beside his chair and pulled out a sheaf of papers. "Let's start with that German squadron you mentioned."

"What have you heard?" asked Luce.

"I received this confidential cable three nights ago confirming that our boys in Fiji intercepted a wireless exchange between two German warships in the Pacific. It seems they were planning to meet up at Easter Island." He handed two sheets of paper to Brandt, who was seated nearest.

"I'll be damned," said Brandt as he scanned the document. "It's our old friend *Dresden*. It looks like she was trying to contact *Leipzig* farther up the coast, and somehow she accidentally got hold of *Scharnhorst*—probably on a bounce. What do you suppose are the odds of that happening?" Brandt handed the papers to Luce.

"Probably about the same as the chances we'd hear it also," replied Luce, who began to read through the information carefully. "Apparently we'll have to take some bad luck with the good." Luce was not surprised at what he read. Although he had not needed confirmation of Admiral von Spee's plans, this certainly provided it. "Hopefully this has already caused a stir at the Admiralty. If they didn't believe that von Spee was headed to South America, they can't make that argument now. Taking that giant step toward Easter Island can mean only one thing."

"Yes," agreed Brandt solemnly, "he's definitely headed for South America, and now he's collecting every other German cruiser in the Pacific. With the addition of *Dresden* and *Leipzig*, he'll have five warships, plus whatever auxiliaries he's brought along."

"Isn't Easter Island still more than two thousand miles from here?" asked Newman, who had finished his pastries and was now sipping tea.

"Yes," answered Luce, "but these transmissions were intercepted eleven days ago—more than a week after von Spee was last sighted in Tahiti. The Germans could cover a great deal of ocean in that time. My guess is that Admiral von Spee is already at Easter Island. Depending upon how long he planned to stay for coaling, provisioning, and waiting for the other cruisers to arrive, he could have been and gone already."

"In which case," said Brandt, "the German squadron could be here within the fortnight."

Luce could hear the apprehension in Brandt's voice, but his face was set in a stoic mask.

Newman looked concerned but perplexed. "But surely this German Admiral wouldn't venture into Chilean waters with all of your Royal Navy ships prowling about, would he?"

"Unfortunately, Mister Newman," replied Brandt flatly, "if you were to look out into the bay at this moment, you'd see *all* of the Royal Navy warships currently stationed in the Eastern Pacific. I'm sure von Spee would love nothing more than to run right into our two isolated cruisers. His squadron could have a bit of target practice and sink us before lunch."

Luce could see that Brandt was becoming more agitated by the minute. The mounting stress of their situation and the danger they now faced along the Chilean coast was wearing on *Monmouth's* captain. "All the more reason we'll be leaving sooner than later," Luce said. "Mister Newman, what information do you have regarding German agents or operations here in Valparaiso? Have you noticed anything unusual recently?"

Newman nodded. "We have seen an increase in the number of cables and communications to and from persons in the German community here. We intercept what we can, but most of what we get nowadays is encrypted. The activity in the port itself has been the most noticeable. Three of the German merchantmen that have been anchored here since the beginning of the war just coaled within the last week. They haven't moved or loaded any cargo, however. Quite odd, really." Newman shifted in his chair, leaning closer. "One of my men also reported some strange activity at two of the local German warehouses down by the wharf. They have accepted several covered deliveries at night, but we have no idea what they might be storing there."

"Could be anything," replied Luce. "It doesn't matter, really. All of this behavior, while unusual, is easily explained. Simply enough, Admiral von Spee has sent word to Berlin that he is headed here—and now the local Germans are preparing for his arrival. They will coal some ships, gather and store crates of provisions, and probably even recruit some reserve seamen. When the time is right and von Spee is close enough, he'll set these plans in motion and begin resupplying his squadron somewhere, somehow."

"They'll also pass on any information they have regarding our whereabouts," added Brandt. "This German admiral has already shown up at Samoa and Tahiti prepared to fight. I doubt he's coming here just for the bratwurst."

"True," said Luce. "With that in mind, Mister Newman, could we borrow one of your telegraph operators for a few minutes? I'd like to send an update to the Admiralty back home."

"Of course, of course. We only have one telegraphist at the moment, but I will make him available to you for as long as you like." Newman paused and raised a finger. "That reminds me, Captain Luce. The only other cable I have for you came in this morning from my counterpart in Rio de Janeiro, Malcolm Robertson. A sharp young man, that." Newman reached again into the attaché case and withdrew a folder and handed it to Luce.

"Yes he is," agreed Luce. "We were in Rio when war was declared, and Mister Robertson did quite a job of helping us prepare and get on our way." He opened the folder and read the brief cable message:

> [*Consular Cable*]
> CAPTAIN JOHN LUCE RN
> HMS GLASGOW
>
> HEARD YOU MIGHT BE ON THE WEST COAST. HOPE THIS MESSAGE FINDS YOU AND YOUR MEN WELL. I STILL OWE YOU THAT HUNTING TRIP. WILL HAVE TO USE A DIFFERENT BIRD DOG. YOU WERE RIGHT THAT DHOBEY IS IMPOSSIBLE. GOOD AT CHASING PIGEONS THOUGH. STAY SAFE.
>
> BEST REGARDS,
> MALCOLM ROBERTSON
> [*End Cable*]

Luce smiled and folded the message, slipping it into his jacket. He and Brandt rose and followed Newman back through the foyer and down the passageway toward the wireless room.

Thirty minutes later, as they rode back down toward the wharf, Luce found himself lost in thought, and Brandt was similarly reticent beside him. The car trundled down the steep cobblestone road, and the harbor below came into view—now brightly illuminated by the late morning sun. The activity in the port had picked up dramatically, and among the boats moving about on the green water, he could see cutters making their way to and from *Glasgow* and *Monmouth* and the wharf. Luce was pleased— apparently Hirst had been successful in securing provisions for the warships.

On the pier, Lieutenant Hirst and two other assistant paymasters had made a makeshift table atop a large wooden barrel and were logging and paying for all of the goods they had purchased from the local vendors. As Luce and Brandt approached, Hirst came to attention and saluted.

"Welcome back, Captain Luce, Captain Brandt," he said, addressing each of the officers. "We're loading the last of it now. We've been rather successful, I'd say. Once the word got out, it seems everyone here with any British ties was eager to help. Many of these fellows have even refused to take payment."

"Well done, Lieutenant," said Luce. "How soon can we be on our way?"

"A few more minutes only, sir," replied Hirst. "We're getting lots of help." He nodded toward the local men who were helping the sailors load the nearby cutters. "Sirs, if you'll take your seats in your respective boats, we'll be pushing off in a few minutes."

Luce turned to Brandt and shook his hand. "See you back at the coaling base, Captain," he said. "Hopefully Cradock will be waiting there for us."

The two captains parted and took their places aboard the cutters, as the men finished loading the last few crates aboard. Lieutenant Hirst and the remaining sailors boarded also, and soon the boats were headed back out across the bay toward the waiting cruisers. By half past twelve, both warships were ready to depart, and Luce gave the signal to the helmsman.

Under the bright mid-day sunlight, the two British warships steamed steadily westward through a slightly choppy sea until Luce could no longer see the hazy green Chilean coastline astern. He then ordered a course change to the south, and with *Monmouth* in her wake, *Glasgow* headed back toward Vallenar.

# TWELVE

*Thursday, October 15, 1914*
*Easter Island*

AT DAWN on their third day at Easter Island, Maerker sipped from a cup of steaming coffee as he looked out from *Gneisenau's* bridge at the bleak rocky coastline, the few weathered buildings of the village, and the stark, treeless slopes of the island beyond. Driving rain pelted the windows of the wheelhouse, and a howling wind churned the waters of the bay, rocking the big warship as she lay at anchor. A gray woolen sky hung oppressively low, and an insidious cold draft crept through the ship's spaces like the tendrils of an invisible vine.

The crews of all the ships of the squadron had been busy since dropping anchor at Easter Island. Both *Scharnhorst* and *Gneisenau* had already coaled—with some difficulty—in the unsheltered bay. Shore parties had confirmed what had seemed obvious even through the driving rain—that this small remote island was curiously barren. Not a single tree grew as far as they could see. The only visible flora were scrubby, pale green lichens; small, twisted bushes; and coarse grasses that clung miserably to the wind-battered hillsides. The small, pitiful village of crude stone dwellings near the harbor was the only portion of the landmass inhabited by humans. Surprisingly, fewer than three hundred people lived on the entire island. Almost all of them were local natives, but a large swath of the land on this side of the isle was a sheep and cattle ranch run by, of all things, an Englishman. Of course, being isolated here, the rancher had no knowledge of the war, and the squadron's paymasters were already making arrangements with him and some of the locals to purchase beef, mutton, and eggs.

Upon their arrival, the morale of the men had been boosted by the fact that the light cruiser *Dresden* had been waiting for them just out of sight of the island — and now was anchored a few hundred meters away. The horrible weather and the necessary tasks of coaling and provisioning had thus far prevented *Gneisenau's* crew from properly meeting and greeting their new compatriots. However, the mere presence of this other German warship — a gray steel emblem of their seafaring brotherhood and of the distant home for which they were all fighting — buoyed the men's spirits.

Maerker noted that because *Dresden* was much smaller than *Gneisenau*, she was pitching and rolling even more dramatically than the larger armored cruiser. Behind him, on the other side of the bay, lay *Scharnhorst* and *Nürnberg*, as well as the squadron's support vessels, all of which were being similarly buffeted by the wind and waves. *Leipzig* was also scheduled to arrive later that day, and Maerker marveled at the extraordinary circumstances that had brought all of these German ships together in such a remote corner of the world.

Here, at this distant rock in the south Pacific, they were now as far away from Europe — and the horrific land war raging there — as they possibly could be. Yet, the war itself, and the roles that these men were still to play in that conflict, weighed heavily on the captain's mind. That morning, a flag signal from *Scharnhorst* stated that as soon as *Leipzig* had anchored, the captains of all the warships were to convene aboard the flagship. With his full squadron finally assembled, the admiral was calling another council of war.

◆

"WHAT DO YOU MEAN, it might take a week to repair it?" shouted Captain Schönberg angrily, his face contorted with rage and becoming increasingly more crimson. "What in God's name was that ignorant asshole thinking when he brought the damned collier alongside so fast? He should swing from a boom!" Schönberg grasped the frame of the bulkhead beside him with such force that his knuckles whitened.

"He claims, sir, that he was following all established protocols," said the young sub-lieutenant meekly. "Captain Holler said that the swells were simply too great, and *Baden* struck *Nürnberg* unexpectedly."

"Horseshit! Holler is no more fit to be a captain than I am to be a ballet dancer," bellowed Schönberg. "When the admiral hears my report, that idiot collier driver will be bailing bilge water and bunking with the rats." He paused, breathing heavily. "Enough of this," he said with an angry wave of his hand. "I want to see the engineering commander immediately."

"Yes, sir," said the sub-lieutenant, plainly relieved to be dismissed. When the captain was in one of these moods, the safest place to be was somewhere else. He saluted and quickly ducked out of the stateroom, heading aft.

Schönberg noticed that his left hand had begun to twitch slightly. To calm his rising anger, he stalked to the wooden cabinet over his writing desk and unlatched a small door. Inside an upholstered compartment was a clear bottle of *Obstwasser* and four slim crystal glasses. He uncorked the bottle, letting the warm aroma of the rich apple- and pear-flavored liquor fill his nostrils. In moments, he knew, his fury would be tempered by the fiery kick of the powerful drink. "Thank God we're not entirely out of luxuries yet, or I would surely go completely mad."

Before he could pour, a knock at the doorway interrupted him. The engineering commander appeared at the threshold and saluted. Schönberg set the bottle roughly back in the cabinet and addressed the officer sternly. "Lieutenant-Commander Menzel, did I hear correctly that it may take you a full week to repair the damage?"

"Possibly so, sir," replied Menzel, who took a tentative step into the cabin. He was a slight, wiry man with dark, thinning hair. He looked apprehensive, as if he had been forewarned of his captain's dark mood. He swallowed hard and continued. "The divers reported that the port screw is slightly bent. We should not use it until it is repaired. Unfortunately, however..." he hesitated.

"What?" asked Schönberg. "Can you fix it or not?"

"Well, yes, but I'm afraid it is a bit more complicated than that, sir."

"How so?"

"This type of repair is difficult to achieve under the best circumstances, sir. Ideally, we should be in port with a proper dry dock facility and the right type of milling machi..."

"Except that we're not in a damned port with any dry docks or machines or anything else here but fucking rocks, and sheep, and rain!" His ire returned swiftly, and his face began to redden again. Schönberg was now standing directly in front of his senior engineer, shouting into his face.

"Precisely, sir," said Menzel as calmly as possible, hoping that he might be able to reassure his captain and reduce the risk that this angry tirade would continue. He took a half step backward and continued. "Our situation here is far from ideal. That is why we will have to cant the ship over to get better access to the propeller."

"Good lord." Schönberg rubbed his temples. "You mean tilt the whole ship?"

"Yes, sir. In much the same manner as we do when we have to scrape the hulls and have no dry dock or ship lift. About fifteen degrees should do it."

"And how long will she remain tilted at that angle?"

"I'm afraid for as long as it takes to complete the repair, sir. It may not be a full week, if we're lucky. Perhaps only five days."

"Five days," repeated Schönberg. "Five days of living in some ridiculous carnival house, tilted over on our side as the wind and waves toss us about in this godforsaken excuse for a harbor. Wonderful." He shook his head wearily. Schönberg turned away from Menzel, walked silently across the stateroom, and slumped heavily into a chair, running his fingers through his closely cropped hair. He muttered aloud, "Will there be no end to the indignities I must suffer on this accursed voyage?"

At that moment, Lieutenant-Commander Engel walked up behind the engineering commander and clicked his heels.

"What is it, Mister Engel?" asked Schönberg, looking up. "What wonderful news have *you* brought for me?" he said wearily.

"Excuse me, Captain. I have another message from the admiral, sir. I thought I would deliver it personally." The signals officer looked apprehensively at Menzel, then at his scowling captain, who was obviously in a terrible humor. Hesitantly, he stepped forward to where Schönberg sat, handed over a folded transcript, then returned to stand by the door, waiting.

Schönberg assumed the message would have something to do with the planned council of captains, scheduled to occur after *Leipzig's* arrival. When he read it, however, he felt the anger welling anew within him.

[*Confidential Signal*]
CAPTAIN KARL VON SCHONBERG
SMS NÜRNBERG

RESPECTFULLY REQUEST YOUR PERMISSION FOR LIEUTENANT OTTO VON SPEE TO BE GRANTED TEMPORARY LEAVE OF DUTY TO JOIN MYSELF, LIEUTENANT HEINRICH VON SPEE, AND CAPTAIN MAERKER ON AN EXPLORATORY SHORE EXCURSION ON OCTOBER 17 AT DAWN FOR APPROXIMATELY EIGHT HOURS.

MANY THANKS
VIZEADMIRAL M. VON SPEE
[*End Signal*]

That goddamned Maerker again, thought Schönberg, seething and shaking his head. How has this newcomer become the admiral's pet? Now even when the old man plans a reunion with his sons, he invites that unkempt fool to go along? Of course, this Maerker must be trying to curry favor by joining their little family outing—why else would he want to go ashore on this miserable dungheap of an island?

From the corner of his eye, Schönberg noticed that the two officers were regarding him warily, perhaps even staring. He realized that he had been muttering audibly. He caught himself and stood.

"Gentlemen," he addressed them both, recovering his composure. "Thank you. You are dismissed."

Menzel saluted and left the stateroom, but Engel lingered expectantly.

"Yes, Lieutenant?" asked Schönberg testily. "Was there something else?"

"Uh, yes, sir. I was just wondering if you wished to send a reply to the admiral."

Schönberg took another measured breath, then exhaled calmly. "Yes, Lieutenant-Commander, I will send a reply. Please send a message to the admiral stating that Lieutenant von Spee will, of course, be granted shore leave for this excursion." He paused, looking coldly at the signals officer. "If that is all, Mister Engel, you are *again* dismissed."

The young officer departed, closing the stateroom door behind him.

Schönberg rose and walked back to the cabinet, where the bottle and glass waited. The fingers of his left hand were now tingling, so he grasped the bottle with his right hand and poured a full glass.

"Perhaps I shall go mad either way," he muttered.

◆

AS HE HAD two months before in Pagan, the admiral convened his latest council in the dining compartment of his spacious stateroom. When everyone was assembled, the officers greeted each other and helped themselves to some fine cognac set out on a side table. Maerker took note of the officers in the room. In addition to the admiral and himself, seven other commanders were present. The familiar faces were Captain Schultz of *Scharnhorst*; Filietz, the admiral's chief of staff; Schönberg of *Nürnberg*; Vogt of *Titania*; and Thierichens of *Prinz Eitel Friedrich*. The newcomers, Captain Haun of *Leipzig* and Captain Lüdecke of *Dresden*, were welcomed warmly by their compatriots. Maerker had met neither man before, but most of the other commanding officers already knew Haun, because he had been part of the squadron for two years—and had departed with

*Leipzig* for North America just a few months earlier. Lüdecke, however, was a stranger to them all. Not only had he been stationed in the West Indies, but he had only taken command of *Dresden* a few weeks before the outbreak of the war. Maerker introduced himself to both captains and congratulated them on their exploits thus far.

Haun was of average height, with wide shoulders and a round face set off by dark eyebrows and a broad smile. He was, by far, the more gregarious of the two. Perhaps, thought Maerker, this was because he already knew almost everyone in the room. He laughed and joked and happily regaled his fellow captains with his tales of the last several months. *Leipzig* had captured or sunk a series of Allied merchant vessels on her journey southward along the Central and South American coast. Haun's biggest prize had been the Union Oil tanker *Elsinore*, which *Leipzig* had encountered off the Coast of Mexico. Haun had originally planned to let the American-owned ship depart unmolested, until his men discovered that her registry was actually British. After this revelation, he had disembarked her astonished crew and had sunk the 6,500-ton tanker with gunfire.

Lüdecke, by comparison, was reserved. Maerker thought he looked to be about as likely a sea captain as Filietz, the admiral's bookish chief of staff. *Dresden's* captain was a small, thin man with light eyes, a prominent nose, and a receding hairline that made him look older than he probably was. Maerker found his quiet demeanor intriguing—and it appeared that Lüdecke was uncomfortable in this gathering of fellow officers.

The meeting was preceded by a sumptuous meal of braised lamb, purchased from the local English rancher the previous day specifically for this occasion. A rich and tasty vegetable stew accompanied the tender meat, and the stewards served bottles of exquisite French wine from the admiral's personal collection. Maerker had not dined with such extravagance since before they had departed from Tsingtao—which now felt like years ago.

During the meal, much of the conversation concerned their now distant compatriot, Captain Müller of *Emden*. According to newspapers that Captain Haun had obtained during his recent stop in Peru, *Emden* was wreaking an inordinate amount of havoc in the Indian Ocean. Müller had already captured and sunk numerous Allied ships and had even attacked and destroyed the British fuel depot at Madras. The British press were writing about him as if he were some sort of old-fashioned pirate, and the Royal Navy were clearly frustrated with their inability to find the lone light cruiser. Further buoying the festive mood in the room was the news that another German warship—SMS *Königsberg*, stationed in German East Africa—had ambushed and sunk an old British cruiser, HMS *Pegasus*, while she lay at anchor undergoing repairs in Zanzibar harbor. *Königsberg* had escaped southward along the east African coast and, like *Emden*, was now also eluding their enemies. The officers cheered and toasted the faraway captains of these two heroic vessels.

When the meal was finished, the admiral stood. Behind him on the wall, large charts had been overlapped and mounted in such a way to show the South American continent and a considerable portion of the South Pacific Ocean. Graf Spee raised his glass, and everyone at the table fell silent.

"To His Imperial Highness, Kaiser Wilhelm," he said, "and to our brave men all over the world who are fighting valiantly for the Fatherland." Everyone at the table repeated the toast and drank, keeping their attention on the admiral.

"This is a proud moment for me, gentlemen," he continued. "Gathered here at this table are the finest, most capable captains in the *Kaiserliche Marine*. Each of you, individually, is a brilliant tactician. You command excellent ships crewed by extraordinary men. Alone, each of you could inflict terrible damage upon the seaborne trade of our enemies, much as our brave Captain Müller has done. However, you are not alone. I believe that God has brought all of us together here, in this far corner of the world, for a noble purpose. When this war began, our orders were to wage cruiser warfare upon enemy merchant shipping, wherever we could find it. Captain Müller took *Emden* off to attack British trade in the Indian Ocean. I chose to keep the rest of the squadron together to ensure our survival and to maximize the amount of damage we could inflict upon our enemies, their trade, and their ability to wage war against the Kaiser. We have traveled across the Pacific Ocean to do just that. Now that we are finally within two week's travel of the South American coast, we have encountered three extraordinary blessings. The first is the safe return of our Captain Haun and *Leipzig*." He turned and nodded to Haun. "Johann, we have missed you." The other officers applauded and raised their glasses.

"The second," continued Graf Spee, "is the welcome addition to our squadron of SMS *Dresden* and her valiant Captain Fritz Lüdecke." Once again, the captains cheered the new arrival.

"The third, somewhat unexpected, blessing is the information that Captain Lüdecke brings with him about the movements and intentions of our enemies. I think it is best that he tell all of you what he conveyed to me earlier today." Graf Spee nodded to Lüdecke. "Captain?"

Lüdecke looked nervous as he stood and addressed the group. "First of all," he began haltingly, "I would like to express my sincere gratitude to all of you for the warm welcome we have received. For *Dresden*, it has been a long, lonely, harrowing voyage from the Caribbean Ocean down around Cape Horn and out here to the South Pacific to make this rendezvous. I feel truly humbled to be in the company of such fine commanders and, of course the esteemed Admiral Graf von Spee." He nodded in deference to the admiral, took a breath, and continued. "As many of you know, we were pursued during the past months by ships of the British Royal Navy. I do not believe that they were ever closer to us than a few days' steaming, but their continued pursuit certainly spurred us onward. Several times during this voyage, we were able to obtain some useful intelligence about our pursuers. From what we were able to learn, among the warships that have been searching for *Dresden* are HMS *Glasgow*, a Town-class light cruiser; *Monmouth*, a County-class armored cruiser; and *Otranto*, a converted auxiliary cruiser that once was a passenger liner. Additionally, these ships are commanded by an admiral named Cradock, whose ship is HMS *Good Hope*, a Drake-class armored cruiser. Although we have been out of touch from the mainland for more than a week, our sources in Punta Arenas believed that at least three, if not all four, of these ships had transited the Strait of Magellan and were planning to continue their search for us along the southern Chilean coast." Lüdecke paused awkwardly and looked at the admiral, as if he was not sure what to say next. "I'm sorry, sir, but I'm afraid we haven't gleaned much more information than that."

"On the contrary, Fritz," replied Graf Spee, standing once again, "that is an extraordinary amount of information—and it should prove to be useful indeed. Thank you, Captain. Please have a seat." Lüdecke sat down, apparently relieved that he was no longer required to speak.

The admiral turned slightly toward the maps behind him. "Captain Lüdecke has done an admirable job of eluding the British pursuit for many weeks. I have no doubt that he has frustrated them all the way to London. Perhaps more importantly, for us, however, is that he has led the Royal Navy into the Pacific—into the very waters that are our destination."

Commander Thierichens of *Prinz Eitel Friedrich*, the youngest man in the room, leaned forward in his chair, his face clouded with concern. "Does this mean, Admiral," he asked, troubled, "that we must now abandon our original plans—our months of careful planning and preparation? Thousands of kilometers of travel? After all, were we not expecting South American waters to be free of British warships, at least initially?"

"Perhaps, Max, but that was never a certainty. Even if we had arrived off the coast of Chile to find unprotected British and Allied merchant ships, that circumstance would have been fleeting. If anything is certain, it is that the British will move swiftly to protect their maritime interests." He smiled enigmatically. "As I said, this new information is an unexpected blessing. Let me show you why."

He took a step closer to the arrangement of maps and indicated the small dot that was Easter Island. "We have assembled here, some thirty-five hundred kilometers from the mainland," he said. He then pointed to the southern Chilean coastline. "We now know that at least three—perhaps four—British warships have moved through the Strait of Magellan and are searching for *Dresden* somewhere along the coast. It is likely that they will sweep north toward Valparaiso as they search." Graf Spee moved his finger slowly northward on the map. "However, we also know that there are no adequate port facilities on this northward route until they reach the small port of Coronel. The British, like us, are constrained by the rules of neutrality. Their ability to operate in this region will be severely limited. They must either bring colliers with them or choose their coaling opportunities in port carefully. Either way, I believe that they are extremely vulnerable while they are operating in this portion of the Pacific."

"Vulnerable?" asked Schönberg, smiling. "Are you saying that we finally have a real opportunity to pursue and attack some Royal Navy ships directly?"

"That is exactly what I am saying," Graf Spee nodded. "These British ships have been hunting *Dresden* for months. Now, perhaps, those hunters will become the prey." He paused and looked at his officers expectantly.

It was obvious to Maerker that most of the other captains were excited by the prospect of actually battling toe to toe with the enemy. The only face that still bore an expression of concern was Filietz's, but he was sour and negative about everything. Maerker himself had to admit that despite the obvious risks, he was excited by the exhilarating possibility that they might finally be able to engage the enemy directly and contribute to the war in such a forceful, tangible way.

Schultz was the next to speak. "Excellent! I cannot wait to get a British warship in our sights. Perhaps we can finally shoot at something other than towed target boats."

"Absolutely," concurred Schönberg. "I, for one, am tired of skulking around from island to island, always hiding and running. We are long overdue for a stand-up fight."

"I agree," said Maerker, "but the trick will be finding them. Our information on their whereabouts is now, what, two weeks old? The British warships could now be almost anywhere along the Chilean coastline. We need to be able to determine their location more precisely so that we can engage them on our terms, rather than just blundering upon them in some hidden inlet and provoking a frantic, unpredictable firefight."

"That's where our friends come in," said Graf Spee. "Through Captain Lüdecke, our agents in Argentina and Chile have already supplied us with invaluable information about the movements of the Royal Navy vessels. We need to tap into that network of information again as we approach the mainland. Additionally, I think we start our sweep here and move southward." He indicated a portion of ocean north of the Chilean port of Valparaiso. "Because the British are so far from a true base of operations, they will probably find it difficult to operate much farther north than Valparaiso. They don't know that *Dresden* is here with us. They believe she is still somewhere along the coast, so they may also need to simultaneously guard the Strait of Magellan to make sure that *Dresden* doesn't try to slip back through behind them. Consequently, they might split their force to try to do two things at once."

"That would be nice of them," muttered Filietz. "Facing only two enemy ships at a time is certainly preferable to four."

"Agreed," said Graf Spee, "but Cradock is no fool. I've met him, actually. Served with him briefly in China many years ago. He's a sharp fellow—and anything but timid, as I recall. Definitely a worthy adversary. If Cradock sniffs out our presence, he'll do what he can to give himself every advantage."

"Do you think they know we're coming?" asked Thierichens.

"Possibly," said Graf Spee. "Although we've tried to keep them guessing as to our whereabouts and our course, they'll have to consider South America as one of our likely destinations. For now, all they know for sure is that *Dresden* has escaped them somewhere around Cape Horn; the last known position of *Leipzig* was off the Peruvian coast a month ago; and *Scharnhorst* and *Gneisenau* were last seen at Tahiti more than three weeks ago."

He turned to the maps again. "I'd like to maintain that imbalance of intelligence and use it to our advantage. One of our supply ships, *Göttingen*, is depleted of her stores. My plan is to send her here, to Coronel, to reprovision, if possible. Her real mission, however, will be to put an ear to the ground and find out the latest whereabouts of the British warships. She should be able to dock at Coronel without drawing too much attention. Also, because she's a non-combatant vessel, she is not bound by the neutrality rules that would force her to leave port in twenty-four hours. She should be able to linger at Coronel for as long as we need her to. I have spoken with her captain, and he is prepared to leave by morning."

Graf Spee looked at Schönberg. "I'd like to send an escort with *Göttingen*, to ensure that she arrives at her destination without incident.

Ideally, I would send *Nürnberg*, but I understand that she is still under repair. Is that correct, Karl?"

"Regrettably, sir," grumbled Schönberg with a resigned nod. "However, I am driving the engineers to finish as quickly as possible. We could be ready to go in as few as three days." He looked expectantly at the admiral.

"That's not soon enough. I'd like *Göttingen* to have as much time as possible to gather information before our arrival. She must leave tomorrow at the latest. No, I'll have to choose another escort." He paused, thinking.

*Nürnberg's* captain said nothing further. Maerker could tell that Schönberg was disappointed. He shook his head in what seemed to be exasperation, and he began gently rubbing his left wrist with his thumb and forefinger.

Graf Spee went on, looking now toward Thierichens. "I generally prefer to use light cruisers for this type of duty, because of their speed. However, I want to keep the newly arrived *Leipzig* and *Dresden* with us for now. Commander, can *Prinz Eitel Friedrich* be ready to go tomorrow morning?"

"Absolutely, sir. We're fully coaled and reasonably well provisioned."

"Very good. Your auxiliary cruiser will accompany *Göttingen* to within fifty kilometers of Coronel. At that point, Commander, break off and let her continue on to port alone. Then head immediately southwest to rejoin our squadron at Más Afuera, which is our next destination. If you are spotted or pursued, however, do not try to rejoin the squadron. Instead put into port in Coronel or Valparaiso—just don't lead the British back to us."

"Understood, Captain," said Commander Thierichens enthusiastically. He was clearly honored by this new assignment.

"I have already instructed *Göttingen's* captain that he is to remain at Coronel until he receives a signal to weigh anchor, leave port, and join us. If all goes as planned, by the time we arrive off the Chilean coast north of Valparaiso, we will know more precisely where our enemies are operating. Then we can start hunting."

◆

THE FOLLOWING MORNING, Graf Spee and his two sons met Captain Maerker at dawn on the bluffs overlooking Hanga Roa bay. For the first time since the squadron had arrived at the island, no rain was falling, although a chill gusting wind raked over the rocky, treeless terrain. With an escort of four armed seamen, they set off hiking in the dim morning light, first across a low narrow saddle near the southwestern end of the island and then inland toward Rano Raraku, one of the island's dormant volcanic craters. As they hiked steadily uphill, they passed dozens of the island's ancient, enormous stone statues jutting from the earth.

Maerker had, of course, read accounts of the island written by European explorers and missionaries who had visited in the past two hundred years. Seeing it in person was something else altogether. The island was nearly barren now, hardly able to sustain the few hundred or so native inhabitants who remained; but once, long ago, this remote place had supported what had apparently been a large, thriving culture. The ancient people of the island, perhaps a thousand or more years before, had carved hundreds of massive stone statues, which they called "moai", from volcanic rock. These primitive people had managed to transport the huge statues to numerous locations around the island and had somehow erected them. Maerker surmised that even using modern technologies and steam-powered equipment, replicating that amount of work would be an extraordinary feat of engineering.

The statues were dark gray giants with exaggerated features—huge broad noses, square jaws, long ears, and thick brow ridges. Some stood 6 or more meters in height. Maerker could only imagine how many tons they must weigh, and many of the moai lay fallen and crumbling. Most of the huge statues they saw near the coast had originally been erected upon long stone platforms, in lines of a dozen or more, spaced no more than a meter or two apart. Most of those statues had fallen over or been toppled, and many lay broken. As they hiked inland, however, they came upon many more haphazardly arranged moai buried up to their shoulders or necks. It looked as if an ancient army of stone giants had been marching down from the mountain when a landslide had thundered down and partially entombed them—fixing them in place. Here they had stood since, staring down from the hills toward the glittering sea for centuries on end.

The officers and men stopped for lunch beside one of the immense stone heads, which even partially submerged in the earth was much taller than Maerker himself. Graf Spee was obviously enjoying this rare time with his sons, and during the hike he had peppered the young men with questions about their duties aboard their respective vessels.

Heinrich and Otto finished their lunches before the senior officers and set off again together toward the summit, chatting animatedly and clearly making the most of their brief reunion. As Graf Spee and Maerker were packing up, preparing to follow the young brothers, the admiral paused and took a deep breath of the cool, damp air.

"Julius, what are your thoughts about the plans we discussed at yesterday's council? Do you have any reservations?"

"I like the idea of sending *Göttingen* ahead to Coronel to sniff around," replied Maerker. "We could certainly use as much information as possible if those British warships are still lurking along the coast. My main concern is our tactical approach when—and if—we do encounter them. I'd like to do whatever we can to gain the advantage early and minimize the danger to our own ships and men."

"Agreed," said Graf Spee.

"For now, we likely have the tactical edge. If Lüdecke's information is correct, the British squadron's order of battle is inferior to ours—on paper at least."

"True. An old *Drake*-class and a County-class armored cruiser, a light cruiser, and an armed auxiliary even together are probably no match for either *Gneisenau* or *Scharnhorst* alone. However, Cradock is a savvy tactician and strategist. I would not be surprised if he has some tricks in his hat for us. The British may have brought more ships through the Strait since *Dresden* last heard anything. If they now have an additional armored cruiser or two, then the scenario could be dramatically different."

"That is what I'm getting at," said Maerker. "Something that you said yesterday intrigued me—when you mentioned that the British might have split their forces. Regardless of their true order of battle, we would do better to pick them off one or two at a time, instead of facing an entire squadron at once. Even in a mismatch, there can be unexpected outcomes."

Graf Spee nodded, waiting for Maerker to continue.

"The British don't know for sure where we are," said Maerker, "or the full makeup of our squadron, correct?"

"Most likely correct, yes."

"What if we led them to believe that there was no squadron?"

"Excuse me?" Graf Spee raised an eyebrow, and his eyes took on a familiar mischievous glint. "What do you mean, Julius?"

"When we get closer to the coast—within wireless range of Valparaiso—we'll want to remain as stealthy as possible. We'll keep our use of wireless transmissions to a minimum—and of course we'll encrypt them if we must communicate in that manner."

"Of course…"

"I am proposing that when we *do* communicate using wireless, we all use only *Leipzig's* call sign. We'll be steaming in from the north, above Valparaiso. The Brits already know that *Leipzig's* last known position was north of there, off the Peruvian coast. If they hear *Leipzig's* call signal, it would seem completely normal for her to have simply steamed farther south along her previous known route. They know that *Dresden* has been operating along the southern Chilean coast, and they will assume that *Leipzig* has moved south to join her. We let the British believe that all of our transmissions are coming from only one ship. That may help hide the presence of our full squadron and perhaps give us the chance to catch one or two of their ships by surprise, especially if they think they're looking for only one light cruiser."

Graf Spee smiled broadly. He placed a booted foot upon the shoulder of the huge, partially-buried moai beside him. "Brilliant, Julius. Brilliant! I like it." He took a long drink of water from his canteen. "If we're lucky and the ruse works, they might split their forces to search for *Leipzig* and *Dresden* separately, which would offer us an even greater advantage. Excellent idea, Julius."

"We'll see how excellent it is when we get to the coast," replied Maerker. "At the very least, it may confuse them a bit and give us another slight advantage."

The mist had coalesced into a steady, driving rain, and visibility was dropping by the moment. A swirling wind sent ripples surging across the grassy hillsides below them. This storm had the look and feel of one that would not blow over quickly.

"Seaman," Graf Spee bellowed to one of the armed men standing some twenty meters away, "find the two lieutenants and inform them that we will be returning to the ships immediately."

"Yes, sir." The seaman set off along the path in the direction that Otto and Heinrich had taken. Graf Spee, Maerker, and the other sailors began walking back down the way they had come.

As they walked, Graf Spee turned to Maerker, still smiling. "You know Julius, you are a gifted captain, and I'm proud to have you under my command. However, I'm beginning to wonder if you're also bringing us bad luck. Every time I take you on a hike, we get rained upon."

# PART THREE

## Coronel

# THIRTEEN

*Tuesday, October 20, 1914*
*Port Stanley, Falkland Islands*

"AT THIS RATE, Grant should break out some oars and have his men row that old crate to Port Stanley," groused Admiral Cradock, fuming. He had just received a transmission from *Canopus's* captain, saying that they were suffering from unexpected engine problems that had further reduced their speed. "It was bad enough when we thought she could make only sixteen knots. What good is a battleship that can steam at only twelve?"

"Not much, sir," agreed *Good Hope's* captain, Philip Francklin.

The two men were standing outside, at the railing atop the flagship's flying bridge, looking out over the bay and Port Stanley's rustic waterfront. Leaden gray skies hung low over the short stretch of weathered buildings that made up the town—as they had each dreary day of their delay here in the Falklands. Aside from a few small local craft, only two other large ships were moored in the bay, the chartered colliers *Benbrooke* and *Langoe*, which had arrived a week earlier from Montevideo.

Both officers were bundled in greatcoats against the seemingly incessant cold and wind. Frigid gusts whistled through the superstructure around them and sang in the wires over their heads. Cradock cradled his small terrier in the crook of his arm, protecting it from the worst of the cold. Francklin had a transcript of the latest wireless message from Captain Grant folded in his hand. "If she were moving any slower, she'd actually be steaming in reverse," he said with a scowl, "while we freeze here with the penguins."

In the nearly three months since Cradock had made *Good Hope* his flagship, his working relationship with Francklin had remained strangely detached and coldly professional. He had found the seasoned captain to be competent but generally aloof—and his interactions with Francklin were often awkward. Cradock could understand some amount of resentment on the part of *Good Hope's* captain—after all, being forced to cede control of one's ship to a flag-rank officer would be a difficult transition. However, such was the way of things in naval service, and Cradock had little patience or desire to coddle a petulant captain whose energies could be better spent elsewhere. The situation was particularly inconvenient as Cradock wrestled with the confounding puzzle now before him.

Fortunately, he had recently made the acquaintance of the governor of the Falklands, William Allardyce. The governor was the same age as Cradock, and his political career had been as colorful as the admiral's military one. The two men had immediately bonded, and Cradock had found in the governor someone in whom he could readily confide. While *Good Hope* lay at anchor at Port Stanley and he waited in frustration for the delayed arrival of *Canopus*, Cradock made a number of shore excursions to visit with Governor Allardyce. Together they had gone goose hunting, and the governor and his wife had hosted two modest dinners for the admiral. Cradock had also found Allardyce to be a competent chess player. They were scheduled to meet again tomorrow—a meeting Cradock realized might be their last.

"We can't wait another week for *Canopus* to drift down here at such a leisurely pace," said the admiral. "Even if Grant thought he'd arrive tomorrow, we certainly cannot be held to twelve knots all the way to Luce's coaling base at Vallenar. Those Germans certainly aren't going to wait patiently while we gather our skirts and powder our noses. We need to join *Glasgow* and *Monmouth* as soon as possible, with or without the battleship." He gestured aft, where a small local supply vessel was tied up alongside the flagship's starboard gunwales. "How soon until the provisioning is complete?"

"It should be done already, sir," replied Francklin, peering aft over the railing to try to observe the goings-on in the boat below. "But everything moves a bit slower here in Stanley, we've discovered. I'll get a status report and see how much more there is to do. At least we've already coaled."

Cradock nodded. "I'd like to leave in thirty-six hours. I have some personal matters to attend to with the governor, and hopefully before we depart, I'll receive a reply from London to my latest request for additional resources. After that, we're on our way—whether *Canopus* can keep up or not."

"Yes, sir," replied Francklin. "We'll be ready to weigh anchor in thirty-six hours."

Behind them, footfalls on steel rungs announced the arrival of a petty officer who reached the top of the ladder and stepped onto the platform.

"Pardon me, sirs," he said. They turned to see that he was a wireless operator. The young man was in his standard uniform, without a coat, and was decidedly underdressed for the damp, cold wind. He shivered but saluted smartly and remained standing at attention.

"Yes, Mister Harris?" asked Captain Francklin.

"A confidential message from London for the admiral, sir," replied Harris, who turned his attention to Cradock. "It's coming in now, sir. You wanted to be notified."

"Of course," said Cradock. "Thank you. I'll be there in a moment to retrieve it."

"Thank you. Dismissed," said Francklin. Harris swiftly retreated down the ladder, heading for the door that led back to the warmth of the wireless room below.

Cradock glanced at Francklin and raised an eyebrow. "Well, Captain, it looks like we've finally gotten word back from the Admiralty. I'm sure this cable will spell out—in no uncertain terms—just what they believe is good for us."

"Wonderful. I do so much enjoy being one of those little painted wooden ships that the First Lord moves around on his big map."

Cradock had to smile. In spite of Francklin's chilly demeanor, he genuinely liked the man. Under any other circumstance, they probably would have been friends.

The two officers made their way down the ladder, which led to the weather deck just aft of the huge oval base of *Good Hope's* command superstructure. This massive above-decks column, relatively near the bow, housed the wireless room and supported the signals bridge, main bridge, conning tower, and the foremast above them. Like the outer hull of the ship, it was sheathed by several inches of steel armor plate and was intended to protect the command functions of the ship for as long as possible against enemy shellfire. Francklin opened the heavy metal doorway that led to the wireless room within, and both officers ducked inside.

The cold howling of the wind outside was immediately replaced by the warm chattering and clicking of the wireless operators and their equipment within. Of the five men on duty, two wore headsets and sat at their wireless consoles. Two more, including Petty Officer Harris, were helping transcribe both incoming and outgoing messages. The fifth man was the leading telegraphist, a lanky officer named Perry. He noted their arrival and immediately stood at attention.

"You have a message for me, Mister Perry?" asked Cradock. He set his dog gently on the deck, and it immediately trotted over to the aft bulkhead near the compartment's electric heating coil and curled up under a metal bench.

"Yes, sir," replied Perry, as he handed a sheet of paper to the admiral.

Cradock pulled a pair of wire-rimmed spectacles from his jacket pocket, adjusted them on his nose, and began to read. The Admiralty's position had not changed. In brief, blunt language, they had simply disregarded his latest request for HMS *Defence* to join his command.

> [*Confidential Cable*]
> ADMIRALTY CONCURS THAT YOU ARE TO CONCENTRATE GOOD HOPE, CANOPUS, MONMOUTH, GLASGOW, AND OTRANTO FOR COMBINED OPERATIONS ON WEST COAST.
>
> STODDART IN CARNARVON HAS BEEN ORDERED TO MONTEVIDEO. DEFENCE ORDERED TO JOIN CARNARVON AND IS TO REMAIN ON EAST COAST UNDER STODDART WHO ALSO HAS CORNWALL, BRISTOL, MACEDONIA, AND ORAMA UNDER HIS ORDERS. ESSEX TO REMAIN IN WEST INDIES.
> [*End Cable*]

Cradock handed the transcript to Francklin, who read it quickly and dispassionately. He handed the page back and said, "As you expected, sir. Nothing new here."

"Just another verse of the same tune," replied Cradock, shaking his head. Addressing the men of the wireless room, he said, "Good work, gentlemen. As you were." He stepped toward the door, which one of the wireless operators opened for him. A swirling eddy of cold air fluttered the papers within the compartment, and Cradock's small dog popped up and trotted purposefully out the doorway before the officers, as if the door had been opened specifically for him. Cradock and Francklin followed the terrier out onto the blustery weather deck.

Cradock scooped the dog up into his arms again and addressed Francklin. "Now that the Admiralty have given me my dose of medicine, I thought I'd wash it down with some brandy. Care to join me?"

Francklin demurred, "Actually, sir. I must check on the provisioning process—to make sure we're ready to go in thirty-six hours. I don't want to linger at this miserable place a moment longer than we must."

"Of course," Cradock nodded. He had not really expected the captain to accept his offer, but he had still thought it worth the attempt.

"Good evening, sir." Francklin nodded, then turned and strode aft.

Cradock watched him go, then began walking toward his cabin. He, too, had much to accomplish in the next thirty-six hours.

◆

FOR *Glasgow* and *Monmouth*, the voyage south from Valparaiso to Vallenar had been uneventful, with only one ship sighted—a British steamer, *Bret*, headed for Punta Arenas. The seas became rougher with each day of the journey, and Luce was grateful for the calm waters of the secluded coaling base when they finally arrived. Luce had directed *Monmouth* to coal from *Maston* first. While those ships were thus occupied, Luce received word from Captain Edwards that two days earlier, *Otranto* had managed to strike a rocky outcropping while maneuvering in the bay. Fortunately, the damage had been minor, but crews in boats were still working near the big passenger ship's port bow to repair some damaged hull plating near the waterline.

Luce and Thompson surveyed the scene from *Glasgow's* quarterdeck. From several hundred yards away, they could clearly hear the pinging hammers of the shipwrights as they worked on *Otranto's* hull.

"Good lord," said Thompson. "That lumbering beast can't even turn about in a lake without knocking something off. Having her with us was odd enough when we were just hunting for *Dresden*. How on earth are we supposed to use her in a real battle?"

"I doubt we will," replied Luce. "She'll be of little use to us, except as an extra set of eyes in a search formation. If a battle ever occurs, hopefully she can get safely far away. I can't imagine Cradock has any real tactical use for her."

"Do we know if he's left Port Stanley yet?"

"No. Our wireless boys still can't pick up the Falklands from here. We'll just have to assume he's already left or will do so soon."

"So, we just wait?" asked Thompson. "That could be another week, perhaps longer."

"Unfortunately so. We should use this time to get everything shipshape. When Cradock arrives, we'll no doubt be back out to sea immediately."

Thompson nodded. "After we've coaled, I'll set the maintenance crews to work. I'll inform *Monmouth* and *Otranto* as well. I'm sure that *Monmouth* in particular could use a few days of cleaning and refitting."

Luce gazed out at the rolling green hills above the shore of the bay. "Another thing, Will. I'm not comfortable just sitting here like some goldfish in a bowl. We don't know when or where the Germans will actually arrive. Although the odds of them finding this place are slim, I'd prefer that old von Spee not surprise us while we're laying here at anchor." He pointed to the nearest green ridge looming above the southeastern shore. "See that promontory? From up there we should have a commanding view of the channel and the ocean beyond. It might be a bit of a climb, but I'd like to set up an observation post, crewed from sunup to sundown. Let's have two signalmen with flags and field glasses on each shift. Draw them from each of the three ships in rotation. Any sign of a vessel on the horizon, and they can let us know with flag signals."

"Good idea," agreed Thompson. "Can't have the Huns catching us with our knickers down. I'll have Hirst set up the scheduling. Anything else?"

"No, I don't think so. We just need to get coaled and then run over every inch of this ship with a spanner and an oil can to make sure we're ready when Cradock arrives."

Luce looked out again at the crews working on the ungainly *Otranto*, then south toward old *Monmouth,* moored beside the collier. Of course, with a squadron like this, he thought, "ready" was a relative term.

With little else to do but wait for the arrival of Admiral Cradock, the crews of *Glasgow, Monmouth,* and *Otranto* addressed maintenance issues aboard each of the ships. Aboard *Monmouth,* of course, the focus was her outdated engineering spaces. Her boilers and condensers were in such a state that Luce agreed to Captain Brandt's request to draw down all of her boiler fires so that more extensive repairs could be attempted. Without any fire for steam, she would be rendered inoperable and vulnerable for at least two days while the boilers were repaired and the condensers thoroughly scrubbed. Luce thought that for now the risk was relatively minor — and this was as good a time as any while they lay, waiting, in the hidden bay.

*Otranto's* shipwrights were still working on her hull repairs, and Captain Edwards took the opportunity to run his inexperienced gun crews through some mock firing exercises. Aboard *Glasgow,* there were no major mechanical issues, so the crew methodically inspected each critical space aboard the ship to ensure that fittings were tight, hinges were lubricated, pressure readings were accurate, welds were solid, and the electrical systems were not suffering from any undue corrosion.

The spotters' position on the nearby ridge was established, along with a system for signaling to and from the ships. Soon the post of "hilltop spotter" became a coveted assignment for the men of all the crews, for it offered a restful break from the shipboard monotony — and an escape from otherwise omnipresent cleaning, scrubbing, and scouring duties. Junior officers from *Monmouth* and *Glasgow* also arranged hunting parties ashore, and some of those forays returned with prizes of geese, rabbits, and even a few small deer.

The weather remained reasonably pleasant, which prompted a number of *Glasgow's* crew to bring their caged parrots up to the weather deck. The tropical birds responded enthusiastically to the fresh air and began chattering and singing to each other loudly. Soon the sound of raucous birdsong on deck became as commonplace as the regular ship's bells announcing each new watch.

Days passed in this fashion, and Luce found himself becoming concerned. The wireless operators still had not heard a transmission from either the Falklands or *Good Hope*. In fact, the signals officers aboard each of the ships reported with some frustration that the hills around this remote bay were confounding their attempts to receive any consistent wireless signals. Occasionally they would catch a snippet of a distant transmission from somewhere, but they could rarely receive more than a few characters before the signal was lost again. Even with this difficulty, the wireless operators were nearly certain that if a transmission were to be sent from within a couple of hundred miles—such as from the approaching *Good Hope* after she cleared the Strait—that they would certainly be able to clearly hear the signal, even within the bay. Until that were to happen, however, Luce had no way of knowing the whereabouts of the admiral, when he might arrive, or if he had even yet departed Port Stanley with *Good Hope* and *Canopus*. Still, because the agreed-upon plan was for him to rendezvous with Cradock at these coordinates, Luce had little choice. He would wait—and while he waited, he knew that somewhere out there, the German squadron was approaching, steaming ever closer by the day.

◆

"THEY'RE NOTHING but bloody bureaucrats, sitting on their fat arses in a musty old building in London, telling someone on the other side of the world how to do their job properly," sneered Governor Allardyce with a shake of his head. "Admiral, it seems your job and mine are not that different after all."

"No, I suppose not, William," replied Cradock ruefully. He took a long draught from his pipe and sent the smoke curling away toward the overcast sky.

Over the objections of *Good Hope's* first officer and master at arms, Cradock had made this last trip to the governor's house alone, enjoying the solitary walk through the small town and up the gradual hillside beyond. He had even left his dog behind in his quarters, which was unusual in of itself. The dinner with the governor and his wife had been pleasant, as usual, and the two men had spent much of the mealtime discussing their favorite hunting locales around the world.

They were now standing on the steps of covered front porch of the understated stone and wood frame house that served as the governor's residence in this lonely and windswept part of the British Empire. Below them were the gray and brown rooftops of Port Stanley, beyond which was the still water of the harbor, where *Good Hope* and now the newly arrived *Canopus* lay at anchor. A collier was already positioned alongside the old battleship for a coaling process that would doubtless last through the night. Past the large warships in the bay, on the narrow promontory of land known as Cape Pembroke, the white column of the lighthouse stood sentry over the entrance to the harbor. As dusk settled over the islands, the twilight was gradually giving way to darkness, and the distant pulse of the lighthouse beacon brightened with each passing minute.

"At least you have men to command and ships to direct and courses to chart," continued the governor. Like Cradock, Allardyce was a slightly built man. He wore a full, gray mustache; and he continually squinted through round, wire-framed spectacles. "In my career in the Colonial Office, I've spent most of my days tidying up diplomatic messes made by those same damned bureaucrats. Truly, I'm little more than a glorified chambermaid. And what's the reward for my labors? Being marooned here on this rock for God-knows how much longer. Do you know what they call me back in London?"

"No, I'm afraid not."

"Apparently, I'm known as the 'King of the Penguins.' It's a wonder my dear Constance takes me seriously at all, let alone any of these local shepherds and farmhands."

Cradock stifled a smile. "It could be worse. At least you're a king of something. I've wondered lately if the Admiralty thinks of me as an admiral or an errand boy."

Allardyce was silent for a moment. He gestured toward the bay with his cigar. "So, this additional ship they've sent you — *Canopus* — she really is useless to you?"

"For my purposes, yes. If she were somewhere else, she could ferry troops or supplies, I suppose. She could act as a training vessel back home. She could escort merchant ships. She might even be able to scare off the odd destroyer or two — as long as she didn't have to chase them anywhere. But against von Spee's new armored cruisers, that old relic simply isn't useful at all."

"I'm afraid I don't know much about warships. To me she looks formidable enough."

"Appearances are often deceiving. Back when *Canopus* was built, she was probably one of the finest ships afloat. But that was a long time ago. Today she's an antique." Cradock sighed wearily. "To make matters worse, this morning, after she dropped anchor, her captain met with me and confirmed that there is something wrong with her engines. He doesn't yet know the source of the problem."

"Can our locals be of some service? Our harbormaster and his men have some experience with ship repair—you'd be surprised how many ships limp into Port Stanley with some problem or another. Of course, most of those vessels are whalers—nothing even half as large as your battleship."

"No, but thank you. I'm sure that Grant's men can sort it out. Unfortunately, the captain says that until they find the problem and fix it, she can still only make twelve knots."

"Does the Admiralty know of this latest development?"

Cradock nodded. "I cabled them earlier this afternoon. With *Canopus* useless for anything but escorting colliers, I asked for *Defence* to be transferred from Stoddart's command to my own. It won't matter, I'm afraid. They have made it abundantly clear that they wish for me to make do with the limited resources I already possess. I have asked them repeatedly for a fast, powerful, modern ship to put up against the Germans. They have repeatedly refused. They're adamant that *Canopus* and her big guns are the only assistance I need."

"If she's repaired, can you make use of her guns?"

"Unlikely. As I said, she's an antique. Even at her best—without a damaged engine—the old crate could probably only make sixteen knots. Those German armored cruisers can both reach twenty-three. In all likelihood, *Canopus* would never get in range to hit the Germans with those big 12-inchers. What's worse is that she'd hold the rest of our squadron to that slow speed as well. So, instead of being our protector as the Admiralty envisions it, she'd more likely bring about our doom."

"Bloody bureaucrats," Allardyce muttered again. "So, what will you do?"

"Well, I cannot change my schedule, regardless of how long the repairs might take. As you know, I leave tomorrow for the Strait. *Good Hope* must join the rest of the squadron as quickly as possible. According to our estimates, the Germans could arrive on the Chilean coast within the next few days. I need to be there."

"What about your battleship?"

"She can stay here until the repairs are complete. Then Captain Grant will depart, escort the colliers along the way, and join us on the other side."

Allardyce frowned, discarded the butt of his cigar, and crushed it with the toe of his shoe. "What if *Canopus* doesn't reach you before the Germans do?"

"In truth," Cradock sighed, "I doubt that it will make much of a difference either way. The Admiralty have ordered us to keep the German squadron from rounding Cape Horn and getting into the Atlantic. Even if we do find the Germans, stopping them will be difficult. Our patchwork squadron will be at a great disadvantage—with or without *Canopus's* guns. About the best we can hope for is that we are able to inflict some damage—enough that they have to put one or more of their cruisers into port, where they will then have to be interned."

"Perhaps this is a foolish question, but must you fight them?"

Cradock frowned, perplexed. "What do you mean?"

"To achieve your purpose of keeping them from getting into the Atlantic, can't you simply loiter about near the Strait and the Cape and deter them from approaching by your mere presence? Even if they are a superior force, surely they must be reluctant to enter a firefight that might cause enough damage to their side that they cannot proceed at all?"

"Truthfully, I believe that they have little to lose and much to gain in a direct battle with us. If we hope to just shoo them away with the threat of possible damage to their ships, we will be sorely mistaken. They've steamed halfway across the world without any logistical support, and they have already come looking for a scrap at both Samoa and Tahiti. No, if we got in their way, I'm sure they would immediately bring the fight to us." Cradock looked out across the bay, where the gathering darkness was consuming the gray outline of *Good Hope*. "Besides, I have no desire to suffer the same fate as poor Troubridge."

"Troubridge?" asked Allardyce.

"Yes, Rear-Admiral Ernest Troubridge. Some two and a half months ago—on the first day of the war, actually—two German warships, the battlecruiser *Goeben* and the light cruiser *Breslau*, were fleeing across the Mediterranean for safe harbor in Constantinople. Troubridge's squadron was shadowing them, just out of gunnery range. He had a standing pre-war order to steer clear of any superior forces, but now these ships were to be treated as the enemy. He found himself in a bit of a bind. *Goeben* alone was more than a match for all four of Troubridge's ships put together, but his new orders were to engage and destroy all enemy naval forces. But instead of attacking the Germans, Troubridge let them go, telling the Admiralty afterwards that in the interests of saving his ships and men, he could not knowingly mount a suicidal attack. The two German ships sailed on, unmolested, to Constantinople and into the waiting arms of the Ottomans—who are sympathetic to the Germans and could very well declare war upon the Allies any day now."

"But surely the Admiralty could see that…"

"The Admiralty immediately removed him from command, and a court of inquiry has already decided to court-martial him. Troubridge is finished—branded a coward and a traitor."

"But what would they have him do in such a situation? Get himself and hundreds of sailors killed?"

"Precisely. The Admiralty preside over a Royal Navy that has ruled the world's seas for two centuries. They simply cannot conceive of a scenario in which a British warship would decline to fight an enemy, regardless of how powerful that enemy might be."

"That's madness." The governor shook his head. "Perhaps your job and mine are not that similar after all."

"I can tell you that I will not have my legacy be one of cowardice or treason. If we're ordered to try to stop the Germans—then by God, I will do my best to stop them."

"Even if it means your life?"

"There are worse fates." Cradock paused and looked directly at Allardyce. "With this in mind, I have a favor to ask of you."

"Of course, Admiral."

"You may not be so eager when you hear my request."

The governor pursed his lips. "Well, then I think I'll need to hear it over another glass of scotch. Care to join me back in the parlor?"

Allardyce led the way back inside. His wife had retired upstairs for the evening and the housekeeper was nowhere to be found, so Allardyce stoked the embers in the fireplace and poured two glasses of liquor. Cradock removed his greatcoat and hung it on a peg near the door, then reached into the breast pocket of the coat and retrieved a leather-bound package. He and Allardyce sat in armchairs before the stone hearth, and Cradock placed the bundle in his lap.

Cradock raised his glass and said, "Governor, you and I have not had much time to get to know one another, but I truly appreciate your genuine hospitality, your counsel, and your friendship. For a man such as myself, those commodities have been hard to come by lately."

"You're a good man, Admiral," replied Allardyce. "I'm fortunate to list you among my friends."

They each took a sip of the smoky liquid, and Cradock continued, "What I am about to ask, I do so reluctantly. It is something I could ask only of a true friend—and even then, I would not obligate you to this task."

Allardyce regarded him in silence, waiting for him to continue.

Cradock untied the package's rawhide thong and partially opened the bundle in his lap, drawing out a sealed envelope. His jaw was set as he began to speak again. "It has become increasingly clear to me that my next voyage could very well be my last. The Admiralty have left me with little choice but to engage a superior enemy despite my inferior forces. If I do, in fact, perish in the attempt, I do not wish for my telling of this tale to die with me." He handed the envelope to Allardyce. "Should you receive word that my ship has been lost, please send this letter to my old friend, Admiral Sir Hedworth Meux. He'll know what to do with it."

"Certainly," replied Allardyce quietly, accepting the envelope.

"There's something else." Cradock unfolded the package, revealing a glittering collection of naval medals and ribbons. On the top was the large gold and silver cross that signified his status as a knight of the Royal Victorian Order. He looked at the governor. "I do not have any family, William. No wife. No children. I'm not sure what would become of these upon my death under normal circumstances—but I'll be damned if I'll just let them sink to the bottom of the sea. If the worst occurs, perhaps you can find someone or someplace who will take these—the Royal Naval College, perhaps." He closed the package and held it out to Allardyce.

The governor took the bundle from Cradock's hands and found it to be surprisingly heavy. He opened his mouth to reply, but found he could not. He paused to collect himself, took a breath, and said, "I am honored, Admiral. I sincerely hope that you will return within a few weeks to reclaim these medals yourself—over another glass of scotch, of course." He paused again before continuing. "If, however, that is not to be, I will ensure that they are delivered to someone who may truly appreciate what—and who—they represent."

"Thank you," Cradock replied with a nod. "If I do not return, I trust you'll still raise a toast in my honor. We can only hope that they have such an appreciation for the finer things in the next life as well." He finished the last of his liquor, stood, and looked out the window toward the darkened harbor. "Governor, I thank you once again for your gracious hospitality, but I must now take my leave. *Good Hope* departs tomorrow at first light. I have a German squadron to find. Please express my sincerest gratitude to the lovely Lady Allardyce."

"I most certainly will."

"Goodbye, Governor." Cradock shook Allardyce's hand.

"Goodbye, Admiral. Godspeed."

Cradock plucked his coat from the peg, shrugged it onto his shoulders, and strode out the door into the cold night air.

Governor Allardyce closed the door behind him. He turned and slowly made his way back to the chair by the fire—with the admiral's leather package still nestled under his arm. It now seemed even heavier than before.

◆

"WELL, our week's holiday here on the scenic Chilean coast has finally come to an end," quipped Luce.

"True," replied Captain Brandt, eyes downcast, his thoughts elsewhere. "We have a war waiting for us out there."

They were standing on *Otranto's* upper viewing deck, having recently finished a delicious breakfast hosted by Captain Edwards. Unlike *Glasgow* and *Monmouth*, which had all but been stripped down to their metal bulkheads and deck plating, *Otranto* had not been so harshly converted for her wartime duty. In many ways, she still resembled the luxurious passenger liner that she had once been. Although her main dining room was now missing its chandelier, her walls were still paneled in rosewood and teak, and her ornate chairs and large dining table were definitely not standard naval issue. Eating their meal of roast wild duck and warm baked bread, especially in the opulent surroundings, helped the wartime tension and fear fade away, if only for a few minutes.

First officers Thompson from *Glasgow* and Forbes from *Monmouth* had joined them for the meal, and they remained in the dining room with Edwards, discussing the impending arrival of Admiral Cradock and *Good Hope*. The long-awaited wireless message had finally arrived several hours earlier, stating that the flagship had transited the Strait and was expected to arrive at Vallenar the following day before noon. The weeklong delay had only increased the edginess among the men, and Luce was relieved that this period of enforced idleness was finally over.

"You know, I was a passenger aboard one of these liners once when I was a child," said Brandt, surveying *Otranto's* lower decks from the railing against which they were leaning. "When I became an officer cadet—before my fourteenth birthday—I traveled from India to England aboard a ship much like this."

"Can't say I've ever had the pleasure," offered Luce. "Just about every ship I've ever set foot on has belonged to the Royal Navy." He could tell that something had changed in Brandt's demeanor—a grim darkness that now clouded the other man's face and seemed to distance him. Although Brandt had expressed his misgivings about this mission numerous times over the past weeks, his mood today was somehow different.

"Other than that one voyage in my youth, it has been the same for me as well." Brandt paused, looking out over the calm waters of the bay to where *Monmouth* lay at anchor. A slight breeze blew gently across the deck, barely moving the pennants that hung above their heads. "I've seen a lot of things in my career," he continued quietly. "Until today, John, only once before was I absolutely convinced that I was about to die."

A flock of dappled white seagulls soared gracefully over their heads, squawking noisily at each other as they winged westward toward the ocean.

"In eighty-nine," Brandt went on, "I was a green midshipman on *Calliope*. We were in Samoa when the cyclone hit."

"I remember reading about it," replied Luce. "An extraordinary story. I didn't know you were there."

Brandt continued. "*Calliope* had been deployed to Samoa when it looked like the Americans and Germans might come to blows over the islands. The Samoans were entangled in a civil war, and the damned Yanks and Germans both sent warships to make a grab for the islands while they were in turmoil. We were ordered there only to observe and keep things from getting too chippy. *Calliope* arrived not long after USS *Trenton* — which made for seven warships and six merchantmen in port when the storm hit. As I remember, in addition to *Trenton*, the Americans had a gunboat and a sloop. The Germans had two gunboats and a training ship. Apia harbor isn't that big, of course, so all of these warships and the merchantmen were packed in like kippers in a tin. Even with the storm bearing down, neither of the two governments would back off for fear that by departing that they would lose their chance to claim the islands as new colonial territory. So, instead of making for the open sea where they could have ridden out the storm, the ships were foolishly kept there in port. Adhering to his previous orders from the Admiralty, Captain Kane kept *Calliope* there in port with them also. On the fifteenth — the Ides of March, as it happened — the cyclone struck."

Brandt stared out over the water and went on. "To this day, I have never experienced anything like that storm. We could barely see anything, with the rain pouring down as if an ocean was falling upon us from the sky. The winds blew straight into the harbor, which is ringed by reefs — so there was no chance of escape. What struck me initially was the noise of it — like a thousand locomotives. Massive waves surged in from the open ocean, and all of these big ships, moored so close together, never had a chance. I saw one of the German ships tossed upon the shore as if it were a child's toy. Two of the merchantmen and one of the warships were immediately dashed upon the reefs. We watched helplessly as all three broke apart and sank in mere minutes. *Calliope* was the largest ship present, but even we struggled against the power of the cyclone. Our captain kept the engines at full speed with our bow into the waves, and still our anchor was losing purchase. We rode against the surge in that manner all day and into the night, as we saw doomed ships to port and starboard get swept toward the reefs or the shore."

"As ships were destroyed and men perished around us, I was not the only one who thought it would be our end. I made my peace with God and waited for the inevitable. Somehow, however, *Calliope* survived that terrible night, although in the darkness another merchantman narrowly missed us as she was swept landward to her destruction. The next morning, with the wind still howling terribly, Captain Kane decided to try to escape. Between us and the only gap in the reef were a sunken American ship and *Trenton*, which was still afloat but taking on water rapidly. We had to maneuver between *Trenton* and the reef—a space not much wider than our beam. Fighting against the waves, we struggled toward the gap, pitching and falling so dramatically that at times I'm certain our propeller was spinning freely in the air. The visibility was so poor that we didn't even realize that we had shot the gap until we were already well clear of the island. The storm raged on for two more days—preventing our return until it had passed." Brandt paused, clearly troubled by the recollection of these events.

"I remember reading that *Calliope* was the only ship to make it," said Luce quietly.

Brandt nodded. "The harbor was a graveyard when we returned. Every ship but ours had been sunk, wrecked, or beached. Half-submerged hulls lay on the reefs. Broken masts reached up from underwater. Debris and bodies floated everywhere. Some survivors had made it to shore, but there were still a few men clinging to the wreckage." Brandt fell momentarily silent.

"Good lord," said Luce. "I can only imagine what that must have been like."

"It was a strange experience, really. It was exhilarating to have survived, but it was horribly sobering to realize that so many men did not—and they were so helpless in their final moments." Brandt exhaled slowly. "For many months afterward, that cyclone returned in my nightmares. After some time, blessedly, the trauma of it began to fade from my memory. I no longer thought about it every day, and eventually the nightmares faded away, too. It has been many years since that cyclone woke me up in a cold sweat—until last night."

Luce was not sure what to say, if anything. This was the most personal conversation that he and his fellow captain had shared.

"Last night's dream was different from the nightmares I once had. All the previous dreams had taken place during the cyclone, as we struggled against the surge in the bay while ships all about us were being destroyed. Last night I found myself on the deck of *Calliope* after the storm had subsided and we had returned to the wrecked harbor. As we slowly maneuvered our way among the broken remnants of the partially sunken ships, I looked up toward the shore. There, standing on the sand beside the massive overturned hull of a great beached ship, was my wife, Beryl. She was wearing only her nightdress, and she was looking out to sea—as if she was waiting for someone. I waved to her and shouted her name, but she couldn't see or hear me. It was as if *Calliope* wasn't there at all—at least not to her. Then, from somewhere up the beach, a man appeared—a naval officer. I didn't recognize him, but he walked up to Beryl and they talked. He draped his coat around her shoulders to keep her warm. She looked out to the sea once more—not seeing me still—then she turned and kissed the man on the lips. He took her arm, and they walked up the beach together—and then they were gone." Brandt fell silent again, staring vacantly out toward the shore.

"Can't say I'd care to have a dream like that myself," said Luce, "although I wouldn't know what to make of it if I did."

"I know what to make of it," said Brandt. "It means that I am about to die."

Luce frowned. "Now, surely you can't..."

"I know this, John. As certainly as I have ever known anything in my life, I know this. I am going to die out here, and Beryl will never see me again." Brandt appeared to shiver, although Luce doubted it was from cold. He leaned in closer to Luce's face and continued, "I am going to die out here, leaving a young widow with four children back in Worthing. My lifeless corpse will go to the bottom of the sea in that rusting relic," he said, dismissively gesturing toward *Monmouth* across the bay. "Then, perhaps a respectable year or two from now—long after the crabs have picked my bones clean—my dear Beryl will become another man's wife."

Luce was stunned by the emphatic bleakness of Brandt's vision. The man was in anguish—over something that had not yet actually happened.

"Now heave-to, Frank," said Luce, attempting to lighten the mood. "Don't start writing your eulogy just yet. I'm sure that Cradock has no intent to widow anyone. As absurd as this fool's errand has been thus far, sending men needlessly to their deaths cannot be part of our plan."

Brandt stared out over the water and quietly replied, "It's not part of anybody's plan, John. It's just what's going to happen."

His words lingered in the stillness of the air, like an ethereal presence hanging over them.

Luce could think of nothing else to say that might help or comfort his fellow captain. The emptiness in Brandt's eyes was a cavernous void of despair, and Luce gladly tore his glance away to watch another flight of seagulls wing their way toward the sea. His thoughts traveled unbidden to Mary, the boys, and their modest brick house in Wiltshire—all so far away—and for the first time in his life, he too wondered if he would ever see them again.

# FOURTEEN

*Tuesday, October 27, 1914*
*Isla Más Afuera, Juan Fernández Islands, Chile*

"HAVE YOU READ *Robinson Crusoe*, sir?" asked the young lieutenant loudly over the thumping noise of the small pinnace's steam engine.

"Yes, Mister Stüben," answered Maerker. "When I was a boy— I recall that it was one of my favorites."

"I haven't had the pleasure, sir, but some of the men were saying that this is the island where it took place. Is that true, sir?"

Above them to the east rose the dark mountainous peaks of Más Afuera Island, a small rocky volcanic isle some six hundred kilometers off the Chilean coast. Brilliant green slopes rapidly rose to jagged black cliffs that towered nearly a kilometer above them. It was a stunning sight to behold.

From Easter Island, Admiral von Spee had chosen this as the squadron's last coaling stop before the final leg of their voyage to Valparaiso. Más Afuera's only residents were the few inmates of a small Chilean penal colony on the far side of the island. The previous afternoon, the German squadron had anchored unseen beneath the cliffs on the uninhabited western shore. The colliers had immediately begun coaling the warships, starting with *Scharnhorst* and *Gneisenau*.

The admiral had called for another council of his captains, so Captain Maerker, accompanied by Lieutenant Stüben and a seaman who piloted the pinnace, were traveling across the choppy bay toward the nearby *Scharnhorst*. Beyond the flagship lay *Leipzig*, *Nürnberg*, and *Dresden*—the last of which was now coaling from *Baden*. Also anchored nearby was *Prinz Eitel Friedrich*, which had arrived a day earlier after successfully escorting *Göttingen* to Coronel. Astern lay *Gneisenau*, *Titania*, and the remaining colliers. The black cliffs above them loomed so ominously huge that they made even the large armored cruisers look curiously small by comparison.

"Actually," replied Maerker, "It was this island's sister, Más a Tierra—some hundred and fifty kilometers east—that was the inspiration for Defoe's story. As I recall, a couple of centuries ago, a Scotsman was marooned there on the other island for several years before he was rescued. His story was quite famous at the time."

"Why didn't we anchor there, sir?"

"This island is virtually uninhabited, but the Chileans have an actual settlement on the other island. We couldn't coal there without being spotted."

"Aren't the Chileans sympathetic to our cause?"

"That may be true, but the admiral is being cautious. No sense running the risk of alerting the British prematurely if we don't have to."

As they neared the immense gray flank of the flagship, the pilot throttled back the engine and deftly brought the pinnace alongside the starboard boarding platform. Assisted by two of *Scharnhorst's* seamen, the boat was tied off and Maerker was piped aboard.

Once again, Maerker was escorted to the senior officers' wardroom—which, like the comparable space aboard his own ship, no longer seemed so unnervingly empty. He realized that they had all become accustomed to the Spartan deprivations of wartime. Since he had last been here, however, Maerker noticed that the admiral had done some additional wartime "redecorating." The bulkhead behind the large table was now nearly covered with large maps and charts. Sheaves of papers, stacks of files, and numerous boxes were haphazardly situated about the room. As Maerker entered, Graf Spee greeted him immediately.

"Julius! Welcome aboard," said Graf Spee warmly with a handshake and a pat on the back.

"Thank you, sir."

"Now all we need is *Dresden's* captain and we may begin," said the admiral, who walked back around the table and began leafing through a stack of documents.

Already seated at the long table were Captain Schultz of *Scharnhorst*; the admiral's chief of staff, Filietz; Captain Haun of *Leipzig* and Captain Schönberg of *Nürnberg*.

Maerker shook each officer's hand and took a seat beside Haun. As Maerker and Haun chatted about the previous week's squadron-wide celebration of the Kaiserin's birthday, Schönberg and Filietz sat silently while they waited.

A few minutes later, Captain Lüdecke of *Dresden* arrived, looking flustered.

"Glad you could brush off the coal dust and join us, Captain," said Graf Spee, looking up with a broad smile.

Lüdecke hastily took his seat. "My apologies, sir. A few minor problems with the coaling."

"I'll bet it was that damned fool Holler on *Baden* again," snarled Schönberg. "He tried to sink *Nürnberg* the last time we coaled. The man is utterly incompetent. If it wouldn't be a waste of a perfectly good torpedo, I'd like to…"

"Now that we are all here, gentlemen," interrupted Graf Spee, "We need to discuss the next leg of our journey. As you know, we are now within two days' steaming of the Chilean coast. My plan is to depart tomorrow morning and set a course for this spot here, eighty kilometers northwest of Valparaiso." On the map behind him, he indicated a spot in the open ocean off the coast. "From there, we should be able to receive wireless messages from merchant vessels and our agents in the port. Furthermore, as you know, I have sent *Göttingen* on to Coronel to load additional coal and, if possible, gather information about any sightings of Royal Navy vessels in the area. She should have arrived in Coronel two days ago. We will attempt to contact her via wireless when we are in range."

"Will we be trying to find and attack the British ships immediately, sir?" asked Schönberg hopefully.

"Soon enough, Karl. We would need to be patient while we determine for certain their order of battle and location. That is why we will lay up momentarily off Valparaiso while we gather further intelligence. I believe we already have the British at a disadvantage. They followed *Dresden* into the Pacific, but they do not necessarily know that we are nearby as well. Cradock's squadron is hunting for a single light cruiser. Accordingly, we are still hopeful that he may have split his forces to continue the search along the coast."

"What if they are all still together, and what if they now have additional ships since the time of our last intelligence reports?" asked Filietz with unveiled skepticism.

"Both are possible, of course," acknowledged Graf Spee. "For now, we will develop a battle plan based on what we do know. If circumstances force us to change our plans, then we will alter our approach as necessary. Most of you should already be familiar with the known ships of the British squadron, but I believe an in-depth review would be prudent." He picked up a thick leather-bound manual, opened it to a page near the middle, and set the book on the table in front of the officers. He pointed to the diagrams on the opened pages. "From what we know, this is Admiral Cradock's flagship, HMS *Good Hope*. She is an older *Drake*-class armored cruiser, capable of twenty-two or twenty-three knots. Her primary armament is two 9.2-inch guns, each mounted singly in a turret—one forward of the command superstructure and one aft of her fourth funnel. Her secondary armament comprises sixteen 6-inch guns in casemates along the hull."

"This is an extremely antiquated design," commented Maerker, wondering why an admiral would choose such an old and obsolete vessel for his flagship. "How can they possibly fire these 6-inchers in any sea greater than two meters?"

"They probably cannot," answered Graf Spee. "In any case, I hope to render her secondary battery irrelevant regardless of the sea conditions. If we can maneuver to keep the fight at a range where only the 9.2-inchers can reach us, our greater numbers of heavy guns should provide overwhelming superiority in weight of shell."

"Only *Scharnhorst* and *Gneisenau* can fire at those ranges," said Haun. "Regardless of how old she might be, our light cruisers cannot trade punches with this ship."

"True, Johann. You will not be expected to. If we encounter *Good Hope* operating on her own, our armored cruisers will pursue and engage her, and the three light cruisers will immediately be dispatched to locate the rest of the enemy force. If *Good Hope* is accompanied by all of her fellow warships, we will fall into standard battle order, with *Scharnhorst* in the vanguard, then *Gneisenau*, then each of the light cruisers in turn. Our armored cruisers will engage *Good Hope* and *Monmouth*, and the light cruisers will attack the rest of the British line."

"Isn't *Monmouth* a County-class cruiser?" asked Schultz. "I've toured one of those—it was HMS *Kent*. If so, she's just as obsolete as that flagship."

The admiral reached over and turned to another bookmarked page showing diagrams of the Royal Navy's County-class armored cruisers. "Correct, Felix. *Monmouth* has no main battery of guns at all. She carries fourteen 6-inch guns in nearly identical casemates to *Good Hope*. I've always thought that this was one of the worst warship designs the British ever set afloat. As with *Good Hope*, if we can keep her within the range of our main guns but outside the range of her 6-inchers—around ten thousand meters—we should be able to strike her with impunity. Her speed is probably also in the twenty-two-knot range—comparable to our armored cruisers—so continual maneuvering to maintain the necessary distance will be critical."

"I doubt those old ships can still make their designed speeds," said Captain Schultz with a confident sneer. "Depending upon sea conditions, we should be able to maintain that distance without a problem."

"Perhaps," said Graf Spee, "but bear in mind that Cradock is an excellent commander. He's surely well aware of the shortcomings of his armored cruisers. Against only *Dresden*, whom they have been pursuing, his ships are decidedly superior. As soon as Cradock realizes that he is up against *Scharnhorst* and *Gneisenau*, he will act swiftly to minimize his weaknesses. He will either try to close the distance between us to use his smaller guns or he will flee and try to draw one or more of our ships into an ambush or a mismatch. Those ships might be antiquated, but it will not matter if Cradock can bring all of his guns in range. I would rather not try to operate under a constant rain of 6-inch shells." The admiral looked pointedly at Schultz, then at the other captains at the table. "Do not underestimate Cradock or his ships. Our ability to communicate effectively and maneuver precisely as a squadron during battle conditions will be crucial."

"In addition to *Good Hope* and *Monmouth*, they also have a light cruiser in their squadron, correct?" asked Schönberg. "The *Glasgow*, is it? I am not familiar with this ship."

"*Glasgow* is one of the Brits' newer Town-class cruisers," offered Maerker. "An excellent ship—well armed for her size and fast. I had the pleasure of being a guest aboard a Town-class ship for a day when I was *Magdeburg's* captain, just last year."

"Yes, the Town-class cruisers are quite good," agreed Graf Spee, turning to another page in the manual on the table. "Captains Schönberg, Haun, and Lüdecke, you will do well to treat *Glasgow* with extreme caution, should you encounter her without the backup of either *Scharnhorst* or *Gneisenau* nearby. As you can see here, in addition to her 4-inch guns—which are comparable to the batteries carried by each of your ships—*Glasgow* also has two turreted 6-inch guns, which will be able to outrange you. She also may be capable of speeds in excess of twenty-five knots—so she can outrun you as well. Therefore, you are to engage *Glasgow* only if you outnumber her or if one of our armored cruisers is also present. Is that understood?"

"Yes, sir," said Captain Haun. The other two light cruiser captains nodded in agreement.

"The final ship under Cradock's command is an armed merchant cruiser," said Graf Spee. "I can only speculate that this ship is a part of Cradock's squadron only to aid in the search efforts for *Dresden*. She is not a meaningful tactical addition, and I doubt that Cradock will set her against any of our ships. If we encounter this armed passenger liner, we will certainly sink her, but I imagine this ship will be kept far from any real battle."

The admiral stepped back to the chart affixed to the bulkhead behind him. He indicated the route marked from Más Afuera to the designated assembly spot near Valparaiso. He glanced at Maerker, who noted the familiar gleam in Graf Spee's eyes as he continued. "From this moment onward, stealth and surprise will be our greatest advantages. Our Captain Maerker has conceived a brilliant plan to help hide us from our enemies. As we approach the coast, we will be instituting a new, temporary wireless communications protocol to help hide our presence from the British. They already assume that *Dresden* is in the region and *Leipzig* is somewhere along the west coast of the Americas. They know that *Dresden* is hiding from them and would be unlikely to give away her position by using her wireless. As far as they know, *Leipzig* could still be farther up the coast—where she was operating freely and brazenly for weeks. If the British hear *Leipzig's* wireless signal, they will naturally assume that she has simply steamed a bit farther south along the coast. Therefore, until further notice, all ships of our squadron will use only encoded wireless transmissions and will use only *Leipzig's* call signal. If we can keep the Brits guessing—and keep them believing that the only German warship operating in the area is *Leipzig*—we may be more likely to catch them off-guard."

"An excellent plan, Admiral," offered Captain Haun.

Most of the captains nodded and voiced their approval of the plan—all except Schönberg, who remained curiously and coldly silent. Maerker saw that even the usually dour Captain Filietz was also smiling, so what was wrong with Schönberg? Maerker noted that this was just the latest in a series of instances where he had observed a subtle but undeniable hostility from *Nürnberg's* captain. There was something dark and brooding about the man that perplexed Maerker. He got the distinct impression that Schönberg disliked him. Maerker had no idea what he could have done to displease or anger the other captain, but he made a mental note to be wary of him.

"Ensure that the wireless operators on each of your ships follow the new protocol, gentlemen," said Graf Spee. "We depart at first light tomorrow."

◆

"I HAVE TO ADMIT, Will, that it feels good to be on our own again," said Luce to his first officer.

"Agreed. I almost forgot what it was like to steam without a train of plodding museum exhibits in tow."

The two men were standing outside, on *Glasgow's* flying bridge. Patchy clouds drifting across the night sky offered occasional glimpses of twinkling stars beyond. The wind was brisk and cold, but unlike the warmth of the adjacent wheelhouse, the open-air platform offered a measure of privacy for their conversation.

*Glasgow* was steaming north from Vallenar toward Coronel. As expected, *Good Hope* had arrived at the hidden coaling base the day before, along with *South Wales*, a collier that Cradock had chartered in Punta Arenas. Not surprisingly, *Canopus* had not been with the flagship — something about her engine needing repair and being only capable of twelve knots. Supposedly the old battleship was still following along at her glacial pace, bringing with her two more colliers.

After a quick briefing from his captains, Cradock had decided to send *Glasgow* back up to Coronel to check in with the consulate, retrieve waiting messages from the Admiralty, and inquire about any new suspicious activity in the local German community. British officials in Punta Arenas had informed Cradock that German communications traffic had been steadily increasing during the past week, although encryption had thus far foiled their attempts to decipher the nature of the messages. Because of *Glasgow's* speed, she was chosen for this quick dash into Coronel while the rest of the ships remained behind to coal, prepare, and presumably await the arrival of *Canopus*.

Although Luce savored the chance to briefly operate alone, he knew that the danger to his ship and his men was even greater now — with the possibility that the German squadron might appear along the coast at any time.

"I still cannot believe that the best assistance the Admiralty could send us was that old rust bucket, *Canopus*," said Thompson. "They still expect us to find and stop the Germans with this motley little squadron?"

"Apparently so," answered Luce.

"Morale on *Monmouth* is in the pits. It's like a funeral over there. Everyone aboard her is convinced they've had it."

"Unfortunately, it starts with the captain. Brandt's all but decided he's done for. There's no talking to the man."

"It's not just the captain," said Thompson. "Yesterday, after Hirst's meeting with some of the officers and engineers on *Monmouth*, Lieutenant-Commanders Bluett and Lees took him aside. They gave Hirst a sheaf of letters, which he showed to me. There must be a hundred letters in that bundle from officers and men all over *Monmouth* — all of them letters home to wives and families. Bluett and Lees told him that they were sure they were done for, but they believed that because *Glasgow* was so much faster than the other ships, we might be able to get away. They wanted to make sure their wives got their last words and wishes. Damned sobering, really."

"Christ," muttered Luce. *Monmouth* had enough problems as it is, he thought, without adding the corrosive effects of shipwide depression and poor morale. "Hopefully we'll never have to send those letters."

Above them, the clouds had thickened, obscuring the few stars that had been visible earlier. Rain began to fall, at first tentatively, then with greater force. Luce and Thompson returned to the warmth of the wheelhouse to find that Lieutenant Stuart had arrived.

"Good evening, sir."

"Lieutenant. You have something for me?"

"I think so, sir. Something unusual." Stuart frowned. "Perhaps you should come and hear it for yourself."

Luce turned and raised an eyebrow toward Thompson. "You have the bridge, Commander." He followed Stuart down the ladder through the door of the nearby wireless room. This room, situated as it was near the bridge, was small and cramped—offering only enough space for a few people to stand behind the twin consoles where the telegraphists were working.

Stuart stepped up behind one of the operators and tapped him on the shoulder.

The man raised an earpiece of his headset. "Yes, sir?" He was a young man, perhaps nineteen, with a splash of freckles across his nose and cheeks.

"Tanner, can you give the captain a listen to what you've been picking up from our friends up north?"

"Certainly, sir." The young wireless operator detached his headset from the console and depressed a switch. The large, square-faced metal speaker mounted on the bulkhead over the unit popped with static, then immediately began squawking and chirping with wireless signals. Tanner then turned a dial, and the first signal faded—only to be replaced by another burst of more rapid signals. He rotated the dial slightly again, and with a hiss of static found another, fainter tapping pattern.

"These signals, and several more, are all German," said Stuart. "All of them. They're coming from north of us, getting stronger as we go."

"Can you translate any of it?"

"No, sir. Every one of them is encrypted—most of it unfamiliar ciphers—but definitely German. Our guess is that we're hearing merchant ships in the harbor in Coronel, maybe also Valparaiso. They're particularly chatty this evening, sir. We weren't sure who they might all be talking to at this hour, but then we heard something just as strange." Stuart nodded to the telegraphist, indicating that he should explain further.

"It was just a moment, really, sir," said Tanner to the captain. "Only a few seconds—very faint. But it was a German warship."

"How do you know it was a warship?" asked Luce.

"Well, sir, don't know all the odd codes and set signatures those German merchant ships are using, but I know the sound of a *Kaiserliche Marine* Telefunken set when I hear one. It was unmistakable, even as faint as it was."

"Could you get anything from what you heard?"

"No, sir. Unfortunately not. It was just a snippet of a transmission, sir. Nothing identifiable." Tanner lowered his head. "But if I heard it again, I'd know it."

Luce pondered that. This might be their first real indication that the enemy was finally near. The volume of German wireless traffic out of the Chilean ports had definitely increased—and now this stray bit of signal from what likely was a German warship had originated somewhere in the region. This was not a coincidence. "Excellent work, gentlemen. Keep me informed of any further developments."

Luce retired to his cabin. He penned an entry in his log, then decided to write another letter to Mary. In the current climate of gloom and foreboding within the squadron, his letter could easily have been one of fateful and desperate farewell. Instead, he chose to briefly recount their recent stay at Vallenar, the long wait for the admiral, and their renewed search for the German squadron. He finished his letter simply, by inquiring after the boys and stating plainly that he missed his wife and hoped that all of this unpleasant business would be over soon.

The next morning, after his breakfast, he joined his senior officers on the bridge. Among them was Lieutenant Stuart, who had an update from the rest of the night's wireless traffic.

"Good morning, sir. Within the past half hour, we heard that distinctive German naval signal again. This time it was a bit stronger—so we believe we are getting closer to her. Although the transmission was encoded, we were able to decipher the call signal. It's *Leipzig*, sir. From the strength of the signal, she's likely within two hundred miles of us. She only transmitted for about twenty seconds, so she couldn't have been saying much."

"Thank you, Mister Stuart," replied Luce. "Mister Portman, how long until we reach our designated coordinates outside Coronel?"

"Approximately four hours, sir," replied Portman.

"Very well. Mister Stuart, keep us apprised if you hear anything unusual. Inform me immediately if that German warship makes any more noise."

"Yes, sir." Stuart turned and left the bridge.

Outside, the morning light was muted, filtered through low-hanging clouds. *Glasgow* sliced through steel gray swells as she steamed northward at fifteen knots.

"*Leipzig*, huh?" said Thompson, who then turned to the gunnery commander. "What do we know about SMS *Leipzig*, Mister Backhouse?"

"She's one of their *Bremen*-class light cruisers," said Backhouse. "We got a look at *Bremen* herself last year in Montevideo. Three funnels, perhaps two-thirds our size. She's comparable to *Dresden*, but a bit older and not as fast. She can probably do twenty-two knots. Like all the rest of those German light cruisers, she's got a battery of ten 4-inch guns. We're more than a match for *Leipzig*, Commander."

"It's not so much *Leipzig* I'm concerned about," interjected Luce. "It's who else might be out there with her. *Leipzig* began the war somewhere off the coast of Mexico. Her last known position was more than a thousand miles north of here, off the coast of Peru. From the intercepted transmissions of a few weeks ago, we know that *Dresden* made long-range contact with von Spee and was planning to meet him at Easter Island. We don't know if *Leipzig* received the message as well. Whether she did or not, we're now hearing her nearby, perhaps off Valparaiso. She's steamed all the way down here—while *Dresden* made her way around the Cape from the West Indies to join von Spee. None of this is coincidental."

Thompson nodded. "I seriously doubt that both of these German captains have steamed all the way to the Chilean coast just to share *sauerkraut* recipes with their admiral. Gentlemen, make sure all of our spotters have a look at *Leipzig's* silhouette in the book."

"And Mister Portman," added Luce, "when we've reached our point forty miles outside Coronel, prepare to wait there indefinitely."

"Aye, sir."

As they approached the predetermined coordinates near mid-day, the wireless signals continually grew stronger. Twice more, *Glasgow's* wireless room heard *Leipzig's* unmistakable call sign, now no more than one hundred fifty miles away. As Luce instructed, the helmsman slowed and stopped the light cruiser—and there they waited. Laying unseen just beyond the eastern horizon was the Chilean coast and the port of Coronel. Luce had no intention of entering the port if *Leipzig* were truly nearby—for doing so would risk being bottled up in the harbor and losing the speed and maneuverability advantages he would otherwise have against the German cruiser.

Instead, he sent a wireless message to Cradock, informing him of their situation. Cradock replied that *Good Hope*, *Monmouth*, and *Otranto* were preparing to depart Vallenar and would join him in two days' time—and it was up to Luce's discretion as to when he should choose to enter the port to complete his mission.

The next day and a half became an anxious routine of waiting, wondering, and continually scanning the horizon for any sign of funnel smoke. As *Glasgow* kept her position and simply rode the swells just out of view of the coast, the agitation on board was palpable. By now, word had traveled throughout the watches that a German warship's signal had been heard nearby. Although not yet at action stations, the men performed their duties with a heightened sense of vigilance—and considerable trepidation. Although *Leipzig's* signals were heard twice more, the strength of the transmissions had not increased, suggesting that the enemy cruiser was no closer to them. With each daybreak, the seas around them remained empty.

Finally, in the late afternoon of October 31st, Luce decided that with the rest of the British squadron now less than a day away, he could wait no longer—regardless of *Leipzig's* proximity. *Glasgow* once again steamed cautiously into the small port of Coronel.

As they made their way slowly into the outer harbor and dropped anchor, Luce could see that little had changed since their last visit two weeks earlier. In fact, the only obvious difference was the surprising presence of an additional German merchant ship anchored in the port. This new ship appeared to be a collier, and the faded lettering on her stern read *Göttingen*. From where she had come was anyone's guess, but apparently her captain and crew had sought refuge here in Coronel harbor.

Lieutenant Hirst had been chosen to go ashore and make contact with the consulate, deliver mails, send an operational update to the Admiralty, and receive any waiting messages for Admiral Cradock. As several seamen and Hirst's petty officer escort were readying the boat, Lieutenant Stuart arrived on the bridge with a wireless transcript in his hand.

"That new ship, *Göttingen*," said Stuart, "has a wireless aerial, and she wasted no time sending off a message. In fact, the moment we dropped anchor, she started transmitting a repeated signal."

"Did you get a translation?" asked Luce.

"Yes, sir. It was unfortunately quite simple." Stuart read the transcript aloud, "BRITISH LIGHT CRUISER ANCHORED IN CORONEL HARBOR 7:00 PM OCTOBER 31."

"Bloody wonderful," huffed Commander Backhouse. "Here we go again—and this time we know there's at least one German warship close enough to hear it."

"Not surprising, though," said Luce. "The Chileans don't hold the Germans to the neutrality rules like they do with us. As far as that goes,

Coronel might as well be a port along the Rhine. Our presence here was never going to remain a secret. However, I plan to be gone before the Germans or the Chileans can do anything about it. By law, we need to leave port within twenty-four hours. I intend to depart in twelve. That should give Lieutenant Hirst enough time to accomplish his mission—and we can slip away before *Leipzig* or anyone else can arrive to give us trouble."

In the waning twilight, the officers on the bridge watched Hirst's boat heading toward the wharf, as the seamen dipped the oars in near perfect rhythm. Beyond the boat, they could also see crewmen aboard the new German ship observing them with binoculars.

Backhouse frowned and ran his fingers over his moustache. "Let's just hope that twelve hours is soon enough."

◆

FOR MAERKER, finally seeing the cloud-tipped lavender peaks of the Andes Mountains on the distant eastern horizon was a surprisingly emotional experience. They had briefly steamed only close enough to barely see the uppermost reaches of the mountains before adjusting course slightly farther out to sea toward their predetermined rendezvous point. Against extraordinary odds, the East Asia Squadron had escaped from Tsingtao and traversed the entire Pacific Ocean without once being spotted by Russian, French, Japanese, or British warships. They had been both cunning and bold, cautious and daring during their three-month odyssey. Maerker realized that a part of him had been skeptical that they would ever truly reach the South American coast—so to actually see those mountains in the hazy distance brought over him a wave of wonderment and relief. They had really done it.

His exhilaration was short-lived, however, as the realization set in that here along the Chilean coast, they were finally likely to encounter the enemy in force. With that in mind, the admiral had ordered the squadron to assemble some eighty kilometers northwest of Valparaiso. Here, just beyond the sight of land and outside the main coastal shipping lanes, the admiral had immediately begun communicating with contacts on shore— always prefacing those transmissions with *Leipzig's* call sign. Of course, *Gneisenau's* wireless room received the transmissions as well, and Maerker was stunned at the number and frequency of the incoming messages from the coast.

As soon as the faux-*Leipzig* had made her presence known within range of the coast, the squadron's wireless operators were inundated with messages from German agents, consular officers, and anchored merchant vessels from Valparaiso to Coronel. Many incoming messages were of limited use—patriotic words of encouragement or vitriolic screeds against the enemy. However, a few transmissions, once decoded, provided the squadron commanders with useful intelligence.

One of these reports had come from agents down in Punta Arenas. It stated that a British *Canopus*-class battleship had transited westward through the Strait of Magellan, passing Punta Arenas on October 27th. This was a disturbing development, because it meant that the British were reinforcing their known naval assets in the region.

On the evening of the 31st, Captain Maerker called a dinner meeting of his senior officers in *Gneisenau's* main wardroom to discuss the intelligence reports amassed thus far and the latest instructions from the flagship. Seated at the table with the captain were Commander Pochhammer and Lieutenant-Commanders Busch, Petri, Born, and Metz. This was the first formal gathering of his entire senior staff since they had departed Easter Island.

"A battleship?" muttered Pochhammer, shaking his head. "Even with both *Scharnhorst* and *Gneisenau*, we cannot possibly contend with a battleship. Now what will we do?" he asked, plainly distressed.

"Exactly what we have been doing, Commander," replied Maerker curtly. He was not amused by his first officer's chronic melodrama. "We're laying off the coast and gathering information—including intelligence regarding the latest positions of enemy ships in the region. If anything, Mister Pochhammer, you should be glad that we've received this report. We now know that this battleship was at Punta Arenas four days ago. *Canopus*-class ships are quite old and are not particularly fast. This is not a modern battlecruiser we're talking about here. This ship can probably make at most sixteen or seventeen knots." Maerker addressed the senior navigating officer. "Mister Born, assuming that speed, how long might it reasonably take for such a battleship to travel from Punta Arenas to Valparaiso?"

"If they wanted to steam at full speed for the duration of the voyage and burn up their coal supply in one mad dash, perhaps five days," answered Born. "And that assumes they even have that much range, which I do not know."

"Regardless of what her operational range might be, no sane captain would arrive to do battle with empty coal bunkers," said Busch. "No, they'll have to stop somewhere to coal."

Maerker said, "So, she would probably still be another day or so from Valparaiso—*if* she were steaming directly here at full speed *and* had enough coal to get here. I agree, however, that in all likelihood she is not racing toward us at full steam—because as far as we can tell, the British do not yet know we are here. It is much more likely that this battleship has either been tasked with guarding the mouth of the Strait or has been sent to rendezvous with Cradock's squadron, wherever they might be. In either case, just knowing she is now part of the enemy order of battle lets us prepare for her accordingly.

"I doubt that the admiral is interested in a direct confrontation with a battleship, even an old one," continued Maerker. "If they've sent her to guard the Strait, then perhaps we'll just steam around her and leave her behind us. If we must contend with the battleship as a part of Cradock's squadron, then we'll find a way to outmaneuver her and strike her from long range until she withdraws or is disabled."

"Even that sounds risky," said Pochhammer warily. "No one wants to strike a blow for the Kaiser more than I—and God knows I would love to get a British ship in our sights—but a battleship? All it would take is for them to get one lucky hit…"

"I believe that luck favors the better prepared, Commander," said Maerker. Although he had no desire to trade shell fire with a battleship of any vintage, he knew that minimizing fearful speculation among his officers was crucial to keeping their minds focused.

"I am, by nature, a cautious man. I am not prone to reckless behavior, nor would I carelessly risk the lives of any of my men. The East Asia Squadron is the best-trained unit in the entire *Kaiserliche Marine*. Our admiral may be its most capable leader. *Scharnhorst* and *Gneisenau* are extremely formidable warships. If we find this British squadron—even if their old battleship is with them—I will gladly put up our superior training, preparation, gunnery, and tactics against their luck any day." From the resolute nods around the table, he could see that his own confidence was reassuring to them. He glanced toward his senior communications officer. "Mister Petri, with all of those signals coming in, what other news do you have for us?"

Petri flipped through a sheaf of papers in front of him. "As far as we know, the British squadron thought to be operating here off the Chilean coast represents the only known enemy naval presence in the region. We have no indication that the French or Japanese have any assets within several thousand kilometers. Unfortunately, I currently have nothing else at this time about the British ships or their possible locations. Until one or more of them is spotted somewhere, we're still in the dark."

"What of the news back home?" asked Born. "How goes the war?"

"All good, I believe. We'll know more if we can put ashore, get some cables from the *Admiralstab,* and see some actual newspapers, but what snippets I've heard from our local agents sound encouraging. Of course, I cannot say with any certainty, but it sounds like it is but a matter of time before our enemies capitulate."

"Excellent," muttered Pochhammer. "All of them—but especially the British—need to be taught a lesson in humility."

Maerker addressed the engineering commander. "Mister Metz, now that we're contemplating actually going into battle, what can you tell us about the state of our engineering spaces?"

Metz cleared his throat. "Everything is running quite well, sir, considering how long we've been away from a proper port. I'd love to be able to have the hull scraped to get maximum speed out of her, but…"

A knock at the door announced the presence of a young signals lieutenant, who stepped tentatively into the room.

"Yes, Mister Picht?" said Petri testily to his subordinate, annoyed that the young officer had the temerity to disturb a meeting of the senior officers.

"Pardon me for the intrusion, sir," said Picht excitedly. "Your orders were to inform you immediately of any information regarding Royal Navy vessels. We just received an urgent wireless transmission from *Göttingen*. Her captain reports that a single British light cruiser dropped anchor in Coronel harbor within the last half hour."

For a moment, the gathered officers looked at each other in stunned silence. Each face then began to register the real meaning of this development. The light cruiser at Coronel could only be *Glasgow*. This was an unbelievable stroke of luck. The fastest ship in the British squadron was anchored in port, alone and completely vulnerable—for a brief period of time. The question that remained was whether they could get there before *Glasgow* slipped away.

"Thank you, Mister Picht," said Maerker to the lieutenant. "You may return to your post." The young officer left the room, and Maerker returned his attention to his senior staff. He stood as he said, "Gentlemen, prepare the ship to depart immediately for Coronel at full steam."

◆

"YOU'VE CONFIRMED that the transmission was from *Leipzig*?" asked Admiral Cradock as he peered through the glass of the wheelhouse window into the darkness beyond.

"Yes, sir," said the signals officer. "Although the telegraphists cannot yet decipher the body of the message, the call sign is unmistakable—and it's stronger now than before. Either we're getting closer, or she is."

"Excellent," replied Cradock. "If *Leipzig* is operating alone, we may have a chance to surprise her before she can turn tail and escape."

At this early hour, only three other men were on the bridge. He turned to the helmsman. "Increase speed to fifteen knots." Addressing the signals officer and the officer of the watch, he said, "Signal *Monmouth* and *Otranto*. They are to increase speed to match the flagship. Re-plot our course and arrival time, and inform the captain."

Underneath a dazzling array of stars, the line of three warships plowed ahead more rapidly as they steamed northward toward Coronel. A following wind howled around the ship and whipped foam from the growing swells beneath them—revealing specks of white on an otherwise inky black sea.

Still conspicuously absent from their line was *Canopus*, which was now anchored back at Vallenar. She had been approaching the coaling base and was only an hour away when Cradock ordered the departure of the squadron. He had hoped to have the battleship with him as they moved north to Coronel, but a wireless message from Captain Grant indicated that a piston gland was in need of repair. Exasperated, Cradock ordered *Canopus* to remain at Vallenar until the repair was complete—then resume her journey northward to rejoin the squadron.

Cradock's arrival on the bridge had been a surprise to the middle watch officers there. On an otherwise quiet night, senior officers rarely made an appearance at such an ungodly hour. However, Cradock had been sleeping fitfully, so when he was informed of the latest wireless intercept from *Leipzig*, he gladly arose and made his way to the wheelhouse. His terrier had not been as pleased with the unscheduled nocturnal jaunt and was now curled up asleep at the base of the compass pedestal.

The admiral was actually relieved that he was not encumbered by *Canopus*. It was bad enough that *Otranto*—and therefore the rest of the squadron—was limited to a maximum speed of sixteen knots. It would be pointless to try to hunt and trap *Leipzig* with a squadron that could steam at only twelve.

According to the bridge officers' new calculations, they would now reach the designated rendezvous point outside of Coronel just after noon, where hopefully *Glasgow* would be waiting to meet them. With any luck, thought Cradock, Luce will have retrieved messages from the Admiralty—although he doubted that his superiors in London had changed their minds about sending him reinforcements.

Perhaps, he mused, the German squadron had not yet fully come together. If *Leipzig* was operating here alone, maybe she had not yet been able to rendezvous with von Spee and the rest of his warships. This was an extraordinary opportunity to catch one of the German light cruisers by surprise. After *Glasgow* had rejoined the squadron, Cradock would spread the four ships apart to maximize their search area. He would cast a net to try to quickly snare the lone enemy cruiser.

"Lieutenant," he said to the officer of the watch, "have the wireless room send an encrypted message to Captain Luce on *Glasgow*. Give him our revised time of arrival at the rendezvous point. As soon as he is able to leave port and rejoin the squadron, we will initiate our search for *Leipzig*."

"Aye, sir."

"And Lieutenant, have one of the stewards bring me a cup of tea. I have no intention of going back to sleep tonight."

# FIFTEEN

*Sunday, November 1, 1914*
*Port of Coronel, Chile*

DESPITE LUCE'S INTENTION to depart at dawn, *Glasgow* was still moored in Coronel harbor at 8:00 am. The first hours of waxing daylight had been a maddening delay while he waited for Lieutenant Hirst to return from the British consular offices. Instead of slipping quietly out of the port in the half-light of sunrise, Luce had been forced to keep the ship at anchor while the morning progressed and activity in the port rose to its customary bustle. Crews on the nearby moored German merchant ships were once again surveying *Glasgow* with binoculars, and a small crowd of Chileans had gathered on the wharf, presumably to gawk at the British warship. Knowing that hundreds of potentially hostile eyes were upon them and that their presence had been announced via wireless more than twelve hours earlier left Luce feeling exposed and vulnerable.

Without a reliable way to contact Hirst to confirm that his mission had been successful—short of sending another boat and crew to check on him—Luce's concern grew. He simply could not wait much longer and risk being trapped there, should *Leipzig* show up in Arauco Gulf to their west. In anticipation of their imminent departure, he ordered the boilers up to full steam, sending trails of black smoke from the cruiser's four funnels spiraling into the clear morning sky. Finally, at a quarter past eight, spotters saw Hirst and his escort make their way through the assembly on the wharf, clamber aboard their boat, and push off. Within a few minutes, the rowers had traversed the distance from the pier and the boat had pulled alongside the warship's starboard flank. Word then came from below that Hirst was back aboard the ship and the boat was being raised and secured.

"Weigh anchor," said Luce to the bridge officers, who then passed his orders throughout the ship. Fore and aft, men engaged the steam-powered capstans to raise the anchor cables. "Mister Alison, bring her about to port. Slow ahead. We're leaving this place not a moment too soon."

"Aye, sir. Coming about to port. Slow ahead." The helmsman also looked relieved to finally be getting underway. *Glasgow's* propellers churned in the brown water of the harbor and the sleek cruiser began to make her way out of the port.

"Good morning, sir," said Lieutenant Hirst as he arrived on the bridge. "Sorry about the delay."

"I'm glad we didn't have to leave you behind, Mister Hirst," said Luce. "Problems at the consulate?"

Hirst nodded. "A few, sir. Apparently, our visit was as much of a surprise to our consular chaps as it was to the Germans. Firstly, the consul couldn't locate his primary telegraphist for nearly two hours. Then, after they did find him—apparently keeping time with a local girl—and brought him back, there were problems with the cable equipment." Hirst rolled his eyes. "They finally got that repaired, but it then became clear that none of the recently-arrived cables from the Admiralty had been decrypted. The consul and I worked together to expedite the decryption process. I brought back several cables and messages for the admiral. I was also able to send our status update to the Admiralty and drop off our mails and those from *Monmouth*."

"Good work. Anything else of note?"

"Our boys have been keeping an eye on the German consulate, which is less than a quarter mile from our building. Seems Fritz had the lights on all night and there was an unusual amount of activity there."

"I'm glad we could give the local Germans something to do on their Saturday night," said Thompson, who surveyed the town once more as *Glasgow* completed her turn and headed due west.

"We heard *Leipzig's* wireless twice more during the night," said Luce. "Stronger each time. I'm sure that the German consulate was encouraging her to come and trap us here."

"Our consul confirmed," continued Hirst, "what we were hearing as we approached. German communications traffic has increased dramatically over the past four or five days. They're certainly acting like something big is going on."

"Bring her up to ten knots," said Luce to the helmsman. "Set a course due north. Stay on that heading until we're out of sight of the port, then turn west to rejoin the squadron." Luce turned his attention back to Hirst. "Once again, good work, Lieutenant. Be prepared to deliver the admiral's package of cables and messages when we meet up with the flagship. We'll send you over in a boat. Until then, you're dismissed to get a rest and something to eat."

"Thank you, sir." Hirst turned and departed the bridge.

As *Glasgow* steamed out toward the open ocean, her bow rose and fell on the growing swells and whitecaps. The sky was a brilliant blue-gray, with thin wisps of clouds streaking northward.

"Wind and sea picking up," commented Thompson. "Looks like we're in for a rough day."

"At least we have good visibility for now," said Luce. "If *Leipzig* is out there, our spotters should have no problem finding her."

A whistle echoed from one of the pipes. "Wireless room to the bridge," said a hollow-sounding voice from one of the metal cones on the console in front of them.

"Go ahead, Mister Stuart," replied Luce, speaking into a cone marked *Wireless Room.*

"Good morning, sir. Two items to report. First, we heard another German wireless transmission sent just a few minutes ago, again from *Göttingen.* It reads, 'BRITISH LIGHT CRUISER DEPARTED CORONEL HARBOR 9:00 AM NOVEMBER 1'."

"You have to hand it to those Germans," said Thompson. "Certainly are prompt and precise."

"And the second item?" asked Luce.

"As we speak, sir, we're intercepting another encrypted transmission from *Leipzig.* Very close. Strongest signal yet."

"Thank you, Mister Stuart. Inform me if you hear anything else." Luce glanced at Thompson. "Looks like they just missed closing the net on us."

◆

ON *Gneisenau's* quarterdeck, Chaplain Rost had to raise his voice over the wind and the pounding of the waves. "As we go forth on this holy day to do His will, remember the words of the Lord in the book of Isaiah: '*Lift up your eyes on high and behold who hath created these, that bring out their host by number; he calleth them all by name, by the greatness of his might, and for he is strong in power, not one shall fail*'."

Nearly one hundred officers and men had gathered on deck for the chaplain's service. The gathering likely would have been larger in number, had the southerly wind not been so terribly cold. Although the sky was a brilliant clear blue-gray and the sun shone brightly, stinging spray and mist lashed the decks continually as the armored cruiser plunged through the rising swells at fifteen knots. The service had started with the men singing "*Ein feste Burg ist Unser Gott,*" after which Rost had begun his sermon. The chaplain had already been talking for some time, and Maerker could tell that he was only just now hitting his stride.

"As we prepare to meet our foe in battle," continued Rost, "each man among you must look to the Lord for that strength. He will not fail you, and therefore you will not fail."

Maerker reflected on the curious irony of such a martial sermon delivered on All Saints Day. He would not, however, question the chaplain's choice of message or its timing. He considered the preacher to be an essential member of the squadron, and on this day—this otherwise holy day—he believed that the men might need as much bolstering, divine or otherwise, as they could find. He rarely attended the chaplain's services, but this morning—as the squadron steamed rapidly toward the port of Coronel—he had made an exception. Perhaps it was the holy day itself, the previous day's Feast of the Reformation, and the reverence for such solemn rites that his late parents and grandparents had treated with such seriousness. More likely, however, it was the possibility that today they might finally meet their enemy in battle. Maerker had some difficulty believing that God would truly choose favorites in an earthly conflict, but he mused that if God really supported the German side, he would have kept *Glasgow* anchored in Coronel harbor a bit longer.

As expected, as soon as they had received word of *Glasgow's* arrival at the port, the admiral had ordered the five warships of the squadron to set course immediately for Coronel. *Titania* and *Prinz Eitel Friedrich* were diverted with the remaining supply ships to Valparaiso for reprovisioning—after which they were to escort those ships back to the clandestine anchorage at Más Afuera to await further orders. Led by *Scharnhorst*, the squadron had steamed on through the night at the same pace they were now keeping. Barely two hours ago, they had received the transmission from *Göttingen*, announcing *Glasgow's* departure from Coronel. The admiral had sent a wireless message to the squadron immediately, informing the captains that their goal was now to find and trap *Glasgow* near the port before any of her fellow ships could come to her aid.

Rost was now talking about how God had looked over and given strength to the great leaders of the Fatherland in Germany's glorious past. Maerker had heard all of the preacher's inspirational stories about General Scharnhorst and Field Marshall Gneisenau many times before, and he began to wonder how much longer the service might last. After all, he had a warship to command—a warship that was currently barreling headlong toward the last known location of an enemy vessel.

Unexpectedly, a junior officer stepped up next to the captain and saluted. "Excuse me, sir," he tried to whisper so as not to be too obtrusive to the ongoing sermon.

"Yes, Lieutenant?"

"Pardon the interruption, sir, but our spotters have seen some funnel smoke on the eastern horizon."

"Very well, Lieutenant. I'm on my way to the bridge immediately." Maerker stepped out of his place in the assembled congregation and began walking briskly toward the command superstructure. Now *that* is some divine intervention, he thought with a smile.

When he entered the wheelhouse, he found Pochhammer, Busch, and Petri already there. The first officer and gunnery officer were both standing at the port side windows, scanning eastward with binoculars. As Maerker arrived, Petri greeted him.

"Good morning, sir. Smoke on our port beam, twenty kilometers. The spotters think it's funnel smoke from a merchant steamer moving up the coast, but we're too far away to tell for sure."

Busch lowered his glasses. "It's far enough away that only the spotters can see it from up there. Unfortunately, we can't see anything here."

"Well, we certainly cannot divert the entire squadron eastward to confirm the sighting," said Maerker. "We can't risk missing the opportunity to catch their light cruiser operating alone near Coronel. Confirm with the flagship in case they haven't seen this smoke to the east. Perhaps the admiral would be willing to send one of the light cruisers out to have a closer look."

"Yes, sir." Petri relayed the message to the signals bridge. A few minutes later, flag signals from *Scharnhorst* replied, "Smoke on eastern horizon confirmed. *Nürnberg* detached to investigate, twenty knots."

"Do you think the smoke could be from a British ship?" asked Pochhammer.

"Unlikely," said Petri. "We've received no intelligence indicating the presence of any other British ships north of Coronel—and even *Glasgow* could not have steamed this far north in only two hours."

"I don't think the British even know we're here," offered Busch, "and if they did know we had assembled here, they most certainly would not risk splitting their forces in such a gamble. My money's on that smoke being from some local merchant vessel."

"Probably so," agreed Maerker, who looked aft to see the rest of the squadron steaming in line behind them. *Nürnberg*, the last ship in the formation, was four kilometers distant, trailing *Leipzig* and *Dresden*. "Although it is a necessary precaution, my guess is that Captain Schönberg has been diverted for naught." As he watched, *Nürnberg* turned sharply out of the formation, heading east. Black plumes billowed from her funnels as she increased her speed to investigate and identify the source of the distant smoke. "Commander," he said to Pochhammer, "at our current speed, how much longer until we reach Coronel?"

The first officer looked at the map laid out on the chart table and checked the plotted course. "Just under four hours, sir."

"Then we have just under four hours to ensure this ship is prepared for battle."

◆

ABOARD HMS *Good Hope*, Admiral Cradock viewed the scene through the large plate glass windows of the wheelhouse. Half a mile away, *Glasgow*—newly returned to the squadron from Coronel—was, like all of their ships, pitching wildly on the heavy seas. Seamen were securing one of the boats above her port gunwales—having recently abandoned the idea of sending a boat to the flagship to deliver the admiral's messages. The sea was simply too rough to risk lowering a boat. Luce had sent a signal indicating that he was now preparing to have the messages delivered to *Good Hope* in some other fashion.

Cradock had been relieved to finally see Luce's cruiser steaming toward the rendezvous point at about 1:00 pm. The squadron was some sixty miles west of Coronel, and the swells rolling at them from the south were increasing in size with each passing hour. Since dawn, German wireless traffic had increased dramatically—and the transmissions from *Leipzig* were now stronger than ever.

"Whatever Luce comes up with," said Captain Francklin to his right. "I hope he's right quick about it. We don't want to miss our chance to catch that German light cruiser alone."

"Agreed," said Cradock. "Luce is a clever chap. He'll think of something."

"Flag signal from *Glasgow*, sir," said the signals officer, who was also watching the smaller ship through binoculars. "It asks, 'Permission to tow line across your bow. Barrel with messages attached'."

"Go ahead," said Cradock, and the signalmen relayed the message.

*Glasgow* was now moving, coming about on a new heading that would bring her across in front of the flagship.

"I need four men on the forecastle with poles and hooks, on the double," barked Francklin. "Retrieve that line and bring the barrel aboard as soon as you have it."

A team of seamen raced to the bow, assembling on the gunwales to either side. The men were repeatedly drenched as gouts of foaming spray washed over the forecastle, and some of them looked to be having trouble keeping their footing. Despite their precarious position, all of the men leaned over the gunwales expectantly with their hooks. About a hundred yards away, *Glasgow* steamed across the flagship's bow, dragging a grass line. Moments later, one of the men on the starboard gunwale snagged the floating rope and hauled it upward. The other men immediately assisted with hauling up a small wooden cask.

"Well done, Mister Francklin," said Cradock. He addressed the signals officer. "Signal to Captain Luce, 'Maneuver well executed'."

"Aye, sir."

"Please have the contents of that barrel brought to my quarters," said Cradock. "Captain, now it is time to find *Leipzig* so we can cut her off and gobble her up before she can rejoin her squadron. Signal all ships to form a search line, each ship fifteen miles apart. *Glasgow* landward, then *Monmouth*, then *Otranto*. We'll take the western end of the line. When all ships are in position, proceed in search formation north northeast at ten knots."

"Yes, sir."

"I will be in my cabin reviewing the messages from the Admiralty." Cradock turned and left the bridge. His terrier got up from his customary spot in the aft corner of the wheelhouse and trotted after his master. Miserable conditions for a hunt, Cradock thought as he and the dog made their way along the passageway to his cabin. Even aboard a ship as large as *Good Hope*, he could feel the deck rolling and tilting beneath his feet.

A bundle of papers from the consulate—surprisingly only slightly damp—had been placed on his writing desk. He sat and began methodically going through them. Almost immediately, he found the Admiralty's reply to his latest request to have *Defence* added to his command. As he had suspected, their answer had not changed. If anything, the tone was even more curt than before.

> [*Confidential Cable*]
> DEFENCE IS TO REMAIN ON EAST COAST UNDER STODDART. THIS WILL LEAVE SUFFICIENT FORCE ON EACH SIDE IN CASE THE HOSTILE CRUISERS APPEAR ON THE TRADE ROUTES.
> [*End Cable*]

Cradock shook his head. "Sufficient force" to do what, exactly? He pressed some tobacco into the bowl of his pipe and lit it, savoring the woodsy aroma of the smoke. The Admiralty are obviously immovable on this point, he thought. We are to make do with the ships we have, regardless of the true threat that the German armored cruisers pose—and regardless of the consequences should we actually encounter them.

The dog, seemingly sensing his master's troubled state of mind, leapt into his lap and nuzzled against Cradock's hand. He idly stroked the terrier's neck and watched the black ink in the well upon his desk slowly tilt back and forth as the big ship rode the worsening swells. "So be it," he said to himself, glancing out the porthole at the angry green sea. "Make do we shall."

◆

*NÜRNBERG*, which had left the main German squadron to investigate the mysterious trail of funnel smoke to the east, was finally drawing near to the source of that smoke.

"Spotters confirm two single-funnel steamers, fourteen kilometers away, ten degrees to port, sir," said the signals officer. "Heading north, in convoy."

"Single funnels, Mister Engel?" asked Schönberg with an exasperated sigh. "Merchant ships?"

"Apparently so, sir."

"Of course. The squadron finally gets a whiff of the enemy, and instead of joining the chase, we're sent off on this useless diversion." Schönberg had been apoplectic when the admiral's order had sent him out of the squadron's line. He had no choice but to comply, however — assuaging his frustration with the slim hope that the unknown source of the smoke might turn out to be British.

"Your orders, sir?"

"As much as this is utter foolishness, protocol dictates that we confirm the identity of these vessels. In the unlikely event that one or both of these merchants is a British ship, the admiral will want to know." He turned to the young lieutenant at the wheel. "Helmsman, set an intercept course. Maintain twenty knots."

"Yes, sir. Twenty knots."

"Hopefully we can conduct our inspection rapidly and rejoin the squadron before they find the British light cruiser without us," Schönberg muttered. With every passing minute, the southward-steaming squadron was leaving them farther behind.

*Nürnberg*, with her starboard beam now to the wind and driving sea, was rolling crazily through the swells and troughs. The bridge officers were forced to hold onto consoles and bulkheads to keep their balance. Closing the distance to the two ships was taking vastly longer than it should have. Two hours had already elapsed since *Nürnberg* had been detached from the squadron — on a mission that should have taken them a fraction of that time — and only now were they near enough to the ships to make out any details. Schönberg realized that each subsequent moment they spent on this task was a waste of precious time, and he felt his anger and frustration growing.

"Excuse me, Captain," said Engel, who was looking over a message just handed to him by a junior lieutenant.

"Yes?"

"General signal from *Scharnhorst*, sir. The flagship's telegraph operators are hearing more frequent British wireless signals—and they're getting stronger."

"Of course they are, damn it," he grumbled, then took a deep breath to try to calm himself. "Thank you, Lieutenant-Commander. Inform me of any other developments."

The two unidentified ships were now less than a kilometer away. They looked to be a matched pair—both small merchant steamers with black hulls. Each vessel's single funnel had a white and red stripe at the top. They rode low in the water and were struggling in the rough seas, making perhaps five knots.

"Shall I signal them to heave-to, sir?" asked Engel.

"No, don't bother. They might as well be stopped already. Let's just swing around astern of the second ship and have a look. Hopefully we can see where she's from and be done with this business." He raised binoculars but found that the combination of *Nürnberg's* motion and the steamers' rise and fall made identification of any details difficult. "Lieutenant, bring us around aft of the trailing ship, one hundred meters. Ten knots."

"Yes, sir. One hundred meters. Ten knots." The helmsman turned the wheel and *Nürnberg* swung in an arc behind the steamer. After several more minutes, they crossed her stern, and Schönberg could just make out the white lettering on her hull: *Compañía Sud Americana de Vapores, Valparaiso.*

"Chilean ships, sir," said Engel. "Probably carrying…"

"I know they are Chilean ships, Lieutenant-Commander," snapped Schönberg. "Damned useless Chilean ships. Do you know why, Lieutenant-Commander? Because since this fucking war began, I have been cursed to always be at the wrong place at the wrong time. Enough of this!" He turned and glared at the helmsman. "Set a course two-hundred degrees south southwest, twenty knots. We need to catch up to the squadron as quickly as possible."

*Nürnberg* swung southward, once again sailing into the brunt of the still-growing swells. Each time the small warship topped a crest and plunged into the trough beyond, foaming seawater broke over her bows.

"Lieutenant Haas, can you estimate how much of a lead the admiral might have on us now?" asked Schönberg, who was steadying himself against the compass pedestal.

Haas pored over the chart table, making mental calculations. "At the squadron's previous rate of speed, I believe they would now be approximately fifty-five kilometers ahead of us, sir."

"Fifty-five kilometers," repeated Schönberg with a growl. "With seas like this, it could take us hours to catch…"

"Wireless room to the bridge," said an echoing voice from one of the pipes in front of the captain.

"This is the captain. Go ahead," said Schönberg into the cone.

"Urgent message from the flagship, sir. Because of the increasing volume and frequency of British wireless traffic, we have been ordered to return to the squadron immediately."

"Of course we have." Schönberg rolled his eyes. He opened his mouth to say something else but stopped himself. After a pause, he said, "Send a response to the admiral: 'Message acknowledged. Two vessels identified as local merchants. We are fifty-five kilometers astern, heading south southwest at twenty knots'."

"Yes, sir."

Damn it all, thought Schönberg as he looked out over *Nürnberg's* bow pounding through the roiling sea. With the kind of luck I'm having, they will have found the British light cruiser, sunk her, and finished their celebratory party all before we even arrive on the scene. He looked down and realized that his left hand had gone completely numb. With some difficulty, he clenched his fingers into a fist and slipped his hand into the pocket of his coat.

◆

THE BRITISH SQUADRON was now arranged in a search formation, four ships abreast, heading north northwest. *Glasgow* held the easternmost position in the formation, closest to the coast and the port of Coronel. Fifteen miles to the west steamed *Monmouth*, her funnel smoke just barely visible to *Glasgow's* spotters. Fifteen miles beyond her was *Otranto*, then *Good Hope*. In this manner, the admiral hoped to search a swath of the sea some seventy miles across in the hope that they might catch the lone German light cruiser.

"A few more minutes and we'll be fully in position, sir," said Lieutenant-Commander Portman.

"Good," replied Luce. "Soon we'll be running out of daylight. If we hope to find *Leipzig*, we'll have to do it in the next few hours."

Customarily, a following sea would be welcomed, but in these conditions, Luce found little comfort in having the wind to their stern. The swells had grown throughout the day until now, just after four in the afternoon, some of the troughs looked large enough to swallow the ship. As they rode the swells and plunged into the troughs, green water repeatedly broke over the forecastle and sent foaming surges back over the weather deck.

The blue-gray sky was still clear, and the wind had increased—a continual howl through the ship's masts, wires, and superstructure. Luce did not envy the task of the spotters in the foretop, some thirty feet above the bridge. Although those men would have excellent visibility on such a clear day, the spotters' platform offered only minimal protection from the elements, and the mast upon which it was affixed was swaying dramatically as the ship below it rode the heavy, undulating seas.

"*Monmouth* signals she's in position, sir," said Stuart.

"Any word from *Otranto* or *Good Hope*?"

"Not yet, sir."

Luce was particularly concerned for Captain Edwards and *Otranto*. The passenger liner's commercial hull design and immense bulk made her woefully unsuited to these poor conditions. He imagined that the armed liner was being rolled about even worse than any of the warships.

"This sea is truly miserable," said Thompson, steadying himself against the chart table. "It's bad enough now in the daylight. After nightfall, it could get even worse—and certainly harder to navigate. If we don't find this German cruiser in the next couple of hours, we'll probably have to head back to Vallenar."

"True, or fall back to wherever *Canopus* is right now. We could resume the search in the morning, if *Leipzig* hasn't already run off by then."

"Foretop to the bridge," said a voice from one of the pipes. "Funnel smoke off starboard bow. Approximately fifteen miles." The spotter's voice was nearly drowned out by the howling wind.

Thompson stepped to the voice pipe array, selected the pipe marked *Foretop* and replied, "Bridge to foretop. Can you identify the vessel?"

"No, sir. Too far away still. Having trouble keeping anything in view with the glasses in this sea."

"Understood. We'll get a closer look." Thompson turned to Luce. "Perhaps our luck has just changed."

"Maybe so," said Luce. "Or it's another wild goose chase. Helmsman, starboard twenty-five degrees, fifteen knots."

"Aye, sir. Starboard twenty-five degrees, fifteen knots."

"Mister Stuart, signal the squadron that we've sighted funnel smoke east northeast of our position. Moving to investigate."

"Yes, sir."

*Glasgow* turned eastward, now rolling dramatically as more of her beam faced the driving seas. Luce, Thompson, and Backhouse all took up binoculars and scanned the distance ahead. Within a few minutes, they saw a stream of gray-brown smoke hugging the horizon. As the ship rose and fell on the swells, the smoke would appear, then briefly disappear from their view.

"Damn it," groused Backhouse. "We need to get closer."

"Foretop to the bridge," announced the spotter from above. "It looks like multiple funnels, sir. Still too far off to identify."

"Multiple funnels?" said Thompson. "That just may be our German ship."

"I want full steam up," said Luce. "We may need it."

Now they could see the smoke trail consistently, even with the motion of the ship beneath them.

Thompson, the tallest of the bridge officers, craned his neck to get a better viewpoint, while bracing himself on the port bulkhead. "I can see the smoke but… can't quite see the tops of the…"

"Foretop to the bridge. Three funnels, sir. It looks like *Leipzig's* silhouette. Bearing ten degrees. Heading south, distance ten miles." Even with the howl of the wind, Luce could hear the excitement in the voice of the spotter.

"Finally!" exclaimed Backhouse. "About time we heard some good news."

All three officers continued to scan the sea ahead, waiting for a glimpse of the ship themselves. After a few more minutes, *Glasgow* rose upon another swell and suddenly all of them could see the distant but distinctive three-funnel outline of a German *Bremen*-class light cruiser. Just visible on the eastern horizon, she was plunging into the swells on a southward course, dead ahead of them.

They had found *Leipzig*.

"There she is," said Thompson, smiling. "Nice of her to make an appearance before nightfall."

"Action stations!" said Luce.

Bells and klaxons sounded throughout the ship. Men raced to their positions, and the cruiser's gun turrets rotated into action. Luce heard cheering echoing through some of the voice pipes. He realized that the men were releasing months of pent-up frustration, now that they finally had the enemy in sight.

"We need to let the squadron know. Mister Stuart, general signal: 'Enemy light cruiser sighted. Distance nine miles east of current position'."

"Yes, sir," said Stuart.

"Do we wait for the rest of the squadron or engage her now before she can bolt?" asked Backhouse.

"We may be the only ship that can catch her," replied Luce, "especially since she's east of our squadron's search formation. She's too far away for anyone else to join in except maybe *Monmouth*, but she's now more than eighteen miles astern. We'll wait for the admiral's signal, but my inclination is to go after her..."

The voice pipe interrupted the captain. "Foretop to bridge. Two more enemy warships sighted, each with four funnels. Bearing thirty degrees, ten miles."

"*Four* funnels?" asked Thompson. He stepped to the voice pipe and said, "Can you confirm four funnels on those two additional ships?"

The voice pipe was silent for a few moments. "Confirmed, sir," came the reply from above. "Both have four funnels."

Thompson's eyes met Luce's, but neither man said anything.

"I can confirm it now, too," said Backhouse, who had his lenses trained on the eastern horizon. "It's *Scharnhorst* and *Gneisenau*. We haven't just found *Leipzig*; we've found their whole bloody squadron."

Luce felt a chill travel down his spine. He raised his own binoculars. As the ship was lifted by another swell, he saw them come into view. Three ships were now just visible on the horizon, traveling roughly north to south across *Glasgow's* course. Steaming ahead of *Leipzig* were two immense German armored cruisers — definitely *Scharnhorst* and *Gneisenau* — their light gray superstructures and bristling gun barrels brilliantly lit by the afternoon sun.

Dear God, he thought. We've blundered right into them. "General signal, Mister Stuart: 'Three enemy ships in sight. Two armored cruisers and one light cruiser'." Luce turned to the helmsman. "Lieutenant, hard to port. New course two hundred sixty degrees, west by south. We are turning about and rejoining the squadron — full speed."

"Aye, sir. Coming about hard to port. Full speed. New course, two-six zero degrees." He spun the wheel and *Glasgow* began to turn in a tight arc westward, back toward the rest of the British ships. The deck beneath them tilted dramatically in the rolling seas as the cruiser came about, and the bridge officers momentarily lost sight of the German ships now behind them.

"Foretop to bridge. All enemy ships are turning to follow us."

Luce turned to Stuart. "Send a signal to the flagship: 'Being chased by enemy armed cruisers and light cruiser. *Glasgow* rejoining squadron'."

*Glasgow* was now nearly up to full speed, and the funnel smoke of the pursuing German ships began to recede behind them to the east.

"They're jamming us, sir," said Stuart. "Wireless room reports that before we could transmit the last signal, the German ships flooded all bands with noise. We don't know if the rest of the squadron could hear our signal through the chaff."

"Send it again anyway. In a few minutes we'll be close enough to send it by signal lamp, too."

The light cruiser plunged westward through the swells at full steam. Luce scanned the western horizon for any signs of *Monmouth* or *Otranto*. He realized that in the span of a few short minutes, *Glasgow* had been suddenly transformed from predator to prey.

◆

ABOARD *Gneisenau*, a long day of steaming south into increasingly rough seas in the hopes that they might catch a lone British light cruiser had set the crew on edge. At a quarter past four in the afternoon, the German squadron was finally in the vicinity of Coronel, some sixty kilometers northwest of the port. Captain Maerker believed they had missed their chance of finding *Glasgow*, for more than seven hours had elapsed since *Göttingen* had announced her departure from the harbor. Although the wireless operators had continued to intercept strong British wireless signals all afternoon, Maerker knew that *Glasgow* could now easily be two-hundred kilometers away.

The crew had begun their customary late afternoon routines to prepare the ship for the evening and night watches. On every deck, men performed their end-of-shift checks of guns, hoists, fittings, equipment, and machinery. Maerker himself could sense the deflation among the officers and men as they began to realize that this day's urgent race southward had been in vain.

Maerker assumed that the admiral would soon issue new orders to the squadron, and he wondered if they would now remain in the vicinity of Coronel or head back north toward Valparaiso. He scanned the southern horizon again, seeing nothing.

"Wireless room to the bridge," said Lieutenant-Commander Petri's voice through the pipe.

"Go ahead, Mister Petri," said Maerker.

"General transmission from *Leipzig*, sir. Her spotters have seen some smoke to the west."

Turning to peer out the starboard windows of the wheelhouse, he scanned the western horizon, which appeared to be empty. The late afternoon sun was steadily sinking in the western sky before him, casting countless glittering reflections off the roiling surface of the ocean. The glare was brilliant, and despite the clear weather, this was not the best circumstance in which to try to spot a distant ship on the western sea.

Busch selected the voice pipe to the forward spotter's platform above them. "Bridge to foretop. Do you see anything due west?"

After a few seconds came the reply, "Looks like funnel smoke, sir. Distance approximately seventeen kilometers. Can't yet see the ship."

"Perhaps the British cruiser hasn't gotten that far away after all," said Maerker, who could still see nothing to the west. *Leipzig*, trailing more than a kilometer behind their starboard quarter, was likely closer to the mystery vessel—and her spotters apparently had a better view.

"Flag signal from *Scharnhorst*, sir," said a lieutenant. "It says 'All ships raise full steam'."

"Seems the admiral thinks this might be our quarry also," said Busch.

Several more minutes passed, and still Maerker could see nothing but sea and sky to the west. Then, suddenly, there it was—a long, thin smoke trail stretching out over the water from south to north, its source still too far away to identify. He did not realize how quiet the bridge had become until the silence was broken by another voice pipe announcement from the wireless room.

"Wireless to the bridge. *Leipzig* confirms vessel is British light cruiser. Four funnels. Distance fourteen kilometers."

"Battle stations," said Maerker. "Clear decks for action."

They had found *Glasgow*.

The sound of drums thundered through the ship's spaces, followed by electronic buzzers calling the crew to action. Maerker could now clearly see *Glasgow's* gray superstructure and funnels on the horizon. She was headed toward them, nearly bow-on, but as he watched, she began to turn to port.

"She's turning about," said Maerker.

"They've seen us, too," said Busch. "They're running—heading back the way they came."

"Wireless room to the bridge," said Petri through the pipe. "Flagship has instructed us to jam enemy wireless bands. Until instructed otherwise, all of our signals are to be transmitted by flag or signal lamp."

"Proceed accordingly," said Maerker. "Hopefully jamming can keep her from warning the rest of their squadron."

For a few moments, all of the bridge officers could see the distant *Glasgow* as she turned back westward and began to beat a hasty retreat— with plumes of black smoke belching from her funnels.

"Flag signal from *Scharnhorst*," said Born. "A course adjustment to two-hundred fifty-five degrees, west southwest. We are to follow the flagship's lead, battle line formation."

"Understood," said Maerker. "Helmsman, follow the flagship. New course two-hundred fifty-five degrees."

Less than a kilometer ahead of them, *Scharnhorst* turned westward, and *Gneisenau* followed. *Leipzig* fell in behind, followed by *Dresden*, four kilometers farther back. *Nürnberg*, delayed by her earlier diversion to inspect the Chilean steamers, had not yet caught up to the squadron and was still more than forty kilometers away. In the distance, the fleeing *Glasgow* was already lengthening her lead on the pursuing German squadron. Now only the tops of her funnels were visible through binoculars. Maerker was surprised to realize that he was experiencing a sense of elation—the excitement of the hunt and the long-delayed promise of real action against the enemy.

Commander Pochhammer burst into the wheelhouse through the starboard doorway, panting heavily. "We've found the British light cruiser?" he asked breathlessly.

"Yes, Commander," replied Maerker, noting with some amusement that the first officer was now wearing a sidearm holstered at his belt. "I see you're dressed for the occasion."

"Are we in pursuit?"

"Yes, but remember that *Glasgow* is the one ship in the British squadron we cannot catch by speed alone. Unless we can somehow flank her or box her in along the shore, she'll be able to outrun us."

Pochhammer snatched up a pair of field glasses and scanned the western sea. "Damn," he said. "I can't see her. She must be retreating at full steam. Cowards."

"Bridge to foretop," said Busch into the voice pipe. "Can you still see the enemy light cruiser?"

"Yes, sir," came the reply from the spotter above. "Hull down. Nineteen kilometers, heading west southwest."

"Unless we increase our speed, she'll soon be out of sight of our spotters as well," said Pochhammer plaintively. "She will make her escape, and all of this will be for naught."

"Perhaps, but I don't believe she's escaping," offered Maerker. Something about the encounter with the British ship puzzled him. "*Glasgow* departed Coronel harbor earlier this morning, but when we first saw her, she was steaming *from the west*—the open ocean. That means that for some reason, she left the port, steamed more than eighty kilometers out to sea, then turned around and was coming back. Even if that weren't unorthodox, it would be unusual for a light cruiser to be operating out there alone. She may have another ship with her, or the rest of her squadron may be out there as well. She may be rejoining them for safety. If so, we should know soon enough."

The German squadron steamed west southwest, roughly parallel to *Glasgow's* last observed course. The two armored cruisers rose and fell on the angry seas, but Maerker could see that *Gneisenau* was considerably more stable than *Leipzig* and *Dresden*, following astern. The light cruisers were being tossed dramatically by the swells, and their bows were regularly awash in green water.

After twenty minutes of pursuit, Maerker began to wonder if he was right about *Glasgow* rejoining her squadron. Then, suddenly, he was proven correct.

"Foretop to the bridge," said the spotter with obvious excitement in his voice. "Four ships, west northwest. Distance to the nearest ship approximately nineteen kilometers."

"Can you identify any of the vessels?" asked Busch.

"Only the light cruiser, sir. In a few moments, we should be able to see the others more clearly."

Busch glanced at his captain with a respectful nod. "Looks like you were right, sir. We may have caught more than just *Glasgow*."

Maerker scanned the western horizon. He could just see some funnel smoke drifting northward, but not yet any ships.

"Come on, just a little closer," whispered Pochhammer as he, too, looked westward through the glasses. "I want to get a good look at you British bastards before we send you to the bottom of the sea."

For several long minutes, no one on the bridge could see anything but the trails of black smoke in the clear blue-gray sky above the horizon.

"Foretop to bridge. Enemy vessels identified. The light cruiser, two enemy armored cruisers, and what looks like a large merchant vessel of some kind. They are forming up, west northwest, distance seventeen point five kilometers."

"Signal from the flagship," said Born. "All ships raise battle ensigns."

"Finally!" exclaimed Pochhammer, but Maerker could not tell if the commander was excited about raising the battle flags or the fact that the British ships were now visible from the bridge.

Through his binoculars, Maerker caught his first glimpse of the British squadron in the distance. His heart was pounding heavily as he identified them, ship by ship. They were maneuvering into a battle line formation with a *Drake*-class armored cruiser in the vanguard. That would be Cradock's flagship, *Good Hope*, he thought. Falling in behind the flagship was a County-class cruiser that had to be *Monmouth*. Behind her was *Glasgow*, and farther off in the distance, trailing the warships, was an ungainly armed merchant liner. Those four were the only enemy ships in view—and nowhere in sight was the British battleship they had been warned of.

In an instant, he realized what the admiral was probably thinking also.

They had the enemy squadron outmatched.

# SIXTEEN

*Sunday, November 1, 1914*
*Pacific Ocean, 50 Miles (80 kilometers) West of Coronel, Chile*

"CHRIST," muttered Captain Francklin of *Good Hope* as he looked eastward with field glasses. "Luce was right. We've found both of their armored cruisers."

Admiral Cradock did not immediately answer. He, too, was peering through binoculars. The German squadron was approaching from the northeast—the closest ship still some ten miles away. Even at this distance, he could see that the lead armored cruiser—which he assumed was von Spee's flagship, *Scharnhorst*—was flying her black, white, and red battle ensigns. Steaming behind her was *Gneisenau*, equally immense and menacing. The huge, light gray warships were plowing powerfully though the heavy swells, their bows throwing up great fans of foaming spray. Identifying the enemy ships caused him to catch his breath—and for a second, he had trouble believing the sight before his eyes. For months, they had speculated on, wondered about, and dreaded the possible approach of the Germans from Tsingtao. To actually see those ships here, off the Chilean coast, was somehow both surprising and vindicating. He had been right all along.

Then he noticed the funnels and upper works of *Leipzig*, trailing behind the armored cruisers, near the limit of his visual range. In a sickening moment, Cradock realized that the Germans had used some form of wireless trickery to make him think that only *Leipzig* was operating in the area. How could he have been so foolish? He also realized that the other ships of the enemy squadron were out there as well, probably still beyond the horizon. Quite simply, he had been drawn into a trap. The Germans were prepared for battle—and he had a decision to make.

"Action stations and raise the battle ensigns," said Cradock, who turned to the helmsman. "Turn south and assume a new course, one-hundred eighty degrees. Flag signal to the squadron: follow in battle line formation—*Good Hope, Monmouth, Glasgow,* then *Otranto.*" He lowered the glasses. "Send a wireless signal to *Canopus.* Hopefully she can hear us through the jamming. We need to know how far away she is."

"Yes, sir," said the lieutenant standing to his right, who then repeated the order through the voice pipe to the wireless room.

*Good Hope* turned southward, her bow now pointed directly into the howling wind and surging seas. The old warship plunged heavily through the swells, and the decks beneath the men's feet pitched dramatically as they rode over and through the powerful waves. Foaming green water washed over the forecastle, now with enough force that great fans of spray erupted from the forward gun turret as the waves struck the bulbous steel obstacle jutting from the deck.

Half a mile behind the flagship, *Monmouth* fell in behind, matching *Good Hope's* course, followed by *Glasgow.* The cumbersome *Otranto,* which had been having difficulty all day in the rough conditions, had not yet joined the line—and was still attempting to come about some four miles to their northwest.

"They've turned and assumed a parallel southward course, sir," said Francklin, watching through glasses at the distant German ships, now steaming in a line mirroring their own, less than nine miles away. "They're not closing the distance. Looks like they're content to maintain this range for now."

Cradock looked again through the lenses. He could see clearly the first three ships in the German line, as well as funnel smoke from what must be another light cruiser falling in farther behind them. Now there were at least four of them. *Scharnhorst,* in the vanguard, kept to her new parallel southward course and seemed to be matching *Good Hope's* speed of fifteen knots. "Admiral von Spee wants to fight this battle on his own terms," said Cradock. "He'll wait until his entire squadron is ready; then he'll maneuver closer, just within range of his biggest guns—and try to pound us while most of our guns still cannot reach him."

"If we keep heading south," offered Francklin, "perhaps we can keep him at bay long enough to join up with *Canopus.* Her 12-inchers should be able to even the odds a bit."

"Perhaps, but I cannot imagine von Spee will just let us lure his ships onto her guns." Cradock swept his lenses along the German formation, admiring the powerful lines of the two large armored cruisers leading the enemy squadron. They were beautiful ships—and every bit as formidable as he had imagined.

"Wireless to bridge," said the hollow voice from the pipe array to their right. "Reply signal from *Canopus*, sir. She reports a position of 42.20 south by 76.10 west, making nine knots north with colliers *Benbrook* and *Langoe*."

"Lieutenant," barked Francklin to the young navigation officer hovering near the chart table, "how far away is their position?"

The lieutenant plotted *Canopus's* reported position on the map, quickly calculating the distance to their own. He looked up and hesitated.

"Well, out with it, man!" shouted Francklin.

The young lieutenant swallowed hard. "*Canopus* is more than two-hundred fifty miles away, sir."

The bridge fell momentarily silent.

*Canopus* was still more than a full day's steam from their position, and sunset was only an hour away. There was simply no possibility of the old battleship joining the fight.

"The Germans have us outmatched and outgunned, sir," said Francklin. "If we retreat westward now at our maximum speed, we could probably elude them until we're protected by the cover of nightfall."

It was true, the admiral realized. Their odds of prevailing in such a lopsided fight were miniscule—as he had known they would be. Even under the cover of *Canopus's* big guns, they would likely still be woefully overmatched. A hasty retreat now could save most of their ships to perhaps fight another day, at another time—on a day when the odds might be in their favor.

But saving *most of their ships* was not enough.

Cradock paused, then turned to the captain and shook his head solemnly. "If our squadron's 'maximum speed' was limited only by these old engines or those of *Monmouth*, you might be right. Our speed is instead constrained by *Otranto*, which is already steaming near her limit. If we flee at the twenty or more knots it would require for us to escape into the night, we would leave her behind... with them." He nodded toward the German squadron. "I will not abandon *Otranto* to a slaughter."

Francklin had no reply. The admiral was right. They could not abandon the plodding converted liner and her crew to certain destruction and death, even if it meant having to stay and fight a superior foe. He breathed deeply and nodded in resignation.

Cradock looked back over his right shoulder through the rearmost window of the wheelhouse. There, some four miles astern on their starboard quarter, was the cumbersome hulk of *Otranto*, laboring through the heavy seas in an effort to keep up with the three warships. Without her, they might have made their escape. With her, they were forced to stay and fight.

The admiral took a deep breath, and he surprisingly felt an extraordinary calm settle over him.

"If we cannot drag the enemy to our chosen fight," said Cradock quietly, "we shall take the fight to them." He turned back to Francklin. "We will use this setting sun to our advantage. While it sinks behind us, the German gunlayers and spotters will have great difficulty targeting our ships through the glare. While they are blinded, we will turn toward them and close the distance between our lines rapidly—so that we can engage their ships with as many of our smaller guns as possible. Perhaps we can quickly do enough damage to cause them to abandon the fight."

"Sir?" asked Francklin hesitantly. "What if we cannot engage them before…"

"The timing will be critical, Captain. We'll not get a second chance."

◆

"ALL GUN CREWS report that they are prepared for battle, sir," said Busch.

"Excellent," replied Maerker. "Has *Dresden* joined our line?"

"Not yet." Busch briefly suspended his surveillance of the British ships to their west and quickly scanned the sea astern. "She is still two kilometers behind *Leipzig*, but she is closing the gap rapidly."

"The admiral will likely wait until she has fallen in before engaging the enemy," said Maerker. "Although we cannot wait for *Nürnberg*, we'll want both *Leipzig* and *Dresden* to keep their light cruiser and armed liner busy while we engage their armored cruisers." He turned to the first officer. "Mister Pochhammer, is the rest of the ship prepared for action?"

"Yes, sir," replied Pochhammer. "We have full steam up; all loose materiel is stowed or secured, the ship's boats have been filled with water; fire suppression crews are standing ready; and Doctor Nohl in the main infirmary reports that he and his staff are prepared for any potential injuries."

"Very well." Maerker raised his binoculars again to survey the enemy squadron. They had now been steaming on a southward course roughly parallel to the British line for nearly thirty minutes. Less than an hour of full daylight remained, as the brilliant sun sank lower on the western horizon—casting a blinding glare over the churning sea and causing Maerker to squint as he viewed the enemy ships beneath the shimmering golden orb.

Even through the glare, Maerker could see that the looming battle was shaping up as if Admiral von Spee had scripted it himself. When the timing was right, they would maneuver just within the effective range of their largest guns. In their current battle order, *Scharnhorst* would engage

*Good Hope*, her counterpart in the enemy vanguard—flagship against flagship. *Gneisenau* would be tasked with attacking the armored cruiser *Monmouth*, the second vessel in the enemy line. *Leipzig* and *Dresden*, in turn, would target *Glasgow* and their armed liner.

*Monmouth* was an ungainly ship, he thought. She had three funnels rising from a blocky, almost featureless upper deck. Although precise details were difficult to discern at this distance in the brilliant glare, he knew that the guns in the hull casemates along *Monmouth's* flanks would undoubtedly be shuttered and useless in the current heavy seas. At most, the older British ship might be able to train only four to six of her guns upon *Gneisenau*. His ship, by contrast, would be able to direct full salvos of fire at the enemy vessel.

"Signal from the flagship, sir," said Petri. "We are to follow and maneuver to maintain this distance from the British line. No closer than fourteen thousand meters."

"Understood," replied Maerker. Fourteen thousand meters—or about eight and a half miles, as the British would be measuring it—was the current distance separating the two lines of warships. The enemy was still about three kilometers farther away than the outermost range of *Gneisenau's* main battery of guns.

"What are we waiting for?" asked Pochhammer. "Soon it will be dark, and those damned British bastards will be able to escape into the night."

"They can't escape," said Maerker. "We have the advantage of superior speed. The admiral is probably concerned that Cradock will try to force the battle before the sun sets—and while we're still blinded by this glare. We'll need to keep them out of range until the conditions once again favor us."

"After the sun sets," offered Busch to Pochhammer as if he were instructing a cadet, "our spotters will no longer be blinded, but the glow in the western sky should still cast plenty of light for us to aim by."

"And if we're lucky," added the captain, "their ships may be perfectly silhouetted against that dusky sky for some time."

"Perfect conditions for gunnery," said Busch with only a hint of a grim smile.

"Still sounds risky to me," said Pochhammer. "What if..."

"Commander Pochhammer," interrupted Maerker, "are you prepared to take your position in the central station and conning tower?"

"Um, yes, sir," stammered the first officer enthusiastically, coming to attention.

The central station was a fortified chamber in the heart of the ship beneath the main superstructure that supported the bridge. It was the most heavily armored part of the ship, with twenty-centimeter-thick walls of solid Krupp steel. It contained duplicates of the basic controls to steer and drive the ship, as well as voice pipes to communicate with fire control stations and the wireless and engineering compartments. The topmost portion of the central station was the conning tower, a small cylindrical metal chamber—just large enough to accommodate a single standing man—that jutted above the weather deck in front of the bridge. It had thin horizontal slits cut in the armor around its topmost rim, allowing it to function as a secure viewing platform. The purpose of the central station and the conning tower were to provide redundant command and control in case a lucky enemy shell happened to strike the main bridge area. Even if all of the bridge officers were to be killed in such a strike, a handful of officers in the central station below could—while one of them peered through the thin view slits in the uppermost steel shell—still steer the ship and give commands to keep the warship operational.

"Excellent," said Maerker. "Please inform us via voice pipe when you and your officers are safely sealed within."

"Yes, sir," replied Pochhammer with a crisp salute. He was clearly delighted and honored to be assigned this duty. He turned on his heel and strode briskly from the bridge.

Strictly speaking, *Kaiserliche Marine* combat protocol dictated that a senior officer take up station in the central station during a battle. For Maerker, however, getting Pochhammer off the bridge during this critical moment was an even better reason to send him there.

Maerker looked up once again and squinted across the brilliant glittering sea toward HMS *Monmouth.* With or without the glare of the setting sun, he thought, the old British ship was simply no match for *Gneisenau.*

◆

FROM *Glasgow's* bridge, Luce watched as the ominous array of enemy warships, brightly illuminated by the slanting sunlight, steamed southward eight and a half miles to the east. A fourth warship—another light cruiser—had now joined the German line. Her silhouette was familiar to all of *Glasgow's* officers.

"On the bright side," said Thompson, "we've finally found *Dresden.*"

Luce managed a brief smile. "Yes, it's a shame she has all that company with her. I had still been hoping to catch her in more of a one-on-one duel."

"Can Cradock seriously be considering staying and fighting?" asked Thompson. "This would have been dodgy even if we had *Canopus* with us. Without her, it seems like madness."

Luce had to agree. It did seem like madness. The enemy squadron had them outgunned, the heavy seas were the worst possible conditions for the gunners aboard *Good Hope* and *Monmouth*, and soon the darkness would make targeting the enemy ships exceedingly difficult.

A deep trough pulled the ship into its maw, causing the deck to pitch severely forward, then back again. All of the officers on the bridge braced themselves against nearby pedestals and bulkheads to keep their footing. *Glasgow* crested the next huge swell and sank again into the depression beyond.

Luce again thought of how difficult these conditions must be for Captain Edwards and *Otranto* trailing behind them—and he realized at that moment that Cradock intended to stay and fight, despite the odds against them. "We have to fight," he said to Thompson. "If we run, we'd be forced to leave *Otranto* behind. Cradock will never let that happen."

Thompson paused. "You're probably right," he agreed. "Damned ironic, really. *Otranto* keeps us from escaping, but she'll be no use to us in the battle itself."

*Dresden* had now maneuvered to within half a mile of *Leipzig* at the end of the German line. Out beyond the enemy ships, just over the eastern horizon, Luce could just see the gray-green peaks of the Andes Mountains, shrouded in clouds.

"Flag signal from *Good Hope*," said Lieutenant Stuart. "It says, 'Follow in the admiral's wake. Increase speed to seventeen knots'."

"That's our signal, gentlemen," said Luce. "Raise battle ensigns. Prepare to engage the enemy at longest effective range, port side. Gun crews are to aim for the third ship in the enemy line—the light cruiser *Leipzig*—and wait for the signal to fire."

"Aye, sir," said Backhouse, running his fingers through the rusty brush of his moustache, his gray eyes fixed on the enemy targets steaming to the east.

"Wireless to the bridge," said a voice through the pipe. "*Good Hope* has just sent a message to *Canopus* stating, 'I am going to attack the enemy now'."

Luce's chest tightened. His entire career, perhaps his whole life, had been building to this very moment. He knew that his ship and his men were ready. They had trained countless times during the past two years in anticipation of this scenario. Still, the reality that they were now rushing headlong into battle against a full squadron of powerful enemy ships was truly terrifying.

Half a mile ahead of them, *Good Hope* increased her speed and began a gradual turn to port, adjusting her course several degrees eastward toward the German squadron. Luce could see that the admiral was trying to close the gap between the two lines of warships. *Monmouth* followed in turn, then *Glasgow*. The three British cruisers were now steaming faster than *Otranto* could possibly go, and she began to fall farther behind the warships. The sun was sinking lower in the western sky, shining harshly off the light gray hulls and superstructures of the German ships on the eastern horizon.

Luce turned to the gunnery commander. "In these conditions, Mister Backhouse, how close will we need to be to hit their light cruisers with our 6-inchers?"

"Inside ten thousand yards, sir. Although *Good Hope* may be able to fire at eleven or twelve thousand with her main guns, I have no doubt the Huns' armored cruisers can hit us from there. We'll need to get closer to do any damage. Our spotters are having a devil of a time keeping them in our sights—and with this bloody wind and heavy sea, the scopes keep getting crusted over with spray and salt."

"Understood. Keep me apprised of our range to the target ships."

"Aye, sir."

The deck beneath them tilted dramatically again, this time rolling to port. A lieutenant lost his footing and slid a few feet before he was able to arrest himself on the edge of the chart table.

"Foretop to bridge," said the spotter through the pipe. "The enemy ships have increased speed and are edging away eastward."

Luce looked through binoculars and confirmed what the spotter had reported. The German ships, seeing Cradock's attempt to close the distance between the two lines, had also altered course, steering away to port to maintain their distance from the British ships.

"Are they delaying?" asked Thompson.

"I'm afraid so," answered Luce grimly. "Clever chaps. They don't want to give us the chance to hit them from closer range—at least not while the sun is still in their eyes."

Ahead, *Good Hope* increased her speed slightly and adjusted course two more degrees to port, trying once again to set a course that would converge on the German line. *Monmouth* and *Glasgow* followed suit, steaming in as tight a battle order as the powerful seas would allow. Again, the German ships increased their speed and maneuvered farther away, keeping the distance to roughly eight miles. This was futile, Luce realized. The German squadron had a distinct edge in speed and could keep maneuvering away all night if they wanted to.

But the British did not have all night. To the west, the sun had now dipped to the horizon, casting an ominous scarlet glow across the sky. In only a few minutes, the fiery disk would completely disappear—and with it their only chance to strike first at their enemies.

Lieutenant Hirst appeared on the bridge, having finished his last-minute inspection of the infirmary's readiness—in anticipation of the possibility of casualties. "Excuse me, sir," he said. "I have a strange request that I just received as I was making my way back from the sick bay."

"Yes?" answered Luce without taking his glasses off the distant German squadron.

"Remember the parrots we picked up in Rio de Janeiro? The men would like permission to release them."

"Pardon me, Mister Hirst?" This was certainly among the least likely topics of conversation he would have expected at such a time. Luce lowered the binoculars to look quizzically at his intelligence officer.

"The men are fond of the birds, sir, and are concerned about them being in their cages when all of the gunfire begins. Not knowing how… all of this might work out, they'd like the parrots to have a chance to escape."

"Do the men think the parrots can fly the fifty-odd miles to shore?"

"Not certain, sir. They'd just like permission to release them."

Luce shrugged. "Granted. Pipe it throughout the ship." He smiled briefly at the thought that the men, in this dire moment, were thinking of saving their pets.

"Flag signal from *Good Hope*, sir," said Stuart. "The admiral has dismissed *Otranto* from the line. She is to get away to starboard."

"It's about time," said Thompson. "Hopefully we can keep the Germans busy enough that Edwards can get her safely out of harm's way."

Several miles astern, *Otranto's* large bulk visibly slowed, then changed course slightly westward. She was, for now, still within visual range, but she would not remain so for long.

Luce's vision drifted upward to the sky beyond the German ships. To the east, above the mountainous coastline, the deep purple of night was steadily advancing as the sinking sun pulled the looming darkness over the sea like a shroud.

◆

MAERKER was relieved to see the blood red disc of the sun dip below the western horizon. They had successfully maneuvered away from the British for the last forty minutes, preventing the enemy ships from advancing within gunnery range. The western sky was now a brilliant panoply of color, from deep russet to shimmering peach and iridescent purple. He could finally see the British squadron without squinting painfully into the glare, and—as he had hoped—the silhouettes of the enemy cruisers stood out starkly against the spectacularly hued sky.

"Flag signal from *Scharnhorst*, sir," said Petri. "It states, 'Prepare for long distance fighting, battle by starboard'."

"Understood," replied Maerker. To Busch he said, "Our mark is the second ship in their line, HMS *Monmouth*. Have your gunlayers target the forward third of the enemy cruiser. Armor-piercing shells."

"Yes, sir." Busch repeated the order through the voice pipes, instructing the starboard batteries to prepare for the order to fire. In response, the fire control spotters and rangefinders calculated the distance to the target, and the starboard gun crews elevated their barrels so that the outgoing shells could travel at or near their maximum ranges.

Ahead of them, the flagship adjusted her course several degrees to starboard and increased her speed. Maerker ordered *Gneisenau's* helmsman to replicate the maneuver. Instead of turning away, as they had been for most of the last hour, the squadron was now on a converging course toward the enemy line.

"Flag signal from *Scharnhorst*, sir," said Petri again. "The admiral asks if his smoke is disturbing our view of the enemy vessels."

"Reply that our view is clear, Mister Petri." The German squadron was steaming almost directly into the wind, but the smoke from *Scharnhorst's* funnels was drifting past them to port and therefore was of no hindrance to their spotters or gunners.

*Gneisenau's* bow rose and fell dramatically on the swells, and wind-whipped spray spattered the bridge. Although the gunners of the East Asia Squadron were among the best in the *Kaiserliche Marine*, they had never trained in such severe conditions. Maerker knew that hitting their targets would not be an easy task, even with the now-favorable change in the balance of light.

"Range to target?" Maerker asked.

Busch conferred via voice pipe with the lead spotter in the foretop above. "Just under twelve thousand meters and closing," he said.

"Be prepared to fire when we are within eleven thousand meters, but we will wait for the flagship."

"Yes, sir. We'll be ready."

To the west, the British squadron was maintaining its course and was keeping a disciplined line in spite of the heavy seas. They had not turned away or attempted to flee, although Maerker could see that the bulky enemy converted liner had dropped out of formation and was being left farther behind with each passing minute.

"It looks like they intend to stay and fight with their three remaining ships against our four," said Maerker.

"Yes," agreed Lieutenant-Commander Born. "Fortunately, no sign of their battleship. We have them at a disadvantage."

"But only if this twilight holds long enough for us to engage them—otherwise they will slip away in the darkness."

"Eleven thousand meters and closing," announced Busch as the information was relayed to him.

"Flag signal from *Scharnhorst*," said Petri. "It states, 'As flagship fires, engage enemy ships in battle line order. *Leipzig* and *Dresden* to concentrate fire upon enemy light cruiser'."

The two squadrons steamed on southward, edging steadily closer as dusk settled over the roiling sea. The dark silhouettes of the British ships were a bold contrast to the glowing backdrop of gold and magenta in the dying sky. Through the binoculars, Maerker could make out the details of the enemy ships' superstructures and could also see the British battle ensigns fluttering furiously in the driving wind. Visually, the conditions for his spotters and gunners simply could not have been better.

"Ten thousand, five hundred meters," said Busch.

Only ten and a half kilometers away—some six and a half miles. The enemy was now well within the outer range of *Gneisenau's* largest guns. Maerker could feel the tension building among the bridge officers as they waited for long minutes without any sign from the flagship steaming ahead.

"Ten thousand, two hundred fifty meters," said Busch, who walked over to a metal pedestal that supported a basic gunnery targeting calculator—a flat upturned face of moveable concentric dials over which was suspended a hinged metal arm. He adjusted the dials and the position of the arm, confirming the range to target and calculating their current relative speed and bearing. Busch relayed the new calculations to his gun crews through the voice pipe.

Ahead of them, *Scharnhorst's* starboard guns fired—a wave of successive brilliant orange flashes rippling along her flank from her bow to her stern. Rapid hammerblows of sound echoed across the water.

"Commence firing," said Maerker.

"Firing," confirmed Busch, who pulled a metal switch mounted on the console before him.

Electric buzzers sounded throughout the gunnery spaces. *Gneisenau's* starboard batteries fired in sequence from fore to aft with a thunderous roar that rolled throughout the ship. The deck beneath the officers' feet shuddered as the first salvo left the barrels of the guns, sending the initial wave of shells arcing toward the line of enemy cruisers.

"Spotters, watch for the fall of shot," barked Busch into the pipes.

Maerker scanned the expanse of churning black water, waiting to see where their first salvo would fall. He saw flashes of return gunfire from each of the British ships, which had fired in response to the muzzle flashes of the German guns. It would be several moments before those incoming

British shells would arrive. For a few seconds, two waves of artillery shells were streaking through the evening sky toward each other, passing as they arced over the ocean toward their targets.

*Scharnhorst's* shots were the first to fall. A hundred meters from *Good Hope's* beam, a colonnade of tall, foaming splashes erupted as *Scharnhorst's* first salvo exploded in the sea. Two seconds later, a nearly identical picket of foaming columns exploded short of *Monmouth's* flank—the fall of *Gneisenau's* first salvo. Their first shells had not traveled far enough.

"One hundred meters short," yelled Busch into the pipe. "Adjust elevation and prepare to fire." He checked his wristwatch, counting down the seconds until he knew each of the starboard guns would be reloaded, aimed, and ready to fire. He adjusted the dials on the targeting calculator and shouted the revised numbers into the pipes. *Gneisenau's* gun crews had performed these actions in drills countless times during the past months. Under ideal circumstances, the expert German gunnery crews could fire a new salvo every twenty seconds.

Maerker waited anxiously for the incoming shells of *Monmouth's* first return salvo. He was surprised to see only two initial splashes more than a kilometer away, followed by three other foaming explosions bursting near the first in a haphazard pattern. *Monmouth's* smaller 6-inch guns were still far outside their range, and her gunners were—thus far—having difficulty coordinating their fire.

Ahead of them, *Scharnhorst's* guns roared again, sending her next salvo of shells toward *Good Hope*.

"Firing," said Busch. Again, the signal buzzers sounded throughout the ship, and again the guns thundered in their rapid series of blasts that traveled down *Gneisenau's* starboard flank from fore to aft.

Seconds passed as Maerker and Busch watched through binoculars to see where their second wave of shells would fall.

Two tightly spaced lines of splashes rose up from the sea beyond both *Good Hope* and *Monmouth*. The second salvos from *Scharnhorst* and *Gneisenau* had both overshot their targets.

"Seventy meters long," shouted Busch into the pipe. "Adjust elevation. I want the next salvo on the decks of that cruiser!" He checked his watch again, waiting as the seconds ticked away.

◆

"THEY'VE ALREADY FIRED two salvos to our one," said Cradock as he peered into the deepening gloom on the eastern horizon. "We cannot let them outpace us."

"Mister Gaskell," growled Francklin to the gunnery officer standing to his right, "where's my next salvo?"

Gaskell bent over the voice pipes and loudly exhorted his spotters, rangefinders, and crews to get the guns ready to fire again. *Good Hope's* first shells had fallen well short of the mark, while the Germans had already straddled the British flagship with their first two salvos.

Cradock was having difficulty seeing the enemy ships. With the sun now fully set, the visual situation had changed dramatically in a matter of minutes. Where moments ago the German cruisers had been brilliantly illuminated, now they were all but invisible — merely dark smudges against an ever-darkening backdrop of shadows and advancing night sky.

As he peered at the distant, indistinct shadow he knew to be *Scharnhorst*, he saw the orange flashes from her flanks as she unleashed yet another salvo. Now it was three to one. The discipline of the German gunners was impressive. Not only were they able to maintain an extraordinary rate of fire, but each salvo was a precisely executed ripple of gunfire that traveled smartly from the enemy ship's foremost gun to the rearmost in perfect, rapid sequence. He knew that his own inexperienced gun crews could never hope to achieve such precision, and *Good Hope* was old enough that she lacked anything resembling modern fire control. He hoped instead that, with luck, they could quickly inflict a crippling blow to one or more of the German ships and force them to withdraw. As he waited with trepidation for the latest wave of incoming German shells to fall, he finally heard the gunnery officer's pronouncement.

"Firing, port side," said Gaskell as he pressed a series of switches to signal the main turrets and the port gun casements.

*Good Hope's* main batteries, her two turreted 9.2-inch guns, fired again with two great blasts, followed by the lesser reports of four of her 6-inch guns, the only other port-side weapons currently usable in the heavy seas. The remaining casemates, mounted lower on the hull, were being buffeted by the heavy waves and had to remain shuttered, lest the surging seawater pour into the lower gunnery spaces.

Cradock was frustrated by his gunners' slow pace and their inability to use all of *Good Hope's* guns in the heavy seas. Nonetheless, they had gotten off another salvo. Perhaps, he thought, once the gunnery crews got a rhythm going, they would be able to increase their pace to better match that of the enemy ships.

Then the enemy shells struck.

*Scharnhorst's* third salvo was brutally accurate. Although several of the rounds exploded in the water along *Good Hope's* hull, sending towering fountains of water over her decks, four shells struck the British flagship itself.

Near the bow, a falling shell plunged into the foremost port side hawse pipe, severing an anchor chain and exploding a deck below—severely damaging the anchor windlass machinery and rending a ragged hole in the hull plating.

The second shell struck the main weather deck amidships, punching through the armor plate and exploding in the number three coal bunker. Fortunately, the bunker was nearly full, and the mounds of coal within helped deaden the force of the blast, minimizing any damage to the surrounding spaces.

Another round struck the thin metal sheeting atop the aftmost funnel, passing completely through the cylinder of the smokestack before exploding in the air to starboard, raining metal splinters over the quarterdeck. The concussion of the aerial blast shredded the funnel itself—crumpling it inward—and shattered the nearest suspended lifeboat.

The fourth armor-piercing shell was the most destructive. It struck the base of the forward 9.2-inch gun turret mounted on the foredeck directly in front of the bridge. The falling shell penetrated the turret's metal skirt, sliced downward through the cylindrical mount shaft, and detonated beneath the main gun assembly. The white-hot explosion in the confined space instantly incinerated twelve men working in the compartment, and the intense blast ignited the propellant charges in a row of shells stacked in the gun's ready rack. A more devastating secondary explosion burst upward through the gun turret itself, venting an orange and black geyser of flame and fragmented steel—like a volcanic eruption from the forecastle of the warship.

The deafening blast shattered the windows of the bridge and sent a searing shock wave through the wheelhouse, knocking all of the bridge officers off their feet. Steel splinters and shards of torn armor plate rained down over the entire ship.

Admiral Cradock lay dazed upon the bridge deck in total darkness, his ears ringing. He realized that he had actually blacked out for a moment. The ringing in his ears became the ship's blaring fire alarm klaxons. He heard a voice calling to him, and he opened his eyes to see Gunnery Officer Gaskell and a young lieutenant crouching over him.

"Admiral, sir? Can you hear me, sir?" asked Gaskell again.

At least Cradock *thought* it was Gaskell. The man's voice was familiar, but over his face he appeared to be wearing a diabolical-looking red mask.

"Sir, are you injured?" asked the masked officer.

Cradock realized then that the man speaking to him was, in fact the gunnery officer. He was not masked, but he was bleeding profusely from a long gash at the top of his forehead. Rivulets of crimson traced down his face, and fresh drops of blood dripped from his nose and chin. The admiral then became aware that he too was bleeding. He brought his fingers to his cheek and they came away speckled with his own blood. He blinked to clear his vision and looked around.

The interior of the bridge was still mostly intact, but glittering shards of glass covered every surface, including Cradock's uniform. The air reeked of cordite and sulphur, and thick smoke filled the compartment. All seven forward facing windows in the wheelhouse—large panes of glass that had once looked out over the forward turret—had been shattered by the blast. Smoke from a fire burning somewhere on deck gusted in through the warped frames where the windows had once been, borne by the frigid southerly wind that buffeted the ship head-on.

Most of the bridge officers, although temporarily dazed by the explosion, had returned to their duties—but not all of them. Cradock saw the bodies of two men lying nearby. On the opposite side of the wheelhouse, an officer lay slumped in a seated position against the bulkhead. He recognized the man as the duty helmsman, a young lieutenant whose name Cradock did not remember. The officer's head lolled over his chest and dark blood was oozing from somewhere around his nose or mouth. The senior navigating officer had already taken the man's place at the helm and continued to steer the ship through the heavy seas.

Cradock turned to look down at the other body, which lay beside him. The gold bars on the man's shoulder epaulets identified him immediately as Captain Francklin. He lay on his back, staring dully upward, with his mouth partially open. A long, jagged sliver of curved gray metal, like the blade of a crude scimitar, protruded from a horrific wound in Francklin's neck, just under his right ear. The razor-edged arc of steel had been a piece of the forward turret's armor plate, flung outward by the blast. The captain's head had been nearly severed by the blow, and his lifeless body lay in a spreading pool of dark blood.

Cradock realized that Captain Francklin had been standing between himself and the windows when the explosion occurred. Very likely the captain's body had absorbed enough of the blast that the admiral had been spared no more than superficial injuries. Cradock sat up and shook the last of the reverberating daze from his head.

"Admiral," repeated Gaskell, speaking loudly to be heard over the sound of the wind and the alarm bells, "are you injured?"

"No, Lieutenant-Commander," replied Cradock. He glanced again at Francklin's unmoving body, then allowed the two younger officers to pull him to his feet. "Do we have a damage report?"

"The forward turret is gone, sir."

"Gone?" Cradock stepped to the ruined windows and looked out over the forecastle. Below him, where the turret had been just moments ago, was a large charred hole in the deck plating. Flames licked from the opening of the circular chasm, and black smoke poured from somewhere down below. Metal debris lay strewn about the foredeck, but the turret itself was gone—its remnants thrown overboard by the explosion. "Good God," said Cradock. "We need to get that fire put out. If there are any survivors down there, get the wounded to the infirmary immediately."

"Yes, sir. We also have a report of damage to the number four funnel…"

A whistling shriek and a rapid series of detonations announced the fall of another German salvo. Fountains of water rose up around the ship, and the deck beneath their feet shuddered as a shell struck *Good Hope's* armored belt amidships on her hull just above the waterline. All of the bridge officers braced themselves against the bulkheads.

Cradock raised his binoculars to look out at the enemy squadron. The darkness to the east was nearly complete. "Did anyone see our last fall of shot?"

"Terrible visibility, sir. While we were getting knocked around in here, one of the spotters believes our last salvo also dropped short."

They were still too far away. He had to get close enough to reliably hit the Germans with *Good Hope's* secondary battery of 6-inch guns. "What's our range to target?"

"Hard to tell, sir. Our spotters are having a devil of a time. Right now, about all we have to go by are the flashes of their guns. I believe we're about ten thousand yards out."

Cradock knew their situation was becoming increasingly more desperate. The German gunners had found their range and were now striking *Good Hope* with every salvo. He had no idea how much damage the ship had already taken, but it would only get worse unless they could somehow blunt the enemy attack. He had already lost one of his two big guns, severely limiting the flagship's firepower, particularly at long range. "Keep firing at them," he said to Gaskell. "Never mind salvo firing. Tell your crews to fire at will, as rapidly as they can get the guns reloaded." He turned to the navigation officer. "Helmsman, one point to port. Let's get them in range of our smaller guns."

"Yes, sir."

"What of *Monmouth* and *Glasgow*?" asked Cradock of the senior signals officer.

"No response yet from either ship, sir, but spotters report that *Monmouth* is burning."

Cradock needed to see for himself. He walked across the wheelhouse to the exterior starboard door, beside which lay the limp body of the lieutenant. Small dark puncture wounds traced a line across his chest, from waist to shoulder—indicating that he had been struck down by a fusillade of metal splinters. Cradock looked away from the corpse and opened the door. He stepped outside the wheelhouse into the wind. From the starboard flying bridge, he looked aft toward *Monmouth*, steaming a quarter of a mile behind *Good Hope*—and immediately saw that Captain Brandt's ship was in equally dire circumstances. The armored cruiser had been struck multiple times already, and at least three fires raged above her decks—two near the bow and another somewhere amidships. The darkness prevented Cradock from assessing the damage done thus far, but the size of the fires indicated that her situation was already grave. As he watched, one of *Monmouth's* port guns fired, then another. She was still in the fight, but it was only a matter of time before the enemy shells struck a mortal blow.

"Another enemy salvo on the way, sir!" shouted a young signals lieutenant over the roar of the sea and wind.

Cradock stepped back in from the flying bridge, closing the door behind him. "Watch for any return signal from *Monmouth*. We must know how she is faring."

"Yes, sir." A loud boom made the young man flinch, and several other officers grasped nearby handholds in anticipation—but it was just the sound of *Good Hope's* remaining aft 9.2-inch gun firing another round at *Scharnhorst*. Three other guns fired as well, sending a ragged salvo of their own toward the enemy flagship.

A moment later, the mournful whine of more German shells sailing overhead caused all of the officers to once again brace themselves. Explosions in the water straddled the length of the ship, washing her decks in foam. *Good Hope* trembled as a round detonated aft in one of her port side machine spaces and another struck the base of her second funnel, tearing it from its moorings. The smokestack remained erect for a few brief seconds, suspended drunkenly in place by its support wires, before it toppled to starboard in a ruined heap.

"Fire in port engine room," said a lieutenant.

"Get those fires out, on the double!" shouted Cradock. He knew that the fires aboard his ships would act as beacons, allowing the German gunners to aim with accuracy even in almost complete darkness.

"Yes, sir—but the firefighting crews aren't responding. We can't tell if they've been able to access the burning spaces to put any water on the fires." The young man's face was drained of color. He was obviously terrified.

"Let me know as soon as you hear anything from them. Get me an injury report as well." Perhaps it was futile, he thought. He knew that deck by deck, everywhere aboard the ship, the mounting destruction was unraveling the ship's command and control functions. Machinery and equipment were destroyed, officers and men lay dead or wounded, fires raged out of control, and undoubtedly some lower compartments were beginning to flood. Although *Good Hope's* smaller guns were now within range, he knew that her ability to do any significant damage to the enemy ships was becoming more limited with every passing minute.

*Good Hope* was dying.

Across the dark open water to the east, a series of muzzle flashes grimly announced another wave of incoming German shells.

Admiral Cradock felt a strange, unfamiliar feeling seizing his chest like a powerful clenched fist. With some surprise, he realized that the feeling was fear.

◆

"FINALLY!" exclaimed Backhouse, peering out into the darkness through the port side windows of *Glasgow's* bridge. "Our spotters think our last salvo straddled *Leipzig*, but it's damned difficult to see anything out there."

"Understood," replied Luce. "Keep targeting the flashes of her guns. Now that they've brought their 4-inchers in range, things will get dicier for us. We'll need to do some damage quickly." Thus far, *Glasgow* had not been hit, but with every salvo they exchanged with the two German light cruisers, the chances of being struck continued to rise. He turned his attention back to *Good Hope* and *Monmouth* steaming before them, and what he saw was chilling.

Both of the larger British warships were burning. For the past forty minutes, the wickedly accurate German gunners had struck the armored cruisers repeatedly—and splashes from incoming heavy shells continued to erupt around them. Fires burned fiercely aboard both ships, most brightly near their bows, and they were having difficulty maintaining their course in the powerful seas. Only occasionally did one or more of the British guns return fire, and in the deepening darkness, Luce could not see if the big German warships were suffering any damage at all.

From the beginning of the battle, the bridge officers aboard *Glasgow* had watched in horror as *Good Hope* and *Monmouth* endured a withering barrage of enemy shellfire. Salvo after salvo landed near each ship, and explosions bloomed on their decks as some of the rounds struck home. The cumulative damage aboard each of the ships must have been horrific, and Luce wondered how much longer Cradock could keep up the fight. Surely, in these conditions, against such overwhelming opposition, it would make sense for the admiral to disengage and use the cover of darkness to retreat and fall back toward *Canopus*. However, *Good Hope* had not turned away, and in fact she was edging ever nearer to the enemy line. No signals had been seen or heard from the flagship since the beginning of the battle, and Luce wondered if her wireless room and signals bridges were still intact.

The light cruisers *Leipzig* and *Dresden*, bringing up the rear of the German line, had been firing continuously at *Glasgow* since the onset of the battle, but only now were their shell splashes surrounding the British ship. In the darkness, *Glasgow's* spotters were having great difficulty seeing the fall of shot, but the discipline of Luce's seasoned gun crews were doing well to keep their fire accurately directed on the two smaller enemy warships.

"Firing, port side," announced Backhouse.

*Glasgow's* two 6-inch guns and her five port-side 4-inch turrets fired simultaneously, sending another salvo out into the night sky toward *Leipzig*. Immediately, he could see muzzle flashes from two different locations on the distant, black horizon as the two smaller German ships fired back—aiming for the flashes of *Glasgow's* guns.

"Be prepared, gentlemen," said Thompson. "They're getting more accurate by the minute."

Seconds later, half a dozen foaming explosions rose from the dark swells, less than fifteen yards from the ship's port beam. A high-pitched whistling accompanied another flight of shells that arced over the ship, throwing up four more splashes on her starboard side, close enough to send spray over *Glasgow's* gunwales.

"They've straddled us," said Lieutenant Hirst, agreeing with the first officer. "Definitely getting more accurate."

"Captain," said Portman, the senior navigating officer. "*Good Hope* has shifted another point to port—towards the enemy—but *Monmouth* is having problems keeping the line. She's drifted off a bit to starboard. What course do we follow?"

Luce looked across the dark sea toward *Good Hope* and *Monmouth*. The fires aboard the two armored cruisers were like beacons—and he had no doubt that the German gunners aboard *Scharnhorst* and *Gneisenau* were using those fires to easily target the British ships, while the night's gloom enveloped the surrounding ocean completely. Half a mile ahead, *Good Hope* steered a bit farther to the east, trying to close the distance to the enemy battle line—and Luce recognized it as a desperate move, perhaps an attempt to draw within torpedo range. *Monmouth*, sailing less than a quarter mile behind the flagship, had veered off course slightly westward, apparently having difficulty following the admiral.

"Stay on the flagship's line, Mister Portman," said Luce, "but maintain our current speed. *Monmouth* will rejoin the line when she is able." He hoped that was true.

"Yes, sir."

Out in the inky distance, Luce saw the rippling orange muzzle blasts from the big German cruisers once again—as the enemy sent another salvo screaming toward the two wounded British ships. The distance between the two battle lines was not so great now, so the delay before impact was no more than a few seconds. Ahead of them, splashes rose all around *Monmouth,* and Luce could see a tongue of fire rise from her stern. Farther ahead, he saw another similar flash on *Good Hope's* port flank as she was struck again.

Then, suddenly, *Good Hope* disappeared in a massive explosion.

Where the flagship had been moments before, a great white sphere of blinding light appeared. In an instant, nighttime became day, illuminating all of the combative ships in a spectral glare that lit the ocean for miles around. As the initial brilliant flash faded, a colossal orange and red fire cloud rose from the ruined hull of the flagship. A deafening thunderclap rocked *Glasgow's* wheelhouse as the blast's shock wave hammered the cruiser. Decks shuddered and bulkheads reverberated as if a huge drum had been struck upon the ocean. Debris rained down from the darkness above, and small shards of metal pelted *Glasgow's* decks.

The fireball rose into the night sky, towering hundreds of feet over the swells and bathing the sea in a hellish crimson glow. As it roiled and churned above like a blood-red storm cloud, Luce caught his last glimpse of what remained of HMS *Good Hope.* Her blackened, skeletal remains lay low in the water, sinking, with a few small hot spots still glowing, as she drifted slowly eastward into the gloom. The fire cloud above the wreckage curled upon itself and died out, casting the sea back into darkness.

"Good God," whispered Luce. A wave of nausea washed over him.

All of the bridge officers stood silently in shock, their eyes staring into the dark void in the sea where their flagship had disappeared.

"Must've hit the main magazine," said Backhouse.

"Nine hundred souls," said Hirst quietly. "No one could have survived that."

"No," agreed Luce, "I cannot imagine that they did." He swallowed hard; his throat constricted. As shocking and terrifying as that realization was, he did not have the luxury of being able to grieve. Abruptly, he was once again the senior commander of the squadron, and his concern now was to keep the same fate from befalling his own ship and crew, as well as the stricken *Monmouth* and missing *Otranto*—wherever she was now. Out in the darkness, the Germans were firing again, targeting the blazes raging aboard *Monmouth*. Shells again began to fall around her, and Luce could see a splash of flame lick out from her quarterdeck as another round struck the ailing cruiser.

"She's dropped her speed, sir," said Portman.

Ahead, in the gloom, *Monmouth's* wake lessened, as she slowed and began to drift to starboard. They were close enough now that Luce could see the silhouettes of men working on her deck—their forms visible against the glow of the fires they were frantically trying to extinguish. With *Good Hope* gone, *Scharnhorst* had joined *Gneisenau* in targeting *Monmouth*, and now the rain of shells falling around her was nearly continuous.

"Reduce speed by half," said Thompson to the helmsman as he watched the fearsome hail of shells falling about the armored cruiser before them. "We don't want to steam right into that storm."

*Glasgow* began to slow, keeping a steady distance from her burning sister ship ahead. Splashes from falling shells rose all around *Monmouth* now, and two more explosions flashed on her upper works. Her guns were no longer firing.

"We have to help her get away to safety," said Luce. "Mister Stuart," he said to the signals officer, "he may not respond, but signal Captain Brandt to get away to the west. Mister Backhouse, ignore the enemy light cruisers for now. Have your gunlayers target the second ship in the German line— the armored cruiser *Gneisenau*. Perhaps we can distract her long enough for *Monmouth* to put some distance between her and the German ships and escape in the darkness."

"Aye, sir." Backhouse conveyed the new orders to his crews. In moments, they were ready. "Firing, port side," he said.

Once again, *Glasgow's* 6-inch and 4-inch guns fired simultaneously, this time sending a salvo toward the nearly invisible dark shape of *Gneisenau*. Ahead of them, *Monmouth* was slowly turning westward away from the enemy, as the glowing wounds from a score of fires burned within her hull.

◆

"SIR, SPOTTERS REPORT that the British light cruiser is firing on us now," said Busch. "Her first salvo directed at us fell just off our port quarter."

"She's probably trying to draw our fire away from *Monmouth*," replied Maerker." He was surprised and impressed. The captain of the enemy light cruiser was either extremely courageous or stunningly foolhardy. The small, unarmored ship was no threat to *Gneisenau*—and it risked swift destruction against the bigger ship's powerful guns. Attacking *Gneisenau* directly was a maneuver borne of desperation. "No matter," he said to the gunnery officer. "Tell your crews to target the flashes of her guns. We'll silence *Glasgow* soon enough—then we'll find *Monmouth*, wherever she's limped off to."

Busch passed the new targeting orders to the gun crews and came to stand beside the captain. They both peered out into the darkness toward the western horizon, where the last dull purple glow was disappearing from the sky.

*Gneisenau* had been struck only twice thus far. One of *Monmouth's* armor-piercing rounds had penetrated a segment of forward deck armor and drilled into an officer wardroom, creating a half-meter-wide hole in the starboard hull that was allowing the surging waves to seep into the compartment. Shipwrights and carpentry crews were already working to patch the hole. Another shell had exploded in an aft crew compartment, starting a small fire that had been quickly extinguished. Only one slight injury had been reported—a crewman wounded by flying shell fragments from the first hit. Overall, the damage was minor—nearly insignificant, really. As Maerker had expected at the outset of the battle, the contest had been over before it had begun. *Scharnhorst* had pummeled the British flagship until she was obliterated in a spectacular explosion. *Gneisenau* had hammered *Monmouth* into submission, and now the enemy cruiser's guns were silent.

In fact, Maerker realized he could no longer locate *Monmouth* in the darkness. A few minutes earlier, the damaged enemy ship had been marked brilliantly by numerous fires burning along her port flank. Now he could not see a single fire. She must have turned so that her stern was toward them now, and perhaps she had gotten some or all of those fires under control. For the time being, she was effectively invisible.

Now his task was to target the smaller British light cruiser as soon as she revealed herself again.

He had only to wait a few more seconds. A compact cluster of yellow flashes appeared in the distance as *Glasgow* fired at them again.

"There she is," said Maerker.

"Firing," said Busch, pulling the switch on the console. Another staccato cadence of gunfire rippled along the ship, accompanied by a string of bright muzzle flashes as *Gneisenau* unleashed her first salvo against the smallest ship in the enemy squadron.

As they waited for the fall of their shot—with the hope that they would see the flash of an explosion aboard the enemy ship—*Glasgow's* shells arrived.

A line of five splashes breached the surface of the dark water a hundred meters to starboard, well short of their target. Another splash arose just off the stern, only two meters from the hull. The seventh round found its mark. One of *Glasgow's* 6-inch shells struck *Gneisenau's* rear deck turret at its base, tearing through a thick steel flange and exploding between it and the turret's main cylindrical base.

Up in the bridge, Maerker felt the impact of the hit as a dull thud that rumbled through the ship. "That one hit us somewhere aft," he said. "We need a damage report."

After a few moments came word through the voice pipe: "Aft gunnery control to bridge."

"Go ahead, Lieutenant," said Busch.

"We took a hit to the main aft turret, sir. It looks superficial, but the explosion bent the turret cowling pretty badly and may have knocked the central cylinder out of alignment. For now, we can't get the turret to rotate at all."

"Any injuries?" asked Maerker.

"None reported yet, sir."

"Get the engineers to work on it immediately," said Busch. "Report when you have it operational again."

"Yes, sir."

"One lucky hit and they knock out one of our main turrets?" Maerker shook his head. The odds against it were astronomical. He turned to Busch. "Lieutenant-Commander, let's ensure that *Glasgow* has used up the last of her luck this evening."

Busch nodded grimly and checked his watch. "Firing," he said again calmly.

Massed cannon fire again echoed from bow to stern as *Gneisenau* sent another salvo of deadly missiles hurtling toward the enemy light cruiser—the only British ship still in the battle.

◆

THE PIERCING WAIL of enemy shells streaking over *Glasgow* had become a continuous and deafening cacophony. The entire German squadron now had but one target at which to fire, and they were concentrating that fire with deadly accuracy, even in the darkness. Columns of water large and small erupted everywhere around the cruiser as falling shells exploded in the sea nearby—drenching *Glasgow* in foam and pelting her steel hull with thousands of tiny shell fragments.

Beside him, Luce saw Lieutenant Hirst wince and duck as a shell screamed loudly past the bridge and detonated in the sea off their starboard gunwales. The resulting explosion of water and foam was tall enough to drench the windows of the wheelhouse. Luce realized that he, too, was continually flinching as more and more incoming rounds whistled past. He knew that to linger in this position much longer was lunacy, but he had to ensure that *Monmouth* had gotten safely away.

With a sharp crack, a shell exploded somewhere abaft of the bridge, its impact rattling the wheelhouse windows in their metal frames. At least two other enemy shells had already struck—but Luce had not yet received a damage report.

"Wireless signal from *Monmouth*, sir," said Stuart. "Tough to understand all of it through the jamming, but we believe Captain Brandt says we should get away while we can and that we should not attempt a rescue nor should we try to get her under tow."

"Do we still have *Monmouth* in sight?" asked Luce.

"No, sir," replied Hirst. "Her last sighting puts her somewhere west northwest of our position, but she's managed to get most of her fires suppressed, so our spotters cannot see her anymore."

"That's good," said Luce. "If we cannot see her, then neither can the enemy."

A thud echoed through the ship as a German shell struck somewhere amidships. Another shell tore through the second funnel without exploding, splashing into the sea west of the ship. The whistling cries of the falling shells continued, and more columns of water leapt upward from the black swells around them. Luce knew that under such conditions, the lifespan of his ship and his men could be measured in mere minutes.

"Firing, port side," announced Backhouse.

*Glasgow's* guns again sent a salvo toward the enemy, and immediately another series of flashes appeared in the darkness to the east as the Germans targeted the bursts of the British guns.

"We finally have a damage report," said Thompson, who had been conferring with Petty Officer Hobbs. "We've taken a hit in the port side coal bunker, and it looks like the number one ammunition hoist has been damaged. The rest of it is superficial—for now."

"I'd like to keep it that way," said Luce. "If *Monmouth* is away and out of sight, we should break off and find her. Brandt surely needs our help." He addressed the gunnery officer. "Mister Backhouse, cease fire. We certainly cannot sink all four of them, and every time we fire, we're giving them a target fix on our muzzle flashes. We'll use the darkness as..."

He was interrupted by a thunderous explosion aft. A huge gout of foaming spray drenched the sternmost weather deck, and the whole ship trembled with the force of the shell's impact. Several of the bridge officers stumbled sideways as the cruiser was shaken from stern to bow.

"That was a big one," said Thompson, who had braced his lanky frame against a bulkhead. "Might have hit the port engine spaces." He stepped to the voice pipe array and chose the pipe marked *Engine Room*. "Bridge to engineering," he shouted. "Damage report!"

There was no response.

"Helmsman," said Luce, "hard to starboard. Come about to a new course of two nine zero degrees. Let's put some distance between us and the enemy — and see if we can find *Monmouth*."

"Coming about starboard to two-hundred ninety degrees." The helmsman turned the wheel sharply, and *Glasgow* rolled into the severe turn, her decks tilting dramatically as the heavy swells struck her port beam and threatened to capsize the cruiser. All of the bridge officers held onto something as the deck undulated wildly beneath them. Within a few moments, the ship had completed her turn to the northwest, with the huge waves and wind now lashing at them from the stern.

However, something was wrong. Luce could tell that the ship was handling differently now. She felt sluggish, encumbered. That last hit had definitely caused serious damage. They were probably taking on water.

"Engineering to the bridge," said a strained and panicked voice through the pipe. "We've taken a hit near the port engine spaces. Must be near the water line. We can't yet tell how bad it is, but we've already had to seal off a compartment and a passageway because of the flooding."

"Get a crew down there immediately," said Luce to his officers. "Assess that damage and repair as much as we can — on the double. I also want a full injury report from all decks."

*Glasgow*, now damaged herself, steamed into the darkness — toward the last known position of her stricken sister ship. Fewer and fewer incoming shells fell behind them, and soon it became clear that the Germans — no longer able to target the flashes of *Glasgow's* guns — had also ceased fire. Even in the darkness, however, Luce knew the Germans would be hunting them. The enemy had wounded their prey — and like a pack of wolves closing in for the kill, they would pursue the remaining British ships until they found them.

He glanced aft, over their starboard quarter, out across the dark sea toward where he knew the unseen enemy ships were approaching. As he did so, his heart sank. He had hoped to escape under the cover of darkness, but that was not to be.

To the east, just above the horizon, an immense full moon had risen, casting a brilliant silvery glow over the churning sea.

# SEVENTEEN

*Sunday, November 1, 1914*
*Pacific Ocean, 50 Miles (80 Kilometers) West of Coronel, Chile*

IN *GNEISENAU'S* WHEELHOUSE, Lieutenant-Commander Busch scanned the darkness to the west. "No muzzle flashes for several minutes," he confirmed. "Either we've sunk them both, or they're trying to escape without revealing their positions."

"They're both still out there somewhere," said Maerker. "With their flagship gone, it makes sense that the remaining ships would try to flee — but *Monmouth* has taken a severe beating. How many times did your gunners hit her? Thirty or more? She is gravely damaged — I doubt she'll be escaping anywhere quickly. Their light cruiser is another matter. Can our spotters confirm any hits on *Glasgow* before she stopped firing at us?"

"Nothing confirmed, sir. Simply too dark, but the spotters did see explosions that they think may have been impacts upon *Glasgow*."

Maerker nodded. "Hopefully she is wounded and lame as well. Otherwise, we'll never catch her. If any enemy ships are still within a few kilometers of us, the moonlight should reveal them soon enough." He turned to the senior signals officer. "Mister Petri, anything from the flagship?"

"No, sir. No lamp signals, and the wireless operators are still just jamming."

Maerker was concerned that they might be squandering a valuable opportunity. *Gneisenau*, *Leipzig*, and *Dresden* were still following *Scharnhorst's* wake, heading south, as if the enemy squadron were still steaming along their previous parallel course — but obviously they were not. The British flagship, *Good Hope*, was gone — destroyed in an explosion more devastating than anything Maerker had ever seen. *Monmouth* was severely damaged and had turned westward, away from the German line. *Glasgow* had stopped firing and was now effectively invisible—probably also fleeing westward. Now was the time for pursuit, before the enemy could use the darkness to make good their escape. Perhaps the admiral was simply being cautious. The British were cunning opponents, and Admiral von Spee might be waiting to ensure that they were not laying a trap—perhaps maneuvering toward them under the cover of darkness to try to torpedo one of the armored cruisers.

"While we await orders from the flagship," he said to his assembled officers, "I want detailed damage and injury reports from every portion of the ship."

The bridge officers passed their orders to the men under their individual commands. As they were doing so, the wireless operators reported that *Scharnhorst* had suspended its jamming. A few minutes later, Petri received a message from the wireless room, and he read it aloud: "Flagship instructs *Leipzig*, *Dresden*, and *Nürnberg* to sweep west in a search pattern, twelve kilometers apart, at twenty knots. Find any remaining enemy vessels and report any contact. *Gneisenau* and *Scharnhorst* to remain on station until further orders. Jamming to resume immediately."

Finally some direction, thought Maerker. Sending the swift light cruisers made sense, of course. They could more economically pursue the British ships at speed and were less valuable targets, should the enemy actually be laying some sort of trap.

Ahead of them, *Scharnhorst* slowed slightly and began a gentle starboard turn as the admiral prepared to take up a watchful station, slowly loitering in the area to provide support to the light cruisers, if needed. Astern, Maerker could just see *Leipzig* and *Dresden* both peel off the line, heading westward. Although he could not see *Nürnberg*, he assumed that she was also out there, joining the hunt for the remaining enemy ships. Surging swells continued to rock *Gneisenau*, and the chill wind howled across her decks.

"Follow the flagship," he instructed the helmsman, "and match her reduced speed. We will await further orders while the light cruisers hunt them down and mop up."

◆

ABOARD *Glasgow*, spotters, officers, and men alike peered out over the inky sea, anxiously searching for any sign of *Monmouth*. Luce had set a course toward the northwest, hoping to intercept the armored cruiser along her last known heading. They had already been searching for a quarter of an hour with no sign of their sister ship. With each passing minute, tensions among the men rose higher, because they knew that at any moment the enemy squadron could suddenly materialize from the darkness.

"Still nothing," said Thompson soberly. "Thought we would have found her by now. From the looks of her when we last saw her, she could not have gotten far." He paused. "Do you think she's gone under?"

"I hope not," said Luce, "but we're running out of time to find her before the Germans catch us out here just milling about."

Hirst looked up from the voice pipe array. "One of the spotters thinks he sees *Monmouth*, bearing twenty degrees off our starboard bow, distance two miles."

"Helmsman, twenty degrees to starboard," said Luce. "Fifteen knots." The light cruiser steamed northeast, rising and falling on the dark, turbulent sea. The wind was increasing, and whitecaps flashed on the moonlit swells.

After a few minutes of searching the black seascape, they found her.

*Monmouth's* gray bulk loomed out of the darkness a quarter of a mile ahead, like a phantom ship materializing in the moonlight. She was barely moving, making perhaps five knots. As *Glasgow* approached her from the stern and moved up along her port beam, the terrible extent of the damage to the armored cruiser became chillingly clear. The old ship was listing dramatically to port, and her bow was so low in the water that it was almost completely submerged. All of the cruiser's port gun casements were below the surface, and the heavy swells repeatedly sent foaming water crashing over her port gunwales. Two of her four funnels were missing altogether, and the remaining stacks were crumpled and shredded. Large jagged holes gaped in her steel hull and decking—and from many of the black voids emanated a dull red glow from deep within the ship. In several places, the moonlight illuminated trails of smoke curling upward from within the crippled warship. The superstructure supporting the bridge was punctured with holes large and small, and most of her suspended boats had been damaged. The forward turret was the only portion of the forecastle not continuously awash in seawater, and Luce could see that the turret itself had been shattered—a large chunk of its armor plate was missing, like the cracked shell of a great steel tortoise. Although the exterior of the cruiser was no longer aflame, the entire length of the ship was scored by the black scars of dozens of fires.

*Monmouth* was mortally wounded, but she was not without life. The moonlight illuminated numerous sailors as they moved carefully on the steeply canted deck, struggling to repair or patch some of the damaged portions of the ship. They were having difficulty maintaining their footing as the stricken and listing cruiser was rolling heavily in the swells. Hundreds of random objects floated alongside the ship, borne along by the surging sea. As *Glasgow* settled in beside *Monmouth*, the bridge officers could see that floating among the debris were numerous uniformed corpses.

"Jesus," whispered Thompson.

Luce swallowed hard. This was a scene from a nightmare. He knew, instinctively, that *Monmouth* was already lost. He wondered how many of her crew of seven hundred still lived. He took a deep breath and forced himself into action. He turned to the signals officer. "Use the lamp," he said. "Ask her captain, 'Are you all right?'"

"Aye, sir."

Two men out on the starboard signals bridge rotated the large signal lamp toward *Monmouth* and briskly clattered the metal louvers open and shut as they transmitted the captain's query. Using the signal lamp was a risk, but Luce had few options. Even if *Monmouth's* wireless array still functioned—which he doubted—the Germans were still jamming the wireless bands. Flag signals were useless in the dark. He hoped that the shuttered light from the lamp would not be seen by the enemy ships, wherever they might be.

Minutes later, a blinking reply came from *Monmouth's* signal lamp: "MAKING WATER BADLY FORWARD. TRYING TO GET STERN TO SEA."

Luce briefly considered ordering boats to be lowered to pluck off as many of *Monmouth's* men as he could take, but he knew that such a rescue could not happen. Even if the seas were not so rough as to make such an operation extremely hazardous, he knew the approaching German squadron might spot them at any moment. An attempted nighttime rescue of hundreds of men, in towering swells, would take too long and would put all of *Glasgow's* men at grave risk. The best he could do for now would be to try to help *Monmouth* get away. Unfortunately, with *Monmouth's* bow and forecastle awash, affixing a tow line would be impossible. Perhaps, if *Glasgow* could simply escort her farther westward, they might be able to avoid the enemy long enough that the rough seas would eventually lessen and permit a rescue.

"Mister Stuart, send them another message: 'Can you steer northwest? Enemy is following us astern'."

"Aye, sir."

The signalmen outside sent the captain's message using the lamp, and then the bridge officers waited. Long minutes dragged by without any response, and Luce could feel the tension growing with every second.

"Come on, Brandt," urged Thompson under his breath. "Give us something."

There was no response.

"Her engines are dead," observed Backhouse.

It was true. The old ship was drifting now, powerless and at the mercy of the sea. Some of the men clinging to her slanted decks waved frantically at *Glasgow*, but their voices were lost on the wind.

"What can we do?" asked Hirst.

"Probably nothing," said Luce solemnly, "unless she can survive the night without being spotted—and we might then be able to attempt a rescue."

"Foretop to bridge," said a panicked voice from the pipe. "Enemy cruiser sighted to the southeast, off our starboard quarter, approaching us bearing one hundred fifty degrees, distance five miles. There may also be a second one farther south, but I cannot be certain in the moonlight."

"They'll be on us in minutes, Captain," said Backhouse. "Do we stay and fight, sir?"

Luce looked out again at the stricken *Monmouth*. Her tattered white battle ensigns were still flying, fluttering on lines suspended from her tilting mainmast. Customarily, displaying the ensigns indicated a warship's intention to carry the fight to the enemy. This warship, however, could do no such thing. In her current state, the few of her guns that might still be operable would be impossible to target and fire. She was powerless against the sea, and she was powerless against the enemy. Reluctantly, Luce pulled his gaze from the damaged ship and looked over the faces of his senior staff—the distressed expressions of his officers indicated that they all knew what he was about to say. "We must leave her, gentlemen," he said quietly. "At least one and perhaps two enemy ships will spot us any minute now—and where there are two of them, we can assume that all five will arrive soon enough. We cannot battle the entire German squadron. If we linger here and attempt to fight them off, we shall also be destroyed. I will not needlessly sacrifice another man. If the Germans do come upon her, they will see she is lost, and I hope they will do their best to rescue as many of her crew as possible. Alternatively, if *Monmouth* can remain afloat until daybreak without being spotted, we can circle back and rescue her crew." He paused and looked over once more at the listing hulk of the armored cruiser. With a heavy-hearted sigh, he said, "Helmsman, full speed. Due west, course two hundred seventy degrees."

"Aye, sir."

Down below, *Glasgow's* engines rumbled and the cruiser pulled away from the listing *Monmouth*. As the old ship faded into the darkness behind them, Luce could see some of her crew still waving and gesturing wildly at them. Knowing he could do nothing for those poor men left him nearly desperate—but he had to save *Glasgow* from destruction. It was the most anguished moment of his life. "God help you all," he whispered, "and God willing, you will survive the night so that we may return to rescue whoever still lives."

The rest of the bridge officers stood in silence, watching *Monmouth's* ghostly shape disappear from view. In a few brief minutes, *Glasgow* had accelerated to twenty-four knots, at which point her hull began to reverberate—a low, heavy shaking that Luce felt as much in his chest and head as he did through his feet. The hole in the hull rent by the earlier explosion near her stern was affecting the cruiser's seaworthiness and limiting her speed. He maintained their westward course and instructed the spotters to scan the eastern sea behind them for any sign of enemy pursuit.

Somewhere back there, the Germans were still hunting.

◆

CAPTAIN Karl Schönberg of SMS *Nürnberg* could not recall when he had been in a fouler mood—a significant revelation for a man prone to angry outbursts and ranting tirades. He marveled that somehow, yet again, Fate had plotted against him on this execrable voyage—this time spitefully determining that he alone was to miss the entirety of the climactic battle with the British squadron. During the past hour, a dull ache near his temples had become a sharp pain that had entrenched itself behind his eyes. Schönberg seethed and paced back and forth within the cruiser's wheelhouse, muttering to himself. His bridge officers wisely averted their glances and attended to their duties with particularly rapt focus.

*Nürnberg* had finally rejoined the squadron long after darkness had fallen and the battle was already over. During their approach, they had received and listened to *Scharnhorst's* intermittent wireless transmissions, and Schönberg and his men had been able to piece together the preamble of the fight, from the opening encounter with the lone British light cruiser onward through the first sighting of the rest of the enemy squadron. He knew when the battle had been joined, although the flagship's wireless signals had ceased at that time—replaced with incomprehensible jamming noise. Schönberg had been beside himself with frustration, cursing once again his damnable luck at being too far away at that critical moment. Even bringing his ship to her top speed had not been enough to close the distance until the fighting was all but over. In fact, as they finally drew near the squadron, *Nürnberg's* spotters observed a few distant muzzle flashes, and then nothing. The battle had ended.

Not long thereafter, Schönberg received the admiral's wireless command directing the three light cruisers to head west to search for the fleeing British warships. He was suddenly buoyed by the possibility that not all of the enemy ships had been sunk—although surely they were damaged. There was still a chance—albeit a slim one—that *Nürnberg* might yet play a role in the battle.

He ordered a course change to the west and had the helmsman drop the speed slightly to twenty knots to match *Dresden* and *Leipzig*, which were traveling in search formation to the south. Long minutes passed as they steamed into the darkness with the full moon as their only illumination. The light cruiser struggled in the heavy waves, which surged against her port beam and caused the small warship to roll and pitch severely. Schönberg began to worry that once again he was to be cheated out of his opportunity.

The quiet of the wheelhouse was broken by a voice from one of the pipes. It was the spotter in the foretop above. "Possible enemy warship sighted, bearing twenty degrees off starboard bow. Distance three kilometers."

"Can you identify it?" asked Schönberg.

"Not yet, sir."

"Alter course to intercept," said the captain. "Battle stations. All guns depressed to sea level. If this is indeed an enemy warship, we are coming upon her in very close quarters. Prepare for short range fighting."

The helmsman made the slight course correction to the northwest, and all of the bridge officers strained to see anything in the darkness ahead. Within a few minutes, the shape of a vessel began to take form before them, pale and indistinct in the moonlight. It was large—considerably larger than *Nürnberg*. Schönberg initially had trouble identifying the ship because of the extensive damage that had been done to her. Approaching from the vessel's starboard quarter, much of what he initially saw was the stern and aft starboard hull, lifted awkwardly high because her port side and bow were submerged. Even in the darkness, it was obvious that the vessel was severely damaged and foundering. Schönberg ordered the helmsman to slow to five knots. From what he remembered, this ruined hulk most closely resembled the diagrams he had studied of the Royal Navy's County-class armored cruisers, but he had to be certain.

"Starboard searchlights," he commanded. "I'd like to identify this enemy vessel properly. Helmsman, adjust course twenty-five degrees to port and maintain two hundred meters distance. We'll stay astern and avoid her bow area in case they try to launch a torpedo at us. Come around behind her stern and begin a slow starboard turn so we can get a look at her port side. I want to hold there, behind her port quarter."

"Yes, sir."

Sailors activated two large searchlights on the starboard side of the quarterdeck and began to play the harsh, bright beams over the stricken vessel. The wavering disks of light lashed over the length of the ship, and the extent of her damage became much clearer.

It was extraordinary that she was still afloat. As *Nürnberg* maneuvered around behind the armored cruiser, the searchlight beams illuminated the name "*Monmouth*" on her stern. After a few more minutes, *Nürnberg's* course brought *Monmouth's* port quarter into view and the bridge officers got their first good look down the port side of the enemy ship. The damage already inflicted upon the British cruiser was horrific. Dozens of ragged holes, some quite large, marred her deck plating and hull from bow to stern. Her aft wireless mast and two of her funnels were gone. Smoke billowed upward from many of the hideously gaping wounds—evidence of fires still burning deep inside. Her bow was low in the water, fully submerged, and heavy swells washed over her forecastle. At least thirty British sailors were visible either trying to move about on the steeply tilted decks or simply clinging pitifully to portions of the railing. Some of the men looked to be trying to make repairs, although their efforts were certainly futile. *Monmouth's* sailors, apparently recognizing *Nürnberg* as an enemy warship, stared in grim silence as the German light cruiser positioned herself behind the crippled ship.

"Do you wish to signal the flagship, sir?" asked Lieutenant-Commander Engel. "To inform the admiral that we have located the British ship *Monmouth* and report upon her condition?"

"Send no such signal, Mister Engel," replied Schönberg sternly. "For the time being, we shall maintain our wireless silence." He surveyed the scene dispassionately. If the battle had unfolded according to the admiral's plan, this warship would have been engaged by *Gneisenau*. Maerker's big cruiser had pummeled *Monmouth* viciously. So much damage, and yet, this enemy vessel still floats, he thought. What had happened that Maerker could not finish her off? Had *Gneisenau* been damaged and forced to withdraw? Had *Monmouth* simply escaped into the dark? There were several possibilities. Regardless, somehow that fool Maerker had let HMS *Monmouth* escape. Finally, Schönberg realized, Fate had put before him an opportunity previously denied.

"Starboard gun batteries," said Schönberg, "prepare to fire armor-piercing shells at close range on my command. We are going to sink this enemy ship once and for all. Helmsman, prepare to bring us along the enemy's port beam, no faster than three knots."

"The starboard batteries are ready, sir," said the gunnery officer.

"Sir?" interjected Engel, aghast. "Are we to fire on a defenseless ship?"

The other bridge officers paused momentarily in their duties—surprised by Engel's query, which was an unprecedented challenge to Schönberg's authority. Others may have also harbored Engel's concerns, but they remained silent, looking with some trepidation at the captain and the senior signals officer.

"They are still flying their battle ensigns," observed Schönberg, turning toward Engel with a venomous glare. "If this enemy vessel is so 'defenseless', why have they not struck their colors? Probably because they are waiting for us to make some soft-headed blunder. I'd wager that if you and I were having this discussion while viewing her bow instead of her stern, we would see British torpedoes streaking toward us."

"That is, of course, possible, sir—but could it also be possible that they are unable to lower the flags in their current damaged state?" Engel asked. "This vessel will likely sink within the hour. They do not appear to be capable of continuing the fight in any form, sir." He stood stiffly and held his head high, but the corners of his mouth quivered slightly. He clearly realized that he was taking a great risk by questioning his captain in this manner.

"Perhaps, Lieutenant-Commander, you should remain attentive to matters of communications rather than naval combat." Schönberg's voice was a low hiss, and his anger was unmistakable. "You have much to learn about command, especially during wartime. Perhaps you would prefer to give our enemy a sporting chance to blast some holes below our waterline before we fire upon them?"

"Not at all, sir. I simply…"

"You simply have overstepped your position, Lieutenant-Commander. These enemies of the Kaiser are still flying their battle flags—which is evidence of their continued hostile intent. While I have wasted time debating this point with you, they have had ample time to lower their flags and surrender their ship—but you can plainly see they have not done so." He gestured toward *Monmouth's* canted forward mast, from which still flew the cruiser's tattered ensigns, snapping in the driving wind. "Therefore, we will sink this enemy warship and remove the continuing threat that she represents. Is that understood, Lieutenant-Commander?"

"Of course, sir." Engel's eyes were downcast, his demeanor chastened.

"I trust you will not question my orders in the future," said Schönberg. "I will not abide insubordination in any form. Consider yourself fortunate that you are not already in the custody of the master-at-arms." With that, he turned his back on the signals officer, effectively ending the exchange. "Helmsman," he said, "ahead slowly. Maintain distance to target of two hundred meters."

"Yes, sir. Two hundred meters."

*Nürnberg* began to edge forward, rolling on the large swells as she drew alongside the foundering *Monmouth*. The beams of the searchlights played over the ruined hull of the enemy ship. More of the British sailors were emerging above decks, perhaps escaping fires or flooded compartments below. Some of their uniforms hung in shreds, and a few held makeshift bandages over their wounds. They clung to whatever handholds they could find and mutely stared at the German cruiser as she approached. If any of them could foresee what was about to happen, they gave no indication.

"Fire at will," said Schönberg.

"Firing, starboard batteries," replied the gunnery officer.

*Nürnberg's* five starboard 4.1-inch guns roared and spat bright yellow cones of flame. A flurry of explosions burst upon *Monmouth's* aft decks as the first shells struck. Most of the rounds detonated on the exterior of the ship—for even in her crippled condition, much of the old cruiser's armor plate was still too thick for *Nürnberg's* small shells to immediately penetrate. As the German cruiser slowly steamed alongside, her guns fired again and again, hammering *Monmouth's* decks and hull. The pattern of blooming white and orange explosions traveled slowly along her hull from the stern forward, as the German gunners methodically poured shell fire into the drifting ship. British sailors fell or were torn violently from their perches as the repeated concussions devastated her upper decks. Chunks of metal plating, shreds of funnel cylinders, pieces of mast, remnants of tethered boats, and fragments of human bodies were ejected into the sea around the ship. Fires flared up in numerous places, and thick smoke began to obscure the German gunners' view of their target, even with the searchlights illuminating the scene.

When *Nürnberg* had traversed the length of *Monmouth's* hull, Schönberg ordered the helmsman to turn her about and begin another pass. He then directed the port side gunners to commence firing, continuing the grim work begun by the starboard crews. The guns fired repeatedly, sending wave after wave of shells into the burning hulk of the British ship. The repetitive pounding of the muzzle blasts and explosions echoed across the narrow stretch of dark, windswept water.

*Nürnberg* had finished her second full pass, and Schönberg was preparing to order the ship to come about again for a third. Suddenly, in a deafening cacophony of groaning steel and venting steam that was audible over the howling wind, *Monmouth's* immense bulk rolled completely over—her immobile propellers and rudders now pointing incongruously toward the dark sky. With her upper works fully submerged, *Monmouth's* fires were abruptly extinguished, and the remaining smoke was borne away on the wind. Under the searchlights, *Nürnberg's* officers watched as the British cruiser's upturned hull sank lower in the water. For a few moments, her rusted keel rode above the rolling seas. Then, in silence, *Monmouth* slipped beneath the waves and was gone.

The searchlights panned across the area where the ship had been, and all that remained was a sparse debris field, tossed about on the black swells. Among the flotsam were several members of *Monmouth's* surviving crew, some waving and pleading for rescue, others desperately clinging to any buoyant object they could find. In the frigid seas, they would survive for only minutes. Among them floated the torn, lifeless corpses of scores of their shipmates—the ghoulish scene illuminated by the slashing beams of the lights.

Engel turned back from the windows and swallowed stiffly. Addressing the captain, he asked, "Should we lower boats and attempt a rescue of the survivors, sir?"

Schönberg appraised him icily. "I assume you took note of the heavy seas and thirty-knot winds, Lieutenant-Commander? Lowering boats in such conditions would be foolhardy at best. Would you also risk the lives of the Kaiser's brave sailors to try to save a handful of our sworn enemies, most of whom will likely die anyway?"

"No, sir. I would not." Engel stood rigidly and swallowed, with his jaw clenched tightly.

"Instead, I would suggest that you perform a function that actually is part of your customary duties. Have our telegraphists send the following wireless signal to the flagship and the rest of the squadron: 'British armored cruiser *Monmouth* sunk by gunfire at 2200 hours. No other enemy ships sighted. Continuing search westward'."

"Yes, sir." Engel turned and was about to leave the bridge for the wireless room when Schönberg's steel-edged voice caused him to pause.

"After you have confirmed that the message was sent, Lieutenant-Commander, you are relieved of your duties for the remainder of the watch. Designate a replacement to take your bridge position, and then you may return to your cabin. Report to my quarters at 0800 so that we may discuss your future as a member of my staff."

"Yes, sir." Engel nodded stiffly and left the bridge.

Schönberg inhaled deeply, composed himself, and smiled broadly to his remaining bridge officers. "Well done, gentlemen. We have fought and sunk an enemy warship. I am certain that His Imperial Majesty will be immensely proud. Pass on my congratulations to all of your men. Helmsman, set a new course—two hundred seventy degrees, twenty knots. Let us go see if we can find another British cruiser trying to elude us."

*Nürnberg* quickly got up to speed and plunged westward through the dark churning sea. Schönberg scanned the darkness ahead, and he realized that it had been a long time since he had felt so light-hearted.

◆

IF *GLASGOW'S* gunnery commander was experiencing any emotion, Backhouse hid it well under his customary gruff demeanor, as he relayed the message flatly to his captain. "Sub-Lieutenant Hickling confirms the spotter's report, sir. He observed the play of searchlights on the horizon, west-northwest, followed by seventy-five flashes that appeared to be gunfire, then nothing more."

"They found *Monmouth*," said Luce quietly, almost in a whisper.

"And they fired seventy-five rounds into her?" asked Thompson, incredulous. "Jesus Christ. Why fire on her at all, let alone use her for target practice?"

"Bloody barbaric," agreed Backhouse.

"I have no idea," answered Luce. He shuddered at the thought of those men he had seen huddled on *Monmouth's* canted deck, waving and gesturing in the futile hope of rescue. They would have been mercilessly shredded as the Germans poured salvo after salvo into their stricken warship.

"Do you suppose Brandt provoked them by firing off a round as the Huns drew near?" asked Thompson.

Luce shook his head. "I cannot imagine any of those guns still being operable, and they certainly could not be trained upon a target. Her bow compartments also looked to be completely flooded, which would have prevented the launching of her torpedoes as well. No, Brandt didn't provoke it." He paused, thinking for a moment. "Regardless, seventy-five rounds are beyond excessive—and certainly wasteful of ammunition. If the Germans were intent on sinking her, why not do the job with a single torpedo?"

The question hung in the air, and none of the officers offered a reply.

"Nevertheless," Luce continued, "they have not yet found us, and I intend to keep it that way. Mister Portman, plot us a new course, due south, full speed—at least as fast as our damaged hull will permit. I intend to get to the Strait before the Germans can make it there to block our way."

"Yes, sir."

Luce addressed his first officer. "Commander, I'll need a comprehensive damage and injury report from all decks within the hour."

"Absolutely, sir," said Thompson, who stepped to the voice pipe array to distribute his initial set of orders to the officers and men.

"Mister Stuart," said Luce to the signals officer, "We need to get a signal to *Canopus* through the jamming—to tell her what happened and warn her off before she gets any closer. She'll need to turn about and also get back through the Strait as rapidly as she can."

"Certainly, sir. What's the message?"

"For now, send the following: '*Good Hope* and *Monmouth* lost. Our squadron is scattered. Heading south for Strait at full speed'." He added, "Keep sending it until you get a response. Inform me immediately, and I will figure out what else we can tell them."

*Glasgow* assumed her new southward course and steamed on into the night, still buffeted by huge swells and howling winds. A stunned and mournful silence settled over the crew. Not only had their squadron been beaten soundly and decisively in battle, but they had also lost two entire ships' companies, including their admiral. During the past months, many of *Glasgow's* officers and men had forged friendships with their counterparts aboard their companion vessels, and the sudden deaths of so many fellow sailors was difficult to fathom. Throughout the ship, men attended to their duties in near silence as *Glasgow's* crew struggled to understand and accept the day's horrific events.

When he read the damage report, Luce was astounded to see how lucky they had truly been. Although the enemy ships had fired hundreds of rounds at *Glasgow*, she had been struck only six times. Miraculously, not a single man had been injured. Three shells had exploded harmlessly in port side coal bunkers. One round had struck the top of the third funnel but had punched through it without detonating. Another unexploded round had penetrated the deck near the forward turret and had severed an ammunition hoist. That shell had traveled onward through two bulkheads and finally came to rest in Captain Luce's pantry, of all places. The spent and shattered shell fragments had wrecked a portion of his cabin, and toxic fumes were still preventing anyone from entering the compartment.

The most damaging strike, of course, had occurred near the stern, at the waterline on the port side. The explosion had rent a massive hole in the hull, nearly the height of a man and twice as long. Fortunately it had not penetrated the inner armored deck, so the damage had been confined to a single aft storage compartment near the port side machine spaces. Although carpenters and shipwrights could do little to shore up the hole in the exterior hull, they had managed to temporarily seal off the damaged compartment to minimize the chances of flooding the rest of the ship. Still, the force of seawater surging into the weakened space was immense — and at the recommendations of his engineers, Luce ordered the ship's speed reduced to twenty knots. He just hoped that the hull itself could hold together long enough for them to put into a friendly port to assess the damage and, if possible, make some repairs.

Unfortunately, the nearest friendly port was Port Stanley in the Falklands — more than a thousand miles away.

◆

ON *Gneisenau's* bridge, Maerker reviewed the shipwide damage and injury report. *Gneisenau* had indeed fared quite well. She had been struck only four times, and overall the damage was minor. The hole in the forward armored decking, where one of *Monmouth's* rounds had penetrated the officer wardroom, was already sealed. The shipwrights predicted that the compartment would be fully usable again by the first daylight watch. The damage to the aft crew compartment had been minor, thanks to the quick actions of the fire suppression team. The aft 8.2-inch gun turret was still out of order from the improbable hit from *Glasgow*, but the repair crew believed that they would have it functional again within the hour. The fourth strike had glanced off the warship's thick armor plate near one of the starboard flank turrets amidships, leaving only superficial damage.

Fortunately, only three men had been wounded. The initial assessment stated that none of the men's wounds was life threatening, but Maerker would get a more comprehensive report from Doctor Nohl directly.

A wireless operator arrived at the starboard doorway and stood at attention. He exchanged a few words with Lieutenant-Commander Petri, handed over a slip of paper, and was gone as quickly as he had arrived.

Petri scanned the message quickly and handed it to his captain with a smile. "I assume, sir, that you'll want to pass this along to the crew yourself."

Maerker took the paper, which was a transcript of a wireless transmission from the admiral:

> [*General Signal*]
> CONGRATULATIONS TO THE OFFICERS AND MEN ABOARD ALL SHIPS OF THE SQUADRON. YOU HAVE PERFORMED YOUR DUTIES EXCEPTIONALLY WELL, WITH COURAGE AND FIERCE RESOLVE. WITH THE HELP OF GOD, WE HAVE WON A GLORIOUS VICTORY.
>
> GNEISENAU AND NÜRNBERG ARE TO FALL IN BEHIND SCHARNHORST AND MAKE FOR THE PREDETERMINED ASSEMBLY POINT OUTSIDE OF VALPARAISO HARBOR. DRESDEN AND LEIPZIG ARE TO CONTINUE THE SEARCH FOR REMAINING ENEMY WARSHIPS UNTIL FIRST LIGHT, THEN REJOIN COLLIERS AT MÁS AFUERA TO AWAIT FURTHER ORDERS.
>
> VIZEADMIRAL M. VON SPEE
> [*End Signal*]

"Yes, I would," agreed Maerker, who could not help but smile as well. "I don't know which part of this message will cheer the men more—the admiral's congratulations on our victory or the news that we'll finally be putting in at a real port."

Busch chuckled. "Well, sir, I certainly appreciate the admiral's pat on the back. However, the thought that we might get to spend some time ashore with some of our countrymen, tip back a stein or two, and..." he paused and grinned, "...maybe even see a few women is a reward that right now I would value more than a chestful of ribbons and medals."

Maerker laughed and nodded. He stepped to the voice pipe array and made the announcement to as many of the ship's spaces as he could at once, adding his own heartfelt congratulations to those of the admiral. The sound of cheering echoed back through the pipes. Turning to his senior navigation officer, he said, "Mister Born, set a course for the assembly point fifty kilometers outside of Valparaiso harbor, and prepare to follow the flagship."

"Yes, sir."

"Mister Busch," said Maerker, "I think it is only fair to release Commander Pochhammer from his duties down in the conning tower. He and his men have been in there all evening, and unless the engineers have secretly installed lavatory facilities in that little space, I imagine they're all rather uncomfortable."

"Of course, sir," replied Busch, suppressing a smile.

"Mister Born, you have the bridge for the remainder of the watch. I'm going to the infirmary to check on the condition of the wounded men." He paused at the wheelhouse door, then turned back and addressed all of his bridge officers with a satisfied nod. "Well done this evening, gentlemen. As I said to the rest of the crew a few moments ago, you have most certainly made His Imperial Highness proud tonight. I, too, am proud of you. I consider myself fortunate to have you as my staff officers. Hopefully, tomorrow night in Valparaiso I can toast you all properly." He turned and left the bridge.

Half a kilometer ahead of them on the rolling moonlit ocean, *Scharnhorst* began a sweeping turn toward the northeast. *Gneisenau* fell in behind the flagship and matched her speed. Soon *Nürnberg* joined the line as well, and all three cruisers made their way toward the port of Valparaiso.

# EIGHTEEN

*Tuesday, November 3, 1914*
*Valparaiso, Chile*

THE DRIVING WIND and surging seas had finally eased by sunrise, when the sprawling, bowl-shaped port city of Valparaiso came into view from *Gneisenau's* bridge. The contrast of the city's stately older waterfront area and the chaotic jumble of multi-colored buildings clustered on the hillsides above reminded Maerker of some of the seaside Mediterranean towns he had visited early in his naval career. The lush green hilltops ringing the town reached into a morning sky that was a crisp, cloudless blue.

As he scanned details of the city through binoculars, he noticed a small Chilean naval vessel steaming out from the harbor toward the approaching *Scharnhorst, Gneisenau,* and *Nürnberg.* It appeared to be a torpedo boat. One of *Scharnhorst's* small starboard guns fired with a resounding crack—the customary salute upon entering a foreign naval port. One of the torpedo boat's guns fired in return, as did guns from the other Chilean naval vessels anchored in the bay. Maerker was pleased at the warm welcome from the local authorities—it was a marked contrast to their previous anchorages during the past several months. The Chilean torpedo boat turned about and signaled for the German ships to follow. Thus escorted, the three cruisers of the *Kaiserliche Marine* steamed into the outer harbor—completing, at least in ceremony, their long voyage across the Pacific from Tsingtao.

The three German warships dropped anchor in the outermost region of the bay—a reasonable wartime precaution, even though two days earlier they had destroyed or scattered what was likely the only enemy naval presence anywhere along South America's Pacific coast.

Through the glasses, Maerker could see that a large crowd—numbering in the hundreds—had gathered on the wharf to greet the arriving German warships. It was an extraordinary sight. Also, numerous small boats—some steam powered, but most rowed by oarsmen—were converging on the newly anchored cruisers, like a cloud of insects drawn to a lamp's flame. Some of the boats had been launched from the German merchant ships anchored nearby, and others had pushed off from piers along the wharf.

"Should we have the small guns manned or post riflemen at the gunwales, sir?" asked Pochhammer, who was obviously concerned by the sudden approach of so many small vessels.

"I don't think so, Lieutenant-Commander," answered Maerker with a chuckle. "I think they are just part of our welcoming committee. In fact, you should prepare to conduct tours of the ship. I believe that our countrymen would enjoy coming aboard and seeing the inner workings of one of the Kaiser's warships."

"Tours, sir?"

"Absolutely, Mister Pochhammer. It would be shame if those patriotic fellows rowed all the way out here, only to be denied the chance to come aboard. Please make the necessary arrangements."

Pochhammer paused, momentarily nonplussed. "Absolutely, sir," he finally answered. "I'll make the arrangements." He turned and left the bridge, still wearing a puzzled expression.

"General signal from the flagship, Captain," said Petri. "It states, 'All ships prepare to coal and resupply. Shore leave to be granted at the captains' discretion. All ships ready to depart in twenty-two hours.' Also, there's this, sir." Petri handed a sheet of paper to Maerker.

"Thank you, Lieutenant-Commander." The sheet was a transcript of another wireless signal from the admiral.

[*Confidential Signal*]
CAPTAIN JULIUS MAERKER
SMS GNEISENAU


OUR CAPTAINS AND SENIOR OFFICERS HAVE BEEN INVITED TO A DINNER CELEBRATION AT THE DEUTSCHE KLUB AT 1600 HRS. WE WILL ASSEMBLE ON THE PIER AT 1530 HRS. I SHALL REJOIN YOU AND CAPTAIN SCHÖNBERG AT THAT TIME. PLEASE BRING ONE OR TWO MEMBERS OF YOUR SENIOR STAFF.

I WOULD ALSO RESPECTFULLY REQUEST THAT LIEUTENANT HEINRICH VON SPEE BE GRANTED TEMPORARY LEAVE OF HIS DUTIES TO ATTEND THIS EVENT AS WELL. I HAVE SENT A SIMILAR REQUEST TO CAPTAIN SCHÖNBERG, SO THAT I MIGHT HAVE THE OPPORTUNITY TO VISIT WITH MY SONS.

I LOOK FORWARD TO RAISING A GLASS WITH YOU THIS EVENING, JULIUS.

VIZEADMIRAL M. VON SPEE
[*End Signal*]

Maerker was not surprised that the admiral had requested the presence of both of his sons at dinner. International law limited wartime port calls to three combatant ships at any given time, so it was not coincidental that the two ships chosen to accompany the flagship into the port each had one of Graf Spee's sons as a member of its crew.

There was much to do before the dinner hour. The big cruiser needed coal and provisions, and attending to those needs alone would take the better part of the day. Also, the calm water of the harbor offered a rare opportunity for the shipwrights and engineers to finish the repairs begun after the battle. The reality was that although the squadron's mood was celebratory, they were still very much at war. In fact, he realized, their resounding success outside of Coronel might actually make the coming weeks and months even more dangerous for the German squadron. Surely the British would swiftly send more ships to avenge their losses. That sobering thought made him all the more determined to ensure that twenty-two hours from now, *Gneisenau* would be as ready as possible to clash once again with their enemies.

He was also determined to ensure that the bundle of letters addressed to Ilsa would be sent by courier—along with the rest of *Gneisenau's* home-bound mail—to the consular offices that morning.

◆

MOST OF THE DAY was a frenzy of activity. Maerker issued a shipwide notification that all crew members in good standing would be granted limited shore leave—but only after all necessary duties had been completed. The prospect of going ashore in a modern city, with a welcoming German population, was a powerful motivator for officers and enlisted men alike. Coaling operations and the subsequent cleanup were finished in record time. The shipwrights and engineers completed their remaining repair work before noon. Supply officers went ashore to arrange the delivery of provisions. The procession of supply ships from the wharf began immediately and continued on throughout the day.

During this time, junior officers conducted tours of the ship for dozens of German citizens who had arrived on all manner of small vessels. Under Commander Pochhammer's direction, *Gneisenau's* sailors checked the papers of each civilian, to help ensure that British spies could not sneak onto the cruiser. The men and women who did come aboard were still granted only limited access to the weather decks. Those restrictions did little to dampen the spirits of the smartly-dressed visitors, who walked about wide-eyed, chattering happily amongst themselves and peppering the sailors with excited questions.

Maerker spent the day personally inspecting each section of the ship and checking in with officers and watch commanders to ensure they were making good time and were receiving all of the supplies and provisions they needed.

As the dinner hour neared, Maerker finally returned to his cabin near the bridge. Reluctantly, he donned his ceremonial dark blue dress jacket. He was generally uncomfortable with ostentatious attire, and he found this particular version of the naval uniform to be his least favorite. He debated leaving his hat in the cabin and attending the celebration bare-headed, but then thought better of it—not wanting to inadvertently insult anyone by his lack of proper headwear. He reflected on the irony that the last time he had worn the formal double-breasted jacket had been at a reception hosting British Admiral Martyn Jerram in Tsingtao that very summer. How the world had changed in but a few months.

Checking his reflection in the small mirror mounted to the bulkhead beside his cot, he adjusted his starched white collar and determined that his appearance would probably not embarrass anyone—and was therefore satisfactory. Ilsa, of course, would have clucked over him and made any number of fussy adjustments before pronouncing him as being presentable.

Thinking of Ilsa compelled him to open the steel cabinet beside his cot. It was comforting to see the empty space on the bottom shelf where the bundle of letters to her had once resided. He had penned and added to the stack another quick note the night before, recalling the events of the battle and mentioning their planned stop in Valparaiso. After so many months at sea, he was extremely happy that all of those letters had left with the first courier that morning and were now at the consulate, awaiting delivery to Germany. With any luck—perhaps sometime in the next five or six weeks—Ilsa would indeed be sitting in their parlor, opening the first correspondence from her distant husband since before the war began.

Leaving his cabin, he paused briefly in the wheelhouse to formally leave the command of the ship in Pochhammer's hands—along with the responsibility of seeing to the remaining duties before tomorrow morning's departure.

From among his senior staff, Maerker had chosen Lieutenant-Commander Busch to accompany him to dinner—to honor the Senior Gunnery Officer's exceptional performance during the battle. Busch was waiting for him on the quarterdeck, looking much more comfortable in his dress blues than Maerker was in his own. Young Lieutenant Heinrich von Spee was waiting as well, and he came to attention upon seeing the captain.

"At ease, Lieutenant," said Maerker.

"Good afternoon, Captain," said Busch, who was clearly more pleased by the prospect of going ashore than Maerker. "What a scene." He indicated the throng of people along the wharf that had grown throughout the day. More than a thousand people were now gathered, and their cheers and singing were audible even from *Gneisenau's* distant anchorage.

"Indeed," agreed Maerker. "Someone must have passed the word that the admiral was coming ashore."

Below them, beside the aft starboard boarding platform, several of the ship's boats were tied up, and at least fifty of the officers and men were preparing to clamber aboard after the inbound cargo was offloaded. With much of the required shipboard duties now complete, *Gneisenau's* crewmen were eagerly departing the ship for their few hours of leave. At least one-hundred more men were waiting above on the aft weather deck for the next wave of boats to take them ashore.

Maerker, Busch, and the younger von Spee descended the ladder to the platform and were assisted into the largest of the waiting boats—one of the ship's steam pinnaces. This particular boat had already seen considerable use throughout the day and had most recently brought numerous pallets of fresh fruit and vegetables from the dockside warehouses that were still disgorging their contents. A few empty wooden crates remained in the boat, and Maerker chose to sit upon a stack of them. From this makeshift higher perch, he had a better view of the port as they approached. He watched the extraordinary scene on shore as the pinnace chugged landward. People had crowded along every available portion of the waterfront, and some men and boys had even clambered atop bollards and lampposts to get a better view.

As they drew near, the pilot steered the boat toward a pier that had been roped off and was being used as a staging area for distributing supplies and provisions to the German ships. A low floating dock was tethered to the pier, upon which the squadron's paymasters and supply officers were directing activities. On the pier, numerous laborers with wagons and carts unloaded crates, barrels, and boxes.

One of *Scharnhorst's* pinnaces had arrived just ahead of them. At the sight of the admiral stepping up out of the boat, the crowd erupted in a deafening fanfare. From somewhere on the wharf, a band began to play a clumsy rendition of *"Heil dir im Siegerkranz,"* although it seemed few in the assembly could remember the words. With his dress blue uniform, the admiral was wearing a dark blue bicorn hat, trimmed with gold braid and feathers. He was smiling broadly, enjoying this moment of patriotic celebration. Maerker noticed that von Spee had brought with him his chief of staff, Filietz, as well as Captain Schultz.

The pilot brought the pinnace in behind *Scharnhorst's* boat. Sailors secured the lines and assisted the officers as they disembarked. Admiral von Spee strode over to Maerker, who saluted. Graf Spee quickly returned the salute and clasped Maerker's hand.

"Good to see you, Julius," he said. "You as well, Lieutenant-Commander. Your men performed expertly against the British. A fine job all around." He turned and beamed at his son, then embraced the young man, who appeared genuinely surprised. "Welcome to Chile, Heinrich. It has been quite the odyssey."

Captain Schönberg arrived in *Nürnberg's* steam launch a few minutes later. Accompanying him were a lieutenant-commander whom Maerker did not recognize and von Spee's older son, Otto. The admiral greeted them warmly as well, also embracing Otto. Graf Spee then smiled broadly at his assembled officers and stated, "I understand a party is being thrown in our honor. Politeness dictates that we attend." He and the officers then strode up the ramp toward the pier and into the cheering crowd.

◆

LATER THAT EVENING, Maerker received a full report from Commander Pochhammer upon his return to the ship. All of *Gneisenau's* battle-related damage had been satisfactorily repaired. Additionally, most of the necessary engineering work had been finished, although one repair team was still working on a faulty starboard ballast pump. Three dozen eager volunteers with various skills and specialties had been accepted into their ranks, and junior officers were already beginning the new crewmen's indoctrination into shipboard life.

Most importantly, for the first time since they had departed Tsingtao that summer, the ship's refrigerated compartments were once again brimming with food of every imaginable type, and the storerooms were packed with supplies, equipment, and replacement parts.

Maerker noted that the shore leave, although brief, had been a powerful tonic for the mood of the entire crew. As he took a final walk-through of the ship's spaces, he overheard numerous conversations among the men—all discussing what they had done with their few precious hours of leave. All of the men reported having been greeted warmly by the local residents and business owners alike. They had been treated to free drinks, meals, and even complimentary rides on the funicular railroad trams that climbed to the top of the hillsides overlooking the port.

Of course, many men sought word of the war in Europe and had pored over local German newspapers describing the latest developments. For the first time, the sailors had seen maps showing the position of the front lines and the disposition of the troops in the West and the East. While it was heartening to see how far into French territory the German forces had driven, it was sobering that portions of Prussia were still held by the massive Russian armies.

Most of all, Maerker heard stories of the women. After all, the crew had been away from a proper port city for several months. It was only natural for the men's thoughts to be consumed by women. He overheard tales of playful German girls and shy Chilean ladies, each of whom was more beautiful than the last. If even half of the preposterous stories were to be believed, most of Valparaiso's young women simply could not resist the amorous charms of so many dashing and gallant young sailors. Maerker smiled to himself as he finished his rounds, returning to his cabin well after midnight.

He slept for only a few hours, awakening and dressing in time to be on the bridge in advance of their scheduled departure. The sun had not yet risen when the three warships, once again led by *Scharnhorst*, slipped quietly from the port and headed due west upon the dark sea. When the lights of Valparaiso were no longer visible astern, the flagship changed course to the southwest and increased speed to twelve knots.

Maerker left the bridge, stepped out into the brisk sea air, and inhaled deeply. Their next rendezvous at Más Afuera was a full day's steam away, and he realized that beyond that next stop, the admiral had not yet revealed his plan of action, nor any subsequent destination. Once again, they were sailing into the unknown—and despite the brilliant sunrise to the east, he knew they were steaming back into the ominous darkness of war.

# PART FOUR

## Ghosts and Greyhounds

# NINETEEN

*Thursday, November 5, 1914*
*Eastern Mouth of the Strait of Magellan*

CAPTAIN LUCE took another hesitant step forward into the dark, oil-streaked water and was grateful for the high rubber boots provided to him by the engineering lieutenant. He ducked through the low metal doorway and found that he could not raise his head any higher than his current crouched stance. From this awkward position, he surveyed the cramped compartment that had borne the brunt of the explosion from the German shell. Located some thirty feet from the stern—on the port side, at the waterline—it had once been a wedge-shaped auxiliary machine space and storage area. The small compartment was nestled in the space between the main engineering spaces and the outer hull.

Compared to the modest size of the compartment itself, the hole in the exterior hull was enormous. The ragged opening was nearly ten feet long and more than five feet tall at its widest point. The inch-thick steel plates of the outer hull had been rent apart, bowed inward by the powerful explosion—their sharp jagged edges protruding savagely into the compartment. The lower third of the opening was beneath the waterline, and through the hole lapped dark green water that nearly reached the top of Luce's boots. Muted gray daylight shone through the hole and dimly illuminated the space, casting a pattern of dancing, undulating reflections upon the ruined scene within.

In addition to tearing a huge gash in the hull, the impact of the German shell had crumpled the metal support beams and spars within the compartment. Dozens of rivets had been torn free, and the support for what had once been a hanging rack for equipment had been severed. The sagging metal of the ruined assembly above Luce's head kept him from standing fully upright.

Most troubling of all was the damage to the interior bulkhead, which was visibly crumpled and stove inward toward the interior of the ship. Beyond that thin steel wall, Luce knew, was the curved armored deck that protected the main engineering spaces and the port side propeller shaft. He realized once again that his ship had been extraordinarily lucky. Had this round penetrated more deeply before it had detonated, the result would have been catastrophic. Instead, the damage had been limited to this small space.

Immediately after the explosion, engineers had frantically sealed and secured the interior compartment door to keep surging seawater from flooding the ship. For the next several hours, shipwrights and carpenters reinforced the bulkheads of the punctured compartment—wedging timbers and steel rods against its sides and hastily welding metal plates over the bulging and leaking seams. The makeshift repairs had held for the first few days of their flight southward, but as *Glasgow* made her way east through the Strait of Magellan, the leaks had become more pronounced. Finally, heeding the pleas of the engineering commander, Luce had ordered them to drop anchor in a sheltered bay near the eastern end of the Strait. Here, with the waters calm and the threat of German pursuit less likely, the engineers and shipwrights were able to pump some of the water from the space, remove the temporary braces and welded plates, and truly survey the extent of the damage.

The problem was bad enough that the captain had been summoned to see it for himself.

"It's worse than we thought, sir," said the engineering lieutenant, standing immediately outside the compartment door, peering into the space. "First of all, see that bulkhead there?" he asked, pointing to the bent inner steel wall.

Luce nodded. "We're lucky it held and the explosion didn't do more damage."

"Not all of that damage is from the explosion, sir. When we're steaming at more than ten knots, seawater surges in here through the hole. The initial blast warped and weakened the plates, but the water has done even more damage, bending and pushing that bulkhead inward at least four more inches in the past two days. I'm worried that even with it braced on the other side, it could spring a leak and quickly flood the main engineering spaces.

"There's more, sir," the lieutenant continued, directing the captain's attention to the sagging metal above his head. "The damaged overhead has gotten worse, too. Last night we discovered that the deck above this space is now compromised and has detached from the hull joints in two places. In a heavy sea, regardless of how slowly we're steaming, it might come apart completely and collapse—and we could have breaches on two decks simultaneously."

"What can we do to keep her afloat long enough to get to a proper port and dry dock?" asked Luce, who ducked back through the doorway into the passage. He stood upright again with a grimace as he straightened his back and stretched.

"We'll have to try to patch the hole in the outer hull, sir. Unfortunately, we don't have the materials or the capability to properly repair the hull plates themselves, so we'll have to make do. Shipwrights Logan and Smith believe that they can shore up the hole with some of the larger timbers we carry in storage. They would essentially build a wall of wooden beams inside the hull, within this compartment, covering the hole to keep most— if not all—of the water out. They would also brace the overhead to keep it from collapsing. Finally, we would reinstall all of the braces and welded plates that we'd been using around the outside of this compartment—just in case."

"How much time do they need?"

"About twelve hours, sir."

Luce briefly pondered the risk of waiting there, exposed and vulnerable, for half a day and realized he had little choice. Although the German squadron could come barreling thought the Strait or around Cape Horn at any time, *Glasgow* was simply not seaworthy in her current state. The Falklands were still a two-day steam away, and even then, Port Stanley had no ship repair facilities. In fact, the only place along the South American coast that might have adequate dry dock facilities was Rio de Janeiro, which was more than two thousand miles distant—and even then, the Brazilians would likely enforce wartime neutrality rules and prevent Luce from making any significant repairs. He feared that he might be forced to sail on even farther to have the hull properly repaired, perhaps to Gibraltar or even all the way to Portsmouth. In her current state, *Glasgow* would never make it to any of those distant ports. If Luce was to retain any hope of rejoining the war and avenging the losses from Coronel, he knew that he had to make temporary repairs now. Although patching her steel hull with wooden planking was not an ideal or elegant solution, it appeared to be the best option for the time being—and it might work long enough to allow *Glasgow* to limp to Port Stanley and then onward to another port where proper repairs might be possible.

"Go ahead and start," said Luce with a resigned nod. "The sooner we can be back on our way, the better."

Luce exchanged the rubber boots for his shoes and left the aft engineering area with much on his mind. Not only was the damage to the ship more extensive than he originally thought, but he was also worried about the men's morale since the battle. He knew that after all that had happened, he must address the crew. Now that he was forced to pause and make repairs to the ship, this would be his best opportunity to speak to them. He briefly stopped by the bridge and instructed Commander Thompson to muster the entire crew on the aft weather deck in thirty minutes. He then returned to the compartment that was serving as his temporary quarters while the repairs to his actual cabin were completed.

He reflected that even the minor damage to his quarters was an indicator of how lucky *Glasgow* had been. His empty pantry had been wrecked, and a cabinet mounted within his sleeping compartment had been dislodged from the bulkhead. A sheaf of papers on his desk—mostly copies of recent cable traffic—had been scorched by one of the red-hot shell fragments, and the mirror mounted beside his wardrobe was cracked. The repair crews found jagged pieces of the German shell strewn about the compartment, each reeking with toxic fumes from the unexploded yellow powder it had once contained. Had that shell detonated anywhere along its impact path, it could have caused considerably more destruction, particularly to the forward turret's ammunition hoist—and the men working therein. Instead, the damage had been mostly cosmetic, if odiferous.

Of course, the rest of the squadron had not been so lucky. Luce had heard nothing from *Otranto* since she veered away at the beginning of the battle—and he hoped that she had been able to get safely away. *Good Hope* and *Monmouth* now lay at the bottom of the sea, having taken with them more than sixteen hundred souls. The deaths of so many of their comrades weighed heavily upon the officers and men, and Luce could not recall a time when his ship had felt so eerily quiet.

The voyage since the end of the battle had been an unnerving combination of frantic flight and funereal gloom. After seeing the distant muzzle flashes that had marked *Monmouth's* final gruesome moments, *Glasgow* had fled south as fast as her damaged hull would allow. The German squadron continued to broadcast their powerful jamming signals while they hunted in vain for *Glasgow*, and it was several more hours before the light cruiser had steamed far enough south to be out of effective jamming range. Luce was then finally able to get a message through to *Canopus*. Captain Grant replied that he was turning his ship about and he too would chart a new course back through the Strait of Magellan toward the Falklands.

For Luce, the voyage southward was an excruciating exercise in self-doubt and regret. When not commanding on the bridge or inspecting the progress of the few minor repairs that the shipwrights were able to undertake, he kept to his temporary cabin — taking his meals there and writing a detailed account of the battle and the events both before and after. He resolved to have his report ready to send to the Admiralty as soon as they were within wireless range of the Falklands station.

The decision to leave the stricken *Monmouth* weighed heavily upon him. He knew, on some level, that the imminent German pursuit had left him with no choice but to retreat. Still, he ran the scenario through his mind repeatedly — wondering if there had been some alternative that could have perhaps saved some of *Monmouth's* crew. Although each time he came to the same conclusion, acknowledging that he had made the proper decision offered him no solace. He recalled, again and again, the sight of *Monmouth's* sailors clinging to her canted decks. Their desperate, doomed faces returned, unbidden, to his consciousness day and night — haunting him and causing doubt to creep back into his thoughts. He wondered if those wretched images would ever leave his mind. He thought of his last conversation with Captain Brandt, two days before the battle, when they had spoken privately aboard *Otranto*. He recalled the distant, fearful look in the other man's eyes as Brandt had recounted his grim nightmare — and its premonition of his death.

Throughout the restless nighttime hours, Luce would unwillingly re-live brief portions of the battle as they flashed across his mind. Again, he would flinch at the blinding glare of the massive explosion that had torn apart *Good Hope*. Other times, he would hear the menacing shriek of the German rounds passing overhead or the clattering hailstorm of shell fragments pelting *Glasgow's* upper works. He felt, repeatedly, the ominous shudder throughout the ship as the large shell exploded near the stern, rending the huge hole that had nearly sunk them.

The seas became calmer as they steamed southward, and the two-day voyage to the western mouth of the Strait was uneventful. *Glasgow's* wireless operators heard no further indications that the Germans were in pursuit, but Luce was cautious nonetheless. He loitered briefly at the mouth of the Strait, with all hands at action stations, in case the enemy had somehow beaten them there and set up an ambush. No ships of any type — let alone any warships — were sighted for two hours, so Luce gave the order to proceed through the Strait at twelve knots.

As they entered the channel, the wireless operators finally made their first contact with the distant but powerful Falkland Islands wireless station. Luce immediately had the telegraphists dispatch to the Admiralty his report of the battle and its aftermath. He was certain by now that some other account of the battle — undoubtedly from German sources — had made its way to London. His report would help dispel any inaccuracies that the enemy might have conveyed. He also hoped it would give the Admiralty the opportunity to plan their next move, now that von Spee's squadron had virtually no impediment to entering the Atlantic and wreaking havoc upon Allied interests there.

*Glasgow* passed Punta Arenas in the middle of the night, with all of the ship's lights off and her portholes blackened—keeping as close to the far shore as their old charts would safely allow, some twelve miles away, in the hope that her passage would go unnoticed by anyone in the sleeping town. The bridge officers watched the few distant yellow lights of Punta Arenas slip by in silence and were relieved to see no obvious movement or reaction in the port as they passed. As they continued to traverse the channel, they sighted no other vessels. The following day's travel was slower, for the engineers reported increasing leaks in the damaged area of the hull.

As *Glasgow* neared the eastern end of the Strait, the wireless room picked up part of a faint but unencrypted wireless message—most likely from a German merchant vessel—that mentioned the recent presence of von Spee's squadron at Valparaiso Harbor. Luce breathed a bit easier, knowing now that if the German admiral had put in at Valparaiso after the battle, it was highly unlikely that the enemy squadron was yet pursuing *Glasgow* or *Canopus* through the Strait. Without the imminent threat of enemy pursuit, he could now consider his engineering commander's request to stop the ship and inspect the damaged hull.

Now that he had personally viewed the damage, his heart sank. His ship was essentially unseaworthy. She would require significant repairs at a fully equipped dry dock—a process that would likely take weeks.

He buttoned his woolen topcoat, retrieved his hat from behind the door, and left the cabin—heading topside. Commander Thompson, also attired in his formal outerwear, stood beside the railing overlooking the aft weather deck. He saluted the captain and said, "The crew is assembled, sir."

"Thank you, Commander," replied Luce with a return salute. He took his position at the railing and looked aft. Below him, some four hundred men stood silently, shoulder to shoulder, looking up at him in anticipation. The last time he had addressed the crew in such a manner had been back in August, when the realities of war were still an abstraction for these men. The morning was crisp and cold, with a low gray overcast that mirrored the melancholy mood of those assembled below. At this moment they needed him to say something reassuring, something that would help make sense of the fact that two entire crews of men just like themselves had perished just a few nights before.

He had prepared no formal remarks, so he simply began. "Brave men of *Glasgow*," he said loudly, his voice carrying out over the calm waters around them, "today we grieve our fallen comrades, may God rest their souls. Four days ago, in the twilight of All Saints Day, many hundreds of our Royal Navy brethren aboard *Good Hope* and *Monmouth* lost their lives in combat against a powerful and capable foe. During that terrible battle, we lost many friends. We also witnessed acts of extraordinary courage and sacrifice. In addition to the courage of those among the fallen, each of you — the men of *Glasgow* — fought as bravely and selflessly as any soldier or sailor who has ever defended the Crown.

"I am immensely proud of every man here. In the direst of circumstances, in heavy seas, while outnumbered and outgunned, with hundreds of enemy shells raining down around us, you performed your duties with determination and resolve. In every portion of this ship, all of you — officers and men alike — were examples of dedication and unwavering courage."

He paused before continuing. "Still, for the past several days I have been troubled by a question. Why were we aboard *Glasgow* spared while so many of our comrades perished? Was it because we had more experience than the crews of our sister ships? Doubtful, for our experience alone did not keep hundreds of enemy shells from striking us instead of falling harmlessly into the sea. We could attribute it to simple luck, I suppose, and I do believe we were very fortunate — but I do not believe that luck is the entire answer either." He paused again, and his voice lowered — but it was clearly audible in the still air. "I like to think that we survived because our work is yet unfinished."

Luce leaned forward and grasped the steel railing before him with both hands. "Earlier this morning, I inspected the damage to our hull. As some of you already know, our ship will need extensive repairs before we are able to rejoin the fight against our enemies. Our shipwrights will have a temporary solution in place this evening. Unfortunately, we are a long distance from any port where we may effect permanent repairs. Despite that fact, I will do everything in my power to get her properly patched up as quickly as is possible." He raised his voice once more. "Make no mistake — there will be an hour of retribution. It is my hope that *Glasgow* will be present at that hour — for we have a score to settle with our enemies."

Murmurs of agreement rumbled through the assembly below.

"So, take heart in this dark hour," Luce continued. "Today we grieve, but tomorrow, *Glasgow* rejoins the fight!"

At this, the men burst into a spirited cheer — many of them pumping fists into the air. It was the first time Luce had seen smiles among the men since before the battle. He turned to Thompson and said, "Commander, you may dismiss the men." Thompson saluted once again, as did each of the four hundred men below.

Luce made his way back toward the bridge, deep in thought. Like the men under his command, he felt a burning desire to participate in whatever vengeance the Admiralty might have in store for von Spee's squadron. To do so meant that he had to get *Glasgow's* hull repaired without having to steam all the way back to Portsmouth.

◆

AT MID-DAY, Luce received a wireless transmission from Captain Grant of *Canopus*. Because of the old battleship's slower speed, *Glasgow* had actually beaten her to the Strait, and *Canopus* was only now about half-way through the channel herself. Luce informed Grant of *Glasgow's* location and her condition. The two captains agreed that *Canopus* would rendezvous at *Glasgow's* current anchorage and then the two warships would steam onward to the Falklands together. Throughout the day and into the evening, rhythmic sawing of wood and thumping and pinging of hammers echoed from the stern of the ship.

The temporary repairs to the damaged compartment were completed ahead of schedule, a few minutes before midnight. Not long thereafter, Luce was in his quarters when the officer of the watch piped down to him that the approaching *Canopus* had been sighted in the darkness. The captain returned to the bridge and was met there by Commander Thompson. Both of them took binoculars and stepped outside the wheelhouse onto the flying bridge. The southerly wind had picked up during the night, and now chill gusts bit into exposed skin and drove like needles through the officers' topcoats.

Looking though the lenses, the two officers scanned the dark waters of the channel to the southwest. The battleship was traveling without lights, but her pallid bulk was visible in the dim moonlight as she approached, still two miles distant.

"Mister Lyon," said Luce through the open door to the officer of the watch, "have the signalmen use the lamp to send her a message. Tell Captain Grant that we'll be on our way immediately. Then bring us up to steam and prepare to weigh anchor."

"Yes, sir."

*Canopus* was considerably closer now, and both Luce and Thompson could make out more details in the gray half-light—the blunt slab of her prow, her asymmetrical funnels, her masts and low-slung upper works, as well as her two old but massive 12-inch gun turrets. She was a relic from a bygone era of shipbuilding.

"So, what do you think?" asked Thompson. "If this old girl and her big guns had been part of our line at Coronel, how would the battle have gone?"

Luce considered the question—one he had asked himself multiple times during the past few days and nights. "I don't think she would have made much difference, Will. She's not any faster than *Otranto*, so she would have limited our line's speed. The Germans would have been able to maneuver, much as they did, to mostly stay out of her range. About the only thing she might have done is give von Spee enough pause that he delayed his attack long enough for us to slip away in the darkness after sunset."

"Slinking away under the cover of nightfall doesn't sound like Cradock's style," replied Thompson.

A crisp series of bright flashes from the forward flank of the darkened battleship indicated that her signalmen were replying to Luce's message.

"No, I don't think so, either," said Luce. "I think we would have fought them either way. Cradock would have tried to turn our disadvantage to an advantage. He would have kept *Good Hope* in the van, followed by *Canopus*, then *Monmouth*, and then us. He would have attempted to close the distance and engage the two enemy armored cruisers with his two biggest ships, allowing *Monmouth* and *Glasgow* to try to outgun their light cruisers."

"That sounds more like the admiral," said Thompson with a smile and a nod.

"Except that it would not have worked."

The officer of the watch interrupted them by announcing, "*Canopus* asks how seaworthy we are, sir."

"Tell them that we have made temporary repairs but are limited to ten knots," said Luce.

"Aye, sir."

Luce turned back to his first officer. "I think that having *Canopus* with us still could not have won the day, mainly because von Spee is no fool. You saw how he matched Cradock, tactic for tactic. The Germans had advantages over us in speed, range, and weight of shell, not to mention visibility. Like *Good Hope*, old *Canopus* over there is a plodding museum piece. Admiral von Spee would have continually danced away from them both with his big armored cruisers, all the while lobbing salvo after salvo at them. Soon enough, both of our older ships would have been crippled, slowing them down even further. Between us and *Monmouth*, we might have been able to damage one or two of their light cruisers, but even that is a stretch. As we saw, the poor visibility and the heavy seas made for miserable shooting conditions—at least for us. With *Good Hope* and *Canopus* hobbled, the Germans would have been able to pick away at us, piece by piece." He sighed. "In the end, if *Canopus* had been with us, I think that there would just be one more British warship on the bottom of the sea."

Thompson nodded silently.

"If we are to beat this German squadron," continued Luce thoughtfully, "the next time we meet them in battle, we must exceed them in speed, maneuverability, and weight of shell—ship for ship."

"Well, that eliminates creaky *Canopus* from consideration," said Thompson, "as well as just about any other old rust bucket the Admiralty have sitting around in mothballs."

Luce nodded grimly. "Cradock repeatedly asked for bigger, faster, more powerful ships. The Admiralty denied him at every turn. Perhaps now they will be forced to reconsider."

"What you said this morning—about our being present at the hour of retribution—how likely do you think that will be?"

"Truly, I don't know," said Luce grimly. "Regardless of what the First Lord or the Admiralty think, I am convinced that it will be soon, perhaps within a fortnight, that von Spee and his squadron will round the Cape and steam into the Atlantic. When that does happen, if we've been sent on to Gibraltar or Portsmouth to make repairs, we'll never have the opportunity."

The battleship's lamp flashed again. In a few moments, a signals officer stepped out onto the flying bridge. "Sir, *Canopus* asks us to accompany her on her port beam so that she might shield us from some of the wind and sea."

"Quite neighborly of Captain Grant," said Thompson as he followed Luce back into the wheelhouse.

"Agreed," said Luce. He addressed the signals officer. "Tell him we're thankful and are underway. Mister Lyon, weigh anchor."

"Yes, sir. Weighing anchor."

*Glasgow* steamed out into the channel, assuming a position on the leeward side of the old battleship. *Canopus's* bulk did slightly reduce the force of the southerly wind and sea upon the damaged cruiser, and Luce found it comforting to once again be in the company of another Royal Navy warship. Coordinating by lamp, the respective bridge crews brought both of the ships up to ten knots, and together they steamed eastward into the blustery South Atlantic.

◆

THE MEN of *Glasgow* and *Canopus* had never heard so few people make so much noise. Scores of Port Stanley's residents had assembled dockside as the two warships steamed into the harbor. All were cheering. Many of the women were waving scarves or ringing handbells, and some of the men and boys were banging sticks upon pots and pans. The townsfolk had received word of the disastrous outcome of the battle and had turned out to welcome the crew of *Glasgow* back to their adoptive home port. The show of support was a welcome salve for the still-raw emotions of *Glasgow's* crew.

After both ships had dropped anchor, Luce sent a flag request for coal, and the lone collier in port pulled alongside. Nearly fifty of the townsfolk requested—and were granted—access to come aboard and help the grateful crew with the coaling operations. Governor Allardyce also came aboard to speak privately with Captain Luce, expressing his condolences for the losses of the officers and men of *Good Hope* and *Monmouth* and passing along the most recent confidential cable traffic from the Admiralty. Allardyce was particularly saddened by the passing of Admiral Cradock, as the two men had become friends during *Good Hope's* brief stay in Port Stanley in October.

Luce had not yet expected a reply from London to his report of the battle sent several days earlier, but one of the messages handed over by the governor was dated that morning and appeared to anticipate Luce's presence in Port Stanley. It instructed him to immediately make for Rio de Janeiro by way of Montevideo, as soon as *Glasgow* was coaled. *Canopus* was ordered to remain at Port Stanley as a beached, stationary artillery platform, to help protect the port from direct attack—should the German squadron venture into the South Atlantic before other Royal Navy vessels could be dispatched.

Another message that Luce found of particular interest was a more detailed account of Admiral von Spee's recent visit to the port of Valparaiso. It had been drafted by Charles Newman, the British consul in Valparaiso whom Luce and Brandt had met some four weeks earlier. Interestingly, according to Newman, only *Scharnhorst*, *Gneisenau*, and *Nürnberg* had anchored at the port—and none of those three ships had exhibited any obvious signs of battle damage. Neither *Dresden* and *Leipzig* had been seen, and their whereabouts were unknown. Luce held out some hope that one or both of the enemy light cruisers had been damaged in the battle.

Luce reflected again on the Admiralty's new instructions for him and *Glasgow*. The message was curiously brief, and it made no mention of additional orders or deployments. Most likely, all of Britain was reeling from the news of their defeat at Coronel, and this message to him had been hurriedly sent to expedite his return northward while the Admiralty planned its next move. Regardless of what Churchill might have in store for *Glasgow*, the fact that their listed destination was Rio de Janeiro gave Luce the kernel of an idea. He composed two brief messages for governor Allardyce to have transmitted by the Falklands wireless station. The first was to the Admiralty, acknowledging his new orders and estimating *Glasgow's* date of arrival in Rio. The second message was to his old friend, Malcolm Robertson. That second message contained a confidential request that he hoped the minister could fulfill.

Governor Allardyce solemnly thanked Luce and his men for their service and departed, heading off to the wireless station with Luce's messages—after which he planned to meet with Captain Grant on *Canopus* to confer on the planned defenses of the island.

There could be no shore leave for *Glasgow's* crew in Port Stanley, much to their disappointment. Luce's orders were clear. As soon as the coaling was complete, the stokers raised steam again. After a thorough check by the engineers to ensure that the temporary repairs to her hull breach were still holding, the light cruiser made her way out of the harbor. *Canopus* fired a parting salute from one of her small deck guns, and within a few minutes, *Glasgow* was once again steaming out into the open ocean.

◆

AT HER REDUCED SPEED, it took *Glasgow* six days to reach Rio de Janeiro, with one brief stop in Montevideo to coal. As the lush green peaks above the Brazilian capital came into view, Luce reflected on the last time *Glasgow* had made this approach back in July, when the mood of his crew had been so much more buoyant. Of course, that had been before the declaration of war—and the global conflagration of madness that had ensued. Although it had been only four months ago, it seemed as though that previous visit had occurred many years previously. So much had happened since then that Luce could scarcely remember what it had felt like to be anticipating a homeward journey and the end of their commission.

In the early morning, after exchanging customary salutes with the Brazilian warships in port, *Glasgow* dropped anchor in the outer harbor—in much the same spot the ship had occupied when last moored there. The rising sun was already bright in the eastern sky, heralding the beginning of a day much warmer than the men of *Glasgow* had experienced in many weeks.

Minutes after the cruiser's anchors disappeared beneath the calm waters, the wireless room received a message for Captain Luce from the British Ministry. Luce was pleased to see that the message was a request from Minister Robertson to come aboard the ship immediately. Somewhat cryptically, the message ended with the phrase "DON'T GET TOO COMFORTABLE AT YOUR CURRENT ANCHORAGE." Luce had the wireless operators send a reply granting permission. Within forty minutes, the bridge crew spotted a steam cutter approaching the ship.

Minister Robertson was piped aboard, and a petty officer escorted him to the senior officers' wardroom—where Luce and Thompson were waiting. The petty officer closed the door behind Robertson, leaving the three men alone.

"Welcome aboard, Malcolm," said Luce, shaking his hand. Robertson had already doffed his hat, and his cream-colored linen jacket was casually draped over one arm.

"Hello John," replied Robertson with a smile. "Hello again, Commander Thompson." He shook the first officer's hand as well. "Welcome back to Rio de Janeiro, gentlemen. We really must arrange our next meeting under better circumstances. The last time we saw each other, the whole damned world declared war. This time, you've come limping into our port with a big hole in your ship."

Robertson continued soberly. "Please accept my sincere regrets for the losses of your fellow officers and men aboard *Good Hope* and *Monmouth*. I'm truly sorry. I can only imagine what you've all been through." He paused thoughtfully before continuing. "I regret that I never had the chance to meet Admiral Cradock or Captains Francklin or Brandt."

"All good men," offered Luce thoughtfully.

"As are the two of you. I'm glad you're still with us. The first report we heard—through German diplomatic channels, of course—said that your entire squadron had been destroyed."

"Very nearly so," said Luce. "If that big shell had struck us just a few feet off in almost any direction, we might not be here either. We still do not know what has become of *Otranto*."

"I certainly hope she made it safely away as well," said Robertson. He set his hat upon the table. "With regard to your damaged ship, I have some positive news. After I received your cable, John, I made a few discreet inquiries with some friends in the transitional Brazilian government. The timing couldn't have been better, really. This is an election year, as it turns out, and the new Brazilian president who was elected back in March finally takes office today, the fifteenth of November. The last several weeks have been rather chaotic, with all of the transitional mayhem, as you might imagine. The new Brazilian Minister of Marine Affairs owes me a few favors—and it turns out that neither he nor the new president are too happy with the underhanded operations of some of the local German agents since the war broke out. Based on your circumstances, the minister intends to have your warship declared 'unseaworthy and in need of repair'. Under wartime rules, this designation will allow *Glasgow* to stay here beyond the customary twenty-four-hour limit—up to two weeks, actually."

"That's extraordinary," said Luce, marveling at the power of Robertson's diplomatic skills and the seemingly effortless manner in which he employed them.

"Excellent," said Thompson. "Now we just have to figure out how to get her repaired in just a fortnight."

"I'm not quite done, Commander," offered Robertson with a wry chuckle. "Remember that the Brazilian Minister owes me more than one favor. He was also able to make arrangements to have *Glasgow* immediately transferred to the Brazilian navy's floating dry dock in the naval shipyard. A French firm operates the dry dock—with Brazilian labor, of course—refurbishing and refitting the Brazilian navy's destroyers and patrol boats. I've already executed a contract with that firm to have the repairs to *Glasgow* completed within the next ten days."

Luce was momentarily speechless. When he finally found his voice, he said, "Malcolm, much like your Brazilian minister, it seems the list of favors that *I* owe you is growing to the point that I doubt I'll ever be able to repay them."

"Nonsense, Captain. I'm just happy to be able to help a worthwhile cause. Most of my days are spent navigating some ridiculous diplomatic impasse or quagmire, dealing with self-serving bureaucrats who have no incentive to accomplish anything or haven't the courage to try. You and your men, by contrast, risk your lives daily in the defense of the realm—actually *doing* something to win this war. If anything, it is I who owe the favor to you."

"I am extremely grateful," said Luce, who then glanced at Thompson. "We may be back in this fight much sooner than I thought possible."

"On another note," continued Robertson, "I don't mean to sound impertinent, but how long has it been since either of you got a decent night's sleep? If I may say so, you both look as disheveled as this damaged ship you've dragged into port."

Thompson laughed. "Is it really that obvious?"

"I haven't slept much since the battle," admitted Luce.

"Well, I realize that your crew can still bunk on the ship, even while it is dry docked. However, I would be honored to host you both at my residence during your stay."

"We wouldn't want to impose," said Luce. "I'm sure that..."

"No imposition. In fact, as I'm not yet married, I just rattle around in that massive place. I make messes and leave things untidy just so the housekeeper will give me a scolding now and again—somehow feels more like a home that way, you know?" Robertson tilted his head mischievously. "I really must insist. I don't want to have to pull any strings with the Admiralty to compel you both to stay—it just wouldn't look right for a local politician to be ordering Royal Navy officers about. I'll have a legation driver at your disposal, so that you will have immediate access to your ship during your stay."

Luce smiled and looked at Thompson. "Looks like we don't have much of a choice in the matter."

"Excellent!" said Robertson. "I'll have a driver waiting dockside this afternoon. When *Glasgow* is safely ensconced in the dry dock, the car will bring you both over to the residence. My cook does amazing things with the local beef, so bring your appetites with you." He chuckled. "You know, if this lovely weather holds, perhaps we'll even get in that hunt I owe you."

◆

IT TOOK the better part of the day to maneuver *Glasgow* into the dry dock. After Minister Robertson departed on his cutter, Luce allowed a local harbor pilot to come aboard. Then, escorted by two tugboat steamers, the cruiser steamed under her own power some two miles northward toward the main naval shipyards. The floating dry dock was a relatively new acquisition by the Brazilian navy. Although it was not large enough to accommodate massive capital ships such as battlecruisers or battleships, it was spacious enough for *Glasgow* to fit easily within.

As the ship's engineers and the local repair foreman began to work out the technical details, Luce disembarked to visually inspect *Glasgow* from the outside. He had not left the cruiser since before the battle at Coronel, and he was not quite prepared for what he saw when he looked back at his ship from atop the wall of the dry dock. *Glasgow* was almost unrecognizable. Her hull and upper works were streaked with black coal dust, dark gray soot, and crusted salt deposits. Scars and pock marks from the impacts of thousands of small shell splinters marred the painted steel on virtually every surface of the ship. The second of her four funnels had a sizeable hole punched clean through from port to starboard near the top, and each of the other three funnels had been perforated in dozens of places.

Most striking, of course, was the gaping hole near the stern on the port side. It looked even larger from the outside, and again Luce reflected on how lucky they had been to survive. The temporary patch of timbers was still in place, visible through the ragged wound in the steel hull plates. The wooden planks were now thoroughly waterlogged and dark, and Luce wondered how much longer the makeshift barrier might have held—had they been forced to steam onward to Gibraltar or Portsmouth.

When his visual inspection was complete, Luce went back aboard and conferred with the ship's engineers and shipwrights to ensure that they were adequately prepared to assist the local workmen with the repairs.

After his meetings were concluded, he returned to his temporary cabin, where a steward helped him pack two cases of clothing and other necessities that were to be delivered to the British Ministry for the duration of his stay. As the sun sank below the hills to the west, Luce met Commander Thompson on deck and the two of them left the ship together. At the end of the gangplank, two sailors armed with rifles saluted as the officers passed. Minister Robertson had warned that German agents in Rio were even more active now than the last time *Glasgow* had been in port, so Luce ordered a continuous armed watch—to keep the ship secure from the prying eyes of any enemy who might try to sneak aboard while the ship was dry docked.

Robertson had sent two motor cars for them—one for the baggage and the other for the officers. Luce paused a moment before getting in the car. He looked back over his shoulder toward *Glasgow*, suspended so strangely in the dry dock's channel. In the evening shadows, much of her lower hull was now hidden from him, but he saw a brief flash of flame from a cutting torch somewhere along her port quarter. The laborers had already begun their work.

# TWENTY

*Saturday, November 14, 1914*
*Isla Más Afuera, Juan Fernández Islands, Chile*

CAPTAIN MAERKER REFLECTED silently that this was not how he would have chosen to celebrate his forty-fourth birthday. As far as he knew, no one else aboard was aware that it was his birthday, either, which suited him. Under the circumstances, he felt that a boisterous fete would have been inappropriate.

Three kilometers away lay the squadron's support ship *Titania*, anchored in deeper water—rising and falling on light swells under a clear blue afternoon sky. A single small steam pinnace that had been tethered beside her was making its way back toward *Scharnhorst* and the rest of the squadron. Along with the flagship, the remaining vessels of the squadron were again moored in the waters beneath the great dark cliffs of Más Afuera. Anchored out there by herself, *Titania* looked even smaller than usual—vulnerable and alone.

Lieutenant-Commander Busch stood beside Maerker, watching in silence and waiting. Below, on the weather decks fore and aft, dozens of *Gneisenau's* men had gathered at the port gunwales to observe the spectacle. There was nothing boisterous about this gathering. The sailors stood solemnly in small groups, and an eerie quiet descended over the greyhound.

The steam pinnace had traversed about half the distance toward *Scharnhorst* when the scuttling charges detonated. Multiple puffs of black smoke appeared along the length of *Titania's* gunwales, where the force of the explosions deep inside her forced their way upward through vents and deck hatches. A second later, the muffled thumps of the blasts echoed across the water. The small ship shuddered, and her masts and single funnel visibly quivered as shock waves traveled throughout her interior spaces. For a few moments, nothing seemed to happen; then she began to sink.

The decision had been the admiral's. After determining that the next phase of their journey would take the squadron around Cape Horn into the Atlantic, von Spee made a calculated assessment of the seaworthiness of the squadron's support ships. The seas around the Cape were infamously dangerous, with massive, ship-crushing waves; severe, unpredictable storms; and even immense, free-floating icebergs. The lumbering colliers could certainly not accompany the warships around the Cape, so they would fuel the warships somewhere along the Chilean coast before the Squadron headed southward. The colliers would then be sent on through the Strait of Magellan, with instructions to try to make wireless contact with the squadron once again when they reached the Atlantic. With luck, they would not encounter any British patrols and would be able to rejoin the squadron somewhere on the other side to fuel them one last time before the warships and colliers parted for good. Besides the colliers, only two other support vessels — *Prinz Eitel Friedrich* and *Titania* — were still attendant to the squadron.

*Prinz Eitel Friedrich* was a sizeable former passenger liner with considerable coal storage, capable of traversing large stretches of ocean without escort or support. Still, her design was not ideally suited for the rigorous passage around the Cape, so the admiral decided to dispatch her westward toward Samoa, with an assignment for her captain to send out intermittent encrypted wireless transmissions along the way — using *Scharnhorst's* call sign, of course. The admiral hoped that this ruse might mislead the British, French, and Japanese into thinking that the entire squadron was headed that direction. *Prinz Eitel Friedrich* had departed westward the previous evening, with orders to wait four days before beginning to send her false wireless transmissions.

*Titania*, on the other hand, was a small supply steamer with limited range. She had made the long journey thus far only under the protection of the rest of the squadron — and a fair amount of luck in not being forced to steam through any major storms. Were *Titania* to attempt to round the Cape, she would surely founder and sink in the heavy seas. Without a collier, she could not accompany *Prinz Eitel Friedrich* westward. Sending her to a Chilean port was not an option, either, because *Titania* had been attached to the East Asia Squadron for several years and was well known as a *Kaiserliche Marine* support vessel. Faced with these options, the admiral determined that *Titania* had become a liability, and he ordered her scuttled.

The officers and men of *Titania* were given the choice of either transferring to *Prinz Eitel Friedrich* to accompany her on her decoy mission or joining the crews of the warships of the squadron. To a man, each member of *Titania's* crew opted to stay with the squadron. Five of her men and two officers, including Commander Vogt, had been assigned to *Gneisenau*. Captain Maerker was glad to have the young commander on board, and he promptly assigned Vogt to assist First Officer Pochhammer with supply and logistics management. He hoped that the young commander's level head and easygoing demeanor might be a useful example to the often temperamental and rash Pochhammer.

The small ship was then stripped of anything that might be useful to the squadron, such as her guns, ammunition, wireless equipment, supplies, tools, and portable machinery. After the sailors had removed everything of value, Commander Vogt piloted her for the last time into deeper water and anchored her before departing for *Gneisenau*. A demolition crew from *Scharnhorst* placed multiple charges inside *Titania's* hull below the waterline, opened her sea cocks, lit the detonation fuses, and hastily departed the ship.

Now that the scuttling charges had done their work—punching a precise series of holes in the ship's lower hull—the little vessel took on water quickly, as thousands of gallons of brine poured into her holds and interior spaces. At first, she settled slowly in the water, with her stern sinking lower than the bow. After a few minutes, however, a geyser of white foam jetted upward from a ruptured hatch amidships, and *Titania* suddenly rolled over to port—her funnel hovering horizontally above the waves, pointing briefly toward the squadron like an accusatory finger. The ship then sank rapidly, and churning foam closed over her. In moments, the roiling froth disappeared, leaving quiet, unbroken green swells that stretched to the horizon—as if *Titania* had never existed.

Maerker finally took his eyes from the spot where *Titania* had gone under. Below him, on *Gneisenau's* decks, the men were dispersing as the crew quietly returned to their stations and duties. Maerker felt deeply troubled. The morale of the men had already ebbed since their victory at Coronel and the raucous celebrations in Valparaiso. After leaving the Chilean port, *Scharnhorst*, *Gneisenau*, and *Nürnberg* had rejoined *Leipzig* and *Dresden* here at Más Afuera. Unfortunately, they had done virtually nothing since, and more than a week of inactivity while anchored in the shadow of the towering dark cliffs had allowed everyone to reflect upon how isolated and vulnerable the squadron truly was. Maerker had heard muttered misgivings from officers and men alike while the long days passed. He also worried that their delay would give their enemies more of a chance to regroup. The *Kaiserliche Marine* had struck a stunning blow against the mighty Royal Navy at Coronel, but surely now the British would seek swift retribution. While they waited, he sent several ship-to-ship messages to the admiral, asking for a meeting. Curiously, the admiral politely but firmly declined each request and did not call for a council of his captains.

Other than determining the fate of the support vessels, the only other pro-active order von Spee had issued since their arrival at Más Afuera was to dispatch *Dresden* and *Leipzig* to Valparaiso with further communications for the *Admiralstab*. The pair of light cruisers had departed two days earlier, with instructions that they would rejoin the squadron somewhere along the southern Chilean coastline. Still, no order for the rest of the warships to depart was forthcoming, and Maerker began to wonder if the admiral's delay was part of some greater strategy still kept secret from his captains or was an indication that their flag commander was suffering from troubled indecision or wavering resolve.

Now, with crews from every other ship in the squadron watching on, *Titania* had been scuttled. If his own feelings of regret were any indication, Maerker assumed that viewing this sobering event would further erode the morale of the men. Witnessing the sinking of any ship can be troubling for a sailor — for it is a stark reminder of his own tenuous place upon the surface of the ocean. *Titania* had been one of their own, and seeing her go down would surely be troubling to the men.

They had to *do something*, he thought. Sitting here any longer, languishing beneath these oppressive looming cliffs, could serve no useful purpose. He turned his back on *Titania's* final resting place and stepped back into the wheelhouse, followed by Busch. Maerker thought that later that evening he would try again to reach out to the admiral and request a meeting. Perhaps this time, the admiral would acquiesce.

"Signal from the flagship, sir," said Petri, who was looking out toward the nearby *Scharnhorst*.

Maerker turned and saw the series of flags that now fluttered above the *Scharnhorst*. He read the message with relief.

ALL VESSELS MAKE PREPARATIONS TO DEPART BY 0600 TOMORROW, NOVEMBER 15. ROUTE AND DESTINATION TO FOLLOW.

Maerker addressed the other officers on the bridge. "Gentlemen, today's events have been… dispiriting and unfortunate. We'll certainly miss having little *Titania* in our squadron, but we have gained Commander Vogt and his capable officers and men. Additionally, we now have something to look forward to. Take a good long last look at those gloomy cliffs above us. The admiral has given us our orders, and tomorrow we're finally departing this place and continuing our voyage. I believe we'll be headed for an anchorage somewhere along the southern Chilean coast."

"Not a moment too soon," muttered Pochhammer.

Maerker continued. "We weigh anchor at 0600. Everything is to be made ready by 0500, in advance of our departure."

"Understood," nodded Pochhammer. The other bridge officers voiced their assent and began distributing orders throughout the ship.

◆

THE SQUADRON departed Más Afuera as a gray-green dawn bloomed through a low bank of slate-colored clouds to the east. The squadron was led, as usual, by *Scharnhorst*, followed by *Gneisenau*, *Nürnberg*, and the two remaining colliers, *Baden* and *Santa Isabel*. The five ships headed due south, steaming at eight knots, until the towering cliffs were no longer visible astern on the northern horizon. The admiral then ordered a course change to the southeast, taking care to give wide berth to Más Afuera's sister isle of Más a Tierra to the east. Más a Tierra did not have a wireless station, but the admiral could not take the risk that a wireless-equipped vessel might be moored in the port—capable of relaying an alarm before the squadron's guns could neutralize it.

Once out in the open ocean, Graf von Spee relayed the coordinates of their new destination along the southern Chilean coast—the remote and uninhabited Gulf of Penas, some thirteen hundred kilometers south of Coronel. Because the trailing colliers limited the speed of the entire squadron, the voyage took five full days. The seas—although whipped into whitecaps by a brisk southerly wind—presented swells no greater than two meters, and Maerker was grateful for the relatively easy passage.

Two days into the voyage, wireless operators aboard *Scharnhorst* and *Gneisenau* made contact with *Dresden* and *Leipzig*, which were heading southward toward the main squadron after their brief stop in Valparaiso. The flagship made arrangements for a rendezvous at sea, and on November 18th, the two small light cruisers were sighted, approaching rapidly on the northern horizon—briefly causing a panic among the spotters of the squadron until they were positively identified as friends rather than foes. Within the hour, the squadron was whole again, with all five warships and two colliers steaming in formation toward the rugged coast of southern Chile.

The final day of the voyage required them to cross the well-traveled north-south coastal shipping lanes. They traversed the final, riskiest sixty kilometers in the pre-dawn darkness to help avoid being seen, should any ships just happen to be passing by at that time. Luckily, the spotters on the platforms above sighted no other vessels as they entered Chilean coastal waters. At sunrise on November 20th, the East Asia Squadron steamed into the large Gulf of Penas.

During the past few months, they had visited several exquisitely beautiful tropical islands — any one of which could have been considered a paradise. Here before them was a very different landscape, yet of such astonishing grandeur that it almost defied belief. Maerker looked on in awed silence as the squadron steamed slowly northeast into the gulf. Before them, a seemingly endless range of massive, snow-covered mountains filled the farthest reaches of the eastern horizon — their glistening peaks reaching high into the azure morning sky. Before the mountains lay the bowl of a great green valley, at least forty kilometers across, dotted with shimmering blue ponds and verdant marshlands. Flocks of innumerable gray and white wading birds speckled the lush green lowlands for as far up the valley as Maerker could see. The most striking element of the scene before them was the bulk of a massive, brilliant white glacier that descended from the heights like a great frozen cataract. The leading edge of the kilometers-wide glacial fan ended abruptly at the marsh's edge — where it became a crumbling wall of rock and ice, higher and more formidable than any fortress ever built by man.

No less beautiful was the bay into which they steamed, designated on *Gneisenau's* old charts as San Quintin Bay. It was a large fjord of deep blue green water, more than fifteen kilometers long and nearly seven kilometers across at its widest point. The peninsula that made up its southern shore shielded the bay completely from the wind and sea of the gulf and the ocean beyond. Maerker noted that until the bow of the leading warship sent rippling undulations across its breadth, the surface of the bay had been as still as the surface of a mirror. All around them rose steep forested slopes of lush dark green pines. From a cove along the northern shore, a flock of gray long-necked birds took wing, alarmed by the appearance of these large, unfamiliar steel beasts intruding upon their sanctuary.

When all of the ships of the squadron had entered the hidden bay and were no longer visible from the open waters of the gulf, the flagship turned slowly about and maneuvered into a suitable anchorage position, followed by the other vessels. Immediately, flag signals from *Scharnhorst* indicated that the armored cruisers would coal, followed by the light cruisers. *Baden* and *Santa Isabel* came alongside *Scharnhorst* and *Gneisenau*, respectively, and the familiar coaling process began. A subsequent message from the flagship notified the captains of each ship that they were to report the following afternoon for a council with the admiral.

Around noon, with the coaling activity at its peak, Maerker left the bridge and strolled down to the aft quarterdeck to observe the fueling process. Even with the sun at its zenith, the temperature on the weather decks was cool, and he was grateful for the seclusion of the bay, which rendered the air about them virtually windless. Below him, several members of the ship's band, which had not made an appearance since their stay in the Marquesas, were playing a vigorous military march as the men toiled near the coal chutes. Black dust coated much of the stern decking, and most of the sailors below were unrecognizable beneath layers of dark grime. The current labor shift had found their rhythm, and two teams of *Gneisenau's* men were efficiently handling the succession of bulging canvas bags swung over from the holds of *Santa Isabel*. Although coaling was never a pleasant undertaking, he noted that today the men seemed to go about the task with vigor, as if their new surroundings and the prospect of resuming their greater voyage had buoyed their spirits. Behind their soiled face rags, sailors laughed and sang along with the music, and he saw that someone had scrawled an ironic but encouraging phrase in the coal dust upon an outer bulkhead. It read, "Faster! We're more than half-way home. Only 16,000 kilometers to go!"

Maerker was pleased to see that the mood of the crew had improved since their idle delay at Más Afuera. Lieutenant-Commander Busch stepped up beside him. "Excuse me, sir. There is something here you should see."

Maerker looked up and was surprised to see that the expression on Busch's face was deeply troubled. The gunnery officer set his jaw and soberly handed the captain a folded newspaper.

"A boat from *Leipzig* just brought over a stack of these," said Busch grimly. "They collected as many German papers as they could find in Valparaiso."

Maerker wondered what could have caused Busch such dismay. He unfolded the newspaper. It was dated November 11th — two days before *Dresden* and *Leipzig* had called at the port. The front page was dominated by two large headlines in heavy black print. At the top of the page was printed, "JAPANESE INVADERS STORM TSINGTAO – GERMAN COLONY SURRENDERS." Below the fold, in slightly smaller print, was the headline, "VALIANT CRUISER EMDEN SUNK IN BATTLE – SURVIVORS UNKNOWN."

Maerker's heart dropped, immediately banishing his uplifted mood of just moments ago. For the next few minutes, he said nothing as he read both stories in their entirety.

The first article had been cobbled together from British and American news reports, although the German journalists in Valparaiso had attempted to lend the story as much pro-German direction as was possible, considering the circumstances. The fact that the squadron's home port of Tsingtao had been surrounded and blockaded by Japanese and British naval forces for months was nothing new. According to this story, however, during the ongoing blockade of Kiaochow Bay, the Japanese had also begun landing massive numbers of infantry and field artillery just beyond the hills surrounding the colony. At the end of October, Japanese naval and field guns began to shell German positions, as the Japanese and British infantry steadily advanced. According to the newspaper account, the outnumbered German soldiers fought courageously against overwhelming odds, but were simply overmatched. Out of ammunition, with thousands of Japanese troops poised to pour into the colony—likely to inflict unspeakable atrocities upon its inhabitants—the Germans asked for terms of surrender.

Although Tsingtao had been Maerker's home port for only a few weeks before their departure, he felt suddenly orphaned by this news. To his surprise, he realized that in some subconscious portion of his mind, he had envisioned the squadron's triumphant return to the beleaguered German colony after the Kaiser's armies were victorious in Europe. Now that this imagined scenario was rendered impossible, he realized how foolish such a vision had truly been. Regardless of what might happen on the distant battlefields of Europe, there was no longer a German colony in Tsingtao, nor any other German possessions anywhere in the Pacific. The British and Japanese forces had consumed them all like a surging tide over so many sandcastles. The East Asia Squadron now had no home port to which it could return, no true haven outside of Germany itself. They would have to keep moving, hiding, and maneuvering their way across the oceans—until they either finally reached a German port or were destroyed in the attempt.

As depressing as that circumstance was, the newspaper's second headline was even more wrenching. This article was much briefer and had originated from an Australian news bulletin. Again, the German journalists in Valparaiso had made a few patriotic alterations to the story, but the overall effect was no less bleak. The famed SMS *Emden* had been harassing Allied shipping in the Indian Ocean for more than two months, despite a concerted effort by dozens of British, Australian, and Japanese ships to find her. Captained by Karl von Müller, *Emden* had captured or sunk more than thirty vessels, including a Russian gunboat and a French destroyer, and had shelled the large British oil storage tanks in Madras. Only after attacking the British wireless station on the Cocos Islands was *Emden* finally found and engaged by a Royal Navy warship, HMAS *Sydney*. After an hour-long gun battle, the heavily damaged *Emden* was forced aground on Keeling Island. The article noted that the number of survivors from *Emden*, if any, was unknown.

Maerker sighed heavily. "Good God. I would have thought it impossible to fit this much bad news onto a single page of newsprint."

Busch nodded. "In the span of only two days, our home port fell to our enemies and our sister ship was sunk."

"Within the hour, the whole ship will have heard about this," said Maerker, glancing down at the men working in the coal dust below. "I worry that this news may break what little spirit they have built up in the past few days."

"The rest of that blasted paper is no better," said Busch. "I had hoped to read some encouraging news of the war in Europe. However, it says that our armies captured Antwerp but could go no farther. The coast is still held by the British and the French. No news at all about the eastern front. Overall, it appears that the battle lines have moved little in the past month, as if they're content to dig in and wait things out. It makes little sense. We have the most powerful army in the world, but we have yet to crush our enemies decisively? It is looking less likely now that the war might be over by Christmas."

"That always sounded like wishful thinking. On their own, the French would surely have succumbed by now. The British gave them a spine, for a time. We'll have to see how long they can continue to do so."

"There's more," said Busch, gesturing to the paper in Maerker's hands. "They say that the Royal Navy has begun some sort of blockade of German waters. The only positive thing I read at all is that the Ottoman Turks have cast their lot with us. They've already attacked the Russians on the Black Sea."

"With or without the Turks, the Kaiser will find a way," said Maerker, with less confidence than he would have liked. "Although the prospect of us trying to run a Royal Navy blockade in the North Sea sounds less than appealing."

"The North Sea?" Busch shook his head. "I don't know about running any blockades or even making it all the way to the North Sea. Right now, I'd like to focus on getting out of the South Pacific in one piece."

"Agreed." Maerker paused and looked back at the second headline. "It's a shame there isn't more information here about *Emden's* crew. Hopefully there were some survivors—perhaps more likely since she ran aground, presumably in shallow water, rather than sinking out to sea."

"We can hope. Brave men, every one—especially Müller. It took brass ones to sail out there on his own."

Maerker chuckled. "It certainly did. From the sound of it, he had the whole British Empire twisted up in fits as he stayed a step ahead of them, week after week. He's been besting the rest of us in the squadron since he captured *Ryazan* at the beginning of the war. Even with our victory at Coronel, we have a lot of catching up to do to match his numbers." His smile faded and he paused thoughtfully before continuing. "I certainly hope he survived. Someday, I'd like to raise a glass with him."

"I also," agreed Busch.

Below them, the men continued to toil under a thick haze of coal dust. The band had dispersed in anticipation of the coming shift change. Without musical accompaniment, the men had begun to cheerfully sing a bawdy navy song, with two groups alternating to sing the next colorful verse. For that moment, Maerker envied them, because they were caught up in their duties and were still blissfully unaware of either the fall of their home port in Tsingtao or the fate of their brethren aboard *Emden*. Their hearts were not yet heavy with the awful news. Maerker reflected that one cannot appreciate the fleeting comfort of ignorance until it is already gone.

◆

THE ADMIRAL'S long-awaited meeting of his captains took place in the familiar surroundings of *Scharnhorst's* senior officer's wardroom. This was the first such gathering of all the squadron commanders since before the battle at Coronel, which was now three weeks distant. Although a meal would be served later in the evening, the first half of the agenda was devoted to more serious orders of business. The admiral began the meeting with a brief and solemn speech honoring their fallen brothers in Tsingtao and aboard *Emden*, and he recited a brief prayer for the safety of the survivors. For the next full hour, they discussed these developments, their ramifications for the squadron, the greater war effort, and what may have befallen the brave crew of *Emden*.

Moving on after that gloomy discussion, Graf Spee proudly announced that *Dresden* and *Leipzig* had brought official word that the Kaiser had awarded to the admiral and each of his captains the Iron Cross, for their courageous actions at the Battle of Coronel. Furthermore, three hundred additional Iron Crosses were to be awarded to the officers and men of the East Asia Squadron, with instructions that the admiral and his captains could distribute them to whichever crew members they deemed worthy recipients. Under the circumstances, the medals themselves could not be shipped—so for the time being, the awards would be granted verbally and registered in log books, to await the time when each of the deserving recipients could return home to receive his actual medal from the Kaiser himself.

Instead of buoying any of their spirits, the announcement of these awards seemed to have the opposite effect upon the captains. Thus far, Maerker found this council to be more tense than any of their meetings during the past few months. An air of foreboding hung in the room, and there had been no joking or playful banter among the officers. Their original goal of stealthily crossing the Pacific to wreak havoc along the

South American coast had now been supplanted by a new mission—to attempt to make their way across the Atlantic and somehow reach a port in Germany. The capture of their home base in Tsingtao and the sinking of *Emden* in the Indian Ocean crystallized the grave danger that now loomed over them. At the beginning of their long voyage, there had been a sense of adventure and almost reckless bravado within their ranks, but now Maerker could sense that seeds of doubt and fear had begun to germinate in the hearts of his compatriots.

After congratulating each of the men in the room for his recognition from the Kaiser, Graf Spee summarized his recent meeting with the German consul-general and minister in Valparaiso and his other communications with the *Admiralstab* in Berlin. Most of the information he had gleaned concerned known Royal Navy ship deployments and the most recent intelligence gathered by German agents throughout Europe and the Americas. Among the *Admiralstab's* instructions was the order that Graf Spee should attempt to make it home to Germany in whatever manner he chose as appropriate. To assist them in their homeward journey, the German Naval Staff had secretly dispatched three fully laden colliers to the Portuguese-held Cape Verde Islands to await the arrival of the squadron and refuel them for the final leg of their homeward voyage. Berlin still maintained a tenuous and strained relationship with the government of Portugal, which remained neutral—for the time being. However, Cape Verde, in the central Atlantic, was more than eight thousand kilometers from Cape Horn. Not only would that voyage be long and potentially treacherous, but there was the distinct possibility that Portugal would have sided with the Allies by the time the squadron arrived.

"The naval forces arrayed against us will be formidable," said Graf Spee as he leaned over a large map of South America that lay upon the broad wooden table.

The admiral stood on the opposite side of the table from Maerker. To the admiral's left stood Captain Schultz; to his right sat his chief of staff, Captain Filietz—the only man not standing. Filietz wore his customary scowl, and as he sat, he disdainfully regarded the map before him through his spectacles, perched near the end of his nose. On the near side of the table, Captains Lüdecke and Haun stood to either side of Maerker, and Captain Schönberg leaned over the end of the table to their right, also scrutinizing the map.

Graf Spee continued. "Undoubtedly, the news of our victory at Coronel has shaken the very foundation of the Admiralty in London." Upon the map, his index finger slowly traced the outline of the east coast of the South American continent. "Surely now, every major port along the

Atlantic coast will have at least one Royal Navy warship stationed nearby. They will likely have a full squadron positioned to protect the *Rio de la Plata* region and Montevideo, for a great deal of Allied shipping flows through that area. The enemy may have deployed more ships at Rio de Janeiro and Recife to guard the shipping lanes farther up the coast. They may even be guarding the eastern mouth of the Strait of Magellan—hence our plan to instead sail around the Cape. The British will do everything they can to protect their trade in these waters."

"So, how will we choose our targets?" asked Captain Schultz with a frown. "Undoubtedly these waters are rich with potential quarry—but anywhere along the coast, the British may be laying in ambush, just waiting for us to attack a seemingly unsuspecting merchant vessel and foolishly snare ourselves in some sort of trap."

"Targets?" asked Lüdecke cautiously. "If our orders from the *Admiralstab* are to find our way back to German waters, why would we draw attention to ourselves by attacking any merchant shipping in the Atlantic? Should we not instead make haste for home?"

"Our orders didn't say we couldn't make some noise along the way," offered Schönberg with a haughty smile. "I, for one, wouldn't mind sending another enemy warship to the bottom of the sea."

"But can we risk a full-on battle with another British squadron?" asked Lüdecke. "I'm concerned we would be pressing our luck, particularly since the Brits will be ready for us this time."

Maerker thought for a moment, then said, "I agree that we should try to avoid being drawn into another full squadron-to-squadron naval battle. As Captain Lüdecke points out, it is unlikely that surprise will favor us this time. Furthermore, we have already expended roughly half of our ammunition—without the possibility of re-arming anywhere along our homeward route. Prudently evading enemy warships should be integral to our plans. However, we will not be able to avoid conflict entirely, either. We will likely have to capture several vessels on our way to Cape Verde, because the distance is much too great to travel on just the coal we can carry—and we will need to move too fast to drag a chain of colliers with us as we traverse the Atlantic." Maerker noticed from the corner of his eye that as soon as he had begun to speak, Schönberg's brow had knitted into a frown—and Maerker thought he detected an almost imperceptible but continuous shaking of Schönberg's head, as if the other captain was silently disagreeing with him.

Haun nodded. "True. We'll have to capture at least a few merchant ships along the way, just to replenish our coal stores. We cannot guarantee that those colliers in Cape Verde will still be available to us when we arrive. Either way, we'll need coal. It would be foolish for us to try to run a blockade in the North Sea with empty bunkers."

"What about our agents in Argentina and Brazil?" asked Schultz. "Could we contact them and have them dispatch colliers to predetermined rendezvous points along our route?"

Graf Spee shook his head. "The British have a much more robust presence along the east coast of South America than they do here. Their spies are likely watching every ship in every port, particularly colliers. Any collier that headed out to sea would generate suspicion and could be followed—and that collier could bring the Royal Navy straight to us, like dogs following the scent of a butcher's carriage."

"Then we loiter about just outside the shipping lanes," said Schönberg with a matter-of-fact tone. "As we move northward along the coast, we pluck occasional merchant vessels as we would apples from a tree. If one of the enemy's unfortunate warships crosses our path, we simply overwhelm it with our combined firepower and add it to our tally."

"I don't think we should be doing much loitering anywhere," said Maerker. "Once they know we've crossed into the Atlantic, the Brits will send every available ship to hunt us down. From what the admiral has told us, they could have more than a score of warships, plus auxiliaries, searching for us. The Royal Navy will undoubtedly focus its search on the seas just beyond the shipping lanes. A squadron of five German warships in well-traveled coastal waters will be impossible to hide for long. Once we're spotted, they will swarm upon us like sharks on a school of herring, and our chances of escaping and continuing on to Germany will evaporate. We cannot give them a chance to marshal any significant force against us along the route. Haste and unpredictability will be our greatest allies. If they are so intent on protecting their trade along the coast, I believe we should avoid the shipping lanes entirely. Instead, if we were to choose a route farther out to sea and steam more rapidly..."

"Running, running, running!" exclaimed Schönberg suddenly, openly glaring at Maerker. "We've been running since this war was declared. Now that we've made it this far, you would have us hike up our skirts and run home to our mothers? We've bested an entire British squadron once already, without so much as a scratch—yet you seem to have no stomach for another fight. I wonder, Maerker, if wartime command truly suits you."

It was a challenge—and once again Maerker was perplexed by Schönberg's inexplicably venomous hatred toward him. He realized that somehow, *Nürnberg's* captain must view him as a threat, although he could not understand why. This time, however, he would not remain silent on the matter. Disagreeing was one thing—being accused of cowardice was quite another. His eyes narrowed as he turned toward Schönberg and spoke in slow, measured tones. "You seem awfully quick to call someone else a coward, Captain. I find it curious that you are so eager to go spoiling for a fight. Not every British warship that you happen upon will have already been disabled by *Gneisenau's* guns. I will do my best to soften up all of your targets before you blunder onto their sinking remnants, but at some point, you may have to fire at an opponent who can actually fight back."

Schönberg's face flushed, and the fingers of both hands curled into fists. His lips twisted into a snarl, and he growled, "How dare you…"

"Gentlemen," interjected Graf Spee loudly, "Enough! Not a man among you is a coward, and I will simply not tolerate such accusations or the dissention they bring. We have enough to overcome without fighting amongst ourselves." He directed an admonishing glance at Schönberg and crossed his arms across his broad chest. "The reality is that this scenario in which we find ourselves is complicated and treacherous. There simply is no one right answer here. All of us wish to return to our home waters, if that is truly possible. I would certainly like to finish our long voyage before a welcoming crowd in a German port. If that is our destiny, then I will welcome it—at the appropriate time. For now, however, I believe that we can still be a useful instrument of the Kaiser's war machine during our homeward journey."

He uncrossed his arms and once again leaned over the map upon the table. "We cannot make it across the Atlantic to Cape Verde, let alone all the way back to Germany, with only the coal we can carry in our bunkers. We'll need to capture additional fuel—wherever we can find it—along the way." He glanced at Schultz and Schönberg to his left. "I agree that we will need to choose our targets carefully, ideally operating from areas less likely to be actively guarded by enemy warships. However, Julius is correct that prudence—and our reduced ammunition stores—dictate that we attempt to avoid any direct confrontations with Royal Navy warships, if we can."

Maerker could sense that Schönberg still seethed with anger. From the corner of his eye, he could see that *Nürnberg's* captain was rhythmically massaging his left wrist with the fingers of his right hand with such force that the knuckles of his hand were white with tension. He still could not fathom what type of threat he represented to Schönberg, but Maerker knew instinctively that he could not trust him.

Graf Spee paused for a moment, and Maerker thought he saw a hint of a familiar gleam in the older man's blue eyes. "I have been working on a plan," continued the admiral. "Initially, after my discussions with Consul General Gumprecht and Minister Eckert in Valparaiso, I was profoundly disheartened. It appeared that despite our great victory at Coronel, our position was extremely tenuous. We certainly could not retreat back across the Pacific, into the waiting clutches of the British and Japanese. We could not operate along this western South American coast for more than a few months before we were inevitably confronted here by our enemies. If we crossed into the Atlantic to attack merchant shipping along the east coast, we would undoubtedly be steaming into the teeth of the enemy. On top of all this, the *Admiralstab* has instructed us to try to make our way home to Germany. That possibility was tantalizing, but I still felt—and do feel— that we have considerably more to contribute to the Kaiser's war effort before we finally drop anchor back home. I will admit that at first, I honestly did not know which path to take. Then, while we were moored at Más Afuera, I came upon something..."

He plucked a sheet of paper from atop stack of files on the sideboard behind him. "This was buried in the pile of reports and transcripts that our consul general provided to me in Valparaiso. It is a brief note from one of our covert agents in Argentina. Our agent had made the acquaintance of a German pilot serving aboard a whaling vessel that had put in at Buenos Aires for repairs in late October—after calling at Port Stanley in the Falkland Islands. That remote British colony, it seems, had been a regular stop for this whaling ship during the previous six months as they plied the South Atlantic. The pilot made the observation that although the local populace in Port Stanley spoke of regular visits by a Royal Navy cruiser named *Glasgow*, the pilot himself had yet to see a single British warship during any of his calls there." Graf Spee looked up at his captains. "As you know, gentlemen, *Glasgow* is the very same light cruiser that escaped us at Coronel—and which we may have damaged before it fled." He returned his attention to the paper in his hands. "Not only was *Glasgow* absent during this whaling ship's several visits—likely because it had been assigned to the squadron that came hunting for us—but the pilot remarked that he was surprised that Port Stanley and its wireless station had no defenses, even in wartime. This British colony has no garrison, no gun emplacements, no fortifications of any kind."

The admiral set the paper down. "Our enemies have made a critical blunder in the deployment of their naval assets. They are focused on protecting the trade routes and their merchant vessels—they wish to prevent a repetition of the havoc wreaked by Captain Müller upon their shipping lanes in the Indian Ocean. Therefore, it appears that they have deployed all of their warships near the coast and in proximity to major ports. In doing so, they have abandoned the Falklands, which lie only some eight hundred kilometers northeast of Cape Horn—but are nearly sixteen hundred kilometers southeast of Montevideo and the *Rio de la Plata*, where our enemies will likely concentrate their forces. Port Stanley and its wireless station are both critical to British operations in the South

Atlantic. The port also likely has ample coal stocks and food storage. Yet, our enemies have foolishly neglected to protect this outpost."

"Outstanding!" exclaimed Schultz. "We can steam right up to the islands, shell the port and their wireless station, and be on our way before the British Admiralty has any idea what has befallen their colony."

"Actually," said Graf Spee, "I intend to do more than that. I do not wish to just blast the port as we sail past, as we did at Papeete. No, I intend to take the Falklands by force—declaring the islands as captured German territory belonging to the Kaiser himself." To emphasize his point, he brought his index finger downward upon the map as if he were driving it in like a knife—rigidly pointing directly at the Falklands. "Only after we have taken this prize and left it securely defended, then we shall sail on home, to Germany."

For a long moment, no one in the room said anything. Maerker was stunned. To him, the admiral's revelation was as unexpected as if he had told them he intended to capture the moon. Surely, he could not be serious. The other captains seemed equally shocked and were looking toward their commander for confirmation. Graf Spee looked back with what could only be described as a satisfied smirk—but Maerker could tell instantly that the admiral was completely serious.

"Sir?" asked Lüdecke haltingly, breaking the silence. "Do you really mean that we would…"

"I meant exactly what I said, Fritz." Graf Spee's smirk had disappeared, and his jaw was now firmly set—his blue eyes gleamed with energy. "I intend to steam right up to this outpost of the British Empire and take it from them. They have done just that to our colonies at Yap, Samoa, Tsingtao, and everywhere else in the Pacific that once belonged to Germany. Now we shall do the same to them. If the British king was rocked by the defeat of his squadron at Coronel, just imagine how staggering it will be to have sovereign British soil wrested from him by force."

"Brilliant," whispered Filietz softly, his thin voice barely audible in the room's hanging silence. His pale face contorted into something that resembled a smile. "A stroke of pure genius, Admiral. After this, you shall be mentioned in the same breath as your flagship's namesake. The Kaiser will have to commission a new medal just for your exploits."

Maerker had just begun to recover his wits after the initial shock had worn off. He still had trouble believing the admiral was serious about this plan, but he needed to know more. "But how will we hold it after we have captured it? There could be more than a thousand British colonists in Port Stanley alone, not to mention elsewhere on the islands. Those farmers and shepherds may not be trained soldiers, but they know the terrain—and some may be armed. Even landing a force of five hundred men, taking a hundred from each of our ships, might not be adequate to round them all up—and we certainly cannot leave that many of our men behind if we are to continue on our voyage." He looked up at Graf Spee but could read nothing in the admiral's facial expression. He continued, "We must also assume that the British will want their colony back—and will undoubtedly send ships and men to accomplish that. If they swiftly and easily recapture the islands, we will have gained little in the endeavor."

"You are correct, Julius," said Graf Spee with a knowing smile. "We will need some help—not only to take the colony by force but also to keep it after it is ours. I have already set in motion a a multi-faceted plan to address those very concerns." His face became grave, and he leaned forward, speaking slowly and purposefully. "However, not a word of this plan is to be uttered outside this room, gentlemen. Until we have confirmed that we are able to proceed with this attack, I do not want anyone else in the squadron to know, not even your senior officers. For now, we maintain it as a secret. Understood?"

All of the captains cautiously nodded their assent.

The admiral continued. "I dispatched messages with *Dresden* and *Leipzig* when they departed for Valparaiso. Most of those messages were sent to the *Admiralstab*, but a few were directed toward our network of agents on this continent. We will soon discover if the components of my plan will come together as necessary. Firstly, we will need additional ground troops to hold the Falklands colony after we have departed. As you know from our brief visit to Valparaiso, there are dozens, if not hundreds, of reservists and patriotic volunteers among the local German populace. We only conscripted a handful of them as additional members of our crews. Many more remain and may be willing to volunteer for a heroic mission to support us and the Kaiser.

"As we saw when we were in Valparaiso, numerous large German-registered passenger ships are languishing uselessly at Chilean ports. I have requested that our agents select a large, seaworthy, and wireless-equipped liner from among them, preferably one whose absence will not draw too much attention from British consular authorities. If they have followed my request, any available volunteers will have been taken aboard the chosen ship and provided with rudimentary supplies—boots, cold-weather clothing, firearms, and ammunition—whatever our agents were able to scrape together. That ship was then to be dispatched from its current port to our anchorage here. If it was able to depart as scheduled, we should expect it to arrive within the next three days. No one aboard that ship yet knows the nature of their mission, but the captain of the vessel has been given a set of encrypted communication codes so that he can make us aware as he approaches."

"What then?" asked Haun. "Will this passenger liner follow us on our voyage around the Cape? If so, that could be quite hazardous."

"True," acknowledged Graf Spee. "One of the reasons that *Prinz Eitel Friedrich* is no longer accompanying us is that I doubted she could safely navigate the seas near the Cape. I have similar concerns about this passenger vessel. That is why I have asked them to select a robust, seaworthy ship with a seasoned captain. With luck, this liner will be able to accompany us to our next anchorage at Picton Island, then follow on after we have taken the Falklands. Once moored at Port Stanley, the volunteers will disembark and receive deployment orders from our officers. Those conscripts will be the ground force that will hold our new captured possession. Additionally, if necessary, the passenger liner itself can then be repurposed as a prison ship for any captured British colonists."

"But sir," protested Maerker, who was alarmed at just how much planning for this assault the admiral had already considered, "can we expect a shipload of hastily recruited, questionably trained men to be able to hold the islands after we've captured them? Once the British know it has been invaded, they will likely send warships, as well as a troop ship to land well-armed Marines. Without proper armaments or fortifications, our boys will stand little chance against a professional military assault. We would then be leaving these volunteers to their deaths."

"Correct again, Julius. I am not so naïve as to think these conscripts, no matter how patriotic, can hold out for long against a coordinated enemy attack, but perhaps they won't have to. Among the messages I sent were instructions to our agents in Buenos Aires. They have been asked to clandestinely acquire as much weaponry, ammunition, barbed wire, cement, entrenching machinery, canned food, and other supplies as they can find. I have asked them to load those materials aboard one or two chartered, wireless-equipped cargo vessels of non-German registry. Those vessels are to sail for the Falklands, with our agents aboard, as soon as they are fully loaded. If they arrive at Port Stanley before we do, they can simply call at the port and remain there, feigning engine trouble or some such thing. Then, when we take the colony, we will have all the tools at our disposal to fortify it properly—something the British have inexplicably failed to do." The admiral's eyes gleamed with mirth and pride. He had obviously given this plan considerable thought. "It will take the British at least a month or more to deploy a troop ship to the Falklands. If we give our volunteer soldiers the proper equipment, they may be able to put up enough resistance that they can hold the colony for several more weeks or perhaps even a few months. That may be all the time they need. If the

Kaiser can bring our enemies in Europe to terms in that time, which the *Admiralstab* believes is possible, then the British would have to stand down—leaving the Falklands still in our possession."

Maerker was deeply troubled. "Forgive me, sir, but this plan includes a considerable number of speculations. If any one of the pieces does not fall into place exactly as you have envisioned, the entire plan would unravel."

"True enough, which is why we always have the choice of abandoning this plan at any point. I appreciate your caution, as always, Julius. We will proceed for the time being with the attack on the Falklands as our primary plan. As a secondary option, we will bypass the colony entirely and leap forward to the next phase of our journey, which will be to steam across the South Atlantic toward our colony of Southwest Africa. Although our brethren there are beset by South African troops fighting for the British, we still hold the territory. We may even be able to coal at the port of Lüderitz. Even if we cannot, that coast is only sparsely patrolled by our enemies—but a great deal of merchant shipping plies those seas. From there, we can move northward, capturing an occasional ship and its coal as necessary until we reach Cape Verde, which lies only five hundred kilometers off the coast of French West Africa." Again, Graf Spee smiled in self-satisfied pleasure.

The room was again silent as all of the officers absorbed the realities of this extraordinary revelation. Maerker was still stunned, but he resolved to say no more until he could evaluate other elements of the admiral's plan, such as the impending arrival of this passenger liner.

Schönberg broke the silence with a forceful proclamation and a sidelong glance at Maerker. "Well, sir, I cannot speak for some of my fellow captains, but I believe this is a brilliant plan. I support it completely, and I eagerly look forward to planting my boot heel upon the back of the British governor in Port Stanley and raising the flag of the Fatherland on the pole above their colonial offices."

"Thank you, Karl," replied Graf Spee. "Hopefully everything will fall into place and it will come to pass in just that manner." He smiled broadly again and stepped back from the table. "For now, however, I believe that other matters are more pressing. Let us move on into my dining room, gentlemen. We'll see what magic the cooks have conjured up this evening, and I would like to hear whom among your crews each of you will choose to receive the Iron Cross."

CAPTAIN Maerker distributed the awards the next afternoon on *Gneisenau's* quarterdeck. The day was crisp and clear, affording dazzling views of the massive glacier and the mountains looming behind. Dozens of curious brown and white sea birds circled on the breezes swirling above the ship—their calls echoing back and forth across the bay. Virtually every member of the crew was assembled on the weather decks, and they were attired in their sharpest dark blue winter uniforms.

Maerker had given considerable thought to who should receive the Kaiser's prestigious award. He felt that certain members of the crew had been particularly instrumental to their success at Coronel, and he had chosen accordingly. *Gneisenau's* superb gunnery had been the most critical factor of the battle, so the first awards went to Lieutenant-Commander Busch and each of his gunnery officers, and a number of the gunners themselves. Maerker had briefly questioned giving an award to Heinrich von Spee, because he did not want to think he had done so only to curry favor with the admiral. However, Busch had assured him that the young *graf* had performed his duties well during the battle and would be a worthy recipient. Each of the spotters and rangefinders who had been on duty during the fight were also lauded, as were selected other members of the crew, including members of the team that had so rapidly repaired the shell damage to the aft main turret late in the battle. When Maerker had finished and the crew's cheering had subsided, an assistant paymaster had logged the names of sixty-eight recipients in his book.

The admiral had given permission to his captains to grant shore leave as they deemed appropriate. Over the next few days, Maerker allowed nearly every crew member at least several hours of leave, and many of the men went exploring, hunting, and fishing in the beautiful surrounding countryside. As was expected, no one saw any other human beings, but all of the men spoke of the abundant wildlife and the astonishing, pristine beauty of the locale.

Mid-morning on their fourth day in San Quintin Bay, *Gneisenau's* wireless operators notified Maerker that they had heard a strong but encrypted wireless signal that was answered immediately by wireless operators aboard *Scharnhorst*. Minutes later, the flagship hoisted flags instructing *Dresden*—moored closest to the mouth of the bay—to raise steam and move out into the gulf to locate and escort a merchant ship into their anchorage. *Dresden* pulled up her anchors and steamed out of the bay, out of sight around the southern peninsula. Four hours later, she returned, with a modestly sized passenger ship trailing behind. The men of the squadron assembled on the decks of the various ships to view the unusual scene as *Dresden* returned to her original anchorage and the mysterious newcomer turned slowly about and anchored toward the farthest end of the southern shoreline. The liner's hull was predominantly black, with her railings and upper works painted white. She had two masts and a single funnel, and Maerker estimated her length at some one hundred forty meters. He watched through binoculars as she came about, and he could make out the name *Seydlitz* on her stern, as well as "NORDDEUTCHER LLOYD – BREMEN". When asked by his officers about the presence and purpose of this vessel, Maerker answered only that he believed she was being converted to a hospital ship and would be accompanying the squadron for a few weeks for her protection—which was the admiral's official cover story until the reality of his plan was revealed.

The last two days of their stay were spent primarily at leisure, for the admiral believed it might be the last such respite they might have for many weeks. Men continued their shore excursions, and many brought back trophies of wild fowl and small game. Graf Spee visited each of the ships of the squadron, personally congratulating every Iron Cross recipient and ceremonially inspecting the readiness of each warship. He dined with Maerker, Busch, and Petri aboard *Gneisenau*, and the four men enjoyed a game of bridge in the now rarely-used captain's quarters. Although Maerker had wished to privately discuss with the admiral the risks of his plan for attacking the Falklands, he could not do so in the presence of the other officers—so he waited for another time.

The admiral also visited *Seydlitz*, staying on board the passenger liner for several hours. He did not discuss the mystery ship with any of his captains, and no other officers of the squadron were permitted to go aboard. Other than the admiral's single visit, no one else had contact with *Seydlitz*. From time to time, large numbers of men in civilian clothes could be seen milling about on her decks, watching the warships and smoking— but no boats were launched and no one left the liner, even to go ashore.

On the sixth morning after their arrival, the flagship signaled that this was to be their last day at San Quintin Bay. With the warships' coal bunkers full and the colliers unable to follow them for the next leg of their journey, the admiral wanted to try to carry as much additional fuel with the squadron as possible. The colliers were instructed to come alongside each of the cruisers in turn and offload coal in sacks to be stacked in piles upon the weather decks. The ship's crews spent the remainder of the day in this manner as they stacked sack after sack of coal upon the decks, taking care to leave the gun mounts free to traverse their complete rotations. By nightfall, *Gneisenau*, like her sister ships, was a curious sight. Mountains of canvas sacks, bulging with dusty black coal, covered her decks, and the men were busily strapping them down securely in anticipation of the rough seas that surely lay ahead.

On the morning of November 26th, the squadron steamed out of the bay and assembled in formation at the end of the gulf. *Baden* and *Santa Isabel* were to follow on separately, at their more leisurely pace, with instructions to head east through the Strait of Magellan toward the Atlantic. The five warships and one passenger liner steamed out of the gulf into the Pacific. Turning southward at ten knots, the squadron headed on toward Cape Horn. With each southward kilometer that they steamed, the oncoming winds howled stronger and the swells became rougher—and dark gray clouds loomed ominously low over the churning sea.

# TWENTY-ONE

*Saturday, November 21, 1914*
*Port of Rio de Janeiro, Brazil*

"I MUST SAY, John," said Minister Robertson, "They've done an extraordinary job, especially in so few days. She certainly isn't the bedraggled wreck that limped in here not even a week ago." Robertson shook hands with Captain Luce and Commander Thompson. "I was not, of course, present when she was first launched back home, but from a layman's perspective, *Glasgow* looks as though she's about to be floated for the very first time."

"I'd have to agree with you, Malcolm," replied Luce. "I was not present at her launch either, but I cannot imagine that even then she looked as smart as she does now." He and Thompson had just finished a comprehensive tour of the ship that had begun at sunrise, hours earlier. This was to be *Glasgow's* last full day in Rio, so Luce had invited Minister Robertson to come aboard when she was refloated. Robertson had been piped aboard while Luce and Thompson were finishing up their inspections; he had then been ushered to the bridge to await the arrival of the captain and commander. Now the three of them stood in the wheelhouse along with a junior lieutenant, two petty officers, and the local harbor pilot who would briefly take control of the ship as she was refloated and moved to a new anchorage.

"I'd bet a month's pay," offered Thompson, "that she's at least two knots faster now than when she was launched. When the boys on *Bristol* see her, they'll probably mutiny on the spot—and ask for a transfer to our ship." *Bristol* was *Glasgow's* nearly identical sister ship—and the only other Town-Class light cruiser stationed in the South Atlantic. She had been patrolling Caribbean waters until the German threat compelled the

Admiralty to move her farther south. *Glasgow* was to meet up with *Bristol* at their next anchorage.

Luce smiled mischievously. "Good. Perhaps I can finally get a passable first officer."

Thompson rolled his eyes. "Ah, you wouldn't want any of those layabouts from *Bristol*, sir. Not one of them knows his own mainmast from a bilge pump. Besides, if you rid yourself of me, you wouldn't have someone to show you how ducks are supposed to be hunted." The first officer smiled broadly at this jest.

Luce shook his head in mock exasperation and turned to Robertson. "Would you listen to him now, Malcolm? He and I have hunted together for years, and I have consistently bested him on every outing. One lucky day yesterday, and his head has become so swollen that his steward had to fit him with a larger hat."

Malcolm chuckled and raised his hands in a gesture that indicated he wanted no part in their playful squabble.

"Luck?" protested Thompson, shaking his head. "That, sir, was prowess. Such a display of marksmanship that you were simply unable to appreciate it."

"What I do appreciate," said Luce to Robertson, "is your gracious hospitality during this past week. I believe I speak for my addled first officer here when I say that we are most grateful to you. Our stay with you has been a much-needed respite after the events of the past month."

"Agreed," said Thompson, his face now serious. "Malcolm, you have been a most generous host. My sincere thanks to you."

"My pleasure," said Robertson to them both. "I'm glad I was able to do even this small thing for you. As you know, my door is always open for you gentlemen, any time you are in town. Perhaps on our next hunting trip, I'll give both of you a run for your money."

"Of course, it is not only your hospitality for which we are grateful," said Luce. "We owe all of this to you, Malcolm. Because of your intervention, the shipwrights have moved heaven and earth to finish these repairs more quickly than I would have ever thought possible. I cannot see how I'll ever be able to repay my indebtedness to you."

"Nonsense," scoffed Robertson. "As I stated before, there is no debt—except that which I owe to you for all that you and your men are doing for us out there—for everything the men of *Monmouth* and *Good Hope* have sacrificed. That debt I cannot possibly repay."

The previous afternoon, the French foreman of the repair crew had proudly informed the captain that the repairs to his warship were complete, several days ahead of schedule. Luce had already received orders to depart for the Abrolhos rocks the following morning.

Luce's tour of the ship with Commander Thompson had been uplifting. The ruptured aft hull section had been repaired expertly, as had the damaged compartments and passageways within. Even Luce's trained eye had difficulty discerning the repaired portions from the original structure. All other evidence of the battle had been erased. Perforated funnels were now whole; shell damage to decks and coal bunkers was repaired; and every nick, scratch, and hole from the German shell splinters had been patched. The workers had washed every surface, scraped the hull, and had given the entire ship a new coat of paint.

Not only had the local workmen been hard at work repairing all of the battle damage, but *Glasgow's* crew and engineers had worked day and night as well. They had scrubbed the boilers and condensers, checked and tightened every steam fitting, lubricated each moving part, and replaced every worn piece of machinery for which they could find a replacement in the Brazilian navy yard. The crew also brought on board additional supplies, stores, and spare parts. During Luce's morning tour, the engineering commander had stated unequivocally that the ship was in better condition now than during her entire previous service life.

The amazing speed with which the repairs had been completed gave Luce hope that *Glasgow* would yet be able to take part in the hunt to find and stop von Spee's squadron. He had received a confidential cable three days earlier stating that two battlecruisers, HMS *Invincible* and *Inflexible*, under the command of Admiral Sturdee, had been reassigned to the South American station and were already steaming toward the rendezvous point at Abrolhos. Presumably, Admiral Sturdee's mission would be to use his powerful battlecruisers to find and destroy the Germans.

However, Luce was concerned that each additional day of delay gave the German squadron more time to sneak into the Atlantic unchallenged. *Dresden* and *Leipzig* had called at Valparaiso more than a week ago, which meant that if they had rejoined their squadron and steamed directly southward to the Cape, von Spee could be rounding it any day now. Still more troubling were Luce's most recent orders, which seemed to indicate that not only was *Glasgow* to steam to Abrolhos to meet up with Admiral Sturdee, but that all of the other available warships in the South Atlantic were to convene there as well. That meant that even *Defence*, *Cornwall*, and *Carnarvon*, which had been guarding Montevideo and the River Plate area would be pulled off that duty to await Sturdee's arrival. The prospect that the Germans might slip into the Atlantic unchecked—and might even threaten British interests in the Falklands or elsewhere caused Luce to shudder.

Under the watchful guidance of the harbor pilot, *Glasgow*, accompanied by two tugboats, slowly left the dry dock behind, steaming out into the main harbor. When the cruiser reached her designated area, half a mile from the naval shipyard, the harbor pilot relinquished control of the ship to the captain with a crisp salute. Luce ordered that the anchors be dropped, and the pilot departed upon one of the tugs. After a deck-by-deck check of all systems relayed by voice pipe, Luce authorized the approach of the collier and oiler that were standing by.

Fueling the ship took much of the rest of the day, with the last bags of coal swung aboard an hour after sunset. More than a thousand tons of coal and two hundred tons of oil were loaded. The crew then washed *Glasgow's* decks clean of coal dust and made preparations for their morning departure.

After a modest dinner in Luce's quarters—which had also been completely repaired and refinished—the captain and commander bade Minister Robertson a fond farewell, and he departed upon a steam launch. The crewmen on the nighttime watches once again systematically checked every system, section, and compartment upon the ship. By dawn, every department had reported in, and across the board, each had passed inspection.

As darkness gave way to a blooming lavender array on the eastern horizon, *Glasgow* steamed out of Rio de Janeiro's port and headed northeast. As he watched the gathering light shimmer upon the wave tops before the ship, Luce was reminded of their departure from this port in August, on the first day of the war. The atmosphere on board the ship that day had been one of trepidation and concern. Today, his thoughts were of loss, vengeance, and retribution.

◆

AS *Glasgow* made her way to Abrolhos, Captain Luce ordered all departments and watches to perform readiness drills. Although his crew was still the most seasoned and experienced of all the Royal Navy vessels in the region, he wanted to ensure that their near week in dry dock had not dulled anyone's performance. The crew executed all of their drills and exercises with precision and enthusiasm, which Luce took as a good indicator that the men had shaken off their previous malaise. He believed that they, like himself, felt the same energy and passion to get back into the fight and were energized to resume their voyage. His ship was ready. His crew was ready. He was ready.

For the first night since the battle, his sleep was not haunted by nightmarish visions of *Monmouth's* sailors desperately clinging to her sinking hull or of the massive explosion obliterating *Good Hope*. Still, his sleep was not untroubled. In place of the previous dark thoughts, a cold determination had emerged that offered Luce no solace or peacefulness. A sense of desperate urgency gripped him. He knew that each passing hour gave an advantage to the enemy. Each day that elapsed might be the day that the German squadron charged headlong into the Atlantic, either to wreak havoc upon British interests there or to simply slip away into the ocean's vastness and elude them once again. Luce knew that to find and stop von Spee, the Royal Navy would need to immediately deploy all of its available ships to the region near the Cape and the mouth of the Strait in the hope that they might snare the ships of the German squadron as they attempted to slip by. He hoped that his new commanding admiral would share his urgency.

At dusk on November 23rd, *Glasgow's* spotters sighted the familiar yellow glow of the Abrolhos lighthouse beacon to the north. Because numerous other Royal Navy vessels had also been summoned to this spot, Luce directed the wireless room to announce their approach so as not to alarm any of their sister ships that might be near the islands. HMS *Carnarvon* answered the call immediately with a hearty welcome from her captain, Harry Skipwith, whom Luce had known for many years. By the time *Glasgow* had dropped anchor just beyond the reefs, darkness had fallen completely. By the dim silvery light of the quarter moon, Luce and the other bridge officers could see several other ships anchored nearby. The nearest vessel, perhaps half a mile distant, had a silhouette similar to *Monmouth*, which Luce found to be unsettlingly eerie. She was likely *Carnarvon*, which was of another older armored cruiser class similar in appearance to *Monmouth*. Two other ships were less recognizable, but they were probably colliers. Only at sunrise did Luce and his bridge officers appreciate just how many ships were assembled there.

The flaxen glow of dawn revealed an astonishing assembly of ships anchored in the clear blue waters around the islands. In addition to *Glasgow*, five other warships lay nearby. As Luce had surmised, HMS *Carnarvon*, which was Rear-Admiral Stoddart's flagship, lay nearest. Beyond her to the northeast were the armored cruisers *Kent* and *Cornwall*, both of the same class as their lost sister *Monmouth*. To the west lay *Defence*, the newer armored cruiser that Admiral Cradock had unsuccessfully tried to add to his squadron. Anchored due north was *Bristol*, the other Town-Class light cruiser that was *Glasgow's* sister ship. These warships comprised Admiral Stoddart's Fifth Cruiser Squadron, originally tasked with protecting British trade routes in mid-Atlantic waters but now stationed in the South Atlantic—filling the void left by the destruction of Cradock's squadron.

Additionally, two converted armed merchant liners, *Orama* and *Macedonia*, were anchored to the east, each looking as large and ungainly as *Otranto* had been. In attendance to all of these Royal Navy vessels were nine colliers of various shapes and sizes, some quite large, and an oiler—bringing the total number of ships present to eighteen. Seeing this gathering of ships, Luce smiled to himself as he remembered the consternation of the Brazilian lighthouse operator back in August, when only *Glasgow* and her collier had anchored nearby. Surely that poor man must be apoplectic at the sight of so many foreign vessels anchored around his remote home.

Throughout the morning, other messages of welcome came in from the captains of the various warships. *Glasgow* coaled briefly, bringing aboard just enough coal to top off her bunkers once more. Later that afternoon, HMS *Bristol* came alongside and delivered two hundred armor-piercing rounds for *Glasgow's* 6-inch and 4-inch guns—which were identical to her own. The additional shells were most welcomed, particularly by Gunnery Commander Backhouse, who had fretted about being able to replace the more than four hundred shells fired during the Battle of Coronel.

While the crates of ammunition were being brought aboard and stowed in *Glasgow's* magazines, Luce hosted *Bristol's* Captain Fanshawe for dinner in his stateroom. Although much of the conversation involved a somber recounting of the battle and its aftermath, Luce enjoyed the rare opportunity to chat with the commander of another warship of the same class as his own. Luce even took the opportunity to give Fanshawe a tour of the recently repaired portions of the ship—and *Bristol's* captain acknowledged that the work was first-rate.

Luce found the following day to be frustratingly idle, as all of the assembled ships simply lay at anchor under the warm tropical sun. This had been the scheduled date of arrival for Admiral Sturdee's ships, but long hot hours passed without any sign of the battlecruisers. Luce spent much of the day writing reports, attending to various mundane shipboard matters, and reading through the latest cables from the Admiralty and the British Ministry—one of which noted that on the previous Thursday, the wayward *Otranto* had finally docked at Montevideo, nearly three weeks since her last sighting at Coronel. The report stated that Captain Edwards, after being released by Cradock at the opening moments of the battle, had ordered his helmsman to steer due west, farther out into the Pacific, until daybreak revealed no sign of German pursuers. Just to be certain, Edwards steamed westward for another full day before adjusting his course southward. *Otranto* then began a slow, cautious journey down around the Cape into the Atlantic, maintaining wireless silence and always keeping out to sea to minimize the chances that the ship would be spotted and reported by any passing vessel. Edwards then made his way northward, keeping far outside the main shipping lines. Only when the converted liner was short on coal and her crew was threatening mutiny over the lack of rations did Edwards finally risk bringing her in to port—where the local British populace in Montevideo had greeted the ship and her crew warmly. Luce was relieved to receive overdue confirmation that this one other ship of Cradock's ill-fated squadron had survived the horrific battle intact. Luce retired for the evening, and night fell with no sign of Admiral Sturdee's ships.

Early morning on the 26th, spotters noted the appearance of a growing stain of dark funnel smoke spreading across the northeast horizon. A brief wireless transmission to the gathered ships identified the oncoming vessels as Admiral Sturdee's flagship HMS *Invincible* and her sister ship *Inflexible*. As the two battlecruisers drew near, Luce and Thompson joined the other senior officers on the bridge to have a look for themselves.

"Now that," said Thompson reverently, "is what steel was meant to be fashioned into."

Luce took up a pair of binoculars to give the approaching battlecruisers a more thorough inspection. Steaming powerfully in the lead was *Invincible*, the flagship, with *Inflexible* trailing a quarter mile astern. Aside from the admiral's white and red flag flying from the foremast of the lead ship, the two huge gray vessels were identical. *Invincible* and *Inflexible* were each well over five hundred sixty feet long—a hundred feet longer than *Glasgow*—with a beam of nearly eighty feet. Their masts were of the distinctive sturdy tripod design found only upon other modern British capital ships, such as battleships and other battlecruisers. Between those tripod masts rose three stout funnels, and spaced along the length of her weather decks were four rotating armored turrets, each equipped with two massive 12-inch guns.

"They are beautiful," agreed Luce.

Until six years earlier, when *Invincible* and *Inflexible* were launched, there had been no such vessel as a "battlecruiser" in any navy in the world. First Sea Lord of the Admiralty, Jackie Fisher, had commissioned their design because he wanted a class of ship that had the firepower of a battleship matched with speed exceeding that of an armored cruiser. They were designed to steam at twenty-five knots, and their array of heavy guns was more than a match for any opponent smaller than a battleship. These new swift, powerful warships had been nicknamed "Fisher's Greyhounds," and they were as sleek and beautiful as they were deadly.

Gunnery Commander Backhouse, standing to Luce's left, nodded with approval and said flatly, "That German admiral and his fucking squadron have trifled with the wrong bloody empire."

Luce smiled. "Now we just have to go and find them."

The immense battlecruisers dropped anchor beyond the eastern edge of the reef and immediately ran up flags summoning colliers. The two warships had steamed directly from their previous stop at Cape Verde, and their coal bunkers were almost empty. Colliers sidled up beside each of the large ships and began the laborious coaling process. *Invincible* and *Inflexible* were laden with fresh food and supplies from Britain; while the coaling continued, a dozen small boats ferried supplies from the two large warships to the other vessels of the fleet. As noon approached, the flagship ran up another general signal. Each of the warship captains was to convene in four hours aboard *Invincible* for a council with Admiral Sturdee.

◆

THE CAPTAINS gathered in the spacious senior officers' wardroom aboard *Invincible*. Luce had served on a variety of ships during his career, but he had never been aboard a battlecruiser of this class. She was a couple of years older than *Glasgow*, but her condition and overall fit and finish were entirely modern and first-rate. Considering how large a vessel she was, Luce was impressed that her top speed was rated nearly as high as his own light cruiser. This was a warship designed to run down and kill virtually anything afloat.

Although all of the captains were present, as ordered, at the appointed hour, neither of the admirals had yet to make an appearance. The officers mingled among themselves while sharply uniformed stewards walked about, pouring glasses of fine brandy — undoubtedly from Sturdee's private collection. A long wooden table bisected the room, set with fine linens, china, crystal, and silverware for the meal that would follow. Luce knew several of the other captains, particularly Harry Skipwith of *Carnarvon*. Luce had also served with John Allen of HMS *Kent* and Richard Phillimore of the flagship's sister ship, HMS *Inflexible*. He greeted *Bristol's* Captain Fanshawe, whom he had met two days earlier, and introduced himself to the other captains in the room.

"Glad you and *Glasgow* could join our little party," said Skipwith. "I hear that those Brazilians did a bang-up job repairing your ship." Skipwith was a slightly built man of medium height, with black hair, a neatly trimmed mustache, and a broad grin. John had liked Harry from the first moment they met at the academy and could hardly remember a time when he was not smiling.

"They did indeed. I've never seen shipwrights and welders work at such a pace — and with considerable skill. My engineering commander now claims that we have the fastest ship in the entire navy. Of course, with a bit of grog in him, he also claims to be third cousin to the King, so I'm not sure how reliable he is." A steward paused beside the two officers. He was bearing a tray upon which was a crystal carafe of amber brandy. Both captains declined a refill; the steward nodded crisply and moved on. Luce continued, "It's good to be back in the mix again. For a bit there, Harry, it looked as though *Glasgow* might sit out the rest of the war in a dry dock in Portsmouth."

Skipwith gestured to Luce with his brandy glass, suggesting that the two men might share a word in private. They walked over to the port bulkhead, near a porthole that looked out toward *Inflexible*, which was anchored on the gentle swells a quarter of a mile away. A collier was still moored beside the other battlecruiser, and Luce could see booms swinging bags of coal across to the warship's decks.

"Seriously, it's good to see you in one piece, John," said Skipwith. "So sorry about *Good Hope* and *Monmouth*. Too many good men lost."

Luce nodded. "It didn't have to be that way, you know. Cradock asked the Admiralty for more ships, more firepower."

"I know," said Skipwith. He leaned closer and spoke more quietly. "In fact, I heard something about that just a few days ago." He gestured with his head toward the room's forward double doors, behind which the two admirals were still in their meeting. "According to Stoddart, they've pinned our loss at Coronel on Sturdee—and of course Cradock himself."

"Who has?"

"The rest of the Admiralty—Fisher mostly, but Churchill too. Although Sturdee had only been chief of staff at the Admiralty since the start of the war, it seems he wasted little time making himself unwelcome. Fisher hates him apparently—thinks he's an arrogant fool. In fact, it seems everyone in London thinks Sturdee's an intolerable, pompous buffoon. With that loss at Coronel—our first naval defeat in a century—they blame Cradock for the tactical blunders and have fingered Sturdee as the Admiralty's scapegoat. They've sent him out here ostensibly to atone for getting Cradock killed, but really I think they just wanted to be rid of him in London."

Luce shook his head. "Churchill should bear the largest measure of the blame for Coronel. We know how it works at the Admiralty. Sturdee was a paper-pusher. Regardless of what authority he might have held as chief of staff, he didn't have the final word. I've seen the cables. When Cradock asked for help, he was repeatedly denied it—and not by Sturdee. It's a whitewash and a sham." He sighed deeply. "As far as Cradock's share of the blame, he was placed in an impossible position. They offered him only *Canopus*, which was too old and slow to be of any use to us. When we encountered the full German squadron that afternoon, Cradock had only two choices: flee and be branded a coward or stand and fight—and die in the attempt. Anyone who knew Cradock could predict which option he would choose."

"You're right, John." Skipwith was silent for a moment. "At least they've sent *Invincible* and *Inflexible* from the Grand Fleet—something I'd never thought I'd see. Perhaps they are atoning for their *own* blunders and they've finally taken von Spee's threat seriously."

"We can hope," agreed Luce. "And let's also hope that Sturdee takes it seriously as well, because if the Admiralty have just sent him out here expecting him to fail, then this could go very badly for all of us."

Behind them, the forward double doors swung open, and Admiral Sturdee strode purposefully into the room, followed immediately by Admiral Stoddart. All of the captains came to attention, and Sturdee muttered, "At ease, gentlemen." Vice-Admiral Frederick Doveton Sturdee was a small man, with short graying brown hair and deep-set, heavily-lidded eyes. He had a prominent chin and thin lips drawn into a perpetual scowl—and despite his diminutive stature, his uniform appeared to be a size too small for him. His physical movements seemed hurried, as if having to move about the room was a tedious chore that was best accomplished quickly. In contrast, Rear-Admiral Archibald Stoddart, walking gracefully behind him, was taller than Sturdee, slender and impeccably attired, with neatly groomed gray hair. Luce thought that visually they made an odd pair.

Sturdee took a few minutes to quickly greet all of the captains in the room, apparently none of whom he had met previously. When Luce introduced himself and shook the admiral's hand, Sturdee paused briefly and squinted at Luce as though he was assessing the younger man. The admiral said nothing, however, and then moved on to the next captain. Within minutes, he had dispensed with the brief introductions and took his place at the head of the long table in the middle of the room. Stoddart assumed a position to his left.

Sturdee said, "Please take a seat, gentlemen. I promise that I will not bore you with complicated details of our plans—because they are quite straightforward. Then we can move on to what I am assured will be a most sumptuous meal prepared by my chefs."

Although Sturdee remained standing, each of the other men took seats at places along the table, and the stewards fussed about, refilling their glasses. After a moment, when the stewards had retreated and the room had again settled into silence, Sturdee resumed speaking.

"After the regretful losses of so many fine men aboard *Good Hope* and *Monmouth* at Coronel, the Admiralty have seen fit to ensure that the German East Asia Squadron is hunted down and destroyed. To this end, they have sent me, in command of the battlecruisers *Invincible* and *Inflexible*, to find our enemies, wherever they may be hiding, and wipe them from the oceans." He gestured dismissively at the bulkheads around him. "As we know, just this flagship alone has more firepower than von Spee's entire rogue squadron. Having two such battlecruisers provides us with overwhelming firepower. Therefore, the most important part of our task will be *finding* the enemy—for once they are found, we will swiftly annihilate them.

"I have discussed with Admiral Stoddart the disposition of our forces. Because our combined fleet is now led by the two battlecruisers, I have determined that to accomplish our task we will not have immediate need of the armored cruiser *Defence*. Therefore, Captain..." Sturdee paused, apparently not remembering the name of the *Defence's* commander. He looked quizzically toward Stoddard, seated to his left.

"Leatham," said Stoddart quietly.

"Yes, Leatham," repeated Sturdee. "Captain Leatham will be taking her to Cape Town to join the escort squadron there. *Defence* departs at dawn."

Luce glanced over at Captain Leatham, whom he had met only half an hour earlier. The man looked genuinely surprised to hear that he and his ship were no longer needed and were being dismissed to South Africa.

"The remaining ships of the fleet, now under my command, will sail for the Falklands in three days' time, at dawn on the twenty-ninth. Until then, we shall spend the next two full days here at Abrolhos, engaging in formation drills and gunnery exercises."

Luce could hardly believe his ears. Three more days of delay? What could Sturdee be thinking? With each passing hour, the Germans could be closer to launching an attack in the Atlantic, either at the Falklands or at the River Plate. The British ships had already delayed far too long. Although Sturdee was obviously not soliciting opinions from his captains, Luce decided to risk an interruption. "Excuse me, sir," said Luce tentatively. Sturdee paused, looking down the table with his eyebrows knitted into a frown. All of the other officers turned to look at him as well. Luce went on, "Respectfully, sir, the Germans have had three weeks since their stop in Valparaiso to move down around the Cape and steam into the South Atlantic. Every additional day we wait..."

Admiral Sturdee held up a hand, interrupting Luce with a stern look. "Captain, the Admiralty has no reason to believe that the German squadron has yet entered the Atlantic. There have been no sightings of them anywhere south of Valparaiso, and our consular offices report no unusual activity within the German community in Punta Arenas, which was a telling indicator when *Dresden* was operating in the region. Furthermore, a recent wireless intercept report from Samoa indicates that at least some elements of von Spee's group may be headed back westward across the Pacific. He has been known to radically change direction and even split his forces temporarily. In any case, I am confident that we can maintain our current schedule and still be in place to protect the River Plate well before any German warships might consider rounding the Cape. The limited but valuable time we spend here in training during the next few days will ensure that when we do find the Germans, our tactics will be well coordinated and efficient."

Luce was deeply troubled. He felt—somehow *knew*—that Sturdee was making a grave mistake. He was certain that the Germans were much closer than Sturdee or the Admiralty believed. Still, it was also obvious that Sturdee had little interest in counsel from his captains on the matter.

Satisfied that he had squelched Luce's objection, Sturdee continued. "Naturally, when we arrive at Port Stanley, we'll coal all of the ships of the fleet. After that process is complete, using the Falklands as an operational base, we will commence systematically searching for the Germans. We will begin with a sweep along the Argentine coast and shipping lanes from Montevideo to Cape Horn. From there, we will move our efforts through the Strait of Magellan and around the Cape into the Pacific, where I believe most of von Spee's force may still be hiding—somewhere among the thousands of islands and channels along the southern Chilean coast. My plan is to use our two fast light cruisers, *Glasgow* and *Bristol*, as the lead ships in this search effort. They will be followed by the main body of the fleet. The role of *Glasgow* and *Bristol* will be much like that of dogs on a hunt. The light cruisers will find and flush the enemy, then retreat faster than they can be pursued. After the enemy ships have been located and identified, the battlecruisers and the rest of the fleet will then fall upon the Germans and destroy them."

Sturdee paused briefly, looking at the officers at the table as if he were challenging them to ask a question or voice a concern. When no one spoke, he continued. "There will be only one planned deviation from this protocol. If the Germans split their forces during the battle, the two battlecruisers will engage and destroy the large enemy armored cruisers, *Scharnhorst* and *Gneisenau*. The remaining ships of the fleet will engage and destroy the enemy light cruisers, *Nürnberg*, *Leipzig*, and *Dresden*. Is that understood?"

The captains voiced their assent, but Luce said nothing—and no one else appeared to notice his lack of enthusiasm.

"Excellent," said Sturdee with a smile that somehow looked more like a sneer. He motioned to one of the stewards, who briskly left the room. "I am a man of my word. Our meal shall not be delayed a moment longer." He raised his brandy glass. "To King, Country, and the Royal Navy's dominion over the seas."

The officers raised their glasses in unison. An aft door to the room opened, and a phalanx of stewards and cooks swept into the room bearing the first course of the meal—an orange curried soup with steamed vegetables. As they were setting plates and bowls in front of the captains, Admiral Stoddart stood and raised his glass.

"If I may, gentlemen," said Stoddart, speaking to the group for the first time. "I would also like to offer a toast—to the courageous officers and men of *Good Hope* and *Monmouth*. We entrust their souls unto God. May He grant them peace, serenity, and calm seas for eternity." All of the men solemnly returned the toast, and Stoddart took his seat again.

The meal was delicious, as Sturdee had predicted. Luce could not remember when last he had dined in such splendor. In fact, it seemed inappropriately lavish, considering the general deprivations of wartime. Despite the culinary excess, Luce hardly noticed, much less tasted, the various courses as they were served. His unsettled thoughts distracted him more greatly as the evening progressed. He simply could not imagine sitting idly at Abrolhos for several more days while the German squadron lurked out there—somewhere. For all he knew, the enemy could be stealthily entering the Atlantic at that very moment. After a time, he lost his appetite altogether and merely pushed the food about on his plate with his fork.

Immediately after the dessert course was served, Sturdee abruptly stood and announced that he had numerous pressing matters to attend to and would be returning to his quarters. Implied was the suggestion that the assembled captains were dismissed. He wished everyone a good evening and departed quickly through the forward double doors.

Within minutes, all of the other officers, including Admiral Stoddart and Captain Skipwith, were preparing to leave. Luce shook their hands and bade them farewell, but he decided to stay. Luce lingered until only he and *Invincible's* captain, Percy Beamish, remained. Luce had met Beamish only that afternoon. He seemed to be a likeable, straightforward officer, and Luce wondered what he thought of Admiral Sturdee.

"Captain Beamish?" Luce asked. "Do you think I might have a private discussion with the admiral before I leave for *Glasgow*?"

"I don't see why not," answered Beamish with a raised eyebrow. "A word of warning, though. Old Sturdee's a man of set habits. He doesn't care to be disturbed out of turn. He might agree to see you, but he won't be happy about it."

◆

BY HIS ESTIMATION, Luce had been waiting in the passageway outside the door for almost ten minutes. Finally, the young lieutenant-commander reopened the door and stood aside. "The admiral will see you now, Captain," he said.

"Thank you." Luce entered an anteroom that doubled as a small office for the lieutenant-commander, who was Admiral Sturdee's chief of staff.

The lieutenant-commander returned to his desk and motioned toward an open door to the right. "He's right in there, sir."

Luce walked into the modestly-sized room, which was obviously Sturdee's office. One entire bulkhead was covered in shuttered bookcases, filled with dozens of books. Luce was immediately envious, for his crew had offloaded nearly all of *Glasgow's* books in Rio at the start of the war.

In the corner to his left lay a portly cream-colored bulldog upon a folded dark blue blanket. The dog raised his head, opened one large brown eye to regard Luce, and yawned with disinterest. The animal lowered his head and resumed sleeping.

Admiral Sturdee sat at a wooden desk that jutted from the far bulkhead into the middle of the compartment. The desk faced two starboard portholes that currently offered a nighttime view of the Abrolhos lighthouse's amber beacon. A lush blue oriental carpet covered much of the room's floor area. Sturdee wore a pair of glasses and was reading through what appeared to be a sheaf of wireless transcripts.

Without looking up, the admiral asked curtly, "To what do I owe this interruption, Captain Luce?"

"My apologies, sir," said Luce. "I felt it important that I speak with you immediately. Ordinarily, sir, I would not question your orders..."

"But that is precisely what you have come to do, is it not?" said Sturdee, who looked up for the first time and took off his spectacles to regard Luce. "I am not accustomed to being second-guessed by my captains, so I trust this is worth my time." His eyes narrowed as he awaited Luce's reply.

"I believe it is, sir." Luce swallowed hard. "I'm certain that waiting here for another two or three days will be a mistake. The Admiralty is in error if they think that von Spee has split his forces or that he may not venture into the Atlantic. In fact, he and his full squadron may be rounding Cape Horn as we speak, if they have not done so already."

Sturdee looked at Luce quizzically. "We've received no intelligence whatsoever that the enemy squadron is operating anywhere near the Cape or the Strait. When only *Dresden* was hiding down there, we had so many tips and clues that Cradock was chasing his tail trying to find her. If the Germans can't hide a single light cruiser in that region without everyone hearing about it, how in the hell can they be hiding a whole squadron?"

"I think that *Dresden's* captain was inexperienced—and even though he left a number of clues to his passing, he still eluded us. Admiral von Spee will make no such mistakes. He's kept his squadron effectively hidden as he maneuvered across the entire Pacific, despite being sought by three navies. The only times that he showed himself were when his ships arrived suddenly, with overwhelming force—at Fanning, Samoa, Tahiti, and Coronel. In each of those cases, he got away again without leaving any obvious clues as to where he might show up next. He did all of that while pulling a slow train of colliers and support ships. I have no doubt that he could move his squadron around the Cape without us knowing about it."

"What of the wireless signals picked up by our operators in Samoa? They have intercepted a series of messages, getting stronger by the day, using call signs unique to the East Asia Squadron. Why should the Admiralty not take that as a sign that von Spee has doubled back into the Pacific after Coronel and is looking to make mischief farther west?"

"Two reasons, sir," said Luce. "Firstly, why on earth would he brazenly announce his approach to Samoa or Fiji or wherever it is they think he's headed? He has operated in near radio silence for months, and only now does he start giving his position away? I'm not buying it. Secondly, the few times he has shown himself or used his wireless when he knew we were listening, he used deception and misdirection to throw us off. At Samoa and Fiji, he steamed away in the opposite direction to where he was next seen. At Coronel, he had his entire squadron employ only *Leipzig's* call sign to lure us into a trap. If our boys in Samoa are hearing German wireless transmissions getting nearer and stronger, you can bet your rum ration it's a trick."

Sturdee looked exasperated. "Even if your suppositions were correct, it still does not mean that von Spee will come charging into the Atlantic to attack our shipping at the Plate."

Luce nodded. "I agree. I don't think he's planning to attack the Plate at all."

"Then what in blazes do you think he's going to do?"

"I think he's going to make a break for home."

"Did you bring a fortune-teller aboard when you were in Rio, Luce?" asked Sturdee derisively. "How are you so convinced that the Germans are headed not only into the Atlantic, but all the way to Germany—despite the Admiralty's evidence to the contrary?"

"Because it is the only option that makes sense, sir. Admiral von Spee didn't steam all the way across the Pacific, just to turn around and head back the way he came—into the teeth of his enemies. He may have originally planned to harass our shipping along the west coast of South America, but meeting us in battle at Coronel left him with only one real option—now he has to try to make it home to Germany."

"But he won at Coronel—decisively so. Why wouldn't that victory have emboldened him?"

Luce shook his head. "I doubt it, sir. Old von Spee is no fool. He knew a mismatch when he saw one, so he willingly engaged our squadron. He also knows that he'll not get another such opportunity. He's realized that it is only a matter of time before we come looking for him with a force more powerful than his own. His ships' magazines are half-empty, and he has no way of acquiring more shells. Also, with every week that his ships spend out of a proper port facility, their hulls get dirtier and slower. He's likely wearing out equipment and running out of many of the basic necessities aboard his ships. Hell, *we're* running out of them, and we have ready access to supply vessels, reinforcements, and even friendly ports. He's all alone out there. Admiral von Spee knows he's on borrowed time, and he has to try to reach a home port while he still can."

For the first time in their conversation, Sturdee seemed to consider what Luce had said. "Why the hurry, then? Why should we not train for two more days here while we have the opportunity?"

"I think that the Falklands may be in danger, sir."

"If he's making a break for home, as you say, then why would he bother attacking the Falklands?"

"Because he can no longer afford to be held back by a train of colliers. My guess is that he's dismissed them already, before rounding the Cape. He will have to move swiftly, and he'll need coal along the way. Moving up the coast near the Plate is too dangerous, so he'll likely set a course up the center of the Atlantic, away from the primary shipping lanes. Right in his path from the Cape will be the ample coal stores of the Falklands, which he probably knows are lightly defended. With his bunkers full of British coal, he could steam on for another thousand miles or more, and we'd have no way of knowing where he'd turn up next—until his warships appeared on some unfortunate victim's horizon. I'd hate to arrive a day or two late to find Port Stanley a burning ruin."

"Speculation, Luce. All of this is speculation." Sturdee shook his head, but he paused for a moment. "We just got here after an extraordinarily long journey, and you would have us immediately pack up and rush off to the Falklands?"

"Yes, sir," affirmed Luce. "I realize this is just a hunch. I also understand that you would prefer to drill and maneuver with the fleet before we encounter the Germans. Couldn't we do that after we're operating from Port Stanley?"

Sturdee was silent momentarily; then he changed the subject. "I've read your report, of course. Read it a number of times, actually. It was also the subject of some debate at the Admiralty."

"Pardon me, sir?"

"Your dispatch, after the battle—your account of what happened. After reading it, dissecting it, and discussing it, I wanted to ask you a few questions."

"Yes, sir?"

"Why didn't Cradock wait for *Canopus* before attacking the enemy squadron?"

"I think he would have, if *Canopus* had been closer, sir. As it was, she was still a day away. I also think—as Cradock apparently did—that having *Canopus* with us would not have made much of a difference in the outcome. Even with her big guns, she was too slow and unreliable to have been of any real use against the Germans. She would have slowed our line and given the enemy even more opportunities to pick us apart."

"Seems like an awfully rash decision," said Sturdee.

"Respectfully, sir, I disagree. Cradock was placed in a precarious position. If he had fled to join *Canopus*, he would have left *Otranto* to slaughter. Cradock would never have done that. Thus, he chose to stay and fight—and in doing so, he allowed *Otranto* to get away safely."

Sturdee thought about that; then said, "In your report, you made mention of the accuracy of the German gunners. How accurate were they, really?"

"Best damned gunnery I've ever seen, sir. At a range of six miles, steaming in near darkness at seventeen knots into twenty-foot swells, their armored cruisers were hitting *Good Hope* and *Monmouth* with every salvo. Their light cruisers had more trouble striking us in those conditions, but we had the advantage in range. Even with that, they were consistently straddling us. After the big armored cruisers turned their guns on *Glasgow*, we had only minutes to flee before we would surely have been destroyed." He paused for a moment. "I'm still amazed we survived, sir."

"Even so, you went back for *Monmouth*," observed Sturdee.

"Of course, sir."

"I could sense it in your report, Luce. Leaving those men behind was extremely difficult for you."

"Yes, sir," Luce acknowledged. "The hardest thing I've ever had to do. At times... I can still see their faces, sir," he admitted.

"Then how did you know that leaving them was the right thing to do?"

"I'm not sure, sir. I've asked myself that question many times. I had to ensure the safety of *Glasgow's* crew. Had we stayed to attempt a rescue, we probably would have been found and destroyed as well. I'm still not truly convinced that there wasn't some other way."

"Perhaps it was another one of your hunches," observed Sturdee.

"Perhaps, sir," acknowledged Luce quietly.

Sturdee paused silently before speaking again. "Most of us, myself included, can only imagine what that must have been like—to be forced to leave behind a stricken ship with little or no hope that any of her crew could be rescued." Sturdee looked pointedly at Luce, much as he had earlier that afternoon when they first met—as if he was once again assessing the captain for the first time. "I believe that there are different types of courage, Luce. There is courage under fire, courage of conviction, and the courage to make a difficult choice in a dire circumstance. It seems to me that you have all three, Captain."

"Thank you, sir—although it does not always seem that way to me."

Sturdee nodded. "The Admiralty have tasked me with finding and destroying von Spee's squadron. Although neither Fisher nor Churchill care much for me or for how I do things, they have given me wide latitude to accomplish this mission in whatever manner I choose. Because I've worked with that lot, I know I cannot completely trust the Admiralty's assessments of events or their interpretations of the intelligence they receive. They are too great a distance from the action and too distracted by politics. You, however, are the only commander aboard any of the ships assembled here who has actually faced our enemy in battle. I'm more inclined to trust one of your hunches than those of the First Sea Lord. Do you really think that it would behoove us to leave earlier for the Falklands?"

"Yes, sir, I do."

Sturdee sighed. "Very well, Luce, we leave tomorrow."

# TWENTY-TWO

*Sunday, November 29, 1914*
*Drake Passage, South Pacific Ocean, 177 Kilometers West of Cape Horn*

"FLOODING REPORTED in the torpedo compartment, sir," said Sub-Lieutenant Haas, raising his voice to be heard above the roar of the storm. *Nürnberg's* bow crested another huge gray swell and plunged into the swirling trough beyond. Haas was pitched forward toward the voice pipe array, but he managed to brace himself with his hands against the steel console.

"What do they expect? They're in the bottom of the ship," snapped Captain Schönberg testily. He was also thrown forward, but he steadied himself by tightly grasping one of the swiveling metal chairs bolted to the deck of the wheelhouse. "Of course they've got some flooding. Tell them to pump it out."

"They are pumping it, sir," replied Haas. "They report that water pouring in from decks above them is outpacing the pumps."

"Well, they need to pump faster," said Schönberg, exasperated. "I have more important considerations than worrying whether their trousers are getting wet. Five degrees to starboard!" he shouted at the helmsman. "Steer into that oncoming wave!"

"Yes, sir. Five degrees starboard," echoed the young helmsman, who was sweating profusely despite the chill in the compartment. He turned the wheel and the ship's bow nosed slightly southeast as they reached the bottom of the trough and another massive, twelve-meter swell loomed before them.

Schönberg turned back to Haas and said icily, "As for our damp torpedo crew, sub-lieutenant, I assume that the fear of drowning is enough of an incentive for them to pump more efficiently, but tell them that if the water damages the launch mechanisms, I will personally see to it that every man assigned there on this watch is stripped of his rank and put off the ship at our next anchorage."

"Uh, yes, sir," stammered Haas.

*Nürnberg's* forecastle was awash in roiling green seawater as the ship rose up the far side of the trough. Everyone in the wheelhouse held on tightly to handholds, pedestals, and bulkhead supports as the cruiser's bow pitched upward and seemed to slowly crawl up the foaming face of the wave. At the top of the crest, the ship hung there, momentarily perched atop the swell. Then her bow crashed downward again in a dizzying drop that made the stomachs of each of the men lurch. As the cruiser plunged forward and Schönberg's grip tightened on the armrest of the chair, he could just make out, half a kilometer ahead, the stern of *Gneisenau*, steaming in formation before them. Presumably she was following *Scharnhorst*, in the vanguard, but Schönberg could not see the flagship that far ahead through the heavy rain and spray. He also had to assume that behind him, following astern of *Nürnberg*, steamed the rest of the squadron—*Leipzig*, then *Dresden*, and finally, bringing up the rear, the passenger ship *Seydlitz*. Other than occasional glimpses of *Leipzig* behind them, Schönberg had not seen the trailing ships for most of the day. *Nürnberg* had been continually drifting out of the line, despite the best efforts of the duty helmsmen, and the trailing ships were probably also having great difficulty maintaining formation.

He noted that although *Gneisenau* was also pitching and rolling in the heavy seas ahead, the large armored cruiser was much better equipped to handle these extreme conditions than the much smaller *Nürnberg*. Maerker's ship was much steadier in these seas than his own, and he imagined the larger ship's crew was having a somewhat better time of it than *Nürnberg's*—half of whom were probably thoroughly seasick by now. Someday, he thought, I shall be the captain of such a ship, instead of this little sardine tin.

Since their departure from the Gulf of Penas three days earlier, the weather and seas had steadily worsened as the German squadron struggled southward. For the first two days of the journey, they steamed directly into the teeth of the keening wind. With each passing hour, the waves got higher and stronger—and the low turbulent clouds hung over the angry sea like a cloak, obscuring the sky and rendering little difference between day and night. In the early afternoon on the third day, the squadron altered course to the southeast, and the waves now came at them from the starboard bow—each crest seemingly higher than the last. Schönberg was sure that by now almost everything breakable aboard the ship was already broken. As the cruiser pitched and rolled dramatically in the heavy seas, everything not bolted down was sliding around, falling over, and rolling about. Most of the lower compartments on the ship, with the fortunate exception of the magazines, were reporting some flooding, as seawater cascaded down from hatches and openings in the decks above.

The biggest problem Schönberg faced was not inside the ship, however. The dozens of sacks of coal that they had lashed to the weather decks before their departure had altered the cruiser's center of gravity, causing her to be much less stable. Each time a wave struck the ship on or near their beam, *Nürnberg* rolled more dramatically than she would have otherwise, sometimes submerging her gunwales in the white, roiling sea. Already, the waves were well over twelve meters in height. If they got any higher, the ship was at risk of capsizing.

"Lieutenant, what is the wind speed now?" Schönberg shouted toward the navigation officer standing unsteadily to his left. The ship crested another wave and plunged into the churning white trough beyond. The wind was now a constant roar that howled around the superstructure and repeatedly forced sprays of chilling mist through seams in the exterior doorways.

The lieutenant hesitated and rechecked the gauges before him. "Uh…up to sixty-five knots, sir," he said in disbelief. "That's twelve on the Beaufort scale." The winds had picked up steadily during the past hour and were now at hurricane force.

"Good God," said Schönberg. "If we don't get that coal off our decks, we'll be swamped and capsized within the hour." He turned to the communications officer behind him—a relatively inexperienced lieutenant who had been promoted since the recent demotion of Lieutenant-Commander Engel. "Wireless signal to the flagship. Request permission to jettison the exterior coal. Say we are rolling forty-five degrees and are in danger of being swamped or capsized."

"Yes, sir." The young communications officer relayed the message through the voice pipe to the wireless room—having to shout the message and repeat himself to be heard.

Another massive wave, greater than fifteen meters in height, loomed suddenly above them to starboard—a rapidly approaching mountain of foaming white seawater. The helmsman saw it and knew he could not react in time to steer the ship into the oncoming surge. "Brace for impact!" he shouted, before the wave slammed into *Nürnberg's* starboard beam, sending fountains of water over the starboard bulwarks along the length of the ship and nearly submerging the entire cruiser in swirling brine. The cruiser shuddered and groaned with the impact and rolled dramatically to port.

The communications officer lost his grip upon the starboard bulkhead and fell, sliding across the severely tilting compartment. Before he struck the port exterior door, he managed to get his feet in front of him to lessen the impact.

Schönberg noticed that one of the starboard windows in the wheelhouse had begun to crack—the fissures spreading upward from a lower corner like a growing spider web. This was a disturbing indication that the entire ship was undergoing extreme stresses as the powerful seas battered and wrenched the cruiser's hull—pushing, pulling, and twisting the steel from bow to stern with more force than her design engineers had ever envisioned. The constant bludgeoning of wind and sea was taking a toll upon *Nürnberg*, and he knew they did not have much time.

A hollow voice echoed from one of the pipes, but the words were lost in the din. The communications officer regained his footing and scrambled back to his station. He pressed his ear to the fluted opening of the metal tube before him, straining to hear what was being said. "Repeat message!" he shouted into the pipe, then listened once again. "Confirmed," he said. He turned to the captain and announced, "Flagship has granted permission for all warships to jettison the exterior coal, sir."

"About damned time," groused Schönberg. "Mister Haas, assemble three teams: one forward, one amidships, and one aft. They are to go out on deck and cut the restraining lines on those exterior sacks of coal. Toss them over the gunwales after they are cut loose. We can't have hundred-pound sacks of coal sliding around on the deck, smashing everything to pieces, and stopping up the scuppers. Every man is to be tethered securely. Don't lose any idiots overboard. Understood?"

"Yes, sir," replied Haas, who turned and left the bridge, heading down the starboard ladder to the decks below.

For the next half hour, Haas's men worked to cut and jettison the sacks of coal lashed to the deck. As the teams labored in the hazardous conditions, the storm continued to pummel the ship. Wave after wave tossed the cruiser about in a chaotic and gut-wrenching maniacal dance. Schönberg could sense that the storm was worsening, and he hoped that his men could remove the coal before another massive wave capsized his ship or damaged her beyond repair.

After what seemed like an eternity, Lieutenant Haas finally reported via voice pipe that the exterior coal had been jettisoned and that everyone was safe, although two men had suffered minor cuts and bruises and had been sent to the infirmary.

"Let's see how she handles now," Schönberg muttered to no one in particular, but he looked pointedly at the helmsman, who steered the ship into the next immense swell. The cruiser rose up more nimbly over the wave, rolling slightly to port before crashing down into the trough beyond. The effect of the wave was not as severe as it had been before.

Removing the coal sacks had worked.

Thank God, thought Schönberg. We might survive this storm after all. He peered out over the angry sea and again glimpsed the tilting stern of *Gneisenau* steaming ahead. He smiled as he realized that part of him had actually been hoping that Maerker's big ship would be swamped by the waves. He shook his head and willed himself to be patient.

◆

PICTON ISLAND squatted at the eastern end of the Beagle Channel, immediately south of Tierra del Fuego, one hundred kilometers north of Cape Horn. The low, almost featureless island barely rose from the sea at the mouth of the channel, like the gray-green back of a massive beast lurking just beneath the surface. The East Asia Squadron was moored in the sheltered waters near the island after their harrowing voyage around the Cape.

The massive storm had largely blown itself out by the morning of December 1st, leaving only intermittent squalls and biting hailstorms in its wake. The squadron had finally been able to reform and steam at a respectable ten knots once again. Gliding into the relatively calm waters of the channel near Picton Island brought a palpable sense of relief to the crews of the squadron.

All of the ships had survived the trip intact, although the rough passage was not without consequences. Hundreds of items aboard each of the vessels had been broken or damaged in the rough seas. Numerous men had sustained minor injuries—mostly cuts and bruises, burns, and a few broken bones. Some of the ships reported minor leaks and superficial damage that was now being repaired. Most importantly, all of the additional coal that had been piled upon the ships' decks in San Quintin Bay had been lost—jettisoned to save the ships from capsizing. Now, without the colliers, the squadron had enough coal to reach the Falklands but would have difficulty making any other more distant port if they could not refuel. Although *Baden* and *Santa Isabel* had been sent through the Strait of Magellan toward the Falklands, their arrival was far from guaranteed—particularly if they were stopped and boarded by a roving British warship. This turn of events had cast some doubt upon the admiral's plans for attacking the British outpost. Although the squadron could reach Port Stanley, if they had to divert to some other destination for any reason or evade a British patrol, their limited coal supply would become a serious liability.

Admiral von Spee had informed his captains that they would be waiting here for several days while he reconsidered his options. Captain Maerker was hopeful that this unanticipated shortage of coal would cause the admiral to abandon his plan to attack the Falklands and opt instead for a route that would continue more directly homeward. His sense of foreboding about the admiral's plan disquieted Maerker greatly, and the morning after the squadron's arrival at Picton Island, he had awoken from a troubled sleep well before dawn.

Through the portholes across the waters of the channel lay the dark green shores of Tierra del Fuego to the north. Most of the other ships of the squadron were in Maerker's field of view. *Scharnhorst* lay a few hundred meters to the northwest. Moored directly to the north were *Nürnberg* and *Dresden*, and beyond them lay *Seydlitz*, which had also survived the rough passage around the Cape with only minor damage. Only *Leipzig* was currently absent, for she was out on patrol in the waters to the east.

Maerker tried to clear his head by composing a letter to Ilsa. He recounted for her the squadron's recent stay at the beautiful Gulf of Penas—describing in great detail the stunning geology of the place, with its mountains, glaciers, wooded expanses, and verdant marshlands. He also conveyed the terrors of their recent passage around the Cape, as well as the aftermath of that voyage—with broken crockery, snapped wires and lines, injuries to some of the men, and of course the lost coal.

He wished that he could write that the squadron was now certainly homeward bound, but he did not want to mislead her with any false hope. The reality was that he had never felt farther away from home than at that moment—and he wondered if he or any of his officers and men would ever set foot upon German soil again. He sat there, looking out across the water, with his pen hovering expectantly over the paper.

There was a light knock at his cabin door.

"Enter," he said in reply.

A young lieutenant opened the door cautiously. "Good morning, sir. I am sorry to disturb you, but Lieutenant-Commander Petri stated that you wished to be informed of any reported contact with other vessels."

"Yes, that's correct. Have our spotters seen something in the channel?"

"No, sir, but *Leipzig* just reported via wireless that she spotted a sailing ship and is moving to intercept."

"A sailing ship?"

"Yes, sir. *Leipzig* reports that they are in pursuit of a four-masted sailing vessel."

"Thank you, Lieutenant," said Maerker, dismissing the young officer with a nod. A sailing ship? He smiled and thought with some amusement that Captain Haun was apparently having a slow day on patrol duty.

He would later reflect that had he realized the significance of Captain Haun's prize, he would not have been so amused.

◆

THE SAILING SHIP that had blundered within sight of *Leipzig* was *Drummuir*, a thirty-year-old, four-masted, iron-hulled merchant sailing ship owned by Hind, Rolph & Company of San Francisco. She had departed the port of Swansea in mid-September with 2,800 tons of Welsh coal bound for California. *Leipzig's* captain, immediately realizing the importance of her cargo, seized the ship, claiming that the formerly British coal was war materiel belonging to an enemy combatant. *Drummuir's* Canadian captain was irate but could do nothing.

After the sailing ship was towed to the squadron's anchorage at Picton Island, her crew was forcibly removed and transferred to *Seydlitz* under guard. For the next several days, all of *Drummuir's* coal was laboriously offloaded and distributed among the warships.

The capture of the sailing vessel's cargo, to Captain Maerker's disappointment, reinvigorated von Spee's plans for attacking the Falklands. The admiral ordered that all of the cruisers undergo extensive inspections and preventative maintenance in anticipation of the upcoming assault. Not surprisingly, after nearly five months away from any type of proper port facilities, the ships were exhibiting significant signs of wear. The engineers had exhausted their supplies of spare parts of every sort, and even the onboard machine shops could no longer reliably fashion enough struts, plates, spars, fittings, and valves to compensate for all of the squadron's worn and broken parts. *Gneisenau's* engineering commander reported that steam fittings on at least five of the main boilers were now being held in place by makeshift clamps, and the port propeller shaft was intermittently emitting a vibration that his men had yet to isolate and repair.

Of additional concern to Maerker was the fact that until they could dock in a truly sheltered harbor, the ships' hulls could not be scraped of accumulated barnacles. The increased drag of the fouled hulls would limit the speed of the squadron and make them less able to outrun and outmaneuver their opponents as they had at Coronel. Maerker already could tell that *Gneisenau's* top speed had been effectively reduced by a few knots.

While the captain was beset by concern, the overall atmosphere among *Gneisenau's* crew was upbeat. In spite of Graf Spee's directive that the attack plans remain secret, word of the impending raid had leaked out to the crews of all the ships—and the sense of anticipation and excitement among the men was palpable. Maerker chose to keep his misgivings to himself, so as not to dampen the resurgent morale of the crew. He also granted a request from some of the men to go ashore on the nearby island to cut down small pine trees so that the crew could properly decorate the ship for the upcoming Christmas holiday.

Further boosting the men's spirits, the admiral himself toured each of the ships over the next several days while they lay at anchor and coaled, staying for half a day on each warship. He made a point of visiting at length with his sons—Otto on *Nürnberg* and Heinrich on *Gneisenau*. He praised the courage of all of the men of the squadron and promised that a great and glorious victory awaited them.

During his visit to *Gneisenau*, Maerker hosted the admiral for dinner with his senior staff. After the main course, Doctor Nohl surprised everyone by playing classical melodies on the ship's piano, although the instrument was now in dire need of some professional tuning. The evening was a welcome and relaxing change of pace for all of the officers. After dinner, Maerker and Graf Spee also played a game of bridge with Lieutenant-Commanders Petri and Busch. When the card game was complete, the admiral stood and drained the remaining drops of brandy from his glass.

"Time for this old man to turn in," said Graf Spee. "Thank you for your hospitality, Julius. Most gracious as always." He shook hands with each of the officers. "Excellent game, gentlemen. We must do this again at our next opportunity."

Both lieutenant-commanders thanked the admiral, bade him a good evening, and departed. Maerker had not been alone with the admiral in many weeks, and this was his first opportunity to privately express his misgivings about Graf Spee's plans for the attack on the Falklands. "Before you depart, sir, I wondered if I might have a word in private."

"Certainly, Julius. What is it?"

Maerker had determined that being direct with the admiral was his best option, so he simply stated what he was thinking. "Is there a chance that I might talk you out of this attack on the Falklands, sir?"

Graf Spee chuckled. "I suppose there is always a chance of almost anything happening." He looked pointedly at *Gneisenau's* captain and frowned. "I know you're a cautious man, Julius. In fact, it is one of the things I most respect about you. Your measured counsel helps to balance out some of the more… rash views and opinions among my commanders. I believe, however, that in war one cannot always choose the path of least risk. Sometimes we must cast the dice and see which faces come up."

"I agree, of course, sir. Wars are not won by the timid. However, when rolling dice, some bets are unwise, regardless of the potential winnings. We have already come so far, in large part because of our caution and discretion. With the final and most critical leg of our long journey still ahead, a diversion to attack a British installation now seems like madness."

The admiral paused before replying. "Do you think me mad, Julius?" His voice had taken on an edge, and his eyes smoldered a dark blue-gray.

"Of course not, sir. I am speaking only of…"

"It is late, and I am tired, Julius," Graf Spee interrupted, now looking as weary as he sounded. "You will have ample opportunity to express your opinions or alternate plans at the council of captains. I bid you good night." With that, the conversation was abruptly concluded.

Graf Spee summoned a steward, who brought him his coat and hat and sent word to have his pinnace made ready. Maerker walked with the admiral in silence down to the platform where *Scharnhorst's* boat was tied up. Without ceremony, the admiral went aboard.

Maerker saluted as the lines were cast off and the small boat pulled away. Graf Spee returned the salute in a perfunctory fashion and then turned his back and sat down. Maerker watched as the boat steamed across the dark water toward the flagship. He kept thinking of the look in the admiral's eyes just moments earlier—and for the first time he truly wondered if there was madness lurking there.

◆

ON THE MORNING of their fourth day at Picton Island, the admiral summoned the captains of all the warships to the flagship for what was to be the final meeting before the squadron departed for the Falklands. The commanders met once again in the senior officers' wardroom, where a large chart showing the Falklands had been laid out upon the table. As in similar meetings before, Captain Schönberg of *Nürnberg* was aloof and seemingly hostile toward Maerker as he glowered and chewed on the bit of an unlit pipe. By contrast, the other captains, particularly Haun of *Leipzig* and Schultz of *Scharnhorst*, were animated and clearly excited about the prospect of the raid. Lüdecke was thoughtful and quiet, as was his usual demeanor. The men chatted among themselves while they awaited the admiral, and Maerker took the opportunity to reluctantly but graciously congratulate Haun on his capture of *Drummuir*, which had facilitated the refilling of the squadron's coal bunkers. After several minutes, the admiral entered the room with a flourish, trailed by Filietz.

"Good morning, gentlemen," Graf Spee boomed jovially. He smiled broadly and shook hands with each of the captains. Maerker noted that he had never seen such a gleam in the old man's eyes. Before he began, the admiral bade them to sit down at the table where the map was displayed.

"We are poised to embark upon an historic mission," he began solemnly. "The East Asia squadron will soon strike a blow for the Kaiser and the Fatherland that will resonate across the world and rattle the halls of the British parliament. We will land German troops upon the British soil of the Falklands and take from our enemies their only sovereign outpost in the South Atlantic. Even as the Kaiser's armies in Europe are crushing the French, British, and Russians under our boot heels, we will demonstrate that the vaunted Royal Navy cannot protect its possessions abroad. I look forward to clapping the British governor in chains and tossing him into a cell aboard our prison ship, in much the same way that our enemies suffered such indignities upon our governor in Samoa."

He went on to outline the battle plan, from the approach—which would begin under the cover of the pre-dawn darkness—to the initial artillery assault upon the island—targeting the wireless station and any potential gun emplacements—to the armed landings, which would occur in multiple locations within the harbor of Port William and along the peninsula known as Cape Pembroke. After the warships had secured the harbor and the sailors had established a beachhead, *Seydlitz* would steam into Port William with the reserve volunteer soldiers, who would make their landings to secure the town and outlying areas. The initial assault was to take no more than a single day—with the admiral's goal to have the port and town completely secured by sundown. Then, if the two chartered cargo ships with the trenching equipment and additional armament were not yet moored in the harbor, the flagship would contact them by wireless and summon them from wherever they were loitering.

Graf Spee paused and looked at the men seated before him. "I know that some of you have previously expressed misgivings about this plan." He glanced briefly at Maerker. "Now that you have seen the details, I would like to offer this opportunity for any one of you to speak openly about your concerns or offer any alternatives."

Schönberg was the first to speak. "Sir, you have outdone yourself. This plan is as audacious as it is brilliant. I would like to officially request that *Nürnberg* be assigned as the first cruiser to enter Port William after the initial bombardment. With her smaller size and draft, she would be an ideal choice for the first penetration of this enemy waterway. I would not want to risk the flagship—in the event that the channel is partially obstructed or conceals any other hazards. Once within the harbor, our guns can swiftly neutralize any immediate threats and clear the way for the remaining ships of the squadron."

"Thank you, Karl," replied Graf Spee. "I'll consider it."

"Do we know much about these landing sites, sir?" asked Haun, pointing to the locations on the map that the admiral had identified earlier. "Are these shores sandy, rocky, forested?"

"We unfortunately do not know for sure, but we believe that the southern shores along Cape Pembroke are rocky with little significant vegetation. We have reason to believe that there are areas for small boats to land, but our boys will need to be cautious, especially if the seas are rough." Graf Spee then indicated the bay known as Port William and the inner harbor of Port Stanley. "Here," he continued, "are marshy lowlands and sandy shores. The landings within the bay should be much easier. Even if we must land our men under small arms fire from the town, we should be able to disembark and advance rapidly."

"Speed will be critical," agreed Haun. "We'll need to land immediately after the initial bombardment, before the local populace can muster a coordinated defense of the town."

Schultz said, "The smaller guns aboard the ships will providing covering fire while our men land. Our gunners can keep the townsfolk's' heads down while we establish the beachheads."

Maerker glanced among his compatriots and realized that most of them supported the admiral's plan without reservation. Even Lüdecke, whom Maerker knew was also wary of this scheme, said nothing in dissention. After a few minutes, Maerker finally spoke. "As you already know, sir, I am concerned that this plan puts our squadron at unnecessary risk. I still believe it would be circumspect to avoid all British installations, particularly this one, as we head homeward through the Atlantic. The information we were provided about the lack of defenses at the Falklands is now weeks old. The British have had ample time to send ships and troops to defend the port."

"That is true," acknowledged Graf Spee, "but I doubt that the British would suddenly divert valuable military assets to protect this island when they have not done so for months. I believe they are consumed with their search for us — and this is probably the last place they expect us to appear." He paused before continuing. "While I appreciate your concerns, Julius, I intend to proceed with this attack. Scrapping it completely is out of the question." The steely tone of his voice indicated the finality of his decision.

In his peripheral vision, Maerker noticed that Schönberg was barely suppressing a satisfied smile.

Graf Spee continued. "However, I am a prudent man, and I value your counsel, Julius. So let us assume that you are right — and the British have established some sort of defense for the island. If that is the case, how would you revise these attack plans while maintaining the greatest measure of safety for our squadron?"

Maerker thoughtfully scrutinized the map before him. He was deeply disappointed that the admiral was pushing ahead regardless of his concerns, but he appreciated the irony that he was now being asked to modify an attack plan that he opposed more than anyone else in the room. Finally, he spoke. "Unfortunately, we do not know *what* those defenses might be. The British may have only strung up some barbed wire or they may have installed multiple gun emplacements guarding the harbor. They might have a single patrol boat there or a whole squadron of warships."

"Unlikely," scoffed Filietz under his breath.

Maerker ignored him and continued. "Assuming that they have established both land-based defenses and a seaborne presence, our attack plan must be flexible enough to deal with an array of possible scenarios. I don't know that we need to significantly change this entire plan, sir, other than the initial stage. I agree that we should approach the island before dawn, under the cover of darkness—much as we did at Samoa. However, I would propose two changes to your initial plan. Firstly, instead of attacking with the entire squadron in formation, as you have proposed, I believe that most of the squadron should remain some twenty-five kilometers behind, beyond the horizon. Only two ships should make the initial approach, which is where my second change would be implemented.

"Rather than approaching here from the southwest, then turning east along the coast for the bombardment run, I believe our pre-dawn approach should actually take the squadron farther out to sea to the east." He indicated with his finger on the map a semicircular route that looped well to the east of the island and then came back at the coastline westward. "The bay of Port William opens to the east. If the two lead warships are in position out here as dawn breaks, they will have a perfect westward view directly into the bay. Although Port Stanley and its inner harbor would still be screened from sight by Cape Pembroke, we'll be able to see if any ships are moored in the outer bay or if its entrance is blocked or mined."

Maerker looked at the admiral, trying to read anything in his expression. Graf Spee nodded almost imperceptibly but said nothing. Maerker continued. "If our two lead cruisers see any ships anchored in the bay, we can disable those vessels first, before beginning the bombardment run westward along the southern coast. Even if the British have stationed ships there, our sudden appearance at dawn just outside the entrance to the bay will not give them enough time to react effectively. After our lead cruisers have shelled any British warships at anchor, they can then continue their pass westward." He drew his finger in a line that ran west along the island's southern coastline. He indicated a point on the map where the wireless tower was located. "The guns of the two advance cruisers should be able to take down the wireless mast immediately. As they continue their westward course along the shore, we will soon know if the British have any gun emplacements situated along Cape Pembroke. If any such shore batteries reveal themselves, only these two ships will be at risk—not the entire squadron. Once again, two cruisers should have more than enough firepower to neutralize any shore batteries—in the same manner that we quickly silenced the hillside guns at Papeete."

Schönberg interrupted him. "Thus far, Captain Maerker, your plan is little different from the admiral's, except that you are using only two warships initially instead of all five, and in your plan we would be required to steam on a longer circuitous course farther out to sea to come at the target from a different direction. Furthermore, if we are forced to engage enemy warships in the bay before we have brought down the wireless mast, it allows the British that much more time to get an alarm signal out. I can hardly see how any of this is an improvement."

Maerker prickled at Schönberg's smug attitude, but he kept his voice even and measured. "I believe it is an improvement in several ways, Captain Schönberg. First of all, if the British do have a warship laying at anchor in Port William, we had better damn well disable it first, before it can raise steam and clear the bay to engage us in open water—even if the wireless station has to wait. If the British are able to get an alarm message out before we drop the wireless mast, I don't think we've lost much. Regardless, the British Admiralty will have determined within the day that the Falklands station was unresponsive, much as we did when the Yap station went dark. At most we would be buying ourselves a few hours. All of that pales in comparison to the havoc our enemies could wreak if they get a warship out of the port and can engage us at close quarters. Secondly, using two ships instead of five both minimizes the danger to the whole squadron from any shore batteries and would give those Falklands wireless operators less to report about, if they can transmit an alarm. All the British would know is that two enemy warships had attacked—leaving open the possibility that the remainder of the squadron was still elsewhere."

Maerker held his gaze on Schönberg. "Thirdly, shore batteries are not our only concern. The British may have deployed more than just a single warship to protect the island, and some of those additional naval vessels might be patrolling at sea outside the port. If so, we once again put fewer ships at risk during that initial encounter—but our two lead ships may still be able to fall back upon the main body of the squadron, which can then destroy any pursuing British vessels. Finally, it is still possible that the scenario we encounter at the Falklands will make it either difficult or impossible to complete the rest of the mission as planned. If the British have numerous warships patrolling around the island or if they have mined the harbor entrance, we will have to hastily reconsider. We cannot risk a prolonged firefight just to reach the island, nor do we have the proper equipment to rapidly clear a mined harbor to facilitate an armed landing. The element of surprise will be critical. If the two lead ships encounter anything other than an undefended or lightly defended port, they must alert the rest of the squadron, which can then flee before they are spotted." He addressed Graf Spee directly. "And that, sir, may be the ultimate benefit of this modification to the plan. Even if the two lead ships are engaged or damaged and cannot easily escape, the remaining ships of the squadron can flee—perhaps even before they are spotted—thus allowing them to once again disappear before the British can track them down."

Graf Spee nodded thoughtfully. "I think that is a reasonable adjustment, Julius. In fact, it is a measurable improvement. It gives us additional options and may even enhance the element of surprise. Well done." He addressed the whole group. "Do any of you have any comments on Captain Maerker's modified plan?"

"Makes sense," offered Haun. "I like the idea of being able to view all of the bay of Port William as the sun rises behind us. We'll know immediately if any ships are anchored there, and we'll still have the shock and surprise of the initial assault upon the port and the wireless station. It also offers us some flexibility if something does not go exactly according to plan."

"Agreed," said Schultz. "And if the port is undefended, the outcome should be nearly the same as the original plan. After the two lead ships have finished their initial bombardment, they can turn back to enter the harbor and begin landing men. Meanwhile, the rest of the squadron can be there in less than an hour to provide the next wave of landings."

Lüdecke nodded. He looked troubled but remained silent.

Schönberg simply glared, and Maerker wondered if he might actually bite through the pipe clenched between his teeth.

"I still believe these alterations are unnecessary," said Filietz, frowning through his spectacles at the map. "I am certain that the British, in their zeal to search for us elsewhere, have foolishly neglected to protect this outpost. Also, this alteration to the plan will require us to advance our timetable to steam a farther distance around the island but still be in position before sunup. It sounds unnecessarily complicated to me." He paused and glanced at Graf Spee. "Nevertheless, if the admiral is in favor of this approach, then I am as well."

Haun smiled mischievously. "Now the only question is, which two ships will lead the attack?"

Schönberg sniffed derisively. "I also think this change unnecessarily complicates the attack, but I would still like *Nürnberg* to be in the initial pair."

"Fine with me, Karl," said Graf Spee. "*Nürnberg* will be one of the two lead ships. As for the other, I believe we should send one of the armored cruisers in the vanguard. As Julius points out, we could encounter a British warship newly stationed there, and I'd like to ensure that we have enough firepower to repel or sink it, if necessary. Captain Maerker, would you consider leading with *Gneisenau*?"

Maerker sighed and had to smile at the irony. Somehow, he had talked himself into leading the very attack to which he was so adamantly opposed. He nodded in resignation and said, "Certainly, sir."

To his left, Schönberg visibly stiffened, and his knuckles whitened upon the armrest of his chair. He said nothing.

"Excellent," beamed Graf Spee. He leaned over the map once again. "Gentlemen, we have an initial attack plan. Now, let us discuss in greater detail the landings and the assault upon the town and port." He grinned and his blue eyes shone. "On the eighth of December, we take the Falklands."

# TWENTY-THREE

*Sunday, December 6, 1914*
*South Atlantic Ocean, 152 Miles North of the Falkland Islands*

THROUGH BINOCULARS, Captain Luce surveyed HMS *Invincible* from *Glasgow's* flying bridge. The flagship was two miles to the southeast, and although the smoke trailing from her funnels indicated she still had steam up, the huge battlecruiser had come to a complete stop. Under a light gray overcast, the biting southerly wind lashed the tops of the moderate swells into frothing whitecaps and was a chill reminder that they had already steamed back into much harsher climes.

*Invincible* and *Inflexible* had spent the morning engaged in gunnery practice, which had been the first time that the gun crews from either battlecruiser had done so since being deployed to the South Atlantic. For Luce, it had been a day spent in frustrated observation. Although Admiral Sturdee had acquiesced to Luce's request to leave Abrolhos immediately for the Falklands, the lethargic pace of their journey was maddening. Sturdee had insisted that to conserve coal, the fleet should steam no faster than ten knots. *Invincible* had led the procession of five warships and their armed auxiliary on a plodding southward course that had now taken more than a week—much longer than Luce would have preferred. On the second day of the voyage, they were further delayed when Sturdee insisted on practicing tactical maneuvers, including wide sweeping search patterns and contingency plans for splitting the fleet in mid-battle, if necessary.

Then, this morning, on the ninth day of the voyage—with Port Stanley finally within only another day's steam—Sturdee had declared that the two big ships needed to pause and practice their marksmanship. The rest of the fleet idly kept pace some distance away as the two battlecruisers took turns at gunnery practice. *Inflexible's* crew had assembled a target raft, which consisted of linked pontoons beneath a long, tall screen of wooden slats supported by masts. The target was attached to a cable that was played out several hundred yards behind *Inflexible's* stern. Steaming slowly, at only eight knots, *Inflexible* towed the target behind her while *Invincible* moved off to a distance of twelve thousand yards—which Sturdee had declared was his preferred distance for engaging the enemy armored cruisers.

The flagship's practice firings had not gone well. *Invincible* had fired thirty-two rounds—four shells from each of her eight large 12-inch guns. The target had been struck only once. The target raft was then attached to *Invincible's* stern and towed in the same manner for the gunners aboard *Inflexible*. They also fired thirty-two rounds from the same distance—and struck the target only three more times. In fairness, the wooden target's area presented a silhouette that was barely a sixth of the size of one of von Spee's armored cruisers. Still, the battlecruisers' inauspicious first firing drills illustrated how much more practice their gunnery crews would need before these ships would truly become the fearsome killing machines they were designed to be.

Sturdee, in what Luce could only imagine was a fit of frustration and anger, had signaled to the rest of the fleet that the battlecruisers would resume gunnery practice the day after docking in Port Stanley. The message had also indicated that the fleet would be getting underway as soon as the target raft was retrieved and stowed aboard *Invincible*. That, however, had been more than an hour ago, and the target barge still bobbed and drifted more than a hundred yards off of *Invincible's* stern.

"So, what's your best guess as to what they're up to now?" asked Thompson as he surveyed the scene through binoculars.

"Well, now the flagship has two boats in the water near her stern," replied Luce, also scanning with his lenses. "Perhaps a mechanical problem."

"Maybe they're keelhauling the gunnery officers," said Thompson with a grin.

"It looks like they have divers in the water."

"Divers?" Thompson squinted through the glasses. "I'll be damned. You're right."

Luce stepped over to the open bridge door, leaned in, and addressed the petty officer on communications duty. "Mister Hobbs, have the wireless room send a signal to the flagship. Ask if *Glasgow* can be of assistance."

"Aye, sir." Hobbs relayed the message to the wireless room.

Luce received the reply a few minutes later. *Invincible* reported that the tow cable for the target raft had become entangled with one of the battlecruiser's propeller shafts. Divers were working to free the fouled screw so that the fleet could resume its voyage.

"I'd hate to be within earshot of Sturdee right now," said Thompson.

Luce's eyes narrowed. "Another blasted delay. Firstly, the snail's pace of this voyage — as if the urgency I discussed with Sturdee at Abrolhos was of no consequence. Along the way, we actually paused to practice search pattern maneuvers, of all things! Then this morning he has us dally about while his gunners demonstrate their stunning ineptitude. Finally, to top it all off, they can't even reel in the target barge without bungling the operation and delaying us further." He shook his head, fuming. "At least we're still hearing the daily reports from the Stanley wireless station, so we know it isn't yet a smoldering crater."

Thompson was still looking out toward the flagship. "Hey, that looks promising. They've called up the divers and it looks like they're preparing to bring up the boats."

"Not a moment too soon," muttered Luce, who walked back into the wheelhouse, followed by Thompson.

"Another wireless signal from the flagship, sir," said Hobbs. "*Invincible* reports that one of her propellers is still fouled and cannot yet be freed."

Luce leveled a glare across the water toward the flagship. *Unbelievable,* he thought.

Hobbs continued. "The admiral states that the flagship will steam with only three propellers for now. They will repair it at Port Stanley. We are resuming our voyage immediately. All ships are to return to formation."

Luce was relieved. "About damned time."

Two miles away, thick smoke spiraled upward from the funnels of the battlecruisers as they resumed their southward voyage. *Glasgow* and the other warships fell into formation behind the big ships and steamed in formation toward the gray southern horizon.

Finally, Luce thought. By morning we'll be at Port Stanley.

◆

"YOU'RE CERTAIN?" asked Maerker. "We're a full four hours behind schedule?"

"Yes, unfortunately, sir," replied Lieutenant-Commander Born. "I've checked the calculations twice. If the squadron maintains its current speed, we will arrive at the assembly point east of the Falklands at least three hours after sunrise on the eighth."

Maerker shook his head. "If so, we risk being spotted much farther away as we approach. A late arrival would put the entire plan in jeopardy."

Out beyond *Gneisenau's* bow, half a kilometer ahead, steamed *Scharnhorst*, leading the squadron in a tight line, steaming northeast through the churning gray sea. A light rain pelted the windows and reduced the visibility to only a few kilometers. Astern steamed *Nürnberg*, *Leipzig*, *Dresden*, and finally the passenger ship *Seydlitz*.

"The delay this morning really cost us," said Born. "Making up the time in this weather will be challenging."

"Seemed unnecessary to sink her," offered Busch. "That relic had no wireless, and it would have taken her at least two or three days to get to the nearest port." He was referring to the captured sailing ship *Drummuir*, whose remnants now lay on the sea bed less than a kilometer south of Picton Island.

"It would have helped," offered Pochhammer, "if those fools from *Leipzig* had gotten it right the first time."

The plan had been for the German squadron to leave their anchorage at first light, steam steadily through the day and following night, and arrive outside of Port Stanley well before dawn. However, the admiral had ordered that *Drummuir* be scuttled before their departure, which precipitated a series of delays. Firstly, *Leipzig's* crew took longer than anticipated to set the scuttling charges in the emptied holds of the sailing vessel. Then, those charges initially failed to detonate, so the scuttling crew had to return to the ship to reset the fuses. The second attempt was successful, blasting a series of holes in *Drummuir's* keel and drawing the old sailing ship rapidly beneath the waves. As the tops of her masts disappeared from view, the squadron finally set off toward the enemy outpost.

"This pace is our problem now," said Maerker. "Our speed is limited by the blasted *Seydlitz*, but to try to meet our original timetable, we'll need to steam faster than originally planned—even if that means leaving her behind, for now." He turned to Born. "Send a message to the flagship stating our concern, and request that the squadron increase our speed to fifteen knots."

"Yes, sir." Born relayed the message to the wireless room.

Minutes later, the flagship sent a message to the entire squadron:

CRUISERS INCREASE SPEED TO FIFTEEN KNOTS EN ROUTE TO ASSEMBLY POINT. SEYDLITZ MAINTAIN CURRENT SPEED AND COURSE AND AWAIT FURTHER INSTRUCTIONS UPON ARRIVAL AT FALKLANDS.

"Not a moment too soon," said Maerker. "Bring us up to fifteen knots." Ahead of them, plumes of dark smoke rose from *Scharnhorst's* funnels as she accelerated, leading the squadron onward through the mist and rain.

# PART FIVE

## The Falklands

# TWENTY-FOUR

*Monday, December 7, 1914*
*South Atlantic Ocean, Port Stanley, The Falkland Islands*

FOR CAPTAIN LUCE, steaming once again into the inner harbor of Port Stanley was oddly disquieting. The familiar port that had for years been *Glasgow's* home away from home certainly never looked like this. Since their last call here just a month earlier, the townspeople and the crew of *Canopus* had obviously been hard at work. Chains of floating barrels and pontoons, presumably filled with explosives, had been strung across both a portion of the outer mouth of the bay of Port William as well as the narrow inner opening to Stanley's harbor. Wooden palisades ringed the town in concentric layers and extended across the nearby ridges and hillsides. Several of *Canopus's* small deck guns had been taken off the ship and set up as shore batteries at key vantage points overlooking the harbor. Old stone walls that had been crumbling for decades had been newly repaired. In just a few weeks, the sleepy town of Port Stanley had been transformed into a bustling fortified camp.

The most jarring change was the massive bulk of the old battleship *Canopus*, which Captain Grant had beached in the sandy marsh on the southern shore of Port Stanley's inner harbor. Her four massive gun barrels pointed seaward over the low isthmus to the southeast. Here, at last, the old battleship had finally been assigned a duty that suited her. Firmly wedged in place in the sand, the aged warship was a fixed, stable gun platform that might be able to protect the island from any adversaries who might venture within range of her heavy guns.

The low saddle of land where she was beached connected the higher ground of the main island to the west with a narrow rocky peninsula that jutted eastward. The far end of the peninsula, a few miles away, was Cape

Pembroke, the easternmost point on all of the Falklands. There, a seventy-foot black and white lighthouse both warned of the hazardous rocky shore and also served as a beacon to guide ships toward the inlet and bay called Port William and the sheltered harbor and town of Port Stanley.

The strip of land between the grounded battleship and the sea was only a few hundred yards wide and little more than fifty feet in elevation for much of its length, effectively concealing *Canopus's* hull, guns, funnels, and superstructure from any potential observer out to sea. Only her two main masts had been visible above the land, so the masts had been disassembled and set aside. Of course, without the masts, the ship's spotters could no longer direct the ship's gunfire, and the seaward view of the gunners and bridge officers was blocked by the lowlands before them. To replace the missing spotter's platforms, the crew had built a small wooden observation station at the top of Sapper Hill, just west of the town. Crewmen in the structure atop the windswept hill had a commanding view for more than thirty miles out to sea. Sailors and local policemen had lain more than two miles of telephone wire to connect the observation station with the ship. With telephones installed at both ends, the spotters could now help direct the aim of the gun batteries aboard the ship, which could then fire over the spit of land at potential targets beyond.

The British fleet had finally reached the Falklands at noon on December 7th. The battlecruisers *Invincible* and *Inflexible* and the armored cruisers *Carnarvon*, *Cornwall*, and *Kent* dropped anchor in the outer bay, while the two light cruisers, *Glasgow* and *Bristol*, and the auxiliary *Macedonia* moored in the inner harbor. The other auxiliary, *Orama*, was still escorting the colliers from Abrolhos at an even slower pace than the main fleet had taken. Fortunately, two colliers were already in port. Admiral Sturdee ordered that coaling was to begin immediately — with *Bristol* and *Carnarvon* coaling first — and it would continue throughout the remainder of the day and night until each warship's bunkers were full.

Only *Bristol* and *Invincible* reported any significant mechanical issues. *Bristol's* engineers needed to make some engine repairs, so Captain Fanshawe was granted permission to draw down her fires. The flagship still had one fouled propeller, so while she awaited her turn with the colliers, teams of divers from both *Invincible* and *Inflexible* went down to free the tangled screw. While the warships coaled and made themselves ready, *Macedonia* patrolled the mouth of the outer bay of Port William.

Admiral Sturdee called for a brief conference of his captains aboard *Invincible* that evening after dinner. While Luce waited for that meeting, he spent much of the afternoon inspecting the ship and ensuring that she would be ready for the next phase of their operation — hunting in earnest for the German squadron. He also took the opportunity to catch up on a number of cables and reports delivered to the ship by staff from the Port Stanley wireless station. From what he could decipher from the recent reporting out of Europe, the land war was grinding to a stalemate as winter set in. In the west, after more than a month of fighting near Ypres, the front lines had barely shifted, but the loss of life for both the Allies and the Germans had been appalling. In the east, German forces were battling toward Warsaw through heavy snow and bitter cold. They had met stiff resistance from the Russians, who had repulsed the German advance near Łódź, but the Germans were thought to be rallying.

A collier was made available for *Glasgow* by late afternoon, so her crew—as well as a number of the local townspeople—set to the grimy work, which would likely continue past midnight. After taking dinner in his cabin, Luce traveled to the flagship by boat, accompanied by Commander Thompson. The captains of all the other vessels, including Captain Grant of the beached *Canopus*, were in attendance. Sturdee began the meeting by reading two dispatches received earlier in the day, one from the British ministry in Buenos Aires and another from the consular office in Punta Arenas. Both messages noted a curious increase in activity among German merchant ships in port, and the cable from Buenos Aires noted that at least two cargo ships of unconfirmed registry were mysteriously unaccounted for. Sturdee inferred from these reports that such unprecedented activity was unmistakably an indication that von Spee's squadron was to imminently enter the Atlantic. Admiral Sturdee, in his customary aloof and imperious manner, sought no counsel from his commanders. Instead, he painstakingly restated his previous plan to begin searching for the German squadron—as well as his contingency should the enemy ships split up and require multiple pursuits.

According to Sturdee's directive, all of the remaining warships were to be fully coaled by midmorning. Captain Grant had arranged for an early demonstration of his newly installed system whereby the hilltop spotter's station would direct—by telephone relay—the aiming of *Canopus's* big guns toward unseen targets out to sea. After that gunnery exercise was complete, the fleet would depart, heading first for the River Plate region, from which they would begin working their way southward toward the Strait of Magellan and Cape Horn.

Tomorrow, the true hunt would begin.

# TWENTY-FIVE

*Tuesday, December 8, 1914*
*South Atlantic Ocean, 25 Miles (40 Kilometers) Southwest of the Falkland Islands*

THE FIRST VIOLET BLOOM in the eastern sky presaged the imminent dawn and confirmed what Captain Maerker already feared. Despite their increased speed, the squadron had not been able to make up enough lost time.

He peered ahead through binoculars into the predawn gloom. The dark mass of the Falkland Islands loomed on the northeast horizon — still too far away for them to reach before daylight broke over the sea. His carefully formulated plan to have the squadron steam around to the east of the islands before dawn was now rendered impossible. He realized in frustration that they would now have to attack from the southwest and would not have the advantage of being able to see into the outer harbor of Port William during their approach. He hoped that his earlier misgivings were unfounded and that the port would be vacant and undefended.

He turned to Commander Pochhammer, who was also scanning the horizon. "Commander, see to it that the ship is properly prepared for battle — boats filled, loose items stowed, and all hatches secured. Inform the crew that we'll be going to battle stations within the next hour. Those shifts that have not yet had their morning meal should do so now."

"Gladly, sir," replied Pochhammer with a grim smile. "Today will be a good day." Beaming, he turned briskly and left the bridge.

"Mister Busch," said Maerker to his gunnery officer, "Prepare your gun crews for a mix of shore and oceangoing targets. We don't know what we'll find in or around the harbor — so your men may have to swiftly change from shelling the wireless station to targeting an enemy warship, if one appears to challenge us."

"Understood, sir. We'll have a mix of high explosive and armor-piercing shells at the ready for each gun. What's our planned standoff distance for hitting the wireless station?"

"Seven kilometers. That should be far enough away to be out of range of any potential small shore batteries."

"But close enough for us to hit with our 5.9-inchers. At that range, I'd prefer to fire only our secondary battery—and preserve as many of the remaining big guns' shells as we can."

Maerker nodded. "I agree. No sense wasting primary ammunition." He looked out at the dark smudges on the horizon that were the uppermost hilltops of the Falklands. "Because of our tardy arrival, we have lost the element of surprise. If they're watching from any elevation, they'll spot us well before we're in range and they'll be able to get out a transmission of alarm."

"They're probably not expecting us," offered Busch hopefully, "so perhaps no one is watching."

The squadron steamed on steadily toward the islands, which grew larger and more defined as the waxing daylight infused the sky with color. Maerker could see that it was to be an exceptionally clear and sunny morning, without any overcast or fog to impede their visibility. Even the sea was strangely calm for these latitudes, barely rippling under a cold but slight southerly breeze. Although the unusually clear weather would give potential enemy spotters a good view of their approach, these were perfect conditions for the German gunners.

"Flag signal from *Scharnhorst*, sir," said Petri. "*Gneisenau* and *Nürnberg* are detached and are to proceed to target point at eighteen knots. Remaining ships of squadron will continue at current speed and will hold at a standoff distance of twenty-five kilometers."

"Thank you, Mister Petri," said Maerker. "Helmsman, two points to port, assume a parallel course at three hundred meters, and increase speed to eighteen knots.

"Yes, sir. Two points to port, parallel course, eighteen knots," repeated the young lieutenant.

*Gneisenau* swung out of the formation, followed by *Nürnberg*, and began to pick up speed. Dark smoke poured from their funnels and drifted ahead of the ships on the southerly wind. Both cruisers were now steaming alongside the main line of warships, and within moments *Gneisenau* was abreast of *Scharnhorst's* port beam, only a few hundred meters away. A quick series of lamp flashes blinked from the flagship's superstructure, directed at *Gneisenau*. The message read, "GOOD LUCK. WE WILL AWAIT YOUR SIGNAL TO APPROACH."

"Here we go," said Busch. "I'll prepare the gun crews."

"Very well," acknowledged Maerker. "I'll need you back on the bridge in forty minutes." He turned his attention back to the growing landmass ahead, noting that the first sliver of the sun's brilliant orange disc was already pushing above the eastern horizon.

◆

FOR Able Seaman Albert Mattson, dawn could not have come soon enough. His duty shift in the spotter's platform atop Sapper Hill had begun at midnight. He would be relieved in little more than an hour.

This was his second week of such duty, and he was now convinced that there was no colder, more miserable spot upon the entire earth than at the top of that windswept hill. The wooden structure had a roof but only a north wall—supported as it was by four sturdy timber posts. The Falklands were famously windy, with damp, blustery, inclement weather as the norm. Unlike the harbor of Port Stanley, which was somewhat sheltered from the worst of the elements, the newly built observation station was completely exposed to the howling winds and biting cold. Adding to the misery of this duty was the lack of any toilet facilities. To relieve himself, Mattson had to trudge a dozen yards away—usually in complete darkness of course—to squat among some nearby rocks. More often than not, it was raining, which compounded the unpleasantness of the experience. Finally, because the possibility of actually seeing anything out to sea during the nighttime hours, even on a moonlit night, was remote at best, most of the night shift was spent in utter monotony.

The hilltop spotter's duty was usually performed by two men—to increase the chances of seeing something in conditions that often limited their visibility, and to help ensure that the spotters would not fall asleep during their shift. Mattson's partner for this shift was Teddy, a young seaman cadet. Currently, the fifteen-year-old cadet was sleeping soundly on the wooden floor of the platform—wrapped snugly in a gray woolen blanket. The boy had dozed off several hours earlier, and Mattson had decided to let him sleep—preferring the quiet to the cadet's incessant questions and inane observations about everything from naval gunnery to the local sheep.

Although the entire night had been numbingly cold, this morning's weather was uncharacteristically moderate. Rather than the driving winds that usually buffeted the spotters while they huddled and shivered through their shift, only a light breeze curled about the platform and barely ruffled the scrubby grasses of the gray-green heath that blanketed the hilltop. The daybreak was spectacularly clear, and as the brilliant sun bulged over the eastern curve of the sea, the sky took on a rich cerulean hue. The surface of the slate-colored ocean, for as far as Mattson could see in any direction, looked to be as still as glass. It was an odd but welcome change from the usual sullen overcast and howling winds that continually oppressed the island.

Mattson had unfortunately forgotten his gloves when he had started his shift the night before and was grateful that this morning's temperature was more forgiving than usual. Still, he looked forward to ending his shift and taking his morning meal in the comparatively warm and comfortable mess aboard *Canopus*. His mouth began to water at the thought of a plate of hot eggs and biscuits.

As the first rays of sun flooded the island with golden light, he used his binoculars to survey the flurry of activity in the port below. Like his crewmates, he had been astounded the day before to watch the two big battlecruisers steam into the bay at the head of Admiral Sturdee's fleet. To see such an array of might and firepower at this remote outpost was a certain indicator that the Admiralty back home had finally had enough of the elusive and dangerous German admiral who had won the day at Coronel. Surely such an overwhelmingly superior force would make quick work of the rogue enemy squadron—if they could find them.

In the harbor immediately below were moored the light cruisers *Glasgow* and *Bristol*, along with the grounded *Canopus*, of course. Mattson could see that *Bristol* was still undergoing some sort of repairs—a sizeable section of her deck lay open, and men were toiling beneath electric lamps in the machine spaces below. Beyond the harbor mouth, in the larger bay of Port William, were anchored the armored cruisers *Carnarvon*, *Kent*, and *Cornwall*, and the two big battlecruisers, *Invincible* and *Inflexible*, which were still coaling—as the entire fleet had been doing throughout the night. The divers' boat that had been tied up at *Invincible's* stern for most of the night had been pulled up, indicating that they had finally freed her fouled propeller. Mattson scanned outward toward the mouth of the bay and found the auxiliary ship *Macedonia* slowly patrolling there. The former passenger liner looked out of place among the sleek gray warships.

He felt a pang of jealousy as he looked over Admiral Sturdee's fleet. Sometime later today they would be departing, heading toward the coast to hunt for the enemy squadron. He looked away from the harbor and stared wistfully out to sea. Mattson would have gladly joined any one of their crews, even the cumbersome auxiliary, if it meant that he could get back out on the open ocean and do something other than sit, night after night, in a frigid wooden box at the top of a barren hill overlooking nothing but empty ocean.

But suddenly, the ocean was no longer empty.

Something caught his eye to the southwest. Mattson brought his lenses back up, and he scanned that portion of the horizon. He saw it again—a brief flicker of light. At first, he thought his eyes might have been playing a trick on him. As he stared intently at the spot, however, he realized that the flash had been a reflection of sunlight from an otherwise dark mass on the ocean's surface. He continued to watch, and as he did so, the dark mass resolved itself into the unmistakable shape of a ship.

Whoever they are, he thought, he would have to call this in. Beside him was a wooden cabinet, fastened to one of the platform's support posts. He opened the door, revealing a boxy wood and metal telephone that policemen from the town had installed a couple of weeks earlier. A single thin wire from the telephone dropped through a hole in the bottom of the box, followed the post to the floor, and then stretched out over the ground and down the hill. At the other end of the wire was an identical telephone that had been installed in *Canopus's* bridge. Before Mattson reached for the earpiece, he glanced once more back out to sea—and paused.

The shape was more distinct now, even without the binoculars. He raised the glasses to his eyes, and a chill traveled down his spine.

It was a warship.

And it was not alone.

Mattson could clearly see two ships approaching now, still more than twelve miles distant. The first was a large vessel, perhaps an armored cruiser, with four funnels. The second ship was smaller, with three funnels. He was unfamiliar with their lines, but they were most definitely warships.

He gently nudged Teddy's shoulder with the toe of his boot. "You'll want to get a look at this," he said to the boy. Teddy blinked and roused to wakefulness, shivering beneath his blanket. The cadet stood unsteadily and brought his binoculars up to take a look. His eyes widened behind the glasses.

Mattson took another look at the approaching warships. From their bow waves and wakes he could tell that they were moving relatively quickly—more than fifteen knots. He reached into the cabinet, plucked the earpiece off its cradle, and held it to his ear. He briskly rotated the metal crank mounted on the side of the box. Far below, on the bridge of *Canopus*, the other phone was ringing.

◆

JOHN LUCE had taken an early breakfast and arrived on the bridge a few minutes before eight. As he entered the compartment, he was amused to find Lieutenant Hirst and the officer of the watch—a gunnery officer named Foreman—engaged in a spirited discussion about the law of squares, and how that formula may have predetermined the unfortunate outcome of the Battle of Coronel. Both officers bid the captain good morning. He had no sooner returned their greeting when Lieutenant Stuart appeared at the starboard doorway. The young officer's eyes were wide with alarm.

"Sir, *Canopus* just raised a flag signal stating 'Enemy in sight,' blurted Stuart.

Luce stepped out onto the flying bridge and looked over at *Canopus*, nestled in the marshy cove to the southeast. He could see another array of flags being raised above the old battleship's superstructure. He could hardly believe what they said.

"It says, 'Four-funneled and three-funneled man-o-war in sight from Sapper Hill, steering northeast," translated Stuart.

Could it be the Germans? Luce looked again at where *Canopus* lay in her sheltered cove. He then looked out at *Invincible,* still coaling in the bay, with a thick haze of gray-black coal dust hovering above her decks. A spit of land separated the grounded battleship from the rest of the fleet, preventing anyone aboard the flagship from seeing *Canopus* directly. He realized that only *Glasgow* had an unobstructed view of her flags. Unless he relayed the message, the admiral would never see it.

"Mister Stuart, repeat *Canopus's* flag signal immediately."

"Yes, sir!" Stuart relayed the instructions to his men, who began raising the appropriate series of flags.

Luce looked at Hirst. "Lieutenant, get up to the spotter's platform and let me know what you see out there. We need to identify those ships." He hoped the platform would be just high enough for the lieutenant to be able to have a view out to sea over the lowlands to the south.

"Aye, sir." Hirst spun on his heel and sprinted out to the flying bridge, heading toward the ladder that led up to the base of the forward mast directly above them.

"Any response yet from the flagship?" asked Luce.

"No, sir," said Stuart.

The men coaling on *Invincible's* decks toiled on, oblivious to the ominous message fluttering from *Glasgow's* halyards. Perhaps a minute passed as they waited, but to Luce the delay seemed interminable.

Finally, Hirst's voice echoed through the voice pipe from above. He was breathing heavily. "Sir, they're definitely German warships. An armored cruiser—perhaps *Gneisenau*—and one of their light cruisers, either *Nürnberg* or *Leipzig*. Eleven miles to the southwest, steering this way."

The Germans were here.

His pulse quickened. He realized that although their fleet greatly outnumbered and outgunned the two approaching enemy ships, the

British warships were currently extremely vulnerable. All of them lay at anchor in the confined space of the bay and inner harbor, and none currently had enough steam up to get underway. If the Germans could draw within range of the mouth of Port William and fire upon the auxiliary ship patrolling at its mouth, they could sink it there and bottle up the entire fleet within the bay. If the fleet were thus trapped, the firepower and speed of the great battlecruisers would be nullified. In such a scenario, even just those two enemy ships could continue to fire upon the harbor with impunity—for it would be impossible for the British ships to accurately strike back from within the confines of the harbor. He realized with horror that those two German cruisers could destroy the entire fleet before a single ship could make to the open ocean.

"Still no response from the flagship?" he asked. With every minute, the Germans were getting closer to firing range.

"No, sir. With all that coal dust around them, they may not be able to see us clearly."

"Then we need to get their attention." Luce turned to Foreman, who appeared to be frozen in place as he listened, wide-eyed to their exchange. "Don't just stand there. Go fire a gun! If that doesn't work, send a damned boat!"

"Yes, sir!" Foreman snapped into action, racing out of the wheelhouse and virtually leaping down the ladders toward the foredeck below.

"Mister Stuart, get a man on the starboard lamp. When that gun goes off, send the same message directly to *Invincible* by lamp. Repeat it until you receive an acknowledgment."

"Aye, sir." Stuart left the wheelhouse briskly, nearly colliding with Commander Thompson, who had just walked onto the bridge.

"What have we got?" asked Thompson.

"We've got a German armored cruiser and light cruiser approaching from the southwest," replied Luce. "And so far, we can't raise *Invincible*. We're firing a gun to draw their attention."

"Good thinking," replied Thompson. "How far away are the Germans?"

"Hirst says eleven miles."

"Good lord. They'll be in firing range within minutes."

Below them on the foredeck, the three-pound gun fired—its resounding crack echoing across the bay. As the sound of the gunshot died away, Luce could hear the rhythmic clacking of the louvers on the lamp outside, as Stuart and his signalman sent the alarm message directly to the flagship.

In less than a minute, a signal lamp aboard *Invincible* flashed an acknowledgment that the message had been received.

"About damned time," said Luce. "Will, get us up to steam. I want to be on our way as soon as the admiral gives the order."

"On it, sir," replied Thompson.

A series of flags appeared above *Invincible's* superstructure, stating, ALL SHIPS UP TO STEAM. KENT TO SUPPORT MACEDONIA.

The collier that had been tethered beside the flagship pushed off, and Luce could see increasing dark tendrils swirling up from the funnels of the armored cruiser *Kent*. Hopefully within a few minutes she would have enough power to get underway and move toward the harbor mouth, where *Macedonia* still patrolled. All of the other warships began to get up to steam as well, sending great columns of smoke into the morning air.

"We have another message from *Canopus*," said Stuart. "It says, 'Sapper Hill reports more funnel smoke in sight on southwest horizon. Additional enemy ships approaching'."

Luce looked at his first officer. "Raise anchors, Mister Thompson. Let's get out of this harbor."

◆

ON *Gneisenau's* bridge, Captain Maerker and several of his officers had their binoculars trained on the skies above the island to the northeast. The rocky undulating coastal hills prevented them from seeing the harbor or the town of Port Stanley itself, but they could see multiple thick streams of dark, yellow-gray smoke rising above the area where they knew the harbor to be.

"The cowards are burning their coal stocks," said Commander Pochhammer in disgust. "Just like the French fools at Papeete."

"That was always a danger," replied Maerker. "Had we arrived before sunup, we may have been able to hit them before they could react. Now that they've spotted us, they are likely in a panic."

"They've probably already sent out a wireless distress call, too," said Pochhammer sourly.

Lieutenant-Commander Busch frowned. "If so, that will be the last transmission they make. We'll soon be within range of the wireless station."

"All hands to battle stations," said Maerker.

"Yes, sir," replied Pochhammer with a smile. "All hands to battle stations," he repeated, stepping up to the forward console to pass the message along though the ship using voice and electric commands.

*Gneisenau*, trailed by *Nürnberg*, was approaching the predetermined bombardment location just over six kilometers south of a low saddle of land that connected the western highlands with the rocky peninsula of Cape Pembroke to the east. Maerker could now see the tall wood and steel wireless mast jutting up from the rocky coastline ahead. At the base of the mast were two small buildings that comprised the wireless station itself.

Lieutenant-Commander Petri spoke up. "Pardon me, Captain, but our spotters can see the top of a ship's mast moving near the mouth of the bay. They believe it may be an enemy ship trying to escape, sir."

"Understood," replied Maerker. "Signal *Nürnberg* and let them know that after we have shelled the wireless station, we will rapidly move to the harbor mouth to intercept the fleeing vessel."

"Yes, sir," replied Petri.

The multiple columns of smoke above the harbor were getting thicker, and Maerker thought it odd that the British would store their coal in so many different locations.

"Captain?" It was Petri again, this time with a perplexed look on his face. "I think you should hear this for yourself."

Maerker nodded and stepped over to Petri's station. "What is it?" he asked.

Petri leaned over and spoke into the voice pipe before him. "Lieutenant, please repeat what you are observing."

"Yes, sir," came the hollow reply through the pipe, audible to everyone in the now-quiet compartment. "I can see the ship that may be trying to escape. It appears to be a two-funnel passenger liner..."

"The other part, Lieutenant," said Petri in frustration. "Describe what you see in the harbor."

"Yes, of course. Sorry, sir." The lieutenant's voice sounded strained. "I can also see the tops of multiple masts in the harbor, sir. At least six more ships."

Maerker frowned. "Repeat that, Lieutenant. What do you see in the harbor?"

"Multiple ships in port, sir. I can see the tops of a number of other masts. Six or more additional ships. The columns of smoke we're seeing appear to be funnel smoke, sir."

"Can you identify any of them?" asked Maerker.

"No, sir. Not yet."

This was an unexpected development. In none of the accounts and intelligence reports they had read about Port Stanley had they ever heard of that many ships being at the port at the same time.

"We need to identify those ships," Maerker said. He turned to Busch. "You're our identification expert, Johann. Climb up to the spotter's platform and have a look."

"Certainly, sir." Busch left the bridge, heading up an exterior ladder toward the platform above.

"Regardless of what those ships are, we need to inform the admiral of this development. Mister Petri, send a wireless message to the flagship stating that there are multiple unidentified ships in the harbor."

"Yes, sir. Understood," replied Petri, who relayed the message to the wireless room.

Maerker thought again with regret that their current vantage point did not afford a view directly into the harbor. From this location, they were blind to the goings-on in the bay and port.

"Mister Born?" asked Maerker. "How much farther until we reach our bombardment point?"

"Four kilometers, sir. We are now less than eleven thousand meters from the target."

Maerker's plan was to have both ships slow to a stop at seven thousand meters and present their port beams to the target, then unleash a single withering broadside at the station. If that first salvo brought down the mast as intended, they would immediately move onward to the mouth of the bay to cut off the escaping passenger liner. "Very well," he replied to Born. "We will plan to…"

"Captain?" interrupted Busch's voice through the pipe from the platform above.

"Yes, Johann, what do you see?"

"They look like warships, sir. A large squadron of warships in the harbor. Two of them have tripod masts."

"Tripod masts?" asked Maerker, incredulous. "Are you certain?"

"Hard to be certain from this distance, sir, but they look to be tripod masts. That's a distinctive design. I'm not sure what else they could be."

Maerker shook his head, frowning. He was sure this was a mistake but skeptical that his trusted gunnery commander would make such an identification error. "Mister Busch, the only vessels that have tripod masts are British capital ships—battleships and battlecruisers—and the nearest such capital ships should be no closer than the Mediterranean." The thought that the British Admiralty would deploy such modern, powerful ships to such a remote spot in the South Atlantic was preposterous. It was well known that anywhere outside of European waters, the Royal Navy sent only light cruisers and their obsolete, cast-off armored cruisers—such as the motley squadron they had faced at Coronel. Perhaps with his limited view over the ridge, Busch had simply mistaken the masts of some of the enemy's older armored cruisers for the bigger, newer capital ships.

This development did alter their plans, however. With that many British warships in port, a landing and occupation of the colony would now be impossible. They would have to settle for disabling the wireless station and retreating—steaming away faster than the enemy's old armored cruisers could follow. Perhaps then they could turn on their pursuers and destroy them on their own terms, in much the same manner as they had done at Coronel.

"Mister Busch," he continued, "please return to the bridge. We'll need you here when we begin the bombardment of the wireless station in a few minutes."

"Yes, sir," was Busch's reply. "On my way."

Maerker shook his head at their miserable luck. He took no solace in the fact that he had predicted that the British might move to protect the Falklands. All it meant was that once again, the East Asia Squadron had revealed its position to the enemy for little tactical or strategic gain.

Unless…

He walked to the voice pipe array and chose the cone for the forward spotter's station. Busch was on his way back down, but the duty lieutenant would still be there. "Lieutenant, do you still have in sight the two-funneled passenger liner that was leaving the mouth of the bay?"

"Yes, sir," came the hollow reply from above. "But it hasn't actually left the harbor, sir."

Because it's not fleeing, thought Maerker. It's patrolling.

The realization struck him. If they could sink that ponderous guard ship in the mouth of the bay, they might be able to prevent the enemy ships from leaving — effectively bottling up the whole British squadron in the harbor. The enemy armored cruisers would then be vulnerable to bombardment from the sea.

If he could sink that guard ship and trap their squadron, attacking the British warships in the bay would be like slaughtering sheep in a pen.

# TWENTY-SIX

*Tuesday, December 8, 1914*
*South Atlantic Ocean, Port Stanley, The Falkland Islands*

UNDER LUCE'S DIRECTION, *Glasgow's* engineers had gotten steam up quickly, and she weighed anchor within minutes of *Canopus's* first alarm signal. The light cruiser got underway, leaving *Bristol* behind. Off their port beam, Luce noted the flurry of activity aboard their sister ship, as *Bristol's* engineers rushed to reassemble her repaired engine compartment. As *Glasgow* made her way out of the inner port, toward the bay beyond, her crew was buoyed by the cheers of dozens of townsfolk who had quickly gathered on the piers and shorelines to shout their support for the naval vessels.

"Captain Grant and the boys on *Canopus* get to have a different sort of target practice this morning," said Thompson, gesturing toward the beached battleship laying to starboard.

Luce looked over in time to see *Canopus's* two main turrets rotate slightly to the right and stop. Then, in unison, both pairs of long gun barrels protruding from the armored canopies elevated skyward. The muzzles of four massive cannons now pointed up and over the low saddle of land before them—toward an approaching enemy that no one within the harbor could see.

"Hopefully those spotters up on the hill can give them a decent target bearing," said Backhouse skeptically.

The pair of 12-inch guns in *Canopus's* forward turret fired simultaneously, sending twin gouts of orange flame and brown smoke seaward. The blasts echoed thunderously across the port and shook the windows of *Glasgow's* wheelhouse. The old battleship's superstructure shook visibly from the recoil.

Luce realized that it must be extremely difficult for *Canopus's* gunners to hit an unseen target, and that the communications to and from the spotter's platform must be frantic, as they tried to watch for the fall of shot and adjust their aim to compensate.

Moments later, *Canopus's* aft turret rotated slightly to the left, as the crews within responded to instructions to adjust their aim. Then those two guns fired in unison, sending their immense shells arcing out to sea and rocking the port with another deafening thunderclap. HMS *Canopus* had fired the first shots of the battle.

Awed by the display of firepower just a few hundred yards away, *Glasgow's* bridge crew was silent.

Backhouse broke the quiet with a muttered snarl, "Welcome to the Falklands, you fucking bastards…"

◆

ABOARD SMS *Gneisenau*, all hands were at battle stations, but the ship was strangely quiet—as if each man had paused, immobile, in anticipation of the coming order to fire. The big armored cruiser and the trailing *Nürnberg* had nearly reached the designated standoff distance from the wireless station.

"Flag signal to *Nürnberg*," said Captain Maerker. "Full stop. Present port broadside to target. Prepare to fire."

"Yes, sir," answered Petri, who relayed the message to the signalmen.

"Engines full stop and come about thirty-five degrees to starboard."

"Yes sir," replied the helmsman. "Full stop. Thirty-five degrees to starboard."

The throbbing of the warship's large engines ebbed, deepening the eerie quiet. The cruiser continued to coast forward through the calm waters as it slowed, turning slowly to starboard. The ship's port beam was now pointed directly toward the coastal ridge upon which sat the wireless station.

"Port side secondary battery prepare to engage target on land," said Maerker.

"Yes, sir," replied Busch, who now stood at the pedestal supporting the targeting calculator. He worked through the targeting mathematics and relayed aiming instructions via voice pipe to the gunnery officers below. "Distance to target six thousand, nine-hundred meters. Elevation twelve…"

Busch was interrupted by two immense explosions in the water, less than a kilometer off their port quarter. Twin mountains of white foam mushroomed up out of the sea, each towering more than twenty meters in height. A split second later, the sound of the explosions—two impossibly loud concussions—washed over the ship.

"God in heaven!" exclaimed Pochhammer in shock. "What was that?"

The massive mounds of water slowly collapsed back to the surface, leaving a hazy cloud of vapor that hung in the air over an expanding circular cauldron of churning seawater.

"Shore batteries," said Busch. "They're firing shore batteries—and damned big ones, too."

"I didn't see any muzzle flashes," said Maerker. "Where are the guns?"

"I don't know sir," replied Busch. "We should have seen them fire." He swept the coastline with his binoculars. "No sign of them, sir." He stepped up to the voice pipe array and queried the spotters above. "Can you see any gun emplacements or muzzle flashes from the island?"

"No, sir," came the reply. "Nothing in sight."

"Impossible!" exclaimed Pochhammer, sounding both anxious and furious. "Guns of that size? There must be some sign of them."

Suddenly, two more towering columns of foam rose from the water, this time only a few hundred meters off their port beam. Two deafening thunderclaps again hammered the ship. As Maerker watched, awestruck, a large piece of metallic debris from one of those impacts skipped twice on the smooth surface of the sea, tumbling diabolically through the air toward *Gneisenau* at terrific speed. It whined menacingly as it sped toward them, and a dull thud echoed across the decks as it struck somewhere aft of the bridge.

"Damage report," demanded Maerker. "And find me those damned shore batteries!"

"I still can't see anything," said Busch. "Wherever those guns are, they're hidden from our view."

Maerker considered this new development. Somehow, the British had installed at least two massive guns on the island, but no shore batteries of any size were visible. It was possible that the guns were set far enough inland that they could not be seen from *Gneisenau's* current vantage point. Wherever the enemy had hidden them, it was impossible for his gunners to neutralize an unseen target.

"We have a damage report, sir," announced Petri as he leaned over a cone on the voice pipe array, listening intently. "Our number four funnel was perforated by the impact. A hole about two hand spans in width, near the base of the funnel. Minor damage only."

"A lucky hit by a scrap of shell casing," muttered Pochhammer dismissively.

Lucky indeed, thought Maerker. Truly lucky that the round had not exploded on *Gneisenau's* decks. Such obviously massive shells would wreak considerable damage if they found their target. Still, it was a close call that indicated that even more of their original plan was unraveling quickly. He would now have to make a decision. He needed to inform the admiral of this latest development.

"Mister Petri, send a message to the flagship stating that we've been fired upon by large unseen shore batteries. Impossible to target them or return fire."

Maerker did not want to go away empty-handed. The wireless station was already in range, and he also had an extraordinary opportunity to trap the British in their port—if he could get to the harbor mouth and sink the guard ship patrolling there. Assuming the enemy's shore batteries were located somewhere inland, *Gneisenau* might already be at the outermost range of their guns.

"Mister Busch, proceed with our bombardment of the wireless station. Prepare to fire on my order. After the mast is down, we will steam at full speed toward the harbor mouth. Be prepared to engage enemy vessels at close range."

"Ready, sir. On your command."

"Send another message to *Nürnberg*. Tell them to fire when we do."

"Yes, sir," replied Petri. He began relaying the message to the signalmen, who would, in turn, send the flag orders to the trailing light cruiser.

A spotter's voice echoed through the voice pipe from above. "Sir, *Nürnberg* is steering off to starboard."

"What?" Maerker walked to the starboard side of the bridge and looked astern. Sure enough, a few hundred meters behind them, *Nürnberg* had changed course southward. He wondered if she had developed some sort of navigational problem. Then he saw that Schönberg's ship was getting back up to speed. Maerker realized that Schönberg was fleeing. "Unbelievable!" he exclaimed in anger. "I'll have him stripped of his rank for this." He returned to the wheelhouse.

"What are they doing?" asked Busch.

"Leaving us to do the work," replied Maerker with an exasperated sigh. "Looks like the size of those explosions made Schönberg reconsider all of his bravado. Mister Busch, we need to get that wireless mast down. Mister Petri, send a message to the flagship, informing them that *Nürnberg* has left our line without explanation. The admiral can deal with Schönberg later."

Petri relayed the message to the wireless room. The armored cruiser continued to glide slowly forward through the calm waters. The wireless station was now directly off their port beam.

"Mister Bush, range to target?" asked Maerker.

"Six-thousand, two-hundred meters. Port secondary battery prepared to fire high-explosive shells. Awaiting your order, sir."

"Very well…" began Maerker, but he was interrupted by the signals officer.

"Sir, we've received a reply from the flagship," said Petri. "The admiral instructs us to abandon our original mission and fall back toward the main squadron. We are not to attempt to engage shore batteries or enemy vessels in the harbor. Initiate wireless jamming."

For a moment, no one on the bridge said anything, and an eerie silence hung in the air.

"Have your crews stand down, Mister Busch," said Maerker with a sigh. It was over before it began, he thought. Even though he had cautioned against this attack plan from the outset, he felt no satisfaction now that it had to be abandoned. Instead, he was distinctly disappointed that he had been so close to striking a blow but now would have to retreat—and would likely not get another such opportunity.

"Helmsman, get her back up to eighteen knots. New course, one-hundred thirty-five degrees. We're falling back to the main squadron."

"Yes, sir. Eighteen knots, course one three five."

"Mister Petri, tell the wireless room to begin jamming."

*Gneisenau* had to rejoin the squadron, although it was not yet clear to Maerker whether the admiral would try to simply escape over the horizon or ultimately turn back and destroy any armored cruisers that had the temerity to pursue them.

◆

*GLASGOW* was the first British warship to leave the harbor. Only *Kent* was also free of her moorings, but she was lingering near the harbor mouth in support of *Macedonia*. Astern, the rest of the fleet was finally getting underway, with the exception of *Bristol*, whose engineers were still laboring frantically to reassemble her engines.

Luce breathed a sigh of relief when *Glasgow* cleared the mouth of the bay and there was no immediate sign of the enemy warships. The fleet could no longer be boxed in as he had feared. After reaching the open ocean, he brought the cruiser's speed up quickly as he and his bridge crew searched for the enemy ships. They were not hard to find. Multiple dark streaks of funnel smoke on the southeastern horizon indicated the path taken by the fleeing German cruisers. The spotters above reported that they could see five warships retreating to the southeast. Not just two, but five warships. Admiral von Spee's entire squadron was here, and the Germans' lead was less than fifteen miles.

"Helmsman, give me twenty-five knots," said Luce. "Let's close this distance."

"Yes, sir. Twenty-five knots."

"The Germans are still trying to jam us, sir," said Lieutenant Stuart. "But the flagship managed to get a message through. Admiral Sturdee says that *Invincible* and *Inflexible* are leaving the harbor now and will try to catch up to us. We are to observe and report the position of the enemy every five minutes."

"Very well. Report back that we have five enemy ships in sight, bearing southeast, on the horizon. Distance approximately thirteen miles, but we're closing."

The rumbling timbre of *Glasgow's* engines below grew louder as she increased speed—her bow slicing through the calm sea like a sword through vapor. She had always been a fast ship—all of the Town-Class cruisers were—but her recent overhaul in Rio de Janeiro had made her even swifter. Luce was certain that on this bright clear morning in December, there was no faster warship in all the world.

Within minutes, he could clearly see the masts and funnels of the retreating German ships, hull down on the horizon, under the streams of dark gray funnel smoke that drifted behind them. The enemy were moving fast, but not nearly fast enough. He stepped out onto the port side flying bridge to have a look astern to check the status of the rest of the British fleet. He brought up the binoculars and scanned back toward the island.

The sight was awesome.

The two immense battlecruisers, *Invincible* and *Inflexible*, were already clear of the harbor and were steaming powerfully behind *Glasgow*—their flags snapping in the wind. Spiraling gouts of thick black smoke poured from their funnels as they surged through the sea, their bows sending great fans of spray to either side. They were the very embodiment of the Royal Navy's seaborne might—and along with *Glasgow*, they were also now in full pursuit. Behind the battlecruisers steamed the three armored cruisers, *Carnarvon*, *Kent*, and *Cornwall*, trailing in the wake of the massive ships.

As Luce watched, *Invincible* ran up the flag signal for "General Chase," which meant that every ship of the fleet could steam at her highest speed to pursue the enemy. It was an exhilarating sight, and he felt the adrenaline coursing through his body. He heard cheers from the men all over the ship as the message was passed along.

He stepped back inside the wheelhouse and smiled at Commander Thompson. "We can't disobey our admiral, now, can we?"

"Absolutely not, sir," replied Thompson with a grin. He turned to the helmsman. "Let's see what she can do, Lieutenant. General chase—full speed."

"Yes, sir!" replied the helmsman enthusiastically. "Full speed."

The powerful engines throbbed sonorously beneath their feet. Within moments, *Glasgow* was steaming even faster, approaching twenty-eight knots, as she bore down upon the fleeing enemy squadron.

◆

"WE'RE ABLE to confirm it, sir," said the spotter through the voice pipe.

"Tell me exactly what you see," said Maerker, whose pulse was pounding in his temples.

"Six enemy warships in pursuit. The lead ship is a light cruiser, approximately sixteen kilometers astern, followed immediately by two battlecruisers. The remaining three enemy ships are at least three kilometers behind the leaders, but they appear to be older armored cruisers. All enemy ships appear to be at full speed, in direct pursuit."

Battlecruisers.

Maerker took a deep breath. Hearing that word spoken aloud was chilling. He looked astern and raised the lenses to his eyes. He had to see for himself. The clear day and calm seas made for perfect viewing, and the lead enemy ship, a light cruiser, was plainly visible on the northwest horizon. She was steaming rapidly in pursuit, getting closer by the minute. The light cruiser's funnel smoke, drifting behind her, momentarily obscured Maerker's view of the warships trailing behind her. Then the wind shifted slightly and suddenly he could see them.

There they were—two battlecruisers. Their distinctive tripod masts and superstructures were unmistakable. From their lines, they were probably *Invincible*-class ships—very fast and very powerful. Their huge armored hulls surged menacingly through the sea, and above their decks sat multiple turrets bristling with massive 12-inch guns. Just one such warship had enough firepower to sink the entire German squadron, and here were *two* of them. Lieutenant-Commander Busch's original identification had been correct. As unbelievable as it had seemed, the British had truly deployed two capital ships to the Falklands.

The only reason the Admiralty would send these fearsome vessels here was to hunt down and destroy the East Asia Squadron.

Maerker briefly returned his attention to the light cruiser steaming before the battlecruisers, at the head of the enemy fleet. He noted with curiosity that it was a Town-class ship. He could not know for certain, but something told him that this was the same light cruiser that had escaped him at Coronel—HMS *Glasgow*. He remembered the reckless bravery of her captain during the waning minutes of that battle, when the smaller vessel had briefly traded blows with *Gneisenau* so that the stricken *Monmouth* could make her escape in the darkness. Here was *Glasgow* again, fearlessly leading the charge in pursuit of the German squadron. As before, he had to admire the nerve and tenacity of her captain.

*Gneisenau* and *Nürnberg* had nearly caught up to the rest of the squadron. *Leipzig* and *Dresden* were now barely a kilometer off *Gneisenau's* starboard bow, and *Scharnhorst* was three kilometers directly ahead.

Maerker addressed Petri. "Tell our wireless room to cease jamming. It won't do us a damned bit of good now anyway. In case the flagship cannot yet see them astern, send a message to *Scharnhorst* telling them that two British battlecruisers and four other vessels are in pursuit. We'll see what the admiral wants us to do."

Petri nodded. "Understood, sir."

"Johann, my apologies for doubting you," said Maerker to his gunnery officer. "As much as I would rather you had been mistaken, those are, in fact, British battlecruisers."

"No apology necessary, sir," said Busch. "I almost didn't believe it myself. It's unheard of."

Pochhammer, who had been uncharacteristically silent, spoke up, his voice swelling with pride. "This just shows how successful we have been. Our exploits and victories have made the British Admiralty tremble. This is their response—sending these powerful battlecruisers here to try to defeat us."

"The operative word is 'try'," said Maerker flatly. "I have no intention of making it easy for them—nor, do I imagine, does the admiral. For now, we still have a reasonable lead. Tell the men to stand down for the time being—no need to stay at battle stations while we're running."

"Understood, sir," replied Pochhammer. "Standing down." He relayed the commands throughout the ship.

"Message from *Scharnhorst*, sir," said Petri. "All ships are to increase speed to twenty-two knots and maintain southeastward course, following the flagship. We will steam onward until we can find some inclement weather or fog that can help conceal us from the enemy and facilitate our escape."

"Helmsman, twenty-two knots," said Maerker. "Tell them to give it everything they have. Maintain current course."

"Yes, sir. Twenty-two knots."

That was near *Gneisenau's* designed top speed, and Maerker was skeptical that she could match that pace in her current condition, having been at sea for so long without a proper port call.

His fears were realized just moments later, when the helmsman spoke—looking troubled. "Sir? Engineering reports that we are already at our maximum speed, which is barely twenty knots. They are doing everything they can, but the ship just won't go any faster."

"Understood. Tell them to keep trying." Maerker scanned the glittering sea out beyond *Gneisenau's* jutting bow. Not only could his ship not exceed twenty knots, but it appeared that finding the cover of rain or fog would be unlikely. The azure sky was clear as far as he could see in all directions. He thought it was bitterly ironic. This part of the world was infamous for its miserable weather, with sullen overcasts and frequent squalls of frigid rain. Yet, on this day—when they desperately needed inclement conditions—there was not a cloud in the sky.

# TWENTY-SEVEN

*Tuesday, December 8, 1914*
*South Atlantic Ocean, 32 Miles (51 Kilometers) Southeast of the Falkland Islands*

"MESSAGE FROM THE FLAGSHIP, sir," said Stuart on *Glasgow's* bridge. "We are to drop our speed back to twenty-five knots, so that we don't get too far ahead of the battlecruisers."

"There goes the admiral again," replied Thompson. "Spoiling all our fun. We'd have been in firing range within thirty minutes."

"Reduce speed to twenty-five knots," said Luce to the helmsman. "That's all right, Commander. These Germans can't get away from us—not on a day like this. There are too many hours of daylight before dusk and no fog or rain to hide them until then. We may have to wait a little longer, but we'll still get them in range."

Thompson gestured in mock exasperation. "I think Sturdee just doesn't want to have to explain how a light cruiser ran down the enemy squadron and sank them all before he had the chance to use his big, shiny battlecruisers."

Luce smiled. "Something like that."

Although the fleeing German squadron had slightly increased their speed, *Glasgow* had been steadily gaining on them, and the enemy ships were now less than ten miles ahead. The Germans were steaming directly into the wind, and multiple trails of funnel smoke drifted back over the British fleet, occasionally hampering their visibility. Even through the smoke, Luce could now identify all five enemy ships as he scanned ahead with his binoculars. The German ships were not in any recognizable formation, such was their headlong flight. Farthest away, at the head of the small pack, were *Scharnhorst* and one of the light cruisers—which appeared to be *Dresden*. Behind those two steamed *Gneisenau*, then

*Nürnberg,* and finally *Leipzig,* which was lagging half a mile behind the main group and seemed to be struggling to keep up with her sister ships.

Luce roughly calculated the formula in his head. Even considering the reduction in *Glasgow's* speed, they would still be within firing range of the trailing *Leipzig* within the hour.

"General signal from the flagship to the entire fleet, sir," said Stuart. "The admiral instructs that all crews may take their noontime meal."

"No fighting on an empty stomach," said Thompson.

Lieutenant Hirst passed the order along using the voice pipe array. He also requested that some food be brought up for the bridge officers.

"Good idea," said Luce. "We might as well eat now, before the shooting starts."

"Look at them run," remarked Lieutenant-Commander Backhouse, with a grim smile beneath the thatch of his moustache. "They know this isn't the duck shoot they had at Coronel." He trained his binoculars on the enemy squadron ahead and muttered, in a whisper barely audible to those around him. "You can keep running, you Boche bastards, but today there's nowhere for you to hide."

With *Glasgow's* engines reined in, the two battlecruisers steadily gained on her, and within half an hour, *Invincible* was off *Glasgow's* starboard beam, less than a quarter mile away. *Inflexible* was another few hundred yards off the flagship's starboard quarter. As he looked out at *Invincible,* Luce could not help but be awed by her sheer size and power. Thick black smoke poured from her three huge funnels, and her bows flung the ocean aside seemingly effortlessly. As the flagship muscled her way through the smooth slate of the ocean, Luce could see how these battlecruisers had earned their "greyhound" sobriquet. Seeing such sleek, massive, powerful warships at full steam was exhilarating.

On each of the ships, hundreds of crewmen—not wanting to miss their view of the pursuit—opted to grab hastily prepared sandwiches from the messes and return to the weather decks to watch the chase while they ate. At their current twenty-five knot pace, the three British warships inexorably gained on the fleeing German squadron. The enemy ships were still in their ragged cluster, with the light cruiser *Leipzig* trailing the main group by nearly half a mile.

"Signal from *Invincible,* sir," said Stuart. "The admiral informs you that he intends to open fire at sixteen thousand yards."

Luce frowned. Sixteen thousand yards— nine miles— was surely at the outer range limits of the battlecruisers' guns. "What do the rangefinders say?" he asked of the gunnery officer.

After a moment, Backhouse replied. "We're just under seventeen thousand yards to the closest target. That's still a long way off."

"Nonetheless," said Luce to the entire bridge crew, "they'll begin firing any minute now. Action stations!"

◆

ABOARD *Gneisenau*, Captain Maerker had mustered as many of the crew as could be spared, and several hundred men were assembled on the quarterdeck. The sun had reached its peak in the sky and shone brightly upon the gathered mix of dark blue uniforms. In his usual casual style, Maerker had not worn his hat for the occasion, although he carried it in his hand in a grudging acknowledgment of the formality and gravity of the occasion. The cold southerly wind tousled his hair as he looked down at his men from the elevated bridge platform. The crew had been given time for their mid-day meal, but he did not know how many of the men had actually partaken. The mood among them was palpably fearful and somber. Never had he seen such a throng of men who were utterly silent.

He could understand their reticence. He, too, was still feeling the shock of seeing the enemy battlecruisers at full steam in pursuit behind their squadron. Previous thoughts that they might turn back to pummel some overmatched, obsolete armored cruisers were now forgotten. The only chance they had for survival was to run. Of course, with their limited speed, the German squadron was being steadily overtaken by the enemy warships—so even flight might not save them now. He realized that they would soon be fighting a running battle, desperately trying to fend off their pursuers as they sought for some way—any way—to slip away and escape. Now more than ever, his men needed to hear from their captain.

"My countrymen," he began, looking out over the upturned faces of the assembly. "It seems we are to fight our British enemies once again. When last we clashed with our foes at Coronel, we struck a mighty and resounding blow for His Imperial Majesty and the Fatherland. I have never felt such pride as I did on that victorious day. I am proud that the crew of *Gneisenau* performed so exceptionally well. I am proud that each of you men did your duty—not only for your country but for each other. I am proud that you came together—and seven hundred men fought as one."

He gestured casually with his hat back toward the pursuing British fleet. "Today we shall be put to an even greater test. Our enemies are mindful of your skill and bravery. They understand how dangerous you are—how dangerous this warship is. That is why they have assembled this fleet to try to chase us down. Be proud that they regard you with such trepidation. It is a badge of honor that they respect you enough to send such vessels against us." He paused and breathed deeply. "We are now fighting for our survival, and I believe the fighting will be fierce and brutal. I also believe that you are the finest trained and most skilled ship's company in all the world. You are sailors; you are warriors; you are Germans!"

A few scattered exclamations of approval rang out from among the men.

Maerker continued, his voice cutting through the chill wind. "Today, you men of *Gneisenau* will give these Brits a taste of fire and steel. You will show them true seamanship and gunnery. You will give them a lesson in how a naval battle is fought. And, by God, we shall prevail!"

The men cheered lustily. Then, led by the junior gunnery lieutenants, they began to sing *"Die Wacht am Rhein"*. Scarcely had the men begun the second stanza when they were interrupted by two resounding booms astern.

Maerker looked aft, past *Nürnberg,* toward *Leipzig*—which trailed them by nearly two kilometers. Two immense columns of foaming water erupted four hundred meters behind *Leipzig*. The enemy battlecruisers had begun firing.

The men on deck were dismissed, and Maerker headed to the wheelhouse. Commander Pochhammer was already there, along with Lieutenant-Commanders Busch, Petri, and Born, and the duty helmsman.

"Message from the flagship, sir," said Petri as Maerker arrived. "All ships are to raise battle flags."

Maerker nodded. "Raise the flags." He turned to his first officer. "All hands, battle stations."

"Yes, sir," replied Pochhammer enthusiastically. "All hands to battle stations," he shouted into the voice pipes.

Behind them, percussive thumps from four more explosions rolled across the water. Both battlecruisers were firing now, using only their foremost 12-inch turrets—the only guns they could bring to bear on the target fleeing directly before them. Huge splashes rose up from the sea behind *Leipzig*. Thus far, the British gunnery was inaccurate and well out of range. Their shells were falling haphazardly behind the lagging light cruiser, but they were getting steadily closer with each salvo.

Pochhammer squinted as he looked back astern. "I certainly hope we have the opportunity to trade blows with those behemoths. To send such ships to the bottom of the sea would be a triumph that would immortalize us all."

"Perhaps so, Commander," said Maerker wryly, "but right now I'm more concerned about our mortality than our immortality."

Pochhammer did not respond to Maerker's comment. Instead, he stood stiffly at attention and asked, "Permission to man the conning tower and central station, sir?"

Maerker nodded. "Of course, Hans. She's all yours."

"Thank you, sir." Using the voice pipes, Pochhammer hastily notified two junior officers that they were to meet him in the armored compartment below. Then he saluted smartly and left the bridge

Busch raised an eyebrow after Pochhammer's departure. "He seems to have his belt fastened a notch tighter than usual today, sir. Pardon me for asking, but do you think he's, you know… all right?"

Maerker managed a smile. "Truly, I think the Commander is about as well as he's ever been. In fact, if anything, I believe he was born for this very moment. We may find his zeal useful and even necessary in the coming hour."

Two kilometers astern, four more giant columns of foam erupted from the sea, even closer to *Leipzig's* stern than the last explosions. The huge British guns would be in range within minutes.

◆

LUCE LOOKED OUT from *Glasgow's* wheelhouse at the extraordinary sight before him. The three lead ships of the British fleet, *Glasgow*, *Invincible*, and *Inflexible*, were streaking swiftly through the smooth gray sea in pursuit of the enemy squadron. The German ships had not changed course, and their trails of funnel smoke still wafted back over the British fleet. Off *Glasgow's* starboard beam steamed *Invincible*, and beyond her starboard quarter surged *Inflexible*. Both battlecruisers were firing steadily at *Leipzig*, which still trailed the rest of the German ships and was now only eight miles ahead. The long gray gun barrels of the battlecruisers' forward turrets were raised to their maximum elevation and had been firing at approximately one-minute intervals for half an hour. During that time, the ragged fall of shot had been creeping ever closer to the stern of the enemy light cruiser.

Because *Glasgow's* smaller main guns were still far out of range, Luce and his crew were relegated to the role of spectators. Men stood watching at the gunwales on the forecastle below, and the bridge officers viewed the remarkable scene through the wheelhouse windows.

The two great guns in *Invincible's* forward turret fired again, belching jets of orange flame skyward and ejecting billows of thick brown smoke that were immediately carried aft on the wind. A split second later, *Inflexible's* forward guns fired also, and the rumble of the thunderous cannonade echoed across the water.

"That's quite the sight," observed Thompson, speaking to Lieutenant-Commander Backhouse, who stood to his right. The two men were viewing through binoculars, alternately watching the gunfire of the battlecruisers and the fall of shot miles ahead.

Moments later, the shells exploded haphazardly in the water a few hundred yards behind the trailing German cruiser—their scattered detonations hurling four huge but randomly spaced columns of spray into the air.

Backhouse huffed. "Waste of time and ammunition. What daft gunnery officer told the admiral that those guns could throw at more than fourteen thousand yards, let alone sixteen thousand?"

Thompson chuckled. "From the miserable target shooting we saw two days ago on our way down from Abrolhos, I get the impression that neither their gunnery officers nor their gun crews have much experience."

"Bloody embarrassment, that." Backhouse scowled. "Even if they were in range now—which they won't be for another five or ten minutes—I doubt they'd be hitting anything."

Thompson smiled and playfully chided Backhouse. "Tsk tsk, Charles. Do I hear some jealousy? Just because our own guns aren't yet in range isn't reason enough to deride the efforts of those fine fellows over there. They're doing as well as they can, under the circumstances."

"Under the circumstances?" Backhouse looked incredulous. Poor gunnery was no joking matter to the lieutenant-commander. "You couldn't pick a finer day for shooting, Commander. A perfectly calm sea, clear skies, and an enemy is steaming in a damned straight line dead ahead."

Thompson stifled a laugh and decided not to needle the gunnery officer further. "Agreed. Hopefully very soon we'll be in range as well, and I'll look forward to our gunners giving them an overdue lesson in gunlaying."

"Can't happen soon enough," said Backhouse gruffly. "At this rate, with them firing every which way, the admiral's big fancy ships might run out of shells by nightfall, the Boche will have escaped, and we won't have a damned thing to show for it."

To starboard, *Invincible* and *Inflexible* fired again. Thompson and Backhouse scanned ahead, fixing *Leipzig* in their view. In seconds, this latest salvo of shells struck the ocean nearer the target—only a hundred feet away from the red, white, and black flag fluttering at *Leipzig's* stern. A tight pattern of explosions threw up a towering screen of foaming seawater immediately behind the enemy cruiser, temporarily obscuring it from their view.

"They're getting closer," observed Thompson. "And better. Perhaps they won't need you to show them how it's done after all."

"We'll see," said Backhouse. "...now that they're finally in range."

◆

"GOOD GOD, that was close," observed Lieutenant-Commander Busch soberly. "Any minute now, one of those will hit her." He and Maerker were looking astern, watching *Leipzig* through binoculars. The last British salvo had struck just aft of the light cruiser—and the towering white explosions momentarily dwarfed the ship.

"I doubt she'll survive a direct hit," said Maerker. "One of those 12-inch shells might cut her in half." He turned to the communications officer. "Mister Petri, I assume that the admiral and his officers can see this, but in case their view is obscured, send the flagship a message stating that *Leipzig* is in dire peril and the British 12-inch guns have drawn within range of her."

"Yes, sir," affirmed Petri, who relayed the message to the wireless room.

The formation of the German ships, if it could be called a formation, had not changed in nearly an hour. *Scharnhorst* still was in the vanguard, with *Dresden* off her starboard quarter. Then came *Gneisenau*, followed by *Nürnberg* and finally *Leipzig*—all steaming southeast, directly into the wind. The flagship had set the pace at twenty knots, which was as fast as either of the armored cruisers could now steam. The swift *Dresden* could likely go faster but for now was keeping her station near the flagship. *Nürnberg* and *Leipzig* were struggling to keep up, and *Leipzig* in particular continued to drop farther behind the group. If nothing changed, Maerker knew, *Leipzig* would be struck and destroyed in minutes. The only chance they might have to save the light cruiser would be for the smaller ships to break off on one direction while the armored cruisers stayed on their current course. With luck, the enemy battlecruisers would choose to follow the larger quarry—giving the light cruisers a chance to escape.

Four more explosions rose from the sea near *Leipzig*, and this time they were extremely close. Two of the massive fountains of ejected seawater straddled the light cruiser—the falling shells having detonated mere meters from either side of the ship's hull. For a moment, the small warship disappeared under thousands of gallons of airborne spray. Her plunging gray bow reappeared as the mist dissipated—and her scuppers shed torrents of brine that had been thrown upon her decks.

"They missed her…barely," said Maerker. "No visible damage, but those explosions nearly swamped her."

"General signal from the flagship, sir," said Petri. "*Gneisenau* is to change course to port, following *Scharnhorst*, on new bearing forty-five degrees, northeast. Light cruisers are to immediately leave the line southward and try to escape."

The bridge was briefly silent, for every man there understood what that order meant. The two armored cruisers were to make a ninety-degree turn to port, which would inevitably force action with the oncoming enemy battlecruisers. The light cruisers would turn to starboard, steaming southward.

The admiral had decided to do battle with the powerful enemy ships. Maerker knew that this meant potentially sacrificing the armored cruisers — along with himself and his crew — to buy enough time so that the light cruisers might try to escape.

Ahead of them, *Scharnhorst* began her sharp turn to the left, tilting dramatically under full steam. *Dresden*, which had been lingering on the flagship's starboard quarter, immediately turned south, her course rapidly diverging from *Scharnhorst's*. Captain Lüdecke was wasting no time initiating his escape.

"Helmsman," said Maerker, "Maintain current speed. Hard to port. Assume new course bearing forty-five degrees, northeast. Follow in the flagship's wake."

"Yes, sir. Hard to port, new course four five degrees, northeast." The lieutenant spun the wheel, and the big ship muscled into the hard turn.

Maerker steadied himself with a handhold mounted on the port bulkhead as the deck canted beneath him. As *Gneisenau* steamed through the turn, he looked over his shoulder and could clearly see the two light cruisers astern — *Nürnberg* and *Leipzig* — as they also changed direction, steaming away to starboard on a new southward course following *Dresden*. He hoped that the admiral's gamble would pay off and that their pursuers would choose to follow the larger prey. If so, the three other ships might escape safely. Of course, that also meant that his ship and the flagship would be steaming into the teeth of the enemy attack.

*Gneisenau's* course change was complete within minutes, and she leveled out on her new bearing, steaming to the northeast, following *Scharnhorst*. Both armored cruisers were still making twenty knots, and they were rapidly widening the distance between themselves and the three fleeing light cruisers now heading south. The maneuver had allowed the pursuing British fleet to close the distance somewhat, and they too began to change direction. The three lead enemy ships — the light cruiser and the two battlecruisers — also turned to port, assuming a new course parallel to the two German warships. The wind was now blowing across *Gneisenau's* beam from the southeast, and it carried streaming clouds of dark gray smoke from the armored cruisers' funnels toward the British line. Maerker noted that the light cruiser *Glasgow* was no longer leading the British attack and had dropped off somewhere on the far side of the battlecruisers. Perhaps, he thought, *her captain does know when he is outmatched, after all.*

"Message from the flagship, sir," said Petri. "We're to maintain current course and prepare for long range battle."

"Range to targets?" asked Maerker, focusing on the second ship in the British line—the trailing battlecruiser. Undoubtedly, *Scharnhorst* would target the lead battlecruiser, which he assumed was the British flagship. In the brilliant mid-day sunlight, the large enemy ships stood out brightly on the northwestern horizon. He noted the arrangement of their four large turrets—one on the foredeck under the bridge, two amidships between the second and third funnels, and the fourth on the aft deck. All were turned toward the German line, each with a pair of massive gun barrels elevated skyward.

"Twelve thousand, eight hundred meters," replied Busch.

"Target the second battlecruiser. Primary port batteries prepare to fire," said Maerker. Twelve thousand, eight-hundred meters was at the outer limit of their main battery's theoretical range. His gunners had never even conducted drills at such a distance. At this extreme range, he had no way of knowing how accurate or effective their guns would be—or if they could even reach their targets. However, because the enemy might be temporarily blinded by their funnel smoke, this would be an ideal opportunity to score a first hit. In a mismatched battle such as this, striking early and often against the powerful enemy ships—and hopefully inflicting enough damage to force them to withdraw—was the German ships' best hope for survival.

"Yes sir," replied Busch. He checked the targeting calculator and relayed instructions to the gunlayers through the voice pipes. After a moment, he looked up at the captain. "Ready to fire, sir."

"Steady. On the flagship's mark."

Ahead of them, the port side guns of *Scharnhorst* discharged in rapid sequence. A drumroll of heavy gunfire boomed across the water as her guns sent their first salvo toward the British line.

"Fire!" said Maerker.

"Firing." Busch depressed the switches before him. *Gneisenau's* port battery of 8.2-inch guns erupted with a concussive rumble. Orange flames leapt from the long gray barrels and a curtain of brown smoke billowed outward along the length of the warship's hull.

In response, Maerker saw multiple flashes from the battlecruisers' turrets. The enemy ships were returning their fire. He knew that sixteen massive 12-inch shells were arcing toward their line and would fall in seconds.

Several moments after the battlecruisers had fired, *Scharnhorst's* first volley of shells hit the water, throwing up a picket of white explosions four hundred meters short of the enemy flagship's beam. Seconds later, the *Gneisenau's* first salvo also hit the sea, sending up a tightly spaced line of splashes a similar distance from the second battlecruiser's hull.

"Nice opening salvo, Mister Busch," commented Maerker. Your aim was dead-on. We just need to reach a little farther.

Busch was not as impressed. "Four hundred meters short!" he bellowed into the voice pipes. He adjusted the calibration of his targeting calculator and passed the changes to his gun crews. He watched his wristwatch intently, waiting for his crews to reload.

As the German gun crews prepared their weapons, the first incoming British shells struck the water. They were also well short. Sixteen huge fountains rose in a haphazard pattern across the ocean before Maerker's eyes, none closer than two hundred meters off their port beam. The spread of the fall of the enemy shot was broad, stretching from far ahead of *Scharnhorst's* bow to far behind *Gneisenau's* stern. Although the enemy aim was terrible, the effect of the impacts was still astonishing. The explosions were massive, and their concussions washed over the ship like rolling thunder.

"Firing!" bellowed Busch as he depressed the switches again, and *Gneisenau's* guns fired in rapid succession from fore to aft, sending their second salvo toward the enemy.

Maerker peered through the clouds of vapor and smoke that screened his view of the enemy vessels. A line of splashes burst from the sea, three hundred meters short of the target. A similar colonnade of splashes arose before the enemy flagship's hull. The aim was still perfect—but they were still out of range.

"You're getting closer," observed Maerker. "Do we have any more range to play with?"

"We're at outermost range, sir," replied Busch sourly as he again watched the countdown on his watch. "We're using maximum propellant loads. Unless we steer closer to the enemy line, we'll keep dropping short."

◆

AS SOON as the German armored cruisers changed course, Luce knew what to do. The enemy forces had split, and now *Glasgow's* role was to hunt down their light cruisers—leaving the battlecruisers to trade blows with *Scharnhorst* and *Gneisenau*.

*Glasgow* steamed through a tight, looping left turn that took her back around the leeward side of the battlecruisers as they maneuvered into their new track opposite the two enemy vessels. *Glasgow* came briskly about, sliced through the foaming wakes of the big ships, and assumed a southward course behind the fleeing German light cruisers. When the nearly circular maneuver was complete, the battlecruisers were steaming away on *Glasgow's* port side. Clearly visible to the east were the German flagship *Scharnhorst* and her sister ship *Gneisenau.*

Among those in the British fleet, only the officers and men of *Glasgow* had seen the big German cruisers in action before. Luce involuntarily shuddered as he recalled the dread with which he had first identified the array of enemy ships at Coronel. That feeling of unease passed rapidly and was replaced by a determined resolve. That afternoon off Coronel more than a month ago, the British had been at the disadvantage. Today, the Germans were overmatched. It was a day Luce had been quietly anticipating since the sinking of *Good Hope* and *Monmouth.*

For a few minutes, those aboard *Glasgow* had an extraordinary view of the opening stages of the battle between the four big ships. The distant German armored cruisers had the advantage of the lee position, and their thick clouds of funnel smoke streamed out on the wind toward the British battlecruisers. Luce wondered how badly the smoke might affect the accuracy of the British spotters and gunlayers. The Germans took the initiative and fired first. Luce again marveled at the precise discipline of the enemy gun crews. A rapid sequence of muzzle blasts fluttered along the length of each armored cruiser from fore to aft. Seconds later, the two battlecruisers responded by firing a torrent of shells toward the pair of German warships. For a brief moment, the two salvos arced toward each other across the early afternoon sky. The German shells fell first, throwing up a sharply defined picket of splashes well short of the battlecruisers' hulls. Although they were not yet in range, thought Luce, the outstanding German gunnery skills had certainly not eroded since their victory at Coronel. The British fall of shot was much less precise—but was closer to the target than the Germans had been. The German gunners were more accurate and disciplined, but the more powerful British weapons had longer range.

"That won't get the job done," remarked Backhouse ruefully. "Those big 12-inch shells are ship-killers, but only if you actually hit a bloody ship with them."

"Message from the flagship, sir," said Stuart. "It says: CORNWALL, KENT, AND CARNARVON TO FOLLOW GLASGOW IN PURSUIT OF ENEMY LIGHT CRUISERS."

"We're already on it, admiral," said Thompson, who looked out beyond their starboard quarter at the three trailing British warships. Two of them, *Cornwall* and *Kent*, still several miles behind, adjusted their course southward, following *Glasgow.* Despite the orders, *Carnarvon*—lagging much farther back near the northern horizon—appeared to still be heading for the battlecruisers. "Looks like at least *Cornwall* and *Kent* have turned to follow us. *Carnarvon* doesn't appear to be coming along. I think Stoddart wants to stick close to the big boys."

"At least we have *Cornwall* and *Kent*," said Luce. "If the enemy ships split again and run like rabbits every which way, we'll need to portion out the work."

Out to the east, *Scharnhorst* and *Gneisenau* fired again, outpacing the gunners on the battlecruisers, much as they had outpaced the gun crews of *Good Hope* and *Monmouth* at Coronel. The Germans' second salvos were slightly closer than their first, but they were still falling short of the target.

"Dammit," said Backhouse, frowning as he viewed the battle through his binoculars. "All the Germans have to do is nudge it a bit to port, and those shells will be falling on the battlecruisers' decks. Sturdee's boys had better pick up their game. This isn't practice anymore."

The guns of the battlecruisers roared again, spouting jets of flame and huge plumes of brown smoke.

"Hopefully they'll sort it out sooner than later," said Luce, whose attention was now commanded by the three German light cruisers fleeing before him to the south. They were steaming in no discernible line or pattern—they were simply running as fast as they could. *Dresden* was farthest ahead, more than ten miles to the south. *Nürnberg* trailed her by a few miles, and once again *Leipzig* lagged behind her sister ships—little more than six miles ahead, due south. *Glasgow* was steaming ten knots faster than *Leipzig*, which would soon be in firing range.

Backhouse quickly scanned the three ships ahead, then stepped over to the voice pipe array. He spoke into one of the cones. "Range to nearest enemy light cruiser?" he asked the spotter above.

"Just under eleven thousand yards, sir," came the reply.

"What do you think, Will?" asked Luce, who was peering ahead at the distant *Dresden*. "We're the only ship in the fleet that can catch *Dresden*. Do we leave *Leipzig* and *Nürnberg* to the armored cruisers and speed on ahead after her, or do we concentrate on *Leipzig*, since she's almost in range?"

"A bird in the hand?" replied Thompson with a shrug.

Luce nodded reluctantly. Thompson was right. As much as he hated to let *Dresden* speed on ahead unimpeded—increasing the possibility that she might escape—he knew he should press the attack on the nearest ships.

As the senior commander among the captains of this portion of the fleet, it was Luce's responsibility to direct the actions of the armored cruisers. "Mister Stuart, send a message to *Cornwall* and *Kent*. Let them know we are attacking *Leipzig*. Tell them to be vigilant in case one of the enemy ships turns to launch a torpedo."

"Understood, sir," replied Stuart, who passed the orders to the wireless operators.

"Mister Backhouse," said Luce to the gunnery commander. "Prepare to fire at ten thousand yards."

"Yes sir," replied Backhouse.

Thompson grinned and winked at Backhouse. "Now you can show them how it's done."

◆

"WHAT IS the enemy disposition?" demanded Captain Schönberg on the bridge of *Nürnberg*.

Sub-Lieutenant Haas relayed the question to the spotter's station above. Also standing in the wheelhouse were the senior gunnery officer and the duty helmsman.

The spotter's hollow voice echoed back through the voice pipe. "The enemy has split its fleet, sir. The two large battlecruisers have changed course to the northeast and are engaged with *Scharnhorst* and *Gneisenau*. They will soon be out of our sight, sir. Three of the remaining enemy ships, a light cruiser and two armored cruisers, are on a pursuit course following us astern. They are steadily gaining on us. Their light cruiser may already be in gunnery range of *Leipzig*, with the armored cruisers trailing another three kilometers back."

Schönberg took a deep breath to calm himself. The day had begun with such promise, he thought ruefully. He had happily envisioned shelling the enemy wireless station and then triumphantly steaming into the bay to capture Port Stanley. He had hoped this attack would have been an opportunity to demonstrate his bravery and tactical prowess. Of course, his vision had assumed that the British outpost would be lightly defended, if at all. From the moment the hidden enemy shore battery had fired upon them, everything had gone horribly wrong. Clearly, the information they had received about the state of British defenses at the Falklands had been grossly inaccurate. Not only had the Brits sent ships to defend the port, but they had managed to install powerful shore batteries as well. The explosions in the water off their port beam had been unbelievably massive. Had one of those shells struck *Nürnberg*, it surely would have damaged the ship severely—and may have sunk her outright.

His decision to retreat from the island immediately, although admittedly impulsive, had proven to be the correct course of action— validated by the admiral's subsequent order to fall back. The fact that Maerker had briefly lingered within range of the British shore batteries simply showed that *Gneisenau's* captain had little or no tactical sense.

The sight of the British fleet streaming out of the harbor like a pack of loosed dogs had chilled his blood. Particularly terrifying was the identification of the two huge battlecruisers—a fearsome class of warship that Schönberg had previously never seen in person. Suddenly, the East Asia Squadron had become prey—fleeing from very powerful and swift predators. The subsequent revelation that his ship could steam at no more than nineteen knots had sent him into a fit of rage, and he had loudly and angrily threatened every engineering officer with a court martial if they did not wring more speed out of the engines.

The most recent disappointment had been the failure of the admiral's sudden course change to draw off all of the enemy ships. After *Scharnhorst* and *Gneisenau* had turned hard to port, only the two battlecruisers had taken the bait. The rest of the British fleet had simply altered course to follow them south. Schönberg was still being pursued—and *Nürnberg* was still losing ground to her pursuers.

"The British light cruiser is firing on *Leipzig*, sir," said the spotter from above. "They have the range already. Their first shots were near misses, and they are gaining on her rapidly."

"Captain?" asked Haas. "The two enemy armored cruisers are trailing at least two kilometers behind their light cruiser. They are still out of firing range, which leaves their light cruiser alone and vulnerable. Together, *Leipzig* and *Nürnberg* may be able to overwhelm her. We could turn back, and both ships could fire torpedoes or even full broadsides. We might be able to cripple or sink her, then retreat before the armored cruisers can…"

"We will do no such thing, Sub-Lieutenant," growled Schönberg. He looked toward *Dresden*, now nearly five kilometers ahead and widening her lead on her sister ships. Captain Lüdecke certainly was not waiting around in support of his trailing compatriots. He chided Haas. "Captain Haun has not asked for our assistance, Sub-Lieutenant. His job, like mine, is to preserve his own ship—*Leipzig*—and her crew. I will not risk *Nürnberg* on some foolish act of misplaced bravado."

The gunnery officer and the helmsman glanced nervously between Schönberg and Haas but said nothing.

Once again, Schönberg looked south and stared intently at *Dresden*. He realized that Lüdecke's cruiser was currently the safest of the three ships not just because she was swiftest or farthest away. *Dresden* was the safest because two other German targets lay between her and the onrushing enemy. The British would attack the closest target first. An antelope need not be faster than a cheetah, he thought. An antelope only needs to be faster than the slowest antelope in the herd.

Schönberg smiled thinly. "Helmsman, adjust course two points to port."

"Yes, sir. Two points to port."

"But sir," asked Haas with a frown, "won't that that leave *Leipzig* to fend for herself against the enemy?"

"Precisely, Sub-Lieutenant. Precisely."

*Nürnberg* edged slightly to the southeast, diverging from the track taken by *Dresden* and *Leipzig*. Several kilometers astern, the enemy warships continued to gain ground on *Leipzig*, and another flurry of muzzle blasts flared from the forward turrets of the light cruiser.

◆

ABOARD *Gneisenau*, the entire crew was working with extraordinary efficiency. The spotters briskly passed along targeting information and their observations of the fall of shot. The gunnery officers directed the gun crews to adjust their aim after each salvo. The gun crews kept up a blistering pace that allowed them to fire a new salvo every twenty seconds. The communications officers and wireless operators maintained regular contact with the flagship to help the bridge crew anticipate course adjustments and maintain operational cohesion. Down below, engineers prowled the machine spaces, making adjustments, while stokers fed the voracious boilers with fresh coal to keep the engines running with as much speed as they could muster. The entire ship hummed with the cadence of efficient, purposeful activity.

Both *Gneisenau* and *Scharnhorst* had been firing their primary batteries in continuous rhythm. However, at this extreme range, neither Maerker nor the spotters above could determine if their shells were, in fact, striking the enemy ships. Even if they were to score a hit, from this far out the shells would be falling on the enemy ship from a steep angle, so it was hard to guess how much—or how little—damage they might do to the big ships, especially if they struck the heavily armored turrets or the thick armored belt encircling the outer hull. He could not yet see any visible damage to either battlecruiser, but at this distance—with so much funnel smoke, muzzle discharge, and spray from the splashes of incoming shells between him and the target—making out such detail was extremely difficult. He could only hope that his expert gunners could inflict enough damage that somehow they could force the powerful battlecruisers to turn away.

The British gunners, by contrast, had thus far been surprisingly inaccurate. Each salvo from the trailing battlecruiser sent eight huge 12-inch shells at *Gneisenau*. The salvos were not well coordinated, however, and the aim of the enemy battery was inconsistent enough that the fall of shot sometimes varied by hundreds of meters in any direction. Still, the power of those explosions was awesome, and many of the incoming shells were now plunging into the sea on either side of *Gneisenau*, meaning that the German ships were within the effective range of the larger British guns. The detonations ejected mountains of spray—drenching the ship's decks with boiling foam and rocking her hull thunderously. The shells that flew long screamed shrilly as they arced overhead and fell to starboard—a chilling sound that made even the seasoned officers on the bridge wince each time one of the huge deadly missiles whistled past.

Maerker had to assume that the British spotters, rangefinders, and gunlayers were having an even more difficult time accurately targeting the German armored cruisers through the thick smoke that wafted northwest over the seaborne battlefield. The longer that circumstance continued, the better chance the Germans had of evading the deadly fall of shot from the big enemy guns. Soon, he hoped, one or more of *Gneisenau's* shells would strike and inflict serious damage to one of the enemy ship's critical systems, such as her propulsion, steering, or fire control. However, he wondered how long the British would remain in their unfortunate leeward position before they used their superior speed to force a change in direction.

Another enemy salvo was falling all around them—the big shells shrieking downward and plunging heavily into the sea, sending huge plumes into the air. So intent was Maerker on scanning the enemy battlecruiser for *Gneisenau's* latest fall of shot that when the first British shells struck his ship, it caught him completely by surprise.

Two deafening booms shook the wheelhouse, and the force of the concussions caused Maerker to stagger and reach for a bulkhead to steady himself. The entire ship shuddered with the blows. Bracing himself and looking aft, he saw a billowing cloud of black smoke amidships. Hundreds of small white splashes dotted the sea near the ship's beam, where ejected debris from the blast had been thrown outward.

"Damage and casualty reports!" he shouted.

"Yes, sir!" replied Lieutenant-Commander Born, who set about communicating with various areas of the ship to determine what had been hit. Within minutes, they had the answer.

Two of the huge British shells had hit *Gneisenau* directly amidships. One had grazed the third funnel as it arced downward and had exploded on the starboard weather deck right above an 8.2-inch gun casemate. Shell fragments had partially penetrated the armored deck, damaging another, smaller 5.9-inch gun emplacement and tearing into a coal bunker below. The second shell had struck the port bulwark at a steep angle, puncturing the armored plating and exploding just beneath the deck. Some of the deck plating had been bent and warped upward by the blast. Fragments of the shell had torn downward through two more decks below.

Overall, the extensive damage—considering it had resulted from only two incoming shells—was not critical, and crews set to work immediately to try to repair what they could. In the resultant mayhem, the casualty report took longer than usual to compose and deliver. A runner finally delivered a message to the bridge. Lieutenant-Commander Born read it over quickly.

"We have a report from Doctor Nohl, sir," said Born soberly.

*Gneisenau's* port side heavy guns fired another crisp salvo toward the British ships. Maerker paused as the rumbling echoes of the gunfire died away.

"Go ahead, Mister Born."

"Two men were killed outright by the blasts—a deck officer and a junior machinist."

"Do you have names?" asked Maerker.

"Uh, no, sir. Doctor Nohl provided no names in his report."

"Go on," said Maerker.

"Two other men were seriously wounded. A gunlayer has multiple puncture wounds to his torso and is bleeding internally. He is in the infirmary, but Doctor Nohl does not expect him to survive. The other serious injury was to a deck officer—the doctor states that both of his arms were torn off below the elbow." Born grimaced. "He has been stabilized, for now. Three other sailors have been admitted with minor wounds—all are expected to recover."

"Thank you, Lieutenant-Commander," said Maerker quietly. He swallowed hard. Those men were *Gneisenau's* first casualties of the war. He had a dreadful foreboding that they would not be the last.

"They're outrunning us," observed Busch, as he scanned the enemy ships. "They're steaming much faster than we are, and they are steadily moving ahead of our line. I think they intend to use their speed to gain a more favorable wind position and cross us up."

Maerker brought his glasses up to see for himself. "You're right," he agreed. "They've probably had enough of firing blind, and with their speed advantage, they're fast enough to pull it off. We'll need to change course quickly before they cross us and turn *Scharnhorst* into a sieve." The battlecruisers had accelerated eastward ahead of the German line, claiming the sea before them, and were beginning a rapid sweeping turn to the south, which would bring them directly in front of Graf Spee's flagship. If the Germans did not change course, the British ships would likely cross their bows within minutes. This maneuver, known as "Crossing the T" would allow the two battlecruisers to pour full broadsides into the oncoming *Scharnhorst* while limiting the German cruisers to using only their foremost turrets to return fire. It was a clever tactic—ideally suited to a force that had a significant speed advantage over its enemy. Maerker recalled that less than a decade earlier, the Japanese navy had repeatedly used the maneuver with devastating effect at the Battle of Tsushima to utterly crush an entire Russian fleet.

Fortunately, the admiral had seen the danger as well.

Message from the flagship, sir," said Petri. "We're to turn south at full speed, following the flagship, and try to get back out of range of the enemy."

Ahead, *Scharnhorst* was already beginning a sharp southward turn. Maerker addressed the helmsman. "Hard to starboard. Follow in her wake. Full speed."

"Yes, sir. Hard to starboard. Coming about to new southwest course — following in the flagship's wake."

The two armored cruisers turned sharply to starboard, heeling over dramatically at full speed. The wind now raked across their port bows as they headed due south. Maerker looked aft, over *Gneisenau's* port quarter, toward the enemy ships. For the briefest of moments, they appeared to be widening the distance between themselves and their pursuers. Almost immediately, however, it became horribly clear that the British battlecruisers were once again steadily closing the distance.

◆

"FIRING," stated Backhouse flatly. *Glasgow's* gunnery commander was clearly not amused that their first shots had fallen mere feet to either side of *Leipzig's* stern. The forward 6-inch turret and two foremost 4-inch turrets fired again, spouting jets of flame and clouds of brown smoke. Because they were still chasing the fleeing German ship, which lay directly ahead, only those three of *Glasgow's* turreted guns could be brought to bear on the enemy vessel. Thus, they could only fire three shells at a time. *Cornwall*, with her six forward-facing guns, was approaching from behind but was still out of range — which meant that for now, those three of *Glasgow's* forward guns were the only British weapons able to fire at *Leipzig*, steaming some five miles ahead.

All of the bridge officers fixed their glasses on the German light cruiser. A moment later, an orange and black explosion bloomed on *Leipzig's* aft deck as one of the shells struck the enemy ship. Two more plumes of water shot up just aft of her stern.

"I knew you had it in you, Lieutenant-Commander," chided Thompson playfully.

"Well done, Mister Backhouse," said Luce. "Now just keep pounding her until we bring her to heel."

"With pleasure, sir," replied Backhouse, who then barked instructions to the forward gun crews through a voice pipe.

"Spotter's station to the bridge," said the hollow voice from above. "Be advised that *Nürnberg*, the second enemy cruiser in their line, has adjusted course to port."

"Is she turning back to assist *Leipzig*?" asked Thompson. He turned to Luce with a raised eyebrow. "If so, we'll have to contend with two of them in short order."

"No, sir," replied the spotter. "She appears to be continuing her flight—just altering her course to the southeast, diverging from their line."

Luce and Thompson swept their binoculars to the southeast and confirmed that *Nürnberg* had changed course.

Thompson said, "Looks like it's every man for himself. We may have to split up and chase them down individually after all."

Luce nodded thoughtfully. "True, but first things first. We need to take care of…"

Suddenly, ahead of them, *Leipzig* began turning sharply to port, and her full flank rapidly came into view.

"She's trying to get a broadside shot at us," shouted Thompson. "Three points to starboard. Evasive maneuvers."

"Three points to starboard," echoed Hobbs at the helm. The ship altered course slightly to starboard, just before *Leipzig's* flank lit up with a flurry of muzzle flashes.

"Incoming salvo," announced Thompson.

Several seconds later, the shells struck. Three splashes burst from the sea to port and loud booms echoed across *Glasgow's* decks as two of the incoming shells slammed into the ship. A cloud of dark smoke briefly obscured the windows of the wheelhouse before being whisked away by the wind. At least one of the rounds had struck somewhere forward of the bridge.

"All port batteries firing," said Backhouse. Gouts of flame and smoke erupted along the length of *Glasgow* as her two 6-inch turrets and five port side 4-inch turrets fired simultaneously at the enemy cruiser. The roar of the cannonade died away and the muzzle smoke was whipped aft on the wind. Most of the barrage of shells appeared to land short of *Leipzig's* beam, throwing up a line of foaming columns along the enemy cruiser's hull. Two larger waterspouts rose behind the enemy ship.

"Damage report," commanded Luce, who could now see that one of the enemy shells had penetrated the forecastle near the forward turret. A thin stream of smoke drifted from a small scorched hole in the plating on the deck below.

"She's turning again," observed Thompson. "Looks like she fired the broadside to try to buy her some time. Now she's returning to her original course."

Ahead, *Leipzig* was indeed turning back to starboard, resuming her southward flight. The attack had been quick and well executed—and although *Glasgow's* gunners had been able to return fire, they had little time to aim, and all of the rounds from the British salvo had narrowly missed.

Backhouse lowered his binoculars to receive a voice pipe report from one of his gunnery officers. He frowned as he listened intently, then raised his head from the metal cone. "Sir, one of those hits damaged our forward fire control. We're trying to repair it, but for now we've switched to the secondary control."

"Understood," said Luce, once again impressed by the quality of the German gunnery. "Any casualties?"

"None reported."

"Good, what about the second hit? Does anyone know where it struck?"

Lieutenant Hirst spoke up. "Sir, we have casualties in the machine spaces. Engineering reports that the other round penetrated the protective belt and exploded near the port boiler array. A number of men were working right there, but we do not yet have an official injury report. It sounds a bit chaotic down there. The doctor has arrived and the engineers are evaluating the damage to the boilers."

Luce nodded. "Understood. Have Doctor Gilmour provide a full casualty report when he is able. Mister Hobbs, resume our pursuit course. That maneuver likely cost them more ground than it gained."

"Aye, sir. Following in pursuit," said Hobbs.

Luce's assessment proved correct. Although *Leipzig* had scored two direct hits on *Glasgow*, her attacking turn had temporarily slowed the German cruiser and allowed *Glasgow* to further close the distance within five miles. *Cornwall* had also gained ground during the exchange and would soon be in striking range herself.

"Firing," announced Backhouse again.

The three forward cannons roared, and the bridge officers raised their binoculars to watch for the fall of shot. Two of the shells fell short, but once again, one round hit its target. Another bright explosion flashed on *Leipzig's* aft deck—this time accompanied by a plume of venting steam and a shower of dark debris thrown upward by the blast.

"A few more hits like that," observed Thompson, "and she won't be running anymore."

◆

THE SPEED of the battlecruisers was terrifying. As Maerker watched, the two big enemy ships had rapidly made up the distance and had once again drawn nearly alongside the German armored cruisers. They were now only eleven kilometers off *Gneisenau's* port beam. Although the enemy attempt to cross the T in front of *Scharnhorst* had failed, the British now were no longer hampered by the smoke that had limited their visibility during the opening stages of the battle.

The British had improved their view, but they were now closer to the German artillery. *Gneisenau's* gun crews resumed their blistering pace, firing two salvos to every one fired by the British. Finally, Maerker thought he could see bright flashes as their shells fell upon the two battlecruisers. The two lines continued to gradually converge, which would soon bring the battlecruisers into the effective range of the German ships' secondary batteries as well. Lieutenant-Commander Busch seized the opportunity immediately, instructing the secondary batteries to begin firing. Now salvos of both 8.2-inch and 5.9-inch shells were arcing toward the British line. The larger shells sent up pickets of foaming explosions in the water alongside the enemy vessels, while the smaller shells were still dropping well short. Although he was certain that both *Scharnhorst* and *Gneisenau* had each scored several hits, Maerker could not yet see any discernible damage to the enemy battlecruisers.

For the British gunners, however, it was a different story. Although their pace was slower than the Germans', they were no longer impeded by the smoke—and they were now firing at closer range—so their aim was becoming more accurate with every salvo. Another massive shell struck *Gneisenau* somewhere far aft with a rumble—sending tremors throughout the ship.

"Get me a damage report," said Maerker, realizing that the enemy gunners had found their range and could now likely strike them with every salvo, unless *Scharnhorst* and *Gneisenau* could again change course to throw off their aim.

Two more deafening explosions erupted from the sea just off *Gneisenau's* forecastle, sending towering peaks of foaming seawater crashing down over her decks. When the mist cleared, Maerker could see that up ahead, *Scharnhorst* had been struck amidships, with devastating effect. Her foremost funnel was completely gone, and her third was a ragged, crumpled heap that had fallen and now lay draped over the starboard lift boom. A fire raged on her upper deck, sending spirals of black smoke out over the sea. Multiple large pieces of debris began drifting past *Gneisenau* in the flagship's wake. Among the flotsam was the wrecked and partially submerged shell of one of the flagship's steam pinnaces. As it drifted by, suspended eerily just under the surface, Maerker could make out the words "SMS *Scharnhorst*" painted on the small boat's shattered bow.

Lieutenant-Commander Born looked up in distress. "Engineering reports that our starboard engine room has been hit. They've got significant flooding and must shut down the number three engine to make repairs to the compartment." His voice was tinged with fear.

Maerker knew that for the sake of his men, he had to maintain a sense of composure, despite their dire circumstances. "Thank you, Mister Born," he replied calmly. "Instruct them to do whatever they require to control the flooding and get that engine back on line. In the meantime, ensure that the other two engines are operating at the highest possible speed."

"Yes, sir," replied Born, who swallowed hard and relayed the message to the engineering officers.

A flight of enemy shells shrieked overhead and detonated in the sea to starboard. Two more explosions rocked the ship like hammer blows ringing upon an anvil—both rounds had struck the thick armored belt just above the waterline. The big cruiser shuddered under the impacts but continued to steam onward unabated, and Maerker hoped that the fifteen centimeters of steel plating that protected her outer hull could withstand the terrible onslaught.

"Firing!" announced Busch again, depressing the switch before him. *Gneisenau's* port batteries roared in sequence and another precise salvo of primary and secondary shells arced out into the sky toward the British line.

◆

"SHE'S turning again," said Thompson.

Ahead, *Leipzig* had begun another sharp turn to port in a second attempt to unleash a full salvo at her pursuers.

"Three points to starboard," said Luce. "Let's make her pay for it this time."

"We're ready," affirmed Backhouse tersely.

*Glasgow* swung slightly to starboard as *Leipzig* fired another broadside. Simultaneously, *Glasgow's* guns fired again in unison. This time, all of the German shells flew long—whistling over *Glasgow's* decks and detonating in the sea beyond her starboard beam. The British return salvo was more accurate. Three explosions flashed along *Leipzig's* flank, one of which was followed by a secondary detonation that sent a mushroom-shaped cloud of orange and black flame skyward just aft of her third funnel.

"Nice work," said Luce. "She can't possibly keep this up much longer."

"She's turning south again," said Backhouse.

The German cruiser was resuming her southward course, but her latest turning maneuver had again slowed her, allowing the British ships to further narrow the margin between them.

"Get us back on a pursuit course," said Thompson.

"Aye, sir," replied Hobbs.

*Glasgow's* bridge officers heard multiple loud booms echo across the water. A moment later, six fountains of water rose all around *Leipzig*. *Cornwall* was finally in range and was now firing at the enemy ship as well. Luce looked out over the port beam to see that *Cornwall* had drawn nearly even with *Glasgow*, a quarter of a mile away. As he looked at the familiar lines of the aged armored cruiser, he could not help but think of *Monmouth*, which had been *Cornwall's* sister ship. Unlike at Coronel, however, this time the old County-Class cruiser was more than a match for her opponent.

"It's about time they joined the party," said Thompson with a grin, "but I personally thought we were doing just fine by ourselves."

As if not to be outdone by the more heavily armed ship sailing beside her, *Glasgow's* forward batteries fired again. Two of the three shells hit their target, one exploding on the German cruiser's stern and the other slicing through a starboard gunwale and exploding beside the hull.

Now that they had mustered overwhelming firepower against *Leipzig*, Luce wanted to ensure that the other two fleeing German ships could not both escape. *Dresden* was certainly too far ahead to catch immediately—in fact, she was now hull down on the extreme southern horizon, with only the tops of her funnels still visible. *Dresden* might have an insurmountable head start, but *Nürnberg* could still be snared.

"Mister Stuart, send a message to *Kent*. Instruct Captain Allen to break off and pursue *Nürnberg* at full speed."

"Yes, sir." Lieutenant Stuart relayed the message to the wireless room.

*Cornwall's* guns boomed again, and her second salvo was more accurate than the first. Two of her 6-inch shells burst upon *Leipzig's* upper works, ejecting plumes of shredded metal into the air. Backhouse's gunners added their own salvo, with three rounds punching into the enemy cruiser's starboard quarter.

Half a mile behind, HMS *Kent* changed course, turning slightly toward the southeast. Nearly nine miles ahead of her, *Nürnberg* was trying to escape, but already *Kent* was accelerating and closing the distance. Confident that Allen would do his best to run down the fleeing *Nürnberg*, Luce returned his attention to the enemy target immediately before him. A fire was burning on *Leipzig* amidships, and the German cruiser seemed to have visibly slowed. Although she was gravely wounded, *Leipzig* was turning — this time to starboard — to once again engage her pursuers.

"She's trying for another broadside," said Thompson. "They're certainly not just rolling over and playing dead."

"Three points to starboard," said Luce. "Mister Backhouse, prepare to hit her with everything again."

# TWENTY-EIGHT

*Tuesday, December 8, 1914*
*South Atlantic Ocean, 118 Miles (189 Kilometers) Southeast of the Falkland Islands*

MAERKER SWALLOWED and tried to equalize the pressure in his ringing ears. Two more incoming shells had struck the ship just moments before — one of which had exploded upon the foredeck just below the superstructure that supported the bridge. The shock wave from that detonation had staggered the bridge crew and had temporarily deafened everyone in the wheelhouse. The other shell had struck somewhere amidships. At this shorter range, the British gunners were now having no difficulty hitting their targets, and the massive incoming rounds were striking *Gneisenau* with alarming regularity.

"Get me an updated damage and casualty report," said Maerker, coughing as thick greasy smoke infiltrated the wheelhouse. Numerous fires now burned below decks throughout the ship, where penetrating shells had detonated. The smoky air reeked of cordite, sulphur, burning oil, melting rubber, and a stench that Maerker could only assume was burning flesh.

*Gneisenau's* port side gun batteries roared again, launching another salvo at the second British battlecruiser in the enemy line — now no more than eight kilometers to the east. Although he assumed that his guns had hit the British ship repeatedly, he still could not see any obvious signs of damage. He hoped that *Scharnhorst* was having better results, but the enemy flagship was pounding Graf Spee's cruiser relentlessly. In fact, it appeared that *Scharnhorst* had thus far sustained even more damage than *Gneisenau*. As Maerker brought his binoculars up to look at the flagship, he witnessed another huge explosion that obliterated her fourth funnel, shredding it into metallic confetti that swirled into the sky on a roiling column of heat and flame.

That left *Scharnhorst* with only one standing funnel. She was developing a slight list to port and was settling lower in the water. Multiple fires burned throughout the flagship, and she appeared to have incurred some damage to her steering machinery as well. The visible damage to the armored cruiser was horrific, and Maerker could only imagine the destruction that had been wreaked below decks. Still, her guns continued to spit fire at the enemy in angry defiance of her wounds.

As he surveyed the damage to *Scharnhorst*, something caught his eye out to the southeast. He adjusted his lenses to get a better look. Inconceivably, a three-masted, fully rigged sailing ship had appeared, sailing over the horizon directly toward the battling warships. She was a large and extraordinarily beautiful vessel—her hull was painted white, and her white sails shone brilliantly in the mid-afternoon sunlight. So incongruous was the sight that for a moment, Maerker wondered if he was seeing an apparition.

"What do you make of that, Mister Born?" he asked.

The navigation officer took a look and shook his head. "Perhaps a passenger vessel, sir? Looks to be flying a Norwegian flag."

Maerker looked again. "That she does," he confirmed, seeing a red flag with a blue cross fluttering from her halyards. "She's as far from home as we are." He could only imagine what the passengers and crew of that elegant sailing ship must be thinking—as they blundered upon this maelstrom of gunfire and smoke in such a remote corner of the ocean.

Busch spoke up. "Damage report, sir. One of those last incoming rounds hit our port firing station. My officers report that it is no longer functional—the outer bulwark was entirely blasted away, leaving the compartment torn open to wind and sea. At least two of the gunnery officers survived the blast, because they have reported back in from the starboard firing station. We have already adjusted to send commands through the starboard station."

"Well done," said Maerker. "Anything else?"

"The main crew kitchens are gone, sir," said Petri. "At least nine men were killed, but there may have been more."

"Good lord. Get a status report from Doctor Nohl in the infirmary."

"Right away, sir."

Another British salvo struck the sea all around them—the thunderous explosions hurling thousands of gallons of seawater over *Gneisenau's* decks—but miraculously none of those rounds struck the ship.

The airborne mist from the blasts drifted aft on the wind, and Maerker could see that several kilometers away, the white sailing ship had altered course to the east — steering clear of the oncoming battlecruisers. She was soon obscured by smoke and haze, and Maerker lost sight of her.

"Firing," announced Busch again, and the port batteries fired once more at an enemy that appeared to be impervious to harm.

◆

"THREE SHOTS hit *Cornwall*, sir," reported Hirst, who had the nearby cruiser in view through binoculars. "At least one hit her on the armored belt, but I cannot be sure of the others."

Moments earlier, *Leipzig* had taken another sudden turn and had unleashed a new salvo. Rather than aiming at *Glasgow* this time, however, her gunners had targeted the more heavily armed *Cornwall*, which *Leipzig's* captain now probably considered a bigger threat. Both British ships had responded with fusillades of their own. The German light cruiser had been struck four more times, and her middle funnel had crumpled and fallen upon her weather deck.

"Mister Stuart," said Luce, "send a message to Captain Ellerton. Ask if he's all right."

"Yes, sir."

*Leipzig* had resumed her southward flight, although she now steamed at only fourteen knots. Both *Glasgow* and *Cornwall* had no trouble keeping pace. Numerous small fires were burning on the German ship, and Luce could see teams of men working on the weather deck — trying to quench the flames and make repairs.

"Firing," declared Backhouse. *Glasgow's* forward guns boomed again. A shell burst upon *Leipzig's* stern with a bright explosion, bracketed by two tall fountains to either side of the ship. *Cornwall's* forward guns fired again, and a picket of splashes rose along the enemy cruiser's port flank. One shell from *Cornwall's* salvo struck the center of *Leipzig's* rear deck, severing her aft mast at the base. The mast toppled starboard into the sea, carrying with it several flags.

"Reply from *Cornwall*, sir," said Stuart. "Captain Ellerton reports that *Cornwall* has two small holes in a port coal bunker. Otherwise, no damage."

"Good to hear. Send another message to Allen on *Kent*. Ask him his distance to *Nürnberg*." Above the southern horizon, for the first time all day, he could see a thin line of dark gray clouds looming. "Looks like we might get some weather today after all. We'll need to bring the enemy to heel before they can reach that storm front."

◆

ABOARD *Nürnberg*, Captain Schönberg had also seen the developing rainclouds to the south. Finally, there was some hope of escape.

"How close is the enemy cruiser?" he demanded.

The gunnery officer conferred with the spotters above before answering. "Less than twelve kilometers now, sir."

"Goddamn it," he exclaimed. "What's our current speed?" Schönberg cursed his miserable luck. First, the admiral's plan to draw off the enemy fleet had only succeeded in pulling away the battlecruisers. Now his own course change had failed to shake off all of their pursuers. Two of the British ships had continued to follow *Leipzig* and were now shelling her repeatedly—but one of the enemy cruisers had changed course to follow *Nürnberg* and was now steadily closing the gap between the two vessels.

"Seventeen knots, sir," answered the helmsman.

"Now we've slowed to seventeen?" Schönberg was incredulous. He shouted at the helmsman who was only an arm's length away. "We should be able to steam at twenty-three! An hour ago, we were going eighteen. If anything, we should be steaming faster. Have they been doing nothing down there?" He turned to Haas. "Get Menzel on the pipe, immediately!"

"Yes, sir." Haas hailed the engine room, then called for the engineering commander.

The senior engineering officer's voice echoed through the voice pipe, along with the clattering din of the engines. "Menzel here, sir."

"Menzel, what in God's name are you doing?" Schönberg bellowed into the voice pipe. "You were supposed to get the engines to go faster, not slow them down."

"Yes, sir, but..."

"Are you aware that there's a British armored cruiser gaining on us?"

"Of course, sir, and we're doing everything we..."

"You're obviously not doing everything, you incompetent ass! We're going slower, and they seem to be going faster. That's an old County-class cruiser. She's not supposed to be running us down like a hound after a tortoise." Schönberg seethed through clenched teeth. "Do something, Menzel, to get us moving faster! I don't care what you throw into the boilers. Burn the damned stokers, if you have to. Otherwise, if the British don't manage to kill you, I'll do it myself." Schönberg slammed his hand down upon the voice pipe cone and stalked to the front windows of the wheelhouse, fuming. It had not escaped his notice that the armored cruiser so doggedly pursuing him was of the same class and vintage as HMS *Monmouth*, which he had come upon in her stricken condition at Coronel—and which he had summarily sent to the bottom of the sea.

The gunnery officer hesitantly spoke up. "Sir, spotters confirm that the enemy ship has drawn within eleven kilometers."

Schönberg said nothing as he stared through the windows, out over the slate gray sea, toward the distant line of clouds and rain. The squall was still probably more than thirty kilometers away. Although the weather system was moving northward toward them, it would likely be an hour before *Nürnberg* could gain any cover from it. At the rate that the enemy armored cruiser was gaining upon them, they would be within gunnery range in half that time.

◆

SIXTY-FIVE kilometers north from where *Nürnberg* was fleeing from *Kent*, the men of *Gneisenau* were fighting desperately for their lives.

"Engineering reports that two port side boiler rooms are now flooded," said Born. "Boilers number three through six are inoperable, and the engineering commander reports the water is coming in faster than they can pump it out."

"What's our speed?" asked Maerker.

"We're down to sixteen knots, sir," replied the helmsman.

*Gneisenau* had taken a massive hit amidships, below the waterline, and multiple lower compartments on the port side of the ship were now reporting uncontrollable flooding.

"Get more crews down there to help them seal off those compartments and passageways. We have to give the pumps a chance to work."

"Yes, sir," replied Born.

"We're developing a list to port," observed Busch.

It was true, realized Maerker. Slowly but steadily, as more compartments below decks were inundated, the entire ship was canting more and more to port. Already they were heeling over several degrees.

"If the list worsens much more," added Busch, "our port side 5.9-inch guns will no longer be able to fire."

"Understood," said Maerker. *Gneisenau's* wounds were now critically severe. Most of the compartments had suffered some form of damage. The engines were down to two-thirds of their power, fires were burning throughout the ship, and the infirmary had lost count of the mounting casualties. Thankfully, all of the primary and secondary guns were still operational, although the worsening list to port was now threatening to render the secondary batteries on that side of the ship useless.

He peered ahead through the smoke. Somehow the admiral's flagship was still afloat. *Scharnhorst* was under steam, but she resembled a funeral pyre. Fires raged throughout the ship, spewing smoke and angry orange flames from dozens of ragged holes and fissures in her hull and decking. Only one funnel remained standing, and its topmost third had been shot away. She was riding lower in the water and was also listing to port. Maerker noticed that the admiral's flag, which customarily flew from *Scharnhorst's* foremast, was fluttering half-way down its halyard. He hoped that this was because of some battle damage to the lines and not a sign that Graf Spee had perished.

"Mister Petri, send a message to the flagship. Ask why the admiral's flag is flying at half-mast. Has the admiral been killed?"

"Yes, sir," replied Petri, who passed the message to the wireless room.

After a few minutes, Petri read the reply from the admiral. "I AM ALL RIGHT THUS FAR. SEVERE DAMAGE THROUGHOUT SHIP. HAVE YOU BEEN ABLE TO HIT THE ENEMY?"

"Tell him," Maerker replied, "we believe we have struck the enemy repeatedly. Smoke and distance prevent proper observation."

Petri relayed the message, but there was no immediate reply. Another incoming shell exploded against the hull at the waterline near *Gneisenau's* bow, sending tremors throughout the ship. Busch's gunners responded with a full salvo, but with thick smoke now encircling the wheelhouse, Maerker could not see if any of the shells hit their target.

"Another message from the admiral, sir," said Petri, who wore a puzzled expression. "It just says, JULIUS, YOU WERE RIGHT AFTER ALL."

Yes, thought Maerker, unfortunately he had been right. Attacking the Falklands had been a terrible mistake.

The helmsman announced with some trepidation, "Sir, the flagship appears to be turning hard to port. Do we as well?"

Maerker looked ahead to see that *Scharnhorst* was, in fact, turning severely to port. Her new course appeared to be taking her toward the British battlecruisers. Was the admiral trying to close the distance farther to help the accuracy of his gunners?

Petri spoke up. "Another message from the flagship, sir. It says, DO NOT FOLLOW. TRY TO ESCAPE IF YOUR ENGINES ARE INTACT."

Good God, thought Maerker. The admiral is going to try to attack them with torpedoes at close range. He is going to sacrifice *Scharnhorst* to try to save us.

Ahead, less than a kilometer off *Gneisenau's* port bow, *Scharnhorst* was completing her turn and was now on a trajectory that took her directly toward the British battlecruisers.

"Sir?" asked the helmsman. "Our course?"

Several kilometers to the east, bright yellow muzzle flashes lit up along the decks of both enemy battlecruisers as their huge gun turrets began firing concentrated broadsides directly at the oncoming German flagship.

◆

THE SOUND of multiple explosions washed over *Nürnberg*, as HMS *Kent's* first salvo landed less than a hundred meters aft of the German cruiser's stern. Six columns of water rose from *Nürnberg's* wake in a haphazard cluster.

"What's their range now?" barked Schönberg.

"Ten thousand meters," replied the gunnery officer. "Still beyond our range, sir."

"Damn it!" Schönberg paced restlessly within the confines of the wheelhouse. Scattered rain drops began to spot the windows. He looked out hopefully at the storm front, which churned toward them from the southern horizon—but it was still too far away. He glimpsed, far to the southwest, the last traces of funnel smoke from *Dresden* as she slipped under the dark blanket of the storm and was gone. He turned back on the lieutenant. "Have our aft guns fire at them anyway. Maximum elevation."

"Yes, sir." The gunnery officer relayed the instruction to his gun crews. Seconds later, *Nürnberg's* four rearmost 4.1-inch guns fired. The shells fell in a tight pattern of splashes well short of the oncoming armored cruiser's bow. In response, the British warship's forward guns flashed again.

"Tell them to keep firing," said Schönberg. "Eventually those bastards will be close enough that we'll..."

An explosion somewhere aft interrupted the captain, and the bridge officers felt a dull thud reverberate through the decking. One of the British shells had hit the ship on the fantail. Five other shells exploded in the sea to either side of the stern. The enemy ship had drawn within range.

"Get me a damage report!" growled Schönberg. He addressed the helmsman. "Evasive maneuvers. Adjust our course one to three points each way, port then starboard, every minute. Let's not make it easy for them."

"Yes, sir." He turned the wheel, and *Nürnberg* veered slightly to port.

Schönberg decided to get a better look at his pursuer. He opened the port wheelhouse door and stepped out onto the flying bridge. He raised his binoculars and looked back toward the trailing enemy warship, now only nine kilometers astern. The sea, which had previously been unusually calm, was now lashed by the increasing wind and was speckled with whitecaps. The British cruiser's slab-shaped prow plunged through growing swells, throwing arcs of spray to either side. Her funnels disgorged a torrent of black smoke that fanned out behind the warship like the fluttering cape of a charging horseman. This old County-class cruiser was surely steaming at her maximum speed. With every moment, she drew steadily closer.

He knew that he was outgunned and outmatched. Schönberg scanned the gray sky. Only darkness or weather could save him now. Unfortunately, although it was late afternoon, several more hours of daylight remained. The rain was little more than a sprinkling—certainly not yet enough to conceal the ship or facilitate their escape.

*Nürnberg* began a slight turn to starboard as the helmsman executed the next evasive maneuver. Behind them, the British cruiser's gun barrels flashed again, sending another salvo arcing toward the German ship.

Schönberg stepped back inside the wheelhouse, closed the door behind him, and grasped a handhold. "Incoming fire," he announced to the men on the bridge and then felt oddly short of breath. He inhaled deeply and flexed the fingers of his left hand, which he realized had gone completely numb.

◆

"NEW COURSE, two one zero degrees, southwest," said Maerker. "Full speed—whatever that is now."

The helmsman appeared relieved to hear the order. "Yes, sir. Two-hundred ten degrees." He turned the wheel, and the ship turned sluggishly to starboard. "We're only making fifteen knots now, sir."

Maerker nodded but said nothing. He was aghast at the spectacle playing out on the ocean before him. *Scharnhorst* was burning and adrift. The admiral had taken her on a desperate collision course toward the enemy, despite the withering barrage of gunfire coming from the battlecruisers. The British had poured two full salvos into the German flagship, with nearly every shot hitting its mark somewhere. Clusters of explosions had erupted from bow to stern as the storm of armor-piercing shells tore through steel and detonated savagely within the cruiser. The two battlecruisers had then rapidly changed course, steering away in a tight circle that kept them out of *Scharnhorst's* torpedo range—which eliminated any possible chance that Graf Spee might have had to inflict a final blow upon the enemy ships. The British maneuver briefly suspended the bludgeoning that the flagship was suffering—but more than enough damage was already done.

*Scharnhorst* had been struck more than fifty times by the powerful 12-inch shells. Fires glowed from dozens of gaping holes in her hull and superstructure. Thick black smoke billowed upward from the horrific wounds, and intermittent secondary explosions burst from below her decks. Her aft mast was down, and her last standing funnel was riddled with ragged perforations. She had settled even lower in the water, listing severely to port, and began to sink by the bow.

The British warships were still steaming at full speed as they came out of their turn—now once again on the windward side of the German cruisers. Maerker steeled himself—assuming he was about to witness the two great battlecruisers each fire a last, deadly barrage into *Scharnhorst*—but for the moment their guns were silent. The British could also see that she was finished, and they had briefly ceased fire.

The great German flagship was sinking. *Scharnhorst's* bow was submerged, and her decks canted over to port. Her forecastle began to disappear as the ship slid under. Just before the gray-green waves engulfed her forward turret, one of its guns fired a final time—a last futile gesture of defiance. Then the entire burning hull of *Scharnhorst* slid rapidly beneath the surface, disappearing in a churning boil of turbulent foam. A cloud of smoke and steam rose from the sea and was carried away on the wind.

SMS *Scharnhorst*, her crew of more than eight hundred men, and Admiral Graf von Spee were gone.

A somber silence settled over the officers and men of *Gneisenau*. Crewmen all over the ship gazed out at the stretch of empty ocean where their flagship had been just moments before.

"God rest their souls," whispered Petri.

Maerker scanned the sea where the ship had disappeared, looking for survivors who might have escaped as the ship was pulled under. He spotted no one. Even if he had seen some men swimming, he would not have been able to do anything about it, because the British battlecruisers had drawn parallel once more, now some eight kilometers to starboard. They were firing again, and their aim was now concentrated solely upon *Gneisenau*. A dozen huge explosions mushroomed out of the sea around them, as the British ships renewed their bombardment.

"Now what do we do?" asked Born, who was visibly shaken by the loss of the admiral and the flagship.

"We fight as long as we can," replied Maerker. He pointed southward to the approaching expanse of dark gray clouds. "See that squall, Lieutenant-Commander? If we can fend the British off long enough, perhaps we can elude them in the rain until nightfall." Maerker did not believe this was likely or even truly possible, but he felt it necessary to keep up the hopes of his officers.

"Look at the bright side," said Busch to the navigating officer. He smiled reassuringly. "Now we're firing at them with a completely fresh set of guns." He pressed the switches before him, and *Gneisenau's* starboard primary and secondary batteries roared to life. With the exception of the main fore and aft turrets, these were the first shots they had fired in the battle. The starboard gunners were just as accurate as their compatriots on the opposite side of the ship—and now the range to the enemy targets was closer than before. Bright explosions bloomed on the upper deck of the enemy flagship.

"Right on target," commended Maerker. Finally, he had some visual confirmation that their shells were hitting the British vessels.

"A third enemy ship has joined their line," said Busch as he scanned northward.

Maerker followed where Busch was looking and he, too, saw the third British warship as it fell in behind the battlecruisers. She was an older armored cruiser, of the *Devonshire*-class, and she must have been trailing the bigger ships throughout the battle—having only now caught up. Muzzle flashes flared from her decks as this ship also began firing at *Gneisenau*. Her first salvo fell just short of the stern. The addition of this third warship was of little consequence to the outcome of the battle. Maerker knew that just one of the two battlecruisers could certainly finish the job all by herself.

Two more big incoming shells hit *Gneisenau* in quick succession. The first exploded on her starboard flank, punching through the armor of a 5.9-inch casemate and exploding within. The detonation obliterated the entire gunnery compartment, vaporized the four men within, and gouged a jagged void from the hull of the ship where the emplacement had once been. The second shell struck the base of the main superstructure, just below the bridge itself. The deafening thunderclap rocked the wheelhouse severely enough to once again cause all of the bridge officers to stagger and stumble.

"Where did that one hit?" asked Maerker as he shook his head to clear the drone in his ears. Acrid yellow smoke flooded the wheelhouse. The stench of sulphur and cordite assaulted his nostrils and caused his sinuses to ache.

"Right below us," said Petri, coughing.

"Are the wireless operators all right?" The wireless room was below the wheelhouse, within a relatively lightly armored structure abaft of the foremast.

Petri hailed the wireless room. There was no response. "They're not answering," he said.

"Send a runner down there," said Maerker. "See if anyone's been injured."

"There are no runners," said Born. "All of them are on fire suppression or casualty teams."

"I'll go myself," said Petri. "They're my men." He left the bridge, descending the port side ladder.

Another explosion rumbled from astern. The newly arrived third enemy ship had found its range. Several more shells shrieked menacingly overhead before exploding in the sea off their port bow. Raindrops began spattering the windows, but Maerker knew the inclement weather would be too little, too late.

"Firing starboard batteries," announced Busch as he hit the switches again. *Gneisenau's* guns roared. Seconds later, multiple explosions flared on the decks and superstructure of the enemy flagship as more rounds struck their target.

Maerker scanned the leading battlecruiser's gray form with his binoculars. He could see no signs of obvious damage, nor any evidence of fires. It seemed, he thought with chilling dismay, that these big ships were just too heavily armored for the German shells to truly wound them.

After a few minutes, Petri returned to the bridge. His face was pale, and he had what appeared to be a streak of vomit down his trousers. He inhaled raggedly as he stepped back to his station. "They're all gone," he said quietly, staring into the distance. "Direct hit to the wireless compartment. Everyone's dead. Equipment wrecked. The bodies are..." His voice faltered.

"I'm sorry, August," said Maerker. "They were good men."

Petri took deep, measured breaths as he attempted to regain his composure. He rubbed his face and head as if he was trying to drive from his mind the horrific vision of the charnel house that had once been the wireless room. He looked up and agreed simply, "Yes, sir. They were good men."

For a few moments, all of the bridge officers were silent—a somber unspoken acknowledgment that good men were dying all over the ship. *Gneisenau* continued to steam southwest toward the dark gray line of clouds, as the three enemy warships kept pace eight kilometers to starboard. Through the blowing mist, Maerker could see the batteries of all three British warships flashing once again with bursts of yellow flames, as their guns launched another deadly salvo into the afternoon sky.

Maerker turned to the helmsman. "Evasive maneuvers. Let's keep them guessing. If we can dodge them long enough, we may be able to reach that squall line to the south."

"Yes, sir." The young helmsman swallowed hard. Despite his captain's calm, reassuring demeanor, their chances of actually escaping were slim at best. "Evasive maneuvers," he repeated.

*Gneisenau* began to swerve clumsily back and forth, zigzagging as more heavy enemy shells fell into the sea all around them.

◆

TO THE SOUTH, the outlook for *Nürnberg* appeared equally grim. Two rounds from HMS *Kent's* latest salvo struck the German light cruiser at the base of its first funnel—and the resulting dual explosions wrenched the steel cylinder from its moorings and hurled it forward against the main superstructure. The ruined funnel collapsed on the observation deck above the wheelhouse with a tortured squeal of metal scraping against metal.

The pursuing armored cruiser had drawn within six and a half kilometers of its fleeing prey. The British gunners were now striking *Nürnberg* with every barrage.

On the bridge, Captain Schönberg was bleeding from a gash beneath his right eye. Minutes earlier, a falling shell had burst over the foredeck, imploding the windows of the wheelhouse and spraying the bridge officers with shards of glass. Wind, smoke, and rain now swirled into the compartment, and the increased noise made communicating via the voice pipes more difficult.

"I'm certain they're dead, sir," said Haas, who was bent over and listening intently to one of the cones in the voice pipe array. "There's no response." He was referring to the spotters who had been stationed on the platform above them. In the minutes since the explosion that had shattered the windows, the bridge had not heard from either of the spotters.

"We don't need the damned spotters now anyway," said Schönberg, wiping blood from his cheek. "The enemy is so close that we can almost reach out and touch them."

Another explosion rumbled through the ship as an incoming round struck somewhere aft. By Schönberg's count, they had been hit more than a dozen times already. Crews were struggling to quench fires on multiple decks. *Nürnberg's* rear guns had been returning fire, and he believed they had struck the enemy vessel multiple times, but the armored cruiser had not slowed, nor did she show any obvious signs of damage.

He knew that if he did not change tactics, the British warship could simply continue to trail them and pick *Nürnberg* apart, shot by shot. His only chance, it seemed, was to turn and fire a full broadside—in the hope that a lucky shell might hit either the enemy bridge or one of their critical systems.

"Prepare the port side battery to fire a broadside salvo as we come about."

"Yes, sir," replied the gunnery officer. "Preparing port broadside."

Another shell exploded in the sea off the starboard gunwales. The resultant fountain of water erupted so close to the ship that it sent a torrent of frigid spray through the ruined window panes of the wheelhouse. Several centimeters of brine swirled around Schönberg's feet, and his wounded face stung from the salty mist. Another shell exploded in the sea just before the bow, drenching the forecastle.

"Hard to port!" he yelled over the din. "Bring her about to present the broadside."

"Yes, sir," said the helmsman. "Hard to port." He swung the wheel, and *Nürnberg* tilted into the turn.

As they came about to port, Schönberg could see the oncoming British cruiser bow-on, five kilometers away, her thick cutwater plowing powerfully through the whitecaps. Battle flags fluttered from her yardarms, and her six forward-facing gun barrels were pointed directly at *Nürnberg*. "Fire!" screamed Schönberg.

"Firing," echoed the gunnery officer.

Five guns along *Nürnberg's* port side fired as one, spewing yellow flames and a curtain of dark brown smoke that briefly screened the enemy vessel from their view. As the blustery wind snatched the smoke away, Schönberg saw three bright explosions flash upon the enemy ship's bows and upper works. However, the armored cruiser had not altered course to counter *Nürnberg's* maneuver. Rather, the British warship had simply continued to rush onward, directly at the German ship, rapidly closing the distance between them. The enemy was now only four kilometers distant. To his horror, Schönberg saw all of the enemy's forward guns fire at once.

"Hard to starboard!"

"Yes, sir. Hard to starboard." The ship began to turn once again to the southwest, but for a few moments, her entire beam was presented to the enemy. As the range between the combatants had decreased, so had the flight time of the rounds between ships. By the time *Nürnberg's* helmsman had spun the wheel fully to starboard, the incoming British shells had already begun their downward arc.

In a rapid sequence of concussions, four of the six armor-piercing rounds from *Kent's* salvo struck *Nürnberg*. Three shells plunged through the upper decks amidships and detonated in machine spaces below. The fourth struck the aft steering gear below the waterline. Two boilers exploded thunderously, ejecting geysers of scalding steam and shards of shredded steel into the air. The entire hull of the cruiser trembled under the blows, and much of the quarterdeck was immediately engulfed in flames.

"Sir, I've lost steering!" exclaimed the helmsman, who was spinning the wheel with no effect. "She's not responding."

"What do you mean, she's not responding?" snarled Schönberg. He elbowed the helmsman out of the way and tried the wheel himself. It turned freely to starboard, yet the ship continued sluggishly forward in a straight line. Schönberg also noted that their speed was steadily dropping. Already they had slowed to less than ten knots.

"Get me engineering!" he commanded. "What the hell is going on down there?"

Haas hovered over the voice pipe array and attempted to hail the engine room. He looked up at the captain. "They're not answering, sir."

The ship's speed was now only seven knots. At this rate, they would be dead in the water in minutes. He looked out to the northwest to see that the enemy armored cruiser had come about and was presenting her starboard broadside—surely preparing to unleash another salvo.

"Keep firing at them, you dolt!" the captain screamed at the gunnery officer, who appeared to have been momentarily stunned. Schönberg then turned on the helmsman. "And you! If the steering and throttle are not functioning, I have no need of you here. Get down to the engine room and find out what's happening. Report back as soon as you have something useful to tell me."

"Yes, sir," said the helmsman, who seemed relieved to be sent from the bridge into the fiery compartments below. He left the bridge hastily.

Now less than four kilometers away, HMS *Kent* opened fire with a full starboard broadside of nine 6-inch guns. *Nürnberg's* gunners responded with a salvo of their own. Several rounds from each ship found their marks. A British shell punctured the base of one of *Nürnberg's* forward turrets—and the explosion wrenched the turret from its mounting and sent it tumbling overboard. Two more shells punched into the German cruiser's port bulwark and embedded themselves in coal bunkers. Two German shells burst upon *Kent's* armor belt and another struck near the top of the aft wireless mast, severing the topmost third of the tall shaft.

As the sound of the latest wave of impacts faded away, Schönberg noticed an ominous lack of reverberations under his feet. The customary throb of the ship's engines was gone.

"We've lost all engine power, sir," said Haas, scrutinizing the instrumentation. "We're dead in the water."

They were doomed. The realization hit Schönberg like a gust of frigid air. His chest tightened and he had trouble breathing. The numbness in his hand now extended throughout his left arm. Up until this moment, he had truly believed that somehow he would find a way to escape or even prevail. Now, with the cover of darkness still more than two hours away, no other ships of his squadron in sight, and no engine power, all of his possible options were exhausted.

"Sir?" asked Haas. "What shall we do?"

The deck beneath Schönberg's feet wavered as if made of fluid, and the bulkheads and fixtures of the wheelhouse drifted in and out of focus. He blinked his eyes, trying to clear his blurred vision. He took a deep breath and groaned with effort as though a terrible weight was pressing upon his chest. Dizziness and nausea washed over him like a wave. He braced himself against one of the rotating metal chairs as he dropped to one knee, gasping.

"Sir! Are you injured?" Haas was kneeling beside him and had a hand on his shoulder.

Schönberg struggled to bring everything back into focus. His mouth felt dry and he tried unsuccessfully to swallow. What was happening to him? Surely, he could not be swooning like some heat-addled young girl. He pulled on the metal backrest of the chair and tried to stand—but his legs would not move. His frustration and fear boiled over, and a wave of anger coursed through him. He slumped heavily to the deck and looked up at Haas and the gunnery officer.

"Keep firing at them, you asses!" he rasped. "Keep firing until we run out of shells!"

◆

THE RAIN was falling heavily now, and thick clouds roiled above *Gneisenau*. In spite of the rain, numerous fires burned uncontrolled throughout the ship. Most of the pumps were no longer functional, and the fire suppression crews could make little headway against the spreading flames. Even if nightfall were not still two hours away, Maerker knew that while the ship burned, even the cover of darkness could not hide them from their enemies.

*Gneisenau* still steamed southwest, now making only twelve knots. As her lower compartments filled with water, the hull continued to settle lower. The ship was responding more sluggishly to commands as it slipped into a mechanical torpor. The engineers could not repair the damage to the boiler rooms, and the flooding was now threatening the operation of the engines themselves.

The two British battlecruisers maintained a parallel course eight kilometers to the northwest. From there, they continued to pound away at the solitary German armored cruiser. The third British vessel, the older *Devonshire*-class ship, had swung back out beyond the larger warships and was currently out of range to the north.

"Firing," announced Busch in a flat, business-like manner.

The starboard batteries fired with their customary precision, sending a rippling sequence of muzzle blasts smartly from bow to stern. Only the absence of the one destroyed starboard 5.9-inch casemate prevented the gunnery display from being perfect. Maerker noted with satisfaction that even in such dire circumstances, Lieutenant-Commander Busch and his expert gunners had remained composed, efficient, and accurate. However, their rate of fire had greatly decreased because the damage to the interior compartments made the timely delivery of shells and cartridges almost impossible. Eight kilometers away, four bright yellow explosions flared on the enemy flagship's decks as *Gneisenau's* shells hit home.

In response, multiple muzzle flashes sparked from both battlecruisers, as their massive guns returned fire.

"Captain," announced Busch soberly, "my officers inform me that we have no more live shells for the main guns. No AP, no high explosive. The shell rooms are empty. We're down to practice rounds, and we have fewer than fifty of those."

"What about ammunition for the secondary batteries?"

"We have three dozen rounds for the smaller batteries, but no more than that."

Maerker nodded in resignation. This was the end. Despite the expert German gunnery, *Scharnhorst* and *Gneisenau* had failed to inflict enough damage upon the heavily armored battlecruisers to force them to withdraw. Now his gunners were out of ammunition. They could no longer run, they could not hide, and now they could no longer fight. He reached out and reassuringly gripped Busch's shoulder. "Fire the practice rounds until they are gone, Johann. Then we'll need to prepare to scuttle the ship. I'll not allow her to be captured."

"Understood, sir."

The latest British salvo came screaming down upon them. It proved to be the deadliest fusillade of the afternoon. A deafening blast just aft of the bridge obliterated the first funnel, flinging dozens of its ruined pieces overboard into the sea. A second shell pierced the top of an 8.9-inch casemate, destroying the gun mount, killing the crew, and igniting a series of propellant cartridges that had not yet been loaded. A secondary explosion erupted from the ruined gunnery compartment, venting a plume of yellow-brown smoke. A third shell punched cleanly through the forward armor belt below the waterline, exploding within a crew cabin and sending a new torrent of water into the hull, augmenting the copious flooding that was already pulling the ship ever lower in the water. The fourth shell was the deadliest, for it punctured the aft weather deck and plunged down two levels into the crowded infirmary. There it detonated, instantly killing Doctor Nohl, Chaplain Rost, and nearly four dozen wounded men as the massive explosion turned the sick bay into a fiery crematorium. The fifth and final hit of the salvo sliced into the stern of the ship, exploding powerfully below the waterline and severely damaging the main steering gear.

After the rapid series of explosions, tremors rumbled through the ship like aftershocks from an earthquake.

"Dear God," said Petri. "Surely we cannot survive much more of this."

Smoke was now gathering in the wheelhouse and swirling upward from dozens of perforated and burning portions of the deck. Maerker could hear a man screaming in agony somewhere below.

"Sir, steering is no longer responding," said the helmsman.

"Completely? What's it doing?" asked Maerker.

"The rudders are jammed, sir. There is no response to my commands, and we seem to be stuck in a slow turn to starboard."

"Born, get the conning tower on the horn."

"Yes, sir." Born hailed the central station below.

Commander Pochhammer's voice echoed through the pipe. "Central station here, sir. We've got significant flooding that appears to be worsening. Our compartment's integrity has been breached, and we're standing in knee deep water."

"Understood, Commander," said Maerker. "I need you to try to steer the ship from there. Can you pull us out of this starboard turn?" Maerker hoped that the redundant control systems housed in the conning tower might allow them to bypass the steering problems experienced on the bridge.

After a pause came the reply, "Negative, sir. The mechanism appears to be jammed somewhere farther down the system. We're getting no response."

"Understood," replied Maerker dejectedly. This just made matters worse. Now they were slowly but steadily converging on the enemy line — reducing the distance to their guns even more.

Busch quickly recalculated the gunnery formulas and ordered the starboard batteries to fire again, which was to be their last time. The damage to the guns and the fire control systems caused this final salvo to be more ragged than before, but three of the main guns still fired, sending the solid metal practice rounds at the second ship in the British line.

The second battlecruiser answered in kind, sending another barrage at the gravely wounded German ship. Two more British shells pummeled the forward armor belt, punching new holes in the thick steel plating. Another round plunged deep into the hull amidships, exploding in the machine spaces.

The helmsman was ashen. "We've lost engine power, sir. We're decreasing speed."

The big ship was slowing dramatically. Within moments, *Gneisenau* was adrift and dead in the water.

"Enough," said Maerker. He could not allow it to go on any longer. "Cease fire, Johann. If we keep shooting, we'll only provoke them into firing again. We're finished. We're out of ammunition and we can no longer power or steer the ship. No sense getting more of our men killed."

"Yes, sir," replied Busch with apparent relief. He wiped a soot-stained sleeve across his brow. "What do we do now?"

"We need to evacuate the ship—and save as many men as we can. She'll likely sink on her own, but she might need some help. Do you know if we can get any of the torpedo tubes open, in case we need to scuttle her?"

"I'll hail the torpedo officers, sir. Hopefully at least one of them can still respond."

"Commander Pochhammer," said Maerker loudly into the voice pipe. "Get yourself and your men out of there. Prepare to abandon ship."

"Acknowledged, sir," said Pochhammer. "We're evacuating the central station."

With a loud metallic groan, the deck trembled beneath them. The entire ship lurched over several degrees to starboard. All of the bridge officers grasped chairs, consoles, and bulkheads to steady themselves. Fortunately, the ship settled into her new list and heeled no further. Looking out over the forecastle, Maerker could see that the bow was now so low in the water that the starboard gunwales were submerged, and green waves were lapping over the foredeck.

To the northwest, the dark silhouettes of the British ships loomed balefully. Their gun barrels were still raised, but they had stopped firing. Undoubtedly, thought Maerker, they were holding back to ensure that the Germans did not engage in some last desperate piece of trickery with the torpedoes. Of course, what the British could not know was that the only use Maerker had for the torpedo rooms now was to try to employ them as massive seacocks. In any case, Maerker had no desire to continue fighting. Less than an hour earlier, he had watched *Scharnhorst* go under with all hands. He was determined to save as many of *Gneisenau's* crew as he could.

Commander Pochhammer appeared at the top of the port ladder. He was soaking wet from the waist down, and his face and neck were covered in dark gray soot. He stood at attention on the awkwardly tilting deck. "Your orders, sir?"

"Good to see you in one piece, Mister Pochhammer," said Maerker. He addressed the entire bridge crew. "The admiral would be proud of you, gentlemen. It has been an honor and a privilege to serve as your commanding officer. Each of you is a credit to SMS *Gneisenau* and to the *Kaiserliche Marine.*"

Pochhammer saluted solemnly. "The honor and privilege has been ours, Captain." One by one, each of the other men came to attention and raised a hand in salute as well.

As his officers stood there in reverent silence, Maerker regarded each of their grim, determined faces. He returned their salute and said, "Now you must save yourselves and your men. Issue orders to abandon ship immediately. All men overboard!"

◆

FROM *Glasgow's* bridge, Captain Luce looked out at *Leipzig*, less than three miles ahead. He marveled that the German light cruiser was still attempting to escape into the increasing rain and mist, despite the severe damage she had suffered. *Leipzig* could now manage no more than twelve knots. Two of her three funnels were down, as was her main mast. Four of her gun turrets had been destroyed, and multiple jagged holes marred her hull, which now rode significantly lower in the waves. Half a dozen fires burned throughout the ship, and smoke and steam poured from below decks.

Not only was she still fleeing, but she was still fighting. Fortunately, *Glasgow* had not been struck again since the two hits earlier in the battle. The forward fire control system had been repaired. The damage to the boiler room was more severe and was still hampering the proper functioning of one of the engines. More importantly, Luce had received confirmation that there were several casualties from the explosion below.

As he scanned out over the bow toward the fleeing enemy ship, *Leipzig* once again made a sudden turn to starboard. Four of her remaining guns fired in unison. The accuracy of the enemy cruiser's guns was deteriorating—all of the shells whined over *Glasgow*, missing and falling into the sea beyond the ship.

"Spotters station to the bridge!" The voice from above sounded frantic. "We have an injury that requires medical attention."

"Who's injured?" asked Stuart.

"It's Miller, sir," said the spotter. "One of those shells blasted right between me an' him here on the platform. Felt like a locomotive rushed right by us. Missed my shoulder by a hair, but it took Miller's hand off at the wrist! He's bleeding really badly, sir."

"Tie his belt tightly around that forearm," said Stuart. "We'll send someone up to take him to the infirmary."

Thompson addressed Hirst. "Tell Doctor Gilmour that we have another injury on the way."

"Yes, sir."

*Leipzig* was turning again, resuming her southward course.

"Firing," Backhouse announced. *Glasgow's* forward batteries fired again, followed once more by *Cornwall's* guns. Moments later, splashes bracketed the German cruiser and three more explosions bloomed brightly on her decks.

"Looks like she's turning again," said Thompson. "This time to port."

"Again so soon?" said Luce, looking out at the German cruiser, which was coming about to port. Unlike the previous turns—which had only briefly presented a broadside before turning again and resuming course—

this maneuver seemed designed to reverse the cruiser's direction entirely. *Leipzig* had looped around completely and was now headed directly for *Cornwall*. "She intends to fire torpedoes! Hard to starboard!"

The helmsman spun the wheel and *Glasgow* tilted into the turn, veering away from the oncoming enemy ship, which was now less than three miles distant. To the east, *Cornwall* was also turning away while firing her guns at the approaching cruiser. One of the shells hit *Leipzig's* bow dead-on, punching through the steel and detonating next to the anchor windlass assembly.

"Firing port broadside," said Backhouse. "This should make them reconsider that daft idea." Both 6-inch turrets and the five port-side 4-inch turrets roared as one, sending a throaty rumble over the sea. Seconds later, a flurry of shells hit *Leipzig*, as every round of the broadside punched into her hull.

Suddenly, a huge explosion burst from within *Leipzig*. Roiling orange flames and black smoke geysered into the air from a massive fissure amidships—like the eruption of a volcano. Shards of metallic debris rained down upon the sea around the cruiser, and a thunderclap washed over *Glasgow*. When the fire cloud dissipated, *Leipzig* floated motionless, dead in the water. Fires raged from bow to stern, and she appeared to be taking on water rapidly. Her guns were silent.

Yet, still she flew her battle flags. While those flags fluttered on her halyards, it indicated that the Germans considered themselves still in the fight. Only lowering them would signal an official surrender and cease-fire.

"Send a message to *Cornwall*," said Luce. "The Germans have not yet struck their colors. Beware of a torpedo attack."

"Yes, sir." Stuart relayed the message to the wireless room.

"Mister Hobbs, down to eight knots. Keep us beam-on to her as we circle around." Luce wanted to keep a wary distance with his full broadside ready. *Leipzig* had proven to be a tenacious opponent, even when completely outmatched—and he had no desire to fall prey to some last desperate ruse that might get his ship sunk when the battle was essentially won.

"Aye, sir. Eight knots."

"*Cornwall* has replied, sir," said Stuart. "Captain Ellerton asks, SHOULD WE FIRE ON HER AGAIN?"

Luce watched the flames rapidly spreading over *Leipzig's* upper works. The enemy ship was finished. Surely her captain would not stubbornly sacrifice more lives by refusing to surrender. A number of men were visible above decks on the German ship. They were retreating from the advancing flames, but none made any effort to reach the mast that held the battle flags. It appeared that the enemy had no intention of lowering their colors. Luce considered the idea of firing upon a stricken opponent to be nearly unthinkable. Unfortunately, if *Leipzig's* commander still hoped to lure them close enough to fire a torpedo, he would have little choice.

He sighed wearily. "Tell *Cornwall* to hold fast. We will wait as well, but be prepared to fire on her once more—if we must convince her to lower those flags."

"Yes, sir."

Luce turned to the gunnery commander. "Mister Backhouse, ready one salvo with just the 6-inch guns," he said reluctantly. "Hopefully, we'll not need to use it."

"Understood, sir." Backhouse relayed the commands to his gun crews.

For long moments they watched and waited. A few more of *Leipzig's* sailors emerged on portions of the weather deck that were not engulfed in flames. The battle flags continued to flutter above them.

Luce turned to the communications officer. "Mister Stuart, signal *Leipzig* with the lamp. Send the following message: I AM ANXIOUS TO SAVE LIVES. DO YOU SURRENDER?"

Stuart nodded. "Yes, sir." He passed the instructions to his signalmen.

The louvers of the lamps clacked and squeaked as the message was relayed. Long minutes passed with no response. Still *Leipzig* burned, and still her flags flew.

"We have another message from *Cornwall*, sir," said Stuart. They're asking if we should fire torpedoes to finish her off."

"Tell them to hold their fire, for now," said Luce. "C'mon, you damned fools," he pleaded as he looked out at the burning German ship. He knew that if the enemy crew refused to submit, he would be forced to fire on her until she sank.

Suddenly, two green flares shot up from *Leipzig*, arcing high over the sea toward the south.

"I'll take that as their sign of surrender," said Luce with relief. "Tell *Cornwall* that I am closing on *Leipzig* to save as many lives as I can." To Thompson he said, "Prepare to get our boats in the water. Instruct the oarsmen that they are to keep clear of the enemy ship's hull for their own safety. She could explode again or capsize, and I don't want our boys too close. Mister Hobbs, bring us to four hundred yards."

"Aye, sir. Four hundred yards."

*Glasgow* steamed cautiously toward the stricken *Leipzig*, burning even more fiercely than before and now listing severely to port. Luce watched as the few remaining German sailors began jumping overboard into the frigid sea.

# TWENTY-NINE

*Tuesday, December 8, 1914*
*South Atlantic Ocean, 131 Miles (210 Kilometers) Southeast of the Falkland Islands*

*GNEISENAU'S* BRIDGE CREW clambered out of the wheelhouse and down the outer port side ladder. The order to abandon ship had been given, but it remained to be seen how many of the men had heard it, with all of the damage to the voice pipes. The officers were already shouting to the crew to pass along the order, man to man. Captain Maerker was the last officer to leave the bridge compartment, and as he stepped out into the chilly southerly wind, he was shocked to see the destruction that had been inflicted upon his ship.

The first funnel had been destroyed, and its remnants lay strewn about the starboard half of the quarterdeck. The other three funnels were riddled with hundreds of holes and scarred with rusty blotches where the light gray paint had been blasted away. The main mast above him was pockmarked and broken, and all of the flags had been shot away—except for two that still signaled "full speed ahead." Severed lines and halyards swayed in the wind. The decks were littered with debris, mostly unrecognizable shards of metal. The deck plates and bulwarks were gouged with innumerable jagged holes—some smaller than a hand-span's width, others large enough for a full-size lorry to pass through. All of the ship's boats had been damaged or destroyed, and some of their splintered and broken remnants still hung haphazardly from their davits. Fires burned everywhere, on deck and below, and columns of thick black smoke churned upward from the belly of the dying warship. Intense heat from the fires created dancing eddies in the air, warping Maerker's view as he gazed aft toward the stern, which was now nearly submerged.

Rain was falling steadily—having arrived much too late to cloak their attempted escape. Unfortunately, it did nothing to quench the raging furnaces that were consuming the ship from within. The rainfall moistened the debris and soot upon the canted weather decks—making the already dangerous footing even more slick and treacherous.

The ship's list was worsening. Green waves lapped over the starboard gunwales. Small groups of dazed and battered men gathered near the port railings and gun mounts—trying to find purchase on the parts of the ship that were lifted highest from the sea. They were collecting lifebuoys, hammocks, oars, scraps of wood, and anything else that might float. As Maerker made his way clumsily to the tilting deck of the signals bridge, many more men appeared from hatches, doorways, and even holes in the decking. They climbed up into the blustery squall, covered in soot, oil, and blood. Many of the sailors were wounded. He saw one young man, probably a gunner, holding his bleeding head with one hand as he tried to navigate through multiple obstacles on the canted deck. As the gunner turned to step over a fallen spar, Maerker could see that he was trying to keep a large severed flap of his scalp in place. Other men had puncture wounds, burns, and even gruesome amputations—and many stared vacantly at their chaotic surroundings as if unable to comprehend the horror that had befallen them.

Maerker looked out across the darkening sea. The three British ships— the two battlecruisers and the single armored cruiser—held their positions two kilometers away. Their ominous silhouettes, partially screened by rain and mist, were stationary. Undoubtedly, they were waiting for *Gneisenau's* final death throes. He returned his attention to the ruined decks around him. More men were emerging from the shattered interior of the ship. Some were dragging the limp bodies of fallen comrades, and soon the lifeless forms of many men lay sprawled on the decks. Officers walked among the dazed and wounded, exhorting men to move to higher perches and prepare themselves to abandon the ship. Maerker surveyed as much of the ship as he could from his vantage point. By his count, fewer than three hundred sailors were visible above decks—less than half the ship's full complement.

Maerker shouted as loudly as his smoke-damaged throat could muster, in the hopes that everyone on deck could hear him. "Brave sailors of *Gneisenau*, you have fought valiantly, with skill and courage. But now we must abandon our ship. All of you must live to tell this tale of heroism to your grandchildren. Let's hear three cheers for His Imperial Majesty!"

Several hundred weary voices mustered a cheer in response.

Maerker added, "And three cheers for our good and noble *Gneisenau*!"

This brought an even heartier response from the men, some of whom began to sing as they worked their way up to the elevated port gunwales.

Below him, a low rumble sent a shudder through the hull. More compartments were failing and flooding beneath them. They had only minutes left.

"Now, all men overboard!" Maerker gestured demonstratively to the men, indicating that the time had come to leave the ship. "Quickly get as far from the ship as you can!" His orders were repeated by other officers who walked among the sailors, encouraging them to get moving immediately. He shrugged out of his thick woolen jacket and tossed it aside, not wanting to be wearing the cumbersome garment in the sea.

Crewmen began to leap or slide into the water. Those who had been able to find life buoys or some other buoyant object clutched them tightly as they left the ship. Many of the sailors held nothing at all and simply leaped into the sea and began swimming. Some men, already wounded or dazed, floated listlessly in the waves, barely keeping their faces above the dark gray swells.

Maerker, satisfied that his final orders were being carried out as efficiently as possible, made his way down the ladder from the signals bridge to the quarterdeck. The footing was treacherous on the sloping deck, which was slick with rain and covered with debris. He saw Commander Pochhammer leave the ship—pushing off into the waves from a starboard gunwale. Maerker spotted another man in the water who looked like Lieutenant-Commander Born. He hoped that the other bridge officers had also made it safely off the ship. In the chaos, smoke, and rain, he simply could not keep track of everyone. As he surveyed the rest of the weather deck before him, however, he noticed with dismay that too many sailors were still aboard the ship. Some of the laggards were officers or crew chiefs, trying to get the last of their men to leave before they, too, would disembark. Other men were either too severely wounded or too frightened to move. Still others lay immobile—perhaps already dead.

"C'mon, gentlemen," Maerker said forcefully as he walked among them. "No more dallying! Off the ship! That's an order, sailor!" Most of the men complied immediately, jumping or sliding awkwardly into the sea. Some, clearly terrified, required further encouragement. With a loud rumble, the ship lurched again, and a powerful tremor reverberated through the hull. The pit of Maerker's stomach tightened as he realized that whoever remained had likely only seconds to get away. Still, he continued to walk gingerly along the inclined deck, sidestepping flaming holes, cajoling men who clung to railings, and examining prone bodies for any signs of life. He had to save as many of his men as he could.

He clambered over a large curved sheet of metal that had once been a portion of funnel casing, and he nearly tripped over the leg of a man pinned beneath the wreckage. Maerker bent down and grasped the rough edge of the metal, heaving it upward with all of his strength.

"Can you move?" yelled Maerker at the man.

"Yes," gasped the sailor painfully, as he slid awkwardly out from under the casing. "Thank you, sir," he said. He had suffered burns to his head and upper torso, and his face was coated with oil, grime, and caked blood. His tattered uniform indicated that he was a lieutenant.

"You need to get off the ship, Lieutenant. She's going under. Can you stand?"

"I think so, sir." The wounded officer drew his sleeve across his face to wipe away some of the blood and tried to stand on the steeply tilted deck. He wavered, and the captain caught his arm to lift him onto his feet.

Maerker then recognized the young man. He was one of the junior wireless officers. Somehow, he had survived the explosion in the nearby wireless room and had been thrown the fifteen meters or so to this spot, where he had been pinned by wreckage.

"Lieutenant Picht," said Maerker, grasping the shoulders of the dazed and unsteady officer. "You need to get off the ship immediately. Swim as far from the ship as you can, and grab onto anything that floats."

The young officer simply nodded, then turned and half-slid, half-leapt into the sea. Maerker watched as Picht's head bobbed back up to the surface; then the signals officer began swimming away from the ship.

The captain looked around and saw two more prone figures lying nearby. He began picking his way across the debris field toward them. Suddenly, the deck plating beneath his feet erupted in an explosion, as venting steam and flames geysered upward from a ruined compartment below.

Maerker was thrown violently against a steel bulkhead, and he tumbled into a heap upon the weather deck. Searing pain shot through his left leg and ribcage, and his hand came away from his chest coated in bright crimson blood. He winced and saw that his left foot was bent at an impossible angle — his ankle surely shattered.

He grimaced and realized that he was having trouble breathing. He guessed that the force of the blast or the subsequent impact had broken several ribs and may have punctured one of his lungs.

*Gneisenau's* hull shuddered violently, and from below came a deafening groan of tortured metal. The deck tilted more severely to starboard as the great ship heeled over. Maerker realized that the cruiser was capsizing. He began to slide, along with all of the loose material upon the deck. Maerker wanted to jump clear before the ship turned over upon him, but his ruined leg would not move. He saw the gray surface of the sea tilting toward him. The ship was going over.

For an instant, Maerker hung in mid-air as he lost purchase on the near-vertical deck and began to fall. He plunged deeply into the icy water with a shock and momentarily lost his bearings as he tumbled beneath the surface. Bone-chilling cold and ear-splitting noise assaulted his senses. His eyes stung and his popping ears were filled with a cacophonous buzzing. Hundreds of metal fragments, large and small, sank past him into the abyss. Looking up through the filtered green haze, he saw the immense dark bulk of the capsizing ship closing over the water above him like the lid of a massive coffin. *Gneisenau's* decks and superstructure descended and met the surface with a deafening rumble. An underwater shock wave hammered his body, and he tumbled uncontrollably in a maelstrom of swirling foam. He lost his bearings once again, and his lungs began to burn.

◆

THE GUNS of HMS *Kent*, now only three kilometers away, were methodically pounding *Nürnberg*. Barrage after barrage of shells tore into her unarmored flanks, ripped into her superstructure, shattered her decking, and detonated savagely within her interior compartments. Fires raged from every portion of the ship, sending towering columns of flame higher than her funnels had once stood. Yet, still her battle flags flew.

Captain Schönberg tried again to lift himself off the wheelhouse floor, but his body would not obey any of his commands. He sat, slumped against the bulkhead, staring outward toward the port side windows, unable to even turn his head. His breathing was a thin reedy whisper, and the edges of his vision were blurry and indistinct. He realized that he had briefly lost consciousness. His mind turned slowly, and he could not recall the last few minutes.

He could not see Sub-Lieutenant Haas, but he heard him commanding someone to lower the flags to signal their surrender. Schönberg's anger boiled over. "Haas, you mewling, cowardly traitor! Belay that order immediately! If I had my sidearm, I'd kill you where you stand, you shameful excuse for..." He paused, realizing suddenly that he was not actually speaking. In fact, he was making no sound at all. The angry tirade was occurring entirely in his mind.

Haas walked quickly across his field of vision and stood near the windows, looking downward. He seemed oblivious to Schönberg, though the captain lay only two meters away. Haas looked over his shoulder and addressed the gunnery officer, who was still out of the captain's sight.

"The enemy ship has ceased firing, but they may resume unless we strike our colors."

"I dispatched two signalmen to do so," replied the gunnery officer. "With all the fires on deck, I hope they can reach the lines."

Haas nodded. "Issue orders to abandon ship."

Schönberg was incredulous. Abandon the ship? He could hardly believe his ears. Never would it occur to him to simply surrender to their hated enemies. If he had to sacrifice the life of every crewman, he would do so to ensure that the British paid as dearly as possible for their victory.

"What do we do about the captain's body?" asked the gunnery officer.

"We leave it here," answered Haas. "We cannot bring it with us. When the ship goes down, he'll be properly buried at sea. It's the most honorable way."

My body? Buried at sea? Schönberg tried to scream at them both. "I'm not dead, you idiots!" he yelled in his mind, but no sound escaped his lips.

Darkness enveloped him, and he temporarily lost consciousness again.

He awoke to stinging pain from the laceration on his cheek. His vision returned, and he saw he was alone in the darkened wheelhouse. A choking yellow haze hung in the air, but he could not move his head to determine the source of the smoke. Gusts of rain blew in through the broken windows, lashing his skin where it struck.

Schönberg heard distant, familiar voices from somewhere outside, and he heard someone repeating, "Abandon ship!" accompanied by the insistent clanging of a bell.

Abruptly, he became aware of the fire, seeing the dancing orange and black shapes in the periphery of his vision even before he felt it. The shattered wheelhouse was burning. Scorching heat radiated from the bulkheads like the walls of an oven. The conflagration increased in intensity, defying the rain drops that sizzled and popped as they struck the searing surfaces. White hot flames surged up from below, boiling through warped fissures in the ruined deck and licking out along the flooring like the searching tongues of a score of serpents.

Instinctively, Schönberg tried to back away from the approaching flames, but he could not move. He watched in horror as tendrils of fire curled around his immobile feet and legs. First his shoelaces, then the cuffs of his trousers began to smoke. In a flash, the fabric around his lower legs ignited. The pain was excruciating, as flames mercilessly crawled upward along his body, but in his agony, Schönberg could not even scream.

In moments, the raging inferno completely engulfed *Nürnberg's* bridge and superstructure in a swirling vortex of flame. The German cruiser's burning hull settled lower in the water, listing to starboard and sinking at the stern. An explosion erupted amidships, ejecting fiery trails high into the evening sky. Minutes later, the ship heeled completely over and sank rapidly in a foaming, boiling cauldron of steam and smoke.

Across the rainswept water, HMS *Kent* edged forward, and her crew prepared to launch boats.

◆

DIFFUSED gray-green light beckoned to him from above, and Maerker struck out for it, churning frantically up through the water — while his chest hammered in pain and his left leg dangled, useless, below him. He breached the surface and hungrily inhaled, wincing in agony. He gasped and tasted blood in his mouth.

He was barely treading water in what appeared to be a scene from hell. The gargantuan mass of *Gneisenau's* upturned keel jutted from the sea before him, extending thirty meters in either direction. Waves lapped against the mottled rust-colored steel, and in the water along its length, clots of bubbles rose to the oil-streaked surface. All about the capsized hull floated debris of every conceivable sort. Barrels, splinters of wood, and scraps of fabric bobbed on the swells. Bodies were everywhere. Some floated face down, inert, but others showed signs of life. Some men were calling out in panic; others were trying desperately to grasp something upon which they could float.

Maerker was overcome with fatigue. The chill of the water was rapidly draining the heat from his body. His clothing clung to him heavily and made every motion a tortuous chore. His sodden shoes weighed him down, and every breath he drew brought knifing pain to his ribcage.

He spotted an object floating nearby and struck out for it, laboriously swimming with overhand strokes. With a painful lunge, he reached out and slapped it with the fingertips of his left hand. It was a splintered wooden beam, greasy and slippery. After several unsuccessful tries, he was able to grasp the beam and pull it toward him. He heaved his arms over the shaft and hung there, gasping, as he floated and bobbed on the swells.

A gurgling rumble echoed over the water, and he raised his head wearily to see the keel sinking sternward. Her huge mass slid rapidly under the sea, which boiled and foamed as it swallowed her. As he watched, the last curve of her stem slid under the waves, and she was gone. Massive eddies swirled about him, and he was sent briefly spinning. Maerker looked over the oil-sheened swells where his ship had disappeared. Somewhere far below him in the abyss, the ruined hulk of *Gneisenau* would settle in her final resting place. He wondered how many of her crew were still aboard.

The weariness was overwhelming, gnawing at the corners of his vision. Only the frigid water kept him from passing into unconsciousness. His teeth chattered, and he could no longer feel his fingers. Each wheezing breath he took seemed to be more painful and more laborious than the last.

He floated limply on the swells, clinging to his scrap of wood. As he rose upon a swell, he saw the two battlecruisers in the mist to the northwest. Thankfully, the British ships were much closer now—just a few hundred meters away. Crewmen aboard the nearest battlecruiser were lowering boats. Thank God, Maerker thought. Now his men just needed to hang on long enough in the frigid water to be rescued.

He drifted in and out of consciousness, with the jarring pains in his chest and leg repeatedly wrenching him back to bleary wakefulness. Fatigue crept over him like a fever, sapping his remaining strength and making even the slightest motion seem slow and dreamlike.

Less than thirty meters away, the first of the British boats arrived. More boats were following—their oars digging into the water in rapid rhythm. Behind the boats loomed the massive gray bulk of a battlecruiser, wreathed in mist. The nearest wooden boat had "HMS *Inflexible*" stenciled on its gunwales. Four uniformed sailors were rowing, and others were throwing out ropes and life buoys to *Gneisenau's* floating men. He could hear his men calling out weakly to the British sailors.

Another swell washed over Maerker's head, dislodging him from the wooden beam, and he inadvertently inhaled a mouthful of water. He struggled back to the surface, gasping and choking. He willed his arms and legs to move, but he could not feel his extremities to know if they were receiving commands from his brain. Fatigue pulled at him as surely as the water, and an overwhelming sleepiness clouded his senses. He fought to keep his eyes open and his chattering mouth just above the surface.

His vision became hazy, and he had trouble focusing. Now less than twenty-five meters away, he saw—or he thought he saw—two British sailors reach into the water and heave out the limp form of one of *Gneisenau's* men. Then he was certain he saw them help another German sailor clamber aboard the small boat.

A wave of relief coursed through him. His men were being rescued. Maerker thought that he smiled, but he could not be sure. Keep at it, lads, he thought wearily. Don't give up. Save as many as you can.

Maerker' view of the boat suddenly disappeared as a large swell rolled over him, and he was once again submerged. This time, however, he did not struggle—for his arms and legs could no longer move. He looked upward as he sank, and he could see the dark silhouettes of some of his men still floating on the surface above him. The hazy green-gray light steadily dimmed as he descended, and then he was in complete darkness.

It occurred to him that he no longer felt cold. In fact, the sea enveloped his body in a comforting embrace. The pressure steadily increased, and he felt overwhelmingly sleepy.

Motes of light began to flicker in his vision, and for brief seconds they resolved themselves into fleeting, indistinct images. Some of the scenes were familiar to him, and again he thought he smiled. For just a moment, he was certain that he saw a beautiful auburn-haired woman, sitting in a parlor, reading a letter.

And then there was nothing.

# THIRTY

*Tuesday, December 8, 1914*
*South Atlantic Ocean, 209 Miles (336 Kilometers) Southeast of the Falkland Islands*

*LEIPZIG* WAS THE LAST German warship to sink. She had been burning and adrift for more than an hour. During that time, *Glasgow* had launched her boats, and teams of British sailors searched for survivors floating on the increasing swells. The end came as a murky twilight cloaked the sea. With little warning, *Leipzig* suddenly capsized to port, finally snuffing out the fires that had raged upon her decks. Within minutes, the light cruiser's upturned keel slipped beneath the waves, leaving a halo of steam and smoke to mark her passing.

For half an hour more, boats from *Glasgow* and *Cornwall* crisscrossed the debris field, searching for any men in the water. The rain fell more heavily, stippling the undulating surface of the slate-colored sea. *Glasgow's* searchlights played over the area in a largely futile effort to find more floating seamen. Quite simply, there appeared to be very few survivors.

"We have a reply from the flagship, sir," said Stuart. "Both *Invincible* and *Inflexible* have suspended their search for any more survivors from the two sunken German armored cruisers. They are returning to Port Stanley. The admiral asks about the last known position and heading of *Dresden*."

"Reply that we last spotted her more than four hours ago," said Luce. "Hull down on the horizon, heading two-hundred twenty degrees, southwest."

"Yes, sir." Stuart relayed the message to the wireless operators.

"So, she's escaped us again," observed Thompson, shaking his head. "That's the most elusive damned ship in the Kaiser's navy."

"But she's truly on her own now," said Luce. "*Dresden* no longer has the protection of her squadron, and we know most of her previous hiding places." Luce thought for a moment. "You know, her captain seemed to be a smart and cautious fellow. If he's still being smart and cautious, he'll decide to put in somewhere—rather than continuing to run. His best move would be to find a friendly Argentine or Chilean port where he can have her interned."

"You're probably right," Thompson sighed. "Too bad, really. I was looking forward to finally getting that blasted cruiser in our sights."

"Message from *Bristol* to the fleet, sir," said Stuart, looking at the latest transcript sent up from the wireless room. "Seems *Bristol* and *Macedonia* happened upon three German support ships while they were patrolling south of Port Stanley. They were able to capture two of the vessels—colliers *Baden* and *Santa Isabel*. The crews of both ships were taken into custody, and then the colliers were sunk with gunfire. *Baden's* captain confirmed that they were attendant to von Spee's squadron and had orders to rendezvous with him there."

Thompson whistled. "Bad timing for the Germans all around, I'd say."

Stuart continued, "Interestingly, sir, *Baden's* captain also stated that the third German support vessel that got away—a passenger liner—was being used as some sort of troop ship."

"A troop ship?" asked Luce.

"That's what the message says, sir."

"What do you suppose that means?" Luce looked at Thompson quizzically. "Do you think the Germans meant to try to capture or occupy the island?"

"Sounds rather mad to me."

"I agree, but I've heard stranger things." Luce frowned. "Take today for example. What are the odds that our forces and this German squadron would blunder into each other twice—both times in the middle of nowhere?" He shook his head in amazement. "Millions of square miles of ocean all about us and two times in as many months we have found ourselves in the same place at the same time as von Spee's squadron. A thousand different circumstances had to have aligned to make that even possible."

"The flagship has replied, sir," said Stuart. "The admiral acknowledged our report of *Dresden's* apparent escape. We are instructed to pursue her immediately. We are to proceed to the mouth of the Strait of Magellan to prevent *Dresden* from entering."

Luce seriously doubted that *Glasgow* was in any condition to chase after anyone. "What's the latest from Engineering?" he asked.

Portman replied, "Sir, Lieutenant-Commander Shrubsole reports that the two damaged boilers are still inoperable. Repairs will likely take another twelve hours. Until then, turbine number one can only operate at one-third power."

"And our coal supply?"

"Less than three hundred tons, sir."

"That'll get us to the mouth of the Strait," offered Thompson, "but not much farther."

Luce shook his head. "With those boilers offline, we'll only be able to limp along. I'm certain *Dresden* has no such impediments. Hell, she's probably half way there already. We're nearly out of coal. We're also completely out of armor-piercing rounds. Even if we could chase after her, I'd rather not pick a fight with her in the state we're in." He turned to Stuart. "Send a reply to the admiral. Tell him that we have engine damage and are short on fuel and ammunition. Request permission to return to Port Stanley."

"Aye, sir."

Hirst spoke up. "Pardon me, sir. The last of the boats is back aboard."

"How many men did we pull out?"

"Lieutenant Lyon reports that they pulled out only fifteen. Three were found to be dead—their bodies were returned to the sea. The doctor is attending to the other twelve. Most are suffering from exposure, and we're hoping that none of them succumb to the effects of the cold. We should have a full accounting shortly."

Only twelve survivors, thought Luce grimly, from a crew of three hundred. He looked out toward *Cornwall*, which was keeping her station a quarter mile to the east. The last of her boats had also returned, and Luce wondered how many additional survivors they might have rescued.

"Admiral Sturdee has replied that *Glasgow*, *Cornwall*, and *Kent* are to return to Port Stanley, sir," said Stuart.

Luce nodded and looked out once more over the dark, empty stretch of sea where *Leipzig* had disappeared. He addressed the helmsman. "New course, heading three-hundred thirty-five degrees, ahead twelve knots."

"Aye, sir. Three three five degrees. Twelve knots."

*Glasgow* slowly came about and began to make her way northwest. Behind her, *Cornwall* fell into line, and the two warships steamed back toward Port Stanley.

◆

"MILLER'S STABLE, SIR," said Doctor Gilmour. "As you can see, he's sedated. We've stopped the bleeding and sutured the wound. He'll need another surgery before he's done, but he'll make it through."

Signalman Miller lay on the cot, sleeping. His right arm was heavily bandaged, and a mass of white gauze was bound where his right hand had once been.

Luce nodded thoughtfully. "Good work, Doctor." The captain had come down to the infirmary to see the wounded men and speak to the surgeon about their condition. One sailor had been killed when *Leipzig's* shell had exploded in the machine spaces. Three others had been seriously wounded. Along with Miller, that brought the number of injured men in the sick bay to four. Luce was walking along with the Doctor, stopping at each cot to discuss the condition of its occupant. They walked up to the cot of the fourth and final sailor, who also lay unconscious. His entire head and upper torso were covered in bandages, rendering him unrecognizable, and small pink and yellow stains were seeping through the gauze.

"This is Able Seaman Bridger," said Gilmour. "Of the wounded men, he's had the worst of it. He has severe burns to most of his upper body. In several places, the skin and flesh were scorched away to the bone. I'm doing what I can for him, and the hospital in Stanley may be able to do more, but in cases like this, the outcome is almost always the same. Infections and the resulting fevers will likely claim him within the next week."

"Good lord," said Luce, shaking his head. "Thank you, Doctor. Please keep me regularly updated on each man's condition. We'll be back in port by morning, and you can make arrangements for the transfer of these men to the town hospital. I'll have our boys send a wireless message to let the hospital staff know what to expect when we arrive."

The doctor nodded. "That would be helpful, sir." He then addressed one of his assistants. "We have some seepage through Mister Bridger's dressings. Let's keep those wounds as clean as possible."

"Yes, sir," replied the assistant, who brought a tray of fresh dressings over to Bridger's cot.

The captain and the doctor walked to the end of the compartment. "What of the Germans we rescued?" asked Luce. "I'd like to see them next. I understand that some are in pretty bad shape."

"Exposure, mostly," said Gilmour as he opened the fore doorway and stepped into the passageway. Four Royal Marines stationed in the passage came to attention as the captain and doctor appeared. "He stopped before a side door flanked by two of the Marines. "We have them all in this compartment here." Gilmour opened the door, and he and Luce stepped through.

The compartment was a relatively large space customarily used for general storage. A few crates and boxes remained in the room, stacked in a corner, but otherwise it had been cleared to make room for the German captives. Four more Marines stood guard inside. Also there were Lieutenant Hirst, Petty Officer Hobbs, and one of Doctor Gilmour's assistants.

Twelve German sailors were in the compartment. Most of them were sitting on crates or lying on the deck, wrapped in woolen blankets. To a man, they looked haggard and miserable. Many were holding and sipping steaming cups of tea. Two large metal tubs of hot water had been placed in the center of the compartment, and some of the shivering sailors were warming their feet in the basins. A few of the Germans looked up at Luce and Gilmour when they walked in, but they barely seemed to recognize the presence of the captain and the doctor.

Hirst and Hobbs came to attention. They had been speaking with the only German who was standing—a young dark-haired lieutenant. The German officer also came to attention at Luce's approach.

"Good evening, sir," said Hirst. "These twelve are the only living crewmen we could find out there. Five officers and seven men. They were nearly frozen to death—a few more minutes in the water and they'd have been done for." He gestured to the German officer standing beside him." This is Lieutenant Schiwig, one of *Leipzig's* deck officers. He's the only one who speaks a smattering of English."

"Thank you, Mister Hirst," said Luce, who turned to address the German officer. "Lieutenant Schiwig, I'm John Luce. Welcome aboard *Glasgow*."

"Thank you, sir," replied Schiwig quietly.

"How are your men?"

"Most are merely cold, sir. But they are strong; they will recover." He looked over his shoulder to where the medical assistant was attending to another German officer. "However, *Oberleutnant* Weiss has a severely injured hand. He is the worst of us."

"I'll have a look," said Gilmour. The doctor left the captain's side and walked over to where the injured German sat upon a crate. The officer's face was contorted in pain, and Luce caught a brief glimpse of a mangled and bloody mass that had been the man's hand. The doctor and his assistant began to examine the wound carefully.

Luce turned back to Schiwig. "Hopefully our good doctor will have your fellow officer fixed up in no time. I'm certain that you and your men are hungry. We'll have food brought for you."

"Thank you, sir. Your Lieutenant Hirst has already made some arrangements."

Hirst interjected, "Already took the liberty, sir. We should have a hot meal for them down here in a few minutes."

Luce nodded. To Schiwig he said, "I am sorry we were unable to rescue more of your men."

Schiwig sighed heavily. "There were very few of us left at the end, sir. Not many to save."

"I have to ask, Lieutenant, why did your commander wait so long to signal your surrender? Your ship was dead in the water for some time, yet there was initially no response to our queries. I had hoped to send boats to you sooner."

"The flames, sir. Too many fires inside and on the deck. Our captain wanted to lower our flags, but no one could reach them because of the flames. We could not lower the flags, and our wireless was destroyed. We could not signal our surrender. Then they found the flares, and Captain Haun ordered us to abandon ship. We are grateful that you sent boats to rescue us..." His words trailed off into silence.

"Sorry to interrupt, sir," said Doctor Gilmour, who had walked back to where the captain stood. "That German officer's hand is badly damaged. I'm afraid we'll have to amputate at least one finger, and I'll need to perform some immediate surgical repairs so that he doesn't lose the whole hand."

Luce nodded. "Do whatever you need to, Doctor."

Gilmour and his assistant then escorted the injured German officer out the door and down the passageway toward the infirmary.

Luce looked back over toward the remaining German sailors huddled in the compartment. "Mister Hirst, please see to it that we find proper sleeping arrangements for our guests. They've been through quite enough for one day. The least we can do is give them a decent bunk after their meal."

"Certainly, sir. I'll see to it."

Luce addressed the German officer again, "Lieutenant, my sincere condolences on the losses of your fellow officers and men. Your commander was a courageous man, and your crew fought valiantly. I am deeply sorry that we were unable to save more lives."

"Thank you, sir." The German lieutenant saluted crisply. Luce returned the salute, then left the compartment, heading back toward the bridge—his heart burdened and his mind troubled.

◆

A MISTY DAWN revealed a sullen, overcast morning in the Falklands, as *Glasgow* steamed into the outer bay of Port William. As his ship slowly passed the anchored battlecruisers, Luce noted that they bore only slight evidence of the prolonged battle the day before. Much like *Glasgow*, several blast scars and pockmarks marred the funnels and sleek flanks of the big ships, but little other damage was visible. *Glasgow* dropped anchor in Port Stanley's harbor to jubilant fanfare from the gathered townspeople.

A boat arrived within minutes to transport the injured seamen, both British and German, ashore to the hospital. The remaining German sailors were then sent on another boat to *Canopus*—designated as the temporary holding area for all captured prisoners of war. *Glasgow's* crew gave three cheers for *Leipzig's* crewmen as they were escorted into the waiting boat.

The remainder of the day was spent coaling and repairing damage to the ship. Late in the afternoon, *Kent* finally appeared at the harbor mouth. She was the last of the British ships to return. Because her wireless equipment had been damaged in her fight with *Nürnberg*, she had been unable to notify the flagship of her status, and her return was a great relief to the men of the fleet who had wondered what had befallen her.

As the details from the previous day's battle filtered in, the magnitude of their victory became clear. Four of the five German warships of the East Asia Squadron had been sunk. The enemy flagship, *Scharnhorst*, had gone down with all hands—more than eight hundred men, including Admiral von Spee himself. Among the other vessels, *Gneisenau* had performed the most orderly evacuation and had the greatest number of survivors—nearly two hundred. Only sixteen men had been rescued from *Leipzig*—including the twelve that the *Glasgow* had pulled out as well as four more by *Cornwall*. *Nürnberg* had the fewest survivors, at only seven. In total, the Germans had lost more than twenty-two hundred men in a single day. By contrast, the British fleet had very few casualties. Seven men had perished, eighteen were wounded, and the British vessels had almost no damage. Additionally, *Bristol* and *Macedonia* had captured and sunk two of the German squadron's support vessels. It had been an overwhelming victory for the Royal Navy and Admiral Sturdee. Only *Dresden* had escaped, and with her squadron gone, soon she would likely need to put in at a South American port—where undoubtedly, she would be held and interned.

The following morning, the admiral informed all of his captains that the fleet would remain at Port Stanley for two more days to refuel and refit before resuming the search for *Dresden*. Luce granted a well-deserved shore leave for most of his crew. The repairs to *Glasgow's* boiler room were complete by early afternoon, which allowed the men on the engineering crews to enjoy some time off as well.

That evening, Admiral Sturdee hosted a celebratory reception aboard *Invincible* for all of his captains and commanders. He also invited the only two surviving senior officers from the German squadron, both of whom had served on *Gneisenau*. Although both German officers were gracious in defeat, Luce thought that Commander Hans Pochhammer, who had been *Gneisenau's* first officer, seemed rather haughty and defiant. In contrast,

Lieutenant-Commander Johann Busch, *Gneisenau's* senior gunnery officer, was quieter and more reticent. They both spoke quite serviceable English. Curiously, however, the two men appeared not to care for each other's company and spoke little to each other, if at all. Pochhammer spent much of the evening testily debating points of politics with whoever would listen—and engaged in a particularly prolonged exchange with Captain Phillimore of *Inflexible*. Busch, by contrast, listened politely to the discourse but said almost nothing. After the meal, as they were enjoying their last sherry of the evening, Luce approached the German gunnery officer.

"Pardon me, Lieutenant-Commander," said Luce, extending his hand. "I am John Luce, of *Glasgow*. Pleased to meet you."

Busch shook his hand, regarding him thoughtfully. "Johann Busch. The pleasure is mine, Captain Luce."

"I am sorry for the losses of your officers and men, Mister Busch."

Busch nodded respectfully. "Thank you, Captain. And please accept my regrets for the losses of your squadron's crews at Coronel. Unfortunately, such is life for us in the Royal Navy and the *Kaiserliche Marine*."

"Unfortunately," agreed Luce. "As naval men—whether German or British—our similarities likely exceed our differences, and it is regrettable that we must currently meet under such circumstances."

"True." Busch paused for a moment, looking directly into Luce's eyes, before he continued. "My commanding officer, Captain Julius Maerker, would have liked very much to have met you, Captain Luce. In both of our encounters with your ship—first at Coronel, and then... here, two days ago—he was impressed by your bravery and seamanship."

Luce chuckled. "Don't confuse bravery with foolishness, Mister Busch. I'm lucky to be alive. Your gunnery at Coronel was, frankly, the best I have ever witnessed. In that battle, had we lingered in *Gneisenau's* sights for even a minute longer, I'm certain I would not be here today."

Busch managed a thin but gracious smile. "Perhaps so, but the fact remains that Captain Maerker was the most capable commander under whom I have served—and he regarded you as a brave and worthy adversary. I would consider that high praise."

"Thank you. I am sorry that I could not have met him. This war has already claimed too many good men—on both sides." Luce raised his glass. "To Captain Maerker."

"To Captain Maerker," replied Busch, who touched his glass to Luce's with a chime of crystal.

◆

ON THEIR FINAL DAY in Port Stanley, Captain Luce and Commander Thompson attended a solemn funeral ceremony for the seven British sailors who had lost their lives during the battle. More than three hundred officers and men from the ships of the fleet filed into the town cemetery—a gently sloping strip of grassland outside of town that overlooked the calm waters of the harbor. The bleak weather matched the mood of the gathering. Under an oppressive gray overcast, blustery winds whipped sheets of icy rain over the assembled gallery of dark jackets and hats.

Chaplains from both *Inflexible* and *Carnarvon* spoke about the brave men who had passed on and of the sacrifices they had made in honor of their king and country. A single bagpiper played a mournful salute, as seven identical wooden caskets were lowered beside each other into a single large grave excavated from the rocky soil.

After the ceremony, the sailors quietly dispersed, heading to the boats that would take them back to their respective ships. Luce lingered for several minutes longer, watching as a few local men turned spadefuls of earth over the coffins. For a time, the only sounds were the howl of the wind, the patter of rain drops, and the scrape of shovels in the soil. Commander Thompson remained standing by Luce's side, silently respectful of his captain's reflective mood.

It was over, Luce thought. The Battle of the Falkland Islands had been the day of reckoning that he had anticipated for long, anguished weeks. Admiral von Spee's feared East Asia Squadron, which had escaped Tsingtao at the outset of the war, eluded enemy forces for months while traversing the Pacific, vexed the Admiralty into apoplexy, and had soundly defeated Cradock's ships off the coast of Chile, was destroyed—laying broken and littered upon the ocean floor. The British losses from the Battle of Coronel were finally avenged. However, Luce did not feel triumphant. He simply felt weary.

He thought of his injured crewmen in the Stanley hospital who would not be accompanying the ship when she departed the next morning. He thought of the surviving German officers and men, currently incarcerated aboard *Canopus*, who would soon be on their way to prison camps in Britain. Ironically, they would set foot on Luce's home soil long before he would. He recalled his gruesome vision of *Monmouth's* doomed crew clinging desperately to her railings in their final moments. He again saw *Leipzig's* men as they tried, in vain, to abandon their sinking ship as flames consumed her decks. He mourned the thousands of sailors from both nations who had perished in such a brief time. He thought of Admiral Cradock and of Captain Brandt—and even Captain Maerker, whom he had never met.

Although Luce had won this latest battle, he knew that the larger conflict was far from over. For himself and his crew, that would mean finding *Dresden*, wherever she might now be, and continuing to protect Allied trade and British interests in these waters.

The laborers finished their work. With shovels on their shoulders, they trudged back toward the town. Behind them, the unrelenting rain was turning the gravesite into a muddy quagmire.

Luce turned to his first officer. "Let's head on back, Will."

"Gladly," replied Thompson with relief, as he shielded his face from the driving rain. "I don't know if there's a colder, wetter, more inclement place on earth than these blasted islands." The two officers began walking back toward the harbor, where a single steam launch was tied up at the pier, waiting for them.

"Come now," protested Luce with a smile. "We just fought a battle to protect *these blasted islands*, as you call them—which happen to be sovereign British territory. Are you suggesting we shouldn't have bothered?"

Thompson gasped in mock outrage. "Nothing of the sort, sir. Of course we need to protect this beautiful corner of His Majesty's Empire. After all, these islands are home to quite a few of our fine countrymen, not to mention thousands of sheep, some number of penguins, windswept rocks, more sheep, and plenty of year-round rain—except, of course, when it's snowing. Oh, did I mention the sheep?"

Luce laughed. "I know who to recommend if Governor Allardyce needs a local Minister of Tourism."

"As long as I can do the job from Brighton, I'm your man," grinned Thompson.

Out across the harbor, a foghorn sounded from one of the battlecruisers—a reminder to all the sailors of the fleet who might still be ashore that they were to return to their ships.

At the pier, the two Marines waiting with the boat stood at attention and saluted.

"At ease, men," said Luce. "Let's head back so we can get our delicate first officer out of this rain."

The officers clambered into the steam launch as the Marines released the lines and hopped in to join them. The pilot engaged the thumping engine and brought the boat about. As the blustery downpour intensified, the launch chugged slowly out into the windswept harbor. Luce looked out at *Glasgow*, moored less than a quarter mile away. Streams of smoke coiled upward from her funnels—evidence that the engineers were testing her newly repaired boilers. His ship would be ready to depart with the fleet at dawn.

Luce turned to his first officer and said, "Good to see she's up and running, because we do have some unfinished business."

Thompson nodded and smiled. "We'd best get back at it then."

# EPILOGUE

## SMS *Dresden*

*Sunday, March 14, 1915*
*Isla Más a Tierra, Juan Fernández Islands, Chile*

THE CONVOY of three British warships had steamed steadily through the night from the southern Chilean coast. HMS *Glasgow*, in the vanguard, led the armored cruiser *Kent* and the armed liner *Orama* as they swiftly approached the mountainous island of Más a Tierra—Robinson Crusoe Island—from the southeast. The dawn brightened under a cloudless ultramarine sky.

"Spotters confirm no other vessels in sight," said Backhouse. "Clear on all horizons."

"So far, so good," answered Luce. "We haven't spotted a ship in two days. With luck, no one will have warned of our approach." The island's jagged green peaks now loomed ahead, and he scanned the rugged, uninhabited coastline. "Anything on wireless?"

"Nothing for the last four hours, sir," confirmed Stuart.

"If she's here," said Luce, "hopefully we'll catch her idling at anchor."

"I do love a good surprise," quipped Thompson. "How far to the mouth of the bay?"

"Approximately nine miles, sir," answered Portman, looking at the chart before him. "We'll pass those headlands that jut out to the northeast. After we round those mountains, much of the bay should be in view, but it will still be at least two miles distant."

"We'll need to sweep in swiftly to ensure she cannot run," offered Luce. After so many months of searching in vain, SMS *Dresden* might finally be in their grasp.

Astonishingly, *Dresden* had been able to repeatedly elude capture during the months since the Falklands battle. In fact, the last time that anyone had definitively sighted the enemy light cruiser was a few days after the battle, when she had put in briefly at Punta Arenas to coal. Local British officials immediately notified the Admiralty. *Glasgow*, accompanied by *Bristol*, had steamed into the Strait at top speed to try to catch her, but by the time they arrived at Punta Arenas, *Dresden* had already hastily departed—disappearing westward into the convoluted maze of the southern Chilean coastline.

Admiral Sturdee and his battlecruisers were recalled north to join the North Sea blockade, leaving command of the Fifth Cruiser Squadron back in Admiral Stoddart's hands. Because of Luce's seniority and his familiarity with the region, Stoddart had given him command of the search group.

What followed were some of the most frustrating months of Luce's career as he and his ships explored scores of fjords, channels, bays, and river mouths along hundreds of miles of coast as they hunted fruitlessly for *Dresden*. They followed up on dozens of unsubstantiated reports that the German warship had been sighted at a particular anchorage or had made arrangements to meet a collier or supply ship at a specific location. In every case, the reports had turned out to be false or woefully outdated. Days turned into weeks, weeks turned into months, and *Dresden's* whereabouts remained unknown.

Then, in the second week of March, *Glasgow's* wireless room had intercepted a brief wireless exchange between two vessels:

> [*11.3.15.09:22*] JF3420 TO ALDA [*stop*] MEET AT JUAN FERNANDEZ MAR 14 [*stop*] LESS THAN 100 TONS COAL REMAINING [*stop*] CONFIRM [*end*]

> [*11.3.15.09:41*] AX18 ALDA TO JF3420 [*stop*] CONFIRMED [*stop*] WILL MEET AT JUAN FERNANDEZ MAR 14 [*end*]

Luce's interest in the seemingly innocuous messages had been piqued by the fact that *Alda* was a German-flagged cargo ship that had been moored idly in Valparaiso for weeks. Here was a request from an unidentified ship stating only that she was low on coal—and confirming that *Alda* was to meet her at the Juan Fernandez Islands in three days. Something about the exchange gnawed at him. One-hundred tons of coal should be plenty of fuel to traverse the four-hundred or so miles to Valparaiso, so why wouldn't this mystery vessel have just steamed into port to coal? Somehow, Luce knew this was not a coincidence. Could it be that out of desperation, *Dresden's* captain had finally misstepped? If the mystery ship was actually the enemy cruiser, this intercepted call to a supply ship might finally be the key to finding her.

Of the Juan Fernandez Islands, Más a Tierra was the nearest to Valparaiso. Cumberland Bay, on the northwest coast of the island, was the closest thing to a proper port on the island. If *Dresden* was waiting at Juan Fernandez, she would be there.

The three British warships had set off immediately, steaming on through the next day and following night as fast as *Orama* could manage. *Glasgow's* spotters had first sighted the island's southernmost promontory just after dawn. They steamed in a tight line northeast along the island's rocky cliffs and folded emerald mountainsides, until *Glasgow* rounded the outermost point of the headlands.

"There it is, sir," said Portman. "The mouth of Cumberland Bay. No ships yet in view, but we can't yet see the whole bay."

"Action stations," said Thompson. The bridge officers relayed commands to their men throughout the ship. On the foredeck beneath the wheelhouse, the forward 6-inch turret rotated several degrees to port—its barrel directed at the opening of the bay, now only a few miles away.

Cumberland Bay was a broad, mile-wide crescent carved into the coastline. As *Glasgow* sped onward, followed by *Kent* and *Orama*, a large cove came into view—and in it was anchored a single vessel.

A warship.

SMS *Dresden* was moored in the cove, a hundred yards off shore. She was riding high in the water—evidence that her coal bunkers were, indeed, nearly empty. Her colors were flying from her halyards, and thin streams of wispy smoke curled upward from her three funnels—an indication that even though she was low on coal, her captain was keeping up steam in case he needed to flee. A small rustic village of perhaps a few hundred inhabitants was nestled along the shoreline behind it, between the sea and dense forested slope rising behind it.

Despite his confidence that they would find the enemy ship here, Luce was still amazed to actually see *Dresden* laying at anchor. She had eluded him so many times before, that to finally find her was almost as shocking as it was exhilarating.

"Message to *Kent*," said Luce. "Direct her to move to the far end of the bay to ensure that *Dresden* cannot escape."

"Yes, sir," replied Stuart, who passed the message on to the wireless room.

"Range to target, four thousand yards," said Backhouse. "Ready to fire, sir."

"Hold for now," said Luce. "I want to position ourselves so that the village behind her isn't in our line of fire. Helmsman, cut our speed. I'd like to drift another three hundred yards northwest to give us a better angle."

"Aye, sir."

"I'd also prefer to wait to see if she'll surrender on her own. Although she's flying her battle flags, she is still moored in a neutral port."

"Captain Allen asks if he can open fire, sir," said Stuart.

"Tell him to wait for us," replied Luce. "All ships are to hold their positions and wait for our signal."

"Activity on her decks, sir," said Backhouse, who was viewing the enemy ship through binoculars. "At least three of her guns are now pointed in our direction, and the bastards are scurrying about on deck."

"Are they preparing to abandon ship?"

"No, sir. It seems they are rushing to action stations."

"What do you suppose they're up to?" asked Thompson. "Surely they can't reasonably expect to fight us off."

"Delaying," replied Luce. "They're waiting to see if we'll really fire on her while she's anchored in a Chilean port. Her captain is betting that we'll play by the rules and hold our fire."

"So, will we?" Thompson cocked an eyebrow.

Luce looked at his first officer and smiled. "Hell no," he stated matter-of-factly. "*Dresden* has flouted those very same rules for months, with the tacit approval of the Chilean government. If her captain won't willingly offer his surrender, we'll encourage him to do so." He checked to see that their firing position had improved and that most of the structures behind the anchored German ship were no longer in jeopardy. Satisfied that they were now in the best position he could reasonably achieve, he turned to the gunnery officer. "Mister Backhouse, you may proceed."

"With pleasure, sir." Backhouse flipped a set of switches and announced, "Firing, port broadside."

*Glasgow's* guns thundered, spouting jets of flame and billows of brown smoke. The deck beneath the bridge officers' feet trembled. At such close range, a few of the rounds flew high, thumping into the jungle canopy on the shore behind the ship. However, most of the shells found their target. Bright orange explosions burst along the length of *Dresden*. *Kent* and *Orama* opened fire as well. Fountains of water erupted all around the German ship, and more explosions tore apart her superstructure. *Glasgow's* guns fired another salvo, hitting the enemy cruiser with every shell. Staccato blasts echoed across the water. *Dresden's* second funnel shuddered and swayed but remained standing. Fires sprang up in multiple places, wreathing he entire ship in swirls of black and brown smoke. German sailors leapt from the stricken cruiser into the bay and began swimming for shore.

Through the dark clouds, Luce could see her battle flags come down, replaced rapidly by a single white flag. The attack had lasted only minutes. "Cease fire," he said, "and signal the other ships to hold their fire." *Glasgow's* guns fell silent. He squinted through the binoculars at the enemy ship. A series of flags were being raised on *Dresden's* foremast, but shrouds of smoke partially obscured his view. "Mister Stuart, can you or your men above make out that signal?"

Stuart took up a pair of lenses and peered at the burning vessel. He frowned. "It is a bit mixed-up, sir. I think it says, 'Negotiations will be sent'."

"I believe they mean to put a boat in the water," said Thompson, "although the word *negotiations* implies that they have something to offer us."

"The only two things they can offer us are their surrender and their ship," said Luce. "Helmsman, bring us in closer, fifteen hundred yards. Keep us on her beam, in case they have the notion to fire a torpedo."

"Aye, sir. One thousand, five hundred yards, on her beam."

"Mister Backhouse, keep your guns trained on her. If those German turrets so much as twitch in our direction, fire another full salvo at her."

"Understood, sir," said Backhouse with a grim nod.

*Glasgow* maneuvered closer to *Dresden*, stopping less than a mile away in the calm waters of the bay. *Kent* and *Orama* also moved closer, taking up positions that effectively surrounded the anchored German cruiser. Luce could see many men now above decks on the enemy ship. Teams of German sailors were working feverishly to put out her fires. As he watched, a small steam launch with three men aboard appeared around *Dresden's* starboard quarter, making for *Glasgow*. Flying above the craft's single slim funnel was another white flag.

"Get some men on the gunwales with rifles," ordered Backhouse through a voice pipe to one of his lieutenants. "In case these Boche bastards try any funny business."

Within minutes, the launch had traversed the distance between the two vessels. Its pilot brought her about below *Glasgow's* port bow and idled there. During its transit, Luce had left the bridge and made his way down to the forecastle so that he could be within earshot of the boat's occupants. When he stepped up to the gunwale and looked down at the boat, one of the German sailors—an officer—stood up and saluted.

Luce returned the salute and said simply, "State your business."

"I mean to parley, sir," said the German officer. "I am *Kapitänleutnant* Wilhelm Canaris of His Imperial Majesty's Ship *Dresden*. I represent Captain Lüdecke. I am here to negotiate terms." The young German lieutenant had neatly coiffed blond hair and a brilliant, confident smile.

"Terms?" Luce chuckled. He was certain that this 'negotiation' was nothing more than a delaying tactic. "Mister Canaris, I am afraid you are not in a position to negotiate anything. You are outnumbered, outgunned, and unable to maneuver or escape. You must surrender."

"But we are anchored in a neutral port, Captain. By firing upon us, you have violated the terms of the Hague Conventions. You have violated international law, and I am certain that the Chilean authorities..."

"Mister Canaris, I am not interested in a lecture on law or politics. The only *terms* that you and your captain need to be concerned about are these: you will surrender immediately and unconditionally or we will sink your ship where she's moored."

Canaris was undeterred, still smiling. "But surely, Captain, you can see the political delicacy of this situation..."

"You are testing my patience, Lieutenant," interrupted Luce, who found himself liking the German officer despite the man's obvious attempts to stall and delay. "*Dresden* will surrender immediately and unconditionally. All of your officers and men are to disembark and assemble ashore in an orderly fashion, and I will send my men aboard and take possession of your vessel. You are to make no attempt to scuttle or otherwise disable your ship, for she is now the property of His Majesty, King George." He raised his voice and leveled Canaris with a stern glare. "Anything short of that, and I will fire upon your vessel until nothing remains but a blackened husk. Is that clear?"

"Absolutely, sir," replied Canaris with a deferential nod, seemingly chastened. "We will accede to your demands. We will surrender unconditionally." He paused, then said, "If I may, Captain, your attack resulted in the deaths of several of our men. Additionally, we have numerous wounded—some grievously. May we trouble your physicians to tend to their injuries?"

"Yes, of course," replied Luce. "Offload your wounded men as you disembark your crew. I will send my surgeon ashore to see to them, and I will make our infirmary available for any who need treatment."

"Thank you, sir. That is most gracious. I must return and inform my captain of our conversation." He saluted once more, then said something to the pilot, who throttled up the steam engine, turned the boat about, and set back across the bay toward *Dresden*.

When Luce returned to the bridge, Thompson, Backhouse, and Stuart were waiting for him. Thompson asked, "So, do you think they'll actually give up that quietly?"

"No," replied Luce. "In fact, I'm certain that they've been preparing to scuttle their ship this whole time. They'll not let us take her as a prize."

"Can we try to stop them?" asked Backhouse.

Luce shook his head. "If they're intent on sinking her, they'll do so whether we try to stop them or not. I'd rather not risk any more lives— ours or theirs—in the attempt. Just assemble armed shore parties and prepare to launch boats. Keep our guns trained on them for now. Mister

Thompson, please notify Doctor Gilmour that we'll need him to go ashore and tend to some seriously wounded men." He addressed Stuart. "Send a message to Captains Allen and Seagrave. Tell them that we've secured the surrender of the enemy ship and are preparing to go ashore to treat some wounded."

"Yes, sir."

"There go the rats," groused Backhouse as he viewed the German ship through binoculars again.

Across the bay, the entire crew of *Dresden* was assembling on her weather decks. They were abandoning the ship. Although some men were leaving in boats, many were either clambering down ladders into the water or simply leaping over the gunwales and swimming toward the shore. Men still on the ship were throwing crates, boxes, and other items to the men already in the water.

"Lower our boats," said Luce. "I want at least forty armed men ashore within ten minutes. Then we'll send the doctor."

The exodus from the German cruiser was accomplished quite rapidly. In only a few minutes, nearly the entire crew had made it off the ship. Four of *Glasgow's* boats were already approaching the shore, where the defeated German sailors were now gathered—mostly sitting on the ground in small groups. A modest crowd of local villagers had also gathered to gawk at the spectacle.

As Luce watched from *Glasgow's* bridge, he could see no more German sailors still aboard *Dresden*, although he doubted that the entire crew had disembarked. As he looked on, he saw the white surrender flag being lowered.

Backhouse saw it too. "What do you suppose they're up to now, sir?"

"Not sure," replied Luce, frowning.

Then, as they watched, *Dresden's* black, white, and red ensign suddenly appeared as it was raised on the halyard high upon the cruiser's foremast. There it flapped jauntily, in bold defiance of the British ships that surrounded it.

"Those sneaky bastards," muttered Backhouse. "Should we blast them again, now that their damned colors are back up?"

Luce sighed and had to suppress a smile. "No, don't bother. You'd be firing on an empty ship; most of her crew is already ashore. Besides, I have a feeling that in a few moments, she'll be on the bottom of the bay anyway."

They watched as the last two German crewmen still on board—undoubtedly those who had raised the flag—ran across the deck, vaulted over the cruiser's port gunwale, and leapt into the water. They swam furiously for shore and had almost reached the sand when *Dresden* exploded.

The German cruiser's forward magazine erupted in a massive cloud of black smoke and orange flame, briefly lifting the ship's bow and buckling her hull beneath the bridge area. The blast's shockwave sent concentric swells racing across the bay and rumbled thunderously across *Glasgow's* decks. Shards of metal debris rained down upon the water around the ship. The assembled villagers panicked and ran in a chaotic stampede away from the shoreline as a column of roiling smoke rose above the cruiser. In contrast to the frightened locals, the German sailors on the beach let out a loud and boisterous cheer. In their last act of defiance, they had—in a way—eluded the British a final time by preventing the enemy from seizing their ship.

As the rumbling echoes of the explosion died away, Luce could see that *Dresden* was taking on water rapidly, sinking by the bows and listing to starboard. As she settled lower, her crew somberly arranged themselves in rows upon the shore, standing at attention and saluting as if at review. As water lapped over the sinking cruiser's forecastle, her entire crew began to sing *Die Wacht am Rhein*. Seconds later, *Dresden* disappeared—the tips of her masts slipping beneath the churning waters of the bay. As she went under, the crews of the three British ships also let out a cheer.

Luce nodded in satisfaction. He did not care that the Germans had engaged in a final act of trickery to keep him from seizing their ship. Rather, he was relieved that it was now truly over. The last and most elusive of the German cruisers had finally been sunk.

He left the bridge in Thompson's command and made arrangements to go ashore himself to speak to the local representatives of the Chilean government. Although Luce had no regrets about sinking *Dresden*, he still wished to minimize the political backlash of having fired upon an enemy combatant while she was anchored in a neutral port.

Not unexpectedly, as he strode ashore with Lieutenant Hirst and a squad of armed seamen, Luce was immediately approached by several Chilean governmental officials. The town mayor was completely irate. With the aid of Hirst and a local interpreter, they translated the mayor's red-faced tirade. Not only had Luce's ships blatantly violated international law by attacking the German cruiser while she lay at anchor in the harbor, but some of the rounds had flown long and had exploded in the town. By the mayor's count, three houses had been severely damaged, a wooden fence had been knocked over, and an entire chicken coop had been destroyed—along with several unfortunate chickens inside the structure at the time of the attack. Luckily, no villagers had been injured or killed by the errant shells. After much cajoling, Luce was able to significantly improve the mayor's disposition by offering to pay for the damage and distress caused to his village and its occupants — in gold sovereigns.

Next was the matter of the German sailors who were still milling about the beach — kept in some semblance of order by their officers. Because the enemy seamen all now stood upon neutral Chilean territory, the British could not capture them as prisoners of war. That was just as well, thought Luce, because he did not want the hassle of minding and transporting them until they could be shipped back to Britain. He was satisfied to leave them in the custody of the Chileans, who could do with them as they pleased.

The wounded sailors were another matter. The island had no hospital, nor even a true physician. Of the sixteen men who had been injured in the attack, four — including *Dresden's* first officer — were seriously wounded and would require surgery and hospitalization. Doctor Gilmour did what he could initially for each of them, but Luce decided to have all of the wounded German sailors transferred to *Orama*. Captain Lüdecke initially objected, but Luce assured the German captain that his men would be transported immediately to Valparaiso, where they could receive the necessary medical care.

Finally, Luce offered the services of his men to help bury the eight German seamen who had died in the attack. *Dresden's* sailors declined, preferring to conduct the ceremony themselves. With his business on shore concluded, Luce bade farewell to the German captain and his officers and returned to the ship. He was looking forward to sending this particular report to the Admiralty.

His boat pulled alongside *Glasgow's* rear quarter, and Luce climbed the ladder to the aft weather deck. As he came aboard, some commotion to his left drew his attention, and he turned to witness a most unusual sight.

Half a dozen sailors were gathered in a cluster and were laughing and joking about something. They all came to attention as they heard the boatswain's call announcing the captain's presence. Luce could then see that they had been standing around a small pink and brown spotted pig that had a makeshift leash around its neck. The pig was merrily gorging itself on some food in a bowl the men had set out for it. Luce also noted that at least two of the sailors were completely soaked and dripping with water.

"What on earth are you men doing?" Luce asked, both curious and slightly amused at the odd scene.

One of the seamen stepped forward and stood once again at attention. "Beggin' your pardon, sir. After the enemy ship went under, we seen this 'ere porker swim away from the wreckage. Seems the Boche had been keeping 'im on board to butcher 'im. When they abandoned ship, they must've left 'im behind, sir."

A younger man—one of the two sailors who was dripping wet—spoke up. "Sir, we seen the pig swimmin' around, and me and Tommy here decided to go in and get him." He gestured to the other damp seaman, who wore a broad grin. "It took us forever, sir. He's a slippery one. But me and Tommy finally wrestled him aboard." The grinning sailor beside him nodded happily.

"I see," said Luce with a smile. "Now that you men have rescued this wayward pig, what do you intend to do with it?"

"With your permission, sir, we'd like to keep him."

"Keep him?" asked Luce. "Like a pet?"

"More like a mascot, sir. The way we see it, this here pig was braver than all those Germans who abandoned their ship. He stayed on board even after she exploded, and then he went down with her. We think he'd make a fine mascot, sir."

The pig grunted and lifted its head from the now empty bowl. It looked around and regarded Luce briefly before it began sniffing around at the sailors' feet.

"And you men can keep him fed and out of everyone's way?"

"Most certainly, sir," said the seaman expectantly. "We'll make sure he doesn't get himself blown into a pile of pork chops, sir."

Luce found himself laughing. "Well, we no longer have a ship's dog, so I imagine we can find room for a ship's pig. Permission granted."

The men let out a cheer, and the pig cocked its head quizzically.

Luce turned, still chuckling, and resumed walking toward the bridge. He shook his head with a smile. Perhaps the part about the pig would not make it into his official report.

## Author's Historical Note

THE BATTLE OF CORONEL, on November 1st, 1914, was the first British naval defeat in more than a century — the previous loss having occurred at the Battle of Lake Champlain during the War of 1812. The overwhelming German victory at Coronel sent shock waves around the world. By any measure, Graf von Spee's odyssey was an extraordinary achievement. In an era before radar or voice-to-voice radio, he led an entire squadron of warships and auxiliary vessels across the Pacific, without any support, reinforcements, or resupply. Almost immediately upon their arrival in South American waters, the modern German ships engaged and soundly defeated an outgunned and largely obsolete Royal Navy squadron under Rear Admiral Sir Christopher Cradock. Chastened by the tragic losses of HMS *Good Hope* and HMS *Monmouth*, the Admiralty dispatched two swift and modern battlecruisers, HMS *Invincible* and HMS *Inflexible*, to lead the powerful squadron that ultimately destroyed the rogue German ships at the Battle of the Falklands on December 8th, 1914. Historians have long debated Graf von Spee's motivation for steaming toward the Falklands on that fateful morning in December. Some believe that the Germans only intended to shell the British outpost, but compelling evidence exists that Graf von Spee truly intended to capture and occupy Port Stanley.

These extraordinary events during the early months of the First World War get little or no mention in most history courses. Students of military history may not have heard of courageous Captain John Luce of HMS *Glasgow* (who finished his distinguished Royal Naval career with the rank of Admiral). Graf Maximillian von Spee is considerably more famous — the German navy subsequently named three different warships after him — but many have never truly explored the events that garnered him such fame. Few have heard the stories about the many brave officers and men from Britain and Germany who sacrificed, fought, survived, or perished during the Battles of Coronel and the Falklands. This novel is my humble attempt to shine a small spotlight on this largely forgotten chapter of military history.

Any author attempting to write a fictional story about real people from the historical record — whether the subject is Julius Caesar or Julius Maerker — is faced with the challenge of recreating those persons and their thoughts and actions in a way that mirrors the known events but also makes for a compelling, if fictional, storyline. Historians familiar with this period and these events will likely note that I have taken liberties with some of the characters, their motivations, or their actions. In some places, I compressed timelines or eliminated some events altogether to help the flow of the fictional narrative. I hope that after all of my culling, snipping, stretching, and squeezing of the source material, the end result is still a fitting homage to the inspiring real people about whom this fictional account is based.

For those interested in reading nonfiction accounts of these events, I would highly recommend any of the following sources (although many of them are, unfortunately, long out of print):

Robert K. Massie, *Castles of Steel: Britain, Germany, and the Winning of the Great War at Sea* (New York: Ballentine, 2003).

Robert K. Massie, *Dreadnought: Britain, Germany, and the Coming of the Great War* (New York: Ballentine, 1991).

Geoffrey Bennett, *Coronel and the Falklands* (London: Pan Books, 1962).

Geoffrey Bennett, *Naval Battles of the First World War* (London: Penguin, 1968).

Lloyd Hirst, *Coronel and After* (London: Peter Davies, 1934).

Keith Yates, *Graf Spee's Raiders: Challenge to the Royal Navy 1914-1915* (Annapolis: Naval Institute Press, 1995).

Richard Hough, *The Pursuit of Admiral von Spee: A study in loneliness & bravery* (London: George Allen and Unwin, 1969).

E. Keble Chatterton, *Gallant Gentlemen* (London: Hurst & Blackett, 1931).

# Acknowledgments

IN MY LIMITED EXPERIENCE, it takes a village to help write a book. The process to bring this novel from concept to reality required several years of research, writing, editing, and rewriting. I simply could not have done all of that by myself. Along the way, I leaned on many people who humbled me with their willingness to help, their shared passion for my project, and most of all—an extraordinary amount of patience for me and all of my tedious "I'm writing a book" nonsense.

Firstly, I must thank my brilliant wife, Diane, who has read every iteration of this novel—particularly the rough early versions that were a punishing slog. She reads at least six books for every one that I complete, and her keen eye for characters, plot, and pacing were invaluable. She also provided essential ongoing encouragement, particularly during my most discouraged moments.

Our amazing adult children, Colton, Emily, and Kate, each had a role in bringing this novel to life. From their old high school history projects about the First World War that sparked the original idea for this novel, to their patience with reading different versions of the book, they helped with critical insights and support. My late father, the original author in the family, intrepidly tackled an early version of the manuscript and provided helpful insights and suggestions. My mother, another avid reader, has provided continual support, wisdom, and guidance. Our niece, Megan, also boldly volunteered to read and comment on an early draft.

I will attempt to thank everyone else who helped me along the way. Margaret Newman and Graham Dobbin at the Royal Naval Museum provided copies of journals and letters from officers and crew of HMS *Glasgow*. Dr. Lorna Haycock at the Wiltshire Archaeological and Natural History Society provided access to excellent information about Admiral John Luce, as did historian Hans Houterman at unithistories.com. Author and historian Ralph J. Whitehead provided invaluable information about the officers and crew of SMS *Gneisenau*. Paul H. Thomas of the Hoover Institution Library at Stanford University provided critical access to a translation of Commander Hans Pochhammer's 1924 memoir: *Graf Spees Letzte Fahrt: Erinnerungen an das Kreuzergeschwader*. Thanks also to Mauricio

Hermosillo and Aislinn Sotelo at the UCLA Library's Department of Special Collections and Matthew Bailey at the National Portrait Gallery in London for their contributions. My gratitude to Ian Koviak for his masterfully designed cover art. Additionally, all of the members of my ARC Team were unsung heroes in this process, and I appreciate them greatly. Finally, many thanks to my good friend and fellow writer Michael Murbach, for all of his help, editorial assistance, and support.

## About the Author

ROBERT SCHREINER is a former CIA Intelligence Officer. After leaving government service, he embarked on a subsequent career as a consultant and executive in the global private security industry. He is an avid amateur military historian who has traveled the world, routinely sneaking in side-trips to visit ancient fortifications and battlefields. He lives in the Blue Ridge Mountains of Tennessee with his wife, two spoiled cocker spaniels, and an amusingly musical cockatiel.

*The Wolves and the Greyhounds* is his first novel. Visit the author at www.RobertSchreiner.com.

* 9 7 9 8 9 9 0 1 0 4 3 0 3 *